I0727876

Torn Between Hearts

A Love Triangle Romance Collection

Alison Reid

Torn Between Hearts – A Love Triangle Romance Collection

by Alison Reid

Copyright © 2026 Alison Reid

All rights reserved. No part of this publication may be reproduced, stored in a retrieval system, or transmitted in any form or by any means—electronic, mechanical, photocopying, recording, or otherwise—without prior written permission from the publisher, except for brief quotations used in reviews.

This is a work of fiction. Names, characters, businesses, places, events, and incidents are either the products of the author's imagination or used in a fictitious manner. Any resemblance to actual persons, living or dead, or actual events is purely coincidental.

ISBN: 978-1-7645079-1-2

First edition

Independently published

Introduction to...

Torn Between Hearts

A Love Triangle Romance Collection

Love isn't always simple.

Sometimes it doesn't arrive neatly or quietly.

Sometimes it asks you to choose.

In **Torn Between Hearts**, love is complicated by history, loyalty, and desire that refuses to be ignored. These stories are about the moments when the heart is pulled in two directions—when walking away feels just as painful as staying, and choosing love means risking everything.

Each romance in this collection explores the emotional tension of loving two men for very different reasons. A past that won't loosen its grip. A future that promises something more. A choice that must be made—not because it's easy, but because the heart demands it.

Written in the spirit of classic Mills & Boon with modern emotion and depth, these standalone romances deliver slow-burning chemistry, powerful alpha heroes, resilient heroines, and the kind of longing that lingers long after the final page.

There is no cheating.

There are no easy answers.

And every story ends with a hard-won, deeply satisfying happily-ever-after.

If you love emotionally charged romance, impossible choices, and stories where love is tested—and ultimately chosen—welcome to **Torn Between Hearts**.

Enjoy the journey.

Table of Contents

Hearts on the Line

Alison Reid

A complete standalone romance

Previously published individually

Chapter One

The mantel clock had just chimed midnight when the front door burst open with a thud, making Julia Davis jump. From the sunroom, where she'd been curled up with a novel and a blanket, came laughter—loud, slurred, unmistakably male.

She stood, set her book aside, and made her way to the foyer.

"Jesus," she muttered as Joseph stumbled in, one arm slung around the shoulders of a man who looked much steadier but equally amused.

"Jules!" Joseph grinned, arms thrown wide as he nearly tripped over the Persian rug. "You're still up? It's like old times, huh?"

"More like old headaches," she said, stepping forward just in time to stop her older brother from crashing into the hall table. "You're drunk."

"I earned it," Joseph declared, then tilted his head toward the man helping him stay upright. "Blame him. Birthday whiskey. Real expensive stuff. Burns on the way down."

"I told you to stop at three glasses," the other man said, his voice smooth—low and clipped like velvet over steel.

Julia looked up at him then. Daniel Moore.

Exactly as she remembered—and then some.

Tall and lean, dressed in a charcoal-grey suit with the top button undone and a whisper of stubble along his jaw, he looked maddeningly composed despite the hour. His dark hair curled slightly at the collar, a touch unruly compared to the rest of him. But it was his eyes that caught her the same way they always did— an impossible green, sharp and unreadable, like the forest after a storm.

"Julia." He greeted her with a nod that carried both warmth and restraint.

"Daniel." Her voice came out too soft, too careful. She tried to hide the flutter in her chest.

It had been nearly a year since she'd seen him. Maybe longer. But time hadn't dulled her reaction to him. If anything, it had made it worse. More intense. More impossible.

Joseph slumped against the wall, muttering about needing his study couch, then staggered off in that direction without further help. The hallway echoed with the sound of his retreat.

Julia crossed her arms, trying to seem unaffected. "You didn't have to bring him all the way home. I could've gotten a cab for him."

Daniel shrugged one shoulder, his gaze drifting over her in a way that made her hyper-aware of her old hoodie and bare feet. "He insisted. Besides, I owed him a birthday night."

She nodded, unsure what else to say. He was standing in her house, at her front door, and somehow, she felt like the outsider. That was Daniel—always composed, always cool. He could walk into a storm and not come out with a hair out of place.

"Guest room is made up," she said, forcing composure. "Same one as last time."

He gave a small smile, something unreadable flickering across his face. "Thanks."

He made no move to go just yet, lingering in the foyer, his hands in his pockets. There was something else in his expression—hesitation, maybe. Or curiosity.

"I like what you've done with the place," he said after a beat, glancing toward the living room.

Julia blinked. "It's mostly the same."

"No," he said, meeting her eyes for the first time since he arrived. "You've made it warmer."

Her breath caught. For a moment, it was as if the world around them dropped away. As if he saw her—not just the woman who lived here, not just Joseph's kid sister—but her.

She looked down, unsure what to say. This was dangerous territory. They had danced near it before, once or twice, but never crossed the line. Because of Joseph. Because Daniel never stayed long enough.

"You should go to bed," she said, voice thinner than she wanted. "It's late."

He nodded slowly, gaze still on her, but said nothing else as he moved past and disappeared up the staircase.

Julia stood there long after he was gone, her heart beating too fast for the silence he left behind.

The study door clicked shut, followed by a dull thump. Joseph had passed out cold—again. Julia leaned against the stair rail, exhaling as silence finally settled through the house. Her brother's birthday binge was typical but tonight had stirred more than the usual eye rolls and cleanup duties.

Daniel was here.

His presence clung to the air. That scent—cedar and something darker—lingered like a secret whispered too close, too late.

She hadn't seen him in nearly a year. Not really. Not in this house. Not where everything always felt ten shades more complicated.

He'd looked the same and entirely different: still devastatingly handsome, still impossible to read, but tired around the eyes. Older. Lonelier maybe. Or maybe she was just projecting. She always had.

God, Julia. Pull it together.

Five years. That's how long she'd been quietly, painfully in love with Daniel Moore. Her brother's best friend. The man who never stayed long, never looked too closely, never reached for her the way she so desperately wished he would.

But tonight… there'd been something different in his eyes. A flicker. A hesitation. A crack in that perfectly curated armour.

She turned off the hallway light and padded toward her bedroom, the low hum of distant traffic the only sound. The carpet was soft under her feet, and for a moment, everything felt still—peaceful, maybe.

Then she saw him.

Daniel stood at the end of the hallway, near the guest room door, his suit jacket slung over one arm. He'd undone more buttons of his shirt, exposing the hollow of his throat and the slight dip of his collarbone. His hair was messier now, one curl falling onto his forehead.

He looked… disarmed. Unshielded. Like the version of himself he never let anyone see.

"Hey," he said softly, his voice slurred just slightly at the edges. "Why are you still up?"

Julia froze. "Couldn't sleep."

He stepped closer, his green eyes catching the light from the hallway sconces. "That's a shame. You always looked peaceful when you slept."

Her heart stuttered. He remembered that? That one time she'd fallen asleep on the couch during movie night when she was twenty-five, her head accidentally resting on his shoulder. He'd said nothing the next day. She thought he hadn't even noticed.

"I didn't know you noticed," she said carefully.

"I notice everything about you, Julia," he murmured, his eyes never leaving hers.

She laughed softly, unsure whether it was disbelief or fear making her voice tremble. "You're drunk, Daniel."

He stepped closer. "Maybe but I'm not blind."

She backed up slightly, just enough to press against the wall. His arm came up beside her, resting against the doorframe like he needed it to steady himself—or maybe to trap her.

"You've changed," he said, voice low. "You used to hide behind your brother, always watching. Quiet. Sweet."

"And now?" Her voice was barely above a whisper.

He smiled, a lazy, intoxicated thing. "Now you glow."

Her breath caught. This wasn't real. He didn't say things like that. Not to her. Not unless—unless something had shifted.

She should have walked away. Told him goodnight. Kept the line drawn where it had always been.

But she didn't.

"Daniel," she said, trying to sound stern but failing. "You should get some sleep."

He leaned in, eyes flickering between hers and her mouth. "Maybe. But right now…" His voice dipped, dark and velvet smooth. "…I want to kiss you."

And then he did.

His mouth found hers—tentative, hungry, like he'd been holding his breath for five years and finally let it out in a single kiss. His hand brushed her waist, drawing her just slightly closer.

She kissed him back. There was no hesitation. No fear. Only five years of aching need unravelling in a single, breathless collision.

When he pulled back, silence rushed in. Their eyes locked, breaths unsteady, and her heartbeat thundered so loud it felt like it echoed in her bones.

Daniel blinked slowly, like waking from a dream. "That… probably shouldn't have happened."

"Probably not," she whispered, but her fingers still clung to the fabric of his shirt, curling into it like an anchor. He hadn't stepped back.

He stared at her a moment longer—then reached up, brushing his knuckles along her jaw. "But I'm not sorry."

Julia swallowed hard.

When he kissed her again—deeper this time, slower, his hands sliding to her waist—it wasn't a mistake. There was no hesitation, no blurred lines. Just heat. Hunger. Years of tension unravelling in the space of a heartbeat.

As his lips trailed to her neck, he whispered, "I've been wanting to do that for years."

A soft sound escaped her throat, and she arched into him. "Then don't stop."

His breath hitched. "Come with me."

"Where?"

He nodded toward the guest room, his hand slipping into hers. "Bedroom."

She hesitated only a second before she nodded. "Okay."

Their fingers locked, and they stumbled down the hallway together, half-laughing, half-breathless, kissing between steps—against the wall, at the edge of the doorframe—like they couldn't bear the spaces between.

By the time they reached the guest room, Daniel pushed the door open with one hand, the other already sliding up her spine. He kissed her as though he already knew how she tasted in every season of longing—how she smiled when no one was looking, how she'd always only wanted him.

Julia didn't overthink. She didn't second-guess.

She let herself fall—into his arms, into his bed, into the moment she'd dreamed of for so long.

Chapter Two

Daniel's hands were warm against her bare skin—tentative at first, like a man touching something precious for the first time. Something he'd wanted for so long he wasn't sure he had the right to want it at all.

But then Julia arched into him, soft and sure, her breath catching as if she had been waiting too—and everything inside him broke open.

His hesitation dissolved like fog under sunlight. His touch turned surer, bolder—like reverence set aflame. Like he was discovering a map he'd only ever traced in dreams, and now he needed to know every line, every curve by heart.

His fingers skimmed the soft dip of her waist, lingered on the curve of her hip, brushed upward to trace the elegant line of her ribs. He moved like a man savouring a miracle. Every stroke drew a breath from her lips, a shiver across her skin.

When their mouths met again—slower this time, deeper—it wasn't just a kiss. It was surrender. The years of denial, the tension coiled tight beneath the surface, every unsaid word—all of it melted into that moment. Nothing else existed. Not Joseph, not the rules, not the weight of what it meant.

Only them.

The heat between them unfurled in slow, insistent waves—deliberate and consuming, like a fire that had waited far too long to burn. There was no urgency, no rush. Only the aching pull of five years of restraint breaking open, inch by inch.

Whisky lingered on Daniel's tongue, bittersweet and smoky. His stubble scraped lightly along her jaw as his lips wandered—down her neck, across her collarbone, setting trails of fire in his wake. When she whispered his name, her voice trembling with want, he groaned—a low, raw sound that vibrated against her skin.

He pressed his forehead to her shoulder like he was trying to hold himself together.

"Julia…" he breathed her name like a confession, like prayer. "You have no idea what you do to me."

She didn't answer with words.

Her hands slid beneath his shirt, fingers splaying wide across his back. The heat of his skin, the strength beneath her palms—it grounded her, even as everything inside her unravelled. She tugged him closer, until there was no space left between them, only the undeniable weight of him, the certainty of this. Of him.

They undressed each other slowly, reverently—like every piece of fabric was a barrier to something sacred. With every layer that fell away, something deeper was laid bare. Trust. Desire. The kind of yearning that came not just from the body, but from the soul.

When his mouth found the soft swell of her breast, she gasped, arching into him, her fingers tightening in his hair. Her body trembled under the heat of his mouth, under the sheer intensity of his focus.

He touched her like a man starved—like each inch of her was a revelation. His hands roamed slowly, memorising, savouring, drawing sounds from her lips that she didn't know she could make. The tension built inside her, hot and coiling, until she thought she might come undone from his touch alone.

And then—he was inside her.

She gasped, the breath catching in her throat as her body stretched around him, welcomed him, knew him. It felt like release and coming home all at once. Like something that had always been waiting, just under the surface, now finally realised.

They moved together in a rhythm that felt inevitable—like gravity had always been pulling them here. Julia wrapped her legs around his waist, her nails dragging down his back, pleasure rising inside her in waves, relentless and sweet.

"Tell me you want this," Daniel murmured, his voice rough with restraint, eyes locked on hers.

She didn't hesitate.

"I've always wanted you," she whispered, the words trembling with everything she'd held in for so long.

His mouth found hers again, rougher now, driven by the need between them—and when she came, it hit her like a wave breaking against the shore. Her body arched beneath his, every nerve alight, every thought swept away by the intensity of it.

Daniel followed with a shudder, a groan torn from somewhere deep, his body sinking into hers like he was finally letting himself feel.

Afterward, they didn't speak.

He pulled her close, tucking her against him as if afraid she might vanish. One hand rested low on her back, the other curled in her hair, his breath warm against her neck. His body was still damp with sweat, heavy with exhaustion, but his hold on her never loosened.

He drifted first, breathing slow, steady, content.

Julia stayed awake.

She lay there, her fingers drawing soft, invisible shapes against his chest, memorising the feel of his heartbeat beneath her cheek. The scent of him was on her skin—salt and musk and something uniquely Daniel. In the hush of the guest room, with the night pressing close around them, she let herself believe—just for this one stolen night—that maybe this was a beginning.

That maybe he'd finally seen her.

The way she had always seen him.

Later, when he slept beside her, chest rising in slow, steady breaths, Julia lay with her head on his shoulder and let the quiet wrap around them. His arm curled around her waist like instinct. She wanted to bottle this moment. Keep it. Replay it.

She smiled into the dark.

It had finally happened.

Five years of loving him in silence. Of watching him drift in and out of her life like a beautiful storm. And now… this. Something real. Something impossible and perfect.

She turned her face into the curve of his chest. Remembered.

It had started quietly, years earlier. She was twenty-two the first time she realised she was falling for Daniel Moore. It was at Joseph's engagement party—one of the extravagant, over-catered affairs he loved throwing for women who never lasted long.

Julia had been helping in the kitchen, balancing a tray of cocktails with the precision of a tightrope walker, when she spotted Daniel across the room. A redhead hung off his arm—glamorous, dripping in gold, and laughing like she owned the night. Julia doubted the woman even knew her name.

Daniel, in contrast, looked bored. Impeccably dressed in a navy suit that fit him like a second skin, he stood still amid the swirl of conversation, his glass of whiskey untouched. His jaw was tight, his posture polite but distant. He wasn't listening—not really. Not to the woman. Not to the noise.

And then he looked up.

Their eyes met across the crowd, a flicker of recognition threading between them. And he smiled.

Not the lazy, charming smirk he usually wore for effect—but something else. Smaller. Quieter. Real. Like a secret passed through a crowded room meant only for her.

Her hand tightened around the tray, and something in her chest tilted off its axis.

That was the moment she knew.

Not just that she was falling. That she already had. Her heart had never been the same since.

She was twenty-four the summer he taught her to drive stick.

They were out near the edge of the Moore family property—an empty, winding stretch of dirt road surrounded by gumtrees and silence. The old Land Cruiser sputtered and jolted every time she tried to shift gears. Ten minutes in, she flooded the engine.

Daniel laughed, pulling off his sunglasses with a slow shake of his head. "You're trying too hard," he said, that familiar tease in his voice. "You're gripping the wheel like it's a wild animal."

She huffed, cheeks flushed. "It feels like one."

He leaned over then—close enough for her to smell the mint on his breath, the warm spice of his cologne—and gently adjusted her grip. His hand closed over hers, steady and calm.

"Let go," he murmured. "You don't need to control everything. Just trust it'll move forward when it's ready."

She hadn't realised he was talking about more than cars until years later. But the way he looked at her then—calm, unflinching, a hint of something unreadable behind those impossible green eyes—had stayed with her ever since.

And when she was twenty-five, she got the flu.

A brutal, aching, body-wrecking kind that left her wrapped in blankets and too weak to reach the kettle. Joseph was somewhere in the Alps with his latest distraction, out of reception and utterly unreachable.

She hadn't expected anyone to come. But Daniel did.

He showed up on the second day, grumbling about airborne contagions, armed with ginger tea, homemade soup, and enough medication to stock a pharmacy.

He stayed. Sat with her through hours of bad television and even worse movies, one foot propped on the coffee table, arms folded as if he wasn't emotionally invested—until she caught him mouthing the lines to The Princess Bride.

At some point, her fever dragged her under. She drifted off mid-movie, her head accidentally finding his shoulder.

When she woke in the middle of the night—sweaty, shivering, disoriented—his arm was around her. Protective. Solid. Like he'd been there the whole time, just in case.

He never mentioned it again.

And neither did she.

But sometimes, when she was alone, she could still feel that quiet moment in the dark. The weight of him beside her. The impossible hope in her chest that maybe—just maybe—he'd stayed because he wanted to.

Now, in the dim glow of morning, Julia looked at the man beside her and let herself hope.

Daniel had kissed her like he meant it. Touched her like he'd wanted to for years. Maybe Joseph had been wrong. Maybe Daniel wasn't incapable of love—maybe he was just afraid.

But last night, he hadn't been afraid. He'd been hers.

For once, she hadn't been the younger sister, the girl he'd overlooked, the one Joseph always protected. She'd been a woman—a woman Daniel wanted.

And maybe, just maybe, he wanted more.

She slid carefully from the bed, brushing a curl from his forehead as he murmured something in his sleep. He didn't wake.

She lingered in the doorway for a moment, watching him. Naked, tangled in the sheets, brow furrowed in some dream she couldn't follow.

She kissed her fingertips and pressed them to the doorframe.

"Don't screw this up," she whispered, not sure if she meant him—or herself.

And then she left, barefoot and hopeful.

Chapter Three

Daniel woke to the pale gold hush of morning—the kind of light that softened edges and slowed time, like the world itself was still asleep. The room was warm with the residue of sleep and something sweeter—floral, faintly spiced, unmistakably feminine. It clung to the sheets, lingered on his skin, curled in the air like a memory he couldn't quite hold onto.

His body ached in that delicious, slow-burning way that only followed something good. Something real. His limbs were heavy, sated. Like he'd been wrapped in heat, touched deeply, held tightly.

For a long moment, he didn't move. He lay still, eyes half-lidded, letting the sensation hum through him. There was a calm in his chest—strange and unexpected. No hangover. No regret. Just… contentment.

His arm curved naturally to the side, searching—

Nothing.

The space beside him was empty. Sheets tangled and creased, the other pillow faintly indented, holding the trace of someone who'd once been there. And that scent again—vanilla and jasmine, maybe. Soft. Intimate. Familiar in a way that made his breath catch.

He inhaled deeply, trying to draw the memory into focus. But it stayed maddeningly out of reach.

Still, his body remembered.

Flashes sparked at the edges of his mind like the remnants of a dream—warm skin beneath his hands, the press of a trembling voice against his throat, a sigh that sounded like surrender. His name whispered like it meant something.

Julia.

He remembered seeing her last night—really seeing her—for the first time in over a year. She'd always been beautiful, but now… now there was something more. A quiet strength in the set of her shoulders, a confidence behind her dark eyes that hadn't been there before. She looked like a woman who knew exactly who she was—and it had undone him.

He'd always noticed her. Even when he shouldn't.

Especially when he shouldn't.

Joseph had made his stance crystal clear. "She's not a fling," he'd warned. "She is my sister." As if that should've stopped Daniel. As if it had.

But Daniel wasn't blind. Or numb. He'd thought about Julia more times than he'd admit. Imagined what it would be like to pull her close, kiss her breathless, strip that carefully guarded sweetness down to something raw and real.

And last night…

Had he dreamt it again? Maybe. It wouldn't be the first time.

He remembered the way she'd looked—barefoot, flushed from laughter, soft in the glow of lamplight. So close. So damn close. But that had to be where the night had ended. *Didn't it?*

Still, the sensations clung to him like truth. Heat. Softness. The curve of a body pressed perfectly against his. Her mouth—open beneath his. Her breath—a shiver across his skin. Real. Too real.

He frowned and sat up slowly, the sheet slipping low around his hips, cool air brushing across bare skin. The room was silent. No soft breathing. No lingering warmth. Just the unmistakable absence of someone who should have been there.

He dragged a hand over his face, the unease finally catching up to the calm.

He should feel worse. Should be nursing a headache, or guilt, or that usual morning-after detachment that followed nights he couldn't remember. But instead, there was only this strange, steady quiet inside him—like something fundamental had shifted without his permission.

And still… it made no sense.

If anything had really happened—if he'd touched her the way his body insisted, he had—wouldn't she still be here? Wouldn't she have said something? Left something? A note, a sign, anything at all?

No. He must have dreamt it. It had to be just another fantasy—sharper than usual, more vivid than he'd ever dared allow.

But God, it felt *real.*

The dreams about Julia were getting harder to shake. More dangerous.

He scrubbed both hands over his face.

Joseph would kill him if he knew what he had been thinking. What he still thought about. What he wanted. What he couldn't have.

The scent of coffee hit Daniel first—freshly brewed, rich, grounding. He followed it down the hall, dragging one hand through his hair, still barefoot, the hem of his T-shirt sticking slightly to his skin. He felt… better than he had any right to. Better than he could explain.

The kitchen was warm with morning light and the low hum of something cooking. Julia stood at the stove, her back to him, wearing a soft green sweater that dipped low on one shoulder and a pair of loose cotton shorts that made his mouth go dry.

She turned when she heard him, and her face—God—lit up like sunrise. Pure, open joy.

"Morning," she said, her voice a little shy, a little sweet. "You're up early."

Daniel smiled, something easy and automatic. "Smelled coffee."

She laughed, the sound soft and hopeful. "I made extra. Figured you'd need it after last night."

He paused, leaning against the doorway, arms crossed over his chest. "Yeah. About that…" He rubbed the back of his neck. "I, uh… don't remember much. Must've hit the whiskey harder than I thought."

Julia's smile faltered—just a flicker, a crack—but enough to make his stomach tighten.

"Oh," she said. Just that. Soft. Thin.

He frowned slightly, watching her more closely. "Did I say anything embarrassing? I remember us talking for a bit when we came in. You looked…" He trailed off, unsure how to finish the sentence without sounding like a creep.

Beautiful. Touchable. Everything he shouldn't want.

"You don't remember?" she asked—soft, thin, like hope folding in on itself. No accusation. No bitterness. Just… breathless disbelief.

Daniel blinked. "Not really. Just flashes. Vague stuff."

Julia turned away quickly, fiddling with the heat on the stove, even though the eggs were already done. Her hands moved too fast, too precise, like she needed them to be busy.

"I see," she murmured. "You were pretty out of it."

Daniel stepped closer, sensing the shift, though he couldn't name it. "Did I do something stupid?"

There was a long pause before she answered, her back still to him.

"No," she said quietly. "You didn't do anything at all."

She plated the eggs without looking at him, her hands steady now, detached. Her earlier joy—gone. Folded away like it had never existed.

But Daniel felt it. The echo of it. The emptiness that had taken its place.

She passed him a plate without meeting his eyes. "Here. Eat before it gets cold."

He took it slowly, watching her with something hollow gnawing at his chest. She was pulling away. Folding into herself. And he didn't know why.

Because if nothing happened…, why did it feel like he'd just broken something?

The silence between them stretched. Daniel sat with the plate untouched in front of him, fork resting against the edge, his eyes still fixed on Julia.

She didn't look at him. She poured herself a cup of coffee with slow, careful precision, every movement deliberate. Controlled. But he could feel the distance. And it unsettled him more than it should.

And then—

"God damn," came a groan from the hallway. "Who let a truck run me over in my sleep?"

Joseph stumbled into the kitchen, shirtless, his jeans half-buttoned, his eyes squinting against the light like it personally offended him. He made a beeline for the coffee pot, muttering curses under his breath, and poured himself a mug so full it sloshed over the side.

"Morning, sunshine," Daniel said, a little too dry.

"Go to hell," Joseph muttered, taking a gulp like it was medicine. "You could've warned me about that last bottle, man. I can feel my liver filing a restraining order."

Julia gave a brittle laugh—too bright, too fast—and turned toward the sink, mug clutched tightly in both hands.

Joseph didn't seem to notice. He turned, squinting blearily between the two of them. "Why're you both up so early? And why's the air in here so thick?"

Daniel forced a smirk. "That's just your hangover-induced paranoia. Go take a shower."

Joseph ignored him, instead dropping into a chair with a loud groan. "Nope. I live here now. Right here. On this chair. This is my new home."

Daniel chuckled, grateful for the distraction. "I'll mail you your bills."

Julia stood frozen at the sink for a beat too long before she spoke. "I'm going to go… check on the laundry," she said, voice light and pleasant and utterly false.

Neither man answered as she slipped out of the kitchen. But the moment she disappeared around the corner, Daniel's gaze followed her—worried, confused, heavy with questions he didn't know how to ask.

Joseph noticed this time. He narrowed his eyes at Daniel over the rim of his mug.

"What's with that look?"

Daniel shook his head, reaching for his fork again. "Nothing. Just… think I said something wrong last night."

Joseph raised a brow. "To Julia?"

Daniel didn't answer, but the tension in his jaw did.

Joseph grunted, leaning back in his chair. "Well, as long as you didn't touch her, you'll live. She's a big girl. But she's also my little sister. You know the line, man. Don't cross it."

Daniel didn't look up. He speared a piece of egg and tried not to think about warmth, or jasmine, or the aching sense of something lost that he couldn't quite name.

He chewed, swallowed.

Then lied.

"Yeah. Of course. Nothing happened."

Joseph leaned back in his chair with a grunt, stretching one arm across the backrest, the other cradling his mug like it was the only thing keeping him alive.

"God, Jules makes good coffee," he muttered. "Always has. Girl could sweet-talk a bean into roasting itself."

Daniel offered a low laugh, but his heart wasn't in it. His eyes drifted again to the doorway Julia had disappeared through, his thoughts tangled and restless.

Joseph caught the glance and narrowed his eyes, the humour draining from his face. "You good, man?"

"Yeah." Daniel's voice was too quick, too neutral.

Joseph's brow rose, suspicious. "Because you're acting weird. Like… I dunno. Like you've seen a ghost. Or you're about to confess something I'm not gonna like."

Daniel met his gaze then, the briefest flicker of guilt flashing in his eyes before he masked it with a shrug. "I told you; I think I said something wrong last night. She seemed—off."

Joseph gave a half-snort. "She's always off around you."

That landed heavier than expected.

Daniel leaned back in his chair, arms crossed over his chest, suddenly tired of pretending. "You think I don't notice how she looks at me sometimes?"

Joseph went still.

"Don't start," he warned.

"I'm not starting anything," Daniel said. "I'm just saying… she's not a kid anymore."

"I know she's not a kid," Joseph snapped. "Believe me, I've been watching guys stare at her like she's a walking goddamn temptation ever since she turned twenty. But you? You're different."

Daniel arched a brow. "Different how?"

Joseph ran a hand through his hair, exhaling hard. "Because I trust you. Because you know better. Because you've seen what kind of wreckage you leave behind when you screw up. And I won't let her be another casualty."

Daniel flinched, the words cutting deeper than Joseph probably meant.

"I'm not that guy anymore," he said quietly.

Joseph looked at him then—really looked. "Aren't you?"

There was a long silence between them.

Heavy.

Honest.

Daniel's jaw worked. He wanted to say no. He wanted to swear he wasn't still haunted by past mistakes or hiding from real connection. But the truth sat like lead in his chest.

He wanted Julia.

He'd wanted her for a long time.

But she was Joseph's sister. And Joseph was the one person who had never turned his back on him, even at his worst.

"I haven't touched her," Daniel said at last.

Joseph nodded slowly. "Good. Keep it that way."

But Daniel couldn't help the thought that clawed its way up anyway—

What if he already had?

Chapter Four

Julia leaned against the bathroom sink, hands braced on either side, trying to breathe through the hollow bloom in her chest.

She stared at her reflection—eyes wide, rimmed with confusion. Her mouth was still red from where he'd kissed her last night, from where she'd whispered yes against his skin. From where she'd finally, finally let go of everything she'd held back for so long.

But this morning…

Daniel hadn't remembered.

Not the way his hand had cradled her face like she was something precious.

Not the way he'd whispered her name like a secret.

Not the way they'd moved together, breathless and bare, like they'd been trying to erase all the time they'd lost.

He'd looked at her with that easy smile, the same one he wore when talking to strangers. Safe. Uncomplicated. Forgettable.

Her chest tightened.

Forgettable.

That word rang loud in her head, louder than she wanted to admit. He'd touched her like she meant something—but woke up like it had meant nothing at all.

Julia turned on the cold tap and let the water run over her fingers, trying to ground herself. But her skin still hummed with the memory of him. Her skin still hummed where he'd touched her, her heart still fluttering with the lie she'd told herself in the dark.

That maybe this time, it would be different.

That maybe, if he finally saw her—not just as Joseph's kid sister or someone to protect, but as a woman—he'd stay.

But instead, he'd erased her.

The worst part? He'd been gentle. He hadn't dismissed her with cruelty or arrogance. He'd dismissed her with kindness. As if she were fragile. As if he didn't even realise what he was doing.

That kindness cut deeper than any coldness ever could.

She grabbed a towel, drying her hands with more force than necessary, jaw clenched tight against the sting behind her eyes.

She wouldn't cry. Not over Daniel Moore.

Not again.

She'd spent too many years watching him chase women he didn't care about, too many birthdays, too many Sunday dinners pretending she didn't feel a spark every time he looked at her. And now—after one night that had felt like everything—he was already pretending it hadn't happened.

Fine.

If that was how he wanted to play it, she could do that too.

She folded the towel neatly and placed it on the edge of the sink. Squared her shoulders. Raised her chin.

He doesn't remember.

Then she'd make damn sure he would never know she did.

The quiet hum of a car pulling into the driveway broke the late morning stillness. Julia glanced up from her spot in the living room, where she'd been trying—and failing—to read the same page for half an hour.

The front door creaked open, followed by the familiar voice of the housekeeper, Lorna, announcing her return with a brisk, "Morning, dears! Hope you didn't burn the place down while I was gone!"

Julia managed a faint smile as Lorna bustled into the kitchen with the practiced efficiency of someone who'd been running the Davis household for over a decade. The comforting clatter of groceries being unpacked and water set to boil for tea helped steady Julia's frayed nerves, but only just.

Because Daniel was still here.

Still wandering the halls with that maddening air of ease, like the night they'd shared hadn't happened. Like she was the only one who remembered. The only one who felt undone.

She hadn't spoken to him since that morning. She couldn't.

She didn't trust what might come out of her mouth—anger, heartbreak, or worse, hope.

She heard her brother's voice rumble from the hallway as he entered the kitchen. "Hey, Lorna. You're just in time. Julia nearly poisoned me yesterday."

"Lies," Julia called automatically, without looking up.

Joseph chuckled and made his way into the living room, leaning against the doorframe with a familiar, lazy grin. He looked better than this morning—less hungover, more like himself—but he was still rubbing the back of his neck like it ached. "Hey, just a heads-up. Daniel's going to be staying a while."

Julia stiffened, her eyes finally lifting. "What?"

Joseph shrugged. "His penthouse is getting gutted—full reno. Some leak turned into a mould situation. Place is unliveable for the next couple months."

Julia opened her mouth, closed it again.

Two. Months.

She gave a tight nod, eyes returning to her book. "Fine."

Joseph studied her for a beat, his easy expression dimming. "You okay?"

"Of course," she said, too quickly.

He didn't push. Just ruffled her hair like he used to when she was ten and walked back into the kitchen.

Not long after, the sound of an engine stirred outside—deep, expensive, and unmistakably familiar.

Julia rose and stepped out onto the porch, blinking into the sun as a sleek black Jaguar pulled up the winding driveway of the Davis estate. A tall figure stepped out with careless grace, dark hair tousled by the wind, a crooked smile spreading across his face.

"James Giles," she said under her breath.

Her childhood friend—once all sharp elbows, muddy shoes, and mischievous grins—now moved with the polish of inherited wealth and the quiet authority of someone who'd never had to prove himself. The wild boy who used to dare her to climb trees and race bikes through the orchard had traded denim for designer, his lean frame now filled out by tailored suits and the easy confidence of old money.

He lived in the estate next door—Giles Manor, with its manicured hedges and too-perfect gravel drive—though she hadn't seen him much since she'd returned. The past twelve months had been a whirlwind of deadlines and daydreams in Brisbane, working long hours as an illustrator for a children's publishing house. It had been good work, meaningful in its own quiet way, but exhausting too. Coming home was supposed to be a breather. A pause. Not a heartache.

"Jules!" James called, striding across the lawn with that same unshakable swagger she remembered from childhood. His voice carried easily on the breeze, familiar as the sound of cicadas in summer. "Heard you were back. Thought I'd come see if you still remember the boy who used to push you in the creek."

Julia's lips lifted despite herself. "Vividly," she said. "Only every time I find sand in my ears."

He reached her, eyes crinkling as he looked her over. "You look… different. Good different."

They wandered into the garden side by side, the familiar rhythm between them settling in as easily as slipping into a well-worn coat. The late afternoon sun stretched long shadows over the lawn, and the scent of jasmine drifted on the breeze. Julia spoke with quiet animation, telling James about her work in Brisbane—the long hours spent sketching storybook creatures, the bustle of the city, and how what was meant to be a short break back home had stretched into something slower… more uncertain.

James listened with an attentiveness she remembered well. He didn't interrupt. He never had. And that steady presence—his ability to make the world quiet around him—was something she hadn't realised she'd missed.

As they rounded the curved path near the rose garden, the low murmur of voices and a burst of laughter drifted from the patio. Julia's steps faltered. Joseph and Daniel were seated in the shade, beers in hand, their ease and familiarity unmistakable. Daniel looked relaxed—sunlight catching the edge of his jaw, his eyes lifting just in time to find hers.

Julia's smile vanished.

She didn't know what she'd expected—an apology, maybe. A moment of recognition. But there was nothing in his gaze but polite surprise. Distant. Detached. As if last night had never happened.

"Is that Daniel Moore?" James asked, following her line of sight. His voice was low, but the tension in it was unmistakable. "Does he still think he owns the world?"

She didn't answer right away.

"Yes," she said finally. "He's staying here. For a while."

James's head snapped toward her. "Why?" he asked, sharper than before.

"His penthouse is being renovated."

James's jaw tightened just slightly, but his smile didn't slip. Not yet.

"There are hotels," James said flatly, his brow furrowing. "Plenty of them."

Julia folded her arms across her chest, the warmth from before draining away. "You think I had a choice in it?"

James studied her face. "You didn't invite him?"

"No." Her voice cracked a little on the word, and she cleared her throat. "Joseph did."

They stood in silence for a beat, the distance between them suddenly full of unspoken things. Julia looked down at the gravel path, then back toward the patio. Daniel had turned away, laughing at something Joseph said, and it hurt more than she cared to admit.

"I don't care about him anymore," she said softly, though it didn't sound convincing even to her own ears.

James didn't press her. He just opened his arms.

Julia hesitated only a second before stepping into them, letting herself be folded into the warmth of an old friendship. His embrace was steady, grounding—safe in a way she hadn't felt since last night. She closed her eyes and exhaled slowly, telling herself it was just comfort. That it didn't matter that Daniel hadn't remembered. That it didn't matter he hadn't looked back.

But her heart told a different story.

And James, with his arms wrapped tight around her, might have known it too.

Chapter Five

Daniel leaned back in the patio chair, the cold bite of beer barely registering on his tongue. The sun was beginning its slow descent, throwing honeyed light across the yard. Joseph was in full storyteller mode—something about a broken fence and a runaway goat from one of the neighbors' properties. Daniel chuckled at the right moment, but his eyes were elsewhere.

Locked on her.

Julia.

She was in the garden with someone—tall, polished, wearing confidence like an accessory. Daniel didn't recognise him at first, but then the guy turned slightly, and it clicked.

James Giles. The childhood friend. The neighbour.

The competition.

Daniel's fingers tightened around his bottle.

They looked… easy together. Like no time had passed. Like the last year of silence hadn't happened. Like she wasn't the girl who'd been haunting the edges of his thoughts more than he cared to admit. And when James opened his arms and Julia stepped into them without hesitation, something sharp twisted in Daniel's chest.

Jealousy wasn't an emotion he entertained often. Usually, if someone wanted something he had, he let them try to take it—confident they wouldn't succeed. But this was different. Julia wasn't something to be possessed.

She was—

She was his regret.

One he couldn't stop thinking about.

"Careful," Joseph said beside him, voice casual but knowing. "You keep scowling like that, people'll think you've got a problem."

Daniel didn't look at him. "I do have a problem," he muttered. "That guy's a prick."

Joseph let out a short laugh. "He's harmless."

"No. He's calculated." Daniel's tone sharpened. "And way too eager to wrap his arms around your sister."

Joseph's smile faded. His mouth hardened. "So what? You've got a problem with James now?"

Daniel finally turned to face him. "I'm saying I don't think he's good for her."

Joseph leaned back, expression unreadable. "And you are?"

Daniel said nothing. The unspoken accusation sat heavy between them.

"Look," Joseph said more quietly, "Julia's a grown woman. She can decide who's good for her or not. If she wants to make things official with James, I wouldn't be surprised. They've known each other forever."

Daniel's jaw flexed. "That would be a mistake."

Joseph snorted. "And why's that, huh? Because you suddenly care?"

Daniel looked back to the garden. Julia had stepped away from James now, her hand brushing his arm as they laughed about something. The sound of it drifted across the lawn and curled tight in his gut.

"I'm just saying she deserves better," he said lowly.

Joseph gave him a long look, then set his beer down with a quiet clink.

"No," he said. "You don't get to say that. You don't get to play protector when you've never been the guy who stays. You treat women like options, Daniel. Julia's not that."

"I know," Daniel said, voice tight.

"Do you?" Joseph leaned forward, eyes hard. "Because I mean it—she is off-limits. Always has been. You want to chase models and heiresses and bored divorcées, go for it. But not her. Not my sister."

The silence stretched, brittle and dangerous.

Daniel looked down at the condensation trailing his bottle. His throat felt dry, despite the beer.

"Understood," he said.

But the flicker in his chest—the defiance, the ache, the memory of her skin beneath his hands—didn't go away.

And he wasn't sure he could pretend forever.

The garden path crunched under Julia's sandals as she and James made their way toward the patio. Jasmine floated on the cooling breeze, and the sky was flushed in orange blush. From a distance, Daniel and Joseph looked relaxed—drinks in hand, easy laughter fading as she approached.

But she felt it the second Daniel looked up.

That tension. Immediate. Coiled.

His eyes locked on hers for just a moment, then flicked to James, narrowing. His posture shifted—subtle, but unmistakable. The lazy sprawl stiffened into something alert.

Annoyed.

She ignored it.

"Gentlemen," James greeted, smiling smoothly, always a breath away from smug. "Hope we're not interrupting the riveting goat story."

Joseph grinned. "James Giles. Still allergic to fun?"

"I'm plenty fun," James replied, slipping a hand into his pocket. "Just selective."

Joseph barked a laugh. "Want a drink?"

"No thanks. I'm actually here for something else."

Daniel watched him carefully, his expression unreadable—but cold.

James turned to Julia. "I was hoping to steal Jules away for dinner. Thought she might be tired of eating with her brother."

Her heart jumped—half nerves, half impulse—but she didn't hesitate.

"Sure," she said lightly. "Why not?"

Daniel's jaw ticked.

Joseph gave a low whistle. "Look at that. She said yes. Careful, mate, you might have to actually try."

James grinned at her, then flicked his eyes—deliberately—to Daniel. "I don't mind a little competition."

Julia didn't miss the way Daniel's grip tightened on his beer bottle, knuckles white. His eyes stayed on her now, sharp with something too complex to name.

Regret? Jealousy? Possessiveness?

Whatever it was, she refused to let it sway her.

"Pick me up at seven?" she asked James, tone breezy—as if Daniel's presence didn't matter. As if the weight of his gaze didn't make her heart race.

James nodded. "It's a date."

As he walked off with confident swagger, Joseph nudged Daniel with a smirk. "You don't like him, do you?"

Daniel didn't answer.

Julia didn't stay to hear what he might say. She turned and walked inside without a backward glance.

If he didn't remember what happened between them, then he didn't get to be angry.

Not now. Not ever.

Upstairs, Julia stood in front of the mirror, smoothing the cream dress over her hips. It clung in all the right places—sophisticated, elegant—but with a whisper of defiance.

She wasn't dressing for anyone.

Or so she told herself.

Her long chestnut hair fell in soft waves, freshly brushed and touched with gloss that caught the lamplight. Her brown eyes—usually kind, open—were lined tonight in smoky bronze. Unreadable.

For once, she wanted to be seen. Not overlooked. Not forgotten.

She misted jasmine along her collarbone—soft, familiar, unmistakably hers. The same scent that had lingered in Daniel's bed the night he forgot everything.

The doorbell rang downstairs—sharp, punctual. James was right on time.

Her heart fluttered—half nerves, half anticipation—but she lifted her chin and stepped into the hallway.

Daniel was there.

Leaning against the balustrade like he'd been waiting. His gaze swept over her—slow, stunned, far too intimate. For a moment, neither of them spoke.

Then he straightened, blocking her path.

"You look…" His voice caught. "Nice."

She raised a brow. "Thanks."

He hesitated. "Just… be careful with James, okay?"

Julia blinked. Then a bitter laugh slipped out. "Seriously?"

"I'm not joking, Julia. He's not who you think he is."

"And you are?" she shot back, stepping past him.

His hand curled gently—but firmly—around her arm.

"Don't go," he said, voice low. "Not with him."

Something in her snapped. She yanked her arm away.

"You don't get to say that," she hissed. "Not after the way you treat women."

His mouth parted, as if to protest—but he didn't. Couldn't.

Her voice softened but cut deeper. "You don't care. But you want to protect me?"

"I just—"

"No, Daniel." She turned away. "You don't get to care halfway."

She descended the stairs without another word, heels clicking against polished timber.

At the front door, James was waiting—smile in place, keys in hand.

And Daniel?

He was still standing at the top of the stairs.

Fists clenched.

Watching her go.

Chapter Six

The restaurant James chose was tucked behind a row of heritage buildings—charming, candlelit, quiet. The kind of place where couples lingered over shared desserts and fingers brushed across white tablecloths. Julia recognised the atmosphere for what it was.

Intentional.

She followed the maître d' to a corner booth, heels soft on the plush carpet. James walked beside her, that easy smile in place—the one that had always been just a little too sure of itself.

"Hope you're hungry," he said as they sat. "They do the best lamb in the state. Maybe the country."

"I thought you said you were *selective* about your fun," she teased, scanning the menu.

"I am. That's why I only bring beautiful women to places I actually like."

Julia arched a brow. "Smooth."

He winked. "Effective?"

She didn't answer—just smiled, then turned her focus to the wine list.

Over the course of the meal, James was everything Julia remembered from their childhood—witty, polite, well-read, and comfortable. He filled the silences with light stories, teased her gently when she ordered dessert before finishing her meal, and asked her questions that made her feel seen. Respected.

And yet… something in her stayed cautious. Not because of anything James had done—but everything he wasn't.

He wasn't Daniel.

James reached across the table, brushing his knuckles against hers.

"I've really missed this, Jules."

She looked up, startled from her thoughts. "What?"

"This," he said, nodding toward their empty plates and shared laughter. "Time with you. We were always good together, weren't we?"

Julia offered a cautious smile. "We were kids, James."

"Sure," he agreed. "But we grew up. And now… I think maybe it's time we stopped pretending this doesn't mean something." He paused, then leaned forward, voice gentler. "I want to date you, Julia. Seriously. No pressure, no games—I just want to see where this could really go."

Her fork stilled on the plate. She wasn't surprised. The signs had been there—his attentiveness, the lingering touches, the way he looked at her like she was already his.

But the weight of his words still landed.

She hesitated.

Not because James wasn't wonderful. He was. He was exactly the kind of man any woman with sense would want.

But she wasn't any woman.

And lately, she hadn't had much sense.

Still, she reached for her wine glass, took a slow sip, then met his eyes with quiet honesty.

"We'll see where it goes."

James smiled—wide, bright, and deeply satisfied. He reached for her hand again, this time with confidence.

"That's all I ask."

Later that evening, the drive back to her family home was quiet, but easy. James had one hand on the wheel, the other resting casually on the gearshift. Soft jazz drifted through the car—something smooth and old-school—and Julia leaned her head against the window, watching the familiar streets slip by in a blur of headlights and moonlight.

When they pulled into the driveway, the porch light cast a golden glow over the front steps. James got out without a word and walked her to the door. There was no rush, no pressure—just the calm comfort of someone who knew her history and wanted to be part of her future.

She opened the front door, stepped inside, then turned back to face him.

"Thanks again. Dinner was lovely."

"I had a really good time tonight," James said, his voice low and sincere.

"Me too," Julia replied, and she meant it.

He held her gaze for a beat longer, then leaned in—slowly, deliberately—his eyes dropping to her lips before returning to hers. He was giving her a chance to pull away. She didn't.

The kiss that followed was soft at first, tentative. His hand rose to her cheek, warm and steady, and the kiss deepened—still gentle, still unhurried. Affectionate. Earnest.

But when his fingers slid toward the curve of her jaw, brushing skin that still remembered someone else's touch, something inside her recoiled.

Julia pulled back.

James paused, searching her face. He wasn't angry. Just surprised.

"Too soon?" he asked, voice a quiet murmur.

She nodded, breath catching. "Just… not tonight."

His smile returned, softer now, touched with patience. "Whenever you're ready."

She offered a small nod, grateful. "Thank you."

He stepped back, reluctant but composed, the pause between them stretching like a question neither wanted to ask.

"Text me when you're free again?"

"I will," she said, her voice barely above a whisper.

She watched him retreat down the path, then gently closed the door behind him. The latch clicked softly into place, echoing through the stillness of the hallway.

A silence that wasn't entirely hers.

Not anymore.

Unseen by James—but not by her.

Because Julia knew, even before she looked up, that they weren't alone.

Daniel stood on the balcony above, half-swallowed by shadow, arms crossed, jaw set tight. Watching.

Their eyes locked—just for a moment, but it was a moment too long.

His expression didn't shift. He didn't say a word.

But the silence?

It screamed.

Julia exhaled slowly, gathering herself, then started up the stairs.

He was still there when she reached the landing.

"Did you have a nice time?" he asked, voice low and strained.

"I did, thank you." She moved to walk past him.

His hand shot out, not rough, but firm—stopping her.

"Don't go out with him again."

Julia stilled. Then met his gaze, calm but unwavering.

"James and I are dating now."

The words landed with quiet finality. And though her voice was soft, they cut deeper than a shout.

Daniel didn't respond right away. Just looked at her, like he was trying to find something he hadn't realised he'd lost—until now.

She stepped past him without another word.

This time, she didn't look back.

Daniel watched her go.

Her words echoed in his chest like the crack of a door slamming shut. 'James and I are dating now.'

He didn't move. Didn't speak. Couldn't.

The hallway light cast soft golden edges across the top of the staircase, where Julia's silhouette disappeared into the dark. And yet Daniel stood frozen—still tasting the bitterness of that moment, of how final it had felt. Not angry. Not loud. Just… done.

She hadn't said it to provoke him.

That was the worst part.

She meant it.

His fingers flexed at his sides. He could still see her standing at the door, flushed from the night, lips slightly parted from James's kiss. A kiss that should never have happened.

Not because James wasn't good enough.

But because he wasn't ready. And she'd stopped waiting.

Daniel pressed a hand to the back of his neck, trying to breathe past the ache building behind his ribs. This wasn't jealousy. This wasn't possession.

This was loss.

And he had no one to blame but himself.

Julia closed her bedroom door behind her with a quiet click.

The room was dim—lamplight golden, soft—but her pulse still hadn't settled.

She leaned back against the door for a moment; heart beating faster than it should have. From James's kiss. From Daniel's eyes. From the minefield she'd just walked through.

She wasn't angry.

Just tired.

Tired of feeling like she had to defend her choices. Like every step toward healing was some silent betrayal.

But tonight, had felt good. James had been kind, respectful, thoughtful—everything Daniel used to be before he became cold and closed-off. And it had been real. Not fireworks and chaos—but quiet comfort. Gentle warmth.

And yet, standing in the stillness of her room, she didn't feel quite as steady as she wanted to.

She crossed to the dresser, touched the edge of the frame that held an old photo—her, Joseph, and Daniel, taken one summer long ago. Back when everything had been simpler.

Her reflection stared back at her in the glass—older now, sharper around the edges.

You made a choice, she reminded herself.

But that didn't stop her from whispering into the empty room:

"I wish he remembered their night together."

Chapter Seven

Three weeks. That's how long James had been orbiting closer—texts, dinners, that ever-tightening presence.

Daniel had asked her—more than once—to stop seeing him. His words had ranged from calm to clipped, but Julia had refused to engage. She hadn't answered him then, and she still wasn't answering him now.

Instead, she let James in.

And James, once merely attentive, had started inserting himself more and more into the corners of her life.

More messages. More calls. More casual "Just thinking of you" drop-ins that always aligned a little too perfectly with her schedule. Her lunch breaks, her errands, even her standing coffee run. At first, it had felt flattering. After so long feeling overlooked by the one man who made her feel everything and nothing at once, part of her had clung to the steady warmth James offered. Needed it, maybe.

But even comfort, when poured too generously, could start to feel like drowning.

"This place just opened last week," James said, steering her by the elbow toward a sleek café tucked beneath a canopy of flowering gums. His hand was light, but there was insistence behind the gesture. "Thought it'd be fun. Just us."

Julia smiled, polite and practiced. "Didn't you have meetings today?"

He waved the question away like a pesky fly. "Pushed them. You're more important."

She didn't argue, but the words lodged in her ribs like a splinter. She wasn't used to being prioritised. And yet, the way he said it—like she was a reward, not a choice—made her stomach twist.

The café was charming. The food was fine. The conversation flowed easily enough. James was charming, no question—witty, observant, good at making people feel like they were the centre of his orbit. But every time her phone buzzed—once from Joseph, twice from Mary—he glanced toward the screen before she could. Not suspicious exactly. Just… aware. Like he was keeping mental tabs. Like each notification was a small challenge he hadn't expected to share her with.

After lunch, he walked her to the car. His hand found the small of her back—again—and lingered there. Familiar. Almost territorial.

"You should come to that gallery opening tomorrow," he said. "They've got a new collection from that artist you like—what's his name? The one with all the weird geometry."

She blinked, surprised he'd remembered. "James, I don't know. Tomorrow's—
"

"It's settled," he cut in, that easy grin fixed in place—but tighter now. "I'll pick you up at seven."

Settled.

The word rang through her like a quiet alarm. She hadn't agreed to anything. But somehow, she'd been dismissed from her own decision.

She didn't push back—just nodded faintly and looked away. Her reflection caught in the car window: eyes dulled, lips pressed in a neutral line.

Not no.

But definitely not yes.

She climbed into the driver's seat, offering a parting smile that felt more like a reflex than a choice—automatic, like fastening a seatbelt. James leaned in through the open window, pressing a soft kiss to her cheek, his fingers brushing along her arm with that same practiced gentleness he always used—like he was reading from a script he'd memorised.

That was as far as Julia let him go.

A kiss here. A hug there. Enough to keep things pleasant, not enough to make promises.

Lately, though, he'd begun pressing for more. Little hints dropped in between compliments. Lingering touches that edged past comfort. Invitations that carried more weight than the words themselves.

But Julia wasn't ready.

She wasn't even sure she would be—could be—with James.

His touch held no threat—but it carried weight. A quiet, constant pressure. A quiet, steady push that felt like it was always waiting.

As she shifted into reverse and pulled away, she caught a glimpse of him in the mirror—standing on the sidewalk, hands in his pockets, watching her leave.

Just watching—like someone counting backward from a moment he planned to own.

Like he was memorising something he didn't want to forget. Or maybe... cataloguing something he wanted to control.

The rest of the day, Julia moved through her tasks with a vague sense of detachment. She answered messages, reviewed design updates for a project she was finalising, even FaceTimed with Mary, who immediately clocked something was off.

"You look pale," Mary said, frowning. "Are you eating?"

"I'm fine."

"You don't sound fine."

"I'm just tired."

That was half true.

The other half sat in her stomach like lead. Not nausea. Not exactly. Just… a growing sense of being unmoored. Dizzy in waves. She'd blamed it on stress, or hormones, or the endless tightrope walk between Daniel's silence and James's constant presence.

But in the quiet moments, when her hand slipped to her abdomen, she couldn't ignore the shift in her body.

Something was off.

Not sick exactly.

But definitely not right.

Two days later, she was supposed to have dinner with James. But Mary had landed back in town—and when your best friend showed up unannounced after months abroad, dinner dates could wait.

Julia messaged James to cancel, a quick:

Hey—can't make it tonight. Mary just arrived. Rain check?

His reply came almost immediately.

Seriously?

No emojis. No softness.

She stared at the screen, thumb hovering. He hadn't even pretended to hide the irritation.

Julia sighed and tossed her phone aside just as the front door swung open—without ceremony, as always.

And just like that, a whirlwind of perfume, designer heels, and unapologetic energy swept into the room.

"Tell me you have wine," came the familiar voice, rich with mock despair. "Or at least something stronger than this sad little airport espresso."

Julia turned—and the weight of the week fell off her shoulders.

"Mary?" she breathed, already smiling.

Mary Collins stood in the doorway, impossibly tall, sun-kissed and glowing, hair in loose, careless waves that probably took an hour to perfect. A vintage trench hung from one shoulder, oversized sunglasses pushed up onto her head, and red lipstick still flawless despite fifteen hours of international travel.

"Don't just stand there gawking, Jules," Mary said, striding in like she owned the place. "Hug me before I cry."

Julia crossed the room in seconds and threw her arms around her best friend. "You're actually here."

Mary squeezed tight, then leaned back and studied her. "God, you look tired. Still stunning, but like… emotionally wrecked. So, who do I kill first?"

Julia laughed. It felt good. "Start with the patriarchy. Work your way down."

"Sounds like a Tuesday."

They settled on the couch, feet tucked under them, a bottle of wine open between them before the hour was out.

"I've missed you," Julia said softly.

"I missed you more," Mary replied, brushing hair out of Julia's face. "You've been way too quiet lately. And don't think I haven't noticed the strategic vagueness in your texts."

Julia hesitated, then sighed. "Things have been… complicated."

"I gathered. Joseph's cryptic texts. Daniel going full ghost. And don't get me started on James." She took a long sip of wine. "So. Talk. Or I swear I'll do a deep dive and start calling people."

Julia smiled, but it faltered. "James and I are… seeing each other."

Mary lowered her glass slowly. "You're joking."

"I'm not."

"Julia. No. Come on."

"He's been kind," Julia defended, softer now. "He's been there. He listens. He cares."

Mary tilted her head. "You're trying to convince me—or yourself?"

Julia didn't answer.

Mary leaned back, exhaling hard. "I've never trusted him. Something about that 'nice guy' thing feels like a mask he wears too well."

"He hasn't done anything wrong," Julia insisted, but her voice lacked conviction.

"Yet," Mary replied. "There's a difference between being loved… and just being wanted."

Julia blinked, heart clenching.

"He doesn't challenge you. He absorbs you. There's a difference."

For a long time, neither of them spoke. The silence stretched, but it wasn't uncomfortable.

Mary was the only person who could hold up a mirror and make Julia look without flinching.

Finally, Julia whispered, "Daniel saw us. Kissing."

Mary's brow arched. "And?"

"He was furious. But he wouldn't say it outright. He just... stood there. Watching. Judging. And then told me not to see James again."

Mary scoffed. "Of course he did. God forbid someone else value you when he can't even figure out how to."

Julia's voice cracked a little. "I told him I was dating James. And then I walked away."

Mary reached over and took her hand. "I'm proud of you."

"Even if I'm making the wrong choice?"

"Especially then. Because it means you're choosing for you. And that's step one."

Julia gave a small laugh, eyes misty. "You always come back right when I need you."

"Dramatic entrances are my specialty."

Mary leaned over and clinked their glasses. "To doing whatever the hell we want."

Julia smiled, leaning into her friend's warmth. And for the first time in weeks, she felt something shift.

Not relief.

But maybe... resolve.

Chapter Eight

The storm didn't come all at once. It started with a flutter.

A skipped morning coffee. A headache that lingered at her temples longer than it should have. A tightness in her chest that no amount of deep breathing could release.

Julia told herself it was just stress. Work. James. The silence from Daniel that had begun to echo in strange, unwelcome ways.

But when she stood in front of her bathroom mirror that morning, pale and flushed all at once, the truth clawed through denial and wrapped cold fingers around her spine.

Her hand drifted to her abdomen, resting there like a question.

She didn't need a test to know.

Not anymore. The knowing lived in her bones now, undeniable.

Later that week, the storm finally touched ground.

It was a Friday evening, and the city was dipped in gold—the last blush of daylight slanting across the plaza outside the gallery.

Daniel hadn't planned to come. Joseph had dragged him out of the house with promises of whiskey and small talk he didn't have to contribute to. He wasn't in the mood for conversation, but he needed distraction. Anything to silence the loop in his head: Julia's laughter, the way she looked at James now, the way she used to look at him.

He spotted her instantly.

Across the room, near the abstract pieces she always gravitated to—bright colour and fractured shapes—Julia stood, laughing. Not a small laugh. A real one. Her head tilted back, her eyes crinkled at the corners. She looked lit from the inside.

And James stood beside her, too close, a hand hovering at the small of her back like it belonged there.

Daniel felt it before he could name it.

Heat. Tightness. A strange punch to the gut.

Jealousy.

He blinked, shaken by the rawness of it. It wasn't new—this feeling—but tonight it was undeniable.

James leaned in, whispering something in Julia's ear. She smiled, softer now. Her gaze drifted briefly across the room—and landed on Daniel.

She froze.

Just for a second. Long enough for their eyes to lock. Long enough for the warmth to flicker.

Then she looked away.

And so did he.

Julia didn't hear a word James said after that.

Daniel's face—stern, unreadable—kept flashing in her mind. Not cold. Not angry.

Wounded.

For the first time since she'd started seeing James, she didn't feel safe in his presence. Not unsafe in the traditional sense—but exposed. Watched. Caged.

And under it all, the weight of the secret growing inside her pressed harder.

Mary's voice echoed in her ears: 'Being wanted and being loved are not the same thing.'

She reached for her drink, but her hand shook.

James noticed. "You okay?"

Julia forced a smile. "Just tired."

"Let me take you home," he said—too fast, too eager.

She nodded. But inside her chest, the storm cracked wide open.

She knew—without question—she couldn't keep doing this.

Not to herself.

And not to the man whose child she carried.

The next day, Mary didn't even wait for the wine to breathe before pouncing.

"You look like you've seen a ghost," she said, eyeing Julia over the rim of her glass. "Or like you are one."

Julia tried to smile. It wavered, then collapsed. She set the untouched glass of wine down carefully, like any sudden movement might shatter her completely, and pressed her hands to her face.

Mary didn't speak. She just waited—the kind of silence that only came from someone who knew the shape of your pain before you spoke it aloud.

Finally, Julia whispered, "I'm pregnant."

The words dropped between them like a thunderclap.

Mary blinked. "Okay. Okay. Deep breaths. Please don't tell me it's James's."

Julia nodded once. "It's Daniel's."

Silence.

Then Mary exhaled, softly but not gently. "Jesus, Jules."

"I know."

"Are you absolutely—?"

"I counted. It happened that night. The night he doesn't remember." Her voice broke.

Mary sat slowly, the gravity pulling her down like a weight. "Does he know?"

Julia shook her head.

"Are you going to tell him?"

"I don't know," she admitted. "He can barely look at me lately. And now with James—"

Mary groaned. "Oh God, please don't bring up James right now. He gives me hives."

Julia almost laughed, but it came out watery. "It's not like I planned this."

"I know," Mary said, softer now. She reached across the couch and squeezed Julia's hand. "But you don't have to go through this alone."

"I haven't even figured out how I feel about it yet. How am I supposed to tell anyone else?"

"Start by telling the one who deserves to know. And then," Mary said with quiet steel, "you let me deal with the ones who don't."

The next evening, Julia stood by the kitchen window, staring blankly at the garden as she typed out the message.

Hey, I'm really sorry. I'm not feeling great tonight—going to have to cancel dinner. Rain check?

She hit send before she could second-guess herself.

The reply came less than a minute later.

You okay? Want me to bring something over?

She didn't respond. She couldn't.

Instead, she turned off her phone, hoping that silence might be enough.

It wasn't.

Twenty minutes later, James was at her front door, knocking like he had every right to be there.

She opened it slowly, her expression unreadable. "James, I told you—"

"You didn't sound like yourself." He stepped past her into the entryway. "I was worried."

Julia closed the door behind him with a sigh. "You shouldn't have come."

He turned to face her, searching her face. "What's going on?"

She didn't answer right away—just walked into the living room, her steps slow and deliberate. He followed, watching her closely.

Once they were both seated—her on the edge of the armchair, him tense on the couch—she finally spoke.

"I can't see you anymore."

The words dropped like a stone between them.

James blinked. "What?"

"I'm sorry. I just… I can't do this."

His brows furrowed, confusion giving way to something sharper. "Julia, where is this coming from? I thought things were going well."

She shook her head. "They're not. Not for me."

"That's not an answer." His voice grew louder, disbelief hardening into frustration. "You said you felt safe with me. That I was the one who showed up when no one else did."

"I did feel that way," she said quietly, eyes downcast. "But things have changed."

James stood now, pacing a tight line across the carpet. "You're not even giving me a reason."

"I don't owe you one," she said, her voice tired, brittle.

James stopped pacing. "You're throwing us away for what, Julia? Is this about Daniel?"

Her silence answered him louder than any words could.

His eyes widened. "Unbelievable. After everything I've done—after the way he treated you?"

"Stop." Her voice cracked like a whip. "This isn't about what you've done. It's about what I need. And this"—she gestured vaguely between them— "isn't it."

He exploded then. "You've got to be kidding me! You let me in. You let me think this was going somewhere! And now you just shut the door?"

"I never promised you anything," she said, her voice flat, exhausted. "And you never asked what I wanted."

The tension in the air was so thick it felt like the room itself was shrinking.

And then—

"What the hell is going on?"

The voice came from the hallway. Joseph.

Daniel followed a second later, eyebrows drawn tight, posture tense.

James turned, his chest heaving. "Ask her. She just told me it's over—with no reason, no warning."

Joseph's eyes flicked to Julia, his jaw tightening. "Is that true?"

James spun back to her. "Tell them, Julia. Tell them why. Say it."

Julia's mouth opened—but nothing came out at first. Her heart pounded, pulse echoing in her ears.

Then suddenly, the words burst from her like a storm breaking through.

"Because I'm pregnant."

Chapter Nine

Silence dropped like a bomb.

The room felt vacuum-sealed, every breath ripped out of the air.

James stared at her like she'd grown another head. "You can't be. We haven't—" His voice cracked. "We didn't… you and I never…"

Julia lifted her eyes slowly. Her face was pale, but her voice didn't shake.

"I know."

A beat passed—sharp, cold, final.

"It's not yours."

The words slammed into James like a body blow. He staggered a step back, his mouth opening and closing, searching for logic where there was none.

"What the hell does that mean?" he asked, quieter now but somehow more dangerous. "Well, whose is it?"

Silence stretched again—longer this time. Thicker.

Julia's gaze shifted past James, past Joseph, to Daniel.

She looked straight at him.

And said nothing.

She didn't need to.

Daniel didn't move. He didn't speak. He didn't even blink.

He just stood there, staring at her, as if the floor had disappeared beneath his feet and he hadn't hit the bottom yet.

Joseph's voice came next, low and tight with disbelief. "Wait—"

Then louder, slicing through the silence like a blade.

"You're saying it's his?"

He turned to his best friend, eyes blazing. "You slept with my sister?"

Daniel jolted at the accusation, his brow furrowing in confusion. "What? No. I didn't—why are you saying this, Julia?"

Julia's throat worked around the lump rising there. "Because it's true."

A beat.

Then—

Joseph moved.

One second Daniel was standing, stunned and still, and the next he was slammed hard against the wall, Joseph's forearm pressed into his chest, pinning him in place.

"I told you she was off-limits," Joseph growled, eyes wild with fury. "I told you—"

"Joseph, stop!" Julia surged forward, trying to pull him back.

"I didn't sleep with her!" Daniel shouted, shoving Joseph off with both hands. His chest heaved as he turned toward Julia, wide-eyed, pleading. "Tell him, Julia. Tell him it never happened."

But Julia didn't move. Didn't speak.

That silence was its own confession.

"You don't remember?" Joseph roared, his fury rising like a wave. "That's your excuse?"

Daniel looked between them, stunned. "When?"

Julia's voice was barely a whisper. "The night of Joseph's birthday."

Daniel froze. His mouth parted like he was about to say something—but no words came. Then his eyes narrowed, distant, searching.

Suddenly, something clicked.

His expression changed—shock overtaking confusion.

"That was real..." he whispered, more to himself than anyone else. "I thought—it was a dream."

The colour drained from his face. He stumbled back a step, like the truth had physically knocked the air from his lungs. He shoved both hands into his hair, pacing now, like the walls were closing in.

"I was drunk that night. I remember flashes, bits and pieces—but I thought it was just a dream. Something my mind made up to torture me. I didn't know."

James stood frozen near the couch, unmoving, unblinking, like a bystander at the scene of a car crash. "You two... had a night?" His voice was hollow. Dazed. "Are you kidding me?"

Julia wrapped her arms tightly across her chest, bracing against the rising heat in the room. "Yes. One night. It wasn't planned. It just... happened."

James let out a breath that sounded more like a scoff. "And now you're pregnant," he said, half-laughing, half-breathless with disbelief. "Of course. Jesus, Julia."

"I didn't know until a few days ago," she snapped, turning toward him. "And I tried—I tried to make it work with you, James. I wanted something simple. Safe. But *this*—this changes everything."

"No, it doesn't," James said quickly, taking a step toward her. His voice softened—too much. Too rehearsed. "We can still be together. I'll raise the baby. With you. We'll figure it out."

Julia flinched at the sound of that—we. The word hit her harder than his outburst would've.

"No," she said.

And beside her, unexpectedly—firmly—Daniel echoed, "No."

The sound of them in unison cut the air like a blade.

James's face twisted. "So, what, now you're a couple?" he hissed. "One night and suddenly he gets everything. The baby, you—after I've been there every damn day?"

"You were there, James," she said quietly. "But you were never it."

Joseph moved between them, shoulders squared, trying to process the chaos—his best friend, his sister, the betrayal threading through all of it.

"You knew how I felt," he said, voice tight, trembling with restrained rage. "About him. About you two. And you still—God, Julia. How could you?"

Daniel finally turned to Joseph, the guilt raw on his face. "It wasn't supposed to happen. I never meant for this."

"But it did." Joseph spat the words. "And now she's pregnant. And everything's screwed."

A heavy silence fell again. The kind that burns in the chest.

Then Daniel, voice hoarse, asked, "How far along are you?"

"Four weeks," Julia replied, her eyes on the floor.

Daniel did the math—fast.

"That lines up with…," he murmured. "With… that night."

She nodded, not looking at him. Her hands trembled.

"And you didn't tell me because—?"

"Because you didn't remember, Daniel," she said softly, lifting her eyes to his. "You acted like nothing happened. Like I was invisible. You looked right through me."

He winced, the shame carving itself across his face. "I didn't mean to."

"But you did," she said.

Daniel opened his mouth, but no words came. There was nothing left to defend. No easy fix.

Joseph turned away, running a hand over his jaw like he was holding himself back from breaking something. Or someone.

James just stood there, small now—cornered by truth, by rejection, by reality.

No one said anything.

The air felt thin.

And somewhere in the silence, a fracture splintered through the room—quiet but deep.

Not a clean break.

A warning.

This wasn't over. Not even close.

The silence still hung like a heavy curtain when Daniel finally turned to Julia, eyes filled with something between resolve and desperation.

"We'll get married," he said.

It wasn't a question.

Julia blinked.

"No," she said instantly.

And right beside her, like a reflex, James's voice rang out: "Absolutely not."

They said it in perfect unison—different tones, same answer.

Daniel flinched.

He looked from one to the other, confused, frustrated. "What do you mean no? Julia—this is my child. We can make this work. It's the right thing to do."

Julia stared at him, a bitter smile curling at the corner of her lips. "Right for who, Daniel? You? Joseph? Society?"

"It's not about them—it's about us," he said, stepping forward. "We made a mistake, but this is a chance to do the right thing. A real family. I want to—"

"No, you don't," Julia interrupted, her voice calm but cutting. "You want to fix it. Patch it up. Pretend you're not terrified. But that's not love, Daniel. That's guilt."

Daniel's jaw tightened. "You think I don't care?"

"I think you care about what this looks like. And I think a part of you still sees me as Joseph's little sister you weren't supposed to touch."

Julia let out a slow breath, then met Daniel's eyes—softer now, but unshakeably firm.

"I'm carrying your child, yes. But that doesn't mean I belong to you. We're not getting married just because of this."

Daniel opened his mouth. "But I—" he began, reaching for her, desperation edging his voice.

She took a step back, spine straightening. "No, Daniel. If I ever marry, it'll be because he loves me—and I love him. Real love. Not guilt. Not obligation. Not some knee-jerk reaction to a consequence neither of us planned for."

His hand dropped uselessly to his side.

For a moment, he looked like a man who'd just been disarmed—still standing, but winded.

And for once, Daniel Moore—who always had an answer, a strategy, a way out—had nothing to say.

Silence fell again.

But this time, it wasn't charged with rage or chaos. It was thick with finality.

Julia turned and walked out of the room, her steps quiet but unwavering.

Daniel didn't follow.

Behind him, Joseph exhaled sharply—less like a sigh, more like a fuse lighting.

"I can't believe you did this," he said coldly. "I trusted you, Daniel."

Daniel flinched, but didn't look at him.

Joseph's voice dropped lower. Harder. "I told you she was off-limits. I warned you. And still—you touched what wasn't yours."

Daniel turned his head slightly, jaw clenched. "She's not yours, either Joseph."

That only seemed to fuel Joseph's fury. "No. She's my sister. And you're supposed to be my best friend."

There was a long pause—no defence, no excuse.

Just Daniel, staring at the floor like it might give him an answer.

Joseph shook his head slowly, disgust and betrayal thick in his voice.

"You were supposed to help me protect her. Not break her."

Then he walked out too, leaving Daniel alone in the silence he'd created—surrounded by good intentions, terrible timing, and the mess love had made.

James stepped forward, his jaw tight, eyes locked on Daniel.

"I'm not going anywhere," he said flatly. "Just so you know."

Daniel turned slowly to face him, his gaze sharp, voice low. "You're not raising my child."

James smirked, but there was nothing amused in it—just defiance. "We'll see."

The silence between them was electric, the kind that dared one of them to make the first move.

Daniel took a step closer, his height and presence bearing down. "You think this is some kind of competition? That if you just hang around long enough, Julia will forget who the father is?"

James didn't flinch. "I think she needs someone who's actually been there. Who's shown up. You didn't even remember sleeping with her."

Daniel's fists clenched at his sides. "That doesn't mean I don't care. I do. And I will—"

"No, you won't, you throw women away like they are disposable," James snapped, stepping up. "You don't get to push me out just because you suddenly remembered what you lost. Julia will see I'm the right choice."

"No, she won't," Daniel bit back, voice tightening. "That's my child. And I won't let you play house with what isn't yours."

James's expression darkened. "Julia will decide that. Not you. And until she tells me to leave—I'm staying."

The room vibrated with unspoken threats, past wounds, and the cold, hard truth of two men who wanted the same woman—but only one had a piece of her future.

Neither moved. Neither blinked.

Then James turned and walked toward the door, pausing just long enough to look back. "We'll see how this plays out, Moore. And just so you know…"

He smiled, sharp and dangerous.

"I always play the long game."

Then he was gone.

Daniel didn't move. Couldn't. He was already playing his own long game—but for once, the outcome wasn't in his control.

Chapter Ten

The door clicked softly shut behind her, but it might as well have slammed.

Julia leaned against it for a moment, eyes closed, one hand pressed to her abdomen like she was trying to hold herself together. The silence up here was different—no longer suffocating, just… hollow. The kind of quiet that follows a storm but promises another one is coming.

She moved to the bed, collapsed onto it without bothering to change, and stared up at the ceiling. Her chest felt too tight. Her ribs, too small. Not again. Not yet. She didn't cry.

She reached blindly for her phone, thumbs clumsy, vision blurred.

Can you come? Please.

She didn't need to say more.

Mary was already halfway down the block when the message came through. She didn't bother with parking properly—just rolled into the driveway, threw the car into park at an angle, and climbed out in four-inch heels. The door slammed behind her, loud enough to make her flinch.

She stormed up the steps two at a time.

The front door was unlocked. The hallway beyond was dim, heavy with the kind of silence that follows wreckage.

And there—leaning against the wall like it was the only thing keeping him upright—stood Daniel Moore.

Their eyes met. Mary froze on the threshold.

"I'm not in the mood for you," she said flatly.

"I figured," Daniel murmured.

She didn't blink. "So why are you still standing here?"

He exhaled slowly, rubbed the back of his neck. "Because I don't know what to do. I thought I'd wait."

"Wait?" Her laugh was sharp and without humour. "Wait for what? For her to forgive you? For this to magically make sense?"

His jaw tightened, but he didn't respond.

Mary stepped closer, her voice low and cutting. "You don't get to play the tortured hero now, Daniel. You humiliated her."

He looked up sharply. "I never meant to—"

"She was happy that night," Mary continued, eyes flashing. "Happy that you finally saw her. Happy that—for once—she wasn't invisible to you. And then she woke up to a man who didn't even remember it happened."

Daniel's face twisted like her words physically hurt him. "I care about her. I always have."

Mary stared at him for a long beat, then shook her head. "You have a funny way of showing it."

"She's Joseph's sister," he said quietly. "He told me to stay away. That she was off-limits."

"And you've always done what Joseph wanted?" Her voice rising like disbelief was the only thing holding her together. "God, Daniel. You're a grown man. With all your money, all your power—and you still need permission to feel something?"

He swallowed hard, silence stretching like wire between them.

Mary leaned in, her tone cold steel. "Let me be clear. I don't care what happened between you and Joseph. I don't care if Julia forgives you or not. But I will stand by her—no matter what she decides. Even if it's James she ends up with."

Daniel's eyes darkened. "James isn't right for her."

"Maybe not. But he remembers her." She stepped back. "And right now, that matters more than your guilt."

She didn't wait for a response—just turned, heels clicking against the hardwood as she made her way upstairs.

Julia didn't move when the door creaked open.

Mary walked in, quiet now, and sat gently beside her.

"I'm here," she said softly.

That was all it took.

Julia turned into her best friend's arms, and this time—finally—she cried.

Daniel sat on the bottom step of the staircase long after Mary disappeared upstairs. The house was quiet now, too quiet—like the stillness after a storm when everything looks intact, but nothing feels the same.

His head dropped into his hands, elbows on his knees, the weight of the night pressing down hard. But it wasn't tonight that haunted him.

It was that morning.

The morning after Joseph's birthday.

He remembered walking into the kitchen, hair still damp from the shower, the ache of too much whiskey lingering in his bones. And then—

Her.

Julia.

She had been standing at the stove, her back to him, wearing a soft green sweater and a pair of loose cotton shorts that made him want to take her in his arms.

She turned when she heard him, and her face—*God*—lit up like sunrise.

Soft, bright, unguarded.

"Morning," she had said, her voice just a little shy, a little sweet. "You're up early."

Not flirtatious.

Not casual.

Just… happy.

The kind of happiness that only comes from feeling chosen.

From waking up beside someone you've wanted for so long and finally, finally knowing they feel the same.

The kind of smile that says, last night meant something.

He remembered standing there, bleary-eyed and hungover, rubbing the back of his neck as he asked, "Did I do anything stupid?"

That's when it happened.

The light drained from her face.

Gone. Just like that.

Like it had never been there at all.

But he felt it—the echo of her joy, the weight of what replaced it. That aching silence. That look.

Like she'd been hit and didn't want him to see where it hurt.

He hadn't known what to make of it then. He blinked at her, confused, poured himself a coffee like the room hadn't just shifted under his feet. She stood frozen for a beat, then mumbled something about doing some laundry—and walked out like her skin no longer fit.

Like the kitchen was too loud.

Like he was too loud.

And he still didn't get it.

Not then.

But now?

Now he saw it with brutal clarity.

That smile—so soft, so true—had been for him. For them. Because to her, that night had been real.

And to him?

He'd treated it like a question mark. Like a blur.

Like a dream he couldn't quite remember.

And nothing had ever hurt more than knowing her joy had been genuine—while his memory had been missing.

He remembered waking up with a warmth in his chest and a softness in his body, the kind that came from feeling good. He remembered flashes—her hand in his hair, her breath on his skin, the way she whispered his name like a secret.

And he'd chalked it up to another dream.

Another cruel dream.

Because he'd had them before—plenty of them—fantasies built on years of restraint, of denying what he wanted because Joseph had asked him to. Because Julia was off-limits. Because friendship came with rules, and he'd always been so damn good at following them.

Except that night.

He hadn't followed anything.

And Julia—God, Julia had felt everything.

His fingers curled into fists.

She had been happy.

For a moment, she had everything she wanted.

And he'd stood there like a clueless idiot, not even realising he'd finally crossed that line. Not remembering the one thing she'd probably held close to her heart.

The truth of it gutted him.

All these years, he'd told himself he couldn't. That it was better this way. That his care for her was distant, manageable, something he could keep boxed up behind loyalty and logic.

But now he knew better.

He'd always wanted her.

And he'd hurt her in the worst way—by making her believe she'd imagined it meant something only to her.

By forgetting.

Daniel leaned back against the stair rail and stared up at the ceiling, trying to breathe through the pressure in his chest.

He remembered her now.

Every second.

Every sound.

Every sacred, stolen moment.

And it wasn't a dream.

It was real.

It was her.

It was them.

And he'd let it slip through his fingers like it meant nothing.

But it had meant everything.

It had always been Julia. Even when he pretended it wasn't. Even when he tried to bury the feelings, to erase them, to drown them in distractions and one-night stands and women whose names he barely remembered.

But none of them were her.

No one ever came close.

He'd spent years trying to forget her—because Joseph said to. Because she was off-limits. Because being her protector's best friend meant toeing the line, no matter what his heart wanted.

But Mary was right.

He hadn't just obeyed Joseph. He'd hidden behind him.

Like a coward.

He let someone else decide his fate—and hers.

And he'd hated himself for it more than he ever admitted.

But not anymore.

Chapter Eleven

Daniel turned on his heel and went looking for Joseph, striding through the house with purpose until he found him in the study—standing by the window, a half-drunk glass of whisky in hand, his silhouette rigid against the dim light.

Joseph didn't turn around when Daniel entered. "What do you want?"

Daniel shut the door behind him. "We need to talk."

"I think you've done enough," Joseph replied coldly, eyes fixed on the street beyond the glass.

Daniel stepped closer. "Maybe I have. But you're going to hear me out."

Joseph turned now—slow, deliberate—and looked him dead in the eye. "You slept with my sister. You lied to me. You forgot it even happened. What could you possibly say that matters now?"

"I didn't lie," Daniel said, his voice low but firm. "I forgot, yes. But I didn't lie. And I didn't mean to hurt her. I swear to God, I didn't."

Joseph laughed bitterly, short and sharp. "You always said you weren't the relationship type. And I believed you. Because I watched you, Daniel. I saw how you treated the women you slept with. They never lasted long. Never meant a thing."

Daniel's jaw flexed. He looked down, then back up, eyes burning. "And do you know why that was?"

Joseph didn't answer. He didn't need to.

"Because none of them were her." Daniel's voice cracked slightly, but he didn't stop. "Because I compared every single one of them to Julia. And they all came up short."

Joseph's brow tightened, the whisky glass trembling slightly in his grip.

"I tried to move on. To be who you expected me to be," Daniel continued. "But every time I looked at her, I saw everything I couldn't have. Everything I wanted and didn't deserve. And I told myself walking away was the right thing. The honourable thing. But all I did was break her. And myself."

He paused, his voice rough with truth. "I've been in love with your sister for years, Joe. I just never had the guts to say it."

Joseph's silence was colder than anger.

Finally, he said, "And now what? You think a few regrets make this better? You think saying you love her erases the fact that you forgot her—forgot her, Daniel?"

"No," Daniel said quietly. "Nothing erases that. Nothing ever could."

The room was still for a long beat.

Then Daniel added, voice low, certain:

"But I'm not running anymore. I'm not hiding. I love her—and I'm going to prove it. Not for your approval. Not because I expect anything in return. But because she deserves everything. And for once, I'm going to be the man she deserves."

Joseph didn't flinch, but his expression hardened. His grip on the glass tightened, knuckles whitening.

"You say that," he said quietly, "but you treated her worse than any other woman you've been with."

Daniel stiffened. "That's not true."

Joseph's eyes flashed. "Isn't it? Tell me—have you ever forgotten that you slept with any of them? Even when you were drunk?"

The question hung in the air like smoke. Heavy. Toxic.

Daniel opened his mouth, then shut it again.

Because the truth was.

No.

He hadn't.

Not once.

Not ever.

But Julia…

Julia, the one woman who meant something, the one he'd fantasised about for years—she was the one he forgot. The one whose heart he'd unknowingly crushed with a single, careless morning-after question.

And now, finally, Daniel understood what that meant. What it must've felt like for her. That radiant smile, followed by the devastation of realising she'd been nothing more than a blank space in his memory.

He swallowed hard, shame burning its way down his throat.

"I thought it was a dream," he said at last, voice hoarse. "One of the ones I've had about her for years. It didn't feel real… because I couldn't let myself believe it was. That she would want me."

Joseph stared at him for a long time.

"I don't care what your dreams were," he said coldly. "All I care about is the reality you left her with."

Daniel's jaw tensed, his voice low—raw.

"I will regret that for the rest of my life."

Joseph didn't turn. Just stared out the window, his silhouette sharp against the fading light.

"That's the thing about regret," he said quietly. "It doesn't change a damn thing."

Daniel took a step closer. "I didn't mean to hurt her."

"But you did." Joseph's voice cut sharper now. "You hurt her worse than any man ever has. And the worst part? You didn't even know you were doing it."

Silence thickened between them. Then Joseph turned slowly, eyes cold and steady.

"It doesn't matter what you say now, Daniel. She's never going to forget that."

A pause. Then, softer but no less damning—

"I don't even know if she'll ever forgive you."

Daniel didn't speak. Couldn't.

Because he wasn't sure either.

And that, more than anything, gutted him.

Joseph's voice was quiet now—tired, almost worn thin by the weight of everything that had unravelled. He turned away from the window and looked Daniel in the eyes.

"She's the only family I have left," he said, steady but thick with emotion. "I promised I'd protect her when our parents died. She was only seventeen. Just a kid. And I asked you to help me protect her."

Daniel nodded once. "I know."

Joseph's eyes darkened, the memories flickering behind them. "She was devastated when they were killed. Completely shattered. I've never seen someone try so hard to smile through pain that deep. And I swore I'd never let anyone break her like that again."

He stepped forward, voice rising—not in anger, but in pain. "That's why I said she was off-limits. Because you told me—*showed me*—you didn't want anything real. No relationships. No attachments. You made it clear you didn't want to be tied down. And I couldn't let her be just another name on your list."

Daniel's gaze dropped, shame creeping up his spine.

Joseph's jaw clenched. "I don't know what's going to happen now. None of us do. But I meant what I said—I will stand by Julia. No matter what she decides. Even if that means you and I… are done."

The air between them shifted, the finality of those words like a fault line cracking between them.

Joseph shook his head slowly; regret carved into every line of his face. "I never wanted it to come to this."

Daniel swallowed hard, feeling the weight of a friendship cracking under the pressure of love, betrayal, and consequence.

And for the first time, he truly understood the cost.

Daniel's voice was low, but there was steel beneath it. A fire that hadn't been there before.

"It's not going to come to that," he said. "I'm going to convince her I'm the right man for her. Not out of guilt. Not out of obligation. Because I want her. Because I care about her—more than I ever admitted. More than you realise."

Joseph didn't speak at first. He just stared at him, eyes searching Daniel's face for any sign of the man he'd grown up with—the friend he trusted like a brother.

Finally, he nodded, just once.

"I hope so, Daniel," he said quietly, the words catching slightly in his throat. "Because losing you—not just as a friend, but as my brother—would destroy me."

The silence that followed wasn't sharp or final this time.

It was just heavy—with the weight of what had been, what could be lost, and what still might be saved.

Mary just held Julia as she cried—silent, steady, unflinching. She didn't offer empty words or try to stop the tears. She let her best friend fall apart in the safety of her arms, knowing that sometimes the breaking was part of the healing.

When the sobs finally began to fade, Julia pulled back—eyes swollen, cheeks damp, breath catching in little hiccups.

Mary brushed a tear from her cheek and asked gently, "Tell me the truth… what do you want to do? Do you want this baby?"

Julia nodded, voice trembling but sure. "Yes. And not because it's Daniel's… because it's mine."

Mary's lips lifted in the smallest smile—soft, protective, proud.

"Okay," she said, reaching for Julia's hand. "Then we prepare for me to become an aunty."

That made Julia laugh—quiet and broken at first, but real. The sound cracked through the tension like sunlight after rain.

Mary smiled, relief softening her features. "There she is."

Julia wiped at her face, still laughing through the tears. "God, you're going to be the most over-the-top aunty, aren't you?"

Mary lifted a brow. "Please. That kid's going to have better fashion than both of us by the time it's two."

They both laughed then—this time together—and for the first time all day, Julia felt like maybe she could breathe again.

Joseph knocked gently on Julia's bedroom door.

Mary opened it, her eyes narrowing briefly before softening.

"Can I have a word with Julia?"

"Of course. I was just leaving." She turned to Julia and kissed her cheek. "I'll be back tomorrow."

"Thanks," Julia said quietly.

Joseph stepped inside and sat on the edge of the bed beside her. The room was quiet, the tension between them like a third presence.

"I'm sorry," Julia said after a long moment.

Joseph shook his head. "No. Don't. You have nothing to apologise for."

"I do," she said softly. "You were only trying to protect me."

"I've known for a long time that you cared about Daniel," he admitted. "I should never have stood in your way."

Julia looked down at her lap, voice barely above a whisper. "You weren't wrong to try."

Joseph turned to face her. "Julia—"

"I thought I knew what I was doing," she interrupted. "But I didn't. I thought what happened between us meant something to him… and it didn't. Not the way I thought it did. And that… it broke something in me."

Her voice wavered, but she pressed on.

"I'm not saying I don't feel anything for him. I do. I just don't know what any of it means anymore."

Joseph's expression was pained, his voice low. "You don't have to figure it out right now."

"I know," she said, forcing a small smile. "But it's hard to sit here and feel this… mess inside me. Because a part of me wants to scream, and another part—" she hesitated, "—another part just wants him to come in here and fix it all."

Joseph's eyes softened.

"I hate that he hurt you."

"So do I," she murmured. "And I don't know if I'll ever be able to forgive him. Or trust him. I don't even know if I want to."

He nodded slowly, taking her hand.

"I just want you to be okay," he said. "You don't have to forgive him. Or love him. Or make any decisions yet. But whatever you do, I'll stand by you."

Tears stung her eyes, but she blinked them back. "Thank you."

Joseph gave her hand a gentle squeeze. "You take all the time you need. And if he wants to be part of your life, he's going to have to prove he deserves it."

Julia didn't respond at first—just looked down at their hands, her heart aching with the weight of everything unsaid.

But for now, that was enough.

Chapter Twelve

Julia had just stepped out of the shower. She was walking from the ensuite to her bedroom, tightening the belt on her bathrobe, when a soft knock sounded at the door.

Daniel's voice, quiet.

"Can I come in?"

She froze, then hesitated—her hand instinctively tightening the robe around her.

"…Yes."

The door creaked open. Daniel stepped inside slowly, closing it behind him with care.

He looked at her—standing there in her robe, damp hair clinging to her neck, pale and guarded.

"Why are you here, Daniel?"

He swallowed hard.

"Because I needed to say I'm sorry. To your face. Not through someone else. Not later. Now."

Julia looked away. Her voice trembled.

"You don't even remember it. Do you have any idea how humiliating that was for me?"

He stepped closer, carefully.

"I know. And I hate that I made you feel that way. I hate myself for it."

"I'm not just one of your girls, Daniel. I thought…" Her voice cracked. "I thought it meant something."

"It did," he said quietly.

She scoffed, bitter.

"You didn't even know it happened."

"I thought it was a dream," he said, voice thick. "I've had them about you before. For years."

Julia blinked—caught off guard—but said nothing. He continued.

"You were always off-limits. I kept telling myself that. I thought if I crossed that line, I'd lose everything—Joseph, you, any part of myself I respected. So, I kept my distance. But that night… everything I'd buried surfaced. And when I woke up—" he shook his head, "—my mind just shut down. I couldn't let myself believe it had actually happened."

Julia's voice was barely a whisper.

"You shattered me."

Daniel nodded slowly.

"I know."

She finally met his eyes—hers glassy, guarded but burning with something he couldn't name.

"I want to be part of this baby's life, Julia. I know I don't deserve it. But I want to try. Whatever you'll allow me to give—I'll give it."

She looked at him long and hard, her voice calm but edged.

"I don't know if I can ever forgive you. But I won't stop you from being in your child's life."

Daniel didn't flinch.

"You don't have to forgive me. Not now. Maybe not ever. I just want to be here. However you'll have me."

She looked at him—truly looked—and for a flicker of a second, he saw something soft. Something familiar.

But then she shook her head.

"I need time. I don't trust you."

He nodded, no protest, no desperation.

"Then I'll wait. As long as it takes."

He began to back away—slow, respectful.

"I'm not going anywhere, Julia. Not this time."

He slipped out, closing the door gently behind him.

Julia sat on the edge of the bed, heart pounding in the stillness.

And for the first time in days, she didn't feel completely alone.

The next morning, after breakfast, the doorbell rang.

Joseph and Daniel had gone out. Julia was in the kitchen with Lorna, lingering over her second cup of tea.

Lorna started to rise. "I'll get it."

Julia stood, robe loosely tied, her hair twisted into a lazy bun. She still held her half-empty mug. "No, I've got it."

Lorna gave her a warm nod. "Okay, love."

Julia padded to the door, not expecting anyone. She pulled it open cautiously—and froze.

James stood on the porch, casually dressed in jeans and a crisp white button-down, his hair slightly windswept like he'd walked rather than driven. In one hand he held a bouquet of soft white lilies, in the other, two takeaway coffee cups and a brown paper bag.

His smile was warm. A little sheepish.

"Peace offering," he said, lifting the coffees. "And flowers, because showing up empty-handed after being an ass isn't really my style."

Julia blinked, taken off guard. Her lips parted as if to say something, but nothing came.

Then, quietly, she stepped aside.

"Come in."

James entered, moving with a gentleness she hadn't seen in him for a while. His eyes swept over the room like he didn't quite recognise it anymore, though he'd been there many times.

From behind, Lorna gave him a pleasant smile.

"Morning, James."

Then, with a knowing glance to Julia:

"I'll leave you two to it."

She disappeared down the hall, her footsteps light.

James placed the coffees on the bench, then turned and offered her the bouquet.

"I remembered you liked lilies," he said softly.

She took them, surprised by the memory—and the thought.

"Thank you, you're sweet."

He smiled again, more subdued this time.

"I came to say sorry. Properly. I didn't handle yesterday well."

Julia looked at the lilies in her hands, unsure of what to say.

James didn't press. He simply stood there, quieter than she was used to, like he was making room—for her feelings, her silence, her uncertainty.

And somehow, that made her want to listen.

"They're not roses," he said. "Thought you might be tired of grand gestures that don't mean anything."

She looked at the bouquet again, touched. "They're beautiful. Thank you."

He watched her move toward the sink to grab a vase, then cleared his throat.

"About yesterday…"

She didn't look at him, just focused on trimming the stems. "You don't have to explain."

"I do," he said gently. "Because you deserved better than that."

She paused, the scissors in her hand still. Slowly, she turned to face him.

James stepped closer but kept his distance.

"Hearing about you and Daniel—I won't lie, it knocked the wind out of me. Not because of what happened… but because of how much I hate the idea of you hurting like this. And I reacted like a jealous idiot instead of a friend."

Her brow softened. "You were surprised. It's okay."

"No," he said firmly. "It's not. You needed support, and I made it about me. I'm sorry."

Julia studied him for a long moment. He looked sincere. Regretful. And something in his eyes—a quiet steadiness—reassured her.

"What happened between you and Daniel," James said carefully, "that's not what defines you. Or how I feel about you. None of it changes who you are, or what you mean to me."

She exhaled slowly. "Thank you."

"I meant it when I said I care about you. And if you'll let me… I'd really like to be here for you now. No pressure. No expectations. Just someone in your corner who's not going anywhere."

For a moment, she hesitated.

Then she nodded.

"Okay."

His smile was small but real. "Good. Because I brought cinnamon scrolls, and I know you've been pretending to enjoy that gluten-free bread Mary keeps sneaking in."

That made her laugh—an actual laugh—and some of the tension in her shoulders eased.

"You're awful."

"I'm charming," he corrected smoothly, already moving to unpack the box of pastries. "And today, I'm all yours. You need to vent, cry, binge terrible reality TV? I'm here."

She took a sip of coffee and sat at the table.

"Reality TV and pastries sound perfect."

James grinned, sliding a plate toward her. "Then perfect is what we'll do."

And as he sank into seat beside her, laughter still lingering in the air, Julia dared to think—maybe today could really be this simple.

Maybe he had no secret agenda. Maybe today could just be… simple.

She rose with a small smile.

"I'll just go get changed, and we can start our day."

Upstairs, she pulled on a pair of soft denim shorts and a fitted T-shirt, tied her hair into a neater ponytail, and came back down to find James already curled up on the couch, remote in hand and pastries laid out like a feast between two old friends.

They settled into the living room, sinking into the comfort of each other's company.

Reality TV played in the background—loud, ridiculous, addictive. They laughed at the drama, rolled their eyes at over-the-top confessions, and reached for buttery croissants with sticky fingers and full hearts.

At one point, James started tickling her sides—just like he used to when they were kids, and she needed cheering up.

She squealed, twisting away, giggling uncontrollably.

"James! Stop!"

But he kept at it, grinning, playful and teasing.

And then—the front door clicked open.

Joseph and Daniel stepped inside.

The laughter died instantly.

Julia sat up straighter, adjusting her shirt, her face still flushed from laughter. James casually slung an arm along the back of the couch, a pleased, smug look settling on his face—as though he'd just claimed a little victory.

Joseph's brows lifted, and then he smiled—genuinely, warmly.

His little sister was laughing again. That was all that mattered.

Daniel, on the other hand, froze.

His eyes locked onto Julia, then shifted to James—taking in the cozy proximity, the scattered pastries, the fading echo of laughter.

And though he said nothing, his expression hardened.

He didn't look happy.

Not jealous exactly—but something deeper. A quiet storm behind his eyes. Regret. Frustration. Maybe even fear.

And Julia saw it.

Just for a second, before she forced herself to look away.

Chapter Thirteen

It had been two weeks since Daniel learned he was going to be a father.

Two weeks of recalibrating every thought, every instinct, every piece of himself around that single, monumental truth. He hadn't pushed Julia—he'd promised himself he wouldn't. Instead, he'd done what he could: listening, showing up, being present without demand. Trying, in whatever small ways she allowed, to be her friend again.

Some days, that felt like enough.

Other days… like today… it wasn't.

They were sitting outside on the patio—Julia curled up in one of the cushioned chairs, a light throw across her lap, her hands cradling a cup of ginger tea. Daniel sat opposite, coffee untouched in his hands, more focused on her than anything else.

She looked pale, tired. But still beautiful. Always beautiful.

He opened his mouth to ask how she was feeling when the sliding glass door creaked open behind him.

"I hope I'm not interrupting," came James's voice, smooth as ever, laced with a kind of smugness Daniel could feel without even turning around.

Julia looked up. "Hi, James."

Daniel forced himself to stay still, to stay civil, as James stepped onto the patio holding a small box wrapped in brown paper.

"Brought you those biscuits you like," James said, placing them on the table beside her. "Figured they'd help with the nausea."

Daniel bit the inside of his cheek. The timing was always just a little too perfect. Every time he and Julia seemed to find a moment of quiet, of closeness, James would materialise—like a shadow that wouldn't leave.

And every time Daniel caught his eye, James gave him that same damn look.

A faint smirk. A slight lift of his chin.

Like a message carved in silence: I told you I wasn't going anywhere.

Daniel didn't rise to it. Not today.

He just leaned back in his chair, eyes returning to Julia. "Let me know if you want to go for a walk later," he said calmly, voice low and even. "It's supposed to be a nice afternoon."

Julia looked at him, her expression softening for a moment. "I will. Thanks, Daniel."

James settled beside her without invitation, already launching into a story from work, his voice easy and familiar. But Daniel wasn't really listening. He didn't need to hear the words to understand the intent.

He stood after a few more minutes, offering Julia a small smile. "I'll be around if you need anything."

"Okay," she said gently. "Thanks."

He nodded once and walked back into the house, letting the door close quietly behind him.

He wouldn't fight James for her.

Not with words. Not with one-upmanship.

He'd already wasted too much time pretending he didn't love her.

This time, he'd let his actions speak louder than any smug look ever could.

Julia watched Daniel disappear through the sliding door, the glass glinting with the afternoon sun. There was something steady about him lately. Careful. As if he were always holding his breath around her.

James leaned back in the chair beside her; one arm draped casually over the side.

"He's really leaning into the fatherhood thing, huh?" he said, his tone light but not quite neutral.

Julia didn't look at him. "He's trying."

James gave a soft huff, half amusement, half disbelief. "Trying," he echoed. "Yeah. I guess that's one word for it."

She turned her head then, brows drawing together just slightly. "What's that supposed to mean?"

He lifted his hands in mock surrender. "Nothing. Just… Daniel Moore isn't exactly known for sticking around once the novelty wears off. He gets bored, Jules. You know that."

Her stomach tightened, but she said nothing.

"I'm just saying," he added, lowering his voice, like he was confiding something. "You don't have to settle for breadcrumbs from a guy who's spent the last ten years treating you like a revolving door."

"That's not fair," Julia said quietly.

James tilted his head. "Isn't it? I mean, where was he before the baby?"

Julia looked down at her tea. Her hands had gone still.

James leaned closer. "You know I've always been there. You didn't have to ask. I showed up because I wanted to. Not because I felt guilty. Or obligated."

"James," she warned gently.

But he pressed on, his voice softer now, edged with something almost tender. "I'm not saying this to hurt you. I'm saying it because I care. I've seen the way he looks at you when he thinks no one's watching—and I've seen the way he looks when he wants something he can't have. You've always been the challenge, Jules. The forbidden. Now that it's real? Now that it's messy?" He let that hang in the air, like he didn't need to finish the sentence.

Julia's heart thudded unevenly.

"I just don't want you to get hurt again," James finished.

There was silence between them for a long beat.

Then Julia spoke, her voice low, uncertain. "Neither do I."

James nodded, that same familiar smile tugging at his mouth—gentle, patient. Almost victorious.

"I've been reading about pregnancy," he said casually, as if they hadn't just skirted the edges of something sharp and unspoken.

She glanced at him, a flicker of surprise softening her face. "Oh, have you?" Her voice held a trace of amusement, but she sounded impressed.

He leaned back slightly, playing it cool. "Yeah. Just wanted to understand what you're going through. You're due for your first ultrasound soon, right?"

"Yes," she nodded, resting her hand protectively on her belly. "In two days."

"Is Daniel going with you?" he asked, tone light—too light.

Julia hesitated, eyes flicking away. "I haven't asked him yet."

James gave a thoughtful nod, the corner of his mouth lifting in that quiet, understanding way he'd perfected over the years. "Well, you know I'd love to be there for you."

She turned to look at him, surprised again—but this time unsure. "Thanks. I'll keep that in mind… but I do have to ask Daniel."

"Of course," he said quickly, holding up his hands in mock surrender. "I get it. Just… here if you need me. No pressure."

His voice was soft, almost reverent, like he was offering more than just support. Like he was offering himself.

She didn't know why she did it—maybe out of gratitude, maybe out of guilt.

But her hand moved to his.

"Thank you, James. That means a lot."

He smiled again, eyes locking on hers, and for a moment, the air between them stilled.

"You'll never have to go through this alone," he said quietly.

And though she smiled in return, something inside her shifted—uncertain, uneasy.

Because James always said the right things.

And it was getting harder to tell if it was love… or something else entirely.

She used to know the difference. But now, every word from James sounded like comfort… and control.

That night, the dining room was quiet save for the soft clink of cutlery and the occasional hum of conversation. The chandelier above cast a warm glow across the long table, where Julia, Joseph, and Daniel sat for dinner.

Julia pushed her food around her plate more than she ate it. Across from her, Daniel sat relaxed—at least in posture—but his eyes kept drifting to her, watching her with that quiet intensity he seemed to wear around her now. Protective. Attentive. Present.

She glanced at Joseph, who was telling some story about a supplier mishap, then turned back to Daniel. He met her gaze instantly, his fork paused midair.

"I have my first ultrasound on Friday," she said, her voice calm, measured. Then, after a beat, "I haven't asked anyone to come yet."

Daniel straightened slightly, his full attention on her now. "Okay…"

Her lips parted, hesitant at first, but she pushed through it. "Do you want to be there?"

For a moment, silence hovered.

Then his whole face lit up—genuine, unguarded. His eyes softened, and a slow smile broke across his mouth. "Yes. Please."

Joseph's fork paused with a soft clink against the plate.

Daniel didn't notice. Or maybe he did and chose not to react. His eyes never left Julia's.

"I'd really like that," she added, her voice just above a whisper. Something in her chest loosened when she said it.

Daniel nodded, his smile still there, quieter now. "Then I'll be there."

Beside them, Joseph took a sip of his wine, his jaw tight as he glanced between the two. "Well. That's settled then."

Julia's eyes dropped to her plate, heart thudding. But for the first time in a while, the weight she carried didn't feel like hers alone.

Chapter Fourteen

The engine hummed softly beneath them, a steady rhythm that filled the silence between scattered words. Julia sat curled in the passenger seat of Daniel's sleek black SUV, one hand resting gently over her belly, the other gripping the hem of her cardigan. Outside, the morning sun filtered through the windshield, casting golden streaks across the dashboard.

"You warm enough?" Daniel asked, glancing over.

"Yeah, thanks."

He turned back to the road, jaw tight, fingers flexing on the wheel. He was calm on the surface, but she could feel the nervous energy radiating off him in waves. It mirrored her own.

"You sure you're up for this?" he asked after a beat. "I can slow down if you want to stop, take a breather."

Julia gave a soft, almost amused smile. "I'm not running a marathon, Daniel. Just growing a human."

He exhaled a laugh, tension easing in his shoulders. "Right. Sorry. I just… I don't know the rules. The handbook."

"There isn't one," she said quietly. "If there was, I'd have already burned it."

That earned a smile from him. "Fair."

The silence returned, but it was softer now—more companionable than awkward. She watched the trees whip past outside, summer just starting to give way to early autumn. Everything felt like the in-between—summer fading, something new just beginning.

"I didn't expect to ask you," she said after a while, eyes still on the window.

"To come today?"

She nodded.

He waited a moment, like he wasn't sure how much space to give her. "But you did."

"Yeah," she murmured. "I did."

Daniel's hand shifted on the gearstick. "You don't have to explain, Jules."

"I know."

She hesitated, fingers twitching on her lap.

"I just… wanted someone who would be there because they wanted to be."

He glanced at her again—this time longer. "I'm here because I want to be. You don't ever have to question that."

Something in her tightened, then loosened all at once. She nodded, biting her lip.

They turned into the medical centre parking lot, the building squat and familiar in that clinical, comforting way. Daniel parked, then turned off the ignition. For a moment, neither of them moved.

"Whatever happens in there," he said gently, "you won't be alone."

Julia looked at him. The sunlight caught the edge of his face—made his features softer, less guarded. She didn't answer right away. Just reached for the door handle.

"I know," she said finally. "Thank you for coming."

Daniel got out first, then came around to her side without hesitation, opening her door. She stepped out slowly, pausing when she was on her feet.

And then, without thinking, she slipped her hand into his.

Daniel didn't flinch. He just wrapped his fingers around hers and walked with her into the building—two people not quite together, not quite apart, bound by something fragile and enormous.

Hope.

The clinic was quiet that morning—muted voices, the soft shuffle of footsteps, the occasional beep of machinery behind closed doors. Daniel and Julia sat side by side in the waiting area, their fingers still loosely linked between them.

Julia's grip had tightened slightly since they checked in.

He didn't mention it. Just held on.

A nurse in light blue scrubs appeared at the doorway, holding a clipboard. "Julia Davis?"

She stood, and Daniel rose with her. The nurse gave a kind smile. "Right this way."

The room was dimly lit, calm. A monitor was angled beside the bed, and a slim cart held neatly arranged instruments. Julia climbed onto the examination table slowly, adjusting the paper gown over her hips. Daniel stayed close but hovered uncertainly near the chair by the window.

"You can come closer, you know," she said, voice soft but with the smallest smile.

He moved to her side instantly, settling onto the stool beside her and reaching for her hand again. She didn't hesitate this time.

The technician came in moments later, cheerful but efficient. "Alright, let's take a look, shall we?"

Cool gel spread across her abdomen, and Julia flinched slightly. Daniel squeezed her hand in response.

Then, the room fell into silence as the wand slid across her skin and the grainy image appeared on the screen.

Daniel's breath caught.

There, on the monitor, was something small and shadowed and impossibly alive. The technician clicked a few keys, adjusting the angle, and then the shape sharpened. The curve of a head. A flicker.

"There's the heartbeat," she said, pressing a button. The sound filled the room—fast, rhythmic, impossibly steady.

Julia's lips parted. She stared at the screen, her eyes shining with something unreadable.

Daniel couldn't take his eyes off it. Off that sound.

He'd seen a lot of extraordinary things in his life. He'd built empires. Closed deals worth millions. But nothing—nothing—had ever hit him like that.

That heartbeat.

That tiny, pulsing proof of existence.

His child.

He looked at Julia. She was still staring at the monitor, unmoving, her expression stricken and awestruck all at once.

"Hey," he whispered. She turned to him slowly.

"You okay?"

She nodded, but a tear slipped down her cheek.

Daniel reached up and wiped it away with the back of his fingers, his touch feather-light. "We're really doing this," he said.

Julia let out a laugh that trembled on the edge of breaking. "Yeah. We are."

The technician took a few more measurements, printed out a strip of images, and handed it to Julia before wiping away the gel. "Everything looks perfect so far," she said kindly. "Congratulations."

They were alone again a moment later.

Julia looked down at the printouts in her hand—black and white, and grainy, but somehow the most beautiful thing she'd ever seen.

Daniel's voice came low beside her. "Can I… keep one?"

She glanced at him, startled. Then nodded, tearing off the top photo and handing it over.

He took it carefully, like it might shatter in his fingers.

"I'll frame it," he said.

Julia blinked. "Really?"

"Yeah," he said. "Might put it right next to all my other accomplishments. You know—remind me what actually matters."

She stared at him.

And for the first time in weeks, she felt something like certainty begin to bloom beneath the fear.

Daniel held the door open for Julia as they stepped out of the clinic into the soft midday sun. The weight of the morning still lingered between them—not heavy, just real. Tangible. A new shape to their connection neither of them dared name just yet.

"So…" he said, glancing sideways at her as they reached his car. "Do you want to grab lunch? I know a place with a quiet courtyard and absolutely no James in sight."

Julia gave a small laugh, already reaching for her seatbelt. "That sounds suspiciously perfect."

He grinned. "It might be."

The restaurant was tucked away behind a bookshop, all weathered stone and soft jazz floating through shaded outdoor tables. Ivy crawled up the walls and filtered the sunlight like lace.

Julia sat across from him, sipping lemonade, the ultrasound pictures tucked safely into her bag beside her. For the first time in a while, she looked… lighter. The worry was still there, but it wasn't pressing down as hard. Not today.

Daniel was animated, relaxed in a way she hadn't seen in years. He was telling a story—something about one of Joseph's less-than-stellar attempts at cooking during university—and Julia found herself laughing more than she expected.

Their food had just arrived when a flash of movement caught her eye. Tall. Elegant. Familiar.

"Mary?" Julia blinked.

Across the courtyard, Mary Collins—impossibly chic in high-waisted trousers and a silk blouse, sunglasses perched on her head—turned mid-step and beamed.

"Jules!"

She crossed to them quickly, heels clicking softly on the stone, arms already open. "I knew that was you—I'd recognise that laugh anywhere."

Julia stood, pulled into a quick, affectionate hug. Mary turned to Daniel next, arching a brow with amused approval.

"Well, well… Daniel Moore. This is unexpected."

Daniel gave a short laugh, standing to offer her a quick, polite hug. "Mary."

"Are we…?" She glanced between them, lips quirking. "Is this a thing again, or am I interrupting a ceasefire lunch?"

"Just lunch," Julia said smoothly, though her cheeks were warm.

"Mm-hm." Mary slid into the third seat without asking, placing her designer bag on her lap. "I'm actually meeting someone here for a work chat. Milan shoot in four weeks—might be out there for a whole month." She waved a hand casually, like it wasn't a big deal.

"That's amazing," Julia said, meaning it.

Mary shrugged like it wasn't, but the sparkle in her eyes said otherwise.

Then she leaned in. "But never mind Milan—how did it go?" Her eyes darted meaningfully to Julia's bag. "Was today the day?"

Julia hesitated, then pulled out the ultrasound printout, sliding it across the table like it was sacred.

Mary gasped, one hand flying to her heart. "Oh my God." She picked up the strip delicately, her smile stretching wide. "Look at this little peanut! This is my niece or nephew in there!"

Daniel chuckled. "Your enthusiasm is unmatched."

Mary didn't take her eyes off the image. "You better believe it is. I am going to be the most extra aunty you've ever seen."

Julia laughed, the warmth of it curling in her chest. "I don't doubt that for a second."

Mary looked between them then, and for a moment, her tone softened. "I'm glad you went together."

Daniel met her gaze, steady. "So am I."

Mary gave a small nod, then glanced at her phone as it buzzed on the table. "That's my meeting—boring contracts and talk of weather-light makeup. But I'll call you later, okay?"

"Please do."

She stood, then leaned over and kissed Julia's cheek. "You look happier," she whispered. "Don't question it too much. Just let it in."

And with one last wink at Daniel, she was gone.

Julia sat back, her fingers absently brushing the corner of the ultrasound picture.

Daniel reached across the table and stilled her hand with his.

Their eyes met.

"Still up for dessert?"

She smiled. "Absolutely."

Chapter Fifteen

Julia lay curled on her bed, one leg tucked beneath the other, her fingers drifting over the edges of the ultrasound picture that sat beside her on the duvet. The rest of the house was still, shadows stretching long across the hardwood floor as twilight sank through the windows. The lamp on her nightstand glowed softly, painting everything in warm, honeyed light.

Her phone buzzed beside her.

Mary.

She didn't hesitate—just smiled faintly and picked it up.

"Hey," she said, voice low and calm.

"Took you long enough," Mary replied. "I was about two seconds away from calling in a wellness check. Do I need to break into your place with gelato and threateningly loud affection?"

Julia laughed, the sound surprising even herself. "I'm okay. Just… been sitting here. Thinking."

"Thinking," Mary echoed. "Right. That thing you do where you overanalyse everything until you spiral into a tangle of what-ifs."

Julia didn't argue. She didn't have to. Mary had known her too long.

"It was a big day," Mary continued more gently. "You're allowed to feel a little shaken."

Julia stared at the ceiling, voice soft. "It didn't shake me like I thought it would. It grounded me. In this weird, quiet way."

There was a pause on the other end of the line.

"Because he was there?" Mary asked.

Julia's lips parted, but no words came right away.

"I didn't expect him to come," she said finally. "And when he said yes, I almost regretted asking. Not because I didn't want him there, but because… it felt too important to offer to someone who might not stay."

"But he did stay," Mary said. "He was all in. I saw it. He looked like a man seeing his future for the first time and realising it didn't terrify him."

Julia turned onto her side, fingers absently tracing the edge of the sonogram. Her chest ached—not in the way it used to, hollow and uncertain—but in a way that felt heavy with meaning.

"He asked to keep one of the pictures," she said quietly.

"Of course he did," Mary replied, warmth in her voice. "He's probably staring at it right now."

"He said he'd frame it. Put it next to his other accomplishments."

"Okay, that's either wildly romantic or just peak Daniel Moore—a little corporate, a little sentimental, totally sincere."

Julia smiled into her pillow. "It felt real. The whole day. For the first time, this didn't feel like something I was doing alone."

"You're not," Mary said. "Not anymore."

There was another beat of silence before she added, "He looked at you like you were already a family."

Julia exhaled slowly, eyes drifting shut. "It scares me to want that."

"It's okay to be scared," Mary said. "But don't shut the door because of it. You don't have to know how it ends, Jules. Just keep turning the pages."

Julia gave a soft, aching sound of a laugh. "You've been reading too many of my books."

"I'm your best friend. It's practically my job."

Julia stayed quiet for a moment, eyes fixed on the dim outline of the picture in her hand.

"When do you leave for Milan?"

"In four weeks. I'll be there for two weeks maybe longer if the campaign expands. But I'll call. I'll send illegal snacks and curse the Wi-Fi. I'll be here, even if I'm there."

"Promise?"

"Promise."

Julia swallowed, her voice low. "Thanks for today."

"You don't have to thank me," Mary said. "I'm going to be the coolest aunty in the Southern Hemisphere. This is just the beginning."

Julia's lips curved slightly. "Love you."

"Love you too, Mama."

The call ended, and the room settled back into stillness. Julia set the phone aside, then slowly pulled the ultrasound photo to her chest, holding it there like a secret she was finally ready to protect.

Outside, the sky faded into navy. Inside, something deeper had shifted— something quiet, brave, and just beginning to take root.

Later, across the hall—

Daniel closed the bedroom door behind him with a quiet click, the soft latch echoing in the stillness. The house had settled for the night—no footsteps creaking down the hallway, no murmurs of conversation drifting through the walls. Just silence. And the steady, patient ticking of the old clock on the landing.

He leaned back against the door, exhaling slowly—like he'd been holding his breath all day without realising it. Now, finally alone, it escaped him in a long, quiet sigh.

The room was familiar. He always used this one when he stayed at the Davis family home. Same clean lines, same neutral walls. It wasn't his space, but it had become routine. Temporary. Like everything else.

His apartment would be ready in two weeks—the renovations nearly done. A place of his own again. But instead of relief, all he felt was a knot tightening low in his chest.

What if, when he left, the distance between him and Julia grew again?

What if being across the hall was the only thing keeping them tethered?

James lived nearby. He was always around. Always convenient. Daniel could see it—how easy it would be for Julia to choose what was familiar, what was safe. James loved her. He'd made that clear. Probably had for years.

And Daniel had been too damn blind to do anything about it.

He shrugged off his jacket and draped it over the back of the chair, then reached into the inside pocket. The ultrasound photo was still there—folded neatly, carefully protected like something precious.

He drew it out and sat on the edge of the bed, elbows resting on his knees. The image looked even smaller now, the edges curling slightly. But the shadowed form at the centre of the paper—blurred and beautiful—was unmistakable.

His. Hers. Theirs.

He stared at it in the quiet, his thumb tracing along the edge of the printout like it was something fragile. Sacred.

That heartbeat still echoed in his mind. Fast, steady, alive. That single sound had changed something fundamental in him.

He rubbed a hand across his face. He wasn't sentimental. Or at least, he hadn't been. But now? That sound—that life—had cracked something open in him. And in its place grew something terrifying. Something hopeful.

He placed the photo gently on the bedside table, careful to align it just right. Somewhere he'd see it first thing every morning. Last thing every night.

He loved Julia. He ached for her. Knowing she was just across the hall made it worse. Made it impossible to ignore how badly he wanted to be near her—with her—not just for the child, but for everything they could have been… might still be.

He turned off the lamp and padded into the ensuite, flicking on the dimmer switch. The soft glow cast a golden hue across the mirror.

He barely recognised the man staring back at him.

There was something different now. Softer. Quieter around the edges. Less armour.

Julia had let him be there today. Chosen him. And over lunch, it had almost felt like… like they were a couple on the cusp of something real. A family.

He splashed water on his face, the cold jolt grounding him. Then he leaned on the sink, head bowed, hands braced against the porcelain.

He didn't know what came next.

Didn't know how to undo the years he'd spent keeping everyone at a distance. Didn't know if she would ever fully trust him with what mattered most.

But he knew this—he would keep showing up.

Every day.

For her.

For the baby.

For the life blooming in the quiet, tender spaces he never thought he deserved.

He dried his face, turned off the light, and slipped beneath the covers. The room was cool. Still not home. But the photo on the bedside table caught the moonlight just enough to shine.

And for the first time in a long, long while, Daniel Moore fell asleep with something dangerously close to peace—not knowing that across the hall, someone else had too.

Chapter Sixteen

The scent of fresh coffee lingered, blending with the soft clatter of dishes from the kitchen. Morning light streamed through the dining room windows, painting golden rectangles across the floorboards. Julia had just finished breakfast and was clearing the table when the doorbell rang.

She glanced toward the front door, her stomach tightening slightly.

James.

She didn't have to guess—it was the kind of timing he was known for. Reliable. Predictable. Always showing up like clockwork.

"Hey," he said when she opened the door, eyes sweeping over her face with quiet concern. He held a bouquet of soft yellow tulips in one hand and a bakery bag in the other. "Thought I'd check in. How'd it go yesterday?"

Julia stepped aside to let him in. "You didn't have to bring flowers."

"I wanted to," he said simply, handing them to her. "And croissants. Still warm."

She gave him a soft smile—polite, tired. "Thanks. Come in."

They sat on the couch, James watching her with that familiar intensity. Not possessive, exactly—but close. Protective in a way that made her weigh every word before she spoke.

"Well?" he prompted gently. "You okay?"

Julia reached for the envelope on the coffee table. She slid the photo out and handed it to him without a word.

James stared at it, his expression shifting from curiosity to something deeper. His thumb brushed lightly over the image, almost reverently.

"Wow," he said after a moment. "That's… real."

Julia nodded, her voice low. "Yeah. Very real."

James looked up at her, emotion flickering behind his eyes. "I wish I could've been there."

Julia offered a small, soft smile and glanced away. "I had to ask Daniel. You know that, right? I needed to do it with the person who'll be there every step of the way."

His jaw tightened, just barely. "Yeah. I get it."

She gave him an apologetic smile, gentle but firm.

"How was Daniel?" he asked after a beat—too casual to be innocent.

Julia didn't flinch. "He was there. From the moment I asked him. And he was… happy."

James looked back down at the photo, his fingers brushing the grainy edge with a tenderness that didn't quite reach his eyes. The warmth on his face faded, replaced by something quieter. Measured. Almost solemn.

"I'm happy for you, Julia. Truly." His voice was steady, but there was weight behind it—something unspoken coiled in the pause that followed. "If you believe he's ready to be there for you—forever—then I'm happy for you."

The words landed softly—but their edges were sharp. There was no malice in his tone. Just softness. Care. But beneath it all, a thread of warning.

Like he was asking her to think again. To be sure. To remember.

Julia didn't speak right away. She watched him, her gaze steady, searching his face for what wasn't being said.

She took the photo back from his hands and set it carefully on the table beside her. "I believe in what I saw yesterday," she said softly. "That's enough—for now."

James nodded, but the smile he gave her was shadowed—gentle, yes, but tinged with something mournful.

"I wish I could've been the one," he said suddenly, his voice barely above a whisper. "I've loved you for a long time, Julia. I think part of me always has."

Her breath caught, but she didn't interrupt.

"I didn't say anything before because I thought you'd come to me when you were ready," he continued. "But I think I waited too long. And now…"

He hesitated, then looked up at her with eyes that were clear and open and utterly sincere.

"I still want to build a life with you. I want to marry you. Raise this baby together. I know it's not what you expected to hear—but I had to say it. Before you go too far down a road that might not lead where you think."

Her breath caught. Once, this would've been everything. But the weight of what she wanted had shifted—and she wasn't sure James saw that.

Julia blinked, stunned into silence. Not because it was unexpected—but because it still mattered. Because once, she'd imagined it too.

But now?

Now everything felt heavier.

Realer.

And Daniel's face—his hand reaching for hers, his voice when he heard the heartbeat—flickered behind her eyes like a flame refusing to be snuffed out.

She swallowed. "James…"

He held up a hand gently. "You don't have to say anything now. I just needed you to know. I'm not going anywhere. Whatever happens—I'll be here."

His words settled between them like the slow hush before a storm.

And in the distance, Julia could almost feel the weight of a decision beginning to shift.

In the quiet of the study, morning sun lit up the bookshelves along one wall. Daniel stood with his hands in his pockets, the tension in his shoulders at odds with the calm around him. Joseph sat in the leather armchair, coffee mug in hand, eyes fixed on his friend with the same focus he used on high-stakes contracts.

"You want to marry my sister," Joseph repeated, not a question—an assessment.

Daniel nodded. "Yes."

"And this isn't about the baby?"

Daniel met his gaze squarely. "It's about her. It's always been about her. The baby just made me realise how much I can't stand the idea of not building a life with her."

Joseph leaned back in his chair, arms crossed, a slow frown settling over his face. "You know I never wanted you anywhere near my sister like that, right?"

Daniel didn't flinch. "I know. But I should've stood up to you—told you how I felt a long time ago. Before everything got so… complicated."

Joseph's eyes sharpened. "You hurt her, Daniel. Badly."

"I know." Daniel's voice dropped, the words heavy. "I live with that. Every day. I didn't trust what we had back then—not the way I should have. But I see it now. And I'm not running anymore. I want her. And I want this family."

Joseph stared at him for a long moment, his expression unreadable.

"You love her?"

"Yes," Daniel said without hesitation. "Completely. And I'm not waiting around just to watch her slip away to someone who's already at the door."

Joseph's gaze narrowed. "So, this is about James."

"It's about Julia," Daniel said firmly. "About making sure she knows I'm all in. I want to marry her, Joe. Not because she's pregnant. Not because of guilt or pressure. But because I'm in love with her. And I'm ready to build a life with her."

Joseph pushed up from his chair, exhaling through his nose as he paced the length of the study. When he turned back, his expression was harder now. Protective. Grounded.

"If you hurt her again—"

"I won't," Daniel cut in, voice steady. "But if I ever do… you have my full permission to break my nose."

Joseph didn't blink. "I'll do more than that. I don't care how long we've been friends or how much money you've got. I'll bury you."

Daniel's mouth twitched into something like a grin—but it didn't quite hold.

He knew this wasn't over. Not until Julia said yes. And right now, James was still out there, reminding her of what safe used to feel like.

Timing mattered now.

More than ever.

The hallway was quiet, the kind of hush that came after breakfast when the day was still settling into itself. Daniel stepped out of Joseph's study, the door clicking softly shut behind him. He was halfway to the stairs when he saw James coming down the hallway, coat slung over one arm, phone in hand.

They locked eyes.

James slowed, then stopped altogether.

Daniel folded his arms across his chest, brows lifting slightly. "Didn't think you were still here."

James gave a faint smile, polite but not warm. "Just came to check in. See how the ultrasound went."

Daniel's jaw flexed. "Convenient timing."

James glanced toward the closed door of the living room, then back. His smile thinned. "We had a good talk."

There was a beat of silence between them—long enough for tension to bloom in the air like a warning.

Then James added, tone mild but deliberately placed, "I asked her to marry me."

Daniel stopped dead, the words hitting like a punch to the ribs—sharp, unexpected, breath-stealing. For a second, all he could do was stare.

"You what?" he said, voice low.

James tilted his head, still calm. "I asked her to marry me."

Daniel stepped forward slightly, shoulders tightening. "And what did she say?"

James held his gaze, unreadable. "She didn't say yes."

Daniel's jaw clenched.

"But she didn't say no either."

Daniel stared at him, breath steady, heart anything but.

James adjusted the cuff of his shirt with careful precision, then looked up. "You're not the only one trying to build a future with her. Maybe don't forget that."

And with that, he gave a nod and moved past Daniel, his footsteps measured, unhurried.

Daniel stood still for a long moment, pulse roaring in his ears. Behind him, the study door remained closed. Ahead, the living room, where Julia was just a few steps away.

But everything suddenly felt further than it had just minutes ago.

Much further.

Chapter Seventeen

Julia sat on the couch, arms wrapped around her knees, staring at the ultrasound photo on the coffee table. The morning light filtered through the curtains, soft and golden, but nothing in her chest felt warm. Just tangled. Conflicted.

When Daniel stepped into the room, she didn't look up right away.

"I figured I'd find you here," he said gently.

She said nothing. Just kept her eyes on the grainy image in front of her—the tiny shape that had become the centre of everything.

He crossed the room slowly, stopping a few feet away.

"I ran into James," he said.

Julia's breath hitched—so small, most wouldn't notice. But Daniel knew her. He saw it.

"He told me he asked you to marry him."

Julia didn't speak. She looked down at the photo, smoothing a crease that wasn't really there.

"He said you didn't say yes," Daniel continued. "But you didn't say no either."

Still no response.

"Julia."

Finally, she looked up, and the hesitation in her eyes felt like a slap.

"I didn't know what to say," she said quietly. "It caught me off guard."

"You should've said no," Daniel said, his voice low. Not angry. Just… hurt. "That should've been immediate."

"I didn't want to hurt him."

Daniel stepped closer, something raw behind his eyes. "What about me?"

That landed.

Julia's eyes snapped up to his, sharp with pain and something else—something wounded.

"I was in that room yesterday," Daniel said, his voice hoarse. "I saw our baby. I heard the heartbeat. I held that photo like it meant everything—because it does. And I thought you felt that too."

"I did," she whispered, her voice barely holding.

"Then why the hell is James proposing to you—and you're not slamming the door in his face?"

Her jaw tightened. "Because just wanting to be part of this baby's life doesn't automatically mean you get me with it."

Silence stretched. The weight of her words landed between them, heavy and final.

Daniel stepped back like she'd struck him. "You know I love you."

"Do I?" she shot back, eyes glinting with accusation. "Do I really, Daniel?"

His mouth opened, but no words came.

She stood now, her voice low but fierce. "You didn't even remember making love to me. You don't remember the night this child was conceived. And I'm supposed to believe I matter more than anyone else ever has?"

His chest rose and fell with the force of his breath, emotion tightening every line of his face.

"I didn't think it was real because I was drunk. I didn't admit it to myself because I was a coward. But don't you dare question what I feel for you now."

Her expression wavered, but she held firm. "I don't know how I am supposed to forget that. How can I not question it."

Daniel moved closer, his voice raw. "What I feel for you is not obligation. This is everything. I'm sorry I didn't believe that night was real. But I remember that night—I do. Every second of it. You were mine. And I've been yours for a hell of a lot longer than either of us ever admitted."

Julia looked up at him, the silence thick between them.

"I'm not James," he added. "I won't ask for your hand just to win some twisted race. When I ask you to marry me, it'll be because you believe in me enough to say yes. For real."

She blinked fast, her breath shaky.

"I'm not just here for the baby, Julia," he said. "I'm here for you. All of you. And I'm not giving up on us."

Her arms stayed wrapped around herself, protective. But her eyes—those beautiful, guarded eyes—didn't look away.

The doorbell rang.

Daniel rose from the couch, jaw tight as he crossed the room. He'd been pacing most of the afternoon, restless. Julia was out with James—again—and it gnawed at him like a splinter under the skin. Something about James felt wrong. Slippery. Like a mask that never fully dropped. Daniel didn't trust him. And he hated the idea of Julia being pulled into whatever web the man was spinning.

He opened the door.

Jenna Giles stood there, all glossy lips and high-end perfume. Her blond hair was styled to perfection, her dress a little too tight, a little too strategic. She was beautiful—yes—but in a curated, showroom kind of way. A product of salons and filters. Not like Julia. Julia's beauty was quiet, effortless, something you felt before you even noticed it.

"Daniel," Jenna said, her smile wide and bright. "So good to see you."

He arched a brow. "Jenna. What are you doing here?"

"I was looking for James," she replied, stepping forward just enough to suggest she was coming in, whether invited or not. "He said he might be here this afternoon."

Daniel frowned. "He's out. With Julia."

Her smile faltered for half a second—so quick it almost passed unnoticed.

"Ah," she said lightly. "Well, would you mind if I waited?"

Daniel stepped back reluctantly, gesturing toward the living room. "Suit yourself."

Jenna sashayed in like she owned the place, her heels clicking across the hardwood floors. She perched on the edge of the couch, crossing her legs with deliberate poise, then looked up at him with those calculating eyes.

"You know, it's been ages since we talked properly," she purred.

"I didn't realise we ever did talk properly," Daniel said dryly as he crossed to the sideboard. He poured himself a drink without looking her way—and without offering her one.

Jenna let out a laugh—too loud, too bright, too rehearsed. "Always so guarded. No wonder Julia's drawn to you."

He glanced over, unimpressed. "What's that supposed to mean?"

She tilted her head, all faux innocence. "Just an observation. You've got that… intense, brooding thing going. Girls eat that up."

Daniel narrowed his eyes. "Why are you really here, Jenna?"

"I told you—I need James for something." She crossed one long leg over the other and added casually, "Mind if I have a drink?"

He hesitated, then poured a second glass and handed it to her. She took it with a smile that didn't reach her eyes.

Daniel sat at the opposite end of the couch, sipping his scotch in silence. He'd just set the empty glass down on the coffee table when a ripple of sound echoed from the hallway.

Laughter.

Then Julia's voice, light and unguarded, drifted in—warm, familiar.

James answered with something low and smooth—his signature tone, too polished to be real. Daniel tensed immediately. That voice made his skin itch.

Jenna's eyes flicked to the door—and lit up.

"Perfect timing," she whispered.

"What—?"

She pounced.

In a blur, she crossed the short distance, practically throwing herself into his lap. Before he could react, she straddled him, one hand sliding up his chest as the other cupped his jaw. Then her lips crashed onto his.

Daniel froze.

Not from desire.

From sheer, stunned disbelief.

James's car pulled into the driveway just ahead of Mary's, the afternoon sun casting long shadows across the front lawn.

Julia stepped out of the passenger side, a soft smile tugging at her lips as Mary parked and quickly got out. Without hesitation, Mary crossed the path and pulled Julia into a tight hug.

"I was hoping for a girls' night," she said warmly, eyes flicking past Julia.

Her gaze landed on James, sharp beneath polite indifference. "Hello, James."

He gave a slow nod. "Mary."

Julia chuckled. "A girls' night sounds like bliss. James just took me to lunch."

"I hope you're looking after my girl," Mary said, slipping her arm through Julia's.

James answered smoothly, "Of course. She's very precious."

Julia was still laughing as they stepped inside, rummaging through her bag at the living room entrance—until Mary stopped cold.

"What the hell?" she said, her voice laced with disbelief.

Julia looked up—and froze.

There on the couch was Jenna Giles, straddling Daniel, her hands buried in his hair as she kissed him like she belonged there.

For one agonising heartbeat, no one moved.

Then Daniel jerked back, shoving Jenna away just as the trio entered the room fully.

Julia stood there, eyes locked on them, her smile vanishing. Her expression flickered—open, confused, then suddenly guarded, brittle.

James gave a soft chuckle; eyebrows raised in manufactured surprise. "Well. Didn't mean to interrupt."

"Julia," Daniel said instantly, taking a step toward her, his voice taut. "This isn't what it looks like—"

"Oh, come on, Daniel," Jenna said with a lazy laugh behind him, casually straightening her dress. "No need to be shy. We've always had chemistry."

Daniel spun toward her, fury crackling just under his skin. "Don't lie. You kissed me. I didn't—"

James slid smoothly into Julia's space, the model of calm reassurance. "It didn't look one-sided."

His shoulder brushed Julia's like he had every right to be there.

Julia blinked, her eyes meeting Daniel's. She looked like she'd just stepped off solid ground.

Her mouth opened—then closed again.

She said nothing.

But her silence sliced deeper than any accusation.

Her spine stiffened as she turned. Not in anger—but in self-protection, like she was already bracing for the fallout.

"Julia, wait—" Daniel surged forward.

But Mary was faster.

She stepped into his path, planting a firm hand on his chest. "No, you don't. You stay away from her."

Daniel's jaw clenched, every muscle in his body tense, torn between explanations and regrets.

Mary didn't move. She stood between them like a shield, her jaw tight, eyes full of fire. "Not today, Daniel. You have done enough."

Behind him, Jenna sat back with a smug little smirk, eyes gleaming with satisfaction.

Daniel didn't look at her.

Couldn't.

His eyes were still on the door Julia had just walked through—on the woman he loved disappearing into the arms of the one man he didn't trust.

And the worst part?

She hadn't looked back.

Chapter Eighteen

The afternoon air was crisp with the scent of distant eucalyptus and sun-warmed stone. Julia sank onto the cushioned bench on the terrace, her shoulders hunched. James sat beside her, slipping an arm around her back like it was the most natural thing in the world.

"You don't have to say anything," he murmured gently, leaning close. "Just let yourself breathe."

Julia stared straight ahead, blinking quickly. Her face was a mix of disbelief and shame, her jaw clenched tight to keep it all from spilling out.

"I can't believe I nearly fell for it," she said finally, her voice cracking. "He sounded so sincere. I thought…"

James gave a low hum, nodding. "That's the problem with men like Daniel. They make you feel seen—until they don't."

Julia didn't answer. She simply dropped her head in her hands, her elbows braced on her knees, shoulders curling in as if she could fold herself small enough to disappear.

James tilted his head toward her. "He had you convinced, didn't he? That you were different. That this time he meant it."

Julia let out a soft, bitter laugh. "I'm such an idiot."

"You're not an idiot," James said smoothly, his voice a velvet balm. "You're trusting. That's not a flaw, Julia. It's what makes you… you."

He brushed a lock of hair from her cheek. She didn't flinch—but she didn't lean in.

From the open sliding door behind them, Mary stepped out onto the terrace, her arms crossed loosely. She took one look at Julia's pale face, and her voice softened.

"Are you okay, sweet?" she asked, walking over.

Julia looked up, and something in her eyes cracked. "No," she whispered. "I feel like the world just shifted. And I'm the last one to know it already moved."

Mary knelt in front of her, placing her hands gently on Julia's knees. "You didn't do anything wrong," she said firmly. "Whatever that scene was in there, it wasn't about you. It was about someone trying to twist things."

James gave a polite, almost sympathetic nod. "Daniel's clearly not as stable as he lets on. And Jenna—well, she's never been subtle."

Mary's eyes flicked to James. "Neither are you. You just wear it better."

James raised his eyebrows in mock offence. "Come now, Mary. I'm only trying to help."

"I'm sure you are," she said. But her gaze lingered.

He kept his smile in place, easy and smooth. "Look, I get that you're protective. I respect that. But Julia deserves someone who's going to be there. Really there. Not someone who runs when things get messy."

Julia rubbed at her temple, exhaustion bleeding into every line of her face. "I just need… time to think."

"Of course you do," James said, rubbing small circles along her back. "I'll stay as long as you need me. You don't have to go through this alone."

Mary's stomach turned. It was too practiced, too rehearsed—like he'd said those words in a mirror.

But Mary was watching him now—not just his words, but the way he said them. The slight tension in his jaw when Julia mentioned Daniel. The way his eyes flicked to the ultrasound photo, just a little too long. The calculation behind every gentle gesture.

And something… didn't sit right.

She stood slowly. "I'll make us some tea," she said, voice light. "I think we all need something warm."

She met James's eyes as she stood.

They stared at each other for a beat too long.

Then Mary turned, her pace calm but her instincts on high alert. Something was off with James Giles. She could feel it in her gut.

And she wasn't going to ignore it.

Not this time.

Golden light faded through the kitchen windows, casting long shadows over the quiet room. Mary stood at the counter, pouring boiling water into a teapot, her movements sharp and focused. She didn't look up when she heard footsteps behind her.

Daniel.

He stepped in quietly, but there was nothing casual about his presence. His hands were in his pockets, jaw set, eyes dark and unreadable.

"Is she okay?" he asked, his voice low.

Mary didn't turn around. "She will be."

A beat of silence passed.

Then she said, "You've got about sixty seconds to convince me that what happened back there wasn't what it looked like."

Daniel exhaled hard, leaning against the doorway. "It wasn't. Jenna showed up looking for James. I told her he was out. Next thing I know, she's on top of me like we're in some twisted soap opera."

Mary turned slowly now, finally meeting his eyes. "You didn't stop her."

His expression hardened. "I froze. I didn't kiss her, Mary. I didn't want her. You know that."

"I know what I saw. And more importantly, I know what Julia saw."

Pain flashed in Daniel's eyes, quick and raw. "I didn't even get the chance to explain."

"No. Because James swept in like some knight in tailored armour and walked her out before you could say a word."

Daniel straightened, frowning. "You noticed that too?"

Mary nodded slowly. "I've been watching him all afternoon. He's too smooth. Too perfect. The way he hovers near her. The way he always just happens to show up when she's at her most vulnerable."

She turned back to the teapot, but her voice dropped, edged in steel.

"And the way Jenna showed up today? It felt orchestrated. Like he knew exactly what was about to happen."

Daniel's eyes narrowed. "You think he planned it?"

"I think he's playing a long game," Mary said. "And right now, Julia's the prize."

Daniel moved further into the room, his fists clenched at his sides before he could stop himself. "He asked her to marry him."

Mary's head snapped up. "He what?"

"Yesterday morning. She didn't say yes… but she didn't say no, either."

Mary let out a breath. "God."

Daniel rubbed his jaw. "I can't prove anything, but something's wrong with him. The way he looks at her—it's not love. It's obsession."

Mary nodded grimly. "That's exactly what I've been feeling. He's always charming, always in control. But there's something behind his eyes. Like he's measuring everyone. Plotting."

"She won't see it," Daniel said. "Not yet."

"No," Mary agreed. "Not until it's too late."

She turned back to him, her voice low and urgent now. "We need to be smart about this. If we go at him directly, Julia will shut down. She won't want to hear it. She's too shaken, too confused."

Daniel nodded. "Then we find proof. We pull the thread."

She handed him the cup, her fingers lingering a second too long. Then her eyes lifted to meet his—steady, searching.

"Do you love her?" she asked softly.

Daniel didn't hesitate. "More than anything."

Mary gave a small nod. That was all she needed.

"Then we do this," she said. "For her."

They stood there in silence, no more words needed. The steam curled between them, warm and fragile—but the air had shifted. Something colder loomed beyond the quiet kitchen walls, pressing in like a coming storm.

Because James Giles wasn't going to let Julia go—not without a fight.

And this time, they were ready for it.

Julia sat still on the edge of the bed, fingers locked tight in her lap. She didn't tremble—but it took everything not to. Her voice when it came, was soft, brittle. Not angry. Just hollow.

"I know it wasn't him."

Mary looked up from where she stood near the window, arms folded. "You're sure?"

Julia nodded. "He looked at me like he'd been blindsided too. And he would never... not like that. Not in my house."

Mary studied her, then crossed the room and sat beside her. "So, what are you thinking?"

"I'm thinking... Jenna set it up." Julia shook her head. "But I don't understand why. What would she even gain? She doesn't want him. She barely knows him."

Mary snorted softly. "Want him? No. But ruin something good for you? That's more her style."

Julia looked at her, brow furrowed. "That's just spite."

"Exactly." Mary leaned back against the headboard; one leg tucked beneath her. "Jenna thrives on control. On being the centre of everything. She doesn't need to want Daniel—just knowing she could mess with your happiness for five seconds is probably enough to satisfy whatever twisted need she's got."

"She waited until I came in," Julia said slowly.

Mary said flatly. "Classic ambush. She makes the move, you walk in, your heart breaks. She wins."

Julia let out a shaky breath. "God, that's messed up."

Mary offered a faint, bitter smile. "It's Jenna. Messed up is her love language."

"I feel stupid for even reacting," Julia whispered. "I let her get to me."

"You're not stupid." Mary reached over, gave her hand a gentle squeeze. "You've been through hell and back with trust. This just hit you in the worst possible spot."

Julia was quiet for a long moment. Then she asked, "You think Daniel knows it was a setup?"

"I think he suspects," Mary said. "But knowing him, he's also blaming himself. Because that's what good men do when women like Jenna throw themselves at them—they feel guilty for being in the same room."

Julia gave a tired laugh, wiping at the corner of her eye. "He did look like he wanted to disappear."

"Because he probably did."

Julia leaned her head on Mary's shoulder. "I hate that people like her are still in our lives."

Mary rested her cheek against Julia's hair. "She won't be for long. Not if I have anything to say about it."

For the first time that evening, Julia let her eyes close. Just for a moment. Just long enough to feel steady again.

The terrace overlooked manicured gardens, where twilight settled like a silk shawl over stone fountains and trimmed hedges. The Davis estate stood visible beyond the trees—so close, it felt like a shadow waiting to be stepped into.

Jenna leaned against the iron railing, a glass of rosé dangling between her fingers. "That went well," she said, her voice light, but there was satisfaction beneath it. "She looked like someone cracked her ribs open."

James stepped out from the French doors behind her, a glass in hand, dark amber liquid catching the dying light. "She needed to see Daniel for what he really is."

Jenna laughed softly. "Is that what he is? Or just what you need him to be?"

He didn't answer right away. Instead, he walked to stand beside her, his eyes fixed on the Davis property beyond the trees. "Thank you," he said finally. "For what you did today."

She raised an eyebrow. "I kissed a man who had the charm of a brick wall. You're welcome."

James smirked. "You did more than that. You created doubt. It's all I needed."

"You're playing a dangerous game, brother." Jenna sipped her wine, her eyes flicking sideways. "You think once Julia's angry enough, hurt enough, she'll just run to you?"

"I don't need her to run," James said coolly. "I just need her to stop looking back."

Jenna turned to face him now, one hand on her hip. "And when she finds out? Because let's be honest—she will. She's not stupid."

He met her gaze with unnerving calm. "By then, it won't matter. She'll see that I've been the one constant in her life. The one person who never gave up on her."

Jenna scoffed. "That's not love, James. That's obsession with good PR."

"Call it what you want," he said, sipping his drink. "But she's safer with me. And deep down, she knows it."

They stood in silence for a moment, the tension between them like a tight string waiting to snap.

Then Jenna tilted her head. "So, what happens now?"

James gave a faint smile. "Now… we wait. Let the storm settle. And when it does, I'll be the one standing beside her."

She clinked her glass lightly against his. "Just don't forget—I played my part. If this goes south, I'm not going down with you."

"You won't," he murmured, eyes still locked on the Davis estate.

"She'll never know what hit her."

"You really think she'll forgive you once she finds out everything?" Jenna asked.

Chapter Nineteen

The house was quiet. Shadows stretched long and soft across the hardwood floor as Julia padded down the stairs barefoot. The cool air brushed her skin, lifting the hem of her oversized sleep shirt. She crossed into the kitchen, the faint hum of the refrigerator the only sound, and opened it slowly.

She stared at the rows of bottles and containers, eyes unfocused, then reached for a small bottle of juice. She unscrewed the lid and took a long, slow sip straight from the bottle, the sweetness catching in her throat.

But it didn't drown the ache blooming behind her ribs.

Her mind slipped, unbidden, to the image still scorched behind her eyes—Daniel and Jenna, locked in that kiss. Jenna's hands curled around his collar, his arms stiff at his sides. He hadn't pulled her in… but he hadn't pushed her away either.

Julia closed her eyes and pressed the cold bottle against her forehead.

She wanted to scream. Cry. Rage.

She knew Daniel hadn't kissed Jenna—that it had been Jenna who reached for him—but the image still burned behind her eyes. And worse, it hurt.

But instead of fury, all she felt was a hollow splintering inside her—a slow, quiet cracking, like something precious had broken… and the pieces no longer fit.

He'd told her she was different. That what they had mattered. And she had believed him. God help her, she had.

A whisper of movement in the dark pulled her eyes toward the window, but it was nothing—just the curtain lifting in the night breeze. She set the juice down and leaned both hands on the countertop, bracing herself.

Her mind shifted—reluctantly, like it didn't want to go there—to James.

The proposal.

It had been quiet, almost sweet. No dramatic gestures. Just him.

'I still want to build a life with you. I want to marry you. Raise this baby together.'

And now, standing here in the middle of the night, she knew.

She couldn't marry him.

James was comforting, constant. Dependable, even. But something in her pulled back from him—like instinct. Like a warning she couldn't name.

He was too perfect, too present. Always there. Always watching.

He wasn't her person.

Daniel was.

God, she loved him. Even now—especially now—that love lived inside her like breath: constant, involuntary.

But Daniel didn't do roots. He did distance. Charm. Fleeting sparks of emotion that vanished behind the same invisible wall she'd spent years trying to scale.

What if she never got past it?

What if no one could?

She knew that little kissing scene in the living room was all Jenna's doing. It reeked of calculation.

Julia exhaled slowly, her hand resting protectively on her stomach.

Maybe this wasn't about Daniel. Or James. Maybe it was about her.

Maybe she'd raise this child alone.

A single tear slipped down her cheek, warm and quiet.

She wiped it away quickly.

Not because she wasn't scared.

But because somewhere, deep inside the ache, a small thread of strength was beginning to pull taut.

She wasn't alone.

Not really.

She had Joseph and Mary.

She had herself.

She had this baby.

And maybe—just maybe—that would be enough.

The soft glow from a single lamp pooled across the stairwell, casting long shadows as Julia padded toward the bedroom, one hand pressed against the small of her back. She was tired in a way that felt cellular—tired of thinking, of smiling for everyone else's sake, of pretending she had it all under control.

Her foot had just touched the bottom step when she saw movement.

Daniel.

He was coming down the stairs—barefoot, shirtless, hair tousled from sleep. They both froze.

A heartbeat passed.

Julia looked away first. "I was just heading up," she said quietly.

"Couldn't sleep," he murmured. "Thought I'd get some water."

She gave him a polite, tight smile and started up a step.

Daniel didn't move. "Julia... about this afternoon—"

She stopped, still facing the stairs. "It's okay. I know it was Jenna."

"You do?" His voice was cautious, almost disbelieving.

Julia turned just enough to meet his eyes. "I'm not an idiot, Daniel. I know you can't stand her. And she's never liked me."

Daniel's shoulders eased a fraction. "Thank you," he said, almost a whisper.

Julia gave a small shrug. "I'm sorry I reacted at all. I should've known better."

"I get it," he said gently. "It caught me off guard too."

Silence settled again—thick, unspoken things hanging in the space between them. Then Julia took another step up.

"Goodnight, Daniel."

He nodded slowly. "Goodnight."

She took another step.

Then—sharp pain.

Sudden. Low. Deep. Twisting.

Julia gasped and clutched her abdomen, her hand flying to the banister as her knees buckled slightly.

"Julia?" Daniel's voice snapped into urgency as he stepped toward her, hands catching her elbows. "What is it?"

"I… I don't know. Just a cramp, maybe—" She winced, the pain stealing her breath.

"Come on." His arm slipped around her back, gently steadying her. "Let's get you upstairs."

She let him guide her, her pride overridden by discomfort. He didn't ask questions. Didn't hesitate. Just helped her into her room, sat her down on the edge of the bed, and knelt in front of her, searching her face.

"Breathe. Where does it hurt?"

She placed a hand low on her stomach. "Here. It's easing off… I think it's okay now."

Daniel didn't look convinced. "You should lie down."

She nodded and slowly eased back onto the pillows. He pulled the blanket up over her and lingered there, kneeling at her bedside.

"I'll stay until it passes."

She didn't argue.

"Thank you."

Minutes passed in silence—his presence quiet but grounding.

Eventually, the pain faded into a dull ache. She closed her eyes, letting herself drift in the hush of the moment. His hand rested lightly on the blanket above her knee. Not possessive. Not desperate. Just… steady.

It was later—how much later, she didn't know—when she felt it.

A warm dampness.

Julia sat up slowly, heart pounding. She shifted under the covers—and saw the smear of blood.

Panic surged like a tidal wave.

She pressed a hand to her mouth, willing herself to stay calm. But her body moved before her thoughts caught up. She slipped out of bed, pulled on her robe with trembling hands, and padded across the hall barefoot.

She stood in front of Daniel's door, breath shallow, hand trembling as she lifted it to knock.

Once.

Twice.

The door opened almost instantly.

Daniel was still awake. Shirtless. His eyes landed on her—wide, alert—and immediately darkened with concern.

"I need help," she whispered, voice breaking. "Daniel… I'm bleeding."

He didn't speak.

He just moved.

In one fluid motion, he stepped forward, slid a steadying hand under her elbow, and guided her gently into his room.

"Sit down," he murmured, his voice low and firm.

She sank onto the edge of the bed, legs shaky, and watched as he moved quickly—grabbing a T-shirt, pulling on jeans. No wasted motion. No questions. Just calm, controlled urgency.

And for a moment—just a moment—Julia let herself lean into him.

When he was dressed, he crouched in front of her, hands warm on her arms.

"Okay. Let's go."

She stood—but as she did, another cramp gripped her, sharp and sudden. She gasped, doubling slightly.

Daniel caught her.

"I'm losing it," she whispered, panic rising like bile. "I don't want to lose my baby."

"Julia," he said firmly, catching her gaze. "Don't think like that. We're going to the hospital. Right now. You're not alone."

Her eyes filled. She tried to hold it together, but the fear was too loud. Tears spilled down her cheeks as she nodded, allowing him to guide her down the stairs and out to the car.

The drive was a blur of city lights and shallow breathing, her hand gripping the seatbelt like a lifeline.

Daniel said nothing, but his hand reached for hers at every red light. And didn't let go.

At the hospital, nurses moved quickly, gently, ushering her into an exam room. Daniel stayed just outside the curtain—close enough to hear her breathing, far enough to give her space. When the doctor arrived, he stepped back and waited, pacing.

Eventually, a nurse emerged.

"She's stable. We're monitoring her overnight as a precaution," she said calmly. "The bleeding's slowed, and the cramping has eased. But we'll keep a close eye."

Daniel exhaled for the first time in what felt like hours.

He sat in the stiff hospital chair beside her bed, watching the rhythm of the foetal monitor like it was the only thing tethering him to the earth.

By morning, Julia was still resting, the worst of it behind her.

He stepped out quietly and pulled out his phone.

First, he called Joseph.

Then Mary.

His voice was calm. Steady. But when he glanced back through the glass window set in the door—catching sight of Julia's pale face, her fingers curled protectively around her belly—he felt that familiar fear creeping in again.

She hadn't chosen him.

Might never choose him.

And yet, none of that mattered now.

Right now, all that mattered was keeping her safe.

And protecting the fragile heartbeat still pulsing inside her.

The hospital room was dim, quiet except for the steady beep of the foetal monitor and the soft hum of early morning traffic outside the window.

Daniel sat in the chair beside Julia's bed, slouched forward slightly, elbows resting on his knees, her hand cradled gently between his own. He hadn't slept. Not really. He couldn't bring himself to close his eyes—not while every inch of him was tuned to her breathing, every second waiting for movement, for proof that she was still okay.

Then, at last, her fingers twitched.

Her eyes fluttered open.

He straightened instantly, his voice low and warm, filled with gentle relief.

"Hi, sweetheart… How are you feeling?"

Julia blinked, dazed for a moment, then slowly turned her head toward him.

"Better, I think," she murmured. "The pain's gone."

His shoulders dropped slightly, just enough to betray how much tension he'd been carrying.

"The doctors will be in soon," he said softly. "They want to keep you through the day, just to be safe."

She looked down then—only just now noticing their hands. His thumb was grazing the back of hers, careful, rhythmic.

He lifted her hand and pressed a kiss into it. His lips lingered.

She flinched. Pulled back.

"Don't, Daniel."

His eyes flicked up, startled, but not angry. Just… confused. Wounded.

"Why?" he asked gently. "I love you, Julia."

She turned her head away, jaw clenched.

"No, you don't," she whispered.

"You just feel responsible. That's not love."

He sat back, blinking, like her words had knocked the air from his lungs.

"That's not true," he said quietly.

"Yes, it is," she insisted, her voice tight. "You don't get to break my heart and then act like it didn't happen. You don't get to show up now and call it love just because I'm carrying your child."

"I'm here because I care," he said, leaning forward again. "Because I do love you. Not out of guilt. Not because of the baby. I've loved you for years, Julia. I just—I buried it. I pushed it down. Because I was scared. Of what it meant. Of what I could lose."

She looked at him then, eyes raw and rimmed with exhaustion.

"But you did lose it. You lost me."

Daniel didn't move. Didn't argue.

"I know."

She swallowed hard. "You don't get to fix it with bedside vigils and whispered confessions."

"I'm not trying to fix it," he said. "I know I can't. Not with one night in a hospital chair."

He rubbed his hands over his face, then looked at her with something fragile in his gaze.

"But just so you know. I'm not going anywhere. Not now. Not tomorrow. I'll show up every day if that's what it takes."

She looked away again, and this time her voice cracked.

"I don't want to need you."

"I'm not asking you to."

A long silence followed, filled only by the steady rhythm of machines and the weight of everything unsaid.

Finally, she let out a breath.

"I'm tired, Daniel."

"I know."

"I'm scared."

He nodded, eyes wet.

"I am too."

They didn't speak for a while after that. He didn't reach for her hand again. Just sat there—quietly, humbly—with his elbows on his knees and his heart in his throat.

And Julia lay back against the pillow, one hand over her belly, the other curled near her mouth as if trying to block out the sound of her own thoughts.

She hadn't unlocked the door.

But she left it slightly ajar.

And maybe, one day, she'd let him in.

Chapter Twenty

The sun was barely up when the hospital room door creaked open.

Julia stirred at the sound, eyelids fluttering. Daniel stood from the chair beside her bed, shoulders tense. He'd been sitting like that for hours—silent, watching her breathe.

Mary slipped in like a gust of Parisian wind—designer boots, messy topknot, yesterday's eyeliner. She paused the moment she saw them: Julia pale but resting, Daniel hovering protectively nearby.

Her eyes narrowed.

"What happened?" she asked, voice low but urgent.

Daniel stepped back, giving her space.

"She had some bleeding overnight," he said evenly. "They think it was a threatened miscarriage. She's stable now, but they're keeping her for observation."

Mary didn't look at him. Her eyes were fixed on Julia as she crossed the room in three long strides and sat on the side of the bed.

"Oh, honey…" Her voice softened as she brushed a strand of hair from Julia's forehead. "You scared the hell out of me."

Julia's lips parted into the ghost of a smile. "Sorry. It scared me too."

Mary took her hand and squeezed it gently. "You're okay now. That's what matters. You and the little one are still here. That's a win, all right?"

Julia nodded, tears burning behind her eyes.

Mary glanced over her shoulder at Daniel. Her expression cooled a few degrees. "You can go get coffee or something. I'll stay with her."

Daniel hesitated. "I don't want to leave her alone."

Mary arched a brow. "She's not alone. I'm here."

He exhaled slowly. "Right. I'll just… be outside if you need me."

He didn't wait for permission—just gave Julia one last look, then slipped out, the door clicking softly behind him.

Mary watched him go, then turned back to Julia, her voice dropping.

"You okay with him being here?"

Julia closed her eyes for a moment. "I didn't know who else to go to last night. I was scared. He helped."

Mary softened again, stroking Julia's arm. "Of course he did. He should have helped. That's the bare minimum."

There was no venom in her tone—just fierce loyalty.

Julia looked at her, voice quiet. "He stayed all night."

Mary sighed. "Yeah, well. That's nice. But one long night doesn't fix everything."

"I know," Julia whispered.

Mary kissed her knuckles. "You don't owe him anything. Not love. Not forgiveness. Just take care of yourself right now. That's all you need to do."

Julia nodded again, a fresh tear slipping down her cheek.

Mary reached for the tissue box, dabbing it away.

"I've got you," she said softly. "We've got you."

And as Julia sank back into the pillows, hand curled gently over her belly, a fragile sense of safety settled around her. Mary at her side. Daniel waiting outside. Everything else could wait.

Daniel stood in the sterile hallway, arms folded, pacing the narrow strip of linoleum just outside Julia's room. The early morning buzz of the hospital filtered in—soft footsteps, low voices, the distant murmur of a rolling gurney—but all he could focus on was the closed door in front of him.

Mary had been inside for almost twenty minutes. He'd heard their quiet voices—hers comforting, Julia's low and strained—but couldn't make out the words. Still, knowing she wasn't alone brought a small measure of peace.

The door finally opened with a soft click.

Mary stepped out, pulling the door gently behind her. She looked tired but composed, arms crossed over her chest as she closed the gap between them.

"She's okay," she said before he could ask. "Still shaken, but better."

Daniel nodded once, jaw tight. "Thanks."

Mary tilted her head, her eyes narrowing as if she was about to say something else—but then her gaze shifted down the hallway.

Footsteps.

Two men approached, walking side by side—one moving with purpose, the other with quiet confidence.

Joseph.

And James.

Daniel stiffened.

Mary's brow arched sharply as she followed his gaze. "Oh," she said, not amused. "Him again."

Daniel didn't respond—his entire body had gone still.

Joseph reached them first, concern in his expression as he looked past Daniel to the door. "How is she?"

"She's better," Mary replied. "Resting. She will be glad you're here."

James stayed back a few paces, hands in the pockets of his tailored coat, gaze fixed on the floor like he was waiting for permission to enter. When he finally looked up, it wasn't at Joseph—it was at Daniel.

Daniel stepped toward him, blocking the door just slightly. "What the hell are you doing here?"

James didn't flinch.

"I went to see Julia. To make sure she was okay after yesterday," he said calmly. "Ran into Joseph on the way. He told me what happened. I came with him."

Daniel's jaw ticked. "She doesn't need an audience."

James took another step forward, his gaze level now, voice low but sure. "I'm not the one that shouldn't be here."

Then, after a beat, he added—directly, deliberately, "You better get used to it, Moore. I'm hoping Julia will marry me. Because I do love her."

A silence fell between them, taut and electric.

Mary let out a low whistle under her breath. "Well, damn."

Joseph, ever the mediator, held up a hand. "Okay, that's enough. This is not the time or the place. Julia doesn't need a pissing contest in the hallway of a maternity ward."

Daniel's eyes hadn't left James. "She's not a prize to win."

"No," James said evenly. "But she is someone worth fighting for and remembering."

Daniel exhaled through his nose, slow and controlled. "You need to leave, before I throw..."

Mary stepped between them, palms out like she was diffusing a bar fight. "Alright, both of you. Cool it. She's in there trying to keep her body from falling apart, and you're both out here with your egos out."

Her voice dropped. "If either of you push her right now, I swear I'll personally throw you both out."

That sobered them.

James nodded once, backing away from the door. "I'll wait. When she's ready, I'll speak to her."

He looked at Daniel one last time, softer now. "This isn't about us. It's about what she needs. And I trust her to know the difference."

Then he stepped aside, letting the tension simmer as he took a seat on the bench across the hall.

Daniel stayed where he was—shoulders rigid, heart pounding—but he didn't speak again.

Joseph muttered something about coffee and stalked off toward the vending machines.

And Mary?

She stood in the centre of it all, arms crossed, eyes sharp.

The door creaked open with a soft click, and Julia turned her head on the pillow.

Joseph stepped inside, cautious and quiet, as if afraid any sudden movement might undo the fragile peace she'd just reclaimed. His tall frame filled the doorway, hands shoved deep into the pockets of his jeans, brow furrowed beneath sleep-mussed hair.

"Hey," he murmured.

Julia gave a tired smile. "Hey."

He crossed the room in a few slow strides and sat in the chair beside her bed—the one Daniel had vacated a while ago.

"You okay?" he asked, voice low.

"I think so. The cramps stopped. The doctors said the baby's heartbeat is steady."

Joseph nodded, but his jaw worked, tension simmering behind his eyes.

"I should've been here sooner," he said. "I was with a client in the city and left my phone on silent like an idiot. I didn't even see the missed calls until Daniel rang again."

Julia shook her head gently. "You don't have to explain."

"I do," he said, eyes locking with hers. "You're my little sister. And you scared the hell out of me."

She smiled faintly, then blinked hard, fighting the sting behind her eyes. "I scared myself."

He reached out and touched her hand—awkward but sincere. "I'm glad you're okay. That the baby's okay."

"I am too."

There was a pause. Joseph shifted in his seat, clearly weighing something.

"Listen... James is here."

Julia's brow creased. "What?"

"He came to the house, just as I was leaving. I told him what happened, and he insisted he come with me." Joseph hesitated, then added, "He's waiting in the hallway. Said he didn't want to intrude."

Julia stared at her brother for a long moment, processing.

James. Here.

It surprised her—though maybe it shouldn't. He always had a knack for showing up when she least expected it. Still, the fact that he was sitting out there now, waiting patiently, stirred something complicated in her chest.

She nodded slowly. "Okay. Let him in."

"You're sure?"

"I'm sure."

Joseph stood, his expression unreadable. Protective, as always, but respectful too. "I'll send him in. If you need me—"

"I know where to find you," she said gently.

He nodded once, gave her hand a squeeze, and turned for the door.

As it closed softly behind him, Julia shifted in the bed, adjusting her hospital gown and smoothing her hair back with a trembling hand. Her heart thudded unevenly as she stared at the door, waiting.

For the man who had always felt like safety.

For the man who now wanted more.

The door eased open with a soft click, and Julia lifted her gaze.

James stepped in quietly, his usual confidence softened by worry. His suit jacket was gone, shirt sleeves rolled up, tie loose around his neck. He looked like he'd come straight from work and hadn't slept since.

"Hey, sweetheart," he said gently, his voice low and warm, familiar like an old song. "How you feeling?"

Julia blinked, momentarily stunned by how much emotion was packed into that single question. Her throat tightened.

"Better," she said softly. "Tired."

He nodded, stepping closer to the bed but not touching her, not crowding her. Just… there. Present. Steady.

"I came as soon as I heard. I didn't want to stay away if you needed something."

Her eyes flicked to his face. "I didn't know you knew."

"I didn't, until I saw Joseph," he said. "He told me what happened. I asked if I could come."

James gave a dry smile. "He's still not my biggest fan, but he knows I care about you."

She glanced down at her hands. "It was a scare. A bad one."

"I know." He hesitated. "I wanted to punch something when I heard."

That pulled a faint smile from her. "That's very caveman of you."

"Yeah, well. You scared me, Jules."

His voice broke slightly on her name, and Julia looked up, startled by the rawness in his eyes.

He stepped closer then, just a little, and finally reached out—tentative—taking her hand in his.

"I know there's a lot going on. I'm not trying to push my way in. But you know I love you. I have for years."

Julia's heart thumped once, sharply.

"James…"

"I'm not asking for anything right now," he said quickly. "Just—let me be here for you. However, you'll have me."

She stared at him; torn between the comfort he offered and the storm still spinning inside her.

"I don't know what I want," she whispered.

"I know." He squeezed her hand gently. "But I do. And it's you."

She didn't pull away.

But she didn't answer either.

And for James, that seemed to be enough—for now.

Chapter Twenty-One

The door clicked shut behind James.

Silence settled over the corridor like a held breath.

Mary exhaled sharply through her nose, arms folding tight. "He just shows up. Again."

Joseph glanced at her. "What's that supposed to mean?"

Daniel's gaze flicked to Mary, wary.

She didn't answer right away.

Daniel did—quiet, measured. "It means this isn't the first time he's appeared when Julia's vulnerable."

Mary's head tilted, jaw tight. "He's got a gift for timing. Always seems to know when she's cracked open just enough to let him back in."

Joseph frowned. "You think he's manipulating her?"

Mary shrugged. "I think he knows exactly what he's doing."

Daniel said nothing, but his shoulders had gone rigid, hands buried deep in his pockets.

Joseph studied them both, picking up on the charged silence between their words. Then he shifted his weight, voice too casual. "James also told me about Jenna."

Daniel's head snapped up.

Joseph held his gaze. "Said Julia caught you kissing. That true?"

Daniel opened his mouth. "It wasn't me."

"I know," Joseph said flatly, cutting him off. "You can't stand her."

Daniel blinked, caught off guard.

Joseph's voice dropped. "You've hated her since that crap she pulled with Julia a couple of years ago. When she said—and I quote— 'I can't stand how everyone loves you.'" He shook his head. "She's a vindictive bitch. I don't even need to ask."

Daniel's jaw flexed. Then, finally, a quiet, "Thanks."

Joseph sighed and ran a hand over his face. "Still doesn't explain why she was even at our place."

"She said she needed to see James. Claimed it was urgent and insisted on waiting for him."

Mary rolled her eyes. "Women like Jenna don't go quietly. They linger. Stir the pot. Always think they've got one last power move."

Joseph's gaze drifted back to the closed door, where Julia lay just a few feet away—caught in the middle of everyone's mess. Too close to too many ghosts.

"If he's trying to hurt her," Joseph muttered, "he'll have me to answer to."

Daniel's voice was low, steel beneath it. "You'll have to get in line."

Mary's stance softened slightly. "Julia will figure it out. She always does."

Joseph looked between them both. "Yeah. I just hope it doesn't break her in the process."

The three of them stood in silence then, the air thick with quiet tension and bruised loyalty.

From behind the door, James's voice floated faintly through—low, careful, familiar.

And inside, Julia listened.

Inside, the hospital room was quiet again.

Joseph had slipped out first, a parting squeeze on Julia's shoulder and a promise to call later. Mary had kissed her forehead and left with a glare in Daniel's direction that said, don't mess this up. And James—well, James had offered one last lingering glance before the door clicked shut behind him.

Now it was just Daniel.

He stood near the window, hands shoved in his pockets, watching the early afternoon light crawl across the floor tiles. The shadows shifted slowly, the silence stretched between them—not awkward but filled with unspoken things.

Julia let her head sink deeper into the pillow. Her body felt like it had been wrung out and hung up to dry. She didn't speak. Neither did he.

Then, a soft knock.

The doctor stepped in with a clipboard and a reassuring smile. Late thirties, calm, the kind of presence that made Julia feel marginally more stable by sheer osmosis.

"How are we doing?" he asked gently, approaching the bed.

"Tired," Julia murmured.

"Understandable," he said, flipping through her chart. "But your vitals are good. Baby's heartbeat is strong. Bleeding has stopped. We'll keep an eye on things going forward, but for now..." he looked up and smiled, "you can go home."

Relief swept through her in a wave. She hadn't realised how tense she'd been until that moment.

"Thank you," she whispered.

The doctor nodded. "You'll need rest. Proper rest. No stress, no lifting, no long walks, no chasing after anyone."

Julia let out a soft laugh. "I'll try."

Daniel straightened by the window, stepping closer now, his gaze fixed on the doctor. "What does she need at home?"

"Minimal stimulation. No stairs unless necessary. Stay hydrated, light meals, and above all, keep her stress levels down. Anything flares up—cramping, spotting, pressure—she comes straight back in. No exceptions."

Daniel nodded like he was committing every word to memory.

The doctor gave Julia a final smile, scribbled something on her chart, then turned and left as quietly as he'd entered.

Silence fell again.

Daniel stepped to the side of her bed, eyes softer now.

"I'll bring the car around," he said quietly. "We'll get you home."

Julia looked up at him, her voice barely a whisper. "You don't have to do that."

"I know," he said simply. "But I want to."

Something in his tone—steady, no strings, no expectations—made her chest ache.

"Daniel…"

He crouched slightly, so he was at her eye level. "Just rest, Jules. Let me take care of the logistics. One less thing for you to worry about."

She swallowed thickly, a knot forming in her throat.

"Okay."

He stood again, brushing a knuckle softly over her blanket-covered hand before stepping back. "Ten minutes. I'll be right outside."

And then he left—quiet as ever—leaving Julia to breathe in the hush, her hand resting protectively on her belly, and for the first time since the night before, to imagine the idea of peace.

Daniel guided her gently down the hospital corridor, one arm steady around her waist, the other carrying her small overnight bag. She leaned into him just enough to feel supported—not weak, but grateful. Outside, the sun was climbing higher, a soft breeze brushing against their skin as they crossed the car park.

He opened the passenger door, helping her ease into the seat with infinite care.

"Okay?" he asked, one hand resting on the edge of the door, eyes searching hers.

Julia nodded. "Yeah. Just tired."

He didn't respond, just gave her that small, grounding look before shutting the door and circling to the driver's side.

The ride was quiet, peaceful. No music. No questions. Just the rhythm of tyres on asphalt and the occasional glance between them.

When they reached the house, Daniel cut the engine and was out of the car before she could even reach for the handle. He came around and opened the door, then helped her to her feet, letting her lean on him as they slowly ascended the porch stairs.

As they reached the front door, it opened before he could knock.

Lorna stood there, eyes wide with relief. "Oh, thank goodness you're okay. I was so worried!"

Julia managed a tired smile. "Thank you, Lorna. I'm feeling much better."

"I'll bring a tray up shortly," Lorna said, stepping aside to let them in. "Soup, tea, something light."

Daniel gave her a grateful nod and helped Julia up the stairs—slowly, carefully, her steps measured. He never let go of her, one arm around her waist, the other ready in case she faltered. When they reached the landing, she paused, breath catching just a little, and he waited, patient as stone, until she was ready to keep going.

He opened the bedroom door and helped her inside.

It smelled like her—soft linen and lavender. The curtains had been drawn to let in the afternoon light. Everything felt still and safe.

She moved toward the bed, and he guided her the last few steps.

"Julia," he said quietly, his voice catching on her name.

She turned to him, her hand still resting lightly on his arm.

"Yes?"

He couldn't hold back anymore.

The need to feel her—to anchor himself in her—had been pressing on his chest like a weight. Not being able to touch her the way he wanted, to hold her like she was his… it was driving him mad.

He leaned in, slowly, carefully, giving her every chance to step away.

But she didn't.

His lips brushed hers—featherlight at first, more breath than contact, a question held in the hush between heartbeats. Her lips parted with a breath-soft reply— uncertain, hesitant… but not a no.

And something inside him—something tight and aching—broke open.

He deepened the kiss, only slightly, his hand rising to cradle her jaw. It wasn't hunger. It was relief. It was home.

And still… she didn't pull away.

His arms slid around her waist, drawing her gently to him. Her hands gripped the front of his shirt—clutching, steadying—like she needed something solid in the whirlwind of everything. Her forehead rested against his chest for a moment, as if the world felt quieter there.

They stayed like that. One breath. Then another.

Then she tilted her face up, her voice a whisper. "What was that for?"

Daniel looked down at her, eyes soft but steady. "Because I love you, Julia."

Her breath caught.

"I want to be with you," he continued, voice low, thick with emotion. "I know I messed up—I know I hurt you. But I remember that night. Every part of it."

His thumb brushed a strand of hair from her cheek, his gaze never leaving hers.

"The way you looked at me… the way you said my name like it meant something. The way you touched me like I was more than just a mistake. That doesn't disappear, Julia. Not for me."

Her hands fisted tighter in the fabric of his shirt, her eyes shimmering with unshed tears.

"But how do I know this isn't just about the baby?" she whispered. "How do I know I won't be another name on a long list? Set aside once the shine wears off?"

Daniel's jaw tightened, but his voice stayed soft, steady. "I'm not here because of the baby, Julia. I'm here because of you. The baby just made it impossible to keep lying to myself."

He stepped closer, his hands cradling her waist like she might break—or bolt.

"You're not like the others. God, I tried to move on. I compared every woman to you and none of them came close. They weren't you. They never could be."

He exhaled, eyes searching hers.

"I've been in love with you for years, Julia. I just didn't know how to admit it. Not to you. Not even to myself."

She pulled back a little, her arms dropping away from him, her breath catching like it hurt.

"I don't know, Daniel," she said, voice trembling. "I want to believe you… but I don't know if I can."

And just like that, the distance between them wasn't physical—it was made of years of silence, and fear, and something that felt dangerously close to hope.

He pulled back just enough to see her face, his thumb brushing lightly along her cheekbone.

"You probably don't remember," he said softly, "but we were at one of Joseph's engagement parties. One of many."

A small smile tugged at the corner of his mouth.

"I was standing near the bar with a redhead. Can't even remember her name. I was so bored I was counting the ice cubes in my drink."

Julia let out the faintest laugh, but he wasn't finished.

"Then I saw you come out of the kitchen. You were wearing that pale blue dress, the one with the little buttons down the front. You looked like spring had walked straight into the room."

His voice dropped, full of something old and tender.

"You made me smile. And when you looked up—you smiled back. Like maybe you saw me. Really saw me."

He paused; eyes locked on hers.

"I wanted to walk across that room right then and tell you everything I was feeling. But I didn't. I was a coward. I let the moment pass."

Julia's breath caught, eyes glistening.

"And I've thought about that smile more times than I can count," Daniel said, his voice low and raw. "It was the beginning, even if I didn't know it yet."

She stood there for a moment, heart thudding, her fingers still curled lightly in the fabric of his shirt.

"I remember that night," she whispered, voice trembling. "I remember it exactly."

His eyes searched hers.

"It was the night I realised…" Her voice broke slightly. "The night I knew I was in love with you."

Daniel's breath hitched.

"Julia… I—"

A knock cut through the quiet.

She startled slightly and stepped back from his arms, her gaze flicking to the door.

"Come in," she called, her voice steadier than she felt.

The door eased open, and Lorna stepped in, balancing a tray of soup and warm bread with practiced care.

"Here we are," she said, her voice full of genuine warmth as she crossed the room. "You need to eat."

Julia offered a soft smile; her emotions tucked just beneath the surface. "Thank you, Lorna. I will."

Daniel took the tray from her, setting it gently on the bedside table while Lorna gave Julia's hand a motherly pat.

"I'll leave you to eat in peace. Holler if you need anything."

And just like that, the moment was gone—but not forgotten. It lingered in the hush that followed, delicate and unfinished, hovering like a breath between them, waiting for its return.

Daniel stepped back, his eyes lingering on her face, reading the emotion flickering just beneath the surface.

"I'll let you rest," he said softly, his voice low, careful. "You need space… and soup."

A faint smile touched her lips, but she didn't speak. Didn't need to.

He reached for the door, pausing just before opening it.

"I meant every word, Julia. Nothing's changed that."

And then he was gone, the soft click of the door the only sound left in the room.

Julia stood there, unmoving, her pulse fluttered at the base of her throat. One hand rested protectively on her belly; the other still tingled from where he'd held her, as if his touch had left an echo on her skin.

The soup sat beside her, warm and fragrant, untouched.

But her hands stayed still.

Her heart was too full—brimming with feelings she'd buried too deep, for too long.

And yet… her head pulsed with caution. With all the reasons she should hold back.

Love had never been simple with Daniel.

And now, with so much on the line, it was anything but.

Chapter Twenty-Two

It had been a week since Daniel kissed her.

One soft, earth-shifting kiss that unravelled everything she'd been trying to hold together. And yet… nothing since. Not a single hint that he might do it again.

Julia leaned against the kitchen counter; her fingers curled around a lukewarm cup of tea she hadn't touched. The late afternoon light filtered in through the window, golden and soft, catching in the strands of her chestnut hair. She watched the garden swaying outside, but her thoughts weren't on the roses or the breeze.

They were upstairs. Or down the hall. Or wherever Daniel happened to be.

He'd been careful this week—thoughtful, attentive, always asking if she needed anything, if she was feeling okay. He'd stayed close enough to be noticed, but never too close. Like he didn't want to push. Like that kiss had been a moment he regretted… or worse, one he'd already forgotten.

And it was driving her insane.

She pressed the cup to her lips, pretending to drink. Maybe it would've been easier if he'd pulled away and said he was sorry. Maybe then she could've moved on—forced herself to accept that she'd always be Joseph's sister to him. But instead, he kissed her like he'd meant it. Like she meant something.

And now… silence.

Her phone buzzed on the bench beside her. She glanced down. James.

Again.

She ignored it.

She'd managed to avoid him most of the week, feigning fatigue and lingering recovery. It wasn't entirely a lie—she had been tired, and rest had been necessary—but the truth went deeper. She wasn't ready to face him. Wasn't ready to say the words that needed to be said.

She couldn't marry him.

Even if Daniel never touched her again, even if he walked out of her life tomorrow, she still couldn't accept James's proposal. Not out of guilt. Not out of comfort. Not out of a desperate bid for safety. It wouldn't be fair—to him or to herself.

She rinsed her cup in the sink, the sound of running water the only noise in the quiet kitchen. With Daniel out for the evening and Joseph away for a few days, she'd eaten dinner with Lorna at the bench, sharing quiet conversation and warm soup.

Now the house had settled into stillness.

Julia climbed the stairs slowly, cup in hand, her thoughts tangled and relentless. She paused at her bedroom door, fingers curling around the knob.

And then—

A floorboard creaked behind her.

She turned.

Daniel.

He stood a few feet away, dressed in jeans and a grey button-down shirt, sleeves casually rolled to his forearms. Barefoot, as always. His dark hair was damp, curling slightly at the edges, like he'd just stepped out of the shower.

He stopped when their eyes met, then offered her that faint, sideways smile— the one she was starting to crave like air.

"Hey," he said, voice low and rough at the edges.

"Hey," she replied, softer than she meant to.

He stepped a little closer—but not close enough. Not nearly.

"You okay?" he asked, studying her face. "You've been quiet today."

Julia hesitated. "I'm fine. Just… thinking."

His gaze didn't move. "Anything you want to talk about?"

Yes. Talk. Kiss. Touch. Anything. Everything.

But the words stuck in her throat.

She swallowed. "The doctor called this afternoon."

His brows lifted slightly. "Is everything okay?"

She nodded. "Yeah. More than okay. I'm cleared. No more restrictions."

Daniel's expression shifted—his eyes darkened slightly, not with concern but something deeper, something unspoken. "That's good," he said, his voice quieter now. "You must be relieved."

"I am." She gripped her doorknob tighter. "It feels like I can finally… breathe again."

He nodded once, slowly. But something in the air between them had changed. It had weight now. Heat.

"You look…" he paused, eyes raking over her face, her posture, her presence, "stronger."

Julia let out a breath, small and steady. "I feel it."

Another step from him. Closer. Not close enough.

"You've been avoiding James."

She blinked. "How do you—?"

He tilted his head, giving her a half-smile. "You flinch every time someone says his name."

She didn't deny it. Couldn't.

"I haven't… told him yet."

Daniel's voice softened, careful now. "Told him what?"

Julia looked down at her hands, then back up at him. "I can't marry him."

A beat passed. Then—

"You should tell him."

Her head snapped up. "Why?"

His jaw tightened. "Because he's not the one you want."

Her breath caught.

"You kissed me," she whispered. "And you haven't said a word about it since. Do you regret it?"

"No." His voice was low, and gravel edged. "I haven't stopped thinking about it since."

"Then why pull away?"

"I didn't want to push you," he said. "Not after everything you've been through."

He stood a few feet away, torn between restraint and longing, the battle clear in the tight set of his jaw.

She stepped forward, closing the last sliver of distance.

"You didn't push," she murmured. "You retreated."

Daniel's gaze dropped to her lips, lingered, then returned to her eyes. "And if I don't want to retreat anymore?"

Her heart pounded against her ribs. "Then don't."

He exhaled sharply, like he'd been holding it in for days—maybe longer. His hand lifted, tentative but certain, brushing her cheek. She leaned into the touch like it was home.

And then he kissed her.

Not like the first time.

This kiss was deeper. Intentional. Starving.

Julia wound her arms around his neck as he pulled her close, his hands firm at her waist. The kiss turned urgent, wild with everything they'd held back. Every sigh, every brush of lips, burned with weeks of longing.

Everything else—James, the uncertainty, the ache of waiting—fell away.

It was just him. Just this. Just them.

He backed her gently against her bedroom door, one hand splayed beside her head, the other slipping under her shirt to the bare skin at her back. She shivered at the contact, breath hitching as she pressed against him.

He broke the kiss, forehead resting against hers, both of them breathing hard.

"Tell me to stop," he whispered, voice ragged. "If you say it, I will."

She shook her head, barely more than a breath. "Don't."

His eyes met hers—dark, intense, searching. "Are you sure?"

She cupped his face, her thumb stroking his cheek. "Yes."

He kissed her again—slower this time, deeper, like he was memorising her. She reached behind and turned the door handle, and they stumbled inside.

The room glowed softly in the lamplight—familiar, warm. But nothing about this moment felt ordinary.

Daniel stood still, watching her, his chest rising and falling with restrained emotion.

"I've wanted you for so long," he said quietly. "I can't believe it's really happening."

His fingers slid into her hair, drawing her closer. He kissed her again, soft and reverent. Yet desire pulsed between them, building with every touch. Julia responded instinctively, her arms around his neck, her kiss growing deeper—hungrier.

Heat surged between them, raw and consuming. She felt his body press against hers, the tension between restraint and surrender pulling tighter.

He broke the kiss, lips brushing her ear. "Tell me you want me."

Julia's voice was breathless. "I want you… please, Daniel."

He trembled against her, exhaling a broken sound. "God, I want you too."

He settled onto the edge of the bed, guiding her into his lap, kissing her with new urgency. His hands moved to the buttons of her blouse, slipping it open with aching slowness. When the lace beneath came into view, he groaned softly and brushed his thumbs across the delicate fabric, eyes darkening with need.

"Daniel, please," she whispered, arching toward him.

He unclasped her bra, letting it fall away, then dipped his head. His mouth found her breast, his tongue circling, tasting, worshiping. She gasped, fingers threading through his hair.

"You're incredible," he murmured. "I've never wanted anyone like this."

His hands slid to her hips, lifting her, guiding her to stand. He eased off her pants, his hands lingering as he revealed each inch of skin. She stood before him, bare and breathtaking.

"You're beautiful," he said, reverent.

He pulled the covers back and lifted her effortlessly, laying her down before joining her. He shed his clothes with quiet urgency, then stretched out beside her, kissing her again—slow, deep, consuming.

His mouth began a trail down her body—along her collarbone, between her breasts, over her stomach—until he reached the delicate heat of her thighs. He parted her gently, reverently, his mouth finding her with devastating tenderness.

"Daniel… oh," she gasped, her fingers clutching the sheets.

He moved with purpose, his tongue teasing, his mouth worshiping. Pleasure built fast—sharp, spiralling, unstoppable. "You taste like heaven," he whispered against her skin, and then he sent her over the edge with a final, perfect flick.

She shattered, crying out his name, her body trembling beneath him. When the waves of pleasure faded, he kissed his way back up her body, settling between her thighs, eyes locked on hers.

"Tell me again," he murmured, voice thick.

"I want you, Daniel. Please."

With a groan, he positioned himself at her entrance and eased into her slowly, deeply. Julia gasped, her hands gripping his back.

He began to move, gentle at first, letting her adjust, then deeper, more certain. "Wrap your legs around me," he murmured.

She did, anchoring him, moving with him.

Their bodies found a rhythm—fluid, intimate, powerful. With each thrust, each gasp, they climbed higher. Her nails scraped lightly down his back.

"Daniel… please—don't stop," she breathed.

"I'm right here," he whispered, pressing a kiss to her cheek, her jaw, her mouth. "I've got you."

Pleasure coiled tight inside her, ready to explode. Then she broke, clinging to him as waves of ecstasy tore through her. Her cry tore from her throat as her body convulsed around him.

Feeling her release, Daniel groaned deeply and surrendered to his own, his body shuddering with the force of it as he emptied into her.

They collapsed into each other, breathless, trembling, wrapped in warmth and wonder.

He kissed her, slow and lingering. "You… are everything."

She smiled against his lips, eyes fluttering shut.

Wrapped in his arms, her head resting over his heart, Julia finally felt it—peace.

Maybe the storm had passed. Maybe this—Daniel—was her home.

Chapter Twenty-Three

Daniel stirred just as the first light of morning slipped through the curtains, casting soft gold across the room.

Julia lay nestled in his arms, her back pressed against his chest, his arm draped over her waist, palm resting possessively over her stomach. The warmth of her skin, the scent of her hair—it grounded him in a way nothing else ever had.

Slowly, his hand slid lower, fingers trailing across her belly until he reached the heat between her thighs. He explored her gently, finding her soft and ready, even in sleep.

A soft gasp escaped her as her hips instinctively shifted back against him. "Mmm," she murmured, her voice husky with sleep.

His lips brushed her earlobe. "Morning," he whispered.

"Morning," she echoed, her voice barely above a breath.

His free hand slid under her body, curving around to cup her breast. He rasped his thumb over the peak, feeling it tighten beneath his touch.

"Oh… Daniel," she moaned, pressing herself more fully against him.

He chuckled low in her ear, breath warm on her skin. "Do you want me to stop?"

Her response was immediate. "No. Don't stop."

His fingers moved with exquisite precision, coaxing her toward pleasure with steady, knowing strokes. Her breathing quickened, her body trembling against his until she cried out, her release cresting in a wave of sensation that left her breathless and pliant in his arms.

He kissed the curve of her neck, then shifted behind her, guiding himself to her entrance. He paused just long enough for their breathing to align—then he pressed into her in one slow, deep thrust.

"Daniel!" she gasped, her body arching instinctively.

He groaned, one hand anchoring her hip as he withdrew slightly, then pushed in again, harder, deeper.

The morning sunlight bathed them in warmth as they moved together—slow and unhurried, like they had all the time in the world.

Daniel kept a steady rhythm, every thrust a blend of tenderness and need, his arm tight around her, anchoring them together. Julia's soft gasps filled the quiet room, her body pliant, welcoming him, craving him.

When he felt her begin to tighten around him—those delicate muscles clenching in pulsing waves—he pressed his lips to her shoulder and whispered, "That's it, sweetheart. Let go."

She cried out softly, her release rolling through her with trembling intensity. "Oh… yes…"

Her name was a groan on his lips as he buried his face in the curve of her neck, his pace shifting—deeper, faster, more urgent now. The feel of her, the sound of her, the way her body held him—he was undone.

With one final, hard thrust, he surged into her and let himself go, a low, ragged moan breaking from his chest as he found his release.

For a long moment, neither of them moved. Their breathing slowed, their bodies still joined, held in a haze of warmth and closeness.

Daniel pressed a tender kiss to the back of her shoulder, then another to her neck, his hand splayed protectively over her stomach once more.

"I could stay like this forever," he murmured against her skin.

Julia's hand covered his, fingers threading through his. "So could I."

Silence settled between them again, soft and warm, like a cocoon. The morning light filtered in through the curtains, bathing the room in a gentle glow. Outside, birds stirred in the trees, but inside, time stood still.

Then, his voice—low, hesitant. "Julia."

"Mm?"

He hesitated. "My penthouse will be finished by the end of the week."

She stiffened just slightly, enough for him to feel it. He noticed. He always noticed.

"Oh. Okay," she said carefully, trying to keep her voice light. "I bet you're looking forward to being back home."

Daniel exhaled slowly, brushing his lips against her skin again. "I want you to come with me."

A pause.

He held his breath.

Julia turned in his arms, propping herself on one elbow. The sheet slipped down her shoulder, forgotten. Her eyes searched his, wide and full of quiet surprise.

"Really?"

His hand cupped her face, thumb stroking along her cheekbone. "Yes. Not just for a night, or a weekend. I want you there. With me."

She blinked, emotions flickering across her face—uncertainty, wonder, something close to fear… and something closer to hope.

"I know it's soon," he added gently. "And I'm not asking you to give up anything. I just—when I think about being there without you, it feels… wrong. Empty."

Her throat worked around the knot rising there. "Daniel…"

"I love waking up with you," he said tenderly. "I love falling asleep with you. I want that every day. But only if you want it too."

She reached up, resting her palm against his heart. It thudded steadily beneath her fingers, strong and real.

"I never thought you'd ask," she whispered.

Relief broke across his face, pure and unmistakable. He pulled her into his arms and kissed her—slow, deep, certain.

When they finally pulled apart, she smiled. "But just so you know… I still get the bigger closet."

He laughed, the sound warm against her lips. "Deal."

And for the first time in a long time, the future didn't feel like something to fear.

It felt like something to run toward—together.

They spent the day wrapped in each other, more relaxed than either had been in months. The world outside seemed to pause, the usual weight of unspoken things and looming responsibilities somehow suspended.

They moved through the hours like a couple who'd done this for years—effortless, easy. They made love with slow reverence, the kind that left them tangled in sheets and laughter. They cooked eggs together—badly—and ordered lunch instead. At one point, Julia tried to fold laundry, only for Daniel to pull her into his lap and distract her with kisses until the clothes lay forgotten.

They lounged on the couch, half-watching a movie neither could name. Her head rested on his chest, fingers idly tracing patterns on his shirt, while his hand stroked lazily down her arm.

At one point, Julia tilted her head back to look at him. "Shouldn't you be at work?"

Daniel gave her a lazy smile, the kind that made her heart flutter. "I own the company. I can have a day off if I want to."

She smirked. "And is that how this works? Billionaire perks?"

"That," he said, kissing the tip of her nose, "and excellent delegation."

The soft hum of the afternoon lulled around them, warm and content.

But by late afternoon, the weight returned.

Reality, waiting patiently outside their bubble, came knocking.

Julia sat on the edge of the bed, brushing her fingers through her hair. Daniel leaned in the doorway, arms crossed over his chest, watching her.

"Are you sure you want to do this today?" he asked gently.

She nodded. "It's time."

He hesitated, then pushed off the bed and crossed to her. "Do you want me to be there?"

Julia looked up at him. There was concern in his eyes, but not jealousy. Not possessiveness. Just support.

She gave a small, sad smile. "No. I think that wouldn't be a good idea."

Daniel crouched in front of her, hands resting lightly on her knees. "You don't have to protect me."

"I'm not," she said softly. "I just… I don't want to humiliate him. Or hurt him any more than I have to. Seeing us together—he deserves better than that."

Daniel nodded, pressing a kiss to her knuckles. "Then I'll wait here."

"I won't be long."

As she stood and reached for her jacket, he caught her hand.

"Julia?"

"Yeah?"

"If he says anything that makes you feel unsafe, or pressured—call me."

"I will." She leaned up and brushed a kiss to his cheek. "Thank you… for everything."

And with one last look, she stepped out of the bedroom door.

It was time to end one chapter, before she could truly begin the next.

The doorbell rang just as Julia reached the bottom of the staircase.

She paused, her hand tightening briefly on the railing before she walked to the front door and opened it.

"Hi, James."

He stood there in a crisp white shirt and pressed slacks, his hair slicked back too neatly, as if he'd spent an hour trying to look effortless. The smile he offered was tight, strained—his eyes far colder than his voice.

"Julia," he said smoothly. "You're looking well. I'm glad you're feeling better."

"Thanks. I am." She stepped aside. "Come in."

He followed her down the hallway, the sound of his shoes sharp on the floorboards. As he went to sit in the living room, Julia remained standing. She didn't want this to feel like a conversation between equals. Not now.

"I have to tell you something, James," she said before he could settle into the armchair. Her voice was steady, but her hands trembled at her sides.

"I can't marry you."

He stopped mid-motion. Slowly, he stood up straight again, his eyes fixing on hers. There was a flicker—dark, quick, furious. Then it vanished, replaced by a false calm.

"What?" he asked, low and tight.

"I've thought about it. Really thought about it. And the answer has to be no."

He blinked, as if trying to process her words. "But… Julia, I love you."

"I know," she said quietly. "And I care about you. But I don't love you. Not the way I should."

His eyes narrowed. "Care? That's it? That's all I am to you now?" His voice pitched higher. "After everything I've done for you?"

"We're not right for each other," she said firmly. "This was a mistake."

His jaw clenched, the muscles ticking violently. "This is about *him*, isn't it?"

She hesitated.

"Don't insult me, Julia. It's Daniel. Just say it."

She didn't answer.

His temper snapped. "That's it," he growled, stepping toward her. "You're throwing away me—everything we've had—for Daniel bloody Moore?"

Julia instinctively stepped back.

"I can't believe this," James raged. "You led me on. You let me think we were building something real, that we had a future! And now you just—what—change your mind because Daniel saunters back into the picture?"

"I gave you my answer," Julia said, lifting her chin despite the quiver in her voice. "And I don't owe you anything more than that."

"Oh, so I'm just a mistake now?" he snarled. "And him? He's what—your fairy tale? Some billionaire fantasy who's going to swoop in and magically fix your life?"

He was pacing now, his steps erratic, his breathing ragged. His hands were clenched into fists.

The heat in the room shifted—dense, suffocating.

"James, I think you should go."

He turned sharply, his voice a blade. "No. You don't get to stand there and play the victim. You don't get to smile and bat your lashes and walk away like I didn't matter. I waited for you. I was here while he was off with other women!"

Julia backed toward the armchair, gripping it for balance.

His eyes darkened. "What, you think Daniel's your knight in shining armour? Is that what this is?"

"James," she said quietly, her throat dry, "please leave."

He stepped closer. Too close. She could feel the tension pouring off him like static. "You don't see it, Julia. He's not going to stay. He's going to get bored—because that's what he does. And when he does, don't come crawling back to me."

"Leave," she said again, this time her voice breaking. "Now."

"Or what?" he hissed. "You'll scream? Cry? Call for your billionaire boyfriend to come rescue you like a helpless little—"

"Step away from her."

James froze.

Daniel's voice cut through the room like a shot.

He stood in the doorway, his stance wide, fists clenched, eyes burning. He was calm—dangerously calm.

Julia's entire body sagged with relief.

James turned, his expression incredulous. "Of course," he muttered, hands flinging outward. "Of course you're here. Like a goddamn stray dog. Always hanging around. Watching. Lurking."

Daniel took one slow, deliberate step forward. "You're going to walk out that door. Now."

"Or what?" James sneered.

Daniel didn't move, didn't raise his voice. But the tension rolling off him was volcanic. His next words were cold steel.

"If you ever raise your voice to her again, if you ever come near her again, I swear to God, I will make sure you never get the chance to hurt another woman."

James's mouth opened, but no words came. His face twisted, furious, impotent.

He looked at Julia—who now stood behind Daniel, her eyes wide, her hand to her chest—and saw something in her expression.

Fear.

Disgust.

Finality.

James let out a bitter, humourless laugh. "She's not worth it," he spat. "You'll see."

Daniel took another step forward. "Get out."

James stormed past them both, slamming the front door so hard the walls seemed to rattle.

The silence that followed felt deafening.

Julia sank onto the couch, legs trembling. Daniel crossed the room in two strides, kneeling in front of her.

"Are you okay?" he asked carefully, his hands gently cupping her face.

She nodded, but her eyes shimmered with tears. "I just… I didn't expect that. He's never been like that before."

"You don't have to explain," he said, brushing her hair from her face. "He showed who he really is. He won't get near you again. I promise."

She took a shaky breath and gripped his wrists.

"You always show up when I need you."

He leaned forward and pressed a kiss to her forehead. "Always."

Chapter Twenty-Four

The house was quiet.

Too quiet.

Daniel stood near the tall living room windows, one hand resting against the cold glass, the other cradling a tumbler of untouched scotch. Outside, the streetlights stretched down the road—bright, unblinking, indifferent. Somewhere in the distance, a siren wailed—sharp, fleeting—and then, silence again.

Behind him, Julia slept curled on the couch, her face tilted toward him. Even in rest, a faint crease marred her brow.

He hated that.

He'd held her after James left—long after her sobs gave way to trembling silence. She hadn't spoken much, only clung to him like a woman trying not to shatter. And he hadn't let go.

Now, with the storm passed and the door closed, Daniel should have felt relief. Satisfaction. Maybe even triumph.

But all he felt was rage.

Quiet. Controlled. Lethal.

James had crossed a line.

Daniel exhaled slowly, jaw locked tight. It hadn't just been the confrontation. It was the way Julia had looked when Daniel stepped between them.

Not angry.

Not annoyed.

Afraid.

That image replayed in his mind like a broken reel: her wide, stricken eyes… the way her breath caught… how her voice cracked when she said his name.

He closed his eyes and leaned his forehead against the glass.

It wasn't just about this afternoon. It was everything. The pregnancy. The pressure. The isolation. And through it all, she hadn't asked him for anything.

But she should have.

And it gutted him to realise she hadn't trusted him to carry the weight with her.

Not fully.

Not yet.

He turned, gaze softening as it fell on her—small, quiet on the couch, one hand curled near her face, the blanket tucked around her like armour.

Something in his chest twisted.

So strong. And still so breakable.

He set the scotch on the windowsill and crossed the room. Sitting on the edge of the couch, he studied her for a long moment before brushing a lock of hair gently from her cheek.

She stirred but didn't wake.

Good. She needed rest. After everything she'd endured—everything he'd missed—she deserved peace.

Carefully, he lifted her into his arms. She murmured something against his neck, words blurred and soft but leaned into him instinctively. He held her closer, breathing in the faint scent of her shampoo, grounding himself in it.

The line between protection and control was thin. He knew that. He'd walked it before—crossed it, even. Too distant. Too cold. Too careful.

But this was different.

Julia wasn't someone he wanted to possess.

She was someone he wanted to build with.

Grow with.

Bleed for if he had to.

She stirred again, softer this time. "Daniel?"

"I'm here," he murmured, pressing a kiss to her temple.

He carried her upstairs to her room, pushed open the door with his shoulder, and laid her gently on the bed. Then he slipped in beside her and pulled her into his arms.

Her face pressed into his chest, fingers curling into his shirt.

Daniel exhaled and kissed her forehead—longer this time, firmer. A vow.

"You're the strongest woman I know," he whispered. "And you're mine."

She made a soft, broken sound.

"I'll never look at you any way but this," he said, voice low and certain. "With love. With respect. And the promise that if anyone ever treats you like that again… they won't walk away."

He felt her breath hitch—then ease. Her body softened against his, like something inside her had finally unclenched.

And something shifted in him too.

Quietly. Finally. Entirely.

There was no going back. Not from this.

Not from her.

He would love her. Defend her. Choose her—every day.

No more walls. No more running.

Because he wasn't just in love with Julia Davis.

He was hers.

Completely.

Warmth.

That was the first thing she noticed.

Not the kind left behind by tears or panic, but something deeper. Steadier. A warmth that settled beneath her skin and into her bones. The kind she hadn't felt in a long, long time.

Her cheek rested against a solid chest, the steady rhythm of a heartbeat echoing beneath her ear—slow, grounding. The soft cotton of a T-shirt brushed her skin, and an arm—Daniel's—was draped around her waist, holding her in place.

Anchoring her.

She didn't open her eyes. Not yet.

If she kept them closed, she could pretend nothing had happened.

No confrontation.

No fear.

No memories she didn't want to revisit.

But reality, cold and unrelenting, pushed in anyway. The night returned in flashes—James's voice, sharp and pleading. Daniel, stepping in without pause. His body between hers and danger.

A shield.

Her shield.

Her fingers curled into his shirt. She hadn't meant to fall asleep. Hadn't expected her body to give out the way it had.

But she'd been unravelling.

And he had held her together.

She opened her eyes slowly. Morning light filtered through the curtains, painting soft gold across the room. Daniel lay beside her, still asleep, facing her. His features were softer in rest, the tension in his jaw eased. One hand remained on her hip, gentle and protective, even now.

A lump formed in her throat.

She loved him.

So much it hurt.

And yet—she'd been so scared he wouldn't stay.

That's what fear had told her.

But he had.

He would.

He hadn't flinched when she fell apart.

Hadn't demanded answers or explanations.

He'd just been there. Steady. Solid. Safe.

Her heart thudded gently.

She shifted slightly, studying him through the quiet. The faint stubble along his jaw. The crease between his brows that didn't quite disappear, even in sleep. He carried tension like armour, but beneath it, she could feel the softness. The part of him he rarely showed.

Daniel Moore was a man of restraint. Of control.

A man built from edges and walls.

But last night, he'd offered her more than just protection.

He'd given her choice.

He hadn't demanded her trust.

He'd earned it.

Her hand moved instinctively, brushing lightly over his chest. He stirred, lashes fluttering as he blinked awake. His eyes found hers immediately—alert, then softening.

"Hey," he murmured, his voice rough with sleep.

"Hey," she whispered back.

For a long moment, they simply looked at each other.

No urgency.

No expectations.

Just breath and warmth and the fragile beauty of something changing between them.

She reached up and placed her palm on his cheek. "Thank you."

His brow knit slightly. "For what?"

"For staying." Her voice caught. "For… everything."

He shook his head, just once. "You don't have to thank me, Julia." He brushed a strand of hair behind her ear. "You never have to thank me for loving you."

Her breath hitched.

"I was afraid," she said, barely more than a whisper.

"I know," he replied, no judgment in his voice.

She closed her eyes, pressing into his touch. Letting it sink into the cracks she didn't want to carry anymore.

"I'm tired of being afraid," she whispered.

"Then don't be," he said softly. "You don't have to do this alone anymore."

When she looked at him again, there were no walls in his eyes. No distance.

Just him.

All of him.

No more fear.

She nodded, her chest tightening with something unfamiliar.

Hope.

He leaned in and kissed her—soft, sure. A beginning, wrapped in tenderness.

When they parted, she exhaled slowly, grounding herself in his presence. In the feel of his hand, his breath, the promise of something real.

She didn't know what came next.

But for the first time in a long time, she wasn't bracing for heartbreak.

She was ready to believe.

Because Daniel wasn't just staying.

He was choosing her.

And this time—she was choosing him too.

Chapter Twenty-Five

The early morning hush of the Davis estate wrapped the house in stillness, broken only by the gentle rustle of leaves outside and the faint chirp of birds greeting the new day. Golden light streamed through the tall windows of the guest bedroom, casting a soft glow over the room.

Daniel stood near the window, dressed in dark slacks and a crisp white shirt, still unbuttoned at the collar. He was slipping on his watch when he heard the quiet creak of the mattress behind him.

Julia stirred beneath the covers, hair tousled from sleep, one arm reaching instinctively for the warmth he'd left behind.

"You're already up?" she murmured, voice husky with sleep.

He turned, his expression softening the moment he saw her. "Yeah. I didn't want to wake you."

"You didn't," she said, pushing herself up on one elbow. "Everything okay?"

Daniel crossed back to the bed, sat on the edge, and brushed a strand of hair from her face. "I have to fly out this afternoon. Singapore. Just for a couple of days. It came up last night—meetings I can't push."

Julia blinked, disappointment flickering in her eyes before she caught it. "Oh. That's soon."

"I know." He cupped her cheek. "I was hoping you'd come with me."

Her lips parted slightly, surprised—and visibly torn. "Singapore?"

"I thought it could be good for both of us," he said, his thumb brushing her cheek. "A change of scene. A little space from everything here."

She smiled faintly. "It sounds amazing. But..." She sat up more fully, her expression apologetic. "I have that meeting with the publisher in Sydney— Friday morning. Remember? They're reviewing my portfolio for that illustration contract."

Daniel nodded, already expecting it, but the pinch of disappointment still tugged at his chest. "Right. I remember."

"I wish the timing were different," she said, searching his face. "I really do."

He leaned in and kissed her forehead, lingering there for a moment. "I get it, Jules. I want you to take that meeting. Your work is important too."

Her fingers curled lightly around his wrist. "You're not mad?"

He huffed a soft laugh. "Of course not. I'm proud of you."

She exhaled, relief flooding her features. "You'll be back before the weekend, right?"

"Friday night, if everything goes smoothly."

"Then maybe we'll have that quiet weekend after all."

Daniel smiled and leaned down, pressing a kiss to her lips—slow, sure. "It's a date."

As he stood, she caught his hand. "Text me when you land?"

"Always," he said, squeezing her fingers. Then, after a pause, "We'll talk to Joseph when I get back. About you moving into the penthouse."

Her expression softened. "Okay."

And just like that, the moment settled between them—quiet, steady, full of promise. They were both chasing something that mattered. But for the first time, they weren't chasing alone.

The Sydney sunlight spilled across the sidewalk as Julia stepped out of the publisher's building, the contract folder clutched to her chest and a bright smile playing on her lips. The meeting had gone even better than she'd dared to hope. They wanted her—her art, her voice, her perspective. They'd offered her the contract on the spot.

She couldn't wait to tell Daniel.

Sliding into the back seat of the waiting town car, she exhaled slowly, letting herself sink into the soft leather as the driver pulled into traffic. The steady hum of the city blurred around her, but inside, her thoughts were loud and vivid.

She missed him.

Three days—how could it feel like a lifetime? Daniel had called her every morning before his meetings, his voice still thick with sleep and affection. At night, he talked her through her day, asking questions, listening, just being there—even from across the ocean. And in between, the texts never stopped. Short ones, long ones. A picture of the skyline. A joke he knew she'd laugh at. The words I miss you typed so often they'd etched themselves into her heart.

She scrolled to his last message now:

Boarding soon. Final inspection when I land. Then home. Finally.

A second text had come a few minutes later:

Can't wait to hold you.

She hugged the folder tighter, her heart full.

The penthouse. Their new start. He was heading there straight from the airport to do the final walkthrough with the builder. He'd told her it was nearly perfect—just a few last touches before it was ready. Before she could step inside and finally begin that next chapter with him, without hesitation or hiding.

And then… he'd come back to her.

She glanced out the window, the city slipping past, her reflection soft in the glass. So much had changed in just a few short months. Her life, her art, her sense of herself. And Daniel—God, Daniel—had become the centre of a calm she hadn't realised she was still searching for.

A soft, contented breath escaped her lips. By tonight, she'd be in his arms again.

And this time, she wasn't bracing for the fall.

She was ready for the landing.

Together.

The Davis estate was quiet, sunlight pouring through the tall windows and spilling across the polished floorboards. Julia sat curled on the living room sofa, a throw blanket draped over her legs, her fingers absently playing with the edge of it. A gentle smile tugged at her lips as she glanced at her phone again.

Still no update.

Daniel had landed in Sydney over two hours ago, texting her when he touched down.

At the penthouse now. Just a few things to sort out. Then I'm coming straight to you.

That had been nearly ninety minutes ago.

She wasn't worried—Daniel would have let her know if something was wrong. More than likely, the final inspection had taken longer than planned. Or maybe he'd gotten caught up making sure every last detail was perfect before he brought her there.

Still, her heart buzzed with anticipation.

It had only been three days, but it felt longer. And now, knowing what waited ahead—their fresh start, the penthouse, the future they were slowly stepping into together—she couldn't help the quiet thrill running through her.

She looked up when she heard the front door open.

"Hi, gorgeous."

Mary breezed in like a gust of Parisian wind, sunglasses perched atop her head, effortlessly chic in a fitted blouse and dark jeans. She grinned as she crossed the room.

Julia stood, meeting her halfway with a warm hug. "You're back!"

"You first," Mary said, holding her at arm's length. "You're glowing."

Julia laughed. "I feel great."

Mary raised a brow. "Let me guess—Daniel just landed?"

"He did," she said, cheeks flushing a little. "He went to the penthouse for the final inspection. I thought he'd be back by now, but he probably got held up."

Mary smiled knowingly. "He'll be here soon. You've looked like a cat on hot bricks waiting for him."

Julia shrugged but couldn't stop the giddy smile tugging at her lips. "It's just been a really good week. The publisher offered me a contract, I've had actual sleep, I'm drawing again… and Daniel and I—things are really good."

Mary's smile softened. "I can see that. You've got peace written all over you."

Julia tucked her hair behind her ear, heart full. "Joseph got back last night. He said I looked healthy, and I told him Daniel, and I had sorted things out."

"And?"

"He said all he wants is for me to be happy." Her voice dipped slightly. "I didn't tell him about the move yet. Daniel wants to be with me when we do."

Mary nodded, understanding. "That's fair. You know your brother—he'll take it better with Daniel standing beside you."

"That's what I said," Julia murmured, sinking back into the couch. "It's not that I think he'll be upset. I just… want it to feel like we're all on the same page."

Mary dropped onto the armchair across from her and undoing the strap of her heels. "You're nesting. Mentally, emotionally. It's a good sign."

Julia laughed softly. "Is that what this is?"

"Definitely. And the fact that you didn't pounce on him the second he landed is some serious restraint."

Julia smirked. "Give me another ten minutes, and I might drive to the penthouse myself."

Mary stretched, grinning. "I'd pay to see that."

They both laughed—and just then, Julia's phone buzzed on the coffee table.

Her heart leapt as she snatched up the phone.

"Speak of the devil," Mary said, kicking off her shoes. "Want me to clear out?"

Julia didn't answer.

The message glowed on the screen:

I think we should reassess.
Don't think this move is a good idea.

Chapter Twenty-Six

Julia stared at the message, blinking.

Once.

Twice.

Her breath caught.

What…?

She was still staring at the screen, the glow of the text burning into her eyes. Her fingers tightened around the phone.

"Jules?" Mary's tone shifted. She was already halfway across the room, her easy smile fading into concern. "What is it?"

Julia finally looked up, confusion shadowing her face. "He… he just texted me. He said we should reassess. That he doesn't think the move is a good idea."

Mary's brows pulled together, and she reached for the phone. "Let me see."

Julia handed it over, her hand trembling slightly. "I don't understand. We talked about this. He was excited. He said he'd…."

Mary scanned the message, then looked at her. "This isn't like him."

"No, it's not." Julia folded her arms tightly across her chest, as if holding herself together. "Unless something happened."

Mary handed the phone back. "Call him."

Julia hesitated, her thumb hovering over the screen.

Mary's voice softened, but it was firm. "Jules. Don't spiral. Call him."

With a shaky inhale, Julia pressed the button and lifted the phone to her ear.

It rang once.

Twice.

Three times.

"Come on, Daniel," she whispered.

Four rings. Five.

Then it clicked.

The call connected.

But no one said anything.

"Daniel?" Julia said, sitting up straighter. "Hey. Are you there?"

Silence.

She frowned. "Daniel?"

Still nothing. No background noise. No breath. No voice.

Just… silence.

Julia pulled the phone back to check the screen. The call was still connected.

Her heart kicked hard in her chest.

"Daniel?" she said again, louder this time, her voice brittle.

A faint rustle.

Then the line went dead.

She stared at the screen.

Call ended.

"What happened?" Mary asked, already on her feet.

Julia looked up slowly. "He answered. I think. But he didn't say anything. And then the call just… ended."

Mary's eyes narrowed. "That doesn't make sense."

"No," Julia whispered. Her hands had gone cold. "It doesn't."

She stood abruptly, phone clutched tight in her hand as she paced to the window. "He always answers. Even if he's in a meeting, he texts. Something. And he was supposed to be here—almost an hour ago."

Mary grabbed her phone. "Okay. I'm calling him."

She did. They both watched the screen.

Calling Daniel Moore…

Ring.

Ring.

Ring.

Then click.

Mary hung up. "No answer."

Julia's phone buzzed again.

A new message.

She stared down at it.

Stop calling. I'm done. I realised I can't do this with you, Julia.

Her breath hitched.

The room tilted slightly, her chest tightening as she read the words again—each one a jagged cut across her heart.

Her voice came out small. "He… he changed his mind?"

Mary shot up straighter, frowning. "What?"

Julia didn't look up. She couldn't. "He's done. That's what it says."

Mary reached over and gently took the phone from her, reading the message silently. "No. No, this—" She shook her head. "This isn't him."

But Julia wasn't hearing her. Her thoughts were already spiralling.

He'd been so loving before the trip. Attentive. Gentle. They'd made plans—talked about the future. He told her he wanted everything with her.

But what if… what if the space made him rethink?

What if he'd gotten cold feet?

Her voice cracked, barely holding together. "Maybe he just realised it was too much. The baby. The drama with James. Me."

Mary's eyes flashed with disbelief. "Julia, stop."

She did.

Or tried to.

Her mouth pressed shut, but her mind kept racing. Spinning. Pulling her under.

"This is what he's done in the past," she whispered. "He bolts when it gets too serious."

Mary's shoulders stiffened, but she didn't argue. She sat beside Julia and grabbed her hands tightly. "No. Not this time. Not with you."

Julia's voice broke. "This is what Joseph was scared of. So was I."

The tears came then—hot and fast, streaking down her cheeks before she could stop them. She turned her face away, ashamed of how much it hurt. Ashamed of how much she'd let herself believe.

Mary pulled her closer. "Breathe, Jules. Just breathe."

But it was like something inside her had cracked open.

"He said he'd never leave me," Julia choked. "He promised he'd stay. That we'd build something together."

"I know."

"I believed him." Her voice collapsed into a sob. "I really believed him."

Mary wrapped her arms around her, pulling her into a tight hug. "You weren't wrong to. I saw him, Jules. I saw how he looked at you. That man was in it—all the way."

Julia clung to her. "Then why is this happening?"

Mary's voice was low but steady. "Because something's wrong. This isn't Daniel. Not the man you know. Not the man I saw you with."

Julia's tears slowed, her breathing shaky and uneven against Mary's shoulder.

"Whoever sent that message," Mary continued, "wanted to break you down. Wanted to make you feel abandoned."

Julia pulled back slightly, her expression crumpled and confused. "But who would do that? Why?"

Mary's eyes hardened. "That's what we're going to find out."

Julia blinked, tears still shining in her lashes. "You really think he didn't send it?"

"I know he didn't."

"How?"

Mary met her gaze with absolute certainty. "Because I know what love looks like, Julia. And Daniel Moore? That man loves you."

Julia stared at her a moment longer… then slowly nodded, swallowing hard.

A spark of something flickered behind the fear.

Doubt.

Hope.

Determination.

Mary said softly. "Let's think. Who would he have been with? The builder, right? Maybe we can call the site?"

Julia blinked, her mind snapping into motion. "Yes—yes. I have the project manager's number. He gave it to me a few days ago in case we needed updates."

Her hands fumbled as she unlocked her phone, scrolling through contacts with unsteady fingers.

"There," she murmured, spotting the name. She hit dial and stood, pacing as it rang.

Mary hovered beside her—tense, quiet, steady. Watching. Ready.

On the third ring, a voice picked up.

"Hello? Paul Greene speaking."

"Hi, Paul—it's Julia Davis. Daniel Moore's partner. He had a final walkthrough with you at the penthouse this morning?"

"Yes, of course," Paul said warmly. "Everything went really well. Daniel was happy with how it turned out—said the place looked perfect."

"Is he still there?" Julia asked quickly, breath catching in her throat.

"No," Paul replied. "He left just over an hour ago. Said he was in a hurry to get home to you."

Julia's heart slammed once in her chest.

Home to her.

Paul kept talking, but the words blurred around the one that mattered: left. Daniel had finished at the penthouse. He'd been on his way. And that was over an hour ago.

"Thank you," she managed, forcing her voice steady. "Thanks, Paul."

"Anytime. And congratulations again—it's a beautiful place. He seemed really excited."

She ended the call and slowly lowered the phone.

Mary caught her expression instantly. "He left. Didn't he?"

Julia nodded, her voice barely a whisper. "An hour ago."

A beat passed in silence—her heart pounding like a drum in her ears.

Mary straightened. "Then something's not right."

Julia gripped the phone tighter.

No.

This wasn't cold feet.

This wasn't Daniel bolting.

This was something else—something off.

Julia stood frozen, her mind whirring with dread and disbelief, the phone still clutched in her hand as if it could suddenly make sense of it all.

The front door clicked open.

Joseph's voice echoed down the hall. "Jules?"

He stepped into the living room, jacket slung over one shoulder, his expression easy—until he saw her face. And then Mary, standing beside her, tense and silent.

His eyes narrowed instantly. "What's wrong?"

Mary spoke before Julia could. "We think something might've happened. Daniel's messages—they don't sound like him."

Joseph's gaze snapped to Julia. "Show me."

Wordlessly, she handed him the phone. Her hands trembled.

He scrolled, reading the messages, his brow furrowing deeper with each line.

Then he shook his head. Firm. Certain.

"These aren't from Daniel."

Julia's voice cracked. "How do you know?"

Joseph looked up, his tone steady but sure. "Because I know him. He might have flaws—maybe even been unsure in the past—but he's never been a coward. He always ended things face to face, even when it was messy. He would never break up with you over a text."

Julia's throat tightened. "But what if—?"

He cut her off gently but firmly. "And he loves you, Julia. It's obvious. I've known him for over fifteen years. I've seen the change in him."

He handed the phone back to her.

"Something's wrong here. But it's not what you think."

Mary nodded, crossing her arms. "That's what I said."

Joseph turned toward the hallway, already moving. "I'm calling in a favour. Let's find out where he is—now."

Julia sat down slowly, her heart still racing, but now—finally—she wasn't spiralling alone.

They were going to find him.

Chapter Twenty-Seven

Joseph strode down the hall, phone already in hand. He paused at the edge of the kitchen island, scrolling to a contact.

"Who are you calling?" Mary asked, trailing behind him.

"Ethan Hart. He's with Cyber Crimes. He worked a case for me two years ago—guy's a genius with digital forensics. If anyone can trace where those messages came from, it's him."

Julia stood in the centre of the living room, still gripping her phone. "You really think someone else sent them?"

Joseph looked at her over his shoulder. "I'd bet my life on it."

He hit call. Two rings, then—

"Joseph," came a smooth, alert voice on the other end. "You don't call unless there's trouble."

"There's trouble," Joseph said flatly. "I need a trace run on a phone number. Urgent. Personal."

A pause. Then, "Send it through."

Joseph nodded, already typing. "I'll forward you a thread. I need to know where the messages came from—IP, device ID, everything you can get. And fast."

"Give me ten minutes," Ethan replied.

"Thanks."

Joseph ended the call and turned to the women.

"He'll start running it now."

Mary exhaled in relief. "Good. While he's doing that, I say we retrace Daniel's steps—he left the penthouse, but didn't make it here. Something happened in between."

Joseph nodded. "Agreed. He drives a black Mercedes, right?"

"Yeah," Julia said. "The new one. He just had it serviced."

Mary reached for her keys, already moving toward the door.

Joseph stepped in front of Julia, his hands coming to rest gently on her arms. "We're heading out now. I'll have Ethan trace his phone's last known location as soon as he gets a signal."

Julia hesitated, her eyes flicking between them. "Should I come with you?"

Before Joseph could answer, Mary stepped in, her voice calm but firm. "No, Jules. Stay here. In case he comes back—or calls. We need someone here, someone he trusts."

Joseph nodded in agreement. "You're the anchor, Julia. If he can, you're where he'll run."

Julia swallowed hard, her hands clenched at her sides, but she gave a shaky nod. "Okay… Just bring him home."

"We will," Joseph said quietly. "No matter what it takes."

She gave a reluctant nod.

Joseph moved to the door. "I'll call the second I know anything."

He stopped just before stepping out, looking back at her. His voice was softer this time. "Try not to worry. We're going to find him, Julia. I promise."

She nodded; eyes damp but determined. "Be careful."

Joseph sat rigid in the passenger seat, Mary behind the wheel, eyes focused, jaw tight. The city had melted away behind them, swallowed by the heavy silence between them. Now the only sounds were the low hum of the engine and their breathing, taut and measured.

Fifteen minutes later they turned into the underground car park.

"There," Joseph said, pointing. "That's Daniel's car."

Mary pulled in sharply. The vehicle sat neatly in its usual spot, undisturbed.

Both of them jumped out.

Joseph's gaze swept the area—and stopped. "Wait."

Near the driver's side door, a small metallic glint caught the light.

He crouched down, reaching for it.

Daniel's keys.

"What the hell?" he muttered, holding them up. "Why would he drop his keys?"

Joseph's phone buzzed, he checked his screen—Ethan. He answered immediately.

"Talk to me."

Ethan's voice came fast and clipped. "The texts were sent from Daniel's actual phone. No spoofing. It's the real deal. And it's still switched on."

Joseph straightened, adrenaline shooting through his system. "Where is it?"

A pause.

"That's the weird part," Ethan said. "I triple-checked. GPS puts it at your place."

Joseph blinked. "What? Are you sure?"

"Positive. It's been stationary for about ten minutes—pinging right off your home Wi-Fi and nearby towers. The signal's solid."

Mary turned sharply toward him. "Your house?"

Joseph's face went pale. "Julia's there."

Mary was already dialling. "She would've called if he showed up—"

The call rang out. No answer.

Mary frowned. "That's not right. She'd never ignore a call right now."

Joseph's jaw clenched. His voice was tight with barely controlled fury. "Then whoever has Daniel's phone is inside my home. With my sister."

On the other end of the line, Ethan's tone dropped, all business. "At first, I thought Daniel just left it behind. But listen—the last text wasn't sent from your exact address. It pinged from just down the road, thirty minutes ago. From the property next to yours."

Joseph froze.

Ethan continued, "Then the signal moved. Closer."

Joseph's stomach turned to stone. "James. It has to be. He's got Daniel's phone... and now he's with Julia."

"Exactly," Ethan confirmed grimly. "You think he's dangerous?"

"I didn't think so," Joseph muttered, his voice dark. "But now? I'm not taking any chances."

Mary, who'd been pacing by the driver's door, stopped cold. Her voice sliced through the air like a blade. "We need to go. Now."

Joseph was already moving. "Get in. Drive like hell."

Silence settled over the house like a warning after Joseph and Mary left.

Julia sat curled on the edge of the couch, Daniel's last message still etched into her thoughts like a wound. She'd tried calling again—no answer. Tried texting—nothing.

She chewed her lip and stood, pacing toward the kitchen when—

Ding-dong.

The doorbell.

Her heart kicked. Hope surged for a split second.

She ran to the door and flung it open.

James.

Her breath caught.

One hand leaning against the doorframe, his tie loosened, eyes unreadable— but there was something in his eyes that made her spine go stiff.

"James," she said, voice tight. "What are you doing here?"

He gave her a slow, knowing smirk. "Just checking on you. Seeing if everything's okay."

Her stomach turned. "This… isn't a good time."

"Oh, I can see that." His eyes scanned her face. "Looks like he already left you."

She narrowed her eyes. "What?"

"Daniel," James said, stepping forward.

She tried to block the doorway, but he used the movement to wedge his shoulder in and force his way past her.

"James!" she shouted, turning to follow him inside. "You can't just barge in!"

He didn't stop until he was in the middle of the living room, he turned slowly to face her. "Come on, Jules. Don't look so surprised. You and I both knew it wouldn't last."

She stared at him, heart hammering. "Why are you here? Really?"

He shrugged. "I just had a feeling he would have bolted by now. It looks like I'm right. Things got a little too serious?" His eyes flicked toward her stomach, cold and calculating. "Maybe a little too serious for a man like Daniel."

Her chest tightened. "He didn't leave me."

James tilted his head. "Didn't he?"

"Don't," she snapped. "Don't pretend you care."

"I do care," he said quietly, almost mockingly. "You just never wanted to believe it."

She stepped back, her voice dropping. "Did you have something to do with this?"

His smile faltered, just for a second.

Julia caught it—and the chill shot straight through her veins.

"I mean it, James," she said, backing up farther. "What did you do?"

He looked amused again, but there was tension creeping into his posture now. "You're upset, Julia. Grasping at anything. I get it."

"No." Her voice trembled, but her spine stayed straight. "You came here too quickly. You knew too much. Daniel's phone is missing, and now you're here asking questions like you know exactly what happened."

His gaze flickered. "You think I'd go that far?"

Julia didn't blink. "I think you've wanted to get him out of the picture for a long time. Daniel loves me."

The silence between them stretched tight, electric—then snapped.

James moved.

Fast.

Julia barely had time to gasp before he lunged, grabbing her arm and shoving her backward.

She stumbled, hitting the couch, her body pressing into the cushions as he came down over her, pinning her with his weight and fury.

"Don't believe what he tells you," he growled, his face inches from hers, breath hot and furious. "He doesn't love you! You know he was never going to stay!"

"Get off me!" Julia cried, twisting beneath him, panic rising like wildfire in her throat.

But James only tightened his grip on her wrists, slamming them down on either side of her. "I waited," he snarled, eyes flashing. "I watched him take everything. And you let him."

Tears welled in her eyes—fuelled not by pain, but fury. "You're insane."

His face twisted, lips curling into something between a sneer and a plea. "No. I'm the only one who's ever been here. The one who actually loves you."

"You don't *love* me," she spat, her voice trembling but unbreakable. "You want to *control* me. You want to *own* me."

For a breathless second, something flickered in his eyes—something unhinged. The mask cracked.

And then he lunged.

His mouth crashed down on hers, hard and desperate.

Julia jerked her head to the side with a strangled cry, but he grabbed her jaw, fingers digging in, forcing her still. His weight crushed her, his knee wedging between her thighs.

"Get off me!" she screamed, thrashing, legs kicking, fingers clawing at whatever she could reach. "James—stop!"

He caught her wrists again, pinning them above her head with one hand, his other anchoring her down. "He left you," he hissed, his breath hot and frenzied. "I knew he would. He was never going to stay. But I—I would've. I always would."

"You did this," she gasped, her eyes wild. "You planned all of this—"

Another brutal kiss silenced her, ripping the words from her mouth. His hand tangled in her hair, yanking her head back as his body pressed harder into hers. Tears burned down her cheeks.

"No one gets to touch you," he breathed against her skin, his voice dark and trembling. "Except me."

Julia choked on a sob. Her strength was fading—but she kept fighting, her body bucking beneath him, desperate to break free. Her legs kicked wildly. Her nails scraped at the back of his hands. But it wasn't enough.

His hand slid down her body, groping her breast, then lower. She bucked harder, but he pinned her with his weight. She felt him harden against her, and nausea surged.

She felt it—his arousal—and bile surged in her throat.

"No—no, please—" she gasped, her voice cracking.

His fingers fumbled at her skirt, yanking it higher.

Terror closed in, thick and suffocating. Her limbs weakened, her vision blurred. She squeezed her eyes shut, a sob catching in her throat.

Please, she begged silently. Someone. Please…

The front door exploded open.

The crash shook the house.

Footsteps pounding down the hallway.

Then—

"JAMES!" Joseph's voice tore through the house like a war cry. "GET AWAY FROM HER!"

Chapter Twenty-Eight

James froze, but only for a second—just long enough for Joseph to launch forward, grabbing him by the collar and yanking him off the couch.

Julia gasped for breath, curling in on herself. Everything felt muffled—distant—until Joseph's shout cut through the haze.

Joseph slammed James into the hardwood floor.

"You thought you could put your hands on my sister. I swear to God, I will kill you—" Joseph's fist cocked back, but Mary was suddenly there, pulling Julia up and out of the chaos.

"Julia, look at me," Mary said, voice urgent, holding her friend's face in both hands. "You're okay. You're safe. I've got you."

James groaned, coughing as Joseph dragged him toward the front door like dead weight.

Joseph didn't stop until he had him pinned against the hallway wall.

"You sick bastard," he growled. "You thought no one would come? You thought you'd get away with this?"

James barely managed a word before Joseph dropped him to the ground and whipped out his phone, his voice clipped and shaking as he called.

"Police. Now. Attempted assault. Forced entry. 14 Heathridge Lane, Double Bay. Send someone fast."

He stood by the door, looming over James like a sentinel, unmoving until sirens split the silence.

Back inside, Julia trembled violently in Mary's arms.

"I couldn't stop him," she whispered, her voice barely audible. "He wouldn't listen. He said... he said I belonged to him."

Mary's arms tightened around her. "You don't. You never did."

Julia nodded, her body still wracked with tremors, voice barely above a whisper.

"He knows where Daniel is."

Mary's brow furrowed. "Did he tell you that?"

Julia swallowed hard, her hands gripping the edge of the couch.

"No... but think about it—how else would he know Daniel was gone already?" Her voice strengthened with every word. "He came here acting like he knew everything. He knew I was alone. He knew Daniel hadn't made it here."

Mary's expression darkened. "Jesus."

The wail of sirens grew louder—swelling into the street like a promise—and moments later, the door burst open again.

Police Officers streamed inside, their heavy boots thudding against the floorboards as they entered the hallway.

They stopped at the sight—Joseph still kneeling on top of James, holding him firmly to the floor, blood on both of them.

One officer stepped forward, hand resting near his holster. "Step back, sir. We'll take it from here."

Joseph exhaled hard, his hands shaking as he slowly released James and stood. "He forced his way in. Attacked my sister."

James coughed, a twisted grin curling at the corner of his bloodied mouth. "You don't know anything."

Joseph's eyes flared. "I know you used Daniel's phone. And I know you're going to tell us where he is."

The officers moved in, grabbing James by the arms and yanking him upright. "You have the right to remain silent—"

"He won't stay silent," Julia said from down the hall, her voice cutting through the room like glass. She was standing now, supported by Mary, her expression tight and unyielding. "Not when he finally has someone to listen."

James's head snapped toward her, fury igniting in his eyes. "He took everything from me! Everything! And you let him!"

"No," Julia said, her voice calm now. Ice-cold. "You did that to yourself."

Joseph turned to the nearest officer. "You need to question him—now. He knows where Daniel Moore is. He said just enough to prove it."

The officer nodded, radioing through. "We'll take him in. Start digging."

As they dragged James toward the door, he thrashed once—just enough to lock eyes with Julia.

"I should've been the one," he snarled. "Not him."

Joseph moved like lightning, placing himself between James and Julia. "And you never will be."

The door slammed behind them, leaving only the heavy silence in their wake.

Julia's legs buckled, and Mary caught her.

Joseph turned, crossing the room in two steps. "You were right," he said softly, cupping the back of her head. "He knows more than he's letting on. And we're going to find out exactly what."

Julia's voice was muffled against his chest.

"Just find him. Please. Just find Daniel."

Joseph met Mary's gaze over her shoulder, his expression grim.

They would. Or they'd tear the city apart trying.

Meanwhile… miles away—unseen and alone—

Daniel stirred.

The first thing he registered was pain—a sharp, blooming ache at the base of his skull. Then the cold. The floor beneath him was hard, damp. Concrete, maybe. The air stank of mildew and motor oil.

His eyes fluttered open, and even the low light stabbed at his head like knives.

Where the hell am I?

He tried to sit up—but a sudden tug stopped him. His wrists were bound. Rough rope bit into his skin, tied tight to the chair he was slumped in.

Panic flared in his chest, fast and burning.

He blinked again, trying to focus. The room was dim, lit by a single hanging bulb overhead. Shadows stretched across crates and rusted tools along the walls. A warehouse. Industrial. Abandoned, by the look—and the smell—of it.

His mouth was dry. A trickle of blood ran from his temple down to his cheek.

Think. What happened?

He remembered walking to his car… a sting at the back of his neck… then darkness.

A noise—metal scraping concrete—made him twist his head toward the far wall.

A door creaked open.

Daniel squinted, heart pounding as footsteps echoed across the floor. A figure emerged from the shadows.

A man.

Late forties.

Thin, wiry build.

Leather gloves.

Calm.

He lit a cigarette with surgical precision, like this was just another day at the office.

"Well," the man said, exhaling slowly. "Look who's awake."

Daniel glared at him. "Who are you?"

The man gave a half-smile. "You don't need my name. You just need to sit there and behave."

Daniel strained against the ropes, the coarse fibres biting into his wrists as he twisted. His jaw clenched, muscles taut with fury. "You're making a big mistake."

The man across from him didn't flinch. He leaned back against a splintered crate, perfectly relaxed, as if he had all the time in the world. "I'm not the one who made the mistake," he said, his voice calm. Amused. "You did. Getting involved with the wrong woman."

Daniel's blood turned to ice.

"This is about Julia?"

The man didn't answer. Just gave a slow smile, one that didn't reach his eyes. He took a drag from his cigarette, then let the smoke curl from his lips like a sigh. "Can't say I blame you, though. She's something, that one. Real prime."

Daniel's eyes narrowed, fury sparking in their depths. "You've been watching her."

"Oh, not just her," the man replied, tapping ash onto the floor. "You too. For a while now. Nice routine you've got—estate, drivers, security. Almost impressive."

Daniel's heart pounded. Julia. The baby. Every instinct screamed at him. This wasn't random. This was calculated. Targeted.

"If you touched her—" he growled, straining harder against the ropes, pain shooting up his arms.

The man raised an eyebrow. "Me? No, I'm not the one she needs to worry about." He smiled again—mocking, deliberate. "I'm just here to keep you out of the way."

Daniel's breathing went shallow.

"Until it's too late."

Silence pulsed like a second heartbeat. Daniel froze, the words hitting him harder than any blow.

Then, low and deadly quiet, he said, "You'd better pray they don't find me."

The man chuckled, unfazed. "They're not looking in the right place. That's the beauty of misdirection, Mr. Moore. While they're busy chasing shadows, the real show has already started."

But Daniel wasn't listening anymore. His mind had already shifted into survival mode. Calculating. Tracking every second.

Because Julia was out there. Unprotected.

And if anything happened to her—

He would burn the world to the ground to make them pay.

The sterile hum of fluorescent lighting filled the stark, windowless room.

James Giles sat at the metal table, handcuffed, shoulders slouched with calculated ease. A faint smear of blood still marked the corner of his mouth. Across from him, Detective Marla Griggs took her seat, setting a thick case file down with a thud.

She studied him for a long beat.

"You've had a hell of a day, Mr. Giles."

James didn't answer. He tilted his head, eyes flicking toward the one-way mirror. Calm. Arrogant.

Marla opened the file and slid a photograph across the table—Daniel's car, in the underground carpark.

"We found this in the parking garage. You recognise it?"

Still no answer.

She slid another—Daniel's phone, time-stamped, showing the message sent minutes before the alleged assault.

"You had his phone on you when we arrested you," she said plainly. "Unlocked."

James offered a slow shrug. "Found it. Maybe he dropped it."

"Convenient," Marla said, voice crisp. "So, you just happened to be walking around Joseph Davis's estate, picked up Daniel Moore's phone, then broke in and assaulted Julia Davis?"

"She let me in," James said, voice low and tight.

"She told us otherwise. And the bruises say otherwise." Marla leaned forward slightly. "We have enough to charge you, Mr. Giles. Attempted sexual assault, unlawful entry, and obstruction. But you and I both know that's not the worst of it."

James's jaw twitched.

Marla slid another photo forward—Daniel's GPS data, highlighted in red. "Daniel's phone pinged just down the street from Joseph Davis's home before it was brought inside. That message you sent from his number. That was staged; to make her think it was Mr Moore."

She let that sink in.

James said nothing.

"We know Daniel Moore never left his apartment building willingly. We also know his car is still parked at his building and his keys were left on the ground. So, here's what I think—someone jumped him. Took him. And you were involved."

James gave a dry chuckle. "You think I kidnapped him?"

"I think you know exactly where he is," Marla said. "And unless you want to be the one holding the entire bag, now's the time to speak up."

James finally looked at her, eyes narrowing. "You don't know what he's like. What he's done."

Marla stared back, unfazed. "This isn't about what you think he deserved. It's about what you did."

Silence.

She let it linger, heavy and sharp.

Then she stood.

"If something happens to him—and we find out you were the one who could've prevented it? You'll be charged accordingly. And if someone else is involved, you better hope we get to them before they decide you're a liability."

James said nothing. But something had changed in his expression—a flicker of uncertainty behind the arrogance.

Marla left the room without another word.

In the hallway, she exhaled and turned to the waiting officer.

"Hold him. No calls, no visitors. He's hiding something. Let's find out what before it's too late."

Chapter Twenty-Nine

The bulb overhead swayed slightly, casting shadows that jittered across Daniel's bruised face. The ropes bit deeper into his wrists with every tug, but he didn't stop. Couldn't.

Pain didn't matter. Julia was out there, pregnant with their child.

He tested the bindings again. Rough rope. Sloppy knots. His captor might've been confident, but he was careless.

Daniel closed his eyes for half a second, focused on the rhythm of his breathing, and pulled the way his military instructor had once taught him—twist, tighten, slide.

The rope gave an inch.

Footsteps echoed in the distance again. The man was pacing, distracted. Good.

Daniel kept working the rope, each movement sending a bolt of pain through his wrists. Blood warmed his fingers.

The door creaked open again.

"I told you to behave," the captor said, stepping into the room.

Daniel relaxed his arms, wrists still half-bound. "I'm sitting, aren't I?"

The man gave a humourless smile, tapping ash into a rusted paint can. "You don't get it. You're just leverage. You don't matter."

Daniel stared at him. Calm. Cold. "That's where you're wrong."

The man stepped closer, the cigarette dangling loosely between his lips. "Big words from a man tied to a chair."

Daniel waited until he was just close enough—then struck.

He exploded upward, shoving the chair back with all his weight. It smashed into the man's legs. He stumbled with a grunt, the cigarette flying from his mouth.

Daniel twisted hard. The ropes snapped.

He surged up, pain screaming through his limbs, and threw a punch that connected with the man's jaw. The crack echoed through the warehouse.

The man staggered back, reaching for something under his jacket.

Daniel didn't wait.

He dove behind a stack of crates, rolling just as a click echoed—a switchblade flicking open.

His heart pounded.

No exit in sight. No weapon. No time.

The man stalked around the crates slowly, blade gleaming in the overhead light.

"You just made this a hell of a lot harder on yourself."

Daniel's eyes flicked upward—to a rusted pipe just above him. If he could—

He sprang up, grabbing it with both hands, swinging his legs like a pendulum. At the peak of the arc, he kicked out, feet slamming into the man's chest.

The knife skittered across the concrete.

Daniel dropped, landed hard, and scrambled for it.

Fingers closed around the handle just as the man lunged.

Daniel turned, slashing blindly. The blade caught flesh. The man howled and fell back, clutching his shoulder.

Daniel didn't stop. He ran—past crates, broken pallets, through the darkness—until he reached a heavy service door.

Locked.

Of course.

He jammed the knife into the rusted latch and wrenched it sideways. Metal screamed, then snapped.

The door flew open.

Cold air hit him like a shock.

Daniel stumbled into the night, lungs burning, blood on his hands.

Behind him, the man's roar echoed like a promise.

Daniel didn't look back.

He was going to find Julia.

He had to find her.

The house was too quiet.

Julia sat curled on the living room couch, a blanket wrapped tightly around her shoulders. Her eyes were fixed on nothing, unblinking, her body still trembling with the echoes of fear.

Mary sat close beside her, one arm looped around Julia's shoulders like a shield. She hadn't left her side since the police took James away.

The front door creaked open.

Heavy footsteps. Then Joseph's voice, low and tense.

"She's in here."

Julia didn't look up.

Detective Marla Griggs stepped into the room, her navy blazer still buttoned, hair slicked back in a tight knot. She carried a leather notebook, but her eyes were sharper than anything she wrote down.

She paused, taking in the scene—the wreckage of the woman curled on the couch, the loyal friend clinging to her, and the furious brother pacing like a lion denied a kill.

"Ms. Davis," she said gently. "I'm Detective Marla Griggs. I know this has been an incredibly difficult day."

Mary's eyes narrowed. "Cut to it."

Joseph stood just behind the detective; arms folded tightly across his chest. "What did he say?"

Marla shook her head. "Nothing useful."

Julia's lips parted. Her voice, when it came, was dry as ash.

"He won't tell you where Daniel is, will he?"

"No," Marla admitted. "We've got him on assault, breaking and entering, obstruction—and more than enough to hold him. But when it comes to Mr Moore, he's clammed up. Acting like he's the victim."

"He isn't," Joseph growled. "He planned this. The message from Daniel's phone, the timing, the break-in. He wanted Julia alone."

"He keeps repeating that Mr Moore *'took everything from him,'*" Marla said. "He's fixated. Possessive. That kind of language—honestly? It worries me."

Julia's arms tightened around herself.

"I told you he knew where Daniel was," she whispered. "He came here like he knew. Like he'd already won."

Marla's gaze softened for a moment, but only for a moment.

"We're running GPS traces and checking nearby surveillance. But right now? He's not giving us anything. If Daniel's still out there somewhere—hurt, restrained, unconscious—time matters."

Joseph ran a hand through his hair. "So what? We wait?"

Marla turned to him. "No. We pressure him. We dig. We look at any associates, any hired muscle, offshore contacts, burner phones. If he had help—and it looks like he did—we'll find the link."

Joseph stepped forward. "What about releasing something to the media? Getting the word out?"

Marla hesitated. "If he's being held by a professional, exposure might make him harder to reach—or speed up a timetable we don't want accelerated. But I'll consider it."

Julia looked up, her voice thready but firm.

"Just find him. Please."

Marla gave a firm nod. "We're doing everything we can."

She turned toward the door, and Joseph moved to walk her out.

"We'll be in touch," she said over her shoulder.

"Thank you, Detective," he replied, his voice low.

Silence settled once she was gone.

Julia sat frozen for a beat, then her shoulders trembled. Silent tears spilled down her cheeks.

He was alive. He had to be.

She didn't know how she knew—only that she did.

And no matter how broken she felt, no matter how much darkness clung to the edges of her heart—

She would find the strength to hold him again.

The streets were quiet—too quiet.

Daniel staggered through the alley, one hand pressed to his ribs, the other still gripping the bloodied knife. His breath came in ragged gasps, fogging in the cold air.

Each step lit his spine with fire, but he kept moving.

His shirt clung to his back with sweat and blood, and his eyes burned from the warehouse dust and the dry sting of adrenaline. He had no idea how long he'd been unconscious—or how far he was from help.

A flickering streetlamp buzzed overhead.

He blinked up at it, squinting at the faded signage:

"Foundry Lane – No Through Road."

Come on. Think.

The industrial district sat a few suburbs from the city. He'd driven past it countless times. But on foot, disoriented and bleeding?

He could've been on the moon for all it mattered.

He reached the edge of the alley and leaned against a graffiti-covered dumpster, trying to slow his breathing.

Phone. He needed a phone.

But who would he call? Julia? No—he wouldn't risk James or whoever that bastard was tracing it. He needed to reach Joseph.

A movement down the block—a man exiting a petrol station, phone in hand.

Daniel pushed off the dumpster, teeth clenched and crossed the street like a drunk man staggering out of a bar. His knees almost gave out when he reached the man.

"Hey—hey, mate—wait," Daniel croaked.

The guy turned, startled. "Whoa, are you okay?"

Daniel held up both hands, blood dripping from his fingers. "Not gonna hurt you. Just—just need to borrow your phone. Emergency."

The man took a step back, eyes wide. "You're bleeding."

"I know," Daniel rasped. His voice was barely audible, raw from exhaustion. "Please. It's urgent. Call Joseph Davis. I'll give you the number. Or Mary Collins. She's a model. She'll answer."

The guy stared at him like he'd wandered out of a warzone.

But he didn't run.

Daniel staggered, one hand braced against a post to stay upright. "Tell them… Julia's not safe. James… he's not working alone."

The man hesitated, then slowly pulled out his phone and handed it over. "Here. Use it. But you should be calling an ambulance."

Daniel took the phone with trembling fingers, blood smearing across the screen. His vision swam.

He dialled.

Ring.

Ring.

Then— "Joseph Davis."

Relief slammed into him like a wave. "It's me," Daniel choked out.

A beat of silence. Then, sharp, stunned— "Daniel?! Where the hell are you?"

"Industrial district somewhere. I got out. Listen—Julia's in danger. I think it's James, he isn't working alone. He hired someone. I've been held since yesterday. It was planned. All of it. Julia's not safe. Are you with her?"

Joseph's voice hardened instantly, shifting into command mode. "Julia's safe. I got to the house just in time. James tried to assault her."

Daniel's knees buckled. He dropped to the curb, phone pressed tight to his ear. "Is she… is she okay? God, I swear, if he touched her—"

"She's shaken. But unharmed. Mary's with her. She finally managed to fall asleep about fifteen minutes ago."

Daniel let out a shaky breath. "Thank God."

"Where are you? I'll come get you."

Daniel turned his head, spotting the street sign through the haze. "Foundry Lane. Off Carrington. There's a servo on the corner. I'll be near the bench out front."

"Got it. Don't move. I'm on my way."

The line clicked dead.

Daniel handed the phone back with bloodied fingers. "Thanks, mate."

"You sure you don't want to call an ambulance?"

Daniel shook his head. "No. Not yet. There's somewhere I need to see first."

He slumped down fully onto the curb, heart pounding. The knife he'd taken from the warehouse clattered beside him. His hands trembled in his lap, muscles screaming in pain.

But for the first time since waking up in that concrete hellhole, a sliver of hope broke through.

He whispered her name into the night sky—like a prayer, like a vow.

"Julia. I'm coming home."

Chapter Thirty

The house was still.

Too still.

Joseph stepped quietly into the living room, careful not to let the door creak or his boots thud too hard on the floorboards. Julia was still curled on the couch, one arm tucked beneath her cheek, the blanket pulled high around her shoulders. Her breathing was slow. Steady. Thank God.

In her condition, this kind of stress was dangerous.

Mary glanced up from the armchair across the room, her body instantly alert. Joseph gave a small nod and beckoned her over with a curl of his fingers.

She rose without a sound.

He leaned close and whispered, "Daniel just called."

Mary gasped under her breath, eyes wide. "Oh, thank God. Is he okay?"

"Not sure of his condition, but he escaped. I'm going to get him now."

Mary followed his gaze to the couch. Julia hadn't stirred.

Joseph's expression softened for a fraction of a second as he looked at his sister. Then it hardened again, resolve snapping back into place. "If she wakes up— keep her calm. She doesn't need another surge of panic."

Mary nodded, placing a reassuring hand on his arm. "Go. I've got her."

Without another word, Joseph turned and slipped out the door.

Foundry Lane was barely more than a scar of broken asphalt and silence. The streetlight above the servo flickered weakly, casting a jaundiced glow over the bench just outside the station.

Daniel sat hunched over, one arm cradling his ribs, the other braced on his knee. His head hung low, face streaked with sweat and blood—but his eyes snapped up the moment he heard the engine.

Joseph pulled up fast and killed the lights. He was out of the car in two strides.

"Jesus, Daniel," he muttered, taking in the blood-streaked shirt and ghost-pale skin. "You look like hell."

Daniel managed a dry, broken laugh. "Feels worse than it looks."

Joseph crouched beside him. "Can you stand?"

"I can try."

With Joseph's help, Daniel slowly pushed to his feet, biting back a groan. His knees shook, but he didn't fall. Not yet.

"Hospital?" Joseph asked quietly, steadying him with a firm grip.

Daniel shook his head. "No, I have to see Julia first—she needs to know I'm okay."

"She's safe. Sleeping. Mary's with her."

Relief softened the lines on Daniel's face, just for a heartbeat.

Joseph guided him to the car, opened the passenger door, and helped him in. "I've got you now."

As the car pulled away from the curb and melted into the dark streets, Daniel closed his eyes.

The front door clicked open.

Mary was on her feet in an instant, hurrying down the hallway. When she saw him—really saw him—she froze for a second. Daniel looked like he'd crawled through fire. Blood on his shirt, dirt and dried sweat on his skin, a jagged bruise on his temple.

But his eyes… his eyes were clear.

"Daniel," she breathed, voice breaking.

He opened his arms, and she stepped into them without hesitation. Her hug was fierce, almost painful.

"I thought—God, I thought we'd lost you."

"I thought so too," he said, his voice rough but steady.

She pulled back, eyes glassy, but managed a small smile. "She's in the living room. Still asleep."

Daniel glanced past her. "She's okay?"

"She will be. She's been asking for you in her sleep."

Something inside him broke and mended at the same time.

Mary squeezed his arm gently. "I'll give you two some space."

And with that, she turned and disappeared down the hallway, leaving the house in a hush.

Daniel stepped into the living room.

The lights were dimmed low, casting soft shadows across the quiet room. The house was still, hushed, as if holding its breath.

Julia lay curled on the couch, wrapped in the familiar cream throw she always reached for when she needed comfort. Her chestnut hair spilled over the cushion, tangled and soft. Even in sleep, her face was pale, lips parted slightly, a faint crease between her brows betraying the unrest she couldn't quite shake. As if her body was resting, but her mind hadn't yet been given permission.

Daniel stepped into the room and paused.

His heart clenched.

He crossed the space slowly, every movement careful, reverent. When he dropped to one knee beside her, it was instinct—not ceremony, not habit, just the weight of love and helplessness pressing him low.

That's when he saw them.

Faint, but unmistakable.

Bruises.

Dark smudges along her jaw, like fingerprints branded into her skin. As if someone had grabbed her. Held her there. Hurt her.

A cold fire ignited in his chest. His hand curled into a fist before he could stop it.

James.

If he ever saw that bastard again—if he got within arm's reach—he didn't trust himself not to finish what Joseph had started.

But then his gaze returned to her.

To Julia.

And rage gave way to something heavier. Something worse.

Guilt.

He should've been there. Should've stopped it. Protected her. That was his job—his vow.

He reached out slowly, brushing a strand of hair from her temple with trembling fingers. She stirred faintly, a soft sound escaping her lips, but didn't wake.

"I'm here now," he whispered, the words catching in his throat. "You're safe. I swear it, Jules. No one will ever hurt you again."

He stayed there beside her, not moving, watching the rise and fall of her breathing—waiting for the fear in her to settle.

And swearing, with everything in him, that he would never let her feel this broken again.

"Julia," he whispered, brushing a strand of hair from her cheek.

She stirred, brows twitching, lashes fluttering. "Mm?"

"It's me," he said gently. "I'm here."

Her eyes blinked open.

For a moment, she didn't move. Didn't speak. Just stared at him like she couldn't quite trust what she was seeing.

Then—

"Daniel?"

His name left her lips like a breath, a sob, and a prayer woven into one fragile sound.

He nodded, his voice hoarse with emotion. "I made it back."

She bolted upright, gasping, and threw herself into his arms. Her hands clutched at his shirt, shaking. "You're bleeding—Daniel—oh my God—"

"I'm fine," he whispered, burying his face in her hair. "I'm here. I made it back to you."

She drew back just far enough to cradle his face in her palms, her eyes darting over every bruise, every cut, like she was trying to memorise him—rebuild him in her mind.

"I thought I lost you," she breathed.

"You didn't," he said softly. "You never will."

Her tears broke free, and she wrapped her arms around his neck, anchoring him to her with everything she had.

"I love you, Daniel," she whispered, her voice trembling. "Thank God you're back in my arms."

He held her tighter, heart full to bursting. "It's the only place I ever want to be."

Then he pulled back, just enough to search her eyes. "Julia… James didn't hurt you?"

A flicker of fear crossed her face—raw and immediate. "Joseph got here just in time."

Relief and rage warred in his chest. He brushed a strand of hair from her cheek, his touch trembling. "Thank God."

His jaw tightened, eyes dark with fury. "I swear to God, if I ever see him again—."

She reached for him gently, her fingers finding his face, her touch steadying the storm in him. "I don't want to think about him anymore," she whispered. "He's not worth another second."

Then she leaned in and kissed him—softly, deliberately—her lips brushing his like a promise. His breath caught. The world blurred. He closed his eyes, letting the moment wrap around him like a balm he hadn't realised he needed.

"Neither do I," he murmured, forehead resting against hers. "I just want you. Safe."

Her gaze dropped to the blood on his shirt. "We need to get you to a hospital."

He opened his mouth to argue, but the sharp throb in his ribs made the decision for him.

"Okay," he exhaled, his voice ragged. "But only if you stay with me. I don't want you out of my sight."

The sterile scent of antiseptic clung to the air, sharp and clean. Daniel sat on the edge of the hospital bed, his shirt gone, his torso bruised. A dull ache radiated through his ribs and shoulders, but the painkillers were beginning to take the edge off.

The doctor snapped off his gloves and gave Daniel a final once-over. "No fractures," he said, his tone professional but faintly impressed. "You're lucky. A few deep bruises, torn muscle tissue, and plenty of surface cuts. You'll be sore for a while, but you'll make a full recovery."

Daniel gave a tight nod. "Thanks, Doc."

The doctor turned to Julia, who hadn't moved from her chair beside the bed. Her hands were clasped in her lap, knuckles white. "He needs rest for the next several days. No heavy lifting, nothing strenuous, and those cuts need to stay clean and dry."

"I'll take care of him," she said quietly, her eyes locked on Daniel's face.

The doctor gave a short nod, then moved toward the door. "You're free to go home when you're ready."

He stepped out and pulled the door gently shut behind him, leaving a hush in his wake.

Daniel exhaled slowly, his body aching but his spirit lighter. "No fractures," he said, voice low. "That's something."

Julia reached across the bed and laced her fingers through his. "Thank God."

He gave her hand a gentle squeeze, then slowly reached for his shirt, lifting it with care. Pain lanced through his ribs as he eased it over his shoulders, his jaw clenched against the sharp throb of bruised muscles. The movement made him wince, breath hitching through his teeth.

Julia was there in an instant—steady, silent—her hands already helping, guiding the fabric over his back with tender precision. She said nothing, but the worry in her eyes spoke louder than words.

"You sure you're up for this?" she asked, worry shadowing her eyes.

Daniel offered a faint smirk. "I've survived worse."

But she didn't return the smile. "You scared the hell out of me," she whispered.

He rested his forehead against hers for a heartbeat, closing his eyes. "I wasn't scared for me."

She leaned into him, anchoring him without saying a word.

They were just reaching for the door handle when it suddenly swung open with a soft creak.

Detective Marla Griggs stood in the threshold, her gaze sharp but calm.

"Mr. Moore," she said, nodding once. "Before you go, I need a minute of your time."

Daniel sighed and nodded, settling back onto the edge of the hospital bed. "Of course."

Julia hovered, but he gave her hand a squeeze. "It's okay. I'm good."

"I'll wait just outside," she said reluctantly, then stepped out and closed the door behind her.

Marla approached, pulling a small notepad from her coat. "I won't keep you long. I just need to clarify a few things."

"Shoot."

"We have Mr Giles in custody, obviously. He's still refusing to give a full statement, but his phone and financials are giving us more than he has. There's a payment that went through last week to a known enforcer—ex-military, freelance. We believe that's who held you."

Daniel's jaw tightened. "Makes sense. The guy knew what he was doing. Sloppy rope work, but everything else."

"We're also looking into a possible safe house James used for communications— if you can recall anything else about the location where you were held, it could help."

Daniel nodded slowly. "Industrial district. Old warehouse. High ceilings, rusted beams, some kind of machine parts stacked in the back. I think it was near Foundry Lane—maybe off Carrington."

Marla scribbled quickly. "That narrows it down. We'll send a team."

She looked up then, her voice dropping a notch. "What you did—getting out the way you did—that probably saved your life."

"I wasn't thinking about that," Daniel said quietly. "I was thinking about her."

A beat passed.

Marla nodded once. "We'll be in touch. But for now—go home. Rest. Be with the people who matter."

Daniel gave her a tired smile. "I plan to."

The detective opened the door, and Julia reappeared instantly, slipping an arm around Daniel's waist.

"Take care," Marla said before disappearing down the hall.

As they stepped into the corridor together, Daniel leaned into Julia more than before—drawing strength from her, not just physically but in every way. And in his eyes, something steady had returned.

He was going home; with the woman he loved.

Chapter Thirty-One

Sunlight filtered through the curtains, soft and golden, casting a warm glow over the room. The house was still, wrapped in the hush of late morning.

Daniel stirred, his eyes opening slowly to the weightless quiet. His body ached—deep, lingering bruises humming beneath the surface—but the pain was distant now, dulled by sleep and the woman nestled in his arms.

Julia.

Her back was pressed to his chest, her breath warm and even against the hush. One of his arms was wrapped around her, the other resting across her belly, his hand splayed protectively over the small curve of her abdomen. Flat still—but not for long.

He closed his eyes again and let himself feel it. Her warmth. The rise and fall of her breathing. The barely-there movement of her fingers curling around his forearm in her sleep. This… this was everything.

This was home.

He brushed his lips softly against her shoulder, breathing her in, as a thought settled deep in his chest.

This was where he wanted to be—for the rest of his life.

Not just with her. Not near her.

Bound to her.

Julia was the only woman he had ever loved. The only one he would ever love. And lying here now, with her wrapped so trustingly in his arms, he realised something he should've seen all along.

He'd asked the wrong question.

He never should've asked her to move in with him—not like it was some trial run. Some halfway step toward something more.

What he should have asked…

Was forever.

Julia stirred against him, her body stretching slowly in the morning light. A quiet hum left her lips as she shifted, her hand coming to rest over his on her stomach.

"Mmm… you're awake," she murmured, voice sleep-rough and soft.

Daniel smiled against the back of her neck. "Didn't want to move. Not with you like this."

She turned slightly, just enough to look up at him over her shoulder. Her eyes were still heavy with sleep, but there was peace in them. Safety.

"I was dreaming about you," she whispered. "That you never made it home."

His heart clenched. "I did," he said gently. "And I'm not going anywhere."

He pressed a soft kiss behind her ear, lingering there, letting the silence wrap around them like a second blanket.

Then his voice dipped low—steady, sure.

"Julia…"

She shifted fully now, rolling onto her back to face him. His hand stayed on her belly, and hers settled gently over it, anchoring him there—grounding him.

She didn't speak, just looked up at him, her gaze calm, open, and unwavering.

So many things crowded his chest, too big for words. He hadn't wanted a trial run. Not a temporary arrangement or a halfway step.

He didn't want almost or someday.

He wanted to wake up like this—every day. To build a life with her that didn't involve contingency plans or unspoken fears.

He wanted forever.

But if forever was what they were building, he owed it to her to get it right.

And that meant waiting. Just a little longer.

"I've been thinking," he said quietly, brushing his thumb along her knuckles. "About all the ways I got it wrong before."

He paused. "Would it be okay if we stayed here… in this house… for a bit longer?"

Julia didn't hesitate. Her fingers curled around his. "If that's what you want. I just want to be with you. No matter where we are."

His heart pulled tight in his chest. He leaned in and kissed her—slowly, reverently—like a vow not yet spoken aloud.

He would ask the right question soon.

But she deserved the best version of that moment—of him.

And the way he felt right now—bruised, raw, still healing—it wasn't the time.

Not yet.

And in the quiet that followed, their hands stayed joined over the place where their future had already begun to grow.

The sun had just begun its slow descent, casting long, golden fingers across the quiet curve of the private garden behind the Davis estate. The air was soft and warm, fragrant with jasmine blooming along the old stone path, mingling with the crisp, earthy undertone of eucalyptus drifting in from the trees beyond.

Everything felt still. Unburdened. The kind of peace neither of them had known in far too long.

They had remained here—at the Davis estate—ever since the night Daniel came back to her. That night, two weeks ago, he'd returned bruised and bloodied but breathing. Alive. Part of staying had been necessity; he hadn't been in any shape to leave. But the deeper truth—the one he hadn't dared speak aloud—was that he couldn't bear to take her back to his home. Not yet. Not until she returned as something more.

His fiancée.

His wife.

His always.

Because Julia wasn't just the woman he loved. She was the centre of every hope he'd ever held. The home he didn't know he'd been searching for his entire life.

In the time since, the world had started to settle back into place—but not without consequence.

James had been formally charged—multiple counts that couldn't be buried or bought away. Not even his money, nor his connections, could shield him from the weight of what he'd done. His legal team had splintered under the pressure, the media had turned ruthless, and Daniel had made sure the truth found the people who needed to hear it. He hadn't sought revenge—but he hadn't extended mercy either. James had made his bed. He could lie in it.

Daniel had made his choices, too.

One of them was waiting now—just beyond the trees. A newly purchased estate, not far from here, tucked behind wrought iron gates and a long drive lined with cypress trees. A place built not just for beauty, but for safety, for permanence. For family.

For Julia.

He would show her—once she said yes. As soon as he could call her his forever.

He had already taken steps to ensure her safety, steps he hadn't thought necessary until it was nearly too late. Their security had been overhauled—quietly, thoroughly. Julia now had a full-time driver who doubled as a trained bodyguard. Daniel had increased surveillance across every property he owned, added redundancies, closed every gap. There would be no more blind spots. No more chances taken with her life.

He'd come far too close to losing her.

And he would never—never—let that happen again.

Across the garden, Julia stood barefoot in the grass, the hem of her soft cream dress fluttering just above her knees. The breeze lifted her chestnut hair in gentle waves, tumbling it down her back like silk. Her eyes were closed; face tilted to the sky as if soaking in every drop of peace the moment offered. She looked ethereal—untouched by the weight of the past, full of light despite all they had endured.

Daniel stood at the edge of the patio, silent, drinking her in like she was the last beautiful thing left in the world. His heart pounded against his ribs, steady and fierce, like a drumbeat calling him forward.

This was it.

The moment he had imagined and rewritten in his mind a thousand different ways.

And yet… none of them came close to this.

Because she was here. With him. Alive. Stronger than ever.

She hadn't seen him yet.

He took a step forward, then another.

And when her eyes finally opened and met his—calm and clear and unmistakably his—he knew there would never be a more perfect time.

Not because it was extravagant or planned down to the minute—but because it was real. Honest. Whole.

He walked slowly toward her; the ring box tucked in his jacket pocket. When she turned at the sound of his footsteps, her face lit with the kind of smile that knocked the air clean out of his lungs.

"Hey," she said, soft and sweet. "You've been quiet."

"I've been thinking."

She arched a brow playfully. "That's never a good sign."

He chuckled, stepping closer. "Maybe. Or maybe it's finally the opposite."

Julia tilted her head, reading him like only she could. "You look serious."

Daniel took her hands in his. His voice, when it came, was steady. Intentional.

"I've had everything I could ever want in life, Julia—wealth, power, control. But none of it meant anything. Not really. Not until you."

Her breath caught, eyes wide but unblinking.

"You showed me what it meant to fight for something real. To come undone and still choose love. You made me feel worthy of being seen, even when I was barely holding it together." He paused, his voice growing quieter. "And now, every time I look at you… I see the rest of my life."

He released one of her hands, reaching into his jacket. Her eyes followed the motion, lips parting as he sank to one knee in the grass.

The ring caught the sunlight like a promise—simple, elegant, timeless.

"Julia Davis… will you marry me?"

She froze for a breath—only a breath—and then nodded so fast her tears spilled over.

"Yes," she whispered. Then louder. "Yes."

He slipped the ring onto her finger with trembling hands, and as she dropped to her knees to kiss him, it wasn't with ceremony or performance—it was with reverence.

Her hands framed his face, her voice breaking. "I didn't think I'd get this. Not with you. Not after everything."

He wrapped his arms around her, holding her close. "You were always the endgame, Julia. I just needed to grow into the man who deserved you."

She smiled, her forehead resting against his. "You are."

The wind rustled the trees. The garden hushed around them. In that stillness, nothing else existed—just the two of them, whole, healed… and finally home.

Epilogue

Seven months later....

The hospital room pulsed with quiet tension—the kind that settles just before everything changes forever. Soft afternoon light filtered through the blinds, casting long, pale stripes across the polished floor, but the air inside was anything but calm. Machines beeped softly. The scent of antiseptic lingered faintly. Nurses moved with quiet efficiency, voices low, but every sound seemed to echo in the silence between contractions.

Julia clung to the edges of the hospital bed; her body coiled with pain. Sweat gathered on her brow, sliding down her temples, and her hands gripped the rails with white-knuckled desperation. Another contraction surged through her like a rising tide, violent and unstoppable. She cried out, her body curling inward, every nerve ending on fire.

Just months ago, everything had been different—simpler, quieter. Four weeks after his proposal, she'd walked down a rose-lined path in the back garden of the Davis estate, Daniel waiting for her beneath a white arch woven with jasmine and eucalyptus. He'd offered her everything—grand venues, designer gowns, a guest list of hundreds. But Julia had only smiled, taken his hands in hers, and said the only thing she wanted was to be his. No fanfare, no spectacle. Just Daniel. Just forever.

Their wedding had been small, intimate, wrapped in the quiet beauty of promises meant to last. No press. No performance. Just love, vows whispered like secrets, and the feeling that they were finally—finally—where they were always meant to be.

Afterward, they moved into the estate Daniel had quietly purchased before the proposal—an elegant, sun-drenched property nestled among rolling hills and wild gardens. Julia had fallen in love with it the moment she stepped onto the front verandah, barefoot and laughing, the breeze catching the hem of her dress.

Their life together had begun in that place, calm and beautiful. Her pregnancy had been uneventful—no more threats, no late-night emergency calls. Just quiet anticipation and days filled with laughter, soft music in the evenings, and Daniel marvelling at the way she carried their child with such grace and quiet strength. He often found himself watching her in awe, fingers brushing her swelling belly, unable to believe that someone so fierce, so kind, was carrying his child—their future.

Now, that future was about to arrive.

Julia cried out, her voice cracking with pain. Daniel was there—instantly. At her side, fingers entwined with hers, the other hand bracing her back as she leaned forward, chest heaving.

"You've got this, sweetheart," he murmured, his voice hoarse with emotion. "You're almost there. Just breathe."

"I am breathing!" she gasped through clenched teeth, her voice fraying at the edges. "This baby is trying to tear me in half!"

Daniel managed a small, shaky laugh. "He's just eager to meet you. Who could blame him?"

Her glare was blistering, but it faltered with the next wave of pain.

The nurse leaned in, adjusting the monitor. "Almost fully dilated. You're so close, Julia. Just a little longer."

Julia leaned back, chest rising and falling, eyes closed as she fought for control. Daniel pressed a kiss to her damp temple, his voice low and reverent.

"I love you," he whispered. "No matter what happens in the next hour or the next lifetime—you are my whole world."

She didn't speak—couldn't—but her hand tightened around his in response, and that was all he needed.

Outside the window, the light shifted, softening toward gold. Inside, everything was building—toward a moment that would shatter their lives into something new. Something beautiful.

Their son was almost here.

And nothing would ever be the same again.

A nurse adjusted the monitor beside them. "She's fully dilated. Doctor will be here in a moment. Let's get ready to push."

Julia gave a breathless laugh that turned into a sob. "Daniel… I'm scared."

He leaned in, pressing his forehead to hers. "I know. But you've already done the hard part, sweetheart. You carried him. You protected him. Now we meet him."

Tears spilled from the corners of her eyes. "I just want him safe."

Daniel's voice thickened. "He will be. He's got you for a mother."

The doctor entered then, calm but focused, snapping on gloves. "All right, Julia. We're going to bring this little boy into the world now."

The next thirty minutes unfolded in a blur of pain and power. Julia's voice echoed off the walls—cries of agony and effort—and Daniel never once let go of her hand. He whispered to her, counted with her, anchored her through every push, every scream, every breathless pause. Her fingernails dug into his palm. He didn't flinch.

And then—

A sound.

A cry.

Not hers. His.

High-pitched, furious, and perfect.

Julia collapsed back against the bed, sobbing as the doctor lifted a squirming, red-faced baby into the air. "Congratulations," she said, her voice warm. "You've got a beautiful, healthy boy."

Julia's chest rose and fell with broken sobs of relief and wonder. "He's here… oh God, he's really here."

Daniel couldn't move. Couldn't breathe. Could only stare at the tiny miracle being wrapped in a warm blanket by the nurse. "He's—he's everything."

When they placed him in Julia's arms, her whole body softened. She looked down at her son like she was seeing the stars for the first time. Her fingers traced his impossibly small hand, his miniature mouth, the hint of dark hair already damp on his head.

Daniel knelt beside her, speechless, watching her cradle their child. Their son.

"Do you want to hold him?" she asked, her voice trembling with emotion.

He nodded but couldn't speak. Could barely blink. When she passed the baby into his arms, Daniel felt something inside him shift—crack open and overflow. The weight of his son was impossibly light. And yet… heavier than everything else in his life combined.

The baby squirmed and let out a tiny, sleepy sigh.

"Hey, little man," Daniel whispered. "I'm your dad."

Julia smiled, exhausted but radiant. "He has your mouth."

Daniel glanced at her, his throat tight. "He has your strength."

They were quiet for a long moment, soaking in the warmth, the wonder, the miracle of what they'd created together.

Then Daniel looked down again, his voice low and reverent. "Welcome to the world, Nathan John Moore."

Julia reached out and touched her son's cheek, her touch featherlight. "Our beginning," she whispered, eyes never leaving their son.

Daniel leaned down and kissed her—soft, slow, full of every unsaid word.

In that small hospital room, with one perfect baby between them, the world felt complete.

He brushed a thumb across Julia's cheek, then gently placed Nathan back in her arms, lingering a moment longer to watch them—mother and child, his whole heart in two pieces.

"I should go get Joseph and Mary," he said with a soft smile. "If I don't, Mary will kill me."

Julia let out a breathless laugh, the weight of labour already dissolving beneath the joy. "Especially if Joseph gets to hold him first."

The End

Kept Promises

Alison Reid

A complete standalone romance
Previously published individually

Chapter One

Stephanie Vale was twenty-five and, according to her friends, beautiful. They admired her tall frame, the sleek fall of her long blonde hair, and the vivid blue of her eyes. But Stephanie wasn't so sure. Beauty, in her experience, was fragile—dependent on perception, subject to the shifting opinions of others.

And the man whose opinion should have mattered most always seemed to hold it just out of reach.

Ryan Carter, her boyfriend of three years, could be wonderfully charming. He was brilliant in court, magnetic at parties, and the kind of man people turned to when they needed a clever remark to cut through tension. With her, he could be thoughtful, affectionate even—dropping by her office with her favourite coffee or sending flowers just because. But alongside the gestures came remarks that landed sharper than he likely realised.

When she dressed with care for a dinner or gala, Ryan would glance her over and call her "passable." Sometimes he even used it as a nickname—Passable— always with that crooked, playful grin, as though it were harmless, a private joke meant only for them.

To everyone else, she was stunning. Strangers turned heads, friends whispered admiration, compliments trailed her wherever she went. But from him, she only ever got passable.

Most days, she laughed along, convincing herself it was just his humour, his way of keeping her grounded. But in the quiet places of her heart, the word lodged deep. Each barb left a small bruise, wearing at the confidence she worked so hard to hold together, until sometimes she wondered if maybe that was how he truly saw her—adequate, never exceptional.

That morning, she had chosen her sharpest navy suit, pairing it with a silk blouse that softened the lines. She painted her lips with a discreet rose shade and gathered her courage the way some women gathered pearls. By the time she crossed the marble-floored lobby of Grayson Global and stepped into the elevator, she had rebuilt her armour piece by piece.

The thirty-seventh floor opened into a cathedral of glass and steel, sunlight gilding polished surfaces. The hum of conversation, the tap of keyboards, the brisk shuffle of assistants—it all blended into a symphony of precision. And at its centre was the man who orchestrated it all: Trey Grayson.

Her boss.

Her billionaire.

Her undoing if she wasn't careful.

He was a legend in the business world, the kind of man whose name carried weight in boardrooms and headlines alike. Six months ago, she had walked into his office for an interview. Five minutes later, he had hired her as his executive assistant.

"You think ahead," he'd said, his eyes steady, assessing. "I need that."

Now, every day, she walked a careful line between professionalism and the treacherous awareness of the man himself. Trey Grayson was tall, broad-shouldered, devastatingly handsome in a way that felt unfair. His dark hair always looked effortlessly styled, his tailored suits impeccable. But it was his eyes—deep brown, steady, unflinching—that unsettled her most.

He didn't just look at people. He saw them.

Stephanie smoothed her skirt as she walked toward her desk outside his corner office, determined to ignore the flutter in her stomach. It wasn't attraction, she told herself. It was nerves. It was respect. Anything but the dangerous truth.

Her phone buzzed. A text from Ryan lit the screen:

Dinner tonight. Keep it simple. Don't need you turning heads, sweetheart. You know I like you best when you don't try so hard.

Her throat tightened. He probably thought he was being protective. Maybe even sweet. But to Stephanie, it was just another reminder that her beauty—her very self—existed only in the space he permitted.

She locked the phone and set it face down, forcing a steady breath. This was her life—one part competence and ambition, one part compromise and silence.

"Ms. Vale."

She looked up—and froze.

Trey stood at the threshold of his office, a file in hand, his gaze trained on her. The air seemed to shift with his presence, pulling everything into sharper focus.

"Yes, Mr. Grayson?" she managed, her voice calm though her pulse thundered.

"I reviewed the projections you prepared for the Sydney expansion." He stepped closer, lowering his voice so only she could hear. "They were sharp. Precise. You caught flaws my senior team overlooked."

Stephanie blinked, caught off guard. Praise from Trey was rare, and when it came, it was deliberate—meant to carry weight.

"Thank you," she said softly.

The corner of his mouth curved, not quite a smile, but enough to set her heartbeat racing. "Don't thank me. Just keep doing exactly what you're doing."

With that, he returned to his office, leaving only the faint trace of his cologne and a hundred unspoken questions.

Stephanie pressed her palm flat against the desk to steady herself. Ryan might call her passable. But Trey Grayson had just made her feel seen. And that—dangerous as it was—was a feeling she wasn't ready to let go of.

Three years earlier, when she first met Ryan, he had seemed like everything she should want. Successful, charming, the kind of lawyer who could command a room with little more than a smile. In those early months, he'd been all sweetness—flowers at her office, surprise weekend getaways, telling her she was the most beautiful woman he'd ever seen.

But once she moved into his sleek apartment, six months after they started dating, kindness eroded slowly, like stone worn down beneath relentless rain. Compliments gave way to critiques disguised as humour. Affection shifted into condescension.

Her friends noticed the change in her too. At first, they'd liked him—witty, confident, endlessly social. But over time, they saw the subtle ways he chipped at her: jokes that left her quieter, looks that made her straighten her dress as though she'd failed some invisible test.

Rebecca, her best friend since college, was the first to say it aloud. Over coffee one Saturday, she reached across the table, fingers brushing Stephanie's wrist.

"Steph," she said gently, "I don't know if you see it, but you hold yourself differently around him. Like you're bracing, waiting for his approval."

Stephanie had laughed, brushing it off. "That's just Ryan. He teases—it's his way."

Rebecca didn't press. She never did. But the worry in her eyes lingered. "Maybe. Just don't lose sight of yourself, okay? You've always been stronger than you think."

It became a rhythm between them: Rebecca's quiet concern, Stephanie's practiced deflection. No ultimatums, no fights—just the steady persistence of a friend who refused to stop seeing her.

And lately, that persistence had begun to echo louder, because Trey Grayson had unsettled her carefully built world. Ryan chipped away; Trey reinforced. Ryan made her second-guess; Trey made her feel capable. And though she couldn't admit it aloud yet, she was starting to wonder which reflection of herself was real.

The rest of the morning passed in a blur of numbers, phone calls, and back-to-back meetings, the kind of whirlwind pace Stephanie had come to thrive on. Working for Trey Grayson wasn't easy—it demanded sharp instincts, meticulous attention to detail, and a will strong enough not to crumble under pressure. But she wouldn't have traded it for anything.

Trey pushed everyone around him, but never harder than he pushed himself. And Stephanie found that she rose to meet him. Where others stumbled beneath his exacting standards, she seemed to anticipate his needs before he voiced them. He asked for figures; she had them ready. He wanted a client dossier; it was already printed and tabbed. When his schedule shifted unexpectedly, she recalibrated with quiet efficiency.

By late morning, he emerged from his office, jacket slung over one broad shoulder, and handed her a file. "Board wants projections by three. Can you polish this draft?"

Stephanie skimmed the pages and frowned. "The numbers in section three don't match the revenue streams. If you present them as-is, they'll rip it apart."

For a beat, his gaze held hers—steady, assessing. Then the corner of his mouth curved. "Exactly why I gave it to you. Fix it."

Her heart gave an irrational flutter, but she kept her tone crisp. "I'll have it on your desk by two."

He nodded once and disappeared towards the elevator, leaving her with the quiet satisfaction of knowing she had earned his trust. Not just as an assistant, but as someone whose judgment he valued.

By the time her lunch hour arrived, Stephanie felt both drained and strangely energised—the peculiar rhythm Grayson Global always seemed to produce. She carried her salad to the quiet staff lounge and settled by the window, letting the Manhattan skyline steady her.

Her phone buzzed. Rebecca.

How's your day going? And please tell me Ryan's being decent for once.

Stephanie smiled faintly, shaking her head. That was Rebecca—concern wrapped in humour. She typed back quickly.

He's fine. We've got the gala tomorrow night, so I'm bracing myself.

The reply came almost instantly.

Steph… I just want to make sure you're happy. Sometimes I feel like you dim yourself around him. You deserve someone who makes you shine, not someone who leaves you second-guessing.

Stephanie's throat tightened. Rebecca wasn't attacking Ryan, not outright. But she wasn't blind either. She typed back sadder a moment:

I know. It's complicated. I'll figure it out soon.

Rebecca's answer was gentler this time.

That's all I want—for you to feel sure of yourself again. Promise me you'll at least think about it.

Stephanie stared at the screen, her fork forgotten. Rebecca had no idea how close she was to being right. Something inside her had already shifted, something she couldn't name aloud yet.

Because Trey Grayson had made her realise she deserved more—by making her feel seen in ways Ryan never did. Ryan chipped away, often without meaning to. Trey acknowledged, simply and without effort. And the difference between the two men unsettled her more than she could admit.

At precisely one-thirty, Stephanie gathered the freshly polished projections and crossed the outer office to his door. She paused, smoothing her palms down her skirt, and knocked.

"Come in."

His voice was deep, commanding, yet never raised. It carried authority without effort, the kind that could still a boardroom or make grown men scramble to obey.

Stephanie stepped inside, the file clutched in her hands. Trey sat behind his mahogany desk, the city skyline sprawling behind him through the floor-to-ceiling windows. He leaned back in his chair, jacket discarded, tie loosened just enough to suggest he'd been at war with numbers all morning.

"I've corrected the inconsistencies in section three," she said, her tone professional, though her pulse betrayed her. "And restructured the charts so the growth trends are clearer. The board will be able to follow the logic now."

Trey held out his hand, and when she placed the file in it, his fingers brushed hers—light, brief, but enough to make her breath catch. He flipped through the pages with a practiced eye, the only sound the rustle of paper and the faint hum of the city below.

When he looked up, his gaze locked on hers. "You weren't exaggerating," he said quietly. "This is clean. Precise. You've turned a liability into a strength."

Stephanie felt warmth spread through her chest. Praise from Trey wasn't casual. It was deliberate, measured. He never wasted words he didn't mean.

"You make my job look easy, Ms. Vale," he continued, his expression unreadable, though his eyes lingered longer than necessary. "I hope you know that."

Her lips parted, but no words came. For a moment, the air between them thickened with something unspoken, a current she dared not name.

Then, as quickly as it came, the moment was gone. Trey set the file down, the mask of the executive sliding back into place. "Clear the rest of your afternoon. I'll want you in the boardroom at three sharp."

Stephanie nodded, steadying herself. "Of course, Mr. Grayson."

As she turned to leave, she couldn't help the thought that whispered at the back of her mind: with Trey, she felt capable. Valued. Seen.

With Ryan, she only ever felt small.

By three o'clock, the boardroom at Grayson Global buzzed with the clipped voices of executives settling into leather chairs. Polished mahogany gleamed beneath rows of neatly stacked reports, while the city stretched out like a glittering promise beyond the wall of glass.

Stephanie slipped in behind Trey, carrying her own copy of the projections. Though she technically wasn't required to attend board meetings, Trey had made a habit of insisting on her presence. "You see details others don't," he'd once told her. "I need that at the table."

She took her seat at the edge, not with the board, but close enough to take notes and track the flow of discussion. It was a position that gave her a unique view—Trey in command, the board responding to him, and every so often, his gaze flicking toward her as if to make sure she was still with him.

The meeting began in earnest. One executive, Paul Henderson, launched into his usual aggressive commentary. "These numbers don't align with our growth targets," he argued, tapping a chart with his pen. "Section three is all over the place. If we take this to the investors, we'll look incompetent."

Stephanie's pulse quickened. Section three. She had corrected it. She knew it was airtight now.

Trey leaned back, unhurried, then slid the file across the table. "Ms. Vale," he said smoothly, his voice carrying over the room, "why don't you walk us through your revisions?"

Heads turned. Surprise flickered across several faces. An assistant didn't usually speak in a boardroom, not with men who had decades of experience and portfolios worth millions.

Stephanie drew a quiet breath, steadying her hands on the file. "The discrepancies in section three were the result of duplicated revenue streams," she explained, her tone calm, controlled. She flipped to the corrected page, sliding copies toward the nearest members. "I consolidated the data and adjusted the growth model to reflect actual market performance. If you compare the projections side by side—" she gestured, confident now, "—you'll see that the revised version not only resolves the inconsistencies but strengthens our investor position."

Silence settled. Then a low murmur as the executives bent over the numbers. Henderson frowned, tapped his pen again, then gave a short, reluctant nod. "She's right. The correction makes sense."

One by one, heads around the table tilted in agreement.

Across from her, Trey's gaze met hers. No smile, no outward display—but his eyes were warm with something steadier, something that felt dangerously like pride.

"Good," Trey said simply, reclaiming the floor with ease. "We'll proceed with Ms. Vale's revisions. Make sure the investor packets reflect them."

The meeting rolled on, but Stephanie barely heard it. Her chest swelled with a mix of relief and exhilaration. She had spoken. She had been heard. And Trey had been the one to hand her the floor, as though he had known all along she was ready.

When the session adjourned, the executives filed out in clusters. Trey lingered by the head of the table, sliding his jacket back on.

As she gathered her notes, he spoke quietly enough that only she could hear. "You were flawless. Exactly what I expected."

Stephanie's lips curved before she could stop them. "Thank you, sir."

This time, the corner of his mouth lifted in something unmistakable—a smile that reached his eyes. And it was then, more than ever, that she felt the dangerous truth of it: Trey Grayson made her feel like she belonged.

Her phone buzzed against the table, breaking the moment. She glanced down.

Ryan.

Dinner tonight. Don't be late.

The warmth Trey had left in her chest clashed with the chill of the message. Stephanie slipped her phone into her bag, her smile fading as reality closed in.

Belonging with Trey was a dream she could lose herself in. But Ryan was the life she had built—and the one she still didn't know how to escape.

Chapter Two

There was a knock on his office door.

"Come in," Trey called, his voice even.

Stephanie stepped inside, afternoon light spilling over her hair in a golden sheen. She carried her jacket over one arm, her expression composed, though there was always something about her eyes—so sharp, so vivid—that made it impossible for him to look away.

"I'm leaving for the day," she said, pausing just inside the threshold. "Unless you need anything else."

Trey leaned back in his chair, studying her. What he needed had nothing to do with forecasts or strategy decks. What he wanted was infinitely more dangerous—to draw her closer, to see if that steady composure softened when it was just the two of them.

But wanting and acting were two very different things. Especially with her.

"You've done enough for one day, Ms. Vale," he said finally, his voice lower than intended.

She gave a small nod, gathering her jacket. But before she turned, Trey heard himself ask, "You'll be at the charity gala tomorrow night?"

Her gaze lifted to his. Calm. Professional. Yet he thought he caught the faintest flicker of hesitation.

"Yes, sir."

"Will you be bringing someone?" He tried for casual, though the answer mattered far more than it should.

"Yes. Ryan Carter." She hesitated only a moment before adding, "He's one of the company's lawyers."

Of course. Trey knew Ryan Carter. Ambitious. Razor-smart. Too quick with a quip meant to cut. But more than that, Carter carried a name. His parents were pillars of the legal community—respected, influential, the kind of people Trey had crossed paths with at board dinners and charity fundraisers. Their son's career had benefited from their reputation, but he was no slouch in his own right.

It meant Stephanie's connection to him was complicated. It meant Trey had no business letting disappointment pool in his chest.

"Very good," he said at last, smoothing the edge from his tone.

Stephanie offered him a small, polished smile. Professional. Safe. "Then I'll see you tomorrow, Mr. Grayson."

Her heels marked a steady rhythm as she crossed the room, her poise unshaken, every step reminding him why people underestimated her at their peril. She was elegance built on quiet steel.

The door clicked softly shut behind her, the faint echo lingering in the glass-and-steel quiet of his office. Trey exhaled slowly, dragging a hand through his hair, the weight of restraint pressing against his chest.

Ryan Carter. He could already picture him at Stephanie's side—confident, polished, the kind of man who knew how to command a room and keep all eyes on him. Always just a little too quick to claim the spotlight, even when it should have been hers. Trey had seen it more than once, those subtle, almost imperceptible moments when Carter's careless words undercut her. A look. A joke. A dismissal wrapped in charm.

It had stirred something in Trey; he rarely allowed himself—anger. And something more dangerous still.

He forced it down again, the way he always did. Grayson Global could not afford scandal. He could not afford scandal. Least of all one tied to a soon-to-be daughter-in-law of one of his most powerful legal allies, a man whose partnership had bolstered his empire time and again. The risk was too great, the consequences too far-reaching.

And yet.

No amount of discipline, no number of late-night hours spent burying himself in work, could silence the truth pressing harder against him every day.

What he wanted from Stephanie Vale had nothing to do with business. Nothing to do with loyalty, or alliances, or corporate survival.

He had never felt like this about a woman. Not once. He had dated models, entrepreneurs, women whose names and faces carried weight in the same circles as his. He had been pursued endlessly—some drawn by his reputation, others by his money, still others by the simple allure of power. They had all blurred together in a haze of beauty and ambition.

But the moment he met Stephanie Vale; the noise had gone silent.

No one else had mattered since.

He had tried to fight it. God, he had tried. He shoved the feeling into the shadows where it belonged, barricading it behind walls built from discipline, pragmatism, and cold necessity. He told himself it was foolish. That it was dangerous. That desire had no place in the life he'd constructed—precisely balanced, ruthlessly controlled.

But she made a liar of him with every passing day.

Every glance. Every unguarded smile. Every quiet laugh that slipped past her careful professionalism. Each one chipped at the walls he had built, dismantling the fortress brick by brick.

And deep down, he knew the truth.

One day, he wouldn't be able to hold it back. He wouldn't be able to keep it hidden—not from her, and not from himself. The thought should have terrified him. It did. But beneath the fear was something far more perilous.

Exhilaration.

Stephanie stood in front of the full-length mirror, holding the black dress against her body and turning slowly. Simple, yet daring. A slit grazed her thigh—subtle enough to be elegant, daring enough to feel like hers. Tonight, she wasn't playing by Ryan's rules.

Living together didn't mean she had to be at his beck and call. He would meet her at the restaurant, expecting polished, composed, quiet. But Stephanie was done shrinking to fit him.

She slipped into the dress, the fabric smooth and comforting against her skin, then added heels that lengthened her posture and gave poise. A touch of rose lipstick completed the look. When she glanced in the mirror, Stephanie felt something she hadn't in months: ready. Confident. Herself.

Her blonde hair fell freely over her shoulders, and she smoothed the dress at her waist, appreciating how it hugged her figure without constraining her. Tonight, the black dress was understated, careful—but tomorrow would be different.

Rebecca's voice rang in her head, playful and insistent: "You have to try the red dress, Steph! Trust me!" The memory made her smile. Tomorrow, at the gala, she would wear the strapless red dress with delicate sleeves and a daring slit—a dress she would never have picked herself. But Rebecca had been right. It looked incredible. Fierce. Unapologetically bold.

Grabbing her clutch, Stephanie took a deep breath, locked the apartment door, and headed for the elevator. The city lights stretched beyond the windows, sparkling like promise. Ryan would expect polished, quiet, the version of her he preferred. But for once, she would be exactly who she wanted to be.

The restaurant glittered with soft light, glassware clinking in a rhythm of refinement. Waiters moved in elegant choreography, their trays gliding like extensions of their arms. Stephanie adjusted the strap of her black dress, the fabric whispering against her skin, as she approached the corner table where Ryan sat with three colleagues.

He was already half-risen from his chair when he saw her, that practiced smile curving his lips.

"There she is," he said warmly, pulling her chair out with a flourish that drew the eyes of the entire table. "The most beautiful woman in the room."

Heat rushed to her cheeks at the smooth charm of his voice. He kissed her cheek before she sat, his hand lingering just a fraction too long at her waist. It was affectionate—yes—but threaded with that quiet possessiveness she had learned not to question.

The evening unfolded with easy rhythm. Ryan was in his element—polished, witty, the kind of man who could make a waiter feel like an old friend and a CEO feel like the centre of the world. His colleagues laughed easily, charmed by the effortless way he steered the conversation. Stephanie found herself smiling more than she expected, sipping her wine and allowing herself to be pulled along by his charisma.

When one of the men leaned forward and complimented her dress, calling it "classic elegance," Ryan chuckled and draped an arm across the back of her chair.

"She does clean up nicely, doesn't she?" he said, pride in his tone, though laced with teasing.

Stephanie laughed politely, and for a fleeting moment, it felt perfect—the way it used to.

But perfection never lasted.

Later, in the backseat of the Uber, the cracks appeared.

Ryan sat angled away from her, his arms folded, expression sharpened by the rhythm of passing streetlights.

"Elegant, huh?" he said at last, his voice low but edged. "That slit was halfway up your thigh, Steph. Not exactly the impression I want to give my team."

Her jaw tightened. "It's a black dress, Ryan. Elegant, understated—not inappropriate."

"Not inappropriate?" He scoffed softly, shaking his head. "It was over the top. You don't need to show that much to get noticed."

Stephanie turned toward the window, neon lights smearing across the glass. She folded her hands in her lap, her posture tall, her expression calm. She refused to let the sting of his words unravel the fragile confidence she'd felt at dinner.

The driver's eyes flicked briefly to the mirror. Neither spoke again until they reached the apartment.

They rode the elevator in silence, the tension humming between them like static before a storm.

Inside, Ryan loosened his tie with a weary sigh, dropped his jacket carelessly across the sofa, and disappeared into the bedroom without a word.

Stephanie lingered in the kitchen, pouring herself a glass of water. She let her gaze drift across the apartment—floor-to-ceiling windows, polished concrete floors, the Manhattan skyline stretched out like a painted backdrop. It was beautiful, impressive, exactly what Ryan had always wanted. She remembered how excited he'd been the day they moved in; how sure he was that this place meant they had arrived.

She had gone along with his dream. She always had.

By the time she slipped into the bedroom, Ryan was already beneath the covers, one arm draped over his eyes.

"You're going to bed?" she asked softly, careful not to sound accusing.

"Headache," he muttered.

She stood there for a moment, studying him. This was the man who once made her laugh until her sides ached, who had whisked her away on weekend trips and whispered promises of a life bigger, brighter, better. The man who had seemed unstoppable.

She couldn't remember the last time they had made love—really made love. The realisation caught in her chest like a stone.

Still, she turned off the light and slipped into bed beside him, brushing her fingers lightly against his shoulder. He didn't stir.

Staring up at the ceiling, Stephanie exhaled slowly. She told herself it was just a rough patch, that the warmth she remembered was still inside him somewhere. If she stayed, if she held on, maybe she could find it again.

By morning, Ryan was quieter still. He left for work with little more than a kiss on the top of her head, claiming another headache. His absence lingered like a shadow, even after the door shut behind him.

Stephanie dressed deliberately, pressing herself into the day. At Grayson Global, there was no room for hesitation. Her hours filled with projections, calls, client briefs, and the steady rhythm of decisions that demanded clarity.

Work was safe. Work was something she could control.

But tomorrow, at the gala, there would be no hiding—she would be at Ryan's side, expected to dazzle, to smile, to play the part he had chosen for her.

Only this time, she wasn't sure she wanted to play it his way.

By the time Stephanie arrived at Grayson Global, she was already buried in the day's demands. She attacked each task with precision and quiet intensity— projections, client briefs, urgent calls—her mind slicing clean through every problem as though focus alone could silence the echoes of last night. The office hummed around her: the staccato rhythm of keyboards, the low murmur of colleagues, the faint whir of machinery. All of it blended into a background score that matched the purposeful click of her heels across polished marble floors.

Hours slipped by almost unnoticed, the day measured only in deadlines met and emails cleared. When she finally leaned back in her chair to glance at the time, it was already mid-afternoon.

That was when Trey emerged from his office, jacket slung casually over his shoulder, a file tucked under one arm. His presence drew eyes the way it always did—commanding but unforced, as though authority came as naturally to him as breathing.

"You can head out for the rest of the afternoon, Ms. Vale," he said, his voice calm and sure, the kind of tone that steadied more than it directed. "I want you to have time to get ready for tonight."

Stephanie blinked, startled but grateful. "Thank you, Mr. Grayson. I'll see you at the gala."

His mouth curved into something close to a smile, warmth flickering in his gaze. "I'll look forward to it. And don't worry—I know some women take a little longer to get ready. Consider this me being ahead of schedule."

Her laugh came softly, surprising even herself. "Are you saying I'm one of those women?"

"I'm saying," Trey replied smoothly, "that perfection shouldn't be rushed."

The words lingered, and so did the flutter in her chest as he walked past. For the first time all day, the knot of tension in her stomach began to ease.

Stephanie checked the clock. Her hair appointment was at four, which gave her just enough of a cushion. On impulse, instead of heading straight to the salon, she detoured to Rebecca's office. She needed a moment of normal—someone who saw her, heard her, without judgment or expectation.

The real estate firm buzzed with its usual energy. Phones rang, printers hummed, and the air smelled faintly of coffee and fresh paperwork. It was busy, but not overwhelming; the kind of rhythm that had always soothed her, reminding her that life could be steady, simple.

Rebecca looked up from her desk, eyes immediately brightening. "Steph!" she exclaimed, rising to her feet. "And on time, no less. Should I call the papers?"

Stephanie laughed, tension easing from her shoulders. "Barely on time."

Rebecca pressed a coffee cup into her hand. "Now, spill. The dress. The shoes. The whole vibe tonight. And when you're finished getting ready, you have to send me a selfie. No excuses. I demand to preview this masterpiece before you strut into the gala and break hearts."

Stephanie shook her head, warmth tugging at her lips. "You'll be the first to see it. Promise."

They chatted for a few minutes—Rebecca teasing, Stephanie rolling her eyes, both of them laughing until the weight of home felt miles away. Before

Stephanie left, Rebecca gave her a look both playful and serious. "Just remember—you deserve to shine tonight. Don't let Ryan dim that. Not even a little."

Stephanie swallowed past the lump in her throat and hugged her friend quickly. "Thanks, Becs."

Out on the sidewalk again, she hailed a cab, sliding into the backseat as Manhattan's chaos unfurled around her. Through the window, the city blurred into golden streaks of late-afternoon light. She exhaled slowly, letting herself breathe. For the first time all day, the tension in her shoulders loosened—just slightly, but enough.

The hair salon was a sleek, modern space with high ceilings and the faint scent of lavender in the air. Stephanie eased into the chair, letting the stylist drape the protective cape around her shoulders. She ran her fingers through her hair, still soft from the morning wash, and glanced at her reflection. "Just a little volume at the roots and make it shine," she said, her tone casual, though her heart beat a little faster at the thought of the evening ahead.

The stylist nodded, moving with practiced precision. The warmth of the salon, the gentle hum of conversation, the soft music in the background—all combined to create a calm cocoon. For a moment, Stephanie let herself relax, allowing the stress of Ryan and the lingering tension from home to melt away. She focused entirely on the way her hair fell into place, each strand catching the light, framing her face with subtle elegance.

Her phone buzzed. Rebecca's message flashed on the screen:

Selfie soon, or I'll hunt you down!

Stephanie smiled to herself, fingers flying over the screen.

Soon. Promise.

The stylist finished, brushing away the last loose hairs and setting her locks with a soft mist of finishing spray. Stephanie studied her reflection again. The subtle waves caught the light perfectly, blonde shining like polished silk, her eyes framed and alive. She felt… ready. Strong. In control.

Sliding the chair back and settling the cape, Stephanie grabbed her purse and thanked the stylist. Stepping out into the bustling city, the evening air filled her lungs, carrying the scent of street vendors, car exhaust, and anticipation. Manhattan pulsed around her, alive with possibility, every step echoing her growing confidence. The gala, the dress, the evening ahead—it all felt like the first step toward reclaiming a part of herself she had almost forgotten existed.

And for the first time in a long while, Stephanie felt fully, unapologetically herself.

Chapter Three

Stephanie stood before the full-length mirror; the bedroom bathed in the soft golden glow of lamplight. The red silk shimmered like liquid fire against her skin, the strapless neckline daring, the delicate off-shoulder sleeves elegant, and the slit along her thigh unapologetically bold. Rebecca had insisted she try it, and Stephanie had scoffed at first. But now—now she could hardly look away.

She turned slightly, the fabric catching the light, clinging to her curves in a way that felt both dangerous and liberating. For the first time in years, she felt electric. Powerful. Untouchable. Every inch of her reflection radiated confidence she hadn't known she was capable of. Her hands lingered at her waist, savouring the way the dress seemed to armour her in satin and flame.

Her blonde hair fell in polished waves over her shoulders, glossy and luminous as though lit from within. The smoky shadow framing her vivid blue eyes sharpened them into something arresting—magnetic, impossible to dismiss. And the bold sweep of red lipstick, perfectly matched to her gown, wasn't mere ornament. It was a statement, fierce and unyielding.

Stephanie's smile curved slowly, private and knowing. She didn't just look incredible—she felt it, the confidence humming beneath her skin. Tonight, she wasn't disappearing into Ryan's carefully curated shadow. Tonight, she was claiming space, unapologetically stepping into the light.

She angled her phone toward the mirror, snapped a selfie, and sent it straight to Rebecca.

The reply came seconds later.

OH. MY. GOD. 🔥 🔥 *Steph, you're a goddess. Ryan better step aside because you're about to shut down that entire gala.*

Another message followed almost instantly.

Seriously, look at you. Powerful. Gorgeous. You. Don't let anyone dull that tonight—not him, not anyone. Promise me.

Stephanie stared at the words, warmth blooming in her chest. Rebecca's voice, even through a screen, was exactly what she needed: a reminder that this feeling was hers alone, not borrowed or granted by anyone else.

The door clicked open. Stephanie stiffened, then turned, chin lifting.

Ryan stepped into the room and stopped short. His eyes swept over her slowly, and for a heartbeat, there was no sound—only his sharp inhale. "Wow," he murmured, his voice caught somewhere between awe and unease. "Steph… you look… incredible."

Her pulse jumped at the warmth in his tone, but then his expression shifted. His brows drew together, his mouth tightening as he glanced down the long slit at her thigh, then back up to the neckline that bared her shoulders. "It's just… are you sure about this dress? It's a lot. People might… get the wrong impression."

Stephanie arched a brow. "The wrong impression? You just said I looked incredible."

"You do," he said quickly, stepping closer, his hands brushing her arms, lingering in a way that reminded her of the man she'd first fallen for. "God, you do. But this is a gala, Steph. Clients, investors… people who can be judgmental. I just—" He broke off, raking a hand through his hair, frustration shading his concern. "I don't want them looking at you and talking about you behind your back."

Her lips curved, though her voice was steady. "If they're talking, it's because I stood out. Because I made an impression. Isn't that the point?"

Ryan exhaled, tension tugging at the corners of his jaw. He searched her face, torn between admiration and worry. "You're already the most beautiful woman in the room—you don't need a dress to prove it." His hand slipped down her arm, squeezing lightly, almost pleading. "I just don't want them seeing what's mine and twisting it."

Stephanie met his gaze in the mirror, her reflection calm, radiant, undeniable. "Ryan," she said softly but firmly, "I'm not wearing this for them. And I'm not wearing it for you. I'm wearing it for me."

For a moment, he said nothing, his lips parting as though to argue—but then he let out a quiet, resigned laugh, shaking his head. "Stubborn," he murmured, though his eyes softened. "Fine. But don't expect me to stop glaring at every man who stares at you tonight."

Stephanie turned back to the mirror, the silk of the gown whispering around her legs. She lifted her chin, meeting her own reflection—and his in the glass. "Let them stare," she said softly. Then, almost teasingly, she added, "I'm with you, aren't I?"

Ryan's lips curved into a tentative smile, relief flickering in his eyes. "Yes… thank goodness," he murmured, his voice low, meant only for her.

He stepped closer, letting his hand brush hers at the small of her back, a light, grounding touch that spoke more than words ever could. "You look… incredible," he said, softer now, admiration threading every syllable. "But you know… it's bold."

Stephanie felt the warmth of his hand linger, reassuring and protective. She turned slightly to face him, her eyes meeting his in the reflection. "Bold feels good tonight," she said, her smile playful but steady. "And it feels like me."

He nodded, the shadow of wariness still there, but softened by pride and affection. "Then I'll be right here," he said quietly, "keeping you safe in all the right ways."

Stephanie's pulse fluttered—not from fear, but from the unspoken promise between them. She was shining, and he was beside her, careful, loving, and ever present.

The grand chandelier above the ballroom sparkled like a constellation, casting prisms of light across the elegantly dressed guests. Stephanie took a slow, steadying breath as she stepped alongside Ryan. The soft sway of her red gown felt luxurious against her skin, and the click of her heels on the marble floor sounded like a heartbeat in rhythm with her excitement—and her nerves.

Ryan's hand brushed lightly against hers at her back, a subtle but steadying anchor as they made their way through the crowd. "Remember, just follow my lead," he murmured, his voice low, protective but calm. "You look stunning. Everyone's going to notice, and I want them to see you with me."

Stephanie smiled, letting the words settle. There was warmth in the reassurance, a quiet pride in the way he guided her through the throng.

It wasn't long before they reached a corner of the room where Ryan's parents were already talking with other guests. Their eyes immediately found Stephanie, lighting up.

"Stephanie! You look radiant," his mother said, stepping forward and taking both of Stephanie's hands in hers. "Absolutely perfect. Ryan is lucky to have you by his side."

His father nodded, a broad, approving smile spreading across his face. "You've brought out the very best in our son. We couldn't be happier."

Stephanie's cheeks flushed, but the warmth she felt was genuine, not just the kind she received out of courtesy. She laughed softly, squeezing Mrs. Carter's hands. "Thank you so much. It means a lot to hear that."

Ryan's parents lingered on her with unabashed admiration, asking after her work, her interests, and even teasing lightly about her courage to take on Ryan's stubborn streak at home. Stephanie found herself laughing at their easy charm, relaxed in a way she hadn't expected.

Ryan stayed close, subtly shifting so that his presence was always at her side. If a hand lingered too long on her arm, his shoulder subtly moved to intercept it. If someone leaned in for a closer look, Ryan's angle shifted, a light but unmistakable signal that she was his. It wasn't possessive—it was careful, affectionate, protective.

"See?" he murmured quietly as they exchanged pleasantries with a guest. "They like you. They really like you."

Stephanie's smile deepened, and she nodded, brushing a loose strand of hair behind her ear. "I like them too," she whispered back.

For the first time that evening, Stephanie felt at ease, enveloped in a circle of warmth, acceptance, and subtle protection. She didn't notice the tall figure across the room, Trey Grayson, watching her from a distance—his expression unreadable, his gaze steady, measuring. She had no idea that every laugh, every graceful movement, every small moment of her confidence was being catalogued, quietly, deliberately.

Ryan's parents lingered for a moment longer, exchanging a few last words of admiration before Ryan gently guided Stephanie through the crowd. "Come on," he said softly, slipping his hand into hers. "Let's enjoy the night. Together."

Stephanie let herself squeeze his hand in return, heart lighter, aware of the protective rhythm in the way he moved beside her. With him, she felt seen, cherished—and for tonight, she belonged in the light.

Trey leaned against the marble railing on the mezzanine, a crystal glass of scotch in his hand that he hadn't touched in minutes. The amber liquid caught the light, casting fractured shadows across his fingers, but he barely noticed. His attention wasn't on the glittering chandeliers above, or the steady hum of strings from the quartet in the corner, or the polite ebb and flow of conversation rising from the crowd below.

It was on her.

Stephanie Vale.

She appeared at the top of the staircase with Ryan at her side, and for a moment the world seemed to narrow until nothing else existed. Her blonde hair caught the light like spun gold, tumbling in soft waves over her shoulders. The red gown she wore was bold but sophisticated, hugging her curves in a way that suggested elegance rather than ostentation. The slit along her leg flashed as she moved, a teasing whisper of daring that made Trey's chest tighten.

She was… breathtaking.

His breath stalled as he watched her descend into the swell of the ballroom. Conversations seemed to dim around her, or maybe that was only his perception, because his focus had narrowed too sharply to notice anything else. She greeted Ryan's parents with a laugh, her smile radiating warmth, lighting the air around her with a glow that was impossible to look away from. There was an ease in the way she carried herself, a natural confidence threaded through every step and gesture. It wasn't rehearsed, wasn't deliberate—it simply was.

Ryan's hand brushed hers now and then, casual to the untrained eye, but Trey saw the truth beneath the surface. It was a claim. Subtle, deliberate, an invisible boundary drawn with every touch. No one was allowed too close. Stephanie was shielded—not in a harsh or domineering way, but with a quiet precision that reminded Trey of a chess player always thinking three moves ahead.

Trey's jaw tightened, the muscle flexing once as he drew in a breath meant to steady him. This was Ryan Carter's night, Ryan Carter's domain. Not his. He had no business watching her with this kind of hunger.

And yet he couldn't look away.

Every tilt of her head, every glimmer in her eyes when she laughed, every gentle touch that revealed both kindness and composure—she pulled at him. Not like the women he had known before, not with practiced charm or curated allure, but with something rarer. There was fire in her, yes, but also vulnerability—an honesty in the way she existed in the world that made her magnetic.

He lifted the glass to his lips, though the scotch burned unnoticed on his tongue. Attraction in the workplace was dangerous. Desire for someone tied to a man like Ryan Carter was perilous on a scale he couldn't afford. He had built an empire on control, on knowing when to move and when to restrain, and this— this reckless pull—was the one temptation he could not allow.

But denial was beginning to feel like a lie.

From where he stood, he saw how Ryan's parents lit up in Stephanie's presence, how quickly and effortlessly she drew them in. He saw how Ryan's hand lingered on her lower back, how protective he remained even in public. To most, it would read as devotion. To Trey, it looked like possession. And the thought unsettled him more than it should have.

His fingers flexed around the glass, the liquid sloshing against the cut crystal. Every instinct told him to look away, to turn his focus back to the business associates waiting for him downstairs, to bury this want in the same vault where he kept every other dangerous impulse.

But he didn't. He couldn't.

Stephanie Vale had a gravity unlike anything he had encountered, a force that tugged at him no matter how he resisted. And for the first time in months— perhaps years—Trey allowed himself to acknowledge the truth he had buried too long.

He wanted her. Not just her laughter, not just her intelligence, not just the warmth that seemed to seep into everyone around her. He wanted *her*. Entirely.

And tonight, in this room crowded with allies, enemies, and expectations, he knew one thing with searing clarity.

He would have to fight every ounce of himself to stay out of her orbit.

Trey lingered at the edge of the ballroom, glass in hand, his posture relaxed but his focus anything but. To anyone watching, he looked the part of the composed host, surveying the glittering sea of tuxedos and gowns, ensuring everything ran smoothly. But the truth was simpler—and far more dangerous.

His gaze never left her.

Stephanie Vale moved through the crowd with a quiet grace that seemed to draw light to her. Conversation flowed easily around her, laughter spilling in soft ripples as Ryan guided her with the subtle, steady touch of his hand at her back. The red gown she wore clung in all the right ways. Every tilt of her chin, every sparkle in her eyes when she spoke—it was all intoxicating.

He didn't mean to watch so intently. But every time her lips curved in amusement, every time her fingers brushed Ryan's arm as she leaned in to listen, something in him tightened. She wasn't just beautiful—she was magnetic. Her movements weren't rehearsed or polished for effect; they were simply hers, natural and effortless, and that made them impossible to ignore.

Still, Trey forced himself to track the distance. Ryan at her side. Ryan's hand on her back. Ryan's presence, steady and protective. To the room, it was a picture of devotion. To Trey, it was a reminder. She belonged in someone else's orbit tonight.

And yet… deep down, he couldn't shake the sense that she didn't.

A familiar pair entered his periphery, and he straightened automatically, years of practice snapping his composure into place. Sofia and Peter Carter. Ryan's parents. Polished, warm, a couple who could command respect with ease. Trey stepped forward, extending a hand in greeting.

"Mr. Grayson," Sofia said with her characteristic brightness, her diamond necklace catching the light as she smiled. "It's good to see you again."

"Pleasure, Mrs. Carter. And Mr. Carter." Trey inclined his head toward Peter, his voice smooth, professional. "Always an honour."

They exchanged the usual pleasantries; words Trey had spoken a hundred times in a hundred different rooms. But the moment Sofia's gaze shifted toward Stephanie—chatting animatedly with Ryan a few steps away—something sharp twisted in his chest.

"I hear Ryan's dating my executive assistant," Trey said lightly, letting the words roll out as if they were nothing more than a neutral observation.

Sofia's expression softened, eyes brightening. "Oh, yes. Stephanie is wonderful. Hopefully, one day soon, she'll be our daughter-in-law." Her tone carried no edge, no agenda—only genuine affection for the woman she clearly admired.

Peter chuckled, his voice carrying the warmth of pride. "Fingers crossed. Ryan couldn't do any better. She's clever, poised, and she clearly makes him happy."

The words landed with the weight of inevitability. Trey forced a polite smile, nodding in agreement, but his stomach coiled tight. Peter was right—painfully right. Stephanie was everything a man like Ryan deserved. Brilliant. Gracious. The kind of woman who lit up a room without even trying.

And yet every fibre of Trey wanted her for himself.

His gaze slipped toward her again, drawn as if by gravity. She threw back her head in laughter, the sound cutting clean through the murmur of the crowd. The gown swayed as she shifted, a sweep of red silk that caught more than a few glances from others in the room. She had no idea—no idea that every glance she gave, every effortless smile, unravelled him a little more.

"She is a remarkable woman," Trey said at last, his voice even, professional, though the undercurrent was impossible to miss. "Brilliant. Poised. He is… very lucky."

Peter's expression softened further, pride deepening the lines around his eyes. "Yes. Extraordinary. We're thrilled Ryan found someone like her."

Trey inclined his head, his face the picture of composure. But inside, the words gnawed at him. Lucky. Yes, Ryan was. But not him. Not his. And the knowledge burned, bitter and unrelenting.

He lingered only a moment longer before excusing himself, weaving back into the crowd with the same steady grace he always carried. But as he moved, his eyes betrayed him, drawn one last time to her across the ballroom.

Stephanie Vale.

Every instinct warned him to stay away. Every instinct demanded he remember his place, the consequences, the danger of even a single misstep.

And yet every part of him wanted to step forward—wanted to claim her as his, no matter the cost.

Chapter Four

Trey drifted through the ballroom with practiced ease, exchanging handshakes, clasping shoulders, delivering smiles that conveyed warmth without ever breaking his composure. To anyone else, he looked every inch the host and power broker—attentive, controlled, unshakable. But every path he took, every polite detour, angled him back toward the same view.

Stephanie.

She moved through the room as though she belonged to it, not claiming space but somehow filling it. Her laughter spilled easily, warm and unforced, and each ripple of sound seemed to pull him off balance. Ryan's hand rested at her lower back, the touch light, subtle—a quiet claim. It wasn't domineering, wasn't meant to trap her. It was careful. Protective. Attentive. The kind of gesture that signalled devotion without words.

And yet it made Trey's chest tighten with something sharp.

Stephanie's smile lingered on colleagues as she inclined her head in greeting, her warmth so genuine it softened even the most reserved expressions. Every compliment she received seemed to brighten her from within, her presence drawing admiration like a flame draws moths. But each time someone drifted too close, Ryan's cues—his hand, his placement, his subtle pivot—reminded the room where she belonged.

With him.

Trey's jaw flexed as he caught her laughter again, this time at something Ryan murmured, private and low. She tilted her head toward him, eyes alight, and Ryan answered with a smile that was entirely his own—content, assured, claiming.

The sight struck Trey harder than he wanted to admit.

It wasn't just that she was beautiful. Plenty of women were. It was everything else. She was captivating, intelligent, magnetic in ways that had nothing to do with her gown or the way her hair caught the light. Her sharp wit slipped into conversation with ease, her humour disarming and soft all at once. She had that rare quality—an ability to make people feel seen, important, as though they were the only one in the room. Trey knew what that was worth. He knew how rare it was.

And it made him want her all the more.

He paused near the edge of the ballroom, drink forgotten in his hand, watching as a well-dressed stranger angled himself toward Stephanie. She smiled politely, listening, but Trey noted the flicker of discomfort just before Ryan shifted forward. A subtle step. A redirect. A hand reclaiming its place at her back. The intruder drifted away without fuss, leaving Stephanie free, untouched.

Protective. Careful. Thoughtful.

Trey couldn't deny the appeal. He could even respect it. But respect didn't quiet the ache inside him—it only sharpened it. Because he wanted that closeness for himself. He wanted to be the one shielding her, the one she leaned toward, the one whose smile she returned without hesitation.

Her laugh rang out again, richer this time, and a few heads turned in their direction. Trey felt it like a blow. She didn't realise—how could she? She had no idea what she was doing to him. No idea that each smile, each tilt of her head, each unguarded laugh made him want to close the distance, take her hand, pull her against him and keep her there.

For him. Only him.

He adjusted his jacket, smoothed his expression into neutrality, and turned to greet another guest with the same polished composure he had worn all night. But beneath it, desire simmered hot and low, coiling through him with every stolen glance.

Each time Ryan's hand guided her, each protective step, it burned. Not out of spite—Trey knew Ryan cared for her, and in some ways that only made it worse. Because Ryan's care was real. And still, Trey wanted to take it for himself.

She was Ryan's tonight. She belonged to Ryan.

And still… he couldn't look away.

Trey couldn't stay away any longer. He pushed through the glittering swell of the crowd, his stride deliberate, measured, yet purposeful, every step weighted with intent. Across the ballroom, his gaze locked on them—Ryan positioned just slightly ahead, his hand resting at the small of Stephanie's back, protective, precise, a quiet claim that tightened Trey's chest.

Stephanie's laughter rang out, soft and melodic, threading through the hum of conversation and music. The sound struck him like a spark, igniting a coil of longing he had fought to suppress. She was radiant, effortlessly so, every movement fluid, every gesture magnetic. The red gown clung to her curves with sophistication, the slit along her leg adding a daring flourish without ever seeming deliberate. And though Ryan's touch marked her as his, Trey couldn't shake the thought that she didn't belong in anyone else's orbit tonight.

Ryan noticed him first.

"Mr. Grayson," he said, voice polite but firm, tension flickering in the set of his jaw. His hand brushed against Stephanie's in a quiet assertion of connection. "Good to see you."

Trey inclined his head, acknowledging the courtesy. "Ryan." His gaze shifted fully to Stephanie. "Stephanie," he said, low, smooth, the words warm with intent, "you look… stunning."

Her cheeks flushed, and she looked down for a fleeting moment, caught off guard by the weight behind his attention. Ryan's protective instincts stirred immediately—a subtle tightening of his stance, the half-step forward, a shadow of watchfulness in his posture.

"Thank you," she murmured, her voice a mixture of shyness and delight, her pulse betraying her calm exterior.

Trey's eyes held hers a heartbeat longer, drinking in the tilt of her head, the curve of her lips, the effortless poise she carried. He extended a hand toward her. "May I have this dance?"

Stephanie glanced at Ryan. His jaw flexed, measured, protective, a silent question hanging in the space between them.

"You want to dance?" he asked, voice steady.

"I do," she replied, lifting her hand to meet Trey's. A brief hesitation passed, then she allowed herself to be led toward the dance floor.

Ryan's eyes narrowed fractionally, a subtle tension in his shoulders, but his hand stayed lightly at her back, a tether he refused to relinquish. Trey didn't notice—or, more accurately, he didn't care. His focus was entirely on her.

As Trey guided her to the centre of the floor, the music enveloped them, soft and melodic, carrying a world that felt theirs alone. He leaned closer. "You move like you belong out here," he murmured, steady, confident.

Stephanie laughed softly, light and unrestrained, turning her head as she matched his rhythm. A few curious glances flicked their way, but Trey didn't flinch. Ryan's tension was palpable, but it only sharpened the thrill that pulsed through him.

"You're laughing too much," Trey teased, his voice low, intimate. "We might draw attention."

Stephanie tilted her head, a playful spark lighting her eyes. "And you call me out for laughing? Mr. Grayson, this is a gala, not a lecture hall."

He smirked. "Ah, so I'm a lecturer now? Perhaps I need a title that fits the severity of your crimes."

Her laughter rang out clear and warm. She pressed a little closer, teasing. "Mr. Grayson, I don't know if I can survive the severity of your wit."

He paused just enough to catch her gaze, his own darkening with intent. "You know," he murmured, softer now, "since you're already in my arms…" The words hovered, a subtle invitation. "…perhaps you could call me Trey."

Stephanie blinked, caught off guard, then allowed herself a mischievous smile. "Trey?" she repeated, testing the syllables.

A faint spark of satisfaction flared in his chest. "Yes," he said, the simplicity of the name filling the space between them. "Just say it."

"Trey," she whispered, the sound playful yet deliberate, letting it roll off her tongue.

He caught the word like a secret meant for no one else. A slow, satisfied smile curved his lips. "I like that," he murmured, husky with approval. "Say it again."

"Trey," she repeated, her laughter mingling with the music, light and intoxicating.

He drew her a fraction closer, spinning her gently before letting her settle against him. "Perfect," he murmured, low and intimate, just enough for her to hear. "You have no idea how beautiful you are, Stephanie."

She tilted her head back, laughing softly, a sound like a ribbon of music weaving between them. "And you, Trey, have no idea how distracting you are either."

For a few timeless moments, they moved together—laughter, warmth, whispered words—the rest of the world blurred to a haze of light and sound. Ryan's presence at the edges of the room was a distant echo; here, in Trey's arms, Stephanie moved with a freedom she hadn't realised she craved.

The last notes of the waltz lingered in the air, applause rippling across the gala floor. Trey held her a heartbeat longer than necessary, letting the heat of her proximity sink in, memorising the curve of her shoulder, the tilt of her chin.

Reluctantly, he guided her back toward Ryan.

Ryan rose immediately, drawing her close, the faintest edge of possessive ease in the way he pressed her into his side. Trey's jaw tightened, an instinctual irritation rising despite himself. The subtle pressure of Ryan's hand, the effortless claim he made, set Trey's pulse racing.

He forced his gaze elsewhere, adopting a mask of composed civility. "Thank you, Stephanie. That was… wonderful," he said smoothly, every word carrying weight beneath the surface.

"Of course, Mr. Grayson," she replied, cheeks still tinged rose.

Ryan's eyes narrowed, a curt nod sealing the unspoken line. "Glad you enjoyed it," he said, tone polite but clipped, steel wrapped in velvet.

Trey exhaled subtly, every muscle coiled with tension he refused to release. That fleeting dance—the warmth of her laugh, the brush of her hand—had penetrated every carefully constructed boundary he maintained. He had touched her world, even if only for a moment. And that moment had changed everything.

Before he could respond, a woman from the gala committee approached, her smile polite, professional. "Mr. Grayson," she said, tilting her head slightly, "I'm sorry to bother you, but one of the ladies who had agreed to participate in the charity date auction has just pulled out. We were wondering—would you, perhaps, consider someone else?"

Her gaze swept lightly toward Stephanie, and Trey caught the implication instantly.

"Stephanie?" he repeated, voice neutral, though inside, his chest constricted, pulse tightening with an almost imperceptible ache.

Ryan stiffened immediately, stepping closer to Stephanie, his posture rigid with protective intent. "Absolutely not," he said, firm and unwavering. "Stephanie isn't participating in that."

Trey raised a brow, keeping his tone calm, even as a thrill surged through him. "Shouldn't it be Stephanie's choice?"

Stephanie blinked, caught between their eyes, weighing her options. "It's for a good cause," she said, her voice steady despite the flicker of tension in her chest. She met Ryan's gaze briefly before glancing at Trey. "I don't mind participating if it helps."

Ryan's jaw tightened, a shadow of concern crossing his features. His hand brushed hers in a subtle, grounding gesture, anchoring her in his presence. "I don't want you going on a date with another man," he said, his voice low, firm, protective.

Trey's lips curved into a faint, measured smile, calm on the surface but charged beneath. "Then perhaps you should bid on her… I might even join in," he said smoothly, his gaze lingering on Stephanie just long enough to make the meaning unmistakable—a subtle dare wrapped in civility.

Stephanie let out a soft laugh, the tension around her shoulders easing, a playful spark lighting her eyes. "If it's for charity, I suppose anyone can, Mr. Grayson," she said lightly, the tease clear, though her tone carried no malice—only amusement and a hint of challenge.

A low growl of frustration coiled in Trey's chest. She didn't call him Trey—not yet—but the memory of her voice speaking his name on the dance floor still throbbed between his ribs. That single word had ignited something fierce, possessive, dangerous. He forced his face back into polite neutrality, though inside he burned to hear it again.

Ryan pressed his lips into a thin line, unease flashing in his dark eyes. "You're serious?" he asked quietly, tone low but not hostile, every inch the protector.

"I am," Trey replied evenly, smooth and controlled, his warmth deliberate, restrained, and undeniably magnetic. "And if it raises money for the cause, what's the harm?"

Stephanie squeezed Ryan's hand, soft and reassuring, her own voice gentle but firm. "It's just one date, Ryan. It's for the kids. I really think I should do it."

He exhaled slowly, tension lingering in his jaw, the rigid edge in his posture softening fractionally as he finally nodded, reluctant yet yielding. Trey's gaze followed every micro expression, every subtle shift in Ryan's stance, betraying the spark of desire he fought to mask behind polished composure.

The gala committee woman beamed, practically glowing. "Wonderful! I'll come get you when it's time. Thank you, Ms. Vale—you're a lifesaver."

As she moved away, the buzz of the gala carried on, but the quiet current between the three of them remained—an invisible thread of unspoken claims, restrained desire, and the magnetic tension that neither man could deny. Stephanie laughed lightly, brushing past Trey with a casual grace that belied the storm she had ignited, and Trey's pulse thudded, taut with restraint.

He had to remind himself to breathe.

She was Ryan's tonight. And yet every part of him wanted to step closer, to stake his own claim, to hear her call his name.

And he knew, deep down, that this was only the beginning.

Ryan spotted his parents weaving through the glittering crowd and straightened, his hand instinctively brushing against the small of Stephanie's back. "Mother, Father," he greeted warmly as Sofia and Peter Carter reached them, his voice calm, measured, protective.

Sofia's eyes immediately found Stephanie, her expression softening into open delight. "Oh, Stephanie, darling—I can't tell you enough how radiant you look tonight." Her gaze lingered, warm and approving, and Stephanie felt the flush of attention rise in her chest.

"Thank you, Mrs. Carter," Stephanie replied, keeping her voice light, a gracious smile lifting her features.

Ryan cleared his throat, a trace of reluctance tightening his tone. "Stephanie has agreed to participate in the charity auction this evening," he said, careful, protective, each word chosen with the precision of a man used to controlling outcomes.

"Oh, how wonderful!" Sofia clasped her hands together, beaming. "That's marvellous, Stephanie. It's for such a worthy cause."

Peter's chuckle was low and good-natured, his gaze flicking between his son and Stephanie with quiet amusement. "Well, Ryan," he said, the teasing note in his tone subtle but unmistakable, "looks like she'll keep you on your toes. A beautiful woman like this—you'll have to treat her right. Then you won't have to worry about her looking at another man."

Stephanie's cheeks warmed instantly, a delicate blush rising, her gaze briefly dropping as she swallowed the flattery.

Trey, standing nearby, lifted his champagne glass smoothly. "Here, here." His voice was measured, controlled, yet his eyes caught Stephanie's just long enough to unsettle her before he tipped the glass and drank. The faintest flicker of heat rose in her cheeks, a blush she couldn't quite suppress.

Moments later, Trey excused himself with effortless charm. "If you'll forgive me—I should check in with the organisers." He drifted into the crowd, expression composed, posture relaxed—but his mind was anything but calm.

He wanted to bid on Stephanie. God help him, he wanted it more than he should. But the reality was unavoidable: if he fought too hard for her in public, it wouldn't be him who paid the price—it would be Stephanie. A boss bidding aggressively on his assistant? The scandal could ruin her, not him. And yet, the thought of letting her slip away into another man's company—someone else claiming her, even temporarily—was unbearable.

He spotted Mrs. Pettigrew, the gala's coordinator, talking quietly with a waiter. Purposeful steps carried him across the room.

"Mrs. Pettigrew?" His voice was smooth, authoritative, low enough to draw attention without raising it.

She turned at once, a warm, practiced smile on her face. "Yes, Mr. Grayson?"

"I need you to handle something for me—very discreetly." His tone left no room for misunderstanding.

Her smile widened, the slight tilt of her head acknowledging deference. "Of course, sir. I wouldn't dream of betraying your confidence."

Trey studied her for a heartbeat, knowing she was right. A single word from him could unravel reputations, topple careers, ignite whispers that no one could contain. She wouldn't dare betray him.

"I want you to bid on Ms. Vale for me," he said at last, voice low, each syllable deliberate, carrying the weight of command. "Anonymously."

Mrs. Pettigrew's brows lifted briefly, but the gesture was fleeting. Her expression softened into something discreet, almost conspiratorial. "Consider it done, Mr. Grayson," she murmured.

He leaned in slightly, enough to make his intent unmistakable, though not overt. "I'll place bids publicly on several women—including Ms. Vale—to maintain appearances. But make no mistake," he added, a sharper edge cutting through the politeness. "I don't care about the cost. I must win her."

"Of course," Mrs. Pettigrew replied smoothly, unwavering. "I'll arrange an anonymous phone bidder on your behalf. It will appear entirely legitimate."

A flicker of relief passed through Trey's chest, though it did nothing to quiet the turmoil beneath. He exhaled slowly, the weight of the decision pressing down on him like a physical force. The act felt like a blade—part relief, part torment. It resembled possession, buying a claim on someone who should be entirely free. And yet, the alternative—seeing another man win her, even for one meaningless date—was unthinkable.

He raked a hand through his hair, forcing composure back into his posture. Tonight, at least, she would remain out of anyone else's reach. Not openly his—not yet—but not theirs either. And in that carefully maintained distance, Trey found the smallest measure of satisfaction: she was close enough for him to watch, to breathe, to anticipate. And that, for now, would have to be enough.

Chapter Five

Stephanie stood between Ryan and his parents; a flute of champagne held lightly in her hand. The warm bubbles tickled her lips as she smiled, her expression easy and genuine, though her chest tightened just a fraction under Ryan's ever-present watch. Sofia's gaze lingered appreciatively on her, and the compliment was repeated, sincere and deliberate.

"You look absolutely stunning, dear," Sofia said warmly, her eyes shining. "And I think it's so admirable you agreed to step in for the auction tonight. Not everyone would be so generous."

Stephanie dipped her head gracefully, the soft blush warming her cheeks. "Thank you. It's for a wonderful cause—I'm happy to do my part." Her words were calm, measured, but a faint flutter of nerves tickled the back of her stomach.

Ryan's lips curved into a short, controlled laugh, though it didn't quite reach his eyes. He tilted his champagne glass toward her, his gaze sharp beneath the polite mask. "Let's just hope she doesn't go too cheap, hm? Wouldn't want people thinking my girlfriend isn't worth much."

The words struck like a blade, subtle but pointed, a quiet reminder of the small, invisible rules he expected her to follow. Stephanie's smile wavered for a heartbeat before she pressed it back into place, cheeks still warming.

Sofia and Peter exchanged a quick, knowing glance, the kind that carried volumes without a single word. Then Peter let out a low chuckle, trying to diffuse the tension with warmth and levity. "Oh, Ryan. I think you've got it the wrong way around. The bidding's going to climb fast with a woman like Stephanie. You'll be lucky if you can afford her yourself."

Sofia reached out, brushing a delicate hand over Stephanie's in a gesture both maternal and reassuring. "He's right, darling. You'll do wonderfully. People see grace when it's in front of them." Her eyes twinkled, subtle pride softening her words.

Stephanie's smile deepened slightly, gratitude flickering across her features. But Ryan's presence remained a tether, his arm pressing lightly against her back. The subtle weight was a quiet assertion—not harsh, not overt, but unmistakable. She could feel the tension coiling in the space between them, a silent reminder to anyone who looked: she was his.

Despite the warmth of her potential parents-in-law's praise and the champagne's gentle fizz, a small, unbidden tension settled in her shoulders. She forced herself to meet Ryan's eyes, offering a polite nod, a practiced acknowledgment of his claim, even as a tiny, rebellious part of her yearned to loosen the invisible leash, to breathe outside the constant vigilance of his gaze.

Stephanie lifted her glass slightly, offering a soft, controlled laugh to punctuate her composure. "Well, then, I'll do my best to make the cause proud," she said, words light but layered with the quiet defiance she carefully buried beneath courtesy.

Ryan's jaw tightened just a fraction, a subtle shadow passing over his features, but he gave no further words. His protective hand remained at her back, steady, deliberate, and Stephanie knew that for the rest of the evening, his presence would be a constant, silent boundary she was expected to respect.

Yet even as she raised the glass and let it glint in the chandelier light, part of her wondered—briefly, dangerously—how it might feel to have someone else's gaze linger on her the way Trey's had earlier, and whether she could ever let herself notice it without consequence.

It wasn't long before Mrs. Pettigrew appeared, clipboard tucked beneath one arm, her smile brisk and efficient. "Ms. Vale, it's time," she said, gesturing toward the stage with gentle urgency.

Stephanie nodded, setting down her glass and smoothing the silk of her gown. She had barely stepped away from Ryan's side when Trey emerged through the throng, his presence cutting cleanly through the crowd—direct, deliberate, impossible to ignore.

"Good luck," he murmured, his voice velvet-smooth, weighted with something far heavier than courtesy.

Her smile faltered, slipping for just a heartbeat. "Thank you. Though..." her gaze flicked back toward Ryan, "...he seems to think I might need more than luck."

Trey followed her glance, his eyes narrowing when they found Ryan across the room. He leaned in, close enough that the faint spice of his cologne teased the air between them. "He's wrong," Trey said, low and steady, each word a promise. "You'll be unforgettable."

Stephanie's breath caught before she managed a soft, genuine smile. "Thank you, Mr. Grayson."

The title grated against him, sharp and unwelcome. Not after hearing his name on her lips, soft and unguarded on the dance floor. But this wasn't the moment to correct her. He inclined his head instead, his composure masking the frustration clawing beneath.

She turned to follow Mrs. Pettigrew, her gown shimmering as she crossed the floor, and Trey's gaze tracked her every step—a silent claim he couldn't voice. Not yet.

Near the stage, three women gathered in the wings, the hum of voices and clink of glasses drifting in from the ballroom.

A striking brunette in emerald silk—Melinda, one of Ryan's lawyers—spotted Stephanie and immediately sidled closer, relief etched across her face. "Thank God," she whispered, flashing a conspiratorial smile. "I'm glad I'm not the only one being roped into this. Makes me feel a little less like I'm on display."

Stephanie's lips curved. "Strength in numbers, right?"

"Exactly." Melinda's wry smile lingered before she cast a quick glance toward the crowd. "Tell me—how's Ryan taking all this? He seems a little…" she hesitated, then tipped her head knowingly, "…possessive."

Stephanie exhaled softly, her own smile turning rueful. "He's not happy," she admitted, her tone calm but resolute. "But it's for charity, and I wanted to do it. He'll come around."

Melinda chuckled, shaking her head. "Men. They want you to shine—just not too brightly."

Before Stephanie could respond, another voice joined them—tentative, almost timid. "I'm so glad I'm not the only one."

They both turned. A redheaded woman in a pale lavender dress edged into their little circle, her hands twisted together. Stephanie recognised her instantly—Rachel, from Grayson Global's accounts section. Her smile was fragile, as though it might break if she held it too long.

"I thought I was going to faint when they asked me," Rachel confessed with a shaky laugh. "I've never done anything like this. I mean—being put on stage like… merchandise."

Melinda chuckled knowingly. "You'll be fine. At least we're all in this together."

Stephanie's expression softened. She reached out, giving Rachel's arm a light, steadying touch. "It's not about us being on display. It's about raising money. That's what people will see—the cause, not just the dresses."

Rachel's wide green eyes shone with gratitude. "You make it sound so easy. I am sure I'll trip over my own feet out there."

Stephanie laughed, warm and encouraging. "If you do, I'll trip with you. No one remembers perfection. They remember heart."

That earned a grin from Melinda, and even Rachel managed a steadier smile. For a moment, the nerves between them eased, replaced by an unexpected camaraderie in the waiting shadows.

But as Stephanie turned her gaze back toward the ballroom, she caught a distant glimpse of Ryan—the intensity of his watchful eyes unmistakable. And though she couldn't see him, another pair of eyes tracked her too, sharp and unyielding. Trey Grayson hadn't stopped watching either.

The emcee stepped aside as Mrs. Pettigrew adjusted her glasses and approached the microphone, clipboard in hand. The ballroom hushed, all eyes turning toward the stage.

"Ladies and gentlemen," she began, her voice warm, smooth, and perfectly practiced, "thank you for supporting tonight's charity auction. We have three remarkable women who have graciously offered their time for a dinner date, all to benefit the children's hospital. Let's meet them, one at a time."

She gestured to Melinda first. The lawyer in the emerald gown stepped forward, offering a polite smile to the audience. Her hands twisted nervously at her sides, but she held herself upright, radiating quiet confidence.

"Melinda Collins is a talented lawyer at Grayson Global," Mrs. Pettigrew said, her tone effortlessly elegant. "She's bright, witty, and promises an evening of lively conversation. Who would like to bid on a dinner with Melinda?"

A ripple of murmurs passed through the audience, paddles slowly raising. Numbers were called, voices overlapping in the excitement of competition. Trey bid discreetly, one of several competing for her attention. When the final bid was accepted, Melinda exhaled—a mixture of relief and exhilaration—and stepped back to the side, her smile trembling with excitement.

Next came Rachel, the redhead from accounts. Mrs. Pettigrew's introduction was gentle, yet enthusiastic: "Rachel Turner is a talented accountant at Grayson Global. She may be new to the company, but she brings infectious enthusiasm and genuine charm. An evening with her promise's laughter, insight, and a refreshing perspective on life."

Rachel stepped forward, cheeks flushed, her hands twisting together nervously. She stole a quick glance at Stephanie, who offered an encouraging nod. "You'll be fine," Stephanie mouthed, and Rachel's tentative smile widened.

The bidding started quietly, steadily building as the audience warmed to the cause. Trey placed a bid, careful but deliberate, his eyes sweeping over the stage, but he remained composed. The final number secured Rachel's date, and she returned to the side, visibly relieved, throwing Stephanie a shy, grateful smile.

Finally, it was Stephanie's turn. Mrs. Pettigrew's gaze lingered on her, admiration flickering behind her calm exterior. "And now, we have Stephanie Vale," she announced, her voice carrying effortlessly across the ballroom. "Stephanie is not only a remarkable professional—executive assistant to Trey Grayson—but a woman whose warmth and intelligence promise an unforgettable evening. Who would like to bid for a dinner with Stephanie?"

A subtle murmur rippled through the room. "We have an anonymous phone bidder on the line for Stephanie," Mrs. Pettigrew added, prompting a faint ripple of surprise.

Stephanie's eyes widened slightly but she stepped forward, her gown shimmering under the stage lights. Shoulders back, chin lifted, a poised smile gracing her lips, she exuded elegance and self-assurance. Each paddle raised, each call of a number, sent a quiet thrill through her, not fear, but exhilaration at being part of something meaningful.

She noticed Ryan among the main bidders. His jaw tightened, his expression protective yet anxious. Her pulse ticked up slightly, aware of the silent warning in his gaze. Then Trey placed his bid, low and measured, making his presence known without a word. Stephanie blinked, a flicker of surprise crossing her face. Ryan caught her glance and shot Trey a sharp, dark look.

The lady at the phone representing the anonymous bidder added a bid, and the auction moved faster, the atmosphere electric with anticipation. Trey didn't take his eyes off Stephanie, even from across the room, his expression carefully composed while a storm of desire and frustration churned beneath the surface.

The bidding climbed steadily, voices overlapping, until the final number was called. Stephanie exhaled, a rush of satisfaction and adrenaline surging through her. The anonymous bidder had won. She offered a small, gracious nod to Mrs. Pettigrew and stepped back toward the side of the stage, heart racing as curiosity pricked her. Who could the bidder be?

Melinda, standing nearby, leaned toward her, a teasing smile playing at her lips. "You must have an admirer if you had an anonymous bidder."

Rachel giggled nervously, glancing at Stephanie and then at the crowd. "And Ryan… he looked like he was about to lose it."

Stephanie's lips curved into a half-smile, a brief easing of tension, though the weight of that revelation pressed on her chest. She could almost feel Ryan's storm behind his restrained expression, and yet, another presence—Trey's— lurking in the periphery, made her pulse quicken.

Mrs. Pettigrew stepped forward, her clipboard tucked under her arm, offering warm thanks to the three women. "Thank you all for your generosity tonight," she said. "Melinda, Rachel—you'll be contacted by your winning bidders over the next week. They'll coordinate with you directly."

She turned her gaze toward Stephanie, her eyes flicking with a hint of intrigue. "And as for you, Ms. Vale… your winning bidder didn't leave a name. He requested to remain completely anonymous, but he'll be in contact with you soon."

Stephanie blinked, a flicker of surprise passing across her face, her hand resting lightly on the silk of her gown. The thrill of mystery mingled with the tension of the evening, leaving her both curious and unsettled. Across the room, Trey's sharp eyes tracked her, unreadable yet charged, while Ryan's jaw tightened subtly, a protective edge framing his otherwise calm demeanour.

Stephanie inhaled slowly, steadying herself. One thing was certain—tonight was far from over.

Stephanie smoothed the fabric of her gown as she descended from the stage, her pulse still thrumming from the adrenaline of the bidding. The low murmur of conversation and clinking glasses surrounded her, but all her attention was drawn to Ryan, standing with his parents, his posture rigid and eyes locked on her with that familiar, unreadable intensity.

"Darling, you were marvellous!" Sofia exclaimed the moment Stephanie reached them, her hands clasping Stephanie's warmly. Her eyes sparkled with genuine pride. "Truly, the way you carried yourself—it was elegant. And for such a good cause!"

Peter chuckled, lifting his glass in a half-toast. "Absolutely. You had half the room bidding, Stephanie. Quite the effect you made."

Stephanie's cheeks flushed, a soft, grateful smile tugging at her lips. "Thank you. It was nerve-wracking at first, but... it felt good to contribute."

Ryan's arm slid around her waist, firm, almost possessive. His smile was polite, almost smooth—but it never reached his eyes. "Yes, well," he said, low and measured, "I suppose the mystery bidder was very generous. Pity he'll be disappointed when he realises my girlfriend isn't quite the prize he thinks she is."

The words lingered between them, sharp as a whisper beneath the hubbub of the gala.

Sofia's smile faltered for a fleeting moment, brows knitting slightly, while Peter cleared his throat, a light chuckle easing the tension. "Ryan..." he said gently, "I think the gentleman knew exactly what he was bidding on. You should be proud she was in such demand. Means you'd better treat her right—keep her happy."

Sofia slipped her arm around Stephanie in quiet solidarity, her eyes flicking toward Ryan with a faint reprimand. "Yes, darling, you were wonderful," she said firmly.

Stephanie's lips curved in a polite, controlled smile, but beneath the surface, Ryan's words pressed like a weight against her ribs. Her gaze drifted almost involuntarily across the ballroom—and there he was. Trey. His eyes found hers instantly, steady, unwavering, stripping away the din of the crowd and the authority of Ryan's claim.

Before she could look away, he moved. His stride was unhurried but purposeful, deliberate in a way that seemed to part the crowd naturally. He stopped in front of her, the faintest curve of a smile tugging at the corner of his mouth.

"Stephanie," he said, low and intimate, meant only for her. "Dance with me."

She hesitated—not from reluctance, but from awareness. Ryan stood mere inches away, his posture rigid, the protective weight of his presence pressing down. Yet something stronger compelled her. Her hand lifted softly, brushing against Trey's. "Yes," she murmured, letting her fingers close around his.

Sofia's delighted laugh bubbled up before Ryan could speak. "Well, darling, you can't very well refuse your boss."

Peter chuckled, lifting his glass. "Especially when he looks like he's not about to take no for an answer."

Ryan's jaw tightened, the arm around her back pressing subtly to remind her of his claim, but she allowed her hand to rest in Trey's, letting his grip—sure, confident, and possessive—guide her across the murmuring crowd to the centre of the dance floor.

The orchestra swelled, filling the space with soft, melodic rhythm. Trey drew her close, his hand resting at the small of her back, pulling her nearer than propriety allowed. Possessively. Dangerously.

Stephanie's breath caught. She tilted her head, a teasing lift of her lips. "Careful, Mr. Grayson—people are watching."

His eyes flashed, mouth curving into the faintest, almost wicked smile. He leaned close, breath brushing her ear. "Trey," he murmured, deliberate, insistent. "Say it."

Her lips parted, the word trembling between defiance and surrender. "Trey."

A dark thrill ignited within him at the sound. He drew her closer, guiding her across the floor with a confidence that left no room for hesitation, no room for the crowd to intrude. Every turn, every dip, every soft laugh she released tightened the coil of desire in his chest.

From the sidelines, Ryan's gaze tracked their every move. His expression darkened, the glass in his hand clutched too tightly, knuckles whitening as a barely restrained tension radiated from him. Sofia and Peter exchanged a subtle glance but said nothing—the undercurrent between the three was too clear, too sharp to comment on without drawing attention.

Trey registered it all: Ryan's simmering fury, the protective instinct in every inch of his posture. Yet he didn't look away. He held her firmly, let the heat of her proximity settle against him, and allowed her fingers to curl instinctively against his shoulder. One flicker of triumph passed through him—a silent acknowledgment that, even if just for this moment, she was his.

He thought fleetingly to tell her then, to claim the truth: that every bid had been his, that no one else had ever truly had a chance. But he swallowed it, keeping the secret close, savouring the tension, the quiet intoxication of mystery. Not here. Not yet.

Instead, he lowered his head, voice silk and steel brushing her ear. "You don't belong to the crowd, Stephanie. You belong right here, in my arms."

Her pulse stumbled. Lips parted as though to protest, yet all that escaped was a faint hitch of breath, betraying her in the way words never could.

And in that moment, beneath the soft glow of chandeliers, amidst the swirl of the gala, it was theirs alone—a stolen universe where glances spoke louder than vows and every movement whispered desire.

Chapter Six

Trey slowed the last turn, the orchestra drawing the song to a lingering, shimmering close. The final note hung in the air, delicate and intoxicating, as he held Stephanie a moment longer than propriety allowed, his hand firm at her back, his gaze locked on hers. For an instant, the world shrank to just the two of them—the swirl of lights, the glittering chandeliers, the hum of polite conversation—all fading into nothing.

Then applause broke out, polite but warm, pulling Stephanie back to the present. Her chest rose and fell with a quiet, shaky breath as Trey finally eased his hold. His hand didn't drop hers, though; he guided her through the press of guests with a natural, unspoken authority, a silent insistence that she remain tethered to him.

At the edge of the dance floor, Ryan waited. His smile was sharp, too tight, the champagne flute in his hand nearly empty. Sofia and Peter stood slightly behind him, both watching with careful restraint—Sofia's lips pressed thin with disapproval, Peter's hand subtly poised to intervene if necessary.

"Thank you for the dance, Stephanie," Trey said smoothly, his voice silk over steel. He leaned close, brushing her knuckles with his lips before releasing her hand, letting the gesture linger just long enough to claim the moment. His eyes never left hers.

Ryan's jaw flexed. "I'm sure *my girlfriend* appreciates the attention, Grayson," he said, voice just loud enough to carry across the floor. "But perhaps you should remember who she came here with."

The air snapped tight, electric, sharp as glass. Stephanie froze, heat climbing her neck. "Ryan—"

Trey's expression remained calm, unflinching, though a spark of challenge glimmered in his eyes. "No one could forget she's with you," he said evenly. "But I asked her to dance. She accepted."

The simplicity of the statement landed like a blade.

Ryan's laugh was brittle, edged with something darker. "Oh, is that how it works now? You ask, she accepts, and suddenly you think you can put your hands all over her? You're her boss, Grayson, not her—" His words snapped off, jaw tightening, as though voicing the thought in full might be dangerous.

Stephanie's eyes widened. "Ryan, stop. You're making a scene."

"I'm making a scene?" he barked, incredulous, jealousy spilling over in a low, heated rush. "You let him touch you like that—in front of me, in front of everyone—and I'm the one making a scene?"

Sofia's sharp intake of breath cut through the tension. "Ryan," she whispered fiercely, stepping forward. "Enough. This isn't the time or the place."

Peter's hand landed firmly on his son's shoulder, a stabilising anchor. "Son, don't," he warned quietly. "You're going to regret this."

But Ryan shrugged off the touch, eyes blazing, voice low and dangerous. "You've wanted her from the start, haven't you? Don't deny it. Every look, every excuse to be near her—hell, bidding on her tonight like she's—"

"Ryan!" Sofia's voice cracked like a whip, cheeks flushed with mortification, eyes darting to the small crowd now watching with rapt interest. "That's enough! You are humiliating yourself. And her!"

Stephanie's throat tightened, a knot of shame, fury, and helplessness tangling in her chest. She tried to speak, but Trey's quiet, controlled voice cut across the storm, steady and precise.

"Careful, Ryan," he said, low, sharp enough to coil like a blade. "The way you're speaking—it doesn't sound like a man protecting a woman he loves. It sounds like a man afraid of losing what he doesn't value."

The silence that followed was razor-sharp, ears straining to catch the undercurrent of accusation.

Ryan's hand clenched around his glass until the crystal cracked with a sharp snap, champagne spilling across his cuff. He didn't even notice.

Stephanie stepped forward, her voice firmer than she felt, cutting through the tension. "This isn't the place for this. Ryan, we're done here."

His head snapped toward her, shock flaring before the jealousy hardened again. "Stephanie—"

But Sofia was already guiding her away, murmuring apologies under her breath, while Peter leaned in close to his son, steel threading his words. "You need to pull yourself together before you ruin more than your cufflinks."

Behind them, Trey's gaze followed Stephanie unflinching, unshaken, though his chest burned from the effort it took to restrain himself. Tonight, had drawn the lines in stark relief. The war between them—the silent, simmering pull of desire and ownership—was no longer quiet.

Stephanie's hand brushed against Trey's just briefly as she passed, a fleeting contact that sent a shock of warmth up his arm. He didn't let himself react beyond the smallest tightening of his fingers, a private, unspoken victory. Ryan's jealousy was clear, raw, and dangerous—but Trey's calm, measured presence reminded everyone, subtly, that the game had changed.

The ballroom continued around them, laughter and music filling the spaces between, but Trey's focus never wavered. Not from her, not from Ryan, not from anything except the knowledge that tonight, boundaries had been tested, lines had been crossed, and nothing would ever be the same again.

Stephanie's eyes burned, the sting of unshed tears making the glittering ballroom blur. She pressed her fingertips lightly against her temple, trying to steady herself, but the lump in her throat made it impossible to draw an even breath.

Sofia stepped closer, her voice soft, gentle, and maternal. "Oh, sweetheart…" She laid a comforting hand on Stephanie's arm. "Don't let his temper ruin your evening. You didn't do anything wrong."

Stephanie shook her head, her voice breaking as she whispered, "I didn't do anything wrong. It was just a dance."

"I know, dear," Sofia soothed, pulling her just slightly into her side, like she would a daughter. "Ryan was out of line. He let his jealousy get the better of him."

Stephanie blinked, a tear escaping despite her effort to hold it in. She quickly brushed it away, offering Sofia a trembling smile of gratitude.

Peter approached then, his brow furrowed, his expression tight but kind. "Stephanie?" His voice was low, careful. "Are you all right?"

She straightened a little, forcing a nod, though her throat was still tight. "I'm fine," she murmured, the words automatic, though they sounded hollow even to her own ears.

Before either of them could press further, Ryan appeared, his expression still stormy, though now layered with a flicker of regret as he saw her eyes. His steps slowed, his mouth opening as though he meant to speak.

Sofia turned swiftly, her voice quiet but firm, cutting through the tension. "Ryan," she said, a warning threaded in his name. Then, more softly, "Why don't you take Stephanie home? She's had enough for tonight."

Ryan hesitated, looking between his mother and Stephanie, his jaw tight. The fight seemed to drain out of him in increments, leaving him standing there, caught between pride and guilt.

Stephanie lowered her gaze, her pulse still hammering. All she wanted was to escape the watching eyes, the whisper of voices carrying across the ballroom.

"Come on," Sofia urged gently, giving Ryan a look that brooked no argument. "Take her home."

Ryan finally nodded, reaching for Stephanie's hand, though she hesitated before letting him take it. Sofia's palm brushed her arm one last time in silent reassurance.

And as Ryan led her away, Stephanie couldn't shake the weight of Trey's gaze still lingering somewhere behind her, steady and unwavering, as though reminding her she hadn't imagined the way he'd stood by her.

The Uber ride was silent, thick with everything unsaid. Stephanie sat pressed against her door, the cool glass of the window grounding her as the city lights slid across her reflection. Ryan sat beside her, shoulders rigid, his hands clasped tightly in his lap.

The driver hummed along to the radio, oblivious to the storm brewing in the back seat.

Ryan's voice finally broke the silence, low and sharp. "You didn't have to say yes to him."

Stephanie turned her head slightly, her brows lifting. "It was a dance, Ryan. Nothing more."

He let out a humourless laugh, his jaw tightening. "Nothing more? He held you like he owned you. Everyone saw it."

Her breath caught, but she forced calm into her tone. "What everyone saw was me being polite. I wasn't about to cause a scene in front of your parents, or in front of the entire ballroom. Do you really think that would've been better?"

Ryan's eyes burned into her profile, but she kept her gaze fixed on the blur of streetlights racing past. "You smiled at him," he muttered, bitterness threading the words. "Like he was the only one in the room."

That stung, sharp and unfair. She finally turned, meeting his gaze head-on. "I smiled because it was easier than making things worse. The only person who made a spectacle tonight was you."

His jaw tightened, the accusation landing with an unexpected weight. The air between them seemed to shrink, pressing in with a suffocating intensity. Even the hum of the engine and the quiet thrum of the city outside felt distant, as if the world had narrowed to the taut space between them. The driver glanced briefly in the rearview mirror, sensing the unspoken storm brewing in the backseat.

Stephanie's voice softened, though a tremor betrayed her hurt. "You keep seeing threats where there aren't any," she said carefully, each word deliberate, fragile. "I don't know what else I can do to make you believe it's you I'm with—not anyone else. Mr. Grayson is my boss, not your competitor. He... he has no claim on me beyond the office."

Ryan's chest rose and fell sharply, tension coiling and uncoiling with every breath. His hands flexed in his lap, knuckles white against the dark leather, and he didn't answer right away. He just stared ahead, gaze fixed somewhere outside the window but seeing nothing, letting her words settle around him like heavy stones. Each syllable pressed against him, impossible to ignore, yet impossible to release.

The car slowed as they pulled up to the curb outside their apartment building. Stephanie exhaled shakily, bracing herself—because she knew the silence wasn't an end. It was only the beginning of another fight.

From across the ballroom, Trey's gaze followed them like a hawk, sharp and unrelenting. Ryan's hand closed possessively around Stephanie's, guiding her toward the grand exit, and she moved with that effortless grace that made him ache. But Trey saw it—the fleeting, almost imperceptible dip of her shoulders, the quick, furtive lift of her hand to brush at her cheek.

Tears.

A muscle twitched in his jaw. The sight of her hiding something so raw, so undeserved, struck him like a fist to the chest. His blood hammered in his temples, his knuckles whitening around the stem of his glass. Every instinct screamed—close the distance, wrench Ryan's hand from hers, knock some sense into the man. In his mind, the image flashed vividly: Ryan sprawled across the polished ballroom floor, stunned, humbled, finally aware of the consequences of his arrogance.

But Trey didn't move. Not yet.

He forced a slow, measured breath, locking down the storm threatening to break loose. He had far too much to lose—and worse, so did she. Stephanie didn't need a public scene, didn't need the humiliation of his wrath on top of everything else. Not tonight.

Still, he never tore his eyes away. The sight of her leaving, arm in arm with Ryan, twisted something deep inside him, dark and relentless. He lifted his untouched champagne, muttering under his breath, a vow meant for no one but himself:

"One day, Carter… you won't get to walk away with her."

He tipped the glass back. The bubbles bit at his tongue, but they did nothing to quell the fire raging in his chest. Only someone who truly knew him would notice the tension in his shoulders, the almost imperceptible tremor in his grip.

"Mr. Grayson."

The familiar, composed voice drew him from the whirlpool of his thoughts. Sofia and Peter Carter stood before him, their expressions measured, the warmth of earlier replaced with something heavier—discomfort and cautious remorse.

"We wanted to apologise," Sofia said softly, eyes holding a quiet honesty. "Ryan… he behaved poorly. That isn't how we raised him, and it certainly isn't how a woman like Stephanie deserves to be treated. Especially in front of you, and everyone else here."

Trey's jaw flexed. He set his glass aside, inclining his head with a careful, controlled calm. "There's no need. It wasn't me who bore the brunt of it."

Peter exhaled slowly, a weighty sound that spoke of regret and paternal responsibility. "Still," he said quietly, "it reflects on us as his parents. Stephanie is a remarkable woman. She should have been celebrated tonight—not made to feel small."

Something shifted in Trey's chest. Rarely did anyone acknowledge a woman's worth aloud, not with conviction and clarity. He found himself nodding once, deliberately, though the memory of her trembling behind the composure she wore still burned at him.

"She handled herself with grace," he said low, certain. "More than most would've managed under the circumstances."

Sofia's lips pressed into a soft, sad line, her hand brushing Peter's arm in quiet solidarity. "That girl has a good heart. We only hope Ryan realises it before he drives her away."

Trey's gaze darkened fleetingly. The words left his lips smooth, precise, with a weight that carried unspoken meaning. "Some lessons aren't learned until it's too late."

For a moment, the air held, razor-sharp. Sofia's eyes searched his, perhaps seeing more than he intended, glimpsing the silent storm behind the carefully composed exterior.

Peter cleared his throat, a grounding gesture that ended the moment. "We appreciate your understanding, Mr. Grayson. Truly."

Trey inclined his head once more; civility etched into every line of his face. But as the Carters drifted back into the crowd, his thoughts betrayed the mask he wore.

He wasn't interested in understanding.

He was only interested in ensuring Ryan Carter would never have another chance to hurt her—not physically, not emotionally, and certainly not by underestimating the depth of the bond he already knew existed between them. Stephanie would remain untouchable, if not for everyone else, then for him, until the day came when Trey could claim what had been his to protect all along.

And he would wait.

The elevator doors slid open with a soft ding, and Ryan held the door for Stephanie, his jaw tight, fingers brushing hers in a gesture that felt more possessive than reassuring.

Stephanie stepped inside first, the familiar scent of the apartment—a mix of polished concrete, faint vanilla, and Ryan's cologne—washing over her. She set her clutch on the console table and kicked off her heels, exhaling softly.

Ryan followed, coat dropping to the floor with a muted thud. His eyes never left her, dark and intent, a muscle in his jaw flexing, betraying the tension he'd carried since the gala.

Stephanie sank against the wall, hands brushing the silk of her gown. "I didn't do anything wrong," she murmured, voice low, eyes glistening with unshed tears.

Ryan's fists clenched at his sides, his frame taut. "I know," he said, though the words were tight, distant. "But that doesn't mean I liked seeing it… all of it."

Stephanie shook her head, a faint, bitter smile tugging at her lips. "Ryan… you can't control how people see me. Or what they bid."

"I don't care about the bidding," he snapped, the edge in his voice sharp enough to cut. "It's him! Trey—dancing with you, holding you… I don't want anyone else near you!"

Stephanie flinched, pressing her hands over her eyes as though she could shield herself from his words—and from the storm of emotion behind them. "Ryan… please," she whispered. "I'm with you. But I can't live in fear of what someone else thinks or does. You can't—none of us—control everything."

He exhaled sharply, stepping closer, brushing a loose strand of hair from her face. "I just… I hate feeling like I can't protect you," he admitted, his voice rough with the strain he'd been holding back.

Stephanie's fingers curled against his chest, grounding herself, her eyes catching his with unwavering clarity. "You don't have to protect me from everything, Ryan. I'm not yours to shield. I'm me. And I still choose you."

He closed the distance, forehead pressing against hers, the storm in his gaze tempered by the warmth only she could draw out. "I can't help it," he murmured, almost a confession, almost a plea.

Stephanie let herself smile softly through the lingering tears, leaning just enough to rest against him. "I know," she whispered, voice gentle but firm. "I love that you care. But I'm not fragile, Ryan. Not tonight, not ever. And not for anyone—even him."

They lingered in the quiet apartment; the tension softened into a fragile truce, the city outside shimmering with indifferent light. Stephanie sank onto the sofa, heels discarded, silk pooling around her like liquid moonlight.

Ryan remained near the window, coat dangling from one arm, jaw tight, eyes dark and stormy as he studied her. For a long moment, he said nothing, drinking in the curve of her shoulders, the flushed warmth of her cheeks, the faint glimmer of tears lingering in her eyes.

Finally, he crossed the room, voice low and almost pleading. "Stephanie… when I saw Trey with you… dancing… it wasn't just jealousy. It's fear. Fear of losing you."

Stephanie lifted her gaze, steady, unwavering, though a quiet ache threaded through it. "Ryan… I am with you. Not anyone else. But you can't cage me either. That's not love—it's possession. And I need you to remember that."

He ran a hand through his hair, pacing, frustration radiating in every movement. "I can't help how I feel. Seeing him holding you—like you were his—" He stopped, letting the words hang, sharp and unfinished.

Stephanie scooted closer, careful, measured, brushing her fingers along the tense line of his arm. "Look at me," she said softly. "I'm here. With you. That doesn't make me fragile—or up for auction. That was for charity. And tonight, I'm not yours to shield. I can stand in the world myself. But I'm not blind to what's coming either."

Ryan exhaled sharply, lowering onto the sofa beside her, leaving a careful space between them. "I hate feeling powerless when it comes to you."

She touched his hand, letting her fingers linger over the tight, tense knuckles. "You can't control everything, Ryan. You can love me, protect me when I need it. But I'm not a possession. And neither of us can pretend forever that fear or anger can hold what isn't meant to be forced."

The room fell into a heavy, softened silence, punctuated only by the distant hum of the city. Ryan leaned closer, pressing a kiss to her temple. "God, I love you," he murmured, voice rough yet sincere. "I just... I get so scared. Sometimes I just can't help myself."

Stephanie's lips curved gently, reassuringly, though a shadow of sorrow threaded through her warmth. "I know," she whispered. "I love you too. But fear doesn't get to decide for us. And neither does desire, Ryan—not forever."

He finally let his hand cover hers, fingers intertwining, their warmth grounding them. The city lights stretched across the apartment, gold and silver stripes dancing across the floor. The night's tension hadn't vanished—it had merely shifted, a quiet truce at best. Stephanie knew, deep down, that the truce was fragile, a temporary pause before the inevitable. But in this moment, she would remain with him, tender and resolute, even as the unspoken truth lingered between them: their time together was running out.

Chapter Seven

Stephanie lay awake in the darkened bedroom, the city lights filtering through the curtains like distant stars, casting a cold, silver glow across the room. Ryan slept beside her, his steady breathing intended to be comforting—but tonight even that familiar rhythm felt alien, heavy with an unspoken distance. He murmured something in his sleep, soft and meaningless, yet it grated against the fragile tension coiling in her chest.

Another headache, he had muttered earlier—his excuse for retreating into silence—but the ache she felt was sharper, deeper, and it had nothing to do with a migraine. Her thoughts, as they had so often lately, drifted to Trey. She could still feel the weight of his hand at the small of her back, the steady, deliberate guidance through the ballroom. The memory of his eyes holding hers—the intensity, the warmth, the way they seemed to see her—made her heart stutter in ways Ryan's gaze never had. Every glance, every brush of his fingers, had ignited a fire she hadn't realised she'd been starving for.

By contrast, Ryan's presence pressed against her like a binding weight. His sharp words, the subtle edge in his smile, the possessiveness he wielded in public— they had always made her feel protected, secure even—but now that very security felt suffocating, almost suffocating in its demand. She had told herself and him she loved him, and perhaps she did—but it was a quiet, muted love, safe and familiar. It offered comfort, not the spark, the electricity, the pulse that left her breathless and yearning. Trey did that. Trey awakened something raw, urgent, and undeniable in her, and that terrified her as much as it thrilled her.

Guilt curled in her chest, a coiling, twisting vine that tightened with every thought of him. Wanting Trey while tethered to Ryan felt like a betrayal in its purest sense, yet how could she deny it? Every instinct in her body, every flutter of her pulse, every lingering echo of the dance whispered the truth she could no longer ignore: Trey saw her in ways Ryan never had—or perhaps never could. That truth, once exhilarating, now pressed down on her with a painful clarity.

She hugged her knees to her chest, the silk of her nightgown cool beneath her fingers, tracing idle patterns as if she could map out her tangled thoughts. The gala, the auction, the dances—they had only illuminated what had been simmering quietly all along. Ryan's jealousy, his sharp words, his subtle need to control—it was all beginning to feel less like protection and more like a cage. And Trey... Trey had shown her what freedom could feel like, what desire could feel like.

"I'm so confused," she whispered, the words trembling in the quiet room. "I love him... but I—do I even love him?" Her voice cracked on the last syllable, dissolving into silence that seemed to stretch on forever. She pressed her palm to her face, trying in vain to smother the heat in her chest, to erase the longing

Trey had stirred with a single touch. She hated herself for craving it, hated how it made Ryan's words cut deeper than they ever had.

The city lights spilled across the bed in soft, cold stripes, and she sank lower into the sheets, caught between loyalty and longing, safety and the sharp, restless pull of something new. She had loved Ryan, or at least she had tried—but Trey's presence had exposed a truth she could no longer ignore. The intensity, the fire, the heartbeat-in-the-throat anticipation she felt for him was unlike anything she had ever felt with Ryan.

She sat in the stillness for long minutes, listening to the city hum, to Ryan's steady breaths beside her, and felt the crushing isolation of being pulled in two directions at once. Her heart had chosen a new path she hadn't dared to acknowledge, leaving her achingly alone even with the man she had once promised herself to. She wondered, quietly, painfully, if she had ever truly understood what love meant—or if she was only now discovering it, in the shadows of another man's arms, and in the fire of a longing she could no longer contain.

Her eyes drifted to the darkened window, the lights of the city distant and untouchable, and she admitted, finally, with a quiet, shivering honesty: she didn't know if her heart still belonged to Ryan at all. And the truth that followed made her stomach tighten, cold and thrilling at once—Trey had claimed something inside her she couldn't give back. Not anymore.

Morning light filtered softly through the curtains, warm and bright, yet Stephanie felt none of its comfort. Ryan acted almost normal at breakfast—too normal—making small talk, asking perfunctory questions, his easy smile barely reaching his eyes. He mentioned a golf game, slipped in a reminder about tee time, and left, leaving the apartment unusually quiet.

Stephanie lingered at the kitchen counter, stirring her coffee absentmindedly, the gala replaying in her mind like a loop she couldn't stop. Finally, she dialled Rebecca.

"Hey, Steph," Rebecca answered, her voice bright. "Everything okay?"

Stephanie hesitated, slow breath. "I… I need to talk. Can I come over?"

"Of course. I'll make some tea," Rebecca replied. "You sound like you need it."

At Rebecca's, she traded silk for loungewear but carried the night's weight in her posture. They sat with steaming mugs, and Stephanie let the words pour out.

"It was… a lot, last night," she admitted. "I don't even know where to start."

Rebecca nodded patiently. "Start wherever you need."

Stephanie recounted the gala, beginning with her unexpected role in the charity auction. "They asked me to participate in a dinner-date auction… for charity. I didn't think much of it at first, but—" she paused, glancing at her mug, "—it became intense. People bid on me, and… there was a mystery bidder who won my date."

Rebecca's brow rose; curiosity tempered with empathy. "A mystery bidder?"

Stephanie nodded, voice dropping. "Yes. And then… I danced with Trey. My boss. And—Rebecca, I don't even know what's happening with me. I've loved Ryan… but last night, I realised I don't know if I love him anymore." She let the words hang, raw and trembling. "And I… I'm attracted to Trey. But I don't think he feels the same—or at least, I don't want to assume he does. I'm not sure what to do with any of this."

Rebecca listened quietly, neither judgmental nor shocked. "Steph… I can see it. Your feelings for Ryan… they've been shifting even before the gala. I've noticed how tense you get around him sometimes, or how your thoughts drift elsewhere."

Stephanie swallowed hard. "So… I'm not imagining this?"

"No," Rebecca said firmly. "You're not. And that doesn't make you a bad person. Hearts are messy, and sometimes they change in ways we can't control." She reached out, squeezing Stephanie's hand. "Face it honestly, with yourself first."

Stephanie exhaled, a tear threatening her cheek. "It's just… everything last night—it was overwhelming. The auction, Trey, Ryan… I felt pulled in two directions, and it's exhausting."

Rebecca nodded. "Normal to feel conflicted. But hiding won't make it go away. You need space to figure out what you want—without guilt."

Stephanie sipped her tea, letting the warmth seep in. "Thank you, Rebecca. I don't know what I'd do without you."

"You'd do fine," Rebecca smiled softly. "But it helps to have someone who sees through the chaos. Just… be honest with yourself, Steph. That's the only way forward."

Stephanie nodded, weight a little lighter, though far from gone. The road ahead was unclear, but for the first time since the gala, she felt a faint spark of clarity— and the courage to face truths she'd been avoiding.

The apartment was quiet when Stephanie returned. The city hummed softly outside, but inside, the air felt heavy. Ryan lay on the couch, one arm over his forehead.

"Ugh… another headache," he groaned, voice clipped with irritation.

Stephanie stopped in the doorway, setting her bag down. "Again? Ryan, maybe you should see a doctor. This can't be normal—almost a month now."

He lifted one eye toward her, frustration flickering. "A doctor? For a headache? Stephanie... don't be ridiculous. It's a headache. I'll be fine."

She bit her lip, trying not to push too hard. "You've had them for weeks. Please... for yourself."

Ryan rolled his eyes, sitting up abruptly. "I said I'm fine! Can we not do this?" His tone left no room for argument.

Stephanie exhaled softly, tension coiling in her chest. "Fine," she murmured, retreating to the kitchen. "I'll just start dinner."

The kitchen was dim, shadows stretching across the counters. Stephanie moved carefully, pulling ingredients from cupboards. The gala, Ryan's simmering temper, her tangled emotions—all pressed on her, making her hands tremble.

Reaching for a jar on the top shelf, she misjudged the movement and struck her forehead against a cupboard corner. Pain burst sharply across her brow. She staggered back, clutching the counter, catching her reflection in the toaster: a dark, angry bruise forming beneath her eye.

"Stephanie!"

Ryan was at her side in an instant, concern cutting through his usual sharpness. "What happened? Let me see."

"I... I hit the cupboard door," she admitted shakily. "It's already bruising."

Ryan's jaw tightened as he scanned her face. "God, that's bad. We need ice. Now." His hands hovered near her cheeks, cautious but protective.

"It's not your fault," she whispered.

"Still... I should've been helping you. I hate seeing you hurt like this."

Her chest twisted at the rare vulnerability in his voice. Resentment flared. "You can't control everything, Ryan. I just want to make dinner without arguing... without feeling like everything has to be managed."

He didn't argue. For once, he only stood close, tense and protective, watching the bruise deepen.

Stephanie pressed an ice pack to her cheek. Ryan's hand hovered, hesitant. Silence stretched until he finally broke it.

"You should rest. No cooking. I'll order takeout."

She started to protest, but he had already moved to the phone. Returning, he set the food in front of her and draped a blanket across her shoulders. "Eat. Then lie down. No arguments."

She obeyed, too exhausted to resist, pressing the ice against her throbbing skin. Ryan watched silently, taut with worry.

By morning, the bruise had darkened, shadows blooming across her cheekbone like ink in water. At the kitchen window, Stephanie studied her reflection, fingertips hovering over the tender skin, tracing the swell of colour that throbbed beneath her touch. The soft morning light made the damage more visible, a stark reminder of the storm that had raged the night before.

Ryan leaned against the counter behind her, arms crossed, the quiet tension in his posture betraying the concern he tried to hide. "It's worse than I thought," she murmured, voice low, almost startled by the honesty.

"It'll fade," he replied quietly, though the furrow in his brow and the tight line of his jaw betrayed a deeper worry. He stepped closer, careful, and brushed the edge of the bruise with a light, tentative touch. "I hate seeing you like this," he admitted, his voice rougher than he intended.

Her throat tightened, the words catching in her chest. "I don't want it to mean something it doesn't. Not about us," she whispered, the confession nearly swallowed by the quiet hum of the city outside.

Ryan exhaled sharply, his jaw flexing, eyes darkening with a raw vulnerability he seldom allowed himself to show. "I'm scared, Stephanie. Scared of losing you."

Her chest ached at the admission, a pang of tenderness colliding with the ache that had nothing to do with concern for him. The bruise throbbed beneath his touch—a pulse-quickening reminder of his jealousy, his sharp words, the way his love had begun to feel less like comfort and more like walls closing in.

Later, alone in the quiet kitchen, Stephanie pressed the ice pack gently to her cheek, the cool relief doing little to soothe the turmoil in her heart. Her mind drifted inevitably to Trey—the weight of his hand at the small of her back, the warmth of his gaze, the slow, steady pull of his presence that left her pulse racing in a way she hadn't felt in years. With Trey, she felt seen, not measured, not controlled. Ryan's love, though intense, had begun to feel possessive, like a cage disguised as protection. Trey's presence, by contrast, felt like air—free, intoxicating, undeniable.

She closed her eyes, pressing the ice pack more firmly against her bruised skin, and admitted the truth she'd been struggling to confront: her heart didn't beat for Ryan the way it did for Trey. Not now, not ever. The clarity was sharp, painful, but merciful in its honesty.

The bruise throbbed again, insistent, reminding her that while physical marks fade, the emotional ones—the fractures, the truths laid bare—would linger far longer. Ryan's love had left a mark, yes, but it had also exposed the impossibility of what she had once believed. And deep down, she knew: the cracks in their relationship, made painfully clear the night before, could never truly be mended.

Her hand lingered over the ice pack for a moment longer, then dropped to her lap, trembling slightly. The city beyond the window hummed on, indifferent, while Stephanie's heart recognised the shift she could no longer deny. Trey had changed everything. And for the first time, she understood that some things—some loves—couldn't be reclaimed once the truth was finally seen.

Monday morning, Stephanie dabbed concealer beneath her eye, layering her navy skirt suit over the lingering softness of her silk nightgown. Control mattered. She couldn't afford to look fragile—especially not after the weekend. Especially not now.

At her desk, she tried to lose herself in spreadsheets, fingers flying over the keyboard, counting, calculating, focusing on something—anything—to drown the ache in her chest. But then—

"Morning, Ms. Vale."

The deep timbre of Trey's voice sliced through the office hum, freezing her mid-keystroke. She looked up, heart hammering against her ribs, pulse leaping.

"Morning, Mr. Grayson," she said tightly, forcing evenness into her tone.

His warm smile never appeared. Jaw tight, eyes sharp, he studied her like he could see through every carefully constructed layer she'd worn to hide the truth. "My office. Now."

Stephanie's throat went dry. "I—"

"Now, Stephanie."

The command left no room for argument. A flush of heat rose beneath her concealer, awareness of how poorly she'd masked herself impossible to hide. She rose, gripping her notebook like a shield, and followed him into his office. Each step echoed in her ears, her heartbeat thrumming in tandem with the click of her heels. Trey had seen through her. Of course he had.

The office door closed behind them with a soft click. Trey set his briefcase down with a deliberate thud and moved toward her. One hand lifted her chin, tilting her face toward the light.

"Did he do this to you?" His voice was low, raw, edged with fury that made the air between them tense.

Stephanie froze, breath catching. "I—I hit a cupboard door," she whispered.

Trey's jaw clenched, eyes scanning her face with merciless precision. "Stephanie," he said, the words sharp as a blade, "don't lie to me. Not about this."

Her lips parted, then closed. Heart hammering, she couldn't look away.

"If he laid a hand on you—if Ryan so much as breathed wrong—you tell me now," he pressed, thumb brushing the edge of the bruise, gaze darkening further.

"I swear… it was an accident."

His hand lingered, hovering like a sentinel, before sliding away, yet his eyes never left hers. "Then why," he asked, softer now but no less intense, "do you look like you're carrying the weight of the world?"

Her throat tightened. "I'm… confused."

"About what?"

Her voice trembled, fragile but urgent. "You."

The silence that followed was electric, charged with everything she'd been too afraid to name. Trey's expression shifted—imperceptibly, yet enough. The edge of anger softened, giving way to something darker, more dangerous.

"Stephanie… do you even realise what you're saying?" His voice was low, rough, tasting the words.

Her chest rose and fell with shallow breaths. She wanted to retreat into confusion, to laugh it off—but the ache wouldn't let her. "I don't know what I'm saying. I just… when you're near me, everything feels different. I can't stop thinking about it."

Trey's jaw tightened, a flicker of something dangerous sparking across his features before he drew back slightly, leaving just enough space to remind her of boundaries he wouldn't cross—yet. Restraint radiated from him, taut and palpable, written in every line of his body.

"Stephanie," he said, voice low, steady, agonisingly careful.

Her pulse thundered. Words hovered between confession and fear. He'd stepped back—of course he had. She had no right to speak her feelings; he was her boss. Shame stung sharper than the lingering bruise on her cheek.

Turning, she let her heels click against the hardwood, gripping the door like a lifeline. "Sorry, Mr. Grayson. Please… ignore what I just said."

"Stephanie—wait," Trey's voice came, rougher now, threaded with frustration and something far deeper.

Her breath caught, but she didn't turn. If she faced him now, she'd shatter.

Finally, he spoke again, measured, gentle, carrying the weight of unspoken truths. "Don't ever think what you feel is something to be ashamed of."

Kind. Nothing more. Nothing she could claim. She nodded stiffly, throat tight for words, and slipped out before her carefully constructed resolve could crumble.

Her steps echoed in the empty hallway. Behind her, Trey's office remained still, the weight of his gaze lingering like smoke. Outside, the world continued as usual—but for Stephanie, nothing would ever feel the same again.

The click of the office door echoed, sharp in the quiet space, leaving Trey standing frozen. His chest tightened, fingers curling into fists at his sides, heart hammering like a warning drum. She had no idea what she'd just done, what she'd unleashed. For the first time in years, he realised the battle wasn't about professionalism—it was about keeping himself from losing control entirely.

He sank into his chair with a deliberate exhale, trying to anchor himself. But the second her words, her confession, replayed in his mind, the anchor slipped. Her voice had trembled, raw and honest. Her eyes had clung to him in a way that threatened to shatter every carefully constructed boundary. All he wanted, more than logic or restraint could allow, was to pull her into his arms and never let her go. To feel her warmth, her pulse against his chest, to banish the confusion and fear that shadowed her expression.

He ran a hand over his face, jaw clenched, trying to steady the storm inside him. He couldn't. Every inch of his body ached with the need to close the distance between them, to claim the moment, to taste the danger of giving in. Frustration coiled with longing, and beneath it all, a darker, sharper edge: a recognition that she stirred something in him he hadn't felt in years, something he didn't intend to surrender to anyone.

The careful part of him whispered warnings he couldn't quite obey: She's scared. She's confused. Don't push. Don't ruin this before it's even begun.

But restraint was a fragile veneer. He leaned back in his chair, the polished leather pressing cold beneath him, yet it offered no comfort. Every quiet second that passed felt like an eternity, every memory of her touch, her gaze, an unrelenting temptation. He envisioned her in his arms, her head resting against his chest, the world reduced to the rhythm of their breaths. That fleeting vision became a mantra he couldn't shake.

He knew he would wait—for her, for the truth she hadn't yet spoken aloud. He would wait for the moment she admitted what she truly wanted. But the anticipation was a fire in his veins, and every professional mask he wore felt like it was melting away.

The dinner date he'd won on Friday night lingered in his thoughts, a neutral battlefield where they could untangle the knots of desire, confusion, and fear. It was a chance to understand the depth of her feelings—and a chance, perhaps, for him to finally give into the temptation that had consumed him since he met her.

And yet, even as he sat there, battling the storm inside him, he couldn't stop the one, simple truth from asserting itself with overwhelming force: all he wanted... was to pull her into his arms, shield her, and never let go.

Chapter Eight

By Wednesday, Stephanie had almost convinced herself she could pretend. Pretend she hadn't let her guard slip on Monday, hadn't bared a fragment of herself to Trey that she'd spent weeks—and maybe months—protecting. Pretend he hadn't seen the faint bruise along her cheekbone, hadn't heard the quiet, almost trembling confession she hadn't meant to share, hadn't stepped back like she was fragile, like he might break if he touched her.

The week trudged forward in a haze of stiff politeness, each interaction a careful negotiation of distance. They spoke in clipped sentences, passed each other in the hall with only the merest acknowledgment. But underneath it all, a current pulsed between them, electric and unrelenting, a second heartbeat she couldn't quiet, no matter how hard she tried.

Late that morning, a male's voice carried down the hall. "Delivery for Ms. Vale!"

Stephanie looked up just as a courier rounded the corner, balancing a vase that seemed absurdly large, the blooms spilling like a riot of colour—roses, lilies, tulips, impossibly vivid. Heads turned. Whispers rippled through the office. She felt her cheeks heat instantly, a flutter of embarrassment and something else she refused to name.

The vase landed with a soft thud on her desk, commanding the space as if it belonged there. Nestled between the stems, an envelope practically called to her. Her fingers trembled slightly as she slid it open, careful not to crease the delicate paper.

Looking forward to Saturday night.
—Your dinner date

Her breath hitched. The charity auction, the winning bid, the dinner… she'd spent days trying to convince herself it was just a formality, that it would be awkward but harmless. And now, there it was, impossible to ignore.

"Quite the delivery," came a voice—low, measured, and dangerously close.

Stephanie's head snapped up. Trey stood in the doorway to his office, one shoulder pressed against the frame, arms loosely crossed. He said nothing else, but the way he looked at her—dark, steady, unflinching—made the air feel suddenly thinner, sharper.

She tucked the card quickly back into the bouquet, fingers brushing the blooms almost reverently, and tried to smooth a loose strand of hair behind her ear. "It's… from the auction," she murmured, voice tighter than she intended.

Trey said nothing. He didn't need to. The silence itself weighed on her, pressing in from all sides. He lingered for a heartbeat, gaze unwavering, unreadable, and then, with deliberate composure, he straightened. The door closed behind him with a soft, definitive click that left her pulse hammering in her ears.

Stephanie exhaled shakily, staring at the extravagant flowers, the chaos of the office around her fading into a dull hum. Her pulse throbbed in time with her own racing thoughts. Every petal, every shade of red and white, seemed to vibrate with possibility—and warning.

Her phone buzzed on the desk. Ryan. She answered automatically.

"I'm flying out Friday morning," he said briskly, clipped and businesslike. "Big client meeting. I'll be gone until Sunday night."

Stephanie blinked, startled. "Oh. That's… sudden."

"Don't worry. We'll talk when I'm back." His voice was distracted, already pulling away, and then the line went dead.

She lowered the phone slowly, staring at the blooms dominating her desk. Relief twisted through her chest—Ryan wouldn't be home. She wouldn't have to explain, wouldn't have to manage his jealousy, his not-so-subtle possessiveness. But that relief was tangled with something else entirely: anticipation, fear, excitement.

Stephanie leaned back in her chair, the soft petals brushing her bare arms as she absently traced the rim of the vase with her fingertip. The roses were beautiful— vivid, perfect—but they did little to quiet her restless thoughts. Saturday night loomed like a shadow; her upcoming dinner date shrouded in mystery. She didn't even know who she would be sitting across from, and yet the question of it barely touched the surface of her mind.

Because what consumed her wasn't the anticipation of a stranger—it was the memory of Trey.

His dark, unreadable gaze lingered in her thoughts, a burn she couldn't shake, seared into her as if he were still standing before her. She didn't know whether to dread that intensity—or crave it. Perhaps both.

Her hand stilled on the vase, a shiver chasing down her spine as she admitted, silently, what she had never dared to say aloud: she had never felt this way with Ryan. Not once. Not with all his charm, not with his easy smile, not even in their most tender moments.

Not like this.

Not like Trey.

And the thought terrified her almost as much as it thrilled her.

The flowers sat before her like a quiet promise. And somewhere in her chest, a new kind of pulse began to stir—quick, unrelenting, and impossible to ignore.

Trey closed the office door behind him, the soft click swallowed by the thick wood, and finally allowed himself the stillness he denied in public. He dropped a file on his desk, loosened his tie just enough to let his shoulders release some of the tension, and leaned back against the polished edge of his desk. The room was quiet; the hum of the city below reduced to a distant pulse. Alone at last, he could let the edges of his control slip, though only slightly.

Everything was unfolding exactly as he intended.

Ryan was gone for the weekend, sent away on a "can't-miss" work trip—a trip quietly arranged through channels carefully vetted and discreet. No suspicion. No loose ends. To Stephanie, it would seem a coincidence, mere circumstance. To him, it was opportunity.

The flowers were the first move—a grand gesture, theatrical yet precise. To her, they were from the mysterious "winner" of the charity auction, a token of curiosity and charm. To him, they were a seed. A way of planting a thought, a memory, a question in her mind: Saturday night is waiting. A night that belonged only to them, and them alone.

He straightened, moving to the window, letting the Manhattan skyline stretch endlessly before him. Lights winked and shimmered like scattered stars, a world alive beneath his gaze. Le Jardin Noir awaited—a private dining room tucked atop the city, secured long ago, a neutral stage where nothing could interrupt, nothing could intrude. No office politics, no watchful eyes, no Ryan's shadow. Just them. And everything unspoken between them, waiting to surface.

But as that thought settled, so did something heavier—a quiet flicker of doubt.

Was he pushing too far? Was it right to orchestrate circumstances without her knowledge, to manipulate the flow of her life so carefully? She deserved honesty. She deserved the chance to choose without the weight of his strategy pressing down on her. And yet… he told himself the truth, the one he couldn't voice even in his own head: this wasn't about control. Not really. It was about creating the space she might never dare to carve for herself.

He drew a long, steadying breath, forcing the guilt down into a tight, manageable knot, schooling his expression into the mask of composure he wore so well. Calm. Precise. Patient. Measured. Everything he did had a purpose, and every choice had been weighed against the potential for risk.

His fingers brushed the smooth surface of the desk, tracing the edge almost unconsciously, and for a heartbeat he imagined her there—her eyes on him, her hand brushing against his arm, the way his pulse quickened in ways no one else had ever caused. Desire, restraint, and anticipation coiled together in that impossible mixture, and he let himself hold onto it, careful not to let it overwhelm him.

Saturday night would be the test. Not just a dinner. Not just another encounter in a world filled with boundaries. It would be the night he stopped being the man in the doorway, watching from a distance. It would be the night he had the chance to be the man she might finally—deliberately—choose.

And Trey, as always, would be ready.

Friday morning, Stephanie kissed Ryan goodbye at the door, her lips brushing his cheek in a gesture both tender and rehearsed. Her smile was practiced, her words carefully measured. She didn't mention the dinner she was expected at the next night. It was only dinner, she told herself, a single evening of obligation—nothing more. She didn't need the stress of another argument, not when the fraying edges of their relationship already felt raw. The bruise on her cheek had faded, the angry purple softened to a faint shadow. Appearance mattered. Pride mattered. And she could not, would not, show up broken.

The truth, however, gnawed at her: she still didn't know where the dinner would be held, who it was with, or what they had planned. Just Saturday night. That was all she'd been told. A mystery. A quiet thrill, almost terrifying, curled in her chest whenever she thought of it.

By the time she arrived at the office, the morning was hushed, the building still half-asleep. The faint hum of fluorescent lights and the shuffle of early risers filled the air. Trey's office door was already open, lamplight spilling across the polished surface of his desk, illuminating the sharp lines of his world. Of course he was already there. He always was.

Stephanie took a steadying breath, clutched the file she carried like a lifeline, and tapped lightly against the frame. "Morning, Mr. Grayson," she said, slipping inside.

Trey glanced up from his laptop. His gaze flickered across her face, a faint, unreadable shadow passing over his features before he carefully folded it into professional calm. "Morning, Ms. Vale."

She crossed the room, placing the file on his desk, the leather folder making a soft thud against the wood. Her fingers lingered for just a heartbeat longer than necessary, though she hadn't meant to. The air between them was heavier than usual, charged with a quiet intensity she couldn't—or wouldn't—name.

"You always know what I need before I ask for it. Thank you," Trey said, closing his laptop just enough to give her his full attention. There was no warmth in his tone, yet the weight of that gaze pressed against her chest.

Stephanie forced a polite, small smile. "You're welcome, sir. Let me know if you need anything else." She turned, ready to retreat back to her desk. For a half-beat, she held her breath, a secret hope that he might say more, linger a moment longer. Something. Anything.

But Trey only inclined his head, the picture of controlled authority. "That's all for now."

Her heart sank, but she plastered a smile on her face and stepped back through the doorway. The click of the door closing behind her seemed impossibly loud, echoing like a punctuation mark on a sentence she didn't want to end.

At Her fingers hovered above the keys, then slid across the keyboard almost without meaning—words forming and blurring in the glow of the monitor. The office around her hummed on, the printer, the distant murmur of colleagues, the clink of a coffee cup. None of it reached her. Her mind kept snapping back to him—Trey—back to the way his gaze had lingered, the quiet, almost reproachful restraint when she'd let herself be honest on Monday. He'd stepped back then, given her space, and the silence that followed felt like an answer of its own.

She told herself she was being ridiculous. Stop reading sparks into polite conversation. Stop wanting a man who, by every sensible rule, could not — should not — want her. She'd been the one to say the truth out loud; he'd had his chance to claim her and instead had pulled away. If that wasn't a sign he didn't want her, what was?

But anger at him shifted into something harder and clearer: anger at herself, at the life that had narrowed into duty and quiet resignation. The tenderness that might once have existed with Ryan had been ground down to habit. He no longer reached for the parts of her that needed reaching. He wanted compliance, not companionship, possession, not partnership.

The thought settled in her like a blade tempered in cold water — bright, precise, unarguable. She drew a long breath, feeling the resolve set behind her ribs. She was done pretending. She would not live by someone else's small, safe rules any longer.

Her gaze wandered to the window, the city unfurling before her in endless lights and motion, a glittering reminder of possibilities she had once refused to see. Somewhere out there waited a choice—a different kind of life, one she could seize if only she dared. Trey had stirred something she thought long buried: the hunger to be seen, to be wanted for who she truly was. And whether or not it was him, one truth had become undeniable—she deserved more than the hollow shell of love Ryan offered. She deserved to be cherished, to be chosen without condition or restraint.

Her hand pressed flat against the desk, steadying herself, anchoring her resolve. The path ahead was uncertain, a leap into the unknown, but clarity burned inside her like a beacon. Never again would she allow herself to be diminished. Never again would she be silenced, possessed, or bound by someone else's control.

Not by Ryan.

Not by anyone.

Not ever again.

At midday, the reception desk buzzed, and a delivery man walked in with a long white box. Stephanie frowned, her pulse quickening as he handed it directly to her. Curious glances flicked her way from a few coworkers as she signed for it.

She opened the lid, and her breath caught. Nestled against crisp tissue paper was a single, perfect red rose. Elegant. Bold. Undeniably deliberate. Tied around the stem was a small cream envelope with her name in neat handwriting.

Her fingers trembled slightly as she slid the card free.

Saturday, 8 p.m.

Private Dining Room.

Le Jardin.

I'll be waiting.

Her heart skipped, heat rushing through her as she traced the words. She lifted the rose to her nose, the delicate scent filling her senses, grounding her in a moment that felt too unreal to be hers.

"Another delivery?"

Trey's voice cut across her thoughts, smooth but closer than she expected. She jumped, spinning in her chair to see him standing in the doorway of his office, one brow arched.

"Oh—" Stephanie clutched the rose to her chest, as though shielding it. "Yes, um… another delivery." Her voice sounded thin, uncertain even to her own ears.

His gaze lingered on the rose for a long moment, precise and unreadable, before lifting slowly to meet hers. The air between them felt heavier somehow, charged with everything that neither of them dared speak aloud.

"Secret admirer?" he asked, voice calm, measured.

"No, sir. Well… I don't think so," she replied evenly, forcing her pulse to slow, trying not to let the quickening of her heart betray her. "Just the dinner date. Letting me know when and where to be."

Trey's lips curved into the faintest of smiles—a subtle, almost imperceptible acknowledgment. "Very good," he said, voice steady, controlled, carrying that quiet authority she always found simultaneously infuriating and magnetic.

Without another word, he turned, the motion fluid and deliberate, leaving no room for argument, and disappeared back into his office. Stephanie exhaled softly, her fingers lingering on the delicate petals of the rose, her heart still racing despite the fact that she had no idea who had sent it.

Well. That proved something. Trey wasn't interested in her—if he had been, there would have been more than a flicker of acknowledgment, more than that slight, controlled smile. A secret admirer, clearly, wasn't him. Disappointment pricked at her chest, but she forced herself to accept the truth. Trey was not part of her personal future.

She needed to move on. Tomorrow night, she would meet this person—the one who had clearly gone to the trouble of arranging a proper dinner date. Maybe they would be interesting. Maybe she would like them. And if she allowed herself to be open, perhaps this was the start of something real, something that didn't come with impossible longing or unattainable hearts.

Stephanie straightened in her chair, setting the rose carefully in its vase, and breathed deeply. Tomorrow was a chance. And she would take it.

Saturday afternoon, a cheerful knock at the door announced Rebecca's arrival. She stepped in carrying a paper bag that smelled of fresh bagels and warm coffee. "I'm here to gossip and help you get ready," she said with a grin, setting the bag down on the counter.

Stephanie laughed softly and pulled her friend into a quick hug. "I'm so glad you're here," she said, relief threading her voice.

They settled at the kitchen table, coffee steaming in their mugs, bagels spread between them. The chatter was easy at first—catching up on work, joking about coworkers—but soon, Stephanie's nerves got the better of her. She took a deep breath, staring into her coffee as if it would give her courage.

"Rebecca... I... I'm leaving Ryan," she said finally, her voice barely above a whisper.

The words hung in the air, heavier than any bagel or mug of coffee. Rebecca set her own mug down, eyes wide but soft with understanding. "Steph... are you sure?" she asked gently, reaching across the table to squeeze Stephanie's hand.

Stephanie nodded, though her chest tightened with both fear and relief. "I've been trying to ignore it, trying to convince myself it's just a rough patch... but it's not. I'm not happy with him. I don't think I've been happy for a long time."

Rebecca's expression softened further, a mix of empathy and encouragement. "Then you're making the right choice. It's terrifying, but it's the right choice. You deserve to be with someone who makes you feel alive, not trapped."

Stephanie exhaled slowly, the weight she'd been carrying all week easing slightly. "I'm scared," she admitted, voice trembling. "But... I can't keep pretending anymore."

Rebecca smiled warmly. "Then let's focus on something fun for today. Dinner tonight—you're stepping into a new chapter, Steph. Let's make sure you feel ready for it."

Stephanie managed a small laugh, taking a sip of her coffee. For the first time that day, she felt like she could breathe—and maybe even smile at what the night ahead might bring.

Rebecca leaned back in her chair, studying Stephanie with a teasing grin. "So… tell me about this dinner date. Who's the lucky guy?"

Stephanie rolled her eyes, though heat crept up her cheeks. "I don't know. That's the thing. He never left his name—just… notes. Flowers. Tonight's all I know." She gestured toward the single rose in the vase on the counter, its petals catching the afternoon light. "It's… strange, isn't it?"

Rebecca tilted her head, a mischievous spark lighting her eyes. "Mysterious and romantic. I like it already. Maybe it's your boss?"

Stephanie muttered, nibbling at her bagel. "Mysterious, yes. Romantic? I'm not so sure. And I know it's not Trey."

"How do you know?"

She sighed, glancing down. "He asked me if I had a secret admirer. He didn't care if I did or not. That should have been enough of a clue. And… I was stupid enough to let it slip on Monday that I had feelings for him. He stepped back. Not shocked, not angry… just uncomfortable. For all I know, this guy could be some forty-something executive with a bad sense of humour who thought he could buy himself some company for the night."

Rebecca leaned forward, eyes sparkling. "Or maybe he's someone who saw you and thought you were worth every effort—and more."

Stephanie's lips curved faintly, though a tug of uncertainty lingered. "It doesn't matter who he is. It's just dinner. I'm not looking for anything… not yet. I just… need a night that's not about fighting with Ryan. A night to breathe."

Rebecca's grin softened into something warmer, more tender. "Then that's exactly what you'll have. And if this mystery man turns out to be awful, you text me one word—bagel—and I'll come rescue you. No questions asked."

Stephanie laughed, a light, genuine sound that eased some of the tightness in her chest. For the first time that afternoon, she felt a little spark of excitement.

Later, upstairs in her bedroom, Rebecca sifted through Stephanie's closet with gleeful determination. Dresses landed on the bed in a rainbow of fabrics while Stephanie stood uncertainly by the mirror.

"Not too much," she pleaded. "It's just dinner. I don't even know who I'm meeting."

Rebecca shot her a look. "Steph, this is about you. Not him. You're dressing for yourself. Something that makes you feel strong and beautiful. That's all."

Stephanie hesitated, then finally reached for a simple yet elegant black dress—a piece she'd always liked but rarely had the courage to wear. She held it up, uncertainty flickering in her eyes.

Rebecca clapped her hands. "Perfect. Classic. Confident. And just enough mystery to match your evening."

For the first time in weeks, maybe months, she caught her reflection and thought… I don't look like a woman weighed down by someone else's shadow. I look like me.

Rebecca stood behind Stephanie with a curling iron in hand, her tongue poking out the corner of her mouth in concentration. "Hold still. One wrong move and you'll look like you stuck your finger in a socket."

Stephanie laughed nervously, staring at her reflection in the mirror. Piece by piece, her friend was working magic—soft curls cascading down, framing her face in a way that softened her features but gave her an elegance she rarely saw in herself.

When Rebecca leaned back to survey her work, she grinned. "There. Effortless but polished. A little mystery, a little glamour. Men will trip over themselves trying to figure you out."

Next came makeup—Rebecca kept it light but deliberate. A touch of shimmer at Stephanie's eyes made the green flecks pop, a sweep of mascara lent her lashes an almost doe-like quality, and the faintest blush brought warmth to her cheeks. The finishing touch was a lipstick the shade of deep rose. Not bold, not flashy, but enough to make her lips look soft and kissable.

When Stephanie finally slipped into the black dress, Rebecca clasped her hands dramatically. "Oh, sweetheart. Ryan Carter who? You look like a woman who knows her own worth. If your mystery man doesn't faint the second you walk in, I'll eat my bagel."

Stephanie glanced at the mirror again, her throat tightening. She did look… different. Stronger. Like the version of herself she wanted to believe in.

By the time the Uber pulled up, the butterflies in her stomach were fluttering so hard she wasn't sure she could breathe. Rebecca hugged her tightly at the door. "You've got this. Go, eat, laugh, maybe even flirt a little. And remember—if he turns out to be a creep—"

"Bagel," Stephanie finished with a watery smile.

"Exactly." Rebecca winked and opened the car door for her. "Now go knock his socks off."

As the car pulled away, Stephanie caught her reflection faintly in the window. For the first time in so long, she didn't just look ready. She felt it.

Chapter Nine

Trey had never been a man to fidget, but tonight the cuff of his shirt had suffered for it. He smoothed it again, tugged at the edge of his tie, checked the time for the fifth time in three minutes. Every detail had been calculated—the private dining room, the soft amber glow of the lighting, the carefully selected wine that would feel effortless, not ostentatious. He hadn't arranged this to impress her with wealth; he'd arranged it so she could breathe. So, they could exist in a world where it was just the two of them, where expectations, titles, and everyone else's opinions could vanish for a few precious hours.

And yet, when the maître d' opened the door and ushered her in, his carefully constructed composure cracked like glass.

Stephanie stepped inside, and for the briefest instant, Trey forgot how to breathe. The soft curls spilling over her shoulders caught the light in a halo of warmth. The curve of her black dress hugged her frame in all the right ways, modest yet daring in the quietest sense. And those eyes—bright, uncertain, luminous—seemed to flicker with something unspoken. She wasn't polished perfection tonight; she was raw, hopeful, herself. And it was devastating.

She paused just inside, clutching her bag to her chest, lips parting slightly as her gaze swept the room and landed squarely on him. Surprise flickered, delicate and fleeting. Of course, she hadn't expected him—of course she hadn't imagined the full extent of his intentions.

Trey rose slowly from his chair, each movement deliberate, measured. He wanted to savour her reaction, the subtle pulse in her throat, the catch of her breath, the way her hands tightened briefly around the bag. He wanted to imprint every detail—the curve of her shoulders, the faint sheen of nervousness on her skin, the way she was both graceful and slightly fragile in a way only he seemed to notice.

"Stephanie," he said, low, steady, every syllable charged with the restraint he'd exercised all week. He stepped closer, close enough to catch the faint trace of her perfume, close enough to see the slight tremor in her hands, the glint of anticipation—or was it doubt? —in her eyes.

"You…" she whispered, almost to herself, gaze flicking between him and the room, searching for confirmation. "It was you?"

He didn't answer immediately. He let her question hang in the air, a delicate thread connecting them across the small space. His gaze softened imperceptibly, yet there was an edge to it—something protective, possessive, undeniably alive.

"Yes," he said finally, his voice low, deliberate, carrying both certainty and something more vulnerable beneath the control. "It was me."

The words hung between them, suspended like fragile glass. Stephanie swallowed, a faint shiver running through her as if the air itself had thickened. Trey took a measured step closer, careful not to crowd her, yet the space between them seemed to vibrate with every unspoken desire he had contained for days—weeks, perhaps.

For a heartbeat, they simply stood there, suspended in the quiet intimacy of the private room. The hum of the city beyond the windows faded into nothing, leaving only the fragile pulse of tension, the silent rhythm of shared breaths. Everything Trey had been holding back—longing, need, restrained fire— pressed against him, whispering a single, undeniable truth: he wanted her closer.

Close enough to feel the warmth of her, the subtle rise and fall of her chest, close enough to let his fingers brush hers if only for a heartbeat. Close enough to finally close the distance he had kept at bay for far too long.

And in that moment, watching realisation dawn in her eyes, Trey knew that every calculated risk, every careful manoeuvre, had been worth it. Tonight wasn't about business, charity, or appearances. Tonight was about her. Tonight was about them.

Her whisper lingered in the air—It was you? —and Trey felt it vibrate through his chest more than his ears.

She stood, clutching her bag like a shield, yet her eyes betrayed her completely. Wide, luminous, shimmering with relief rather than disappointment. That single truth hit him harder than any argument or confrontation ever could. She had hoped it was him. She had trusted, even in the smallest way, that he would be the one.

Trey's instinct screamed to close the space between them, to sweep the bag aside, take her hand, and reassure her that she wasn't wrong to feel what she felt. But he forced himself into stillness. Not yet. If he moved too fast, if he took too much, too soon, he would shatter the fragile trust she had placed in him merely by showing up.

"Yes," he said again, quieter this time, stepping back half a pace, deliberately inviting her deeper into the room. "I thought it was time you knew."

Her breath hitched, delicate and audible. She moved cautiously, like someone stepping into territory they weren't entirely certain they belonged in. Trey pulled out her chair with a soft, deliberate gesture, his hand brushing only the back of it rather than her shoulder. A line he desperately wanted to cross burned through his veins, but he didn't. Not yet.

As he settled into his seat, he allowed himself a moment to study her in the soft glow of the candlelight. The faint shadow of the bruise—mostly faded, hidden beneath carefully applied makeup—was still visible, and it made something primal clench in his chest. Anger, protectiveness, desire—all tangled together— but he forced it aside. Tonight wasn't about Ryan. Tonight wasn't about fury or revenge. Tonight was about her.

"You look beautiful," he said, carefully measured, deliberate, carrying more weight than he intended.

Her cheeks warmed instantly. Her eyes darted away briefly, then returned to his, that delicate flicker of shyness and uncertainty—pleasure even—lighting her gaze. It was enough to unsettle him completely.

Careful, he reminded himself, sinking back slightly in the chair. This isn't about winning. It's about letting her see you.

He leaned back, shoulders relaxing just enough to seem at ease, smile softening into something warmer. "Shall we order?"

But beneath the calm veneer, his heart was a storm. Every second she sat across from him—the tilt of her head, the subtle rise and fall of her shoulders, the way her gaze met his only for fleeting moments—felt like the first step of something that might consume him entirely. Something he wasn't sure he would be able to stop.

Her heart hadn't stopped pounding since stepping into the private dining room. Trey. Her boss. The man she had tried—and spectacularly failed—to push out of her thoughts for weeks, maybe months.

She had half expected to be mistaken. A wrong room. A wrong restaurant. Perhaps it was just her imagination playing tricks. But then he had spoken, calm, steady, deliberate: *"Yes. I thought it was time you knew."*

It had been him. All along.

Now she sat across from him at a table that suddenly felt far too intimate, hands folded tightly in her lap to stop the trembling. Candlelight danced over his face, accentuating the angles of his jaw, the taut line of his shoulders, the quiet command he carried in every gesture. And yet, underneath it all, she thought she glimpsed something more fragile—something restrained, flickering just beneath the surface, as if he were holding back an avalanche of feeling.

"I... I didn't expect it to be you," she admitted, voice trembling, fragile and small in the hush of the room.

His gaze never wavered. Calm. Controlled. Unyielding. "And now that you know?"

She drew in a measured breath, willing herself to sound steadier than she felt. "I don't know what to think," she whispered, hating how uncertain, how exposed, it sounded.

Trey didn't flinch. He didn't rush to fill the silence. He simply leaned back, eyes locked on hers, studying her as if she were the only thing in the room worth seeing, worth understanding.

"Then don't think yet," he said quietly, his voice low, velvety, a tether that anchored her without touching. "Just... be here."

The simplicity of it nearly undid her. No demands. No sharp edges. Just space. Permission. Relief softened her shoulders almost imperceptibly, and she allowed herself a hesitant sip of wine.

The first course arrived, and they ate in companionable silence, the quiet punctuated only by soft clinks of cutlery and the occasional low murmur of polite conversation filtered in from the rest of the room. When he spoke, it was gentle, precise, every word aimed just for her. She laughed quietly at one of his subtle, dry jokes—a sound that startled her because it felt so unguarded, so effortlessly real. She couldn't remember the last time laughter had come so easily.

Then, a small brush. His hand on the table, just inches from hers. Nothing more. Nothing less. And still… it stole her breath. He didn't reach for her. Didn't close the distance. But the mere nearness of him sent a shiver racing through her, awareness blooming in every nerve, setting her pulse alight.

She tried to anchor herself in something tangible—her plate, the candlelight, the soft hum of the city outside—but it was useless. Every time his gaze lingered, every time his voice softened, she felt herself unravelling. Her thoughts scattered, and her carefully constructed walls began to crack.

And yet—for the first time in what felt like years—she didn't want to hold the pieces together.

She let herself lean just a little closer to the warmth radiating from his side, let herself inhale the faint trace of his cologne, let herself notice the way his eyes never left hers, tracking, attentive, patient. Every second with him was a promise she couldn't yet name, a storm she wasn't sure she was ready to weather, and still—she ached for it.

Trey watched her with the same careful intensity, the restraint of a man who wanted everything and nothing all at once. He didn't push. He didn't demand. And yet, the quiet pull between them was undeniable, wrapping around them both like a tether neither had the courage—or the will—to cut.

Her pulse stuttered, her chest tight, and somewhere deep inside, a part of her surrendered, just a fraction, to the inevitable: she was falling, quietly, irresistibly, for him.

Plates cleared, the wine a gentle warmth in her veins, Stephanie felt almost dizzy—not from the alcohol, but from Trey. His presence filled the room, steady, unyielding, and yet far gentler than she had ever expected.

"There's something I need to tell you," he said at last, leaning forward, forearms braced against the table, gaze fixed on hers as though nothing else in the world mattered.

Her fingers stilled around the stem of her glass. "What is it?"

His jaw flexed once before he spoke. "I have feelings for you, Stephanie. Strong ones. This isn't a passing fancy or some distraction—it's real. I need you to know that. And I'm hoping…" His voice roughened, just slightly. "I'm hoping you feel at least some of it too."

Her breath caught, words snagging in her throat. "I…"

He gestured faintly to the room, the flowers, the hush, the candlelight. "This dinner—it wasn't about impressing you. I chose this because I wanted us on even ground. Not me as your boss, not inside an office where walls press too close. Just us. Here."

The pause he allowed was deliberate, weighted, his eyes unwavering. "Monday morning, I stepped back because you needed space. Time to breathe. Time to decide what you want—without me pressing in."

Her pulse thundered, a fragile ache blooming in her chest. "You planned all of this… for me?"

"Not only for you," he said softly, his eyes darkening, vulnerable in a way she had never seen. "For us."

The air between them shifted—thick with unspoken promises, charged with possibility.

Trey rose slowly, his chair sliding back, and extended his hand across the small space between them. "Dance with me."

"There's no music," she whispered, startled.

A smile curved his lips, quiet but devastating. "Then we'll make our own."

Her hand trembled as it slipped into his. The moment his fingers closed around hers, the trembling stopped. He drew her to her feet, steady, unhurried, guiding her into the open space between table and window.

And then she was in his arms. Closer than she had ever allowed herself to imagine, her cheek brushing against the solid warmth of his chest. His hand found her waist, firm but reverent, while his other held hers as though it were something precious.

They moved—barely more than a sway—but it was everything. The city's glow beyond the glass blurred into insignificance. All that existed was the press of his body, the cadence of his breath stirring her hair, the anchoring certainty of his touch.

Her heart thundered. She tilted her face up, caught helplessly by the pull of his gaze.

And then he kissed her.

Not a tentative brush, not a stolen test of boundaries—but a real kiss. His mouth claimed hers with a slow, devastating certainty, stealing the air from her lungs and scattering her thoughts like ashes in a storm. It was deep, deliberate, consuming—the kind of kiss that rewrote everything she thought she knew about herself.

Stephanie gasped softly against him, and Trey answered with a low sound that vibrated through his chest, pulling her closer until no space remained between them. His hand slid lower, anchoring at the small of her back, holding her as though he would never let go.

The kiss was not hurried. It was thorough, patient, an exploration that savoured her. Every stroke of his lips against hers lingered, deliberate, a slow undoing. And with each breath stolen, with each press of his mouth, she fell deeper into something she could no longer resist.

Her fingers fisted in his shirt, clinging as her knees weakened, as if the only thing keeping her standing was the strength of his arms. Heat rushed through her veins, pulsing in her chest, her skin, her very bones.

And yet—beneath the fire, beneath the wild rush—there was something else. Something achingly tender. His mouth softened, coaxing instead of taking, reverent in a way that undid her more than any hunger ever could.

And in that moment—the press of his lips, the gentleness threaded through the passion—Stephanie knew. She had never, ever felt this with Ryan. Not in all their years together. Not once. With Trey, it was as though her heart had only just remembered how to beat.

Her world spun—not with confusion this time, but with a clarity so sharp it hurt. This was what it meant to be kissed. To be wanted. To be seen.

When they finally broke apart, breath ragged, she found herself staring into eyes that mirrored her own shock, her own hunger, her own terrifying relief.

Trey rested his forehead against hers, his breath warm against her lips, as though even now he couldn't bear to put distance between them. His voice came out rough, low, edged with all the restraint he had fought for weeks.

"You have no idea," he whispered, "how long I've wanted to do that."

Her lips trembled, her heart still racing. The truth slipped out before she could stop it, fragile but irrevocable.

"Then we've both been waiting," she breathed. "Because I've never wanted anyone like this… not ever."

The admission hung in the space between them, delicate and dangerous, and she knew with absolute certainty—there was no going back.

Trey held her close, his forehead resting lightly against hers, breath mingling with hers in the fragile space between them. His eyes—dark, searching—burned with something she had never seen so openly in him before. Vulnerability. Hope. Longing stripped of all defences.

"Stephanie," he said slowly, each word deliberate, measured, as though he was afraid to break the moment, "I want… I want to give this—us—a real chance.

I know you're with Ryan. I know it complicates everything. But I'll wait. I'll give you as much time as you need to figure out what you truly want."

Her chest tightened, her throat thick with emotion. The sincerity in his voice, the careful way he held her, the raw honesty shining through his restraint—it made the decision she had been agonising over for weeks feel suddenly lighter. Not reckless. Not shameful. Inevitable.

"Trey…" Her voice wavered, but her resolve didn't. She lifted her chin, needing him to see the truth in her eyes. "I've already decided. I told my girlfriend today—I'm leaving Ryan. I can't… I can't keep pretending anymore. Not with him. Not with myself."

Relief flickered across Trey's face, but it wasn't just relief. It was deeper, richer—like the sudden warmth of sun after a long winter. Yet even then, he didn't rush. He didn't let joy splinter the careful restraint he'd promised her. Instead, he lifted a hand, brushing his thumb gently over her cheek, pausing on the faint trace of a bruise still ghosting beneath her makeup. The tenderness of it undid her more than the kiss had.

"You have no idea how long I've waited to hear you say that," he murmured, voice low, hoarse with the effort of control. "I told myself I'd be patient, that I'd give you space. But hearing you say it, hearing you choose yourself—choose us—it's everything."

Stephanie leaned into his touch, letting the tension of weeks, months, years fall away all at once. The weight of her decision was heavy, yes, but not crushing. For the first time, it felt like release. Like she was finally breathing on her own again.

"I… I'm scared," she admitted softly, her lips brushing his thumb as she spoke. "I've never done this before. I've never just… chosen me."

His hand cupped her face, steady, sure, his gaze locked on hers with unwavering intensity. "Then we'll do it together. Step by step. No rush. No pressure. But right now, you don't have to be afraid. Not with me."

A shaky laugh slipped from her lips, caught between disbelief and relief. "I think I… I can trust you with that."

"Good," he whispered. The word felt like a vow.

He leaned in then, slow and deliberate, not pulling her to him but waiting for her to meet him halfway. And when she did, their lips brushed—not a question this time, not a test of boundaries, but a promise. A mutual acknowledgment that whatever came next, they would face it together. Not as a secret. Not as a mistake. As something real.

Stephanie's chest fluttered wildly, exhilaration and disbelief flooding her veins in equal measure. She could feel the warmth of his body against hers, the steady, grounding rhythm of his heartbeat, the calm assurance in his eyes that matched the yearning she had been trying to bury for far too long.

When they parted, she lingered close, her smile unsteady but genuine. "I... I don't want the night to end," she whispered, half afraid of the admission, half needing him to know.

Trey's hand slid to the small of her back, steadying her, anchoring her against the storm of her own emotions. His lips brushed her temple as he answered, voice a low promise. "Then it doesn't have to. We can go dancing. Walk the city streets until sunrise. Whatever you want."

Her pulse quickened at the invitation, at the freedom threaded through his words. She tilted her head back, meeting his gaze with something almost like wonder. "Dancing," she said softly, the word trembling with anticipation. "I want to dance with you."

A slow smile spread across his face, devastating and tender all at once. "Then that's what we'll do."

Stephanie and Trey slipped into the jazz lounge like two secrets finding their way into the same hidden corner of the city. Nestled between two weathered brownstones, the place was unmarked except for a small brass plaque and a single lantern casting golden light across the steps. Inside, the world shifted—warm amber hues poured over polished wood floors, low chandeliers flickered like candle flames, and the soft scent of aged whiskey mingled with gardenias tucked in glass vases on each table. It felt like stepping back in time, into a world untouched by rush or noise.

A trio played in the corner—a piano, an upright bass, and a saxophone weaving together a melody that was slow, sultry, almost sinful in its tenderness. The sound didn't just fill the room, it wrapped around it, a velvet ribbon drawing people close. Couples leaned together in quiet corners, swaying in rhythms only they could hear, whispering into each other's skin.

But for Stephanie, the room narrowed until it held only one person. Trey.

He guided her onto the dance floor with a confidence that felt both natural and reverent, like he had been waiting for this exact moment. His hand enveloped hers, warm and steady, while his other hovered just at the small of her back before settling, firm but careful. The polished wood was cool beneath her heels, but her skin burned everywhere he touched.

The first step was tentative, a shy test of trust—but then the music found them. The rhythm slipped under their feet, into their bones, and suddenly it felt as though they had done this a hundred times before.

Stephanie's breath caught when his chest brushed against hers. His presence was steady, grounding, yet every turn of his body pressed her closer into a space where there was no escape—and no desire for one. Her fingers curled lightly against his shoulder, tingling with the awareness of his strength beneath the crisp fabric of his jacket. The restraint she had always admired in him seemed to ease, unravelling with every sway, replaced by something more urgent.

And his eyes—God, his eyes. They never left hers. Dark, intent, searing in their honesty, they spoke in ways no words ever had. He leaned closer, not enough to claim, but enough to let her see the desire he no longer bothered to mask. Their foreheads almost brushed, their breath mingled, and her heartbeat thundered so loud she was certain he could feel it.

The saxophone's sultry cry lingered in the air as he finally closed the distance.

His lips found hers—not tentative, not testing—but slow and consuming, a kiss that was equal parts reverence and hunger. He kissed her like she was something precious and yet something he had craved for far too long. Her fingers fisted in the fabric of his jacket, holding on as the room dissolved around them. The city, the music, even the lingering shadow of Ryan ceased to exist. There was only Trey. Only this.

When their lips parted at last, just enough for breath, his forehead remained against hers, his voice low and rough, shaped by restraint that trembled at the edges.

"I want to give us a real chance," he said, each word measured, heavy with meaning. "But I know you're still with Ryan. I don't want to push you. I'll wait. As long as it takes—I'll wait until you know what you truly want."

Stephanie's chest ached at the sincerity etched into his words. She could feel it—the patience, the quiet strength, the promise that he wouldn't take what wasn't freely given.

He drew back just enough to brush a strand of hair from her cheek, his fingers lingering with aching tenderness. "I want you to come home with me," he murmured, soft and deliberate. "But only if you want to. No pressure, no rush. We'll go at your pace. Always."

Her lips trembled, her voice fragile but steady as she lifted her gaze to his. "I... I want to," she whispered, and the honesty of it made her whole body tremble.

Something softened in his expression then, as though a weight he'd been carrying finally eased. His smile was quiet, devastating in its gentleness, curving with reassurance instead of triumph. He squeezed her hand lightly, a silent vow.

"Then let's go," he said simply.

Their fingers intertwined effortlessly, as though they had always been meant to fit. Together they stepped out of the lounge and into the cool night. The city stretched before them in gold and silver, streetlights glimmering like stars scattered at their feet. Stephanie's nerves hummed with anticipation, but beneath the flutter was a steady, undeniable certainty.

For the first time in years—maybe forever—she knew exactly where she wanted to be. With Trey. On her terms.

And as the city whispered around them, she let herself believe in the impossible: that this was the beginning of something real.

Chapter Ten

Trey's penthouse wasn't what Stephanie expected. She'd imagined sleek, sterile minimalism—glass, chrome, and the cold touch of money. Instead, the space was curated with a quiet elegance that surprised her. Clean lines in muted greys and deep blues gave way to warmth—shelves lined with books that looked well-worn, art pieces that felt chosen, not collected, and soft lighting that gave the entire place a lived-in intimacy.

But it was the view that stole her breath. The floor-to-ceiling windows framed the city, Manhattan glittering beneath them like scattered diamonds across black velvet. Stephanie stood just inside, her clutch still dangling from her fingers, staring out as though the skyline might swallow her whole.

"It's… beautiful," she whispered, almost afraid to break the spell.

Behind her, Trey set his keys in a shallow bowl and loosened his jacket, his eyes never leaving her. A small, almost self-conscious smile curved his mouth. "It's home," he said quietly. "But it's better with you in it."

The words, simple and unadorned, caught at her chest.

He guided her into the living room, where low amber light washed over a plush sofa and a coffee table stacked with well-thumbed novels. He busied himself in the open kitchen, grinding beans and pouring hot water, the rich aroma of coffee soon filling the space. The sound of the city outside—the muted hum of traffic, the occasional horn—seemed to fade, as though the walls themselves kept the world at bay.

On the couch, conversation flowed easily, unspooling into confessions neither had meant to share. Between words came kisses—soft at first, tentative, testing. Then longer, deeper, unguarded. Trey cradled her face as if she were breakable, his thumb brushing along the delicate line of her jaw. Every kiss was measured but lingering, unspoken vows whispered against her lips.

When he finally drew back, their breaths mingling, Stephanie rested her forehead to his. Her hand pressed against his chest, feeling the steady beat of his heart beneath the fabric of his shirt.

"Trey," she murmured, voice trembling with both want and resolve. "I want… I would love to make love to you. More than anything. But I can't—not yet. Not until I've told Ryan it's over. I need to do this right."

For a moment, fear clawed at her—fear of disappointment, of rejection, of that familiar sharpness she'd come to expect from Ryan. But Trey's gaze only softened. He didn't falter. He didn't press. His hand closed more firmly over hers, grounding her.

"I get it," he said at last, voice low, rough with restraint. "I don't want to be something secret. Or stolen. I want you when you're ready. Completely. No halfway."

Her throat tightened, emotion swelling sharp and sweet. She kissed him once more, slow and lingering, as if sealing the promise between them.

Hours blurred, woven from shared laughter, whispered stories, and kisses that deepened but never demanded more. The city outside shifted toward midnight, lights blinking against the velvet dark. And still, she didn't want to leave.

Eventually Trey rose, his movements unhurried, deliberate. He held out his hand, his voice lower now, stripped of command, edged with vulnerability. "Stay."

It wasn't an order. Not even a request. It was a plea.

Her heart stumbled, but her decision was already made. She slid her hand into his, letting him lead her down the short hallway into his bedroom.

The space mirrored the rest of his home—warm, thoughtful. Dark wood furniture balanced by pale linens, the bed wide and inviting. Lamps cast a soft glow across the room, blurring the edges into something cocoon-like, safe.

Trey pulled a T-shirt from a drawer, offering it with a crooked smile that tugged at only one corner of his mouth. "So, your dress doesn't get crushed."

When she emerged from the bathroom, the shirt falling loose around her thighs, his eyes softened. His lips curved faintly. "You look a hell of a lot better in that than I ever did."

She laughed, the sound light, nervous, but it filled the room in a way that made his chest ache.

He didn't rush her. Didn't touch until she came closer. Then, with the same reverence he had shown all night, he pulled back the covers and waited. She slid beneath them, her body taut with anticipation, yet tempered by an unfamiliar sense of safety.

When he joined her, there was no heat of demand, no urgency. He simply drew her against him; her cheek pressed to the warmth of his chest. His arm curved around her, strong and protective, his heartbeat thrumming steady beneath her ear like a lullaby meant only for her.

Stephanie exhaled, her body softening, the last of her tension unspooling at last. "This feels… right," she whispered, almost afraid of the truth of it.

Trey kissed the crown of her head, his lips lingering there as though sealing a vow. His embrace was gentle yet unyielding, a fortress and a promise all at once.

"It is," he murmured into her hair. "It always will be."

They hadn't made love that night—but in the way he kept her close, in the way his arm never loosened around her, Stephanie felt more cherished, more wanted, than she ever had in her life. No frantic touches, no demands for more—just the simple, steady truth of him holding her as if she were something precious. Wrapped in his warmth, she drifted into sleep certain of two things: she wasn't alone anymore, and she was exactly where she belonged.

The first light of dawn crept into the room, a pale silver wash that softened the hard lines of the city skyline. The vast glass windows blurred into morning glow, and Stephanie stirred against the solid breadth of Trey's chest. For a moment, she simply lay there, lashes fluttering, her cheek pillowed against him. She listened to the slow, steady rhythm of his heartbeat—an anchor that kept the chaos of her thoughts at bay.

It was so different from waking beside Ryan. With Ryan, mornings were sharp edges and silence, a weight pressing down on her chest before the day even began. But here—wrapped in Trey's heat, his scent, the quiet surety of his presence—she felt unhurried. Safe.

Trey shifted, murmuring low in his sleep, his arm tightening instinctively around her waist. "Stay a little longer," he rasped, voice rough with dreams, husky with a vulnerability she'd never heard from him in the office.

Her lips curved into a smile against his chest, her heart tugging unexpectedly. Tilting her head back just enough, she studied him in the dawn light. His hair was tousled, his jaw shadowed, his mouth softened in sleep. Without the armour of control he wore at work, he looked different—almost boyish, undeniably human.

"I didn't mean to fall asleep," she whispered, a quiet laugh threading through the words.

His dark eyes opened slowly, focusing on her with a steadiness that made her breath catch. "I'm glad you did," he said simply. "I liked holding you."

The raw honesty in his tone sent warmth flooding her chest. She pressed her palm flat against his shirt, feeling the heat of his skin beneath, the strength of the man who had spent the whole night proving restraint was its own kind of power. "It was... the best night's sleep I've had in a long time."

His gaze softened further, his hand sliding up her back as he bent to press a kiss to her forehead—slow, lingering, reverent. "Good. That's all I wanted for you. To feel safe. To rest."

Her throat tightened. No one had ever said that to her before. Not Ryan, not anyone. The simple truth of it pierced deeper than grand declarations ever could.

She lifted her face, her breath brushing his lips, and he met her halfway. Their kiss was unhurried, a tender echo of the night before, carrying a promise more powerful than passion. When he drew back, he rested his forehead against hers, eyes closing as he murmured, "No rush. Whenever you're ready. Whatever you need—I'll be here."

Stephanie's chest ached at the weight of those words. Not heavy—never heavy—but grounding, like an anchor she hadn't even realised she needed. She brushed her fingertips across his jaw, memorising the quiet strength in his face. "I believe you."

They lingered in that cocoon of intimacy, wrapped in each other until the light grew stronger, until the hum of the city below broke into the full rhythm of morning. And for once, Stephanie didn't dread the day. She wasn't steeling herself for another fight, another disappointment. She was simply here. In his arms. Safe. Wanted.

The rich aroma of coffee soon drifted through the penthouse, warm and inviting, coaxing her from the sheets. She stretched languidly, pulling the blanket around her shoulders as she sat up. The sunlight poured gold across the hardwood, catching in her hair, painting her in soft brilliance as though the morning itself conspired to mark her as changed.

And in that moment—quiet, unhurried, impossibly tender—Stephanie knew. Without hesitation, without doubt. She was deeply, irreversibly in love with Trey. And for the first time in years, she could imagine a future not ruled by fear or compromise.

A future where love didn't wound or diminish.

A future where she belonged—unapologetically, completely—at Trey's side.

Trey moved through the kitchen barefoot, sleeves rolled up, each gesture fluid and unhurried as he poured coffee into two mugs. He looked impossibly at ease, so completely at home in his own space that Stephanie paused, watching him with a warmth spreading through her chest that had nothing to do with caffeine.

"You make coffee too?" she teased softly, stepping closer.

He glanced up, mouth curving into that small, knowing smile that always made her pulse skip. "Among my many hidden talents," he said, sliding a mug across the counter. "Cream, no sugar. Right?"

Stephanie blinked, momentarily startled. "How did you—"

"You pay attention to everyone else but yourself," he said simply, leaning casually against the counter. "I've been paying attention to you."

Her cheeks warmed as she lifted the cup, inhaling the rich steam. "That's… unfairly charming," she murmured, her voice catching just slightly.

He arched a brow, amused. "Unfair?"

"Yes," she said, smiling. "Because now I'll never be able to drink bad office coffee again without thinking about this."

His low laugh rumbled through the quiet kitchen, curling around her and settling deep in her chest. "Good. Then I'll just have to make sure you get the real thing more often."

For a moment, they lingered in the gentle hum of morning. The city below stretched quiet, the distant traffic nothing more than a lullaby. Stephanie leaned against the counter, mug cradled in her hands, watching the way the sunlight softened the angles of his face.

"This feels… normal," she admitted softly, almost to herself. "Like waking up with you, drinking coffee, could just be part of my life. And I want that."

Trey set his mug down, closing the short distance between them. His hand brushed over hers where it rested on the cup—grounding, warm, steady. "It can be," he said simply. "When you're ready."

Her throat tightened, but she nodded, feeling the truth of it settle deep inside her. "Then I guess I'll have to get used to good coffee."

His smile was slow, deliberate, the kind that made her stomach flutter and her chest tighten all at once. "And good mornings," he added softly.

Stephanie laughed, light and unburdened, leaning into him for a heartbeat longer. For the first time in years, the day ahead didn't feel heavy—it felt like possibility.

After coffee, Trey unlatched the tall windows, letting in a soft breeze scented faintly with the city's early promise. He glanced back at her with that boyish grin that never failed to disarm her. "Come on," he said, nodding toward the spiral staircase. "Trust me."

Barefoot and curious, Stephanie followed him up to the rooftop terrace. The city spread out around them in golden light, rooftops glinting, glass towers catching the sun in dazzling shards. A blanket was already laid across the sun-warmed stone, a small radio humming softly beside a basket of croissants and fresh fruit from the bakery downstairs. Stephanie laughed, the sound unexpected and light, and felt something loosen in her chest—a worry, a tension, a year's worth of guardedness unravelling.

They ate cross-legged, stories flowing into silences and back again, the music threading through every glance and laugh. Trey showed her the small herb garden he'd coaxed along the balcony rail, plucking a sprig of mint and pressing it into her palm. She closed her eyes at the burst of fresh green, the brush of his fingers against hers lingering longer than necessary, savouring the intimacy of the touch.

As the sun climbed higher, he suggested making lunch together. He admitted he wasn't much of a cook, while she confessed it had been years since she'd done anything beyond the basics. In the kitchen, ingredients piled on the counter, knives and spoons clattered, and laughter spilled out as they chopped, stirred, and argued good-naturedly over seasoning. Tastes were stolen straight from the pan, mock scolding followed, and soon a slightly uneven but delicious meal took shape. When they finally sat down, their plates steaming, they toasted their triumph with exaggerated flair, the simple act of cooking side by side transformed into something unexpectedly joyful, something that felt bigger than the meal itself.

Later, sprawled together on the cool living room rug, the city humming below, a hush settled between them. Trey traced lazy patterns over her palm, grounding her in the stillness, and then asked quietly, "Tell me about your parents."

Stephanie inhaled, her chest tightening as memories spilled over. "They were wonderful," she whispered, voice soft, "supportive, loving… a day never went by when they didn't tell me they loved me."

Trey's gaze stayed steady, patient, encouraging her to continue.

"When I was nineteen," she murmured, throat catching, "I lost them. They'd taken my dog out for a walk… I was away with friends, just a silly weekend— and then I got the call. A driver… speeding… hit them. I wasn't there. Not for them." She swallowed, a fragile smile appearing despite the ache. "Shelley survived, my dog, but she's gone now too. Just… just me."

Trey's hand tightened around hers, fierce in its protectiveness. "I'm so sorry, Steph," he said softly. He drew her closer, arms encasing her as if his presence alone could shield her from every ache of the past. "That must have been unbearably hard."

Resting against his chest, Stephanie let the quiet speak for her, words unnecessary. The afternoon stretched golden, languid, infused with the hum of the city and the sanctuary they had carved together.

They drifted into a doze on the couch, tangled in warmth. Time folded into moments: coffee refills, stolen touches, and a slow dance in the kitchen to a song neither knew. Stephanie pressed her cheek to his shoulder, heart and mind entirely present.

Eventually, the hour edged toward reality. Stephanie's gaze flicked to her phone. "Ryan's flight gets in at four," she whispered, setting down her fork, pulse stuttering. "I should go."

Trey's jaw tightened almost imperceptibly, but he nodded. "I know." He reached for her hand, thumb brushing her knuckles with careful intimacy. "Are you ready?"

She shook her head slightly, throat tight. "Not really. But I have to be."

He pressed a gentle kiss to her lips, slow, grounding, unhurried. "You don't have to do anything you don't want to. You're stronger than you think, and I'll be here if you need me—anytime."

Tears pricked her eyes at the quiet conviction in his voice. She squeezed his hand once more, then pulled back with a shaky smile. "I'll call you."

"I'll be waiting," Trey said simply, and she believed him.

As she stepped out of the penthouse into the soft hum of the afternoon city, Stephanie carried with her not only the weight of the obligations ahead but also the certainty of what waited for her afterward—a world where she could choose warmth, love, and connection without compromise. This weekend, fleeting though it was, had given her that. And it was perfect.

Stephanie let herself into the apartment, the familiar quiet pressing around her like a soft, weighted blanket. She dropped her bag by the door, kicked off her shoes, and went straight for the shower. The hot water pounded against her back, washing away the city grime, the faint trace of Trey's cologne clinging to her skin, and the memory of his arms wrapped around her all night. Every touch, every kiss, every heartbeat pressed itself into her chest, leaving her both flushed and achingly hollow.

By the time she stepped out, steam still curling around her, she had slipped into a simple, soft dress, the kind that felt like an extension of herself. Her phone lit up with a message from Rebecca.

"Bagel????"

Stephanie laughed under her breath, shaking her head at the timing. She waited until she'd settled onto the couch, hair damp and loosely pulled back, before pressing call.

Rebecca answered on the first ring, practically vibrating with excitement. "Well? How did it go? Who was it?"

Stephanie hesitated, then let the truth slip out, a small, dreamy smile tugging at her lips. "It was Trey."

There was a half-second pause. Then Rebecca's voice shot up an octave, shrill with incredulity. "Trey? Your boss? The one you said wasn't interested in you?"

"Yes," Stephanie admitted, cheeks warming despite herself. Just saying his name aloud made her pulse quicken. Her lips curved unconsciously as she remembered the feel of him—steady, protective, present in a way no one else had ever been.

"Oh. My. God." Rebecca practically squealed, the sound vibrating through the phone like pure delight.

Stephanie laughed softly, but the warmth faded quickly, replaced by a heaviness she couldn't shake. She swallowed hard, voice dipping. "I feel terrible, though."

"What? Why? Steph, don't you dare—"

"I do," she said quietly, almost a whisper. "I stayed the night… but we didn't t— well, you know. And it still feels like I cheated on Ryan. It's not fair to anyone."

She sank back into the cushions, guilt tangling with the sweetness of the memory. Trey's warmth still lingered on her skin, a ghost that made her heart ache, but so did the sharp edge of conscience.

Rebecca's sigh crackled softly through the phone. "Honey, no. You didn't cheat. You made a choice in your heart before your head even caught up. And Ryan? He hasn't treated you like a partner in years. Don't punish yourself for finally choosing what makes you happy."

Stephanie blinked back the sting of tears. Her voice wavered, soft and unsure. "Then why does it still feel so wrong?"

Rebecca paused, then sharpened with that familiar, no-nonsense edge. "Okay, let me ask you something—and don't you dare lie to me. When was the last time, honestly, that you and Ryan… were intimate?"

Stephanie closed her eyes, shame prickling at the admission. "Around eight weeks ago," she murmured.

"Eight weeks?" Rebecca's incredulity pierced through the phone. "Steph, come on. That's not a relationship. That's… that's a roommate situation with a side of control issues. No wonder you're confused. You've been starving for affection, for connection. And when you finally got it—from someone who actually sees you—your whole world tilted."

Stephanie bit her lip, a mixture of guilt and relief warring inside her. "You make it sound so simple," she murmured.

Rebecca's tone softened, though it stayed firm. "Because it is simple. You're already out the door with Ryan. Last night just showed you what's waiting when you finally close it."

Stephanie exhaled slowly, heart aching with truth and fear both. "I'm scared, Bec."

"I know," Rebecca said gently, the warmth in her voice steady and grounding. "But you're not alone. You've got me. And Trey? He sounds like he's willing to wait as long as it takes. That's not a man who just wants your body. That's a man who wants your heart."

Stephanie curled into herself on the couch, hands knotted in her lap, the hum of the city outside muted by the thick glass windows. Every tick of the clock pressed heavier against her chest, pulling her closer to the moment she had been dreading, the confrontation she had to face, and yet also drawing her closer to the life she longed to choose.

For a long moment, she simply sat there, letting the memory of last night, the warmth of Trey's arms, and the quiet certainty of Rebecca's words settle over her. It was bittersweet—full of longing and hesitation, but also full of promise.

She was standing at the edge of a choice, and for the first time in years, her heart knew which way it wanted to leap.

At four-fifty, the scrape of the key in the lock jolted through the apartment, sharp as a gunshot. Stephanie's pulse spiked, her breath snagging in her chest.

She rose half an inch from the couch before freezing, her palms damp, her heart hammering like she'd been caught doing something wrong.

The door swung open. Ryan stepped inside, shoulders hunched, movements stiff and jerky. His eyes were bloodshot, his skin sallow under the harsh hallway light. He pressed a hand to his temple the moment he crossed the threshold, his suitcase dropping with a harsh, jarring thud that seemed to echo through the apartment like a warning bell.

"Headache," he muttered, voice clipped and frayed. "Flight was brutal."

Stephanie's throat worked around words she'd rehearsed a hundred times but couldn't quite force out. She finally managed, "Ryan, we need to talk."

"Later," he snapped without looking at her, fingers still digging into his temple. "After a shower. I feel like crap."

Her shoulders slumped, frustration colliding with a sharp twist of guilt. She had built herself up for this moment, had told herself she would be steady, calm, resolute. But already she felt the air draining from her resolve, leaving only a hollow ache. "Fine," she murmured. "I'll wait."

He disappeared down the hallway, the bedroom door clicking shut behind him. The sound landed like a slammed fist against her chest.

She perched on the edge of the couch, every nerve pulled taut, her foot tapping an erratic rhythm against the floor. Each tick of the clock hammered at her pulse, each passing minute stretching into something unbearable. Her mind ricocheted between dread and guilt—Trey's arms around her, his voice promising patience, the quiet warmth of last night—clashing violently with the suffocating weight of this room, this marriage, this silence.

Ten minutes passed. Fifteen. Twenty.

The shower shut off. But Ryan didn't emerge.

Stephanie chewed her lip raw, her thoughts spiralling. Maybe he was stalling. Maybe he knew—somehow. Maybe she'd lose her nerve if she waited any longer.

Her body moved before her mind agreed. She pushed herself up, legs shaky, padding down the hallway like someone creeping toward their own execution. Her stomach twisted, every step a battle between the fierce determination to reclaim her life and the gnawing fear of what came next.

She reached for the bedroom door. Her hand shook against the knob. For half a heartbeat she hesitated, whispering to herself, you have to do this. You owe it to both of you.

Then she pushed.

The door gave way with a soft click.

Her breath hitched—then caught hard, snagging like barbed wire in her chest.

Ryan wasn't standing by the bed, towelling his hair. He wasn't rifling through his suitcase.

He was on the floor.

Sprawled awkwardly on the carpet, one arm flung out, his shirt clinging damply to his skin. His face was ashen, his lips tinged with a bluish grey, sweat plastering his hair to his forehead. His chest rose, shallow and uneven, each breath a rattling struggle.

Stephanie's knees buckled. The conversation, the guilt, the resolve—everything shattered in a heartbeat.

"Ryan!" Her voice cracked, high and strangled, panic clawing up her throat. She dropped to her knees beside him, her hands shaking so badly she could barely reach for him. "Ryan, can you hear me?"

No answer. Just the weak, fluttering rise and fall of his chest.

Her heart lurched violently, slamming against her ribs as fear devoured everything else.

This wasn't the confrontation she had been bracing for. This was something far worse.

Chapter Eleven

"Ryan?" Stephanie's voice broke as she shook his shoulder harder. His skin was clammy, his breathing ragged and shallow. "Ryan, please—wake up!"

Nothing.

Her heart slammed against her ribs, wild and frantic. Panic tore through her veins, sharp and merciless. She scrambled for her phone, her hands trembling so violently she nearly fumbled it onto the floor. Somehow, she jabbed at the screen, forcing the numbers through the blur of tears.

"911, what's your emergency?"

"My boyfriend—he—he collapsed," she gasped, her voice cracking. "He's unconscious, he's breathing but it's not right. Please, we need help now!"

The dispatcher's calm practiced tone was the only thing holding her together. "Stay on the line with me. Help is on the way. Is he responsive at all?"

"No—no, he won't wake up!" Stephanie pressed her palm against his chest, counting the weak, uneven rises. Her tears fell hot and fast, streaking her face. "Please, hurry. Please."

Each second dragged like an hour, stretching into unbearable silence, until—at last—the distant wail of sirens pierced the air. Relief and terror crashed over her at once, leaving her breathless. She bolted to the door, flinging it wide, waving frantically as the flashing lights drew near.

"In here! He's in here!" she shouted, her voice breaking as the paramedics rushed past her into the bedroom.

They moved with terrifying precision—checking vitals, securing an oxygen mask, slipping lines into his arm with rapid efficiency. Their words blurred into medical shorthand she couldn't follow, too fast, too clipped. Her world had narrowed to the sight of Ryan's still face, the faint flutter of his chest beneath the mask.

Within minutes, they had him on the stretcher. Stephanie stumbled after them, her breath shallow, her vision swimming.

"Ma'am, you can ride with us," one EMT said, already yanking open the back doors of the ambulance.

She climbed in, knees hitting the cold metal floor. Her hand found Ryan's limp one, clutching it desperately as if she could tether him to her by sheer will. The doors slammed shut, and the sirens wailed to life, drowning out her ragged breaths.

"Ryan," she whispered, leaning close, her tears dripping onto his damp shirt. "Please. Please hold on."

With her free hand, she fumbled for her phone again, her thumb scrolling until she found Peter's number. She pressed call, her chest heaving.

"Stephanie?" His voice was warm at first but sharpened instantly at the sound of her sob. "What's wrong?"

"Ryan—he collapsed," she choked, barely getting the words out. "The ambulance is taking him to New York Presbyterian."

There was silence for a heartbeat, then Peter's voice, clipped and urgent. "We're on our way. Just stay with him, Stephanie. Don't leave him alone."

The line went dead, leaving only the shriek of the siren and the thundering of her pulse.

The ambulance jolted to a stop. The back doors flew open, flooding the interior with bright, sterile light. Ryan was rushed out, the stretcher bouncing down onto the pavement. Stephanie scrambled after them, nearly stumbling in her haste, her bag clutched to her chest like armour.

Inside, the hospital swallowed her whole. Harsh fluorescents. The sharp bite of antiseptic. Nurses shouting vitals. A doctor barking orders, voice crisp and urgent.

"Blood pressure's crashing—get him to CT now!"

Stephanie reached out instinctively as they pushed him down the hall, but a nurse caught her by the arm, gentle yet firm. "Ma'am, you can't go past this point. We'll take care of him."

Her lips trembled. She wanted to argue, to fight, to insist that she had to be with him—but her voice broke before words could form.

So, she nodded, weak and numb, and let herself be steered into the waiting area.

The plastic chair was unforgiving beneath her, her body shaking too hard to find stillness. Around her, the hospital buzzed with relentless motion—pages overhead, rubber soles squeaking against tile, the steady beep of monitors that mocked her with their steadiness.

None of them belonged to Ryan.

And Stephanie sat with her hands knotted tight in her lap, her tears falling unchecked, as the weight of fear pressed down with suffocating force.

Minutes crawled by like hours, each one heavier than the last. Stephanie sat with her hands locked so tightly in her lap her knuckles throbbed white, whispering silent bargains to a God she wasn't sure had ever listened. Please, just let him be okay. Please. I'll do anything. Just let him live.

"Stephanie!"

Her head jerked up. Peter and Sofia were striding toward her, their faces pale, fear carved deep into their expressions.

She shot to her feet, tears blurring her vision. "They—they took him straight back," she stammered, voice breaking. "He collapsed at home. He wouldn't wake up."

Sofia didn't hesitate; she gathered Stephanie into a fierce embrace, one hand cradling the back of her head like she was a child again. "You did the right thing," she murmured, her own voice shaking. "You got him here."

Peter's jaw was tight, his eyes wet but unshed. "We'll wait," he said firmly. "Together."

The three of them sat in brittle silence, the antiseptic air of the emergency waiting room pressing down like a weight. Every time the double doors swung open, Stephanie's heart leapt into her throat, bracing for answers that never came.

The television mounted high on the wall played some daytime talk show, the audience laughter grotesquely out of place. The clock above the reception desk ticked too loudly, each second stretching out like a blade.

It felt like an eternity before a man in a white coat finally stepped into the room. His expression was grave, composed—the look of someone practiced at delivering bad news.

"Family of Ryan Carter?"

Stephanie bolted upright, her legs trembling so violently she nearly stumbled. Sofia and Peter rose beside her, all three of them frozen, dread crackling in the air.

"Yes," Peter said quickly, his voice strained but steady. He gestured between them. "We're his parents. This is his partner, Stephanie."

The neurologist's gaze shifted to her, warm but clinical, and he gave a small nod. "Please—come with me."

The consultation room was too small, too still. Four chairs, a low table, a box of tissues placed deliberately in the centre like a warning. Stephanie sat with her pulse hammering in her ears, every nerve braced for impact.

The doctor folded his hands, his tone gentle but unflinching. "The scans show a mass in Ryan's brain. It's what we call a glioblastoma—an aggressive form of brain tumour."

The word tumour landed like a fist to her gut.

He continued, calm and precise. "We'll need more imaging to determine its full spread. Glioblastomas grow quickly. Surgery can remove some of the mass, and chemotherapy or radiation may slow the progression. But..." He paused, and his eyes softened. "The prognosis is difficult. On average, with treatment, patients live twelve to eighteen months. Sometimes longer. Sometimes less."

Sofia made a raw, strangled sound, covering her mouth with both hands as sobs broke free. Peter gathered her against his side, his own face a mask of shock, his eyes staring at nothing.

Stephanie couldn't move. Her body felt carved from stone while her mind screamed. Twelve to eighteen months. Not weeks, not days—but not the life Ryan had pictured. Not the life they had spent years talking about.

Her throat closed. Just last night she had been wrapped in Trey's arms, his voice promising patience, a future. Now guilt seared through her chest, sharp as broken glass. *How can I even think of him when Ryan—*

She forced her voice out, hoarse and thin. "What… what do we do first?"

The doctor leaned forward slightly. "The immediate priority is to stabilise him and have a neurosurgeon review his scans. Surgery will not cure this, but it can relieve the pressure and buy time. After that, we'll discuss chemotherapy and radiation. The goal is to give him the best quality of life possible for as long as possible."

He looked at each of them in turn, as though making sure they absorbed every syllable. "I'd like to admit him tonight. We'll run an MRI with contrast, blood work, and neurological assessments. The surgical team can likely see him within the next forty-eight hours. The sooner we act, the better chance he has to remain himself for longer."

"Yes," Sofia sobbed, nodding rapidly. "Yes, whatever he needs."

Peter's throat worked before his voice came, low and rough. "Doctor… when will he wake up? Will he even understand?"

"He's stable for now," the neurologist said gently. "The seizure and collapse were caused by swelling around the tumour. He'll be groggy, but he should regain consciousness. We'll manage his pain, keep him comfortable."

Stephanie dug her nails into her palms, desperate to ground herself as the words blurred into a foreign language—surgery, chemo, radiation, prognosis. All she could hear was that grim refrain: twelve to eighteen months.

The doctor stood. "The neurosurgery team will brief you once they've reviewed everything. For now—when he wakes, go in one at a time. He'll be disoriented, and too much at once could overwhelm him."

Sofia whispered, "Thank you," her voice fractured.

Stephanie nodded faintly, though her throat burned too hot for words. She could only sit there in the suffocating quiet of the room, one phrase echoing endlessly in her mind.

Twelve to eighteen months.

Stephanie slipped quietly out of the waiting area, leaving Sofia and Peter folded into each other's grief. The squeak of nurses' shoes, the soft hum of fluorescent lights, the faint chemical sting of antiseptic—all of it closed in on her as she wandered down the sterile corridor, clutching her cardigan tight around her as if it could hold her together. Her knuckles blanched white.

She pressed her forehead to the cool plaster wall, the chill biting into her skin, and tried to breathe past the chaos storming in her chest. Just hours ago, she had been ready—ready—to tell Ryan she couldn't keep pretending. That she was leaving. That Trey—steady, patient, devastating Trey—was the one she wanted, the one she loved.

And now…

Now Ryan's life was dangling by the thinnest thread.

The realisation hit her like ice water, stealing the air from her lungs. She couldn't do it. She couldn't walk away. Not now. Not when he might never recover, when every day could be measured in dwindling numbers. How could she shatter his heart when he might not have the time or strength left to mend it?

And yet—God, the truth burned inside her like acid—she didn't love him the way she should.

Stephanie's hands curled into fists against her chest, nails biting through the fabric of her cardigan. I care about him. I want him to live. I'll stay. I'll fight with him. But the words I love him—they stuck like stone in her throat, impossible to force out, even in the silence of her own mind.

Her heart, treacherous and aching, drifted back to Trey. To the way he looked at her like she was the only person in the room. To the gentleness in his hands, the quiet certainty in his voice when he promised to wait. Every touch, every glance from him had lit something in her that Ryan never had, not even in the beginning. Trey made her feel seen. Wanted. Alive.

And now the choice before her was unbearable. She couldn't have both. She couldn't betray Ryan—not when his future was suddenly measured in months instead of years. But to deny Trey, to bury what had finally felt like love—real, soul-deep love—felt like cutting her own heart out.

Her legs buckled, and she sank to the floor by the narrow hospital window. Beyond the glass, the skyline blurred in the night, city lights smeared into pale streaks. Inside her chest, longing, guilt, and fear twisted into something sharp, crushing.

Her lips trembled as she whispered into the empty corridor, "I can't leave him… I can't. But I… I don't love him the way I should."

The words hung there, fragile and damning.

And in that brutal confession, she felt the cage slam shut around her. She cared. She wanted him to live. She would stand by him because she couldn't imagine being the woman who abandoned a dying man. But her heart—her unruly, disloyal heart—already belonged somewhere else. And the guilt of that knowledge pressed down on her, suffocating, making her feel smaller than she ever had, torn apart by a love she could not claim and a duty she could not deny.

When Stephanie finally pushed herself upright, her knees wobbled as though they carried decades instead of hours. She steadied against the wall, smoothed the wrinkles from her dress with trembling hands, and forced one long, deliberate breath. It did little to quiet the pounding in her chest. Each step she took down the sterile corridor seemed to echo louder than the last, reverberating with the truth she'd already accepted: she couldn't leave him. Not now. Not when he was so fragile.

Ryan's room glowed dimly when she entered, the fluorescent ceiling light muted to a low hum, machines providing the steady soundtrack of survival. The rhythmic beep of the monitor, the faint hiss and click of oxygen, the soft shuffle of a nurse adjusting IV lines—it all wove into a fragile lullaby of life sustained.

Sofia sat stiff-backed at Ryan's bedside, her fingers clenched white around Peter's much larger hand. Their faces lifted when Stephanie slipped into the room, both pale, worn, and heavy with sleepless fear. But in their eyes shimmered something else, too—a faint, desperate hope, as if her presence alone might bring strength enough for all of them.

Stephanie's throat tightened. She moved softly, carefully, to the other side of the bed. Ryan was propped against the pillows, skin ashen, lips thin and colourless. Even in stillness, he looked weary, as though the effort of drawing breath was more than his body wanted to give. Yet when his eyes flickered open and found hers, a faint spark lit in their dull depths—a flicker of relief that pierced her heart.

"Hey," she whispered, leaning down to smooth back his damp hair with a trembling hand. Her voice emerged steady, though every nerve inside her trembled. "You scared me."

"Sorry." His voice rasped, cracked, the corners of his mouth twitching toward a smile that never fully formed. His hand shifted weakly, the barest attempt to reach for hers. She caught it immediately, folding her fingers around his, as though she could will strength into his veins by sheer willpower.

"It's okay," she soothed, stroking the back of his hand with her thumb. "You just... you just focus on resting now. Let us worry about everything else."

His eyelids fluttered shut again, his breathing shallow but steadier. Still, his grip tightened faintly in hers, a fragile tether that anchored him to her, to them, to life.

Stephanie felt her throat close. She wanted to break—wanted to weep until there was nothing left inside her, to scream at the ceiling for the cruelty of it all, to run down the hall and call Trey just to hear his voice steady her. Instead, she sat there on the edge of the bed, spine rigid with the effort of holding herself together. She stroked Ryan's hand with careful, measured tenderness, as though that small act could hide the storm inside her.

In her mind, unbidden, Trey's image rose—his arms wrapping around her, the warmth of his chest against her cheek, the kiss that had unravelled her so completely she'd finally felt whole. The memory ached deep, sharp, and treacherous. She swallowed hard and forced it down. Trey wasn't hers to keep. Not anymore.

Leaning closer so only Ryan could hear, she pressed her lips near his ear and whispered, "I'm right here, Ryan. I'm not going anywhere."

The words weren't love—not the kind she longed to give, the kind she'd tasted in Trey's embrace. But they were something she could still offer. Loyalty. Compassion. Care.

For now, that would have to be enough.

Stephanie stayed rooted to her place, her hand never leaving his, even as her chest ached with the silent betrayal of a heart that beat for another.

Early Monday morning, Trey stepped through the glass doors of his building with a lightness he hadn't felt in weeks. The usual crush of Midtown—the honking, the rushing crowds, the city's relentless pulse—blurred around him, fading into a background hum. His tie was loosened, jacket draped casually over one arm, and a small, almost shy smile tugged at the corners of his mouth, the kind of smile reserved for mornings that promised something worth waiting for.

He could still feel the ghost of Stephanie's lips against his, the weight of her body nestled against him when she'd slept, the soft certainty in her whispered confession—that she had already decided to leave Ryan. The memory played through his mind in fragments, looping relentlessly, keeping sleep at bay but filling him with a restless, exquisite kind of anticipation.

She was finally choosing herself. Choosing him.

He had told her he'd wait, that he wouldn't go anywhere. But hearing her say the words, hearing the vulnerability and courage in her voice—it had lit a fire he hadn't allowed himself to hope for. He knew it wouldn't be simple. There would be guilt, fallout, the messy unravelling of the life she had lived with Ryan. But they'd navigate it together.

As he stepped into the elevator, Trey ran a hand through his hair, catching his reflection in the polished steel doors. His eyes lingered on the quiet determination etched there. She hadn't called or texted last night. He'd left his phone on the nightstand, waiting for the familiar vibration, but it had remained stubbornly silent. Not that he minded—he understood she needed time, time to process, time to find the right words. Patience. He could give her that.

Still, as the elevator hummed upward, his thumb drifted to his phone again. No new messages. No missed calls. The absence pressed against him in a way that made his chest tighten, but he exhaled slowly, letting the thought soften: she was worth waiting for, worth every moment of uncertainty.

By the time the elevator doors slid open on his floor, Trey's stride had regained its confidence. Stephanie might not be ready today, or even tomorrow—but she would be. And when she was, he'd be there. Always. Without hesitation.

He rounded the corner toward his office, his hand brushing the polished wood of the doorframe, ready to greet her with the small, hopeful smile that had lingered since the night before. But something stopped him cold.

Someone else sat at Stephanie's desk, typing quietly, glancing up as he approached.

"Good morning, Mr. Grayson," the woman said, her tone bright, polite, professional. "Ms. Vale had a family emergency. She won't be in today."

Trey froze for a heartbeat, a flicker of confusion darkening his features. Family emergency? Her voice hadn't come across, hadn't mentioned this. Why hadn't she told me herself? His chest tightened, a sudden weight pressing down.

"Thank you," he said carefully, forcing his voice calm, neutral, clipped. He offered a polite nod and slipped past her, retreating into the sanctuary of his office. The door closed behind him with a soft click, leaving him alone with the hum of the office and the gnawing knot of uncertainty in his chest.

He leaned against his desk, shoulders squared though his stomach twisted with unease. Stephanie wasn't here. And for the first time that morning, the hopeful anticipation that had buoyed him since dawn was replaced by a creeping, insistent dread.

He pulled out his phone, thumb hovering over the screen before typing quickly:

Stephanie, are you okay?

He stared at the screen, waiting, willing it to vibrate. Nothing. No reply.

His mind began to spiral. Had something happened to her? Was she sick? Injured? Or… had she changed her mind? Had Ryan somehow convinced her to stay? The thought made his chest tighten further, a painful squeeze he couldn't shake.

He forced himself to breathe, to recall the words he'd been given, *family emergency*. But Stephanie had no living parents. Her family was gone. A cold, sinking dread curled in his gut. Something was wrong.

Trey's hands tightened into fists at his sides. His pulse thrummed in his temples. Every instinct screamed that he needed to find her, to know she was safe. The city outside could rage and roar—it didn't matter. Right now, all that existed was her, and the gnawing, relentless need to make sure she was okay.

He grabbed his phone again, fingers trembling slightly, and started typing another message, this time firmer, desperate:

Stephanie. Please. Call me. Now.

He hit send, the vibration mocking him with its silence.

Chapter Twelve

It was mid-morning on Monday before Sofia, Peter, and Stephanie finally left the hospital. Ryan remained behind, groggy and swollen from medication, hooked to monitors and IV lines, his body exhausted from the ordeal. Stephanie had stayed by his side through the quiet hours, holding his hand, whispering soft reassurances when words could find no purchase, offering the only presence he seemed to need.

Sofia glanced at her, worry softening her features. "Stephanie, you've been incredible. But you need to get some rest too."

Peter nodded, squeezing her shoulder gently. "We can manage things here for a while. You need a break—come home with us, just for a bit. Recharge. Please."

Stephanie hesitated, torn between the impulse to stay and the nagging awareness of her own limits. Her fingers clenched the strap of her bag like a lifeline. "I… I can't leave him," she murmured, voice barely audible.

"You're not leaving him," Sofia said firmly, eyes locked on hers. "He's being cared for by the doctors. But you need to care for yourself too. Even just a little. Please, Stephanie."

The words were gentle but insistent, like a lifeline tossed into her churning sea of emotions. With a reluctant nod, she allowed them to guide her to the car. She rode in silence, staring through the glass at the city streets sliding past, letting the motion soothe the tight coil in her chest. For now, she could allow herself a pause—Ryan was safe, in capable hands, and she could gather her strength for the battles to come.

When they pulled up at her apartment, Peter and Sofia offered encouraging smiles. "We'll check on him," Sofia said softly. "And we'll call if anything changes. Go inside and just… breathe, even for a moment."

Stephanie managed a faint, grateful smile, the weight on her chest slightly eased, but still heavy. She stepped inside, the familiar click of the door closing behind her feeling both comforting and isolating.

Once inside, she sank onto the edge of her sofa. The apartment felt impossibly quiet without the hum of hospital machines, without Ryan's fragile murmurs, without the lingering antiseptic scent clinging to her clothes. She pressed her palms to her face, trying to steady the storm of racing thoughts, the enormity of everything pressing down like a physical weight.

Her phone lay on the coffee table, forgotten in the chaos of the morning. Slowly, she reached for it, hesitating before unlocking the screen. Two messages blinked back at her—Trey.

Stephanie, are you okay?

Stephanie. Please. Call me. Now.

Her chest tightened. She hadn't even realised she'd cut herself off from the world earlier, turning off her phone in the hospital haze. Now, seeing his name, the care in those eight words twisted her stomach with a mix of relief and guilt.

Her thumb hovered over the screen, heart hammering. She wanted to answer, to tell him she was okay—or at least as okay as she could be—but the truth was a tangle of fear, moral obligation, and heartbreak. Ryan was still in the hospital, fighting for his life, and she couldn't abandon him—not yet.

She pressed her forehead to the cool back of the sofa, whispering to herself, "I can't leave him… not now." The words were both a promise and a condemnation, echoing in her mind with every heartbeat. Trey deserved honesty, transparency, the chance to share her life fully. But that choice could wait—her loyalty, her sense of duty, demanded she stay the course for now.

Her fingers hovered over the keyboard again. She began typing a reply, words forming, then deleting, reforming, torn between the two halves of her heart. She couldn't send it. Not yet. Outside, the city pulsed and roared, unaware of her struggle. Inside, she allowed herself to sit with the quiet, with the impossible weight of love and duty pulling her in opposite directions, knowing that every second she delayed was a second she gave herself to gather the courage she would need to face the truth.

Stephanie exhaled slowly, chest tight, eyes fixed on the screen, letting Trey's concern hang there, a lifeline she wasn't ready to grasp—but one she would, eventually.

For now, she let herself simply be—tangled, human, torn, and painfully aware that the impossible road ahead had only just begun.

A soft knock at the door pulled Stephanie from the haze of her thoughts. She blinked, staring at the door as if it might vanish if she didn't move.

"Steph?" Rebecca's voice called gently, tentative yet insistent.

Stephanie's hand shook slightly as she reached for the knob. When she opened the door, Rebecca's eyes softened immediately, taking in the exhaustion etched into her friend's face—the red rims around her eyes, the pallor, the way she seemed both present and elsewhere.

"Oh, sweetheart," Rebecca murmured, stepping forward and wrapping her arms around Stephanie in a firm, grounding hug. Stephanie sagged against her, letting the warmth anchor her for the first time all morning, as if the embrace could hold together the pieces of her fraying heart.

"I—" Stephanie began, but the words lodged in her throat. She pulled back slightly, rubbing at her eyes, trying to marshal the strength to speak.

Rebecca's concern tightened her features as she reached for Stephanie's hands, holding them gently. "How is he?" she asked softly, her voice steady but filled with care.

Stephanie swallowed hard, the lump in her throat making her words fragile. "They're running tests," she whispered. "He'll need surgery, treatment… it's bad, Bec. Really bad. And…" Her hands clenched at her sides, nails digging into her palms. "I was going to leave him last night. I was ready. But now… I can't. I just… I can't."

Rebecca's brow furrowed, her eyes narrowing with both concern and compassion. "Stephanie… what about Trey?"

Stephanie's chest tightened, a painful knot of guilt and longing twisting inside her. "I can't ask him to wait eighteen months. We haven't even really started. It's not fair." Her voice trembled, and she bit her lip to stop it from quivering. "Even though I… I want him. I love him, Bec, more than I realised. But Ryan… he needs me right now. I can't abandon him—not like this."

Rebecca's expression softened further, understanding flickering in her gaze. "Trey said he'd wait," she reminded her gently, the words like a lifeline tossed across Stephanie's guilt.

Stephanie's fingers tightened around Rebecca's. "I know. I know he would. But it doesn't make it easier. He deserves someone who can be with him fully, not someone torn between love and duty." Her breath hitched, the weight of the impossible choice pressing down on her. "I can't leave him, not now. And I can't make Trey wait for God only knows how long. It's… it's all wrong."

Rebecca pulled her closer again, resting her chin lightly on Stephanie's shoulder, letting her feel the steadiness in her friend's presence. "You're doing the right thing, Steph. Right now, Ryan needs you. And when the time is right… things will find their way. You're strong enough to handle this. Stronger than you know."

Stephanie let herself lean into her friend, the warmth and reassurance grounding her. For a long moment, she allowed herself to breathe, to let the reality of her impossible situation settle over her like a heavy, suffocating blanket.

"I just… I hate feeling like I'm betraying someone I care about," she whispered, the words trembling, raw and unfiltered.

Rebecca squeezed her hand firmly, her voice unwavering. "You're not betraying anyone. You're being human. You're being compassionate. That's enough for now."

Stephanie closed her eyes, taking in the truth in her friend's words, letting herself rest in the small measure of comfort they offered. Even if it hurt. Even if the days ahead were full of impossible choices. For now, she could let herself simply be held—and that, at least, was enough.

Rebecca stayed close, settling into the chair beside Stephanie's bed with a quiet persistence that felt like an anchor in the storm of her friend's exhaustion and guilt. She had offered water, tissues, a hand to hold—anything that might tether Stephanie to the present, a lifeline against the swirling chaos in her mind. Stephanie curled beneath the covers, fingers gripping the soft sheet as though it could shield her from the weight of impossible choices pressing down on her chest.

"Get some sleep, Steph," Rebecca whispered, brushing a stray strand of hair from her forehead. "You'll need your strength for what's coming."

Stephanie nodded faintly, her eyes heavy, the tears from earlier finally draining her energy. Her mind still raced, playing back every stolen moment with Trey—the gentle press of his lips, the warmth of his arms around her, the patience in his gaze, the unspoken promises that had wrapped themselves around her heart. Yet, beneath the sweetness of memory, guilt coiled tight. She couldn't leave Ryan—not now, not when the fragility of his life had been laid bare so brutally.

When sleep finally claimed her, it was shallow and restless, punctuated by flickers of her own racing thoughts. Rebecca stayed, a silent sentinel, keeping watch over Stephanie's fragile rest. She didn't speak, didn't move unnecessarily, only observed, knowing the hours ahead would demand bravery, clarity, and words that could not be taken back.

Stephanie stirred as late afternoon sunlight spilled through the blinds, painting the room in warm, golden streaks. Her throat felt parched, her chest heavy with the memories of panic-filled corridors, urgent doctor's voices, and the relentless echo of hospital monitors. Swinging her legs over the side of the bed, she rubbed at her face and caught her reflection in the windowpane—red-rimmed eyes, pale cheeks, tangled hair—but beneath it all, determination had settled into the line of her jaw.

Her thoughts inevitably turned to Trey. The way he had held her, the trust he had placed in her, the quiet patience he'd offered—he deserved more than uncertainty. He deserved the truth, unvarnished and direct. No text messages. No hesitant calls. No postponing.

Stephanie rose, stretching stiff limbs, and chose a simple, fitted outfit that felt like armour for the confrontation she knew was coming. She paused by the mirror, taking a long breath, steadying the tremor in her hands, and smoothing the fabric over her shoulders.

"I have to do this," she whispered to her reflection. "He deserves the truth."

Rebecca's presence, still lingering in the room, offered a small, encouraging smile. "You're doing the right thing, Steph. Just… be honest. That's all anyone can ask of you."

Stephanie nodded, giving her friend a grateful look. "Thanks, Bec," she murmured, her voice tight with nerves.

Rebecca pressed a gentle squeeze to her shoulder. "Call me later," she said softly, "no matter what happens."

Stephanie watched as her friend left, the city streets blurring past the Uber's windows, and then exhaled, squaring her shoulders. She stepped into her own car, the familiar skyline rushing past her windows as her pulse quickened with each block closer to Trey's apartment.

The sleek lobby loomed, polished and bright, and Stephanie's palms were clammy as she approached the concierge desk. "Hi… I'm Stephanie Vale. Could you let Trey Grayson know I'm here to see him?"

After calling Trey, the concierge's professional smile offered little reassurance. "He asked me to send you straight up," he said, swiping a card at the elevator panel. "Private elevator—right this way."

He guided her inside, swiping again before stepping back, leaving Stephanie alone in the softly lit elevator. The hum of the machinery, the faint scent of polished wood, and the gentle rise of the cabin pressed her nerves tighter with every floor. Each passing level felt like a countdown to the moment she could no longer avoid.

She gripped the railing lightly, closing her eyes for a heartbeat, letting out a slow, controlled breath. One step at a time, she reminded herself. One truth at a time.

The city blurred past the small window, distant horns and the murmur of life below fading into irrelevance. All that mattered now was the door that waited at the top—Trey on the other side, and the honesty she had kept tucked away finally ready to be set free.

Trey sank into the leather chair behind his desk, the city skyline stretching wide through the floor-to-ceiling windows behind him, gold and grey in the late afternoon light. The amber whiskey in his hand barely registered—the bitter warmth lost in the storm of his thoughts. It had been a brutal day: calls blurred together, emails ignored, decisions postponed. All he could think about was Stephanie. *Where was she? Why hadn't she reached out?*

He'd even called Ryan's office, desperate for some clue, some reason for her absence, but no one had seen her. Ryan wasn't there either. The gnawing certainty in his chest coiled tighter with every passing second: she'd changed her mind. She wasn't ready. Maybe she never would be.

The soft chime of the intercom cut through the silence, sharp and immediate.

"Yes?" he said, voice tight, controlled.

"There is a Stephanie Vale here to see you, Mr. Grayson," the concierge replied, calm and professional.

Trey's chest tightened. His pulse skipped. "Send her up," he said without hesitation, standing abruptly. The whiskey rattled faintly in the glass as he placed it on the desk. Every nerve in his body was alive with anticipation and dread.

When the elevator doors opened, he froze. Stephanie stepped inside, her eyes swollen and red-rimmed, her shoulders slumped as if the weight of the world pressed her down. She looked… broken.

She didn't hesitate. Her gaze found his for a fleeting heartbeat before she crossed the threshold and collapsed into his arms. Her body shuddered as sobs tore through her, and Trey's instincts flared. His hands went immediately to her back, holding her as if he could carry every ounce of her pain.

"Steph…" he murmured, low, raw, threaded with emotion. "Hey… I've got you. I'm right here."

Her sobs racked her body, and for the first time all day, he felt the sharp ache of helplessness. She was here, in his arms. And yet, a fragile distance lingered, a chasm he couldn't cross with a hug alone.

"I'm… I'm so sorry," she whispered against his chest, words broken, muffled.

Trey tightened his hold, resting his chin atop her head. "Shhh… don't say anything yet. Just… stay. I'll hold you."

Her grief pressed into him like liquid fire, and he realised she wasn't just overwhelmed—she was torn, carrying burdens he hadn't imagined. Every sob, every quiver of her body, drove home the truth: she wanted to be here, but her heart was split in two.

He pressed a gentle kiss into the crown of her hair, letting his arms encompass her completely. "You're safe now," he murmured. "No one can hurt you here. Not me. Not anyone."

She clung to him as if he were the only solid thing left in her world, and he held her tighter, willing his strength to flow into her, to anchor her even for a moment. The soft click of the elevator doors closing behind them became a protective barrier, the hum of the city fading into irrelevance.

For long minutes, there was nothing but the quiet press of her grief against him, the steady rhythm of her sobs, and the unspoken promise between them: he wouldn't let go. Not now. Not ever.

And in that suspended moment, Trey realised that words could wait. She needed presence, safety, the certainty that she wasn't alone—and he could give her that. He could give everything.

Trey gathered her into his arms again, lifting her effortlessly and carrying her to the sofa. He sat down, settling her on his lap, his hands cupping her back as he held her close. Her sobs wracked her body, shuddering in waves that made his chest ache. Slowly, over minutes that felt both suspended and endless, her tears began to ebb, leaving behind a raw, trembling silence.

She hiccupped, her voice barely audible. "I… I need to talk to you."

Trey's arms instinctively tightened around her, but she gently pushed away, stepping off his lap. He stayed still, eyes locked on hers, steady and patient, letting her gather the courage to speak.

"We can't be together, Trey," she said, her voice trembling yet resolute. "It's… it's not possible."

He froze, the warmth of her body gone but the echo of her presence still pressing against him. "What… why?" he asked, panic threading his tone. "Did you… change your mind about us?"

"No," she said instantly, shaking her head, her eyes meeting his with a flash of pain. After a pause, she added softly, almost reluctantly, "Yes…"

Trey's chest tightened, but he didn't move, didn't interrupt. He let her speak, knowing that whatever came next, he had to listen.

"I… I can't leave Ryan," Stephanie said, her voice trembling, tears spilling freely, her hands clutching the edge of the sofa as if it could hold her upright. "He needs me now. I can't abandon him."

Trey's hands clenched into fists on his lap, urgency threading every movement. "I said I would wait for you, Stephanie. I'll wait until you're ready. You don't have to decide now. You don't have to choose between what's right and what you feel tonight."

Her throat constricted, words catching. "I… I can't ask you to do that. It's too much. You've already given me so much."

"I want to," he said firmly, leaning forward, his gaze locked on hers. "I want to wait. I've never felt like this about anyone, Steph. Not like this. I want to be here for you, no matter how long it takes. You don't have to go through this alone."

Stephanie shook her head violently, a sob catching in her chest. "No… it's not that simple." She drew in a shaky breath, voice breaking. "Ryan—he has a brain tumour."

The words hit Trey like a physical blow. His stomach dropped, his chest tightened, and his pulse raced. The world seemed to shrink to the sound of her voice, trembling and pained, confessing a truth that shattered every fantasy he had allowed himself to hold.

"A brain tumour?" he repeated, disbelief and shock threading every syllable. "Stephanie… oh God…"

Her hands trembled as she pressed them against her face, trying to hide the raw emotion she could no longer contain. "It's aggressive… they don't know how long he has… twelve, maybe eighteen months. I can't… I can't leave him now. Not when he's so vulnerable, not when he needs me."

Trey's mind whirled, the anticipation of finally being with her, the dreams he'd allowed himself, colliding violently with the cruel reality of Ryan's illness. His chest ached with helpless love, the rawness of wanting her and knowing he couldn't claim her yet slicing through him.

"Steph… I get it," Trey said softly, his voice rough with emotion. "I get it. But… I don't care how long it takes. I'll wait. You're worth it."

Stephanie shook her head again, tears streaking down her cheeks, her chest tight with guilt. "It's not fair to you. You deserve someone who can choose you freely… not someone whose heart is torn in two. I couldn't ask you to wait eighteen months while I… while I'm stuck in limbo."

Trey rose from the chair, his knees brushing the coffee table, and crossed the short distance between them. He cupped her face in his hands, brushing a thumb over her trembling cheek. "I don't care about fair," he said, his voice low, steady, unwavering. "I care about you. That's it."

Her lips trembled as she looked away, guilt and longing warring across her features. "I couldn't do it… not to you. Not to Ryan."

Trey's hands tightened slightly on her face, his voice dropping to a whisper, almost pleading. "You're not choosing to hurt anyone. You're choosing to be true to yourself. I'll wait, Steph. I don't care about months or obstacles. I care about you. Nothing else matters."

Stephanie swallowed hard, the weight of everything pressing down on her— loyalty, love, guilt, longing. Her chest ached with the impossible choice before her, yet beneath it all, one undeniable truth shone through: her heart had already made its decision, even if her conscience still fought it.

Her hands slid up, gently enclosing his wrists, and with trembling resolve, she eased his touch away from her face. She stepped back, creating space between them, though it felt like tearing herself in two.

"I can't," she whispered, her voice raw and fragile. "We haven't even begun, and I can't ask you to make that sacrifice. It would destroy me to let you put your life on hold for me. You can't wait, Trey."

His eyes darkened, disbelief flashing across them, and he stepped closer, closing the distance she'd made. "Don't say that. Don't make this choice for me. If I want to wait, if I choose that—why can't you let me?"

Her breath hitched, tears spilling over again. "Because I wouldn't feel right about it. I couldn't live with myself knowing I kept you tethered to me while I'm bound to Ryan's fight. You deserve more than uncertainty. You deserve a love that isn't measured in waiting or hesitation."

Trey's jaw tightened, his hands curling into fists at his sides, the frustration and helplessness coiling tight in his chest. "All I want is you. Half, whole—it doesn't matter. Don't you see that?"

Stephanie shook her head, her heart breaking as she forced the words out. "It matters to me. Because I do care about you, Trey. And that's why I can't let you wait."

The silence that followed was sharp, suffocating. Trey's chest rose and fell with unsteady breaths, the weight of her rejection cutting deeper than he thought possible. And yet, in her tear-streaked face, he saw the truth—she wasn't choosing Ryan over him. She was choosing guilt, loyalty, and sacrifice. And that made it hurt even more.

Stephanie wiped her face with the back of her trembling hand, her gaze darting away. Her voice came out quiet, hesitant. "Do you… do you want me to quit?"

The question lodged in Trey's chest like a blade. He hated that she even thought it—that she was willing to cut herself out of his life so cleanly, to make it easier for him to move on. He swallowed hard, shaking his head firmly.

"No," he said, voice steady though every muscle in him ached. "Don't quit. I couldn't—" His throat tightened. "I couldn't stand not seeing you every day. Don't take that away from me too."

Stephanie's lips trembled, a fragile flicker of relief passing through her. She nodded, turning slightly toward her bag, her movements shaky but deliberate. "I should go," she whispered.

He didn't stop her. He couldn't. He watched her walk toward the elevator, each step pulling her farther from him, the space between them heavy with everything unsaid, everything withheld, everything waiting.

When the soft ding of the closing elevator doors echoed through the apartment, Trey sank back against the sofa, staring at the empty space where she had been. Silence pressed in, suffocating and absolute. His chest ached, his heart thrummed painfully, but beneath the hurt, a quiet, stubborn thread of hope remained. He would wait. He always would.

Chapter Thirteen

He stood frozen, staring at the elevator doors that had swallowed her, his fists clenched so tightly his knuckles ached. Every nerve in his body screamed to chase her, to tear down the walls she was trying to build, to hold her and never let go. But he forced himself to stay rooted, the raw ache in his chest fiercer than any whiskey could dull, sharper than the sting of rejection.

She thought she was protecting him by pushing him away. She thought she could create distance, convince him to let her go. But she was wrong. She didn't get to make that choice for him—not alone.

If she wouldn't let him love her openly, he would find a way to stay. Boss. Friend. Shadow. It didn't matter what shape it took. He would be there, in her life, by her side, no matter how long it took. Because letting her go wasn't an option. Not now. Not ever.

Jaw tight, Trey crossed to the bar and lifted the half-full glass, the amber liquid catching the light. Without a second thought, he poured it down the sink in one sharp motion, the sound of liquid splashing into the basin echoing like finality—and a promise. He didn't need the whiskey to steady him; his resolve had never been clearer.

Stephanie might believe she could shut him out for Ryan's sake, might think she could hold him at arm's length to protect him, to protect herself. But he knew the truth now.

He loved her. Not just the woman who made his world brighter, who stirred something in him no one else had ever touched—but the woman who would sacrifice her own happiness to protect someone else. That kind of heart, that kind of strength… she was worth every single moment of the fight he would have to endure. Every delay, every tear, every moment she wavered between duty and desire—he would wait. He would stay.

Their story wasn't finished. Not by a long shot. And Trey would be there— patient, unwavering, relentless—whether she wanted him to or not. He would be there until she realised what he already knew in his bones: they belonged together, no matter the obstacles, no matter the timing.

He sank into his chair, letting the silence press in, tasting the bitter absence of her touch, but beneath it all, a quiet, stubborn fire burned. Stephanie Vale might have walked away tonight, but he would not—could not—let her go. Not ever.

The next morning, Stephanie sat stiffly at her desk, hands folded so tightly in her lap that her knuckles had gone white. She had done her best with concealer, but the mirror hadn't lied—her eyes were still rimmed red, shadowed with exhaustion and the residue of a night spent wrestling with guilt and impossible choices. She felt fragile, brittle, as if one wrong word could shatter her composure entirely.

The familiar cadence of footsteps echoed down the corridor, precise and deliberate. She braced herself. A moment later, Trey's voice cut through the quiet, smooth but roughened by something he couldn't hide.

"Morning, Ms. Vale."

It should have sounded ordinary, neutral, but it didn't. It carried weight—the ache of unspoken words, the tension of emotions neither of them could fully release. Stephanie forced herself to look up, her lips twitching into a polite, faint curve.

"Morning, Mr. Grayson," she murmured. Her voice was measured, even, but her eyes betrayed her fatigue and the silent storm raging beneath the surface.

For a long, suspended second, he just stood there, watching her. Every instinct screamed at him to move closer, to bridge the distance she had imposed, to reach for the vulnerability he knew she was hiding. But he held himself back, retreating behind the professional veneer he knew she needed.

"How… are you holding up?" he asked quietly, the formality slipping like sand through his fingers, betraying the concern he couldn't suppress.

Stephanie blinked, throat tight, and gave a small, fragile nod. "Trying my best," she whispered, lowering her gaze to the neatly stacked papers on her desk.

Trey's jaw flexed. He wanted—needed—to say more, to reach out, to tell her she didn't have to carry the weight of everything alone. But he held back, forcing his words into the confines of professionalism.

"Clear my morning schedule," he said finally, tone clipped but not unkind.

"Yes, sir," she murmured, eyes still lowered. As he passed her and entered his office, he felt the weight of her silence trailing him, pressing into him like a physical presence. The ache in his chest was almost unbearable. She was here—within reach—but somehow, she had never felt farther away.

Trey shut the office door with a sharp click, a sound that seemed impossibly loud in the otherwise quiet space. He pressed his palms flat against the wood for a moment, jaw locked, before dragging a hand down his face. Seeing her like this—red-rimmed eyes, a brave, forced composure, fragile yet determined—had torn something open in him. She was breaking, and yet she tried to carry it all alone.

He paced to the window, staring out at the city skyline, but all he could see was her. The brittle curve of her lips. The tiny catch in her voice when she said, *Trying my best.* He wanted to go back out there, close the distance between them, take her hand, and tell her she didn't have to pretend—not with him. But she had made her choice. She thought she was protecting him, sparing him, shielding him from the pain she carried. Chasing her now might only push her further away.

He sank into the chair behind his desk, every muscle taut, fists curling against the polished surface until his knuckles ached. She was right there, yet she felt worlds apart. He exhaled sharply, the sound harsh in the stillness of the office, eyes burning as he stared at the skyline he could no longer focus on.

Fine. If she needed distance, he would give her that illusion. If she thought she could push him away, he'd let her believe it. But the truth burned brighter than any pretence: he wasn't walking away. Not from her. Not ever. She could pretend. She could build walls. But he would remain, a steady presence, waiting, fighting for her in every way she would allow.

And when she was ready, he would be there—steady, unwavering, and completely hers.

They carried on as best they could. Trey maintained the careful facade of the detached executive, keeping a professional distance that masked every inch of his restless attention. Stephanie moved through her tasks with her usual precision, every keystroke, every folded corner of a document executed with practiced efficiency. To anyone else, it looked like a normal, uneventful afternoon at the office. But Trey noticed the small fissures she tried so hard to conceal—the slight hesitation before she answered an email, the way her fingers lingered a fraction too long on the keyboard, the faint tremor in her jaw when she exhaled.

By mid-afternoon, Stephanie was buried in emails when her phone buzzed. She glanced at the screen—Sofia. Her stomach tightened immediately, a sharp twist of worry and anticipation.

"Steph, it's me," Sofia said gently, her voice soft and reassuring. "The specialist wants to see us at four. Do you want to be there? Can you get away if you do?"

Stephanie gripped the edge of her desk, trying to steady herself. "I… I do want to be there. I'll… check with Mr. Grayson first."

"Text me if you want us to pick you up on the way—we go right past your building," Sofia added, her tone light but caring.

"Okay… thanks for letting me know," Stephanie murmured, taking a deep, steadying breath.

She rose and walked toward Trey's office, her shoes clicking softly against the polished floor. Her hand trembled slightly as she knocked on the door, forcing her tone flat and professional, though her pulse thudded in her ears.

"Mr. Grayson," she began, standing straight despite the tightness in her chest, "may I leave a little early today? Ryan's specialist wants to meet us at four."

Trey looked up instantly, pen resting in his hand, sleeves rolled, eyes flickering briefly to hers. His gaze was steady, unwavering, yet it carried the weight of every unspoken word, every lingering moment of the night before.

"Of course. Go," he said slowly, deliberately, his voice measured but not without warmth. "That's where you should be."

Stephanie nodded, relief mingling with something heavier she couldn't name. "Thank you."

He leaned forward slightly, lowering his voice so only she could hear, the veneer of the unshakable CEO softening just enough to reveal the man beneath. "If you need more time—days, weeks—take it. Don't worry about this place. I'll make sure it's handled."

Her hands curled into fists at her sides, bracing herself against the intensity of his words. The armour of professionalism hid the ache in his eyes, but not entirely—the patience, the pain, the longing, the unwavering promise all shone through in that quiet moment.

"I appreciate that," she whispered, barely audible.

He nodded, leaning back, forcing the distance, forcing the practiced calm of his role. "Go be with him, Stephanie. That's what matters right now."

Stephanie turned to leave, but Trey's hand curled into a fist on the desk, the subtle motion betraying the tension coiled inside him. Every fibre of him wanted to reach out, to stop her, to pull her back. But he didn't. Not yet. If letting her go—even just for a few hours—was what it took to keep her close, even in part, he would endure it.

As the office door closed softly behind her, Trey remained seated, eyes fixed on the empty space she had left behind. His chest ached with longing and frustration, but beneath it all was a steadfast certainty: he would wait. He would stay. And no distance, no circumstance, would ever change that.

Stephanie followed Ryan into the specialist's consultation room, Sofia and Peter close behind. The sterile scent of antiseptic clung to the air, mingling with the faint metallic tang of fear that seemed to radiate from Ryan. His hand found hers, fingers lacing tightly with hers, grounding both of them. Sofia and Peter settled on either side, their presence a protective buffer, silent but steady.

The specialist's gaze swept the room with calm precision, though his words carried a weight that pressed heavily on everyone. "The scans show an aggressive glioblastoma," he began, voice measured. "With comprehensive treatment—surgery, followed by radiation and chemotherapy—patients can often survive twelve to eighteen months. The exact outcome varies, depending on individual response and adherence to treatment."

Sofia's hand flew to her mouth, muffling a gasp, while Peter's arm instinctively went around her shoulders. Stephanie's heart lurched violently, her chest tightening as she pressed her thumb along Ryan's knuckles in a silent anchor.

"Immediate surgery is necessary," the doctor continued, flipping through the images on the lighted panel. "After surgery, strict radiation and chemotherapy follow. Regular MRI scans and neurological assessments will track progress. Symptom management—medication for swelling, pain, or neurological issues—will be ongoing. We need to admit Ryan tonight. Surgery should be scheduled in the next few days. The sooner we begin, the better his chance of maintaining function and independence."

Stephanie felt her chest constrict. She lowered her head gently against Ryan's shoulder, feeling the faint rise and fall of his breathing. "We'll face this together," she whispered, her voice trembling but determined, a promise she wasn't sure she could keep in its entirety—but one she had to make.

Ryan's eyes flicked to hers, a flicker of gratitude mingling with raw fear, vulnerability peeking through his usual calm exterior. "I… I can do this," he said softly, each word carrying both hope and uncertainty.

Stephanie's thoughts threatened to wander to Trey—the warmth of his hands, the quiet patience he had shown, the hope he had placed in her. She clenched her jaw and forced it down, pressing her lips into a thin line. Not now. Ryan needed her. Every ounce of her focus, every beat of her heart, belonged here, to him, in this fragile moment where love meant presence, not desire.

She straightened slightly, squeezing his hand, drawing a deep, steadying breath. "We'll take it one step at a time," she said, voice low but firm. "You're not alone. We're right here with you—every step of the way."

Peter nodded, his expression tight but resolute. Sofia's grip on Ryan's arm was gentle yet unyielding, an anchor in the storm. And for the first time since the diagnosis, Stephanie allowed herself a sliver of clarity: no matter the sacrifices, the heartache, or the choices she would have to make later—right now, Ryan's fight was hers too.

The doctor adjusted his glasses and leaned back slightly, sensing the weight in the room. "I know this is a lot to take in," he said gently. "We'll guide you through every step. The treatment is aggressive, yes, but with a strong support system, Ryan can maintain his independence and quality of life for as long as possible."

Stephanie pressed her lips to Ryan's shoulder once more, silently vowing that she would be that support, that constant presence—even if it broke her in ways no one could see.

That evening, as Stephanie, Sofia, and Peter left Ryan's hospital room, she promised she'd be back in the morning before surgery. Ryan murmured, "I love you, Steph."

She pressed her lips to his shoulder. "I love you," she whispered, burying her face so none of them could see the guilt twisting her heart.

Sofia and Peter drove her back to their apartment on in near silence. Peter squeezed her hand. "We'll be there at seven in the morning. We'll all go together."

Stephanie nodded, throat tight. "Thanks. I… I really appreciate it."

Sofia smiled. "You've done so much already. Rest when you can, okay?"

Inside, Stephanie showered, dressed comfortably, made a sandwich, and finally messaged Trey:

Ryan's surgery is tomorrow morning. I'm sorry I won't be in. I need to be there for him and his parents.

His reply came instantly:

Thanks for letting me know. I hope all goes well. Look after yourself too, Steph. I'm here if you need me.

Stephanie typed back simply:

Thank you.

She set the phone aside, exhaling slowly. There would be no easy sleep tonight, but at least Ryan—and the people she cared about—would know she was there. That was all that mattered for now.

Stephanie curled up on the edge of the sofa, a blanket pulled tight around her shoulders. The apartment felt impossibly quiet now, stripped of the chaos of the hospital and the presence of Sofia and Peter. She set her sandwich aside, untouched, and let her head rest against the cool leather.

Her mind refused to slow. She replayed the doctor's words over and over— eighteen months if he follows treatment—and the impossible weight of the choice she'd made pressed on her chest. Ryan's life depended on her presence now. She couldn't leave him, not after everything.

And yet… Trey. Every smile, every whispered promise, every stolen moment replayed in her mind. She had wanted him, she loved him, and now she was denying herself the one person who had made her feel whole. The guilt twisted in her stomach like a knife.

Her phone buzzed again, a small reminder that the world outside Ryan's apartment still existed. She picked it up and stared at Trey's message:

If you need anything, just ask.

She whispered his name into the stillness, tears blurring her vision. She wanted to reach out, to call him, to let him know she was alive, that she was thinking of him—but it didn't feel right. Not tonight. Not when Ryan needed her.

Hours passed—or maybe minutes; she couldn't tell. Her body ached with exhaustion; her mind thrummed with anxiety and longing. Finally, the tension in her shoulders eased just slightly as sleep tugged at her.

She tucked the blanket tighter around her shoulders, curling into herself, and let the darkness of the night swallow her. For now, she would rest. Tomorrow, she would be ready. Tomorrow, she would be there for him.

Even if it meant her own heart would have to wait.

The hospital room was quiet, broken only by the rhythmic beep of monitors and the soft hiss of the oxygen machine. Morning light filtered through the blinds, casting pale stripes across the bed where Ryan sat propped against pillows, hospital gown slightly rumpled. His hair was tousled, eyes tired but alert, and a faint, nervous smile played across his lips as Stephanie, Sofia, and Peter entered.

Stephanie moved immediately to his side, sliding into the chair beside the bed and taking his hand in hers. Her fingers laced tightly with his, a silent tether. "Morning," she whispered, voice soft but steady, a fragile attempt at normalcy.

"Morning," Ryan rasped, squeezing her hand weakly. "Thanks for… for being here."

"You don't have to thank me," Stephanie replied, brushing a stray strand of hair from his forehead. "I'm where I want to be." Her words were simple, but beneath them, a storm raged—guilt, longing, and the memory of Trey, all pressed into a quiet knot in her chest. She clenched her jaw, forcing herself to stay present.

Sofia stepped closer, resting a comforting hand on Ryan's shoulder. "We'll all be right here, Ryan. Every step of the way."

Peter lingered near the foot of the bed, arms folded but eyes soft with concern. "The team knows what they're doing. You're in good hands," he said, his voice firm but gentle.

Stephanie leaned closer, pressing her forehead lightly against Ryan's temple. "We'll get through this," she whispered. "You're not alone, okay?"

Ryan's gaze met hers, full of trust and fragile hope. "I love you," he murmured, squeezing her hand once more.

Stephanie's throat tightened, a lump forming as the words landed heavy in her chest. "I love you too," she whispered back, pressing her lips to his forehead and letting her face rest against the curve of his shoulder. She held herself still, careful not to let him see the storm of guilt and longing swirling in her eyes. Each heartbeat reminded her of the impossible choice she had made, the life she had quietly set aside to stay by his side. She didn't know if he sensed it, and she couldn't let him. Not now.

A soft knock at the door drew her attention. The nurse appeared, clipboard in hand, calling Ryan's name gently. "It's time," she said.

Stephanie helped him adjust in the bed, her hand never leaving his. She offered him a reassuring smile, her voice steady despite the ache in her chest. "We'll be waiting when you wake up," she promised, squeezing his hand one last time.

Ryan's eyes lingered on hers, gratitude and fear mingling in the pale morning light. "Thank you… for everything," he whispered, voice fragile, nearly swallowed by the hum of the machines.

Stephanie nodded, holding the promise tightly in her heart. "Always," she murmured softly, letting him slip out of the room with the nurse.

Sofia squeezed Stephanie's shoulder with a quiet strength, and Peter placed a hand on her other arm. "We'll be there the moment it's done," Peter said firmly, grounding her.

Stephanie exhaled slowly, her chest tight, forcing her mind to release the fleeting thought of Trey—the life, the love, the possibility she had let go of. It tugged at her heart, sharp and bittersweet, but she pushed it aside. Ryan needed her fully now, and she would be there, unwavering, even as a part of her quietly ached for what could not be.

Stephanie sat between Sofia and Peter in the stark, sterile waiting room, her hands clasped tightly in her lap. The hum of fluorescent lights overhead and the faint squeak of nurses' shoes against linoleum made her skin crawl with anxiety.

Sofia sat close, her hand occasionally brushing Stephanie's for reassurance. Peter's arm rested protectively on the back of the chair; eyes fixed on the closed door to the surgical suite. All three were silent, the weight of anticipation pressing on them in waves.

Stephanie's phone buzzed. She glanced down and saw a text from Rebecca:

Thinking of you. You're doing the right thing, Steph. I'm here if you need me.

Her chest tightened. She wanted to reply, to explain the jumble of fear and guilt twisting inside her, but she couldn't. She put the phone down, pressing her fingers against it like it could somehow channel her support across the city.

Another buzz—Trey. Her stomach clenched. She opened the message with trembling hands:

Her breath hitched. She stared at the words, torn. She wanted to reply, to tell him she was safe, that she was there for Ryan—but she couldn't. Not yet. Not when every second felt like it counted for Ryan.

Sofia's soft murmur brought her back. "He's going to be okay," she said, though the tight line of her jaw betrayed the worry she didn't voice.

Peter nodded, his hand squeezing hers gently. "We'll be right here when he comes out. No matter what, he's not alone."

Stephanie nodded, swallowing hard, pressing the phone face-down on her lap. Her fingers curled into the leather of her purse. The messages from Trey and Rebecca were lifelines she couldn't use yet—but just knowing they were there gave her a flicker of strength.

And so, they waited. Minutes dragged like hours. Every footstep in the hallway, every muffled conversation, made her heart lurch. Stephanie leaned forward slightly, her eyes fixed on the closed doors, silently willing the surgery to go smoothly, silently willing Ryan to come through this with the life they all hoped for.

The fluorescent lights in the waiting room seemed sharper now, harsher, as Stephanie, Sofia, and Peter hunched forward in their chairs. Every tick of the clock, every distant murmur from the hallway made her stomach twist.

Chapter Fourteen

Hours later, the door at the end of the corridor opened, and a man in a white coat stepped through. His expression was serious, calm, but his eyes carried the weight of what he had seen behind those doors. Stephanie's heart stuttered as he approached.

"Family of Ryan Carter?" he asked.

Sofia and Peter rose immediately, Peter's hand gripping Sofia's shoulder, while Stephanie pushed herself up, clutching her purse as if it could anchor her.

"That's us," Peter said firmly, though his voice was tight. "Is he okay?"

The surgeon gave a short nod. "Ryan's surgery went as planned. The tumour was aggressive, but we were able to remove the majority safely. There were no major complications during the operation."

Stephanie felt a breath she hadn't realised she was holding escape in a shuddering exhale. Her hands pressed to her mouth. "He... he's going to be okay?" she whispered, almost afraid to hope.

The surgeon's gaze softened slightly. "He's stable. He's in recovery now, resting. There will be swelling and some neurological effects to monitor over the next twenty-four hours, but right now... he's safe."

Sofia's shoulders slumped, relief and exhaustion mingling in a sigh. Peter's hand found hers and squeezed it. Stephanie sank back into her chair, closing her eyes briefly, letting the tension drain in small, shaky waves.

The surgeon paused, placing a hand briefly on Peter's shoulder. "We'll monitor him closely. You'll be able to see him soon once he's awake and settled in the ICU."

Stephanie nodded, her throat tight, her heart full of conflicting emotions. She pulled out her phone to send a quick message to Trey and Rebecca:

He's through surgery. He's stable. I'll keep you updated.

A moment later, her phone buzzed—his reply:

Thank God. I'm glad he's okay. Be with him. I'll be here if you need me.

Stephanie pressed the phone to her chest, a bittersweet ache settling in her ribs. She couldn't tell him how much she wanted him. Not when Ryan's life—her responsibility, her devotion—was still so fragile.

Sofia rested a hand over hers. "We'll go see him in a bit," she said softly. "He needs us now."

Stephanie nodded, taking a slow, steadying breath. She couldn't let herself falter—not for Trey, not for Ryan. But she let herself whisper under her breath, a silent promise she didn't say out loud: I'm here. I'm not going anywhere.

Stephanie, Peter, and Sofia stood just outside the glass doors of the ICU, the faint hum of machines and the steady beep of monitors filling the sterile room. Ryan lay in the bed, pale but stable, tubes and wires running gently from his body. His chest rose and fell slowly under the rhythm of the ventilator.

Stephanie stepped closer, her hand brushing the back of his as if to reassure herself that he was really there, really breathing. Peter rested a hand on her shoulder, a quiet anchor, while Sofia stayed at Ryan's other side, her eyes glistening with tears.

"He looks tired," Sofia whispered, voice cracking.

Stephanie nodded, swallowing hard. "Surgery was long. But he made it through. That's what matters."

Peter gave a small, tight nod, his jaw set. "The doctor said he's stable. They'll keep monitoring him closely tonight, but everything went as expected."

Ryan's eyes fluttered open, dim but aware. When he saw Stephanie, a faint, exhausted smile touched his lips. "Hey…" he murmured, voice hoarse, but his fingers instinctively found hers.

Stephanie bent down, pressing her lips to his hand. "Hey, you're okay. You're okay," she whispered, trying to keep her own tears in check.

"I love you," Ryan said softly, squeezing her hand, his eyes never leaving hers.

"I love you too," Stephanie replied, her voice trembling, though she pressed her forehead to his shoulder to hide the guilt in her expression.

Sofia and Peter exchanged a glance; their faces etched with relief and lingering worry. Peter spoke gently, "We'll be right here. You're not alone, Ryan."

Ryan managed a small nod, closing his eyes briefly. Stephanie stayed at his side, fingers intertwined with his, murmuring quiet reassurances and stroking his hand, refusing to let go. The machines beeped steadily around them, a harsh but comforting reminder that he was still here, still fighting, and that they were there with him—every step of the way.

The next morning, ICU was quiet except for the rhythmic beeping of monitors and the faint hiss of the ventilator. Morning light filtered through the blinds, painting the room in pale, sterile stripes. Stephanie sat close to Ryan, her hand still loosely holding his, though he was now fully awake, blinking against the harsh light.

Peter and Sofia hovered nearby, standing protectively at the foot of the bed, their expressions taut with worry. Ryan's hair was damp from the nurse adjusting his gown, and the faint lines of exhaustion traced his face, but he was alert, and that small victory lifted Stephanie's chest with cautious relief.

The door opened softly, and the neurosurgeon stepped in, accompanied by an oncology nurse. He smiled briefly, but the professional gravity in his eyes made Stephanie's stomach knot.

"Good morning, Ryan," the doctor said, pulling up a chair. "How are you feeling?"

"…Tired," Ryan admitted, his voice hoarse. He gave a small, tired smile to Stephanie. "But okay, I guess."

"That's good to hear," the doctor replied gently. He turned to the group. "I wanted to go over the results from the surgery and the next steps for treatment."

Stephanie squeezed Ryan's hand, and he returned the gesture with a weak but grateful squeeze of his own.

"The surgery went as planned," the doctor began, "and we were able to remove a significant portion of the tumour. There are still some areas we couldn't remove safely, but the pressure in the brain has been relieved, which is why you're feeling more stable today."

Ryan nodded slowly, absorbing the words.

"Now," the doctor continued, "to maximise the time we have, we need to follow up with radiation and chemotherapy. If Ryan adheres to the full treatment plan, the prognosis is roughly twelve to eighteen months. That's the typical range for this type of aggressive glioblastoma."

Stephanie felt her chest tighten at the words, but she pressed a reassuring smile to his hand. Ryan's eyes flicked to hers, reading the unspoken support there.

"The treatment will be intense," the doctor said. "Radiation sessions daily for several weeks, combined with chemotherapy cycles. We'll monitor closely with regular MRIs and neurological exams. There will be side effects—fatigue, nausea, potential neurological symptoms—but our goal is to maintain quality of life while controlling the tumour as much as possible."

Sofia's hand gripped Peter's arm, and he gave her a small, steadying squeeze.

Stephanie leaned closer to Ryan. "We're with you, okay? Every step of the way."

Ryan managed a small, grateful smile. "Thank you… I don't know what I'd do without you." He glanced at his parents, then back at Stephanie. "I love you, Steph."

Her eyes stung, but she pressed her lips gently to his forehead, hiding her conflicted emotions from view. "I love you too," she whispered.

The doctor nodded, pulling out a small chart. "I know this is a lot to process. Take some time today, and tomorrow we'll start planning the first radiation and chemotherapy sessions. You'll have a team supporting you the entire way."

Ryan exhaled slowly, letting the reassurance sink in. Stephanie stayed close, brushing a thumb across his knuckles, letting him feel her presence as an anchor in the storm.

Outside the ICU, the world could wait. Here, they were united—a fragile but unbreakable front against the uncertainty ahead.

Later that afternoon, after Ryan had fallen asleep in his room, Stephanie quietly stepped out into the hallway. Sofia and Peter had gone to grab a quick cup of coffee and some air, leaving her a few moments alone to gather her thoughts.

She leaned against the cool wall, phone in hand, and typed a message to Trey:

Ryan is starting radiotherapy in the morning. He is stable for now.

Almost immediately, her phone buzzed with his reply:

Good. I'll be here if you need me.

Stephanie's thumb hovered over the keyboard, the cursor blinking like a silent metronome against her chest. She wanted—no, needed—to text him back, to pour out everything she felt, to lean on him as he had asked. But even as her fingers trembled, a sharp pang of guilt stabbed through her chest, halting her.

Her mind raced back over the last week: the stolen glances, the quiet moments that had made her heart ache, the way he had been patient, steadfast, willing to wait for her, no matter how long it took. And now she understood, painfully, that keeping him close under these circumstances wasn't fair. Trey deserved someone who could choose him freely, without reservation, without the weight of another life tethering her heart.

Her fingers shook, hovering above the keys a moment longer before she finally set the phone down, the silence echoing in the empty hallway. She pressed her forehead against the cool wall, eyes closing as if the pressure could somehow anchor her swirling thoughts. I can't keep him in my life like this, she thought, heart twisting painfully. It's not fair. He deserves to move on… to find someone who can love him completely, without guilt, without waiting.

The hallway was quiet except for the faint hum of the air system and the distant beeping of monitors, a rhythm that mirrored her rapid heartbeat. Stephanie exhaled slowly, letting the tension seep from her shoulders, willing herself to breathe evenly, to regain control over the storm in her chest. She wasn't letting him go completely—not yet—but she needed to create some distance. Not because she didn't love him. Not because she didn't want him. But because love sometimes demanded sacrifice, and sometimes that sacrifice meant stepping back, even when it hurt, so the other person could breathe.

Tears she hadn't realised were falling streaked down her cheeks. She brushed them away and straightened, forcing herself into composure, the weight of her decision pressing down like an invisible hand. With careful, measured steps, she walked back toward Ryan's room, each footfall deliberate. He needed her focus now, her care, her unwavering presence.

Trey… he needed freedom. Freedom to live, to love, to move forward without waiting in limbo. And perhaps, in granting him that space, she could finally allow herself to stay fully present where it mattered most—by Ryan's side, tethered by responsibility, loyalty, and the love that demanded her attention now.

She inhaled deeply, steadying herself, the edges of her heartbreak tempered by resolve. This is where I belong—for now. This is what I must do.

When they stepped back into Ryan's room, the soft hum of the monitors and the faint antiseptic scent wrapped around them, a quiet reminder of the fragility that hung in the air. Sofia moved first, resting a steady hand on her son's arm. Her touch was gentle but grounding, anchoring him against the subtle tremor of the machines. Ryan's eyelids fluttered, heavy and dazed from medication, yet his fingers found Stephanie's and curled tightly around hers, as if she were the one lifeline keeping him tethered to the world.

"Ryan," Sofia murmured, brushing a stray lock of hair from his forehead, her voice both tender and resolute, "when the doctors start treatment, I want you home with us. You'll need the support—and honestly, we'll all feel better knowing you're under our roof."

Ryan gave a faint, weary smile, the corners of his mouth lifting just enough to betray effort. "Mom, I don't need—"

"You do," Peter interrupted gently, voice low but firm, carrying the quiet authority of a father who would do anything to protect his son. "And we do too. This is something we'll face as a family. All of us together."

Ryan's gaze shifted between his parents, taking in the earnestness in their eyes, then softened as it landed on Stephanie. "What about you, Steph? You don't have to—"

"I want to," she said quickly, throat tightening with emotion. Her voice was quiet but unwavering. "I'll be with you, wherever you are. If staying with your parents makes things easier, then that's where I'll be too."

Sofia's eyes glistened, the mix of gratitude and relief clear in her expression. "Thank you, sweetheart. I know it won't be easy, but… it means the world to us to have you there."

Stephanie offered a small, fragile smile, but deep inside, a quiet ache lingered. Living under their roof would mean being fully absorbed into Ryan's world, a life shaped by hospital visits, medication schedules, and treatments. It would also mean pushing Trey further from reach, a part of her heart she had promised to guard yet was now quietly sacrificing. Maybe this was the only way to do right by everyone—by Ryan, by Trey, and by herself.

Ryan squeezed her hand weakly, a soft, grateful pressure that spoke louder than words. "Then it's settled. We'll go home… together."

Stephanie nodded, letting the decision settle in her chest like a bittersweet promise. She would be there for him, fully present, even as a part of her remained tethered to the longing she couldn't yet release.

Friday evening, the house felt different—heavier, quieter, even though every lamp was on and the smell of Sofia's cooking filled the air. Stephanie carried Ryan's overnight bag through the front door, following Peter as he helped his son ease slowly onto the sofa in the family room. Sofia fussed immediately with pillows, making sure Ryan was comfortable, making sure her boy had everything he could possibly need within reach.

Stephanie stood for a moment, unsure where she fit in this picture. She wasn't family, not really. Yet Ryan's fingers reached for hers the second she set the bag down, and that tether pulled her back into his orbit.

"Thank you for letting me stay," she said softly, glancing between Peter and Sofia.

Sofia straightened, brushing invisible lint off the blanket she'd tucked around Ryan. "Stephanie, you don't need to thank us. You're part of this too. Ryan needs you here." Her voice cracked, just a little, before she moved briskly toward the kitchen. "Dinner's nearly ready."

Ryan leaned his head back against the cushions, looking more worn than she'd ever seen him. "Feels like I'm ten again," he muttered with a wry smile. "Mom hovering. Dad watching like a hawk. And you—" he gave her hand a squeeze "—still right here."

Stephanie forced a smile, though guilt twisted in her chest. She sat beside him, keeping her expression steady, even as she felt the weight of Peter's quiet, assessing gaze.

Later, at the dinner table, the dynamic was unspoken but undeniable. Sofia filled Ryan's plate first, then Peter's. Stephanie sat opposite them, eating little, answering their questions when asked but mostly listening. Their stories of

Ryan's childhood, the easy family banter, wrapped around her like a blanket she wasn't sure she had the right to pull tighter.

Afterward, when Sofia insisted she take the guest room at the end of the hall, Stephanie felt both relieved and displaced. She lingered in the doorway before bed, watching as Sofia bent to kiss Ryan's forehead and Peter murmured something low to him. Stephanie followed, leaning down to brush her lips against his cheek.

"I'll be right here if you need anything," she whispered.

Ryan smiled faintly, eyes half-closed. "Don't go far."

"I won't," she promised. But as she walked down the hall, she wondered who she was really making that promise to—Ryan, or herself. Because every step she took away from Trey felt like a lie, and yet here she was, trying to bury that truth in the heart of this family.

Trey's penthouse was quiet—too quiet. The city sprawled endlessly beneath his windows; a glittering expanse of lights that winked like a thousand possibilities he couldn't reach. The hum of traffic far below was muted, swallowed by the height and isolation of his space. He had poured himself a drink hours ago, but the glass sat untouched on the table, amber liquid catching the glow of the lamps, mocking him with its warmth he couldn't summon. Even whiskey, his usual refuge, couldn't dull the gnawing ache inside him.

He let himself sink onto the sofa, phone still in hand, scrolling back through Stephanie's last text until the words blurred into one long, unbearable line: Ryan's surgery is tomorrow morning. I'm sorry I won't be in. I need to be there for him and his parents.

She hadn't needed to apologise. Of course she was with Ryan. Of course she was with his family tonight. That was Stephanie—loyal, steadfast, selfless even when it broke her. And yet, knowing it didn't soften the hollow in his chest. The ache didn't fade—it only deepened.

He imagined her now, seated beside Ryan, fingers laced through his, thumb brushing gently over knuckles. Maybe she was laughing quietly at one of Peter's awkward attempts at humour, maybe smiling through tears as Sofia recounted memories meant to ease Ryan's fear. She belonged there tonight. He knew that with every fibre of his being. But knowing it didn't stop the sting of her absence, didn't keep his heart from twisting in frustration and longing.

Trey rubbed a hand across his face, jaw tight, leaning back into the cushions. Her voice haunted him—the break in it, the hesitation, the trembling as she'd said she couldn't leave Ryan, that she couldn't ask him to wait. That she couldn't be fully his, not yet.

And yet, he couldn't make himself walk away. He couldn't stop loving her, no matter the pain it caused him. She could push, deflect, create distance—but as long as a thread of her remained in his life, he would hold on. Boss, friend, shadow—he didn't care. He'd take whatever she gave, endure whatever boundaries she set. If it meant keeping her close, he would wait, quietly, relentlessly.

The night stretched long and lonely, the city outside glittering with indifferent indifference. Trey sat back, eyes tracing the skyline, heart heavy but resolute. His fingers tightened around the empty glass, knuckles whitening. The world could carry on around him, filled with everything he had ever wanted—but it didn't matter. Because the only thing that truly mattered was her.

And in the silence, he whispered a vow he knew she would never hear, but the walls, the city, the night could hold for him:

"I'll wait, Steph. No matter how long. I'll wait."

He let the words settle, a fragile anchor in the storm of his longing, and closed his eyes, imagining her, holding onto him in the small ways she allowed—and that would have to be enough.

Chapter Fifteen

The weekend passed in a haze of quiet, measured moments. Stephanie and Ryan spent most of it side by side, letting the hours stretch lazily around them, talking about everything and nothing, filling the silences neither of them wanted to confront. On Saturday, they wandered slowly through the Carter estate, Ryan leaning on her arm as the crisp autumn air brushed their cheeks. The gardens were tranquil, almost painfully so, and Stephanie tried—truly tried—to stay present, to notice the soft curve of Ryan's smile, the warmth of his hand as it closed around hers, the way his laugh felt like a tether to life in the midst of uncertainty.

But no matter how hard she tried, her thoughts kept straying. Her mind betrayed her, slipping inevitably to Trey—the memory of his voice, low and intimate; the way he had looked at her as if she were the only person in the world; the ghost of his touch that lingered in her skin. Each memory was a bittersweet ache, a reminder of the life she had almost allowed herself to step into and the man she had promised would wait. Guilt coiled through her with every smile she offered Ryan, twisting tighter each time he squeezed her hand.

By Sunday afternoon, after Ryan had grown weary and retreated upstairs to rest, Sofia found her in the kitchen, the warm light of late afternoon spilling over the countertops. Peter was there too, leaning casually against the counter, the quiet steadiness of his presence grounding her more than he probably realised.

"You should think about going back to work tomorrow," Sofia said gently, her eyes sharp yet kind, the ones that always seemed to see more than she let on.

Stephanie shook her head immediately. "No—I need to be here. Ryan needs me."

"Ryan has us," Sofia replied softly, stepping closer. "You've barely left his side since this all began. You're carrying too much, sweetheart."

Peter chimed in, calm but firm. "And you'll run yourself ragged if you don't find a little balance. Ryan wouldn't want that."

Stephanie opened her mouth to argue, but the words caught in her throat. Part of her longed for the normalcy of work, not just to reclaim routine but... to see Trey. To catch even a fleeting glance, to hear his voice, to feel the faint pull of hope that lingered whenever he was near.

She lowered her gaze, fingers twisting around the mug she held. "I just... I don't want Ryan to feel like I'm abandoning him."

Sofia's hand closed over hers, warm and reassuring. "Being here doesn't mean you can't breathe. And going back to work doesn't mean you love him any less.

You'll be stronger for him if you have something outside of this to hold onto, something that reminds you who you are beyond these walls."

Stephanie swallowed hard, the knot in her chest tightening. Guilt gnawed at her, relentless and persistent, but beneath it, a spark of selfish longing flickered to life. She nodded slowly, almost reluctantly. "Maybe… maybe you're right."

But deep down, she already knew she would go. Not just for Ryan's sake, not just because Sofia and Peter were right. But because a part of her—small, stubborn, human—needed to see Trey. To be near him, even if only for a moment, and to remind herself that there was still a life outside the fragile orbit of illness, a life where she could feel her heart beat for herself as well as for others.

Later that evening, Stephanie perched on the edge of Ryan's bed, the soft hum of the monitors and the faint scent of antiseptic surrounding them. Ryan rested against his pillows, pale but offering her a faint, reassuring smile. She hesitated, twisting her hands together, the simple motion betraying the storm of emotion coiling in her chest.

"Ryan… your mom and dad suggested I go into work tomorrow. Just for a little while," she said, her voice hesitant, almost fragile.

Ryan's brow lifted, a trace of surprise crossing his face. "And… you don't want to?"

"I… I don't know," she admitted, her voice trembling slightly. "I feel like I should be here with you every second. I don't want you to think I'm… abandoning you." Guilt coiled like iron around her ribs, making each breath a little sharper.

Ryan reached for her hand, his fingers lacing with hers. Despite everything, his grip was steady, grounding. "Steph, you've been with me through everything— every appointment, every late night, every fear. You don't have to prove anything to me."

Her throat tightened, tears threatening to spill. "But I don't want you to feel like I'm leaving you," she whispered, pressing her lips together to hold them back.

He gave a small, quiet laugh, a sound fragile but warm. "I'd never think that. I want you to go. To do something normal. To keep living your life, even while all this is happening to me." He brushed his thumb gently over her knuckles, a small gesture of reassurance that made her chest ache. "Besides, you light up when you talk about your work. I'd hate for you to give that up just because of me."

Tears threatened again, and she blinked rapidly, willing them to stay behind her lashes. "You really mean that?" she asked, voice barely above a whisper.

"I do," Ryan said firmly, meeting her gaze. "Go in. Even if it's just for a few hours. It'll do you good. And… it'll make me happy knowing you're still living, still being you."

Stephanie leaned forward impulsively, burying her face in his shoulder. The steady warmth of him pressed against her, and for the first time that day, she let herself exhale. Relief mingled with guilt, twisting in her chest, but she didn't fight it. Because beneath it all, she wanted to go. She wanted to feel a little spark of normalcy, to remember who she was outside these four walls, even as her heart remained tethered to Ryan.

For a long moment, she stayed like that, letting the quiet hum of the room wrap around them, letting the weight of the world settle just enough to remind her that life, even in its most fragile form, still moved forward.

Monday morning, Stephanie smoothed the front of her blouse with trembling hands as she stepped into the Grayson Industries lobby. The familiar hum of ringing phones, the click of heels on polished marble, and the faint, comforting aroma of coffee enveloped her. It should have felt normal, grounding even, but after two days cocooned in Ryan's parents' home—where every movement was hushed, every word measured—it felt almost unreal. The world outside had kept moving while hers had been suspended, fragile and still.

She squared her shoulders and forced a polite smile at the receptionist, feeling the weight of every glance as she passed. The elevator ride upstairs stretched endlessly in her mind. Each floor that ticked by echoed the distance she'd forced between herself and Trey—and yet, a part of her heart had never left him.

When she reached her desk, her breath caught. Her chair was exactly where she had left it, her files stacked neatly as always. But there, in a slim glass vase, stood a fresh bouquet of white tulips. No note. No card. No words—but she didn't need them.

Her throat tightened as she brushed her fingers over the soft, cool petals. He knew. He always knew. Even in the silence between them, even in the distance she'd tried to enforce, he had understood.

Stephanie sank into her chair quickly, blinking hard to clear the sudden mist in her eyes. The hum of the office receded for a heartbeat as the elevator chimed, and then he stepped out. Trey, immaculate in a navy suit, expression carefully neutral, yet his gaze immediately found hers.

For a single, charged heartbeat, their eyes locked, and she saw it all there: the relief, the worry, the longing he had worked so hard to mask.

"Morning, Ms. Vale," he said evenly, his voice smooth, professional—cool enough to hide the tremor beneath.

Stephanie forced a steady inhale, lifted her chin, and met his eyes for a brief second. "Good morning, Mr. Grayson."

The exchange lasted mere seconds, but it felt like an entire conversation passed between them—unspoken, aching, restrained. Trey's eyes flicked to the tulips, lingering on them just long enough before returning to hers. His lips didn't move, yet the message was unmistakable: I'm glad you're here.

Her gaze dropped quickly, afraid he would see too much if she lingered, afraid that her heart might betray her resolve. She pressed her hands to her desk, straightened her posture, and let the world of emails, client calls, and reports wash over her.

Yet nothing felt ordinary. Every time she sensed his presence near, her chest tightened, every step he took across the office floor a quiet pulse in her veins. Every time she caught herself thinking of him—his voice, the warmth of his gaze, the quiet patience in his hands—guilt and duty forced the thought down, burying it beneath a layer of self-imposed restraint.

Still, the tulips remained, white and luminous against the sleek surface of her desk. Silent proof that some truths could not be hidden, some connections could not be erased, and that no matter how carefully she tried, some parts of her heart would always belong elsewhere.

Trey sank into his chair behind the polished desk, the morning sun cutting through the blinds in sharp, angled lines across the floor. He'd already been at the office for over an hour, sifting through the usual flood of emails, reports, and phone calls, but nothing had stuck. Nothing mattered except the soft, controlled way Stephanie had said, "Good morning," when she'd taken her seat. The memory lingered like a quiet echo in his chest.

His office door, normally closed, stood open today, a silent concession to his own impatience. He watched her from across the room, pretending to review a thick report, but his gaze kept drifting. She moved with careful precision—typing, sorting papers, answering calls—but every so often her eyes flicked toward the white tulips on her desk, and each glance tightened the ache in his chest. She was here, physically present, but not entirely herself. The weekend had pulled her heart in a dozen directions, and he could see the residue of it in the subtle tension in her shoulders, the tiny tremble in her fingers as she reached for a pen.

Every small movement spoke volumes. A furrowed brow, a barely audible sigh, the brief tightening of her jaw—each one told him she was carrying more than work today. Guilt. Responsibility. Loyalty. And him.

Trey's hands curled into fists on the edge of his desk. He wanted to cross the office in a single stride, to reach her, to pull her into his arms and tell her she didn't have to carry any of this alone. He wanted to hold her close, even if only for a heartbeat, to let her rest, to let her breathe. But he didn't. He wouldn't. Not yet. He had to respect the boundary she'd drawn, even knowing it was only temporary, even knowing her heart was tugging toward him every bit as fiercely as his toward her.

Because he couldn't force her heart. He couldn't demand she choose him when she was trying to protect someone else. All he could do was wait. Wait, watch, and be ready—patient, unwavering, and steady—when she was finally ready to let herself feel what she truly wanted. And if that took months… years… even a lifetime, he wouldn't walk away.

Trey exhaled sharply and straightened, forcing his shoulders back, trying to push down the ache that threatened to undo him. He lifted a folder from the desk, pretending to read its contents, but his eyes stayed on her. She was brilliant, determined, careful—and hurting. Every line of her posture, every shadow beneath her eyes, screamed of the emotional weight she carried.

He would stay close. Not just as her boss. Not just as a man hopelessly in love with her. But as a constant in her life. A quiet anchor, patient and resolute.

No matter how long it took, he would be there. And when she was ready, when she could finally allow herself to let go of fear and guilt, he would be waiting—steady, unwavering, entirely hers.

That afternoon, Stephanie sat in the quiet hospital waiting area, her hands knotted tightly in her lap. The low hum of the radiotherapy machine carried faintly through the thick doors, a constant, mechanical reminder of the battles waging behind them. Her chest felt heavy, each breath measured, deliberate.

Sofia lowered herself into the chair beside her, moving with careful, deliberate grace, silent but present. Her eyes were soft, observant, and full of unspoken support. Peter paced in the small space nearby, his steps deliberate yet restless, the occasional scrape of his shoe on the polished floor punctuating the stillness. Stephanie tried to focus on her own breath, the slight clatter of the reception desk in the distance, anything to keep her mind from racing.

Half an hour later, Ryan appeared, walking slowly, pale and tight jawed. His gaze avoided hers, locked somewhere beyond the room. The sight of him stirred a sharp ache in her chest. Stephanie sprang to her feet instinctively.

"How do you feel? Do you want water? Something to eat?" Her voice was soft, careful, but quick with concern, like she couldn't bear to keep her hands still.

"I'm fine," he snapped, jerking his arm from her steadying hand. The words cut through her like ice, sharper than the tight line of his mouth or the avoidance in his eyes, yet the sting lingered deeper—because he wasn't really fine.

Stephanie swallowed hard, forcing her voice steady. "Okay… let's just get you home." She kept her tone neutral, hiding the hurt that threatened to flare behind her eyes.

Sofia's gaze lingered on her, quiet and discerning. She read the tension in Stephanie's shoulders, the restraint pressed into the line of her jaw, the way her fingers flexed almost subconsciously. Sofia said nothing, but when she tucked her arm through Ryan's to guide him forward, her free hand brushed Stephanie's wrist in a fleeting, silent squeeze—a gesture that carried reassurance, solidarity, and understanding all at once.

Stephanie met her glance briefly, a faint squeeze of her own in return, acknowledging the unspoken truth between them: she would stay strong, even when it hurt. Even when Ryan pushed away. Even when every instinct inside her screamed to hold on tighter.

As they moved through the hospital corridors, Stephanie stayed close, a quiet shadow beside Ryan. Her heart ached with worry, her mind caught in the delicate balance between care and respect, love and restraint. She reminded herself with every step: right now, he needed her steady, not her panic; her presence, not her frustration.

Even if it meant swallowing the sharp edge of her own fear.

Lunchtime on Tuesday, Rebecca stepped out of the elevator and took a tentative breath, letting her gaze sweep over the sleek, glass-walled office. She had never been here before, and the bright, modern space—with its polished floors, minimalist furnishings, and muted hum of activity—felt simultaneously impressive and intimidating. Spotting the receptionist, she asked politely for Stephanie Vale's desk, then started walking.

When she arrived, Stephanie wasn't there. Rebecca's hands tightened around her bag strap as she glanced about the sleek reception area, torn between waiting or leaving. Stephanie had so much on her plate with Ryan's health; the last thing Rebecca wanted was to intrude. She hovered by the desk, drawing a steadying breath.

A deep, even voice spoke behind her. "Can I help you?"

Rebecca turned—and stopped cold.

He was taller than she expected, broader through the shoulders, his presence carrying an authority that needed no announcement. The cut of his suit framed him perfectly, and even holding his jacket casually over one arm, he looked as though he belonged in command of every space he entered.

This was Trey? Stephanie had undersold him badly. Her friend had mentioned he was handsome, but words hadn't done him justice. He wasn't just handsome—he was striking, magnetic in a way that made Rebecca's breath catch.

"I… uh, I'm looking for Stephanie Vale," she managed, her tone polite though her curiosity slipped through.

"I'm Trey Grayson," he said smoothly, extending a hand. His voice carried the same quiet authority as his stance. "I don't believe we've met."

Rebecca's eyes widened slightly as their hands met. His grip was firm, assured, the warmth of his palm at odds with the cool control in his demeanour. And those eyes—steady, unreadable, yet with a flicker of something that made her pulse quicken despite herself.

"Rebecca—Rebecca Thompson," she said quickly, trying to gather herself. "Stephanie's friend. She's not at her desk right now, I see."

Trey's gaze softened just enough for her to sense a flicker of warmth beneath the otherwise controlled exterior. "She should be back soon," he said, then after a brief pause added, "Would you like to wait in my office? It might be more comfortable than standing here."

Rebecca hesitated, glancing at the minimalist chairs and glass surfaces around her. Then she nodded. "Yes... I think I'd like that."

They walked to his office, the soft click of her heels against the polished floor punctuating the quiet. Inside, the room reflected him perfectly—dark wood, clean lines, understated elegance. Powerful, yet not intimidating. He gestured toward a chair across from his desk. "Please," he said. "Make yourself comfortable."

Rebecca lowered herself into the chair, clasping her hands tightly in her lap. After a long breath, she spoke, her voice quiet but sincere. "I... I wanted to apologise. For everything that's happening with Stephanie. I know it's complicated, and I know the choices she's made affect you too. I just... I felt like I should say it."

Trey studied her, his sharp eyes steady and unflinching, yet thoughtful. He leaned back slightly in his chair, fingers steepled. "I appreciate that," he said quietly. "It is complicated. But I don't blame her—or Ryan."

Rebecca twisted the silver bracelet on her wrist, letting the cool metal anchor her. "I just hate seeing her like this. I've never seen her so torn apart, and I feel... powerless. I don't know how to help. She was going to leave him, Trey. She told me—it was you she wanted."

A flicker of emotion crossed Trey's face—pain mingled with a fragile spark of hope. His gaze dropped briefly to the desk, hand brushing against a pen before he stilled it. "I know," he murmured. "And I'm not giving up on her."

Rebecca shook her head slightly, a rueful smile tugging at her lips. "She won't like that. She thinks you need to move on."

"I can't," he said simply, the quiet conviction in his voice leaving no room for doubt.

The clock on the wall ticked softly, marking out the silence that fell between them. Rebecca leaned forward slightly, her tone softening. "You'll need to tread carefully. If she even suspects you're waiting... it could drive her further away."

"I know," Trey admitted, jaw tightening as he leaned forward, forearms braced on the desk. "That's why I won't say it to her—not now. She doesn't need more pressure, not with everything she's carrying. But she won't push me out of her life either. I'll be here—steady, dependable... whatever she needs me to be. Her boss. A friend. The man in the background. Whatever it takes."

Rebecca's gaze flicked toward the open door as if expecting Stephanie to appear at any moment. Then she met his eyes again, earnest and knowing. "She'll push you away if she thinks you're clinging to something she can't give you right now. She's stubborn—convinced she's protecting you, even if it breaks her in the process."

Trey's mouth tightened, but he nodded slowly. "I know. And I can take it. Whatever distance she needs to feel safe—I'll take it. As long as I don't lose her completely."

Rebecca leaned back slightly, releasing a quiet sigh. When she spoke, her tone was soft but resolute.

"Then you should know something else. Ryan and Steph... they haven't really been a couple in months. Yes, they're still together in name, but that's all it is. He hasn't treated her the way she deserves—not for a long time. They haven't been close, not in any real sense. Honestly, I've been hoping she'd leave him for almost a year now."

Her eyes flicked to Trey, gauging his expression before continuing. "Ryan's not a terrible man, but he's not her person. He stopped cherishing her a long time ago. He hasn't given her the respect, the love, the care she should have. And Steph... she's been shrinking under that."

A shadow crossed Trey's face, sharp and fleeting. His jaw tightened, his hand curling briefly against the arm of the chair before he forced it open again, composure locked back in place.

"Don't misunderstand me," Rebecca said quickly, lifting a hand as if to hold him steady. "I'm not telling you this so you'll pressure her. I'm telling you because you need to understand what keeps her there. It isn't love. It isn't happiness. It's loyalty. And guilt. That's all."

Her tone softened, almost wistful. "She needs someone who won't give up on her. Who'll remind her she's worth more than just sacrifice. If that's you... then I'll support you. But you'll need to play the long game. For her sake."

The hum of the city pressed faintly against the glass, a soft reminder of the world moving on outside their small, heavy bubble.

"I can do that," Trey said at last, his voice steady, quieter than before. "For her—I can do that."

Rebecca's smile was small, touched with sadness, yet genuine. "Then maybe… she's luckier than she realises. And you have my support."

Trey inclined his head, eyes shadowed but resolute. "Thank you."

Before Rebecca could respond, a familiar voice called from the doorway. "Rebecca?"

Both their heads turned almost simultaneously. Stephanie stood just inside the doorframe, surprise flickering in her eyes as she took in the scene before her. Rebecca sat poised, calm and composed, while Trey's presence radiated that familiar mix of authority and unspoken intensity.

Rebecca rose gracefully, her smile warm and inviting. "Ah, there you are. I was waiting for you, and Trey introduced himself."

Stephanie's eyes flicked from Rebecca to Trey, taking in the faint tension that hung between them like a thin veil. Her lips pressed into a small, measured line. "I see," she said, her tone careful, controlled, yet not unkind.

Trey rose from his chair, straightening effortlessly, though his gaze lingered on Stephanie a fraction longer than propriety—or reason—would dictate. "I thought it might be more comfortable for her to wait in here," he explained, his voice smooth, casual, but layered with an undercurrent that only someone paying close attention would catch.

Rebecca gave a light shrug, her smile easy, almost teasing in its warmth. "And I didn't mind. It gave us a chance to talk."

Stephanie's eyes narrowed just slightly, a flicker of curiosity passing across her face. Something unreadable crossed her expression before she offered a small nod. "Well… I'm glad you two met. What brings you here?" Her voice was steady, but Trey caught the subtle tremor in the syllables—an unintentional betrayal of her attention.

Rebecca turned to her, her tone soft but tinged with affection. "Now that you're staying at Ryan's parents' home, I don't get to see you as much. So, I thought I'd come here instead."

Trey's gaze sharpened, shifting subtly back to Stephanie. Her pulse caught. She felt it before she even met his eyes—the quiet, piercing awareness, the unspoken realisation. He hadn't known she'd moved into the Carters' home.

Stephanie forced a calm expression, pressing her hands over the folder in her arms. Her voice was soft, almost measured, but her words carried a weight she couldn't entirely mask. "It… it just made sense. They want to spend as much time with Ryan as possible." She let her gaze drift momentarily toward Trey, as if inviting him to read between the lines.

Trey gave the faintest nod, controlled and minimal, yet his eyes lingered on her, sharp and questioning, as though every unspoken thought danced behind them, daring him to articulate it.

Rebecca's eyes flicked between them, sharp, perceptive, and entirely unflinching. She caught the tension, the quiet undercurrent neither wanted to voice, and gave a small, thoughtful smile. It was the smile of someone who understood the layers beneath the surface—loyalty, guilt, love, and desire—without needing to name them. She didn't speak, but the air seemed to acknowledge her awareness, leaving Trey and Stephanie suspended in a charged, unspoken moment that neither could fully resolve.

For a heartbeat, the room held its breath, a fragile stillness punctuated only by the faint hum of the office around them, before Stephanie finally lifted her chin and stepped fully into the room, signalling a tentative return to reality.

Chapter Sixteen

The days blurred together, each one heavier than the last, stretching Stephanie thin until she barely recognised herself in the mirror. By midweek, the strain was impossible to hide. At the dinner table, the room glowing with lamplight and filled with the comforting aroma of Sofia's roast, she noticed Ryan struggling to cut his meat, his hand trembling slightly with the effort.

Without thinking, she leaned over and began to slice his food into smaller, manageable pieces. "Here… let me—"

"I can do it myself," he snapped, snatching the knife back with a frustrated jerk. The jagged cuts marred his plate, and his glare pinned her in place.

Stephanie's heart tightened, but she kept her voice calm, soft. "Of course. Sorry." She returned to her plate, pretending not to notice the tension in the room or the thin line of disapproval pressing Sofia's lips together. Peter cleared his throat, ready to intervene, but even he seemed to sense it was better to let the moment pass.

The week stretched on, each day folding into the next with quiet battles—stifled frustration, tired smiles, and unspoken words. By Friday night, Stephanie found herself alone in her room at the far end of the hall, the house hushed except for the faint hum of the refrigerator and the occasional creak of settling floorboards. The silence pressed down on her like a weight she could neither lift nor shake.

She replayed every moment from the week—the clipped words, the sharp looks, the subtle tension in Ryan's movements. Each one carved itself deeper into her chest until it was a physical ache, the kind that left her restless even in the stillness.

Her phone sat on the nightstand, glowing faintly with unread messages. She wanted to text Trey. She wanted the comfort of his arms, the steady reassurance in his voice telling her it would all be okay. But she didn't. She had asked him to step back, and he had honoured her request. Even from across the city, his patience reminded her of everything she was denying herself.

And yet the emptiness lingered, raw and insistent.

Because you love him. And you will probably lose him.

Stephanie squeezed her eyes shut against the thought, willing it away. She was doing the right thing—she had to believe that. She had chosen loyalty, care, and presence over desire, at least for now.

Setting her phone aside, she turned off the light and lay back on the bed, letting the darkness fold over her like a heavy, protective blanket. The quiet pressed in, unrelenting, but she let it settle. For now, she could exist in this fragile stillness, drawing what strength she could from it before the storm of tomorrow came calling.

Stephanie was quietly grateful it was Monday morning. The weekend had been a haze of careful routines and muted conversations, punctuated by Ryan's fatigue and the constant vigilance required to get him through each step of recovery. She had tried to be fully present, to anticipate his needs, to smooth out every obstacle—but exhaustion had a way of slipping through even her best intentions, and she could feel it settling into both of them.

By the time breakfast was over, Ryan's steps had slowed noticeably. His hand brushed along the wall for balance as he made his way toward the living room, the edges of his irritation visible in the tight set of his jaw.

"I can do this myself," he muttered, voice sharp but edged with weariness, as Stephanie reached instinctively to steady him.

"I know," she said softly, pressing a calm smile to her face, though her heart ached with the awareness of how fragile he seemed. "But just in case you need a hand."

He snorted, a humourless sound that carried a trace of bite, and she felt it land, a subtle sting she couldn't hide from herself. "I don't need a hand. I need a nap," he said, rubbing at his eyes with the back of his hand.

Stephanie's shoulders drooped ever so slightly, but she kept her tone gentle, nodding in acknowledgment. "Okay... then a nap it is," she murmured, stepping back just enough to give him space while still lingering close, ready if he faltered.

Sofia's gaze swept across the room and lingered on Stephanie. No words passed between them, but her eyes said enough—a quiet, perceptive warning. She saw the strain etched into Stephanie's posture, the subtle tension in the way she moved around Ryan, the way she tried to carry the weight of his recovery without letting it show. Sometimes the loudest caution isn't spoken aloud, it is felt—in a look, a pause, the soft press of a hand on a shoulder.

Stephanie caught the glance, briefly meeting Sofia's eyes. She gave the smallest of nods, a silent acknowledgment. She had noticed too. She was aware of the danger of overextending herself, of letting duty and guilt crowd out her own strength. But she pushed the thought aside for now, focusing instead on the quiet rhythm of the morning and the fragile, tentative peace of Ryan's presence beside her.

By midweek, the tension had seeped further into their daily rhythm, threading itself into every gesture, every glance. Dinner was a muted affair, the soft lamplight casting a warm glow over the dining table, highlighting the pale, tired lines of Ryan's face and the subtle weariness in Stephanie's posture. The aroma of the soup—gentle, light, and meant to nourish—wafted through the air, but it did little to ease the weight that pressed down on the room.

Ryan's fork hovered over his bowl, his frown deepening. "Soup again?" he muttered, the words sharper than intended, the edge betraying his fatigue and frustration.

Stephanie's hand froze midair, the spoon suspended as though time itself had stalled. "The doctors suggested it… to help you keep your strength," she said softly, careful not to let her voice waver.

He shoved the bowl slightly away, a sudden motion that made the liquid ripple. "I don't want soup. I want real food. I'm tired of this." His voice carried more than irritation—it carried the invisible weight of fear, of exhaustion, of feeling trapped in a body that betrayed him.

Stephanie swallowed, the lump in her throat tightening. She wanted to argue, to insist that this was exactly what he needed, that the carefully measured meals were for his own good—but she didn't. She knew that pushing now would only widen the fragile gap forming between them. Instead, she nodded, forcing a small, calm smile. Slowly, deliberately, she spooned another bite toward him. "Okay. I understand. I'll see if we can change it tomorrow."

Sofia's eyes flicked between them, the worry in her gaze barely contained. She noted the tension coiling subtly in Stephanie's neck, the careful restraint in her movements, the way she swallowed hard and set the spoon down after Ryan's sharp remark. She didn't speak—sometimes words would only make the strain heavier—but her silent presence was a gentle anchor.

Peter, seated quietly at the end of the table, let his eyes linger on the two of them for a moment, the faintest crease of concern on his brow. Ryan wasn't being cruel; he was scared, frustrated by the limitations of his body and the uncertainty of the path ahead. But Stephanie, ever attentive, was absorbing it all—every sigh, every flare of impatience, every silent plea hidden behind his tired eyes.

The room fell into a fragile quiet again, punctuated only by the soft clinking of utensils and the hum of the evening. The air was thick with unspoken emotions—guilt, worry, frustration, and an undercurrent of care that neither of them could fully articulate. And in the middle of it all, Stephanie's heart ached quietly, carrying more than her own weight, more than just concern for Ryan. She carried the longing, the guilt, and the hidden love she was trying so desperately to suppress.

By Friday, Stephanie welcomed a brief reprieve from the house. She met Rebecca at the small café tucked into the corner of the Grayson Industries building—a quiet haven from the constant hum of the office. The warm scent of espresso mingled with the sweet, buttery aroma of freshly baked pastries, wrapping around them like a soft, comforting blanket. It was a stark contrast to the tight, silent tension she'd carried all week, a momentary escape from the careful choreography of care she had to maintain at Ryan's side.

"You look exhausted," Rebecca said softly, her eyes tracing the faint lines around Stephanie's mouth and the subtle slump of her shoulders. "Really, Steph. You're doing too much."

Stephanie gave a weary sigh, letting her hands wrap around the warm mug in front of her. A faint smile tugged at her lips, though it didn't reach her eyes. "I'm fine," she said, the words brittle, hollow. "Ryan… he's just… he's having a hard week." Her voice carried the weight of unspoken worry, the endless rotation of hospital visits, medications, and small crises that left her depleted.

Rebecca reached across the table, letting her hand rest briefly over Stephanie's, grounding her. "I know you want to be there for him, but you need to be there for yourself too," she said gently, her voice carrying the warmth of someone who had seen too much of Stephanie's struggle.

Stephanie blinked, swallowing the tight lump in her throat, and let out a shaky breath. "I'll be okay," she whispered, almost more to convince herself than anyone else. She pressed her fingers lightly over Rebecca's before letting go, the gesture a fleeting acknowledgment of the support she so rarely allowed herself to accept.

For a moment, the two of them sat in quiet companionship, the muted hum of café chatter wrapping around them, the clatter of spoons against cups and soft murmurs of conversation creating a fragile sense of normalcy. It was a rare moment of stillness, and Stephanie felt it tug at her—a reminder that life outside Ryan's recovery existed, even if only in fragments.

With a final hug, Rebecca slipped on her coat and headed for the café door, the bell above chiming softly as she stepped into the crisp afternoon air. Stephanie watched her go, feeling a pang of longing for that simplicity, for the laughter and lightness that seemed a world away from the weight she carried. She lingered for a moment, finishing her coffee, savouring the warmth and the quiet before it slipped away.

Finally, she gathered her things, fingers brushing over the smooth surface of the table as if drawing strength from it and headed toward the building lobby. The city noise surged around her once more, brisk and relentless, and she squared her shoulders against it. Outside, the world was moving forward, indifferent to her burdens—but for now, she carried a small, flickering spark of comfort with her, a reminder that she could breathe, even just for a moment.

As Rebecca stepped into the bright, open lobby, her phone tucked securely into her bag, Trey's tall figure immediately drew her attention. He leaned lightly against the reception desk, shoulders relaxed but brows furrowed ever so slightly, eyes flicking toward the elevators with a measured intensity. When their eyes met, he straightened instinctively, smoothing his expression into his usual composed mask—but she could see the faint shadow of concern lingering there.

"Rebecca," he called softly, his voice carrying just enough weight to stop her in her tracks. She hesitated, raising an eyebrow as she turned fully toward him.

"I wanted to talk to you," Trey said, stepping closer, lowering his voice to a careful, almost intimate register. "I'm worried about Stephanie. She… she looks exhausted. And she's been doing too much for Ryan."

Rebecca's gaze softened, tinged with weariness and quiet empathy. "I know," she admitted, voice low. "Apparently, Ryan isn't making it easy for her. She's patient, kind… more than anyone should have to be. But she's carrying a heavy load—physically, emotionally… and alone, mostly."

Trey's jaw tightened, the edges of his mouth pressing into a thin line. "I see. Thanks for telling me." His eyes flicked toward the elevators, as if timing her inevitable departure, then back to Rebecca. "I'll keep an eye on her… discreetly. I won't interfere, but I can't just… let her wear herself down."

Rebecca offered a small, knowing smile, her gaze steady. "Just… don't push too hard. She's stubborn. She'll shut down if she feels pressured if she senses someone hovering. But she'll notice care if it's quiet, patient—if it's genuine."

Trey's lips lifted in the faintest trace of a smile, almost imperceptible, the tension in his eyes giving way to quiet determination. "I can do that," he said, his voice calm, deliberate, but carrying an undercurrent of unshakable resolve. "I'll be there, without her knowing it."

Rebecca nodded, understanding passing silently between them. "Good," she said softly. "Just… be careful with her heart. She's fragile in ways people don't always see."

Trey inclined his head slightly, eyes flicking back toward the elevators as she moved on. He remained rooted where he was, tall and unyielding, yet every line of his posture betrayed a mind racing—calculating how to protect her, support her, and remain a constant presence, all without ever letting her feel the weight of his gaze. The city beyond the glass walls bustled on, indifferent, but inside that lobby, Trey's focus was absolute: Stephanie.

The morning sun streamed through the tall windows of the Carter estate, casting soft golden light across the polished floors and the velvet drapes. Outside, the gardens were awash in autumn fire—crimson maples, amber oaks, the last of the roses clinging stubbornly to their stems. The air carried that crisp, faintly sweet scent that spoke of change, of endings and beginnings.

Sofia's voice broke the hush of the room, gentle but carrying a note of quiet insistence.

"Ryan, why don't you join us? Just a short walk around the grounds." She laid a hand on her son's shoulder, her touch tender, coaxing.

Ryan's eyes flicked toward the door, then hardened, shadowed by something darker than fatigue. "No," he said flatly. "I'm not going."

Stephanie, standing close by, felt the words lodge in her chest. She drew a breath, willing her tone to stay soft. "It's only a short walk, Ryan. Just around the gardens. Fresh air will do you good, and we can go as slowly as you need."

But instead of easing him, her words seemed to strike a raw nerve. His body stiffened, jaw tightening. "I don't need you telling me what's good for me!" His voice rose suddenly, sharp enough to slice through the calm, sharp enough to make Sofia's hand twitch back. "You think I can't handle anything on my own? I don't need a nurse, Steph. I need a life!"

Stephanie's stomach twisted. Her hands knotted at her sides, nails pressing into her palms. "I'm not trying to control you, Ryan. I just…" Her voice wavered, then steadied. "I want to help. You've been cooped up all week, and—"

"Help?" Ryan barked, his tone laced with bitterness. "This isn't help! This is pity!" His voice cracked on the word, his fists clenching at his sides. "You think I can't even take a walk without you hovering like I'm some… some invalid!"

The words struck like a blow. Stephanie's throat closed, her breath catching as though she'd been winded. Sofia moved to her side without hesitation, slipping her hand onto Stephanie's shoulder, firm and grounding. Across the room, Peter stood silently, his arms folded, his gaze heavy with quiet sorrow.

Stephanie fought back the sting in her eyes, forcing her voice into a whisper. "I just want you to be well."

Ryan turned away, his back rigid, his shoulders trembling faintly though his tone came out harsh and defiant. "Well, I am. I'm doing everything the doctors say. Isn't that enough? Can't you just… let me be?"

And before she could answer, he strode down the hall, his footsteps uneven, retreating into the sanctuary of his room. The door shut with a muted thud, leaving a hollow silence in his wake.

Stephanie stood rooted in the hallway, her chest aching with words unsaid, the weight of guilt and frustration pressing hard against her ribs. Sofia's hand remained steady on her shoulder, a silent comfort, but even that touch couldn't stop the tears that burned at the edges of her eyes.

The autumn light spilled across the floor, warm and gentle, a stark contrast to the cold space Ryan had left behind.

By midweek, the strain showed in ways that didn't need shouting to be heard. At Grayson Industries, Stephanie's once-bright presence had dulled. Her emails—usually sprinkled with warmth, even in their efficiency—had turned clipped, stripped down to the bare minimum. Polite, professional, but impersonal.

Trey noticed almost instantly. He skimmed over a message she'd sent to a long-term client, one she usually handled with charm that kept relationships strong. This version read like a cold transaction. No softness. No Stephanie.

The next morning, he stopped by her desk. He didn't announce himself, just leaned against the edge with casual ease that belied the careful thought behind the move. She looked up, startled, the faint shadows beneath her eyes betraying the truth her words rarely did.

"You're doing too much, Steph," he said quietly, his voice carrying that low insistence that always seemed to cut through her walls. "Don't forget yourself."

Her fingers froze on the keyboard. For one fleeting second, she let the concern in his eyes settle on her, let it warm the raw ache inside. Then, just as quickly, she dropped her gaze, pulling the mask back in place.

"I'm fine," she said briskly, too quickly, as if saying it with enough force might make it true. She shifted in her chair, the polite professionalism sliding between them like a shield.

Trey didn't push. He simply lingered a moment longer, watching her with eyes that said more than his words before he straightened and walked away. But the echo of his voice stayed with her, circling her thoughts no matter how hard she tried to silence it.

She bit her lip and focused on the screen, the tulips on her desk catching her eye in the corner of her vision. Don't forget yourself. She wished she could convince herself she was fine. But deep down, she knew his words mattered because they were true.

That same evening, back at the Carter estate, the kitchen glowed in the amber light of the oven. The soft hum of its fan was the only sound until Sofia broke the silence, her hands resting on the counter, her gaze lowered as though she could see Stephanie's weight traced out in the flour-dusted marble.

"She's carrying too much," she said, her voice low, threaded with quiet worry. "Ryan… he's not making it easy for her."

Peter stood opposite her, leaning against the counter with his arms folded. His expression was grave, his silence speaking before his words did. Finally, he nodded. "I've seen it. She's patient, steady—but she's only human. If he keeps pushing her away while leaning on her at the same time…" He trailed off, his jaw tightening.

Sofia exhaled, the sound weary, resigned. "She's not just helping him. She's holding the line for all of us—making sure the house runs, keeping Ryan calm, shielding us from the sharp edges of his moods. She doesn't let herself falter."

Peter's hands tightened where they rested, his voice a quiet vow. "Then we need to make sure she doesn't break under the weight. Because if she does…" He shook his head. "None of us will hold steady."

Outside, dusk painted the gardens in muted strokes of lavender and rose, the last autumn leaves trembling in the wind. But inside, the air hung heavy with tension, exhaustion, and unspoken fear. The cracks in their carefully maintained balance were widening, and they all felt it—whether they admitted it or not.

By the middle of the fourth week, the rhythm of treatment had ground into them all. What had once been carefully managed appointments and hopeful reassurances had shifted into an unrelenting cycle of side effects and weariness. The early energy Ryan had clung to—his stubborn insistence that he could handle it—had slipped away, leaving him hollow-eyed and sluggish. Fatigue clung to him like a second skin. Nausea stalked him from morning to night. And the smallest inconveniences—things he once would have laughed off— now ignited sparks of sharp words.

That evening, the family gathered for dinner, lamplight glowing across the polished table, the rich aroma of Sofia's roast filling the room. Stephanie had tried to fill the silence with gentle conversation—stories of the office, small memories from when she and Ryan had first met, even trivial anecdotes about Rebecca. Anything to push back against the heaviness. But Ryan's patience had worn thin.

"Steph, I don't need a babysitter," he snapped suddenly, his voice louder than usual, the sound slicing through the warmth of the room. "I need space."

The words struck like a blow. Stephanie's spoon froze halfway to her mouth. She lowered her gaze quickly, swallowing against the lump in her throat, her lips pressing into a line as she nodded. "Okay," she whispered, but the softness of her tone couldn't hide the sting.

Sofia's fork hovered above her plate, her face crumpling with quiet worry. Peter shifted in his chair, restless, his mouth opening as if to intervene before he thought better of it. The silence stretched taut across the table, fragile as glass.

After dinner, Ryan retreated down the hallway to his room, leaving the house wrapped in uneasy quiet. Stephanie stayed behind in the kitchen, hands trembling as she stacked dishes into neat piles that didn't need tidying. The clang of porcelain was too loud in the otherwise still space.

Sofia appeared in the doorway, her footsteps soft but steady. "Stephanie," she said gently, her voice carrying both caution and compassion. "Don't lose yourself in this. My son is hurting—but so are you."

Stephanie's hands stilled on the dish towel. She stared at the counter, her throat tightening. "I know," she admitted, barely audible.

Sofia crossed the kitchen, placing a warm, steady hand over hers. "You've been shielding him, trying to carry every part of this alone. But you can't. And you shouldn't. You matter too, darling."

Stephanie blinked rapidly, fighting the tears burning at the edges of her eyes. She forced a small smile that wavered at the corners. "I just… I want to be here for him."

"And you are," Sofia assured, her thumb brushing gently over Stephanie's knuckles. "But being here doesn't mean breaking yourself in the process. You're allowed to feel, too."

That night, when the house had finally gone still and the hum of the heaters filled the corners of her room, Stephanie let the mask slip. Lying on her side in the dark, she pressed her hand against her mouth to muffle the quiet sobs that poured free, tears she had swallowed for weeks. She mourned the sharpness of Ryan's words, the slow erosion of the man she remembered, the gap between the life she had imagined and the one she now lived—heavy with duty, endurance, and the silent ache of everything unsaid.

When the storm of tears finally passed, she wiped her cheeks and lay back against the pillow. One hand rested over her stomach as she whispered into the quiet, a promise even she could barely hear. I won't give up on him. No matter the exhaustion. No matter the hurt. Her loyalty would hold her here, steady as stone.

Monday morning dawned too quickly, and Stephanie felt unusually fragile as she slipped into the office. The contrast jarred her—the hum of phones, the faint hiss of the espresso machine down the hall, the brisk voices of colleagues. Life here moved on with relentless normalcy, while hers had narrowed into hospitals and quiet meals.

At her desk, her fingers hovered over the keyboard, but the words on the screen blurred. Emails stacked like impatient demands, each one small and sharp, but she couldn't seem to gather the focus to answer a single one. Her shoulders slumped, her chest tight with the weight she couldn't name.

Trey walked past on his way to a meeting and paused. He caught it instantly— the tension in her jaw, the slack weariness of her posture, the way she seemed almost swallowed by her chair. For a long moment, he stood there, his gaze holding her with quiet intensity. Then, without speaking, he moved on.

Minutes later, he returned, a warm cup of coffee in hand. He set it down gently on her desk, close enough that she could smell the comforting scent before she even looked up.

Startled, Stephanie glanced at him, her eyes meeting his just as her fingers brushed the cup. Their hands touched—brief, accidental, but enough to spark something alive in her chest, something she hadn't allowed herself to feel in days. Comfort. Understanding.

She cleared her throat, blinking quickly, and managed a small smile. "Thank you," she murmured, trying to sound distracted, careful, professional.

But Trey only gave the faintest nod, his gaze steady, unspoken words flickering in his eyes. *I see you. You're not alone.*

And for the first time in weeks, Stephanie let herself breathe just a little easier.

Later that day, Rebecca coaxed Stephanie into joining her for a quick lunch in the office café. The place was warm and humming with quiet conversation, the air rich with the scent of fresh coffee and the comforting aroma of baked bread. Normally, Stephanie found the café's chatter and bustle grounding, but today it all seemed distant—like she was moving through the motions without fully being there. Still, the presence of her friend was a balm, a reminder that she wasn't entirely invisible.

"You look... exhausted," Rebecca said gently, her hands curling around her latte as though she could draw strength from its warmth. Her gaze swept over Stephanie's face—the pale skin, the dark smudges beneath her eyes, the too-thin frame that told its own story. "And you've lost weight. I can see it, Steph. You're carrying too much on your own."

Stephanie gave a faint nod; her eyes fixed on the foam swirling in her cup. She wanted to answer, to reassure, but words sat heavy in her chest, tangled in fatigue and loyalty she couldn't seem to let go of.

Rebecca leaned closer, lowering her voice to something intimate, almost secretive. "And about Trey," she said softly. "I see it—the way you are around him. And the way he looks at you. He's not pushing, but he's there. Maybe... maybe you should let him. You don't always have to hold the whole world together alone."

At his name, Stephanie's throat tightened, her breath catching on the unspoken longing she carried like contraband. Guilt flared, sharp and punishing—Ryan's illness, Ryan's need for her, Ryan's fragility. But beneath it, dangerously close to the surface, lay the quiet truth she hadn't dared voice: Trey made her feel seen. Safe. Less alone.

Her fingers trembled against the ceramic, her voice breaking on the words. "I... I can't drag him into this," she whispered, her protest thin, unconvincing. "He deserves more than my mess. He... he needs to move on."

Rebecca's brows lifted, her gaze sharpening as she leaned in. "Steph... even you don't believe that," she said quietly, cutting through the excuse with a surgeon's precision. "You say he needs to move on, but your voice—your face—everything about you says you don't want him to."

Stephanie's head jerked up, panic flickering in her eyes. She forced a shaky laugh, a weak attempt at deflection. "That's not true. I just... I care about him, that's all. He deserves someone who isn't... tied down, who isn't breaking apart every other day."

Rebecca's expression softened, but her voice didn't waver. "You're not tied down, Steph. Not really. Ryan doesn't need your loyalty as much as you need your freedom. And Trey—" she paused, studying her friend intently, "—Trey sees you. He wants you. Don't pretend you don't feel it too."

Stephanie's throat worked as she swallowed hard. She tightened her grip on the cup, willing her voice to sound steady. "I do care for Trey," she admitted, low and trembling, "but that's why I can't pull him into this chaos. I won't be the reason he gets hurt. It has to stop with me. He needs… he needs to be free of me, Rebecca. It's the only way."

Rebecca held her gaze, unconvinced, but she didn't push further. Instead, she sat back, lips pressed together, letting Stephanie cling to the fragile wall she'd built around her heart.

When they returned to the office, Trey was already there—quiet, unobtrusive, but unmistakably present. He didn't hover. He didn't demand her attention. Instead, his care appeared in subtle gestures: a fresh cup of coffee left at the corner of her desk, the faintest nod as he passed, the way his eyes lingered just long enough to acknowledge her without pressing. There was a steadiness to him, a quiet patience that both comforted and unsettled her.

Stephanie sank back into her chair, pressing her lips together as she drew in a slow, controlled breath. For the first time in weeks, she entertained a thought she'd pushed away: maybe she didn't have to shoulder everything alone. Maybe it was possible to let someone in, even when the world felt heavy and fragile.

And yet, guilt clawed at her chest. The weight of Ryan's vulnerability at home, his reliance on her for strength she didn't always feel she had, anchored her firmly in place. She had promised to protect him, to be his unwavering support. To step back now—even slightly—felt like betrayal.

Her fingers wrapped around the warm cup Trey had left, the heat seeping through her palms. She lifted it to her lips, and for a moment, the world narrowed to that quiet, steady presence he offered. Not relief. Not escape. Something more delicate, more dangerous.

Hope.

But she shook her head slightly, chastising herself. She couldn't let hope turn into dependence. Trey didn't deserve to be dragged into the chaos of her life, into the guilt and the grief and the mess she carried. He had his own life, his own heart—and she wouldn't be the one to weigh it down.

Still, even as she told herself this, she felt it—a fragile, insistent thread pulling her toward him. And for the first time in weeks, she allowed herself to acknowledge it without immediately pushing it away.

Hope, she realised, didn't have to be a betrayal.

Chapter Seventeen

The final week of radiotherapy had arrived, and with it, the house seemed to tighten around its occupants. The air carried a brittle tension, fragile enough to crack at the slightest wrong word. Ryan's fatigue was heavier now, etched into the hollows of his eyes and the slump of his shoulders, and with the fatigue came a sharpness that flared at the smallest inconvenience. A bowl of soup he didn't want, a gentle suggestion to rest—each became tinder for his irritability.

Stephanie moved carefully, almost like someone navigating broken glass, each step measured, each word weighed before it left her lips. She tried to soothe, to ease, to keep the peace, but her balance was slipping. The more she tried to hold them both steady, the more it felt as though the ground beneath her was giving way.

At breakfast on Monday, Ryan's hand trembled slightly as he reached for his coffee. Instinctively, Stephanie leaned forward, steadying the cup before it could spill.

"Steph, don't," he snapped, jerking it back. His voice cracked with more frustration than strength. "Stop treating me like I'm helpless. I don't need pity!"

The word struck her like a blow. Pity. It echoed in her chest, cutting deeper than all the barbed remarks before. Stephanie froze, the edges of her composure unravelling. Her lips parted, but no answer came—no reassurance, no soft laugh to defuse the moment. Only silence. Her chest felt tight, every breath a struggle against the sting of the word.

Sofia, sitting opposite, exchanged a glance with Peter. The quiet message in her eyes was both worry and warning. She didn't intervene—sometimes the smallest act of love was restraint. Sometimes a single look said more than words ever could.

By mid-morning, Stephanie sat at her desk at Grayson Industries, but her mind was still raw, replaying Ryan's outburst like a bruise pressed again and again. When a minor disagreement over a client report surfaced, something she would normally have smoothed with gentle humour, she snapped.

"Honestly, can we just stick to what I asked?" The sharpness of her voice startled even her. Her colleague blinked, taken aback, and fell silent. Stephanie's pulse spiked as she realised what she'd done. She lowered her gaze, fingers tightening around her coffee mug, shame heating her face.

Later, when her phone buzzed, she barely looked until she saw the name. Trey.

You don't have to answer, just… I'm thinking of you.

Stephanie stared at the words for a long moment; her breath caught in her chest. A fragile warmth spread through her, curling gently against the ache she'd carried all morning. She didn't reply—she couldn't. But she saved the message, anyway, tucking it away like a small talisman. Proof that someone noticed. Proof that someone cared.

That evening, after the house had quieted, Sofia and Peter lingered in the kitchen. The low hum of the refrigerator filled the silence between their words.

"She's withering, Peter," Sofia murmured, her hand pressing against the cool edge of the counter. Her voice carried both worry and sorrow. "And she won't leave him. She's holding on, no matter how much he pushes her away."

Peter leaned back, arms folded, his jaw tight. "I can see it. She's steady, but even steadiness has a breaking point. We have to watch her. If she collapses under this..." He shook his head, unfinished words heavy in the air.

Sofia's eyes softened, though her voice was resolute. "It's hard to watch her sacrifice herself piece by piece. But she's stubborn. Stronger than I ever imagined. She'll endure... even if it means enduring alone."

Beyond the windows, the fading light softened the edges of the Carter gardens, bathing the grounds in muted gold. But inside, shadows lingered in the corners of the house. Stephanie moved quietly from room to room, her footsteps soft but heavy, her thoughts circling endlessly—loyalty, love, exhaustion, each one pulling at her in different directions until she could hardly tell which way was forward.

And still, she carried it all.

By Friday night, the strain finally caught up with her. Ryan had retired early, exhausted beyond words, leaving the house quiet but heavy, as if the walls themselves had absorbed his fatigue and frustration. Stephanie lingered in the kitchen, stacking dishes slowly, her hands trembling just enough that the porcelain clicked softly against the counter. Once the last plate was done, she exhaled, a long, shuddering breath, and moved to her room, closing the door behind her with a careful click.

She sank onto the edge of the bed, curling inward, arms wrapped tight around herself. Tears she had fought back all week slipped freely now, soaking the pillow with their quiet persistence. Her chest ached—not from fatigue alone, but from the relentless weight of loyalty and love that had driven her every choice, every step, every decision.

"I can't... I can't do this wrong," she whispered into the darkness, her voice cracking under the pressure. "I just... I want to help him. I have to be here."

The soft glow of the bedside lamp carved gentle shadows across the room. Stephanie pressed her face into the pillow, letting herself feel the fear, the exhaustion, the frustration, and the quiet, aching longing for someone to see her—not as a caretaker, not as a pillar of strength, but as herself. Someone to hold her, to tell her it would be okay, to carry a little of this burden with her.

She wiped her cheeks, taking a deep, shuddering breath. "I won't give up on him," she murmured, voice barely audible. "No matter what."

The tears faded, leaving a raw ache in their place, but also a quiet, stubborn resolve. Stephanie stayed in the room a little longer, letting herself breathe, letting herself be human. Somewhere in the shadows of the house, she knew that though Ryan's words had cut deep, she would endure. She always had, and she always would.

The first week of chemotherapy brought a different kind of battle. Radiotherapy had left Ryan sharp-tongued and weary, but chemo tore into him like a storm—nausea, vomiting, bone-deep exhaustion that left him fragile and volatile.

On Tuesday night, Stephanie knelt beside the bed, her hand steadying the bucket Ryan clutched, moving with practiced calm as he heaved, time and again. Each sound cut through her, yet she remained composed, her voice gentle, steady.

"It's okay," she murmured, rubbing slow, reassuring circles over his back. "Just breathe, Ryan. I've got you."

His body sagged forward, sweat beading along his temples, limbs trembling. For long minutes, Stephanie stayed there, her knees aching against the hardwood floor, her hand moving in rhythm, steady and patient, a lifeline of quiet endurance.

When he finally collapsed back against the pillow, eyes closed, she set the bucket aside, brushing damp hair from his forehead. Her chest ached at the sight of him so diminished, so vulnerable. Leaning forward, she pressed a soft kiss to his temple. "You don't have to fight alone. I'm here."

But morning brought a sharper reality. As she bent to help him sit up, Ryan's jaw clenched, his eyes opening, alight with bitterness.

"Don't look at me like that," he snapped.

Stephanie froze, hand hovering midair. "Like what?"

"Like I'm some broken thing you have to take care of." His voice cracked, the sting of his words landing with precision. "I don't want your pity."

Her throat tightened, but she forced a faint, calm smile. "I wasn't—"

"Yes, you were." He pushed her hand away, rolling onto his side, curling in on himself. "Just… leave me alone for a while."

Stephanie's chest hollowed, but she said nothing. Quietly, she adjusted the blanket around him, set water by the bedside, and stepped out. The door clicked shut behind her, and she pressed her back against it, letting herself slide to the floor for a heartbeat, letting the tremor in her hands and the ache in her chest register fully.

For the first time, she admitted it to herself: it wasn't just Ryan's illness she feared—it was the slow, painful closing off of him, the way he was shutting her out piece by piece. Each sharp word, each dismissed gesture, felt like a wedge between them, and the knowledge gnawed at her.

Still, she would not speak it aloud. Not to Sofia, not to Peter, not even to Rebecca. She swallowed her exhaustion, her fear, her frustration, and draped her loyalty like a second skin, knowing that endurance—quiet, unacknowledged endurance—was all she had to give.

Two days later, at the hospital, Stephanie slipped away from the treatment ward, letting the sterile smell and the sharp echo of retching—her own, Ryan's, and others'—fade behind her for just a few minutes. The cafeteria offered little comfort: the fluorescent lights buzzed overhead, the coffee carried a bitter tang, and low murmurs of strained conversations filled the space like a constant hum.

She slid her tray onto a table tucked in the corner, movements automatic, almost robotic. She had barely eaten all week, and now even the sight of food churned her stomach. Her own reflection in the glass window startled her: pale skin, dark shadows under her eyes, blouse hanging looser than she remembered. She hardly recognised the version of herself staring back.

"Stephanie."

The voice was quiet, measured, familiar. She turned and saw Trey, standing tall and steady, suit jacket casually draped over one arm as if he had come straight from the office. His gaze softened when it met hers, but he didn't speak further. No scolding, no probing questions, no urging. He simply pulled out the chair across from her and sat, letting the air between them hold its own weight.

Stephanie hesitated for a heartbeat, throat thick, hands curling in her lap. Then she slid into the chair, feeling the rare ease of someone not expecting anything from her but her presence.

The silence stretched, but it wasn't empty—it was grounding, a rare reprieve from the constant pressure she carried. Trey didn't push her to talk, didn't demand explanations, didn't offer platitudes that felt hollow. He just sat, steady and calm, a quiet anchor in the storm of her life.

Her chest ached with unspoken gratitude. She wrapped her hands around the paper cup of untouched coffee, letting the faint warmth seep into her palms. In that small corner of the cafeteria, she allowed herself a moment of reprieve. Her body slumped slightly, shoulders relaxing for the first time in days.

Trey leaned back, gaze unwavering, his expression unreadable yet brimming with something she didn't need words for—protection, patience, understanding. It was a presence that didn't demand, didn't judge—simply existed, and in doing so lifted some of the weight she'd been dragging alone.

When the few stolen minutes ended, Stephanie rose, her movements steadier than when she had arrived. She leaned forward and pressed a soft kiss to his cheek—a fleeting, tender gesture that carried gratitude, trust, and something unspoken between them.

Trey's breath caught, just barely, and for the briefest moment, the corner of his mouth twitched in acknowledgment. His chest tightened ever so slightly, a pulse of longing threading through the calm he so carefully maintained. He didn't move, didn't speak—he didn't need to. The warmth of her lips against his skin was enough, leaving an ache he couldn't quite name but didn't want to ignore.

Stephanie straightened, her chest lighter than it had felt in days. Each step back toward Ryan's ward carried a subtle strength she hadn't realised she still had. Exhaustion clung to her, and the ache in her heart hadn't vanished, but for the first time in days, she felt less alone. For the first time in days, she felt she could breathe—enough to face whatever came next.

And Trey remained behind her, lingering just long enough for the memory of that small, tender kiss to settle into him, a quiet, unspoken promise that he would always be there—even when she couldn't ask for it.

The end of the eighth week came with a heaviness Stephanie couldn't shake. The chemo had stripped Ryan down to shadows—his skin pale, his frame gaunt, his spirit bitter. Nights blurred into days, days blurred into weeks. Stephanie carried buckets, washed sheets, coaxed sips of water, all while keeping her voice gentle and her face calm.

But inside, she was unravelling.

On Friday, the oncologist called them into his office. Stephanie sat beside Ryan, her hand folded carefully in her lap, while Sofia and Peter stood behind them. The doctor's tone was measured, but there was no disguising the truth.

"The chemotherapy isn't having the effect we'd hoped for. The cancer is aggressive, and the response has been minimal."

Stephanie's lungs froze. She turned to Ryan, searching his face. His jaw was tight; eyes fixed on the floor.

"So… what now?" Ryan's voice was flat, brittle.

"We can try additional rounds," the doctor said gently, "but the side effects will intensify. At this stage, it's a balance between quality of life and further treatment."

The words sank like stones. Stephanie felt her throat close, panic pressing against her ribs. But before she could speak, Ryan exhaled sharply, his voice cutting through the air.

"No. I'm done."

The silence that followed was suffocating.

"Ryan—" Stephanie began, her hand reaching for his, but he pulled it back.

"I don't want to spend whatever time I have left sick in a hospital bed," he said, his tone harsher now. "I'm not going to waste it vomiting and being babysat. I want to live while I still can."

Sofia's lips parted as if to protest, but then she stopped, tears brimming. Peter's arm slipped around her shoulders, steadying her.

Stephanie swallowed hard, her heart splintering. "But… maybe it'll work if you—"

"It's not working!" Ryan snapped, turning on her, his voice louder than it had been in weeks. "Can't you see that? I don't want this anymore. I don't want you looking at me like I'm already gone."

The words cut deeper than any blade. Stephanie blinked rapidly, willing her tears not to fall in front of him.

The doctor cleared his throat softly, excusing himself to give them privacy.

For a long moment, no one spoke. Then Ryan stood, unsteady but defiant, and left the room.

Stephanie sat frozen, her chest aching, her pulse roaring in her ears. She wanted to run after him, to beg him to reconsider, but her legs wouldn't move.

Sofia slipped into the chair beside her, her hand folding gently over Stephanie's trembling fingers. "He's made his choice, sweetheart. And now… we'll have to make ours."

Stephanie finally broke, tears sliding silently down her cheeks. She nodded, though the word okay refused to leave her lips.

That night, she lay awake in the dim glow of her lamp, Ryan asleep in his room down the hall, his breathing uneven. Her phone rested on the nightstand; Trey's last text still saved at the top of her screen: *You don't have to answer. Just… I'm thinking of you.*

Her thumb hovered over the message, her chest tightening with longing. She didn't reply. She couldn't. But she read it again, letting it steady her as the reality of Ryan's decision settled like a weight on her soul.

She would stay. She would be loyal. She would carry him through this, no matter how much of herself it cost.

But in the quiet of that night, Stephanie admitted one truth she could never say aloud—

She was already fading.

By Monday morning, the weight of Ryan's decision clung to Stephanie like a second skin, heavy and suffocating. She moved through the office with quiet precision, answering emails, updating files, her face a carefully constructed mask of calm. Inside, she felt hollow, a shadow of herself navigating a world that had lost its warmth.

The elevator chimed, pulling her attention, and she froze.

Near the reception desk, two colleagues whispered conspiratorially, their heads bent over a phone. A name floated over the murmurs, striking her like a physical blow.

"Grayson… Emma Blake… last night…"

Stephanie's pulse spiked. She tried to look away, to focus on her desk, but curiosity pried at her resolve. One of the women tilted the phone just enough, and there it was: a glossy tabloid photo of Trey, immaculately dressed, his hand resting at the small of Emma Blake's back as they exited a high-profile restaurant. Emma's smile was dazzling, meant for the cameras, while Trey's expression was calm, almost indifferent—but his proximity to her was enough.

Her stomach dropped.

She walked past them quickly, heels clicking sharply against the polished floor, the sound echoing her own unease. At her desk, she sat heavily, hands trembling as she pulled her laptop closer. She didn't need to search—the alerts were already there, three news items screaming the same headline: CEO Trey Grayson steps out with international model Emma Blake.

Stephanie stared at the images, throat tight, eyes stinging with heat she refused to acknowledge. Of course. Of course he had moved on.

Her mind replayed their last conversation, his words when she'd told him he had to live his life. She'd been the one to give him freedom, to release him from the quiet tether that bound them. And yet, seeing him with someone else twisted something raw and tender inside her chest.

Trey was handsome, powerful, magnetic. He deserved laughter, late-night dinners, someone whose life didn't smell of antiseptic and sorrow. He deserved happiness.

Her chest ached as she closed the browser, forcing her breathing steady, pressing her lips into a faint, professional smile as a colleague passed her desk. The mask fit perfectly, but beneath it, something fragile had splintered.

She understood it. She even respected it. But understanding didn't dull the sharp sting of grief, the silent ache that gnawed at her ribs.

That night, while Ryan slept fitfully down the hall, Stephanie pressed her face into her pillow, letting tears roll freely for the first time in days. She cried for Trey—the man she had loved quietly, desperately, and for the life she had imagined with him that could never be. She cried for herself, for the unbearable burden of her loyalty, for the love she could never fully claim.

Two griefs tugged at her from opposite ends of her heart, and she had to bear them both alone.

And still, even as her body trembled with exhaustion, she whispered into the dark, almost defiantly, "I'll endure. I always do."

Trey noticed it first on Monday morning. Stephanie's smile—the quiet, secret one she always saved for him—was gone. The one that lingered just a fraction longer in her eyes when they met, the one that had once made the hum of the office feel lighter, vanished.

By Wednesday, the absence had begun to gnaw at him. She moved through the office with precise efficiency, polite and professional, but distant. Her emails were clipped, her tone sharp, almost robotic. She didn't linger in doorways asking questions, didn't meet his gaze across the conference table, and when their eyes did meet, she looked away so quickly it felt like a small rejection, a silent boundary he hadn't crossed.

He told himself it was exhaustion, the stress of Ryan's treatments, the constant strain she had been under. But by Friday, the weight of her silence had become impossible to ignore. Trey couldn't remember the last time she had looked at him without hesitation, without an invisible wall dividing them. And he didn't know what he had done to cause it.

What Trey didn't know—what Stephanie could never bring herself to tell him—was that she had seen the photos. Trey Grayson and Emma Blake, leaving dinner together, smiling for the cameras. She had studied the headlines until the words blurred, trying to convince herself she was happy for him. She even believed she almost was. Trey deserved someone radiant, effortless, a woman who could slip into his world with laughter and ease—not someone tethered to exhaustion, loyalty, and quiet sorrow.

On Thursday afternoon, fate twisted the knife a little deeper.

Stephanie had just returned from filing contracts when she spotted a woman waiting in reception. A woman everyone in the office seemed to recognise instantly. Emma Blake, clad in an elegant cream coat, sunglasses perched atop her glossy hair, radiated effortless charm. Her smile was bright, open, and instantly magnetic.

"Mr. Grayson will be down in a moment," the receptionist called.

Stephanie stepped forward, instinctively polite. "Can I help you? I am Mr. Grayson's executive assistant."

Emma's eyes sparkled as she lowered her sunglasses. "You must be Stephanie," she said warmly, her voice soft but confident. "Trey has mentioned you. I just thought I'd surprise him."

Something in Stephanie's chest twisted painfully. Up close, Emma was more stunning than in any photograph—but it wasn't just her beauty. It was the warmth in her voice, the easy, disarming kindness that made people lean in without thinking. It was effortless, natural, and it hit Stephanie like a silent declaration: this woman belonged here.

"I didn't mean to intrude," Emma continued, leaning slightly forward, her tone conspiratorial, almost intimate. "Trey can be very private about his personal life. I suppose that's why people are always guessing. But he's worth it." She laughed lightly, the sound lilting. "I don't mind letting people think what they want."

Stephanie forced a smile, throat tight, words caught somewhere between her chest and her lips.

A soft chime announced the elevator, and Trey stepped out, expression open, his eyes lighting up until they fell on Emma. For a heartbeat, surprise flickered across his face. "Emma? What are you doing here?"

Stephanie didn't wait. She excused herself with a quiet, polite nod, retreating to the elevator, her pulse hammering, her hands curling into fists at her sides. She told herself she had imagined the implication in Emma's words, tried to convince herself it didn't matter.

But back at her desk, staring blankly at the screen, the truth pressed in with unbearable weight. Trey had moved on. Just like she had told him to. She tried to tell herself she was happy for him. She tried. But all she wanted to do was curl up in a ball, hide, and let the world forget she existed for a little while.

The office hummed around her, indifferent and bright, and Stephanie felt smaller than she had in months. The ache in her chest wasn't just disappointment—it was loss, sharp and unyielding, a reminder of the love she had sacrificed and the man she had lost.

Chapter Eighteen

Trey led Emma into his office, the quiet click of the door closing behind them punctuating the brief distance between Stephanie's desk and his sanctuary. Stephanie didn't look up; her focus remained on her screen, her posture tight, shoulders slightly hunched. Every instinct in him ached to cross that distance, to check on her, to make sure she was truly okay—but he stayed rooted.

Emma slipped off her coat, letting it fall gracefully over the back of the chair, then sank into the seat opposite his desk with effortless poise.

"You didn't tell me you'd still be in town," Trey said evenly, though his mind kept flicking to Stephanie at her desk. The stiffness in her posture, the way she barely looked up—it was a quiet stab to the chest he couldn't ignore.

"I couldn't stay away," Emma replied, tilting her head, a teasing smile curling her lips that was equal parts charm and challenge. "It was great to catch up the other night."

"It was," Trey said politely, though he felt the weight of his own disinterest pressing against the conversation. Emma was undeniably beautiful—bright, engaging, poised—but beauty alone no longer stirred him the way it once had. Not after the way Stephanie had undone him with a glance, with a single fleeting smile that lingered long after it was gone.

Emma crossed one leg over the other, her heel dangling lightly, casual yet deliberate. "You've probably seen the pictures," she said, her tone smooth, teasing. "The press loves to speculate. I don't mind—it keeps me relevant. But I don't want you to think I'm using you."

"I didn't," Trey replied, his voice firm but calm. His eyes met hers steadily. He had seen the photos, the headlines, the tabloid chatter—they were all noise, meaningless. "We went to dinner. That's all."

Emma leaned forward slightly, eyes bright, her tone holding a spark of mischief and invitation. "But it could be more... if you wanted it to be."

For a heartbeat, Trey studied her. She was smart, charming, effortless in the way she moved through a room, the kind of woman most men would fall for without trying. He acknowledged the pull—that shallow, surface-level admiration—but beneath it, his heart was elsewhere. It was tethered firmly to someone who didn't belong to him yet commanded every ounce of his attention.

"Emma," he said gently, letting his voice carry the weight of everything unspoken, "you're remarkable. Truly. But I'm not in that place. And you—" he paused, letting the words hang just long enough to settle in, "—you deserve someone whose heart is fully available. Mine... isn't."

Her smile faltered, a flicker of something unreadable passing across her features before she tucked a strand of hair behind her ear, regaining her composure. "I had to try," she admitted lightly, though her eyes lingered on his, searching for even the smallest trace of doubt she might exploit.

Trey leaned back slightly, steadying himself with a calm he didn't entirely feel. He admired her, respected her, but desire had nothing to do with it. His mind and his heart were consumed elsewhere, quietly, painfully aware of Stephanie sitting only a few feet away—so near, yet so impossibly distant.

Trey returned her gaze, calm, unwavering, offering a quiet kindness that left no room for misinterpretation. "I respect you too much to lead you on."

Emma exhaled softly, letting a small, rueful laugh escape. "Fair enough. You always were the honest type. I'll settle for dinner companions, then. No pressure."

"No pressure," he agreed, though his attention had already begun drifting back toward the space Stephanie occupied.

When Emma left a few minutes later, striding confidently to the elevator, Trey remained at the door. He watched her disappear and yet his thoughts weren't on her. They were on Stephanie—sitting only a few feet away at her desk, her shoulders weighed down by invisible burdens, her eyes focused but distant, her hands tense over the keyboard.

Every instinct in him screamed to cross the room, to reassure her, to ease the weight she carried so silently. He wanted to tell her that she didn't have to do it all alone, that he was there, always, if she would only let him.

If only she would.

By Friday evening, Stephanie's nerves were frayed raw. She stepped into the house, still clutching her handbag, and the sour tang of bile hit her before she even saw him. Ryan was slumped on the sofa, a basin at his feet, his skin pale and waxy, eyes hollowed with exhaustion. Every line of his posture screamed pain, fatigue, and frustration.

"You're late," he rasped, voice jagged with irritation, each word cutting sharper than it seemed he intended. "Where the hell were you?"

Stephanie set her bag down carefully, the soft thud on the floor sounding louder than usual in the tense silence. "Work ran over," she said quietly, trying to keep her voice steady. "I came as soon as I finished."

"You came when it suited you," he snapped, twisting away so his back faced her, shoulders tight and rigid. "You say you want to be here for me, but you're only here when you want to be, not when I need you. Stop hovering. Just—leave me alone."

The words struck deeper than she anticipated, sharper than any anger he'd ever directed at her. Her chest tightened, a hollow ache spreading through her ribs. She felt herself frozen in the doorway, throat constricted, unable to form a response. Her hands trembled slightly as she pressed them together, forcing herself to nod.

"Okay," she whispered, her voice barely audible, a fragile echo in the thick, suffocating air of the room.

For a long moment, she stood there, feeling the weight of his fury and his illness pressing down on her, her own exhaustion battling against the instinct to step closer, to comfort, to steady him. But she knew some things she couldn't fix— not today, not when the world between them had grown so heavy.

From the doorway, Sofia's gaze lingered, her mouth pressed thin. When Ryan stormed off toward the bedroom, muttering under his breath, Sofia reached for Stephanie's hand. Her touch was warm, grounding.

"Maybe," Sofia said quietly, "you should have a night away. Just to breathe."

Stephanie's lips trembled, but she only nodded. She murmured something about staying with Rebecca, kissed Sofia's cheek, and left before the tears could fall.

Rebecca's apartment was already bathed in warm lamplight when Stephanie arrived, the soft glow spilling over familiar furnishings and mingling with the faint, comforting scent of vanilla candles. Before Stephanie could knock twice, the door swung open, and Rebecca swept her into a hug that nearly unravelled her composure entirely.

"I was hoping I'd see you this weekend," Rebecca murmured, pressing her cheek to Stephanie's. "You need a break from Ryan. You've been holding it together too long."

Stephanie tried to lift the corners of her mouth, forcing the calm mask she wore so carefully at home and at work. But the walls she had built over the week crumbled the moment she sank onto the couch. Her shoulders shook, and her voice broke as she whispered, "I can't take much more, Bec. He's sick... he's angry... I know it's not his fault, but—" She swallowed hard, tears finally spilling freely. "I don't know how much longer I can keep being the strong one. He's decided on no more treatment."

"He has?" Rebecca's voice softened, a mixture of surprise and concern.

"The tumour... it's changed him. I don't know what to do." Stephanie's hands gripped the edge of the couch, knuckles white, her chest tightening with helplessness.

Rebecca lowered herself beside her, her fingers tracing slow, comforting circles along Stephanie's arm. "You don't have to do this alone," she said gently. "Let Trey and I help you."

Stephanie's head snapped up, her eyes glimmering with a mixture of pain, disbelief, and something sharper—self-reproach. "Why would I ask Trey?"

Rebecca's brow furrowed, sharp and questioning. "What do you mean?"

With trembling fingers, Stephanie reached into her bag and retrieved her phone. Her breath came in uneven gasps as she swiped to the saved images— the glossy photos burned into her memory. Trey, stepping out of a sleek black car with Emma Blake at his side, flashbulbs illuminating their proximity, their closeness twisted into headlines she couldn't bring herself to read aloud.

Wordlessly, Stephanie pressed the phone into Rebecca's hand.

Rebecca's eyes widened as she scanned the images, her expression shifting instantly from surprise to disbelief, her lips parting slightly. "Steph…" Her voice trembled, thick with both concern and incredulity.

Stephanie hugged herself, fingers clutching at her sleeves. "It's… okay," she whispered, though the words barely grazed the weight in her chest. "He deserves someone like her. Beautiful. Effortless. Not someone who's drowning every single day. I'm… I'm happy for him."

Rebecca's gaze softened, yet there was a steel behind her eyes. She slid an arm around Stephanie's shoulders, pulling her close, holding her steady. "I'm sorry, Steph," she said fiercely. "But we'll figure this out. One step at a time. You're not alone in this."

Stephanie nodded, pressing her face into the curve of Rebecca's shoulder, but the ache in her chest remained, lodged like a stone she couldn't dislodge.

When Stephanie finally turned her face away to wipe at the tears, Rebecca's eyes lingered on the glowing screen. The images were polished, curated— damning, in a way that made her stomach tighten. Trey and Emma, their bodies angled just slightly too close, the press spinning it into the story everyone expected. Yet something didn't sit right. Not after the conversation Rebecca had shared with him, the quiet, unshakable conviction she'd seen in his eyes when he spoke of Stephanie.

Her jaw tightened. Stephanie might be convinced that Trey had moved on, that she had been left behind, but Rebecca wasn't buying it. Not entirely. Not for a second. Not yet.

She held Stephanie a moment longer, a silent vow passing between them. No matter what the photos said, no matter what Stephanie feared, Rebecca would stand in her corner—and she would make sure Stephanie didn't let herself be fooled by appearances.

Monday morning, Stephanie made a quiet, firm decision. She couldn't face Trey—not today, not after the images that had haunted her over the last week. Every carefully constructed illusion of normalcy felt fragile, and she clung to what little composure she had left.

"Why aren't you going to work?" Ryan asked from the sofa, the faint rasp of his voice mingling with the steam rising from his cup of tea. He looked up, eyes bleary but attentive, as if sensing her hesitation.

Stephanie forced a small, measured smile, hiding the tightness in her chest and the ache of disappointment that threatened to overwhelm her. "I thought I'd spend the day with you," she said softly, careful not to let her tone betray the swirl of emotions beneath.

A flicker of genuine happiness crossed Ryan's face, rare and fleeting, breaking through the fatigue that usually weighed so heavily on him. "You're... actually doing that?" His words carried surprise, almost gratitude.

Stephanie nodded, pulling her cardigan tighter around her shoulders as if to shield herself from the vulnerability she refused to voice. "Just us, today," she murmured.

Ryan leaned back, the sofa swallowing some of his weariness, and for a moment, his eyes shone with something lighter, almost mischievous. "Well... alright then. I'll enjoy the company." His words were simple, but the rare warmth in his tone settled over her like a soft weight, a brief respite from the chaos of the past days.

Stephanie poured herself a cup of tea, letting the quiet morning stretch between them. She told herself she was here for Ryan—focused, attentive—but every sip, every glance across the sofa, reminded her of everything else waiting in her mind: the glossy images, Trey's unwavering presence, and the ache of a heart that wanted something it could not have.

And yet, for this small, stolen morning, she allowed herself to be present. To exist only in the soft warmth of the moment, where Ryan's smile—even a small one—was enough to anchor her.

Mid-morning, Rebecca strode into Grayson Industries, her steps brisk, purposeful, though her mind churned with worry for Stephanie. She hadn't known Stephanie was skipping work today—but somehow, it didn't surprise her. Something in the rhythm of the past weeks had whispered that her friend was on the edge, teetering under the weight of loyalty, exhaustion, and heartbreak.

Trey emerged from a meeting just as Rebecca approached. His sharp eyes caught hers immediately, and the controlled tension in his posture deepened— the familiar way he carried concern for Stephanie without ever letting it fully show.

"Rebecca. Have you seen Stephanie?" he asked, voice low, steady, but underpinned with an edge of unease. "She's not in today, and I... I'm worried."

Rebecca's eyes narrowed, and a quiet, simmering anger pressed at her chest. "Worried?" she repeated, her tone sharp, deliberate. "You really had me convinced."

Trey tilted his head, a flicker of confusion crossing his face. "Convinced… of what?"

Rebecca didn't answer immediately. She stepped past him, moving with authority toward his office, and planted her phone firmly on the polished wood of his desk. The screen glared up at him: images of Trey with Emma Blake, leaving a restaurant, flashbulbs capturing their proximity, hands brushing just enough to feed gossip. Another photo showed them stepping from a car, smiles bright, the press's spin implicit in every frame.

Trey's eyes widened slightly, the first trace of realisation softening his controlled expression. There was no guilt, not yet, but a subtle tension, a knowledge that someone else had now glimpsed the same misleading evidence that had tormented Stephanie.

Rebecca's voice softened, though the edge of anger lingered, sharp and uncompromising. "This is what Stephanie saw. Do you understand why she's… not here?"

Trey exhaled slowly, leaning back slightly, letting the weight of the misunderstanding settle heavily on his chest. His jaw tightened as he studied the images, the clarity of the situation pressing uncomfortably against him. "Does she think…" He paused, eyes lifting to meet Rebecca's, realisation striking like lightning. "…she thinks I've moved on?"

"Yes, Trey. Is she wrong?" Rebecca's tone was pointed, though her gaze softened for a fleeting moment, betraying her worry for Stephanie's fragile state.

"Yes," he said firmly, voice low, conviction hardening his features. "Completely wrong. We had dinner—that's all. I saw the photos, but I'm used to the press assuming things. They never tell the full story."

A shadow crossed his face, the memory of Emma's brief office visit tightening his chest. Rebecca's eyes narrowed, sharp and unwavering. "What?"

"Emma came to the office on Friday," Trey admitted, running a hand through his hair, frustration stiffening his shoulders. His jaw clenched, tone clipped and controlled. "She's an old friend, nothing more. Charming, yes—but that's it. Stephanie doesn't know, and I… I can't have her thinking otherwise."

Rebecca's voice left no room for debate, deliberate and commanding. "When Stephanie turns up tomorrow—if she turns up—you tell her the truth. Instantly. No half-measures. No hesitation."

Trey's gaze met hers, solemn, unwavering. "I will," he said, voice low but resolute, each word carrying the weight of a promise forged in patience and quiet determination. Beneath the controlled surface, a flicker of vulnerability lingered—rare, almost startling in a man so accustomed to command.

Rebecca pressed her lips together, drawing in a slow, measured breath before letting it out, steadying herself. "Good," she said, her tone firm yet threaded with worry. "Because she needs to hear it from you—not pieced together from assumptions or gossip. She spent the weekend with me, Trey… and I'm scared for her. Don't underestimate how much she's holding on. How fragile she's become." She paused, letting her gaze drop to the glossy photos in her hand. "She tells me she's happy for you. But I think… this," she gestured sharply, the photos trembling slightly between her fingers, "has cut her deeper than anything else." Another breath, quieter this time. "Ryan has refused any more treatment, and Stephanie… she's struggling. More than she'll admit to anyone."

Trey's jaw tightened, the muscles along his neck coiling with tension. He leaned back slightly, letting the weight of her words settle over him. He could see it all clearly now—the exhaustion etched into Stephanie's posture, the brittle restraint in her smile, the quiet ache she carried alone like a secret she had sworn to protect. Every moment she had misread him, every second she had believed he'd moved on, struck him with sharp regret, mingling with a fierce, protective determination.

He nodded subtly, deliberate, the tension in his shoulders easing just enough to remind him he could breathe—but never fully releasing the weight he now bore. His mind shifted immediately to Stephanie: imagining her walking into the office tomorrow, cautious, guarded, shoulders tense as if bracing for disappointment.

"I won't let her misread me," he murmured, more to himself than to Rebecca, a vow forged in quiet determination. "Not now. Not ever."

Rebecca's eyes softened, the flicker of anger giving way to steady trust. "Then make it count, Trey," she said gently but firmly. "She's spent so long holding herself together for everyone else—now she needs to know someone is holding for her too."

Trey's fingers drummed lightly on the edge of the desk; a silent promise etched into every motion. He didn't need to speak further; the resolve in his eyes said everything. Stephanie would hear the truth from him. There would be no assumptions, no misunderstandings—only clarity. And finally, the support she had been denied for far too long.

Monday had been unexpectedly gentle. Stephanie and Ryan moved through the day with a rare ease, the small routines of morning and afternoon carrying a lighter, almost ordinary rhythm. He didn't snap once, didn't bark at her instructions or resist her gentle offers of help.

By evening, they were laughing together over dinner—small jokes, shared memories, the kind of laughter that felt almost like a balm. Sofia and Peter exchanged relieved glances across the table, their smiles cautious but genuine.

Stephanie poured Ryan another glass of water, brushing a lock of hair from his forehead. "I'm glad we had a day like this," she said softly.

"Me too," Ryan replied, his grin faint but warm, a glimpse of the man he had been before the treatments took their toll.

But the reprieve was cruelly brief. Just minutes after clearing his plate, Ryan slumped forward suddenly, his body stiffening. His eyes fluttered, lips parting in a silent cry, and then his body convulsed.

Stephanie's heart leapt into her throat. "Ryan!" she screamed, rushing to his side.

Sofia and Peter were on their feet instantly, their faces pale with alarm. Stephanie held him steady, panic clawing at her chest as she shouted for someone to call an ambulance. The harsh ring of the phone blended with the sounds of Ryan's seizure and her own ragged breaths.

Within moments, the house was a whirlwind of movement and urgent voices. Stephanie's hands trembled as she cradled Ryan, murmuring his name over and over, willing him to come back to her.

And all the laughter, all the ease of the day, vanished like smoke, leaving only fear, raw and unrelenting.

The ambulance arrived within minutes, its siren wailing through the quiet streets. Paramedics rushed into the house, efficient and calm, but their presence did little to ease Stephanie's panic. She followed closely, gripping Ryan's arm as they lifted him onto the stretcher.

"Ma'am, step back," one paramedic instructed gently. "We need room to work."

She stepped back, her hands trembling as she watched them secure him, her chest tight with helplessness. Sofia hovered nearby, her face pale but steady, while Peter rubbed his hands together, trying to stay composed.

"Will he be okay?" Stephanie's voice cracked as she whispered the question, her eyes refusing to leave Ryan's motionless form.

The paramedic gave her a brief, controlled glance. "He'll be okay. Seizures can happen with his condition, but we're taking him to the hospital for observation. Are you coming with us?"

Stephanie nodded quickly, not trusting herself to speak. She climbed into the ambulance beside Ryan, her hand never leaving his arm. She whispered his name softly, over and over, each syllable a prayer.

The ride to the hospital was a blur of red and blue lights, the cold rush of the city streets outside the windows contrasting with the warmth of Ryan's trembling body against hers. She felt every convulsion, every shallow breath, every silent plea for him to come back to her.

At the emergency entrance, doctors and nurses took over. Stephanie followed them into the sterile brightness, her heart pounding, her chest aching from the terror and relief mingling into something she couldn't name.

Hours later, after tests and monitoring, Ryan finally slept, exhausted but stable. Stephanie sat in the waiting area, her shoulders slumped, her hands clasped tightly around each other. Sofia came over, placing a comforting hand on her shoulder.

"You did everything right," she said softly. "He's going to be okay."

Stephanie nodded, but the tension in her chest didn't release. She had been reminded once again how fragile everything was—the laughter, the ordinary moments, even Ryan's rare calm.

And as she watched him resting in the hospital bed, pale and diminished but alive, Stephanie realised how much she was tethered to him, how much she would endure, and how frighteningly alone she sometimes felt carrying the weight of it all.

Trey had just stepped into his apartment, shrugging off his coat, when his phone buzzed in his pocket. He glanced at the screen, hope flaring briefly—Stephanie? But it wasn't her.

It was Rebecca.

Trey, Ryan has taken a turn for the worse. He's in hospital. Stephanie is with him.

The words hit him like a jolt. His stomach tightened, his heart pounding. Without a second thought, he grabbed his keys, pressed the elevator button.

"Hospital," he muttered under his breath, voice taut with urgency.

The city lights blurred as Trey sat in the back of the limousine, each stoplight a countdown he didn't want to wait for. Stephanie… he had to get there, had to be there for both of them. Every red light stretched longer than it should, every passing car a reminder of the seconds slipping away. His hands fisted on his thighs, knuckles white, and his mind raced, running through every possible scenario—but he knew, deep down, no preparation could steel him for what awaited.

When he finally arrived, the hospital loomed quiet and still against the night sky. He stepped inside, expecting to find Stephanie at Ryan's side, her face drawn but determined, her fingers lightly brushing against Ryan's arm. But the room was empty—save for Ryan, pale against the stark white sheets, breathing uneven yet defiant, eyes bright with that spark of sharp awareness that had always unsettled and challenged him.

"Grayson," Ryan rasped, voice thin but carrying that familiar flicker of wry humour.

Trey's chest tightened, the knot of worry in his stomach tightening further. He pulled a chair closer, settling beside the bed. "Ryan… how are you feeling?"

Ryan gave a broken laugh that dissolved into a cough, and Trey winced at the effort it cost him. "Good… surprisingly good," he murmured, though every word seemed to drain him.

Silence stretched, thick and heavy, filled with the weight of the words neither man wanted to speak aloud. Then Ryan's gaze sharpened, fixing on Trey with a clarity that cut through the fog of fear and exhaustion.

"Listen… I need you to do something for me," he said, voice low, fragile yet commanding.

Trey leaned forward instinctively. "Anything. Just ask."

A faint, tired smile tugged at Ryan's lips, fleeting and brittle. "Look after Stephanie… when I'm gone."

The words hit Trey like a punch to the gut. He blinked, stunned, speechless. "Ryan, I—"

"Don't pretend, Grayson," Ryan interrupted, voice raw but steady. "Am I wrong, thinking you care for her?"

Trey swallowed, his composure faltering. "I… no. You're not wrong. I do."

Ryan gave a small, rasping chuckle, the sound a strange mixture of humour, resignation, and something painfully raw. "I thought so. I think she's in love with you, too. Knew it the moment I saw you two dancing at the charity gala. That's why I… I lost it. I knew I was going to lose her. The way she looked at you… it wasn't the way she ever looked at me."

Trey's hands tightened into fists on his knees, knuckles blanching white, his jaw rigid as a storm of conflicting emotion churned behind his eyes—anger, guilt, longing, and a quiet, unshakable resolve.

Ryan's gaze softened, pity mingling with regret. "It's my fault."

Trey frowned, uncertainty creeping in. "What do you mean?"

"I haven't treated her the way she deserves," Ryan admitted, his voice breaking with the weight of truth. "I took her for granted. Pushed her away when she tried to help. And now… with this," he gestured weakly toward his head, "you start thinking about the things you did wrong. Steph… she's my biggest regret."

Trey's gaze fell to his fists, the confession cutting through him sharper than he'd expected.

"She deserves the best," Ryan continued, forcing strength into his weakening voice. His eyes, bright and clear despite the hollow exhaustion, fixed on Trey with piercing intensity. "Will you look after her?"

Trey lifted his head, his own voice firm, steady, resolute. "Yes, Ryan. I will."

A flicker of relief softened Ryan's features, a shadow of peace settling briefly across his face. "Good," he whispered, his breath hitching. Then, with a faint, mischievous glimmer, he added, "Just... don't be an ass about it like I was."

For the first time that night, Trey's lips curved into a genuine, quiet smile. "I won't," he promised.

Ryan's eyes closed, tension draining from his face as if those simple words were balm enough. His breathing slowed, becoming deeper, steadier, though exhaustion still pulled him toward sleep's fragile edge.

Trey remained in the chair, unmoving, the quiet hum of the machines and the faint scent of antiseptic enveloping him. The weight of the conversation pressed heavily on his chest, a mixture of responsibility, sorrow, and an undeniable awakening of his own heart.

The promise lingered in his mind like a vow carved in stone: protect Stephanie, cherish her, give her the love she deserved.

And, for the first time in a long while, Trey admitted the truth to himself—it wasn't just Ryan's wish.

It was his own.

Stephanie returned to Ryan's room, having walked Sofia and Peter back to their car, and froze in the doorway. The soft click of the door behind her seemed impossibly loud in the quiet space.

"Trey...?" Her voice trembled, barely above a whisper, thick with surprise, restraint, and something she refused to name.

He looked up at her, calm and composed, seated near Ryan's hospital bed. There was a quiet softness in his eyes, an unspoken patience that seemed to wait for her to speak, yet beneath it lay a steady, grounding strength that made her chest tighten. His presence filled the room without a word, filling the air with an intensity she couldn't ignore.

Stephanie's throat constricted. Her heart raced, and every breath felt too heavy. She wasn't ready to confront the man she had secretly mourned while fighting to be strong for Ryan. Her hands trembled at her sides, her voice barely audible as she forced out the words.

"Leave... please."

Trey's expression softened, not with frustration or reproach, but with a quiet, patient understanding—as if he could read the storm behind her carefully constructed composure. His eyes flicked briefly to Ryan, a silent acknowledgment, then returned to her, steady and unyielding.

The pause stretched, each second heavy with unspoken words, before he nodded slowly, deliberately. Every movement—rising from the chair, brushing a hand against its edge—was measured, calm, leaving space for her without pressing.

"I just need to talk to you about—" he began softly, his voice low, almost fragile, the kind of voice that begged her to listen.

"No, Trey. I can't… not right now. Just… leave. Please."

He wanted to argue, to insist she hear him—that he hadn't moved on, that he would wait, patiently, for as long as she needed. But he saw the tension in her hands, the tight line of her jaw, the fragile tremor in her shoulders. He simply nodded, holding back the words, and stepped back.

Stephanie's hands curled into fists at her sides, grounding herself. Her throat was dry, pulse racing, chest tight from the nearness of him. She forced her gaze back to Ryan, pressing her lips into a taut, controlled line, giving a small, stiff nod that tried—and failed—to mask the turmoil within.

Trey lingered a heartbeat longer, eyes softening, offering a silent plea: your walls can fall when you're ready. Then, with the quiet grace that had always drawn her in, he moved toward the door. The click as it closed behind him seemed impossibly loud, leaving behind only the ghost of his presence—and a weight on her chest she wasn't yet ready to lift.

Her gaze fell to Ryan, who stirred slightly, unaware of the tension she carried, and she pressed a hand over hers, drawing in a shaky breath. For the first time all day, she let herself feel the ache, the longing, and the complicated grief that came with loving someone she couldn't claim as her own.

Chapter Nineteen

The days blurred together now. Hospital light, antiseptic, the steady hum of machines—Stephanie barely noticed the passage of time. Monday slid into Tuesday without meaning, and by Wednesday she couldn't recall if she had eaten anything beyond the lukewarm coffee Sofia pressed into her hands.

Ryan slept more than he woke. When he stirred, it was often with confusion or restlessness. The seizures came and went without warning, leaving him pale and trembling, and each time Stephanie's heart lurched as though it might stop with his. She never left his side—not really.

"Steph, go home," Peter urged one evening, his voice gruff with worry as he adjusted the blanket at Ryan's feet.

"I'm fine," she answered automatically, eyes never leaving his face.

Sofia's hand brushed her shoulder, gentle, motherly. "Darling, you're breaking yourself in half."

Stephanie shook her head. "He might need me." That was all that mattered.

That night, while Sofia and Peter stepped out for dinner, Ryan stirred. His eyes opened—clouded, tired, but suddenly sharp.

"Steph?" he whispered.

Her heart jumped. She leaned close. "I'm here."

His hand fumbled against the sheet until she clasped it, holding on tightly. For a moment, he looked at her with the same warmth she remembered from years ago, before the sickness, before the bitterness had taken root.

"I'm… I'm sorry," Ryan breathed, voice fragile.

"Shh, don't," she whispered, throat tight.

"No," he rasped, a flicker of determination in his gaze. "I pushed you away. Over and over. And you stayed. I don't deserve it. But I want you to know— I see it. I see you."

Her chest fractured under the weight of his words. She swallowed hard, blinking back tears. "You don't have to say that. Just rest."

But Ryan's lips curved into the faintest, weary smile. "Let me… just this once."

For a rare moment, Stephanie rested her head on the mattress beside his hand, trembling with the effort to hold herself together.

Later, when Sofia and Peter returned, she slipped into the hallway, leaning against the cool wall, breathing deeply, willing herself not to collapse.

Her phone buzzed in her pocket. She pulled it out, half-expecting a message from Rebecca—but froze when she saw the name on the screen: Trey.

I'm thinking of you.

Her breath caught, sharp and involuntary. For a fleeting second, she almost typed something back—something polite, neutral, safe. But the weight of the photos pressed down on her chest, heavy and unrelenting. Emma Blake's effortless beauty, Trey's easy smile—it all pressed in like stone. She couldn't. Not now. Not when he was finally moving forward, finally living again.

It wasn't fair to complicate that for him. He deserved happiness, unburdened and whole, and she loved him enough to want him to have it—even if that meant it wouldn't be with her.

Turning her face away, Stephanie slid the phone carefully into her pocket, her fingers lingering over the smooth case as though holding on might steady her. She walked back to Ryan's room with measured, slow steps, each one heavier than the last, the unanswered message burning quietly against her heart like a secret she couldn't speak aloud.

The room was quiet except for the rhythmic beep of the monitor and the faint rasp of Ryan's breathing. Stephanie sat close, fingers laced with his, watching every rise and fall of his chest like it was tethered to her own.

His eyelids flickered, heavy with fatigue, then lifted just enough to find her face. "Steph…"

She leaned closer, brushing a thumb lightly across his hand, a small tether to the world. "I'm here," she whispered.

He studied her for a long, fragile moment, the faintest tremor in his gaze betraying his weariness. Then, barely audible, he murmured, "Don't… stop living when I go."

The words stole her breath. Her heart twisted painfully, and tears spilled down her cheeks unbidden. "Don't… talk like that. Please… don't."

His fingers twitched against hers, a ghost of a squeeze, fragile yet deliberate. "You—more than anyone I know—deserve happiness. Promise me."

Her throat burned, words catching in her chest. "I promise." But inside, the promise felt hollow, a fragile lie she barely dared breathe. She was already breaking apart.

Ryan's eyes closed again, a fleeting peace softening his features as though that fragile promise was enough. Stephanie bowed her head, pressing her lips to his knuckles, trying to smother the sob clawing its way up.

The door closed softly, and Stephanie startled, wiping her cheeks hurriedly. Rebecca slipped inside, carrying a paper cup of coffee, her expression warm yet careful.

"I thought you could use this," she murmured, setting it down. Her gaze lingered on Stephanie's pale, tear-streaked face before flicking to Ryan, then back.

Stephanie gave a small, shaky nod.

Rebecca settled on the edge of the spare chair, her voice gentle but steady. "I heard some of what he said. And he's right, Steph. You can't stop living."

"I promised him," Stephanie whispered, her voice hoarse, "but I don't know how."

Rebecca's hand found her shoulder, warm and grounding, squeezing with quiet strength. "Then don't do it alone. You have me. You have all of us. And Trey, too. Even if you don't believe it right now, he hasn't gone anywhere."

Stephanie's eyes stung, and she shook her head, staring down at Ryan's hand still cradled in hers. "Not now," she murmured.

Rebecca didn't press, offering one last gentle squeeze. "One day at a time. That's all you have to think about."

Stephanie nodded faintly, whispering the words as if they might hold her together. "One day at a time."

The room fell quiet, heavy but soft with the weight of care, presence, and unspoken love—each heartbeat a reminder that she was not alone.

The morning light spilled gently across Ryan's room. Stephanie held his hand, trembling despite the calm face she showed the world. His eyes, clearer than they had been in weeks, met hers with surprising sharpness.

"You've been my anchor, Steph," he whispered, faint but steady. "Through all of this... I don't know what I would have done without you."

Stephanie's throat constricted. "You're my anchor too, Ryan. Always."

He gave a faint, tired laugh. "I'm sorry... for everything. For pushing you away. You stayed anyway. I... I needed you more than I could ever say."

Stephanie's hand tightened around his. "You're loved Ryan. Always."

His eyelids fluttered briefly, exhaustion pressing, but there was peace in his gaze as he held her hand one last time. "Promise me something... be happy."

Stephanie swallowed the hollow ache threatening to pull her under. "I promise," she whispered, though inside, it felt like ashes on her tongue.

By nightfall—or the early hours of the next morning—Ryan seized again. The movement was sudden, harsh, unyielding. Stephanie's heart surged into her throat. She called out, voice cracking. Sofia and Peter rushed in, hands shaking as they tried to steady him. But the body they loved was giving way. Stephanie clutched his hand, murmuring his name over and over. Then, with a final, quiet breath, his eyes closed, and the fight left him.

In the days that followed, Stephanie moved with precise, outward composure. She helped Sofia and Peter with every detail of the funeral, coordinated with the hospital, liaised with florists and clergy—all while the gnawing emptiness in her chest grew heavier. She politely declined help from friends; letting herself collapse even for a moment felt impossible.

The morning of the funeral was grey and still. Stephanie stayed close to Sofia and Peter, hand gripping theirs like an anchor. Trey arrived quietly, scanning the room. He spotted Stephanie, rose, and approached cautiously.

"Stephanie…" he said softly.

She stiffened and subtly shifted, placing Sofia and Peter between them. Her jaw tightened, her gaze fixed firmly on the polished floor. She couldn't look at him—not now. She needed to hold herself together, to process her grief without letting the knowledge that she had lost him too, creep in.

Trey's chest tightened, but he held back. He understood, at least in part. Some grief demanded space. He didn't press. Instead, he lingered nearby, silent, patient, ready to step closer when—or if—she would allow it.

Rebecca, observing from across the room, approached him quietly. "Give her time," she said softly. "She's carrying so much—more than you can imagine right now."

Trey nodded, swallowing the ache in his chest. He turned his attention to Sofia and Peter, speaking quietly with them, listening.

"She didn't have it easy," Peter said in a low voice. "Ryan… he made it hard for her. Even loving him, she carried everything—his anger, his pride, his sickness—on her own."

Sofia's eyes flicked toward Stephanie. "She stayed strong for him. Even now, she's trying to stay strong for herself… but it's breaking her inside."

Trey absorbed their words silently. He could do nothing more than be present. He could not rush her. He could not bridge the distance she had built around herself. Not yet.

Stephanie remained close to Rebecca, clinging to her support, her fingers intertwined with Sofia and Peter's. She could not face Trey, not yet—not while she knew she had already lost him. The thought of allowing anyone else in, of letting herself feel in front of him, was too much.

The wake continued around her, voices blending into a dull hum. Trey stayed, quiet and steady, his presence a tether should she ever reach for it. But Stephanie remained locked in her own grief, every step and gesture measured, deliberate, protective of the fragile walls she had built around her heart.

And for now, that distance was all she could manage.

The next morning, the lawyer arrived. Stephanie sat between Sofia and Peter, the folder heavy on her lap.

"Ms. Vale," he said gently, "I'm here to go over Mr. Ryan's estate and his wishes."

Stephanie's hands trembled as she unfolded the papers, the weight of what they contained pressing down like a physical force.

"He left everything to you," the lawyer said quietly, his tone careful, measured.

"I… I can't," she whispered, tears pricking at the corners of her eyes. "I don't want it. I… just…" Her voice broke, trailing off into the ache of disbelief and grief.

Sofia reached out, brushing a strand of hair from her face. "Steph, breathe. Just breathe."

Peter placed a steady hand over hers, grounding her. "We'll help you through this, every step."

"I didn't stay for anything in return," Stephanie said, her voice small, raw. "I stayed because he needed me."

"We know that sweetheart," Sofia said softly, pressing a reassuring shoulder against her.

Stephanie drew in a shaky breath, her gaze falling to the documents in front of her. "Could… could I donate it? Everything… to brain cancer research?"

The lawyer paused, giving a gentle nod. "Absolutely. Your instructions will be followed exactly as you wish."

Relief and grief collided in her chest, a strange mixture that left her breathless. "That's what I want," she whispered, her voice barely audible. "He would have wanted that."

Sofia leaned her head gently against her shoulder. "He would be proud, Steph. Truly proud."

Peter squeezed her hand, his eyes warm. "You're honouring him the way only you could. You're giving meaning to his memory."

Stephanie's gaze drifted to the window, the city beyond a blur of light and shadow. The hollow ache in her chest remained, but for the first time, a flicker of purpose settled in. She could transform her sorrow into something meaningful. Step by fragile step, she could navigate the darkness, guided by love, loyalty, and the memory of the man she had lost.

The next morning, Stephanie stepped into the kitchen, the soft morning light falling across the countertops. Sofia and Peter looked up, immediately noticing the weight in her posture.

"I... I'm going away for a while," Stephanie said quietly, her words careful, measured. "Leaving tomorrow. And when I come back... I'll find somewhere to live."

Sofia's hand found hers across the counter, warm and grounding. "You're always welcome here, Steph. You know that."

Stephanie forced a small, grateful smile, but there was an empty weight behind it. "Thank you. I... I really appreciate it."

Peter shifted, concern tightening his features. "And your job at Grayson Global? Are you—?"

"I'm resigning," Stephanie interrupted gently, letting the words land. "It's... too much right now. I can't handle it."

Peter glanced at her, hesitating. "Does Trey Grayson know?"

Stephanie's throat tightened. She avoided their eyes for a moment, remembering the unreadable expression she'd worn when she last saw him. "He will," she said softly. "I'll tell him. When the time is right."

Sofia's gaze was gentle but knowing. "Take all the time you need, Steph. You don't have to rush anything."

Stephanie nodded, biting her lip to keep the tremor in her voice under control. She felt the familiar pang—the ache of missing Ryan, the ache of leaving Trey unspoken in her heart, of knowing already belongs elsewhere. She had loved and lost in the span of weeks, and every step felt weighted with grief.

"I just... need a moment," she admitted, pressing her palm to her forehead, as though trying to steady herself. "A space to breathe without... without feeling like I'm losing everyone at once."

Peter's hand rested lightly on her shoulder. "We'll be here. Both of us. You're not alone in this, Steph."

Stephanie gave a small nod, swallowing hard. "I know. And... thank you. For everything."

She paused at the doorway, glancing back once, her gaze flicking toward the empty space where she imagined Trey might have been if circumstances had been different. She shook her head lightly, forcing herself forward. For now, she would step away—step back, regroup, and let herself live, even as her heart carried the shadows of what she had lost.

Trey sat behind his desk, eyes scanning the latest quarterly report, but the words swam and blurred across the page. The usual hum of the office seemed distant, muted, as if the world itself had paused. A soft knock at the door pulled him back to the present.

"Come in," he said, striving for calm, but his voice sounded tighter than he intended.

The HR manager stepped inside, her expression polite yet measured, as though she already sensed the storm that might be coming. "Mr. Grayson, I need to inform you that Stephanie Vale has resigned from Grayson Global. She will not be returning."

Trey blinked. The words landed heavier than he expected, like a physical shove in the chest. His stomach dropped, a hollow weight settling low. "She… she's resigned?" His voice cracked slightly, quieter than he intended. He cleared his throat, trying to mask the sudden tightness in his chest, but nothing could hide the jolt of disbelief and dread.

"Yes, sir," the HR manager replied gently, her tone sympathetic. "Her resignation was submitted this morning."

Trey nodded slowly, as if processing the information on a different plane. Each heartbeat seemed impossibly loud, echoing in the sudden quiet of his office. She's gone. She didn't even give me a chance. To explain. To reach her… to fix this. His fists clenched beneath the desk, white-knuckled.

As soon as the HR manager left, he grabbed his phone with a trembling hand. His thumb hovered over her name, almost afraid to hit call, but finally, with a shuddering breath, he pressed it.

Voicemail.

Again. Nothing. Panic flared, sharp and insistent, crawling up his spine. Why isn't she answering? Where is she? He hit redial—still nothing. His chest tightened, the air seeming impossibly heavy.

Finally, he dialled Rebecca.

"Rebecca," he said the moment she answered, his voice taut, raw with anxiety. "Do you know where Stephanie is?"

There was a brief, cautious pause. "I spoke to her this morning," Rebecca said carefully. "She said she would talk to you."

Trey's jaw tightened so hard it ached. "Well… she didn't." His voice came out sharper than he intended, laced with frustration and the ache of helplessness. He ran a hand through his hair, eyes flicking to the window, to the city sprawling below, empty without her. She's out there somewhere, and I can't reach her.

"She'll reach out when she's ready," Rebecca continued softly. "She just… needs some space right now."

Trey leaned back, the leather chair groaning beneath him. Space. Logical, rational, necessary—but it did nothing to ease the raw ache tightening his chest. Space from me? After everything? After all this time? He pressed his fingers to his temples, trying to steady the storm of thoughts clawing at his mind, but they refused to relent, unanswered questions, moments replayed in excruciating detail, words he wished he'd spoken, gestures he might have made.

"She still thinks I've moved on, doesn't she?" he muttered, voice low, almost to himself.

"Yes, Trey," came Rebecca's careful reply. "I think so."

"She didn't even give me a chance to explain," he whispered, each word heavy with frustration and longing. "I just… I wish she hadn't left without a word. I need to know she's okay. I need to know she's… safe."

He turned his gaze to the skyline, the city lights twinkling against the gathering dusk, glittering yet hollow without her presence. Each heartbeat thudded in his chest like a drum, echoing with the absence of her laughter, her warmth, her glance. She's moving on… and I can't stop it. But I won't—cannot—just yet.

The office felt impossibly still, every tick of the clock magnified, every shadow a reminder of her absence. Trey pressed his palms to his face, inhaling and exhaling in slow, measured bursts, forcing himself to steady the tremor that threatened to betray him. He would wait. He would remain vigilant. But the ache—the sharp, insistent, relentless ache—lingered, a phantom wound carved into his chest, unyielding, relentless, a reminder that the fight for her heart had only just begun.

Chapter Twenty

Stephanie had been away for a week. She hadn't told anyone where she was going—her only plan had been escape, even if only for a little while. She'd chosen a small coastal town tucked far from the city's relentless noise, where the air was sharp with salt and the waves seemed to pull the weight from her chest. The inn she'd booked was painted a soft, sun-bleached yellow, its windows framing the horizon like a living canvas. Quiet. Unassuming. Perfect for disappearing.

Mornings began with the soft cry of gulls and the scent of fresh bread drifting from the bakery across the street. Stephanie would walk the shoreline, sand slipping through her fingers as she crouched near the water, the tide hushing against her skin. For the first time since Ryan's illness—and his death—she felt something close to peace.

At the inn, she had met the owners, Margaret and Henry, a warm couple in their sixties whose ease and kindness seemed effortless. Over coffee at the long breakfast table, Stephanie found herself sharing fragments of her story, drawn out by the gentle rhythm of conversation and the quiet hum of the morning.

"I needed to get away... just to breathe," she murmured, stirring her tea, the spoon clinking softly against the porcelain. "Ryan... my boyfriend. He... he passed from brain cancer recently. He meant so much to me. And... it's just been a lot."

Margaret reached across the table, brushing a strand of hair from Stephanie's face with gentle fingers. "Darling, I can see that weighs on you," she said softly, her tone warm and unhurried. "But there's something else, isn't there?"

Stephanie froze, her fingers tightening around the cup. How could she explain? How could she tell a stranger her heart was still entangled with someone else—someone she'd loved in silence while bound to Ryan? But Margaret's gaze was patient, unjudging, somehow safe.

"There is someone else," Stephanie whispered, her voice trembling. "Trey. I love him. We were going to be together, but then Ryan got sick. I couldn't leave him. I told Trey we couldn't... and he said he'd wait. I told him not to. He deserved to be happy. He found someone else. So... I lost him too." The words landed heavy on the table, bitter with shame, and she closed her eyes, trying to stifle the ache.

Margaret's brow creased with concern. "You lost him? Are you certain, darling?"

Stephanie shook her head helplessly, thumb tracing the rim of her cup. "I saw photos of them together." Her voice was fragile, almost a whisper.

Henry, quiet until now, offered a calm, steady smile. "Sometimes our hearts see shadows where none exist. Fear, grief, loneliness—they distort the truth, make it feel permanent even when it isn't."

The lump in her throat loosened slightly, though the ache remained. "I... I don't even know how to feel anymore," she admitted. "Ryan's gone. And Trey... I think I've lost him too, even if I haven't."

Margaret took both of her hands, warm and grounding. "You haven't lost him, sweetheart. Not if you haven't let go, not if he hasn't. But you need to be gentle with yourself. You've carried so much already. Let yourself breathe—even if it's only for a little while."

Stephanie exhaled shakily, her shoulders easing just a fraction. "I don't know if I can. But... maybe here, for a little while, I can try."

Outside, the waves crashed against the shore, relentless and steady. And for the first time in weeks, she felt a fragile tremor of hope. She didn't have the answers yet. She didn't know the truth about Trey, and she might not for some time. But here, in this quiet town, with the wind on her face and the gentle support of strangers surrounding her, she could simply exist—one fragile, precious breath at a time.

The days settled into a rhythm. Dawn walks along the misted shore. Breakfasts with Margaret and Henry, their gentle laughter wrapping around her like a balm. Afternoons spent reading in the sunlit common room or writing letters she would never send. The couple never pressed too hard, but their presence reminded her that connection didn't always have to hurt.

One afternoon, Margaret joined her on the porch, carrying two steaming mugs. She passed one to Stephanie before settling into the chair beside her. "Sometimes," she began softly, "we build walls to protect ourselves. Sometimes we convince ourselves of things because it feels safer than questioning them."

Stephanie stared out at the horizon. "I see him," she whispered. "Trey. With someone else. I assume it's true, and so I grieve. Even though I don't know if there's anything to grieve."

"Do you know for certain?" Margaret asked gently.

Her hands tightened around the mug. "No. But it feels real. And I can't let myself hope it isn't."

Margaret reached over, her touch grounding. "You're punishing yourself for shadows. You've carried enough guilt, enough heartbreak. What would it hurt to imagine—just imagine—that he's still yours?"

Stephanie's breath shuddered out of her. "I... can't. Not yet."

"Then start small," Margaret soothed. "Don't think of forever. Just notice today. Allow yourself a sliver of hope. You deserve even that."

For the first time in months, Stephanie felt her lips curve into a trembling smile. "I'll try."

Henry looked up from his book. "Sometimes trying is enough, my dear. You don't have to fix everything at once."

Margaret added softly, "And if you love this Trey... isn't he worth fighting for?"

Stephanie lifted her cup, the steam brushing her face as she stared out at the sea. It stretched vast and endless before her, a reminder of both her smallness and her strength. For the first time since Ryan's death, she allowed herself to feel it—a flicker of possibility. Trey was worth fighting for. The only question was whether she was strong enough.

At the very least, she owed it to herself—and to him—to ask. To hear the truth from his lips. And if he had moved on, then she would let him go with grace, because he deserved happiness, even if it wasn't with her. But maybe... maybe he wasn't lost. Maybe the life they had paused could still be waiting, quietly, for them both to return.

By the twelfth day, as she folded her clothes into her bag and glanced once more at the sunlit window of her room, Stephanie felt something she hadn't expected—a thread of strength woven through the grief. Fragile, yes, but real. Enough to take her home.

Far across the city, Trey sat in the leather chair behind his desk, the Manhattan skyline stretching endlessly beyond the floor-to-ceiling windows of his penthouse. The city glittered, alive with movement and light, but to him, it felt muted—as though he were watching the world through glass, close enough to see but too far to touch. His laptop screen glowed with the remnants of work he had been attempting to focus on for hours. Contracts, spreadsheets, emails— they all blurred into meaningless lines, words that refused to land.

Stephanie had been gone nearly a fortnight. No calls. No texts. No hint of her presence in his life.

He leaned back, pinching the bridge of his nose, letting out a slow, controlled breath. He told himself he understood. She needed space. Time to process everything—Ryan's illness, his death, the weight of the estate, the unbearable grief that had carved her into silence. He understood it intellectually. But understanding didn't ease the ache in his chest.

Rebecca had called a few days ago, her voice careful, gentle, but with an edge of urgency that only she could wield. She had visited Sofia and Peter Carter, who had told her everything Ryan had done—how he had left his estate to Stephanie, a gesture so in keeping with her own quiet selflessness that she had immediately donated it all to brain cancer research.

So like her. Always giving. Always thinking of others, even when she had so little left for herself. Trey stared at the untouched glass of bourbon on his desk, the amber liquid catching the low light, and felt a sudden pang of tenderness and frustration. That was why he loved her. That quiet, selfless strength, that way she never recognised her own worth.

The apartment was unbearably still without her. He missed the echo of her laughter, the soft cadence of her voice, the subtle way she seemed to fill a room with warmth and quiet light. She had only been there twice, and yet her absence was palpable, tangible. Even the memory of that one perfect weekend they had shared lingered like a ghost in the corners of the penthouse, a private world he could almost touch but never hold.

He remembered her curled against his side on the sofa, the steady warmth of her body pressing into him, as though she belonged there. He remembered her eyes—how they had lit up with passion when she spoke about what mattered to her, softening every word with a natural grace that left him breathless. Those small, unguarded moments haunted him in the quiet hours, when work no longer distracted him and the city outside seemed cold and distant.

His phone sat on the desk, screen dark, taunting him. Again, he reached for it, thumb hovering over her name, every instinct screaming at him to hear her voice, to know she was safe, to know she hadn't truly walked away. But he forced himself to set it down again. If she needed space, he would give it. He had to. Still, every fibre of him rebelled against the waiting, the endless, gnawing ache of absence.

Some might call him mad. He had only known Stephanie for eight months. And of that, they had shared one perfect weekend, one fleeting bubble of happiness that had been almost impossibly intimate without physical consummation. And yet... he loved her. Not with a casual, passing attraction, but with a certainty that startled him. Loved her in a way that made everything else fade—everything but her presence, her laugh, her light.

He loved her loyalty, her quiet, unshakable strength, the way she gave of herself even when life had hollowed her reserves. He loved her kindness, the way she instinctively thought of others first, never expecting return. And yes—he loved her beauty. But not the surface kind that drew stares or envy. He loved the way she lit up a room without trying, the way her presence calmed the restless edges of his life.

He remembered the first time she had walked into his office. He had hired her almost on instinct, without reasoning why. Something in him had refused to let her walk out. And she hadn't disappointed. Brilliant, capable, steady—but it was never just her work. It had always been her.

Even knowing she had been with Ryan had been a weight he carried silently. He had told himself he could handle it, that he could keep his feelings buried.

But he couldn't. The pull toward her was relentless, quiet, suffocating—a longing that grew sharper each day, until denying it felt like denying air itself.

And yet… he never wanted to be the reason for her pain. Ryan's death had left its scars on her. Seeing her grief, her exhaustion, her loyalty stretched thin, had made him ache in a way that was both protective and selfish. He longed to claim her, to love her openly—but only if it didn't hurt her further.

Now, with her gone, the silence pressed down on him like a punishment. He missed her desperately. But beyond the longing, a deeper fear gnawed at him: what if she had already moved on? What if the window had closed before he could even admit to himself what he felt?

Trey's gaze drifted to the skyline once more. The city shimmered in gold and silver beneath the night sky, alive and vibrant—but it might as well have been another world, far removed from the one that mattered most. The world with Stephanie Vale.

And in that silence, he made a vow. No matter the waiting, no matter the space she required, he would remain. Ready. Waiting. Hopeful. Because for the first time in his life, he understood that some loves weren't fleeting—they were inevitable.

Her suitcase was small, only the essentials folded with care, yet it felt impossibly heavy—weighted with grief, questions, and the emotions she had spent nearly two weeks trying not to face. The drive back to the city passed in silence, the hum of the tyres drowned beneath the storm of her thoughts. Ryan. Loss. The hollow ache of goodbye. And always, always Trey—the man she feared she had already lost, the man her heart refused to release no matter how she tried.

When the skyline finally rose before her, glittering and restless against the darkening sky, her pulse quickened. By the time she stepped into the marble lobby of his high-rise, her hands trembled. The concierge hadn't hesitated, hadn't even called upstairs—just smiled knowingly and directed her to Trey's private lift. That alone made her chest tighten. He was waiting. Hoping, perhaps, that she would come.

She told herself again that she had to be here. He deserved to hear her questions, her fears, spoken aloud. He deserved her honesty, even if it cost her everything. Because whatever else had happened between them, she knew one thing to her core—Trey would never lie to her. And if their story was truly over, then she refused to let it end without fighting for the truth.

Chapter Twenty-One

The elevator glided upward, each floor a soft chime, a countdown to whatever awaited her. Stephanie's breath snagged in her throat. Her palms felt clammy, her heart hammering as though it could shatter her chest. What if she had imagined the possibility of this moment for too long? What if reality didn't measure up?

When the doors parted with a whisper, Trey was there in the hallway, tall and steady, his presence filling the space in a way that made the world narrow to just him. Broad shoulders, confident stance, that familiar calm in his gaze—it was a punch to her chest, familiar and overwhelming, achingly missed.

Her feet carried her forward before she even realised, she had moved. The metallic doors slid closed behind her with a final hush, sealing them in a bubble of tense anticipation. For a long, suspended moment, neither spoke. The silence stretched taut between them, alive with all the words they hadn't said, all the feelings neither had dared voice.

Her voice trembled, fragile yet insistent. "I need to know," she whispered, each word carrying the weight of sleepless nights and unspoken fears. "If you've moved on... I would understand."

For a heartbeat, Trey didn't move. Then his expression shifted—surprise first, followed by something deeper, rawer. He drew in a slow, deliberate breath, anchoring himself to the only truth that mattered.

"I haven't," he said, voice firm and resolute. "There's been no one, Stephanie. Not then. Not now. Not since I met you."

Her throat tightened, and the name escaped her lips like reopening an old wound. "Emma..."

His jaw flexed, controlled, but his tone remained steady, unflinching. "We had dinner. That's all. Nothing more. I need you to believe me."

The silence that followed was heavy, but not hollow—it pulsed with truth, steady and unwavering. Stephanie let herself meet his gaze fully, not seeking excuses or pretty reassurances, but the man she had once trusted with her whole heart.

Her breath shuddered, the tightness in her chest loosening in a tremor. A single tear slipped down her cheek, but she searched his face for cracks, for shadows of deceit. There were none—only clarity, unwavering and fierce.

Her lips parted, trembling. "I do believe you. But I put you in a terrible position. I chose Ryan instead of you. Can you ever forgive me for that?"

Trey's eyes softened, warmth threading through the intensity there. His voice was low, rough, tender. "There's nothing to forgive, Stephanie. I understood why you stayed with Ryan. If anything... it made me love you more."

Her breath caught, a fragile gasp. "I thought I lost you."

"You never lost me, Steph," he said quietly, every word a quiet anchor. "Not for a second."

A soft sob escaped her, unrestrained this time, and she pressed a hand to her mouth, as though trying to quiet the noise of months of fear and longing. "It's been so hard," she admitted, voice cracking. "I couldn't drag you into my nightmare."

He stepped toward her slowly, deliberately, as if any sudden movement might shatter her completely. "I was always here. I'll always be here. You just have to let me."

Her hand fell away, leaving her bare before him—raw, tear-streaked, unguarded. Her chest rose and fell with shallow breaths, and her heart thudded like a drum in her ribs. She drew in a shaky inhale, then slowly, tremblingly, she nodded.

"I love you," she whispered, a soft confession that trembled on the edge of vulnerability.

Something inside Trey broke—months of restraint, weeks of aching silence, every night spent wondering if he had lost her forever. In two strides, he was before her, hands framing her face with a reverence that contradicted the storm in his chest.

Stephanie's breath hitched, fingers curling around his wrists as if to steady herself, though it was him who had always been her anchor. And then he kissed her.

It wasn't tentative. It wasn't careful. It was desperate, reverent, full of every sleepless night, every unspoken word, every ache of waiting. Her body melted into his, her hands threading into his hair, clutching at him as if sheer will could prevent him from ever leaving.

Trey's arms circled her waist, pulling her impossibly close, and the world outside—the city, the noise, the weeks of pain—faded into irrelevance. Every exhale, every heartbeat, every brush of lips carried the weight of longing, of survival, of the love neither had dared to name aloud until now.

Stephanie whispered into the kiss, her voice trembling, a fragile confession pressed against him. "Don't ever leave me."

He pressed his forehead to hers, voice rough with need and certainty. "Never. Not ever."

In that moment, the past, the grief, the fear—they all dissolved. There was only this, only them, only a love that had survived every storm and waited, patiently, for its reckoning.

Trey groaned softly against her mouth, pulling her closer still, body trembling with the force of restraint and the relief of finally not needing to. The taste of her, the warmth of her, it was home, it was everything he had waited for.

When they finally parted, breathless, foreheads pressed together, neither willing to let go, Trey murmured, "You'll never lose me. Not now. Not ever."

Stephanie's answer was wet, shaky, but real. "Then don't let me go."

"I couldn't if I tried," he replied, and claimed her lips again, sealing the promise between them. The spark ignited into a fire neither could contain. His hands slid from her face to her waist, pulling her flush against him. Stephanie gasped softly, fingers tangling in his hair, holding on as if she'd been waiting her whole life for this moment.

"Trey…" she whispered, voice trembling with need and relief.

He groaned low, pressing her gently against the wall. His lips left hers only to trail along her jaw, then lower, grazing her throat as though he needed to memorise every inch of her.

"I thought I'd lost you," he murmured, breath hot against her skin, words ragged. "I can't lose you again. Not now. Not ever."

Her hands found his mouth again, pulling him to hers, urgent and sure. "You won't," she promised between kisses, body arching into his. "I can't let you go."

The dam inside her broke. Weeks of grief, fear, and longing poured into every desperate kiss. Trey responded in kind, lifting her as though she weighed nothing, carrying her deeper into the penthouse without ever breaking the connection of their mouths.

He set her down on the cool marble kitchen counter, foreheads pressed together, breaths mingling in ragged bursts.

"Say it," he whispered hoarsely, thumb brushing her swollen lip. "Tell me I still have you."

Her eyes shone with tears, voice breaking but certain. "You've always had me, Trey. I love you."

He kissed her again, without restraint, the reverence and hunger of every movement undoing her completely. Stephanie let herself stop thinking. She let herself feel—him, them, everything they'd almost lost. Arms wound around his neck, lips parting to deepen the kiss. Trey groaned, one hand sliding into her hair, the other firm at the small of her back.

He broke away only to murmur her name, raw, reverent. "Stephanie…"

The sound sent a shiver racing through her. She silenced him with another kiss, tugging at his shirt. He peeled it off in one fluid motion, revealing hard planes of muscle. Her hands roamed across his chest, feeling the steady, pounding beat of his heart.

Trey anchored her hips, lifting her so her legs wrapped around his waist, a breathless laugh escaping her before his mouth claimed hers again—deeper, rougher, burning with months of restrained desire.

He carried her into the bedroom, laying her gently on the bed, lowering himself over her. His hands moved slowly at first, reverent, discovering her as though she were something precious he had nearly lost forever.

Stephanie arched beneath him, alive with need, pulling him down with fierce urgency. As his hands slid beneath her blouse, inching it up, her gasp met his groan.

"Tell me you want me," he whispered, forehead pressed to hers, chest heaving.

Her eyes filled, but her voice was steady. "I've always wanted you, Trey. Only you."

That was all he needed. Clothes fell away, urgency stripping them bare. Skin met skin, and the spark became flame.

Their first joining was slow, aching, reverent—as though neither dared break the fragile beauty of the moment. Stephanie clutched him, tears sliding silently as she gasped his name. Trey kissed them away, soft against her cheeks.

"Always you," he whispered, moving with her, rhythm timeless, inevitable. "Always."

The intensity built until neither could hold back. Passion, grief, and love poured out in one fierce, unshakable release. Stephanie cried out, clinging to him, while Trey buried his face against her neck, shuddering with the force of it.

Afterward, he gathered her close, skin damp, breaths uneven. His hand stroked through her hair, lips brushing her temple.

"I love you, Stephanie," he murmured, hoarse, as though the words had been caged too long.

Her heart swelled, breaking and healing all at once. Meeting his gaze, she answered without hesitation: "I love you too. Always."

In that quiet, tangled embrace, they knew: this time, they would not let go.

They lay facing each other, the early light filtering softly through the curtains. Trey's hand rested on her bare hip, his fingers tracing slow, lazy circles against her skin.

"Rebecca told me Ryan left you everything," he murmured, his voice low, thoughtful. "And that you donated it all to brain cancer research." He leaned forward, brushing a tender kiss to the tip of her nose. "That was a very selfless thing to do."

Stephanie's lips curved faintly, though her eyes grew distant. "I didn't stay with him to gain anything, Trey. Not money. Not security. I stayed because he needed me." Her voice softened to a whisper. "Because I couldn't walk away from him when he was dying."

His gaze held hers, steady and warm. "I don't think anyone would ever question that. Not for a second." His thumb stilled on her skin, pressing gently as if to anchor her. "But giving it all away… that was beautiful, Steph. That was you."

Her throat tightened at the quiet conviction in his tone, but she let herself breathe into it, into him. For the first time in years, the weight of her choices didn't feel like a burden. It felt like love—pure, unshakable, and hers to claim.

Stephanie shifted, easing him gently onto his back. Her body stretched across his chest, her hair spilling like silk over his skin, brushing the planes of his shoulders. Her palms cupped his face, thumbs brushing over his jaw, anchoring herself to him. She leaned down, her lips finding his in a kiss that was slow, tender, reverent—full of months of longing, loss, and unspoken promises.

"Do you know how much I love you?" she whispered against his mouth, her voice trembling with both need and awe.

His hand slid into her hair, holding her close as his lips curved into a faint, aching smile. "As much as I love you," he murmured, voice rough with certainty and longing. "Enough to last a lifetime."

Stephanie's breath caught in her throat. "Definitely," she breathed, sealing her words with another soft, lingering kiss that made him groan against her mouth.

"I'm yours," he said, every word a vow, a confession, a surrender.

She swung a leg over him, straddling his hips, her grin playful yet charged with desire. "And I'm yours," she countered, the teasing glint in her eyes belying the fire in her chest.

His laughter was caught, swallowed by her lips as he kissed her fiercely, fingers tangling in her hair, pulling her impossibly close. Every touch, every shiver, every whispered word between them was charged with the ache of months denied—the longing that had burned quietly in their hearts until now.

Stephanie pressed her body against his, feeling the steady beat of his heart beneath her palm, a rhythm that matched her own racing pulse. He trailed kisses along her neck, low and worshipful, leaving her trembling and breathless, until there was nothing left between them but heat, desire, love, and the sweet, aching release of finally having each other—unrestrained, unbroken, and completely theirs.

When at last they pulled back, foreheads resting together, breaths mingling in the warm quiet of the room, a silence settled over them—heavy with satisfaction, relief, and the fragile joy of closeness. Stephanie's fingers traced the lines of his face, memorising every curve as if engraving him into her soul.

"You feel… like home," she whispered, voice soft and vulnerable, the heat of their connection still thrumming between them.

"And you," he murmured, his thumb brushing over her cheek, "feel like everything I've been waiting for."

Tears pricked her eyes—not from sorrow, but from the weight of finally being seen, finally being loved without restraint. She pressed a lingering kiss to his lips, then rested her head against his chest, listening to the steady thrum of his heart.

"I don't ever want to let go," she admitted, voice muffled against him.

"You won't have to," Trey replied, arms tightening around her, holding her like she belonged there—which she did. In that quiet, warm aftermath, they both understood, this was only the beginning. Love, fierce and patient, had finally found its place between them, and nothing would break it again.

Hours later, after making love and showering together, Stephanie padded barefoot into the kitchen in one of Trey's crisp button-down shirts, sleeves rolled up, the hem brushing her thighs. He followed, tousled and gloriously bare-chested, and together they set about cooking breakfast—bumping shoulders, trading smiles, the air easy and unhurried in a way that felt like home.

As she leaned against the counter, watching him crack eggs into the pan, her expression softened. "I need to start looking for a new apartment," she said quietly. "And... a new job."

Trey stilled, turning his head, one brow arched, spatula poised midair. "A new apartment? A new job? What the hell are you talking about?"

She gave a rueful little smile, though her voice caught. "I can't live with the Carter's, and I quit, remember? You must have replaced me by now."

Setting the spatula aside, he crossed the kitchen in three long strides, the heat of him closing around her before she could even breathe. His gaze locked onto hers, fierce and unyielding. "Stephanie," he murmured, his voice low, threaded with conviction. "I haven't replaced you. Not at work. Not in my life. You already have a job. And I want you here."

Her brow furrowed, though her pulse skittered beneath his nearness. "Here?"

His hand came up, fingers tracing the line of her jaw, thumb brushing the softness of her cheek. His mouth curved into a slow, deliberate smile that made her knees weaken. "Yes here. You belong here with me. Always."

Her breath hitched. "I... I can't just live here."

"Why not?" His tone was rough velvet, his thumb stroking her skin as though he had no intention of letting her go. "I want us to be together."

She shifted, her voice barely above a whisper. "I want to be with you too, but don't you think that it might be... awkward at the office? Or are we hiding this—hiding us?"

His eyes darkened, mouth hovering dangerously close to hers. "Hell no. And why would it be awkward?"

Her heart thudded painfully in her chest, the truth pressing against her ribs like a secret too heavy to carry. "Trey...I'll be dating my boss."

His lips quirked, eyes glinting with unshakable certainty. "Yeah, that's right," he said, stepping closer until she felt the heat radiating off him. "You're dating the boss."

She drew in a sharp breath; frustration tangled with longing. "I'm serious, Trey. People are going to talk. Maybe I should… maybe I should get another job. Something less complicated."

His jaw tightened, but instead of pulling away, he closed the distance, his body braced against the counter, caging her in without touching. "Sweetheart," he murmured, the endearment melting into a low growl. "The last thing I want is distance. I need you close. That means here with me—and at work."

Her pulse raced as his words sank in, threading through every crack in her doubt. "But it isn't that simple. Won't people talk. I don't want it to come between us."

Trey lifted a hand, his fingers brushing the side of her throat, resting against the frantic beat of her pulse. "Let them think whatever the hell they want. I'm not hiding us, Stephanie. Not in my company. Not in my life. I want people to know I love you."

Her breath caught as his thumb stroked slowly against her skin, grounding her even as the world tilted. "You make it sound so easy."

His gaze softened, but the steel beneath it never eased. "It is," he said quietly. "Because I already know what I want. You." He closed the last inches between them until his lips were a whisper from hers, his voice a promise and a vow. "With me. Always."

Her chest constricted at the force of it — desire, fear, relief all tangling into something that made her knees weak. He was asking for everything: no walls, no safety net, just the two of them. And God help her; she wanted it just as fiercely.

Practicality, old and stubborn, rose in her like instinct. "We'll have to tell HR," she said at last, each word steadying her. "There are policies. Appearances matter. This can't just be… private."

His face smoothed into something like relief rather than resistance. "Good," he said. "We'll do it clean. Transparent. We tell them we're together; we file whatever we must — conflict-of-interest, reporting lines — and you stay where you are. Working with me." His certainty wrapped around the plan like armour.

She laid her hand flat against his chest and felt the steady beat beneath her palm. "You really mean that?"

Trey lifted her chin with the gentlest touch. His eyes were bright and fierce all at once. "I mean it. I want you here because I want you — not because it's convenient, not because I can keep you close. Because you're the person I choose, every day. Even when it's hard."

"If you're sure," she breathed, voice trembling with equal parts hope and caution, "then it's on one condition."

"Anything," he said, searching her face.

She swallowed and let the words out. "If it becomes a problem — if it gets messy or ugly — we don't bury it. We don't shut down. We talk. We deal with it, together. No secrets. No running."

Something in his jaw tightened as if her condition had touched something true and tender. He cupped her cheek with a hand that was both rough and reverent. "Okay."

"Promise me, Trey," she whispered, the vulnerability in her eyes raw and open.

His thumb stroked the line of her cheek like a benediction. "I promise you, Stephanie. No running. No hiding. Not ever. Whatever comes, we face it together."

Her breath hitched; the conviction in his voice peeled away the last of her defences. He leaned in, forehead against hers, their breaths mingling in a pause that felt like permission.

"Together," he murmured, voice low and rough with feeling. "Always."

Her fingers rose of their own accord, splaying across his chest to feel the steady thud of him beneath her palm. For the first time in a long time, she let herself believe.

Epilogue

Four months later…

The limousine door swung open, cameras already flashing from every angle, a frenzy of light against the dusk. Trey stepped out first, tall and commanding beneath the strobe of photographers' lenses. He turned immediately, extending his hand—not for the spectacle, though the world would see it that way, but for her. And when his gaze found Stephanie's, the hunger and devotion there belonged to no one else but her.

"Careful," he murmured as he helped her out, his palm warm and steady around hers. Gasps rippled through the press line as she rose beside him, the silk of her gown catching the city lights, shimmering like liquid fire. Trey leaned in, lips brushing the shell of her ear in a whisper that never reached the cameras. "You look ravishing. How am I going to keep my hands to myself tonight?"

Her mouth curved into a teasing smile, her eyes glinting with mischief as flashbulbs popped like fireworks. "You better not keep your hands to yourself."

A low laugh rumbled from his chest, and before he straightened, he pressed a kiss to her cheek—quick enough to pass as casual, lingering enough to make her shiver. The photographers caught it instantly, cameras clicking in a frenzy. But for Stephanie, the world shrank to the warmth of his lips, the soft murmur against her skin. "I love you, sweetheart," he whispered, sincerity threaded through every word.

"I love you too." She slid her arm through his, fitting against him as if she'd always belonged there.

Together they climbed the marble steps, cameras chasing every movement, the crowd of reporters buzzing with speculation. Inside the grand ballroom, the flash and noise faded, replaced by the soft golden glow of chandeliers spilling across polished floors. Waiters swept by with trays of champagne, and beneath the elegant swell of a string quartet, the murmur of conversation wrapped around them like silk.

This evening mattered to both of them. A fundraiser for brain cancer research— an organisation now flourishing with donations Stephanie had helped direct in Ryan's honour. It was more than a cause; it was a promise she'd made to herself, to Ryan, and to the people still fighting battles like his. Trey had insisted they sponsor the event, but Stephanie had insisted it be done quietly, without fanfare.

The past months had not been easy. Working side by side at the company had drawn scrutiny and whispers, some harmless, others sharp with envy or judgment. At first, colleagues had speculated endlessly—some joked about favouritism, others questioned professionalism. Every glance in a meeting, every shared laugh across the office, had felt magnified under invisible scrutiny. They had weathered the stares, the hushed conversations, the polite curiosity, holding steady with quiet determination.

But over time, the chatter had died down. People saw the careful boundaries they maintained at work, the way Trey treated Stephanie with respect, even as their connection was undeniable outside the office. They watched the trust, the tenderness, and the quiet moments that were theirs alone, and slowly, acceptance followed. The CEO and his executive assistant were in love—and it was real.

Tonight was proof of that—proof that their hearts could intertwine without compromise, that their commitment to each other could coexist with their roles, and that love could exist even in the glare of public and professional expectation. Standing together beneath the chandelier glow, Stephanie felt the weight of the past months ease, replaced by the steady certainty of them, together, moving forward—not hiding, not apologising, simply being.

As they crossed the threshold into the ballroom, the soft murmur of conversation and clinking glasses enveloped them. Sofia and Peter Carter appeared, their faces lighting up as they moved toward her.

"Stephanie, love—it's so good to see you." Sofia's arms wrapped around her in a warm, familiar embrace, the kind that carried both comfort and understanding.

Stephanie's smile softened, touched with genuine emotion. "It's wonderful to see you too."

Peter clasped Trey's hand firmly before turning back to her. "You're glowing," he said, a note of pride in his voice. "Ryan would be so pleased to know you've carried his fight forward."

Stephanie's throat tightened, but Trey's arm tightened subtly around hers, grounding her. She drew in a steadying breath and managed a soft smile. "I hope so," she whispered. "This—tonight—it feels like a piece of him is still here."

Sofia's gaze flicked to Trey for a moment, a knowing glint in her eye. Six months ago, at the charity gala, she had suspected the truth—the way Trey looked at Stephanie, the subtle tension, the quiet admiration he tried to mask. It had been impossible to miss, and seeing them now together, Sofia felt a warm relief settle in her chest.

Squeezing Stephanie's hand, Sofia's expression softened. "It's a pity Rebecca couldn't make it tonight," she said gently, a hint of regret in her voice.

Stephanie let out a soft, teasing laugh, the sound light and unguarded. "She was disappointed, but her new fiancé has whisked her away on a tropical holiday. She's not allowed to answer emails or even think about work."

Trey's lips curved into a slow, knowing smile, amusement and adoration flickering in his eyes. He leaned just slightly closer, his voice low and teasing. "I might have to start enforcing that rule myself."

Stephanie's heart fluttered at the gentle heat in his tone. She glanced up at him, her pulse quickening.

Sofia's eyes glimmered with warmth and approval, a tender smile softening her features. "And Ryan would be grateful you didn't stop living in the process. That you let yourself find happiness again."

Stephanie met Trey's gaze, and in that look—fierce, protective, endlessly tender—she felt every unspoken promise and every careful boundary dissolve. Ryan's chapter had closed, but this one was hers to write, and Trey was at the very heart of it. In that moment, all the trials, whispered doubts, and lingering uncertainties seemed distant, eclipsed by the quiet certainty of this new beginning.

The evening unfolded in a glittering blur of gowns that shimmered under the chandeliers, tailored suits, and champagne flutes that never seemed to empty. Guests approached Stephanie with warm smiles—some radiating genuine admiration, others more reserved, offering polite curiosity. She had braced herself for whispers, perhaps even pity, but instead found respect. People acknowledged her resilience, her generosity, and the way she had transformed grief into action, creating something meaningful from her pain.

Trey never left her side. His hand rested lightly at the small of her back, grounding her, his presence a silent shield against the occasional intrusive question. When the chairman of the charity approached, thanking them both for their quiet but substantial support, Trey accepted the accolades with effortless poise—but never without redirecting the praise.

"She's the one who made tonight possible," he said, voice low but unwavering. "This cause... it's her heart."

Stephanie's chest tightened. She wanted to protest, to share the weight of credit, but the look in his eyes stopped her. There was no hint of ego in Trey—he wasn't claiming this for himself. He only wanted the world to see what he already knew: Stephanie was extraordinary.

Dinner passed in courses she barely tasted. Her attention was captured instead by conversations with survivors, families, and doctors who spoke with quiet fervour about their work. Each story carried both sorrow and hope, and with every word, Stephanie felt the weight of her purpose deepen, her grief transforming into something far larger than herself.

When the speeches began, the room fell into reverent silence. A young woman took the stage, her voice quivering as she recounted losing her father to brain cancer. Tears pricked Stephanie's eyes, her fingers tightening instinctively around Trey's hand beneath the table. The memory of Ryan pressed close, raw and unrelenting. For a heartbeat, she wondered if she had been too hasty, if being here—so soon, so fully—was too much.

Then Trey's thumb brushed over her knuckles, slow and steady. The simple touch reminded her she was not alone. She looked up at him, and the quiet, unwavering strength in his gaze held her together. Around them, the ballroom hummed with elegance and life, but for Stephanie, in that moment, it felt like they were in a world carved just for them—a space where grief and hope, love and memory, could exist side by side.

After the applause faded and the music resumed, Trey leaned close, his voice low and magnetic. "Come with me," he murmured.

He led her out onto the terrace, away from the glittering ballroom and the hum of conversation. The night air was cool against her skin, carrying the distant murmur of the city. Overhead, strings of lights glowed soft and golden, casting a warm halo around them. For a heartbeat, it felt as though the world had shrunk to just the two of them.

Stephanie exhaled shakily, leaning against the stone balustrade. "That speech… it brought everything back. Ryan. The nights at the hospital. All of it."

Trey stepped close behind her, his arms encircling her waist, his chin resting lightly against her shoulder. "I know," he said softly. "And it's alright to feel it. You don't have to be strong every second."

Her eyes burned, tears slipping free despite her best efforts. "I don't want to fail you. I don't want my grief to get in the way of us."

He turned her gently in his arms, cupping her face with both hands, his thumbs brushing her cheekbones. His gaze held hers, unwavering and fierce. "Stephanie, listen to me. Grief isn't failing. It's love that hasn't found a place to go yet. And I don't want you to bury it—I want you to share it with me. All of it. The pain, the memories, the hope. I want all of you."

Her breath caught, heart aching at the weight and warmth of his words. "Even when I'm broken?"

"Especially then." His forehead pressed against hers, voice a vow and a promise all at once. "Because I'm not going anywhere. Not tonight, not tomorrow, not ever."

Something inside her cracked open—not in pain, but in release. Tears fell freely now, but so did a trembling, radiant smile. "God, I love you," she whispered.

"I love you too, sweetheart." His lips claimed hers then, soft at first, savouring the moment, then deepening into a kiss that tasted of promise, of safety, and forever.

When they finally pulled apart, the sounds of the ballroom drifted back, faint but comforting—the music, the laughter, the life continuing on. Stephanie leaned against Trey's chest, her hand resting over the steady beat of his heart.

For the first time in months, she didn't feel torn between past and future. She felt present. Whole.

And beneath the canopy of golden lights, with the cool night brushing against them and the city spread out like a glittering sea below, she knew with a certainty as steady as the stars above that she was exactly where she belonged.

The limousine door closed softly behind them, muting the hum of the city as they drove through Manhattan's glittering streets. Stephanie leaned into Trey's side, exhaustion tugging at her, softened by the warmth of his arm draped protectively around her shoulders. The charity gala had left her drained and full all at once—her heart raw with memory but steadied by his steady presence.

When they arrived at his penthouse, Trey led her inside, his hand never leaving hers. The vast windows framed the skyline like a constellation, city lights flickering in a rhythm that felt infinite. But Stephanie's gaze never left him. He shrugged off his jacket, tossing it over the back of a chair, and turned toward her with that look that always made her pulse stutter—a mixture of reverence, longing, and pure love.

"You were incredible tonight," he said quietly, his fingers brushing along her cheek, soft and grounding. "The way you spoke to everyone… the way you listened. Stephanie, you don't even realise how extraordinary you are."

Her chest tightened, but she forced a soft smile. "I only tried to do what Ryan would have wanted."

Trey shook his head, stepping closer until there was no space between them. "No. You did what you wanted. What you believed in. That's what makes it powerful."

Her throat tightened, emotion choking her. "I couldn't have done it without you."

A faint curve touched his lips, though his eyes held something deeper, a quiet fire that made her knees weak. "Sweetheart… there's something I've been carrying for months. Something I've wanted to ask you, but I kept waiting for the right moment."

Stephanie's breath caught. "Trey…"

He took her hands in his, voice steady yet thick with feeling. "When you walked into my office twelve months ago, I knew my life had just shifted. I didn't know how, or why, but I knew I couldn't let you slip away. And then… despite everything—Ryan, your grief, the distance—you stayed in my heart. You still are. You always will be."

Her eyes blurred with tears as he sank to one knee.

"Stephanie," he whispered, producing a small velvet box. The diamond caught the light, brilliant but secondary to the intensity of his gaze. "I don't just want to hold you at night or wake up next to you every morning. I want every moment. Every heartbreak, every triumph, every ordinary day in between. Marry me, sweetheart. Be my wife. Be my always."

Tears spilled freely now, chest heaving with disbelief and love. She had dreamed of this once, told herself it could never be, and yet here he was—on his knee, heart laid bare, asking for forever.

"Yes," she breathed, voice trembling yet resolute. "Oh God, yes, Trey. I'll marry you."

Relief, joy, and awe broke across his face as he slid the ring onto her finger, hands trembling slightly. He rose, sweeping her into his arms, kissing her as though the world outside the windows had ceased to exist.

When they finally parted, foreheads pressed together, breath mingling, his voice rough with emotion whispered, "You've just made me the happiest man alive."

Stephanie laughed through her tears, fingers curling into the fabric of his shirt. "I thought I couldn't be happier. But I was wrong."

Trey grinned, his eyes lighting up with mischief and desire, and lifted her effortlessly into his arms. She pressed close, their laughter mingling as he carried her across the bedroom, every step radiating warmth and strength. He kissed her mid-step, slow and feather-light, the press of his lips sending shivers through her.

When he finally lowered them onto the bed, they tumbled together in a heap of tangled limbs, still laughing, still breathless. His hands traced the lines of her shoulders and back, gentle yet insistent, grounding them in the present. She responded instinctively, letting her fingers explore the warmth of his skin, her lips brushing his jaw, tasting the faint salt of his laughter.

Every heartbeat, every sigh, spoke of relief, of love finally unrestrained, of longing fulfilled. The city lights filtered through the curtains, bathing them in soft gold, but neither of them noticed—they were lost in the quiet rhythm of each other.

Stephanie's breath hitched as he leaned over her, his forehead resting against hers, lips barely brushing, teasing, lingering. "You're mine," he murmured, voice low, reverent.

"And you're mine," she whispered back, a tremor of desire threading through her words.

She let herself melt into him, letting go of fear, grief, hesitation. With Trey, there was no need to hold back. No walls. No boundaries. Only trust, love, and the electric pulse of being completely known.

Wrapped in his arms, pressed close against his chest, Stephanie finally felt what she had been searching for all along. She was home.

The End

Shattered Hope, Stolen Kisses

Alison Reid

A complete standalone romance
Previously published individually

Chapter One

Twenty-five-year-old Aurora Vincent never feared the dark.

She had walked this path from her office to her Sydney apartment a hundred times before, her heels clicking rhythmically against the pavement. The city had always been a part of her—its familiar hum, the distant honk of a taxi, the neon glow of signs reflected in puddles on the pavement. It was home.

But tonight, the air felt different. Heavier. Charged with something unseen.

Aurora wrapped her coat tighter around herself, suppressing a shiver as she glanced up at the nearly deserted street. She didn't usually walk home this late. Her boss had asked her to stay behind to finish a last-minute report, and she—ever the diligent employee—had agreed without hesitation.

Now, she wished she hadn't.

The streets that once felt familiar now felt foreign. The comforting background noise of the city seemed muted, as if the night itself was holding its breath. She forced herself to push aside the unease, blaming it on exhaustion. After all, it had been a long day, and she still had another early morning ahead of her.

Shifting her bag higher on her shoulder, Aurora quickened her pace, her heels clicking faster against the pavement. A few bars were still open, laughter and muffled music spilling out onto the streets. She considered stopping, pretending to be waiting for someone until her nerves settled, but she shook the thought away. She was being ridiculous.

Then came the footsteps.

At first, they were distant, barely noticeable. But as she walked, they grew closer. A deliberate echo of her own movements.

Her pulse quickened.

Aurora turned her head slightly, just enough to glimpse behind her without seeming obvious.

Three men.

Her stomach clenched.

They were a few paces back, their movements slow but purposeful. Maybe it was a coincidence. Maybe they were just heading in the same direction.

Or maybe they weren't.

The pit in her stomach deepened. She wasn't the type to panic easily, but every instinct in her body screamed at her to move. Fast.

She turned onto a quieter street, one that led directly to her apartment complex. If she could just reach the front doors, she'd be fine.

The footsteps followed.

Aurora's breath hitched.

Heart pounding, she quickened her stride, forcing herself not to break into a run. Running would show fear. Running would make them chase her.

But when she heard the pace behind her accelerate, fear gripped her like a vice.

A hand clamped over her mouth. Rough. Unforgiving.

She was yanked backward. Her bag slipped from her shoulder, hitting the pavement with a soft thud.

Aurora thrashed, twisting, kicking—but the hand only tightened. Her scream died against his palm. She fought with everything she had, her nails clawing at the hand restraining her.

"Feisty," a voice sneered in her ear. Hot breath fanned against her skin, thick with the stench of cigarettes and alcohol. "We're going to have some fun with this one, boys."

The other two men laughed, their amusement sending ice down Aurora's spine.

Terror surged through her, raw and suffocating. Instinct took over, her body acting before her mind could catch up. She twisted violently and drove her elbow into the gut of the man behind her.

He grunted in pain, stumbling back. For a brief, flickering second, hope flared in her chest.

But it was short-lived.

Another set of hands grabbed her before she could break free. Stronger. Rougher.

A fist crashed into her ribs.

The impact stole the breath from her lungs. She gasped, doubling over in agony, but there was no time to recover. Another blow followed, then another. A savage strike to her cheek sent her sprawling onto the pavement. The rough concrete scraped against her skin, leaving behind a searing burn.

Dizzy. Weak.

Her vision blurred as she struggled to push herself up, but a heavy boot slammed into her side, knocking the air from her lungs.

She barely had the strength to whimper.

Then, before she could react, weight bore down on her. Someone straddled her, pressing her battered body into the cold ground.

Pain exploded through her skull as he struck her again. And again.

Her head snapped to the side, her swollen lips splitting open, the coppery taste of blood filling her mouth.

"Stop fighting," the man above her snarled. "You won't get hurt as much if you stay still."

"Stay still, sweetheart," another one taunted from above. "Make this easy for yourself."

Aurora refused.

She bucked wildly, kicking and twisting, but it was no use. Rough hands clamped down on her arms, pinning her in place.

No. No. No.

Adrenaline coursed through her veins, but her body wouldn't cooperate. She was too weak, too winded.

Her eyes—now swollen shut—could no longer see their faces, but she could hear them. Their ragged breaths. Their sick laughter.

She felt hands at her waist, fingers tugging at the fabric of her trousers.

Panic clawed at her throat.

"No," she gasped. "Please, stop."

The plea barely made it past her lips before a deep, furious voice shattered the night.

"Get the hell away from her!"

The weight vanished.

The hands disappeared.

Shouting erupted. Footsteps pounded against the pavement, fading into the distance as her attackers bolted into the shadows.

Aurora forced her swollen eyes open, her vision swimming with darkness and pain. A blurry figure rushed toward her, his movements sharp with urgency. She wanted to recoil, but her body wouldn't obey.

A moment passed before she realised, she wasn't alone.

A man knelt beside her. His face was indistinct, lost in the haze of her injuries, but his voice—low, steady, and filled with something she couldn't name— broke through the fear still gripping her.

"Hey. You're safe now," he murmured. "Help is coming."

Safe.

The word barely registered.

Aurora wanted to believe him, wanted to cling to the warmth in his voice, but the pain was too much.

With the last of her strength, she whispered, "Thank... you..."

A single thought flickered through her pain-ridden mind. I don't want to die.

Then the darkness swallowed her whole.

Thirty-two-year-old Dr. Anthony Hardwick adjusted the cuff of his sleeve as he stepped onto the sidewalk, the Sydney skyline stretching high above him. The city still buzzed with late-night energy—cars passing, people laughing outside bars, the occasional wail of a distant siren.

He was on his way to meet an old friend for a drink, a rare night off in his relentless work schedule. But as he passed a narrow alley between two buildings, something made him slow.

A woman's purse lay discarded on the pavement.

His brow furrowed. He bent down, fingers brushing against the worn leather. Then he heard it.

Laughter. Low and cruel.

Then—a muffled cry.

Anthony froze, his sharp instincts kicking in. He turned his head toward the sound and saw them.

Three men.

A woman on the ground.

One of them straddled her, his fists raised, ready to strike again.

Anthony didn't think. He acted.

"Get the hell away from her!"

His voice sliced through the alley like a blade, sharp and unyielding. The men whipped around, startled. The one straddling the woman hesitated—just for a second—before scrambling to his feet.

Then they ran.

Their footsteps pounded against the pavement as they vanished into the night, their laughter replaced by the sound of retreat.

They ran. He barely noticed. His pulse roared in his ears as his gaze locked onto the woman on the ground.

Bruised. Bleeding. Small.

Something dark twisted in his gut. A mixture of fury and helplessness.

Then, like a switch flipping, instinct took over. He surged forward, dropping to his knees beside her.

She was beaten. Broken. Her face swollen beyond recognition, blood streaking her pale skin and pooling beneath her. Her clothes were torn, her pants yanked halfway down her hips. The sight made his stomach turn.

His jaw clenched.

Swallowing back his anger, he reached for her wrist. Her pulse was faint, her breathing shallow.

"Hey," he murmured, his voice gentler now. "You're safe. Help is coming."

She stirred, her lips barely parting.

A whisper—so fragile, he almost didn't catch it.

"Thank… you…"

Then she went still.

Anthony inhaled sharply. No, no, no. He wasn't losing her.

Grabbing his phone, he dialled emergency services, his voice clipped and urgent.

"I need an ambulance. Now. Female, early twenties, unconscious. Severe facial trauma, possible broken ribs. Alleyway off George Street—send someone now."

As he spoke, his eyes stayed locked on her battered face.

Who was she?

What had she done to deserve this?

No one deserved this.

He didn't know her name. Didn't know a single thing about her.

But as sirens tore through the night, drawing closer, he knew one thing for certain.

Whoever she was, he wasn't going to leave her alone.

Chapter Two

Aurora drifted between consciousness and oblivion, pain radiating through every inch of her body. It was everywhere—deep, unrelenting, making even the smallest breath feel like fire in her lungs. Darkness pulled at her, but distant sounds anchored her to reality.

Sirens wailed, sharp and piercing, growing louder with every passing second until they drowned out everything else. The cold pavement beneath her cheek was rough and unforgiving, but she was too weak to move, too shattered to care.

Voices swarmed around her, urgent and commanding.

"We've got a female, mid-twenties. Severe facial trauma, multiple contusions, possible fractured ribs—"

A second voice cut in. "Her name is Aurora Vincent. This must be her purse."

A hand pressed against her wrist, fingers seeking a pulse.

"Aurora? Can you hear me?"

She tried to speak. To say she was still here. That she was fighting. But her lips refused to move. The effort was too much.

The darkness won.

"She's barely responsive. BP is dropping."

Something warm draped over her—a blanket? Hands lifted her onto a stretcher, the movement sending a fresh wave of pain crashing through her body. A soft moan escaped her throat.

"That's good, sweetheart. Stay with us," a paramedic encouraged. "You're going to be okay."

She didn't believe him.

Darkness tugged at her, threatening to pull her under. But she fought it, clinging to the only thing keeping her grounded—the deep voice from earlier. The one that had saved her.

Where was he?

She forced her swollen eyes open just enough to see blurred shapes above her. The inside of an ambulance. A man sitting nearby, watching her, his jaw clenched. His face was a smear of worry, but she recognised him—the stranger who had chased away her attackers.

She wanted to thank him, but the effort was too much. Her eyelids fluttered shut.

The ride to the hospital was a blur of flashing lights and murmured medical terms. By the time they reached St. Vincent's, she was barely hanging on.

The stretcher jolted as they moved her inside. More voices. The beeping of machines. A woman's voice cut through the noise.

"What's her status?"

"Multiple facial lacerations, possible fractures—swelling is severe. She took a heavy beating."

Aurora felt herself being lifted, transferred to another bed. Hands worked quickly, cutting away her torn, bloodstained clothes. She tried to protest, but the words remained trapped in her throat.

"Pupils reactive. Pulse is thready."

A prick of pain in her arm. An IV.

"She's going into shock," someone said. "Get her stabilised."

The voices started to fade, swallowed by the growing darkness.

Aurora let go.

And everything disappeared.

Aurora drifted in and out of consciousness, aware only of distant sounds—the rhythmic beeping of a heart monitor, the soft hum of voices around her.

Her body felt heavy, weighed down by exhaustion and pain. Her face… something was covering her face.

Bandages.

The memories rushed back like a nightmare—the alley, the cruel hands, the punches that had left her gasping for air. Her stomach lurched.

"You're safe."

The voice was deep, steady. She turned her head slightly toward the sound, wincing as pain flared in her ribs.

A man stood at her bedside. Even through the haze of medication, she recognised him. Her rescuer.

"I—" Her voice was barely a whisper, her throat raw.

"Don't try to talk," he said gently. "You need rest."

She studied him as best as she could through her swollen eyes. Strong features, dark hair, a quiet intensity in his expression. Who was he?

As if sensing her question, he hesitated, then said, "My name's Anthony Hardwick. I'm a doctor here."

A doctor. He had saved her. And now, he was taking care of her.

Despite the pain clawing at her body, a strange warmth settled in her chest— something unfamiliar, something safe.

With the last of her strength, she reached out, her fingers trembling as they sought his.

He took her hand without hesitation. The moment their skin met, a jolt of awareness sparked through her, cutting through the haze of agony.

She gave his hand a weak squeeze, a silent thank you, a desperate tether to reality.

Then, the darkness pulled her under.

As soon as Anthony took her hand, he felt it—a jolt of awareness sparking between them. It was fleeting, almost imperceptible, but it was there. A connection. A quiet plea.

She didn't deserve this. No one did.

His jaw tightened as he looked at her bruised, bandaged face. Her injuries were brutal, the work of cowards who had left her broken on the pavement. The thought made his stomach churn with rage.

It had been hours since Aurora arrived at St. Vincent's Hospital. A team of specialists—including a trauma surgeon, neurologist, reconstructive surgeon, and orthopaedic surgeon—had worked swiftly to stabilise her.

Her face was so swollen and bruised that it was almost unrecognisable. Heavy bandages had been applied to reduce swelling and protect her wounds. She had received stitches for deep lacerations, and a nasal splint had been set in place to ensure proper healing.

Anthony had spent the last thirty minutes speaking with her doctors, gathering every detail he could. The prognosis was both a relief and a frustration.

Aurora had suffered extensive facial trauma—multiple contusions, deep cuts, and swelling that masked her true features. They suspected a hairline fracture along her cheekbone, but miraculously, it didn't require surgery. The swelling would take time to subside, and the bruising would last for weeks, but she was expected to make a full recovery in that regard.

Her ribs, however, were another story. Three were fractured—one dangerously close to puncturing a lung. Extensive bruising covered her abdomen and back, clear evidence of repeated blows. A CT scan ruled out internal bleeding, but pain management would be critical. Every breath, every movement would be agony for weeks to come.

And then there was the concussion—moderate, but serious. She had been unconscious for too long. The doctors would be monitoring her closely for any signs of brain swelling or cognitive impairment. For now, she was stable, but the next twenty-four hours were critical.

"She's strong," one of the doctors had told him. "Most people wouldn't have remained conscious after an attack like that. She fought hard. She's lucky you found her when you did. If she'd been left there much longer, she wouldn't have made it."

Anthony had nodded, but the words did little to extinguish the fury burning in his chest.

Anthony's jaw tightened as he looked at Aurora, lying so still in the hospital bed, her face wrapped in bandages, the machines around her beeping steadily. He hoped that whoever had done this to her—whoever had left her broken and bleeding in that alley—didn't get away with it. The thought of them walking free made his blood boil.

He exhaled sharply, running a hand through his hair, trying to calm the storm inside him. But then—

"Anthony, what are you doing here?"

The sharp voice yanked him from his thoughts. He turned, startled to see Mary Moore, his girlfriend, being wheeled into the room. Her arms were crossed tightly over her chest, irritation flickering in her eyes.

"I've been trying to call you for hours," she huffed.

Anthony immediately stood, his concern shifting. "Mary, what happened?" He stepped toward her, scanning her for injuries.

She sighed dramatically. "I fell down the stairs at my apartment block. Twisted my ankle pretty bad."

His brows furrowed. "Do you need surgery?"

"They'll do scans in the morning." She waved a dismissive hand. "For now, I have to stay overnight. And apparently, I have to share a room." Her gaze flicked toward Aurora's unconscious form, her nose wrinkling slightly. "Not exactly thrilled about that."

Anthony glanced between the two beds. It made sense. The hospital was always overcrowded, and Aurora needed close monitoring in the trauma ward. Still, the bitterness in Mary's tone made something twist in his chest.

"Is she your patient?" Mary's eyes flicked back to Aurora, disinterest lacing her voice. As if the woman lying battered and broken was nothing more than an inconvenience.

"No," Anthony said, his voice firm. "I saved her from an attack tonight."

Mary's eyes widened slightly, but just as quickly, the surprise vanished.

"You saved her?" she echoed, tilting her head. "And now you're just... sitting here watching over her?"

There was something in her tone—something close to suspicion.

Anthony crossed his arms. "She was left to die in an alley, Mary. She has no one here. The least I can do is make sure she's okay."

Mary's lips pressed into a thin line. "I just find it interesting that you're here in the middle of the night for a complete stranger."

His patience thinned. "A stranger who would be dead if I hadn't stepped in."

Mary scoffed lightly, rolling her eyes, but didn't push further. Instead, she leaned back in her wheelchair with an exaggerated sigh. "Well, whatever. I just want to get some sleep."

Anthony clenched his jaw, watching as she made herself comfortable. For a nurse, she should have had more compassion. But lately, he'd been noticing things about Mary—little things that weren't nearly as endearing as they once had been. Her bedside manner, it seemed, only extended to those she deemed worthy.

Chapter Three

Anthony stepped into his penthouse, the familiar skyline of Sydney stretching out before him. Floor-to-ceiling windows framed the harbour, the water shimmering beneath the moonlight, but he barely noticed. Exhaustion weighed on him, seeping into his bones. It was past midnight, and he had to be back at the hospital by eight.

He exhaled sharply, shrugging off his coat and tossing it onto a chair. The day had been long—too long. After settling Mary into her room, he hadn't lingered. She had complained about sharing the space, about the hospital food, about how he hadn't answered her calls. The words had rolled off her tongue, one grievance after another, and he had barely mustered the energy to respond.

He ran a hand through his hair. It wasn't just tonight. Lately, being around Mary drained him. They had been together for six months, but something had shifted. At first, she had been warm, affectionate, easy to be with. He had thought there was potential, that maybe, just maybe, she could be the person he built a life with.

But now?

Now, he wasn't even sure he liked her.

Anthony loosened his tie and poured himself a glass of water, staring out at the dark expanse of the harbour. The realisation should have hit harder, but it didn't. It had been creeping up on him for a while—a slow unravelling of the illusion he had convinced himself to believe in.

Mary wasn't cruel. She wasn't terrible. But there was something missing.

Something real.

He rubbed a hand over his face, frustration simmering beneath the fatigue. His job was demanding. As an oncologist, he faced life and death every day. It was gruelling, heartbreaking. But when he got to deliver good news—to tell a patient they were in remission, that they had more time—it made everything worth it.

That was the kind of fulfilment he craved. The kind of depth he needed.

And Mary... Mary didn't fit into that.

Maybe she never had.

Anthony placed his empty glass in the dishwasher, the soft clink echoing in the quiet of his penthouse. The city lights flickered beyond the massive windows, casting a glow across the sleek, modern space, but his mind was elsewhere. Exhaustion dragged at his limbs as he walked into the bedroom, tugging at his tie and unbuttoning his shirt.

Then he saw it.

A dark stain smeared across the crisp white fabric—blood.

Aurora's blood.

His breath hitched, and for a moment, he just stared at it, the deep red stark against the pale cotton. His fingers brushed over the dried stain, and suddenly, the night came rushing back in vivid detail—the alley, the sound of fists meeting flesh, her broken body lying in the dirt. The way her hand had trembled when she reached for him in the hospital.

His stomach tightened.

He had seen his fair share of trauma in the ER, but this was different. He hadn't just been a doctor treating a patient—he had been the one to find her, to pull her away from the brink. And now, standing alone in his bedroom, he couldn't shake the image of her lying in that hospital bed, wrapped in bandages, barely holding on.

With a sharp exhale, he yanked off the shirt, throwing it into the laundry basket as if that would erase the memories pressing down on him. But it didn't.

Instead, they followed him as he stripped down and stepped into the bathroom, the cold tile grounding him. He turned the shower on, letting the water heat up before stepping in, hoping it would wash away the tension knotting his muscles.

As the water cascaded over him, he closed his eyes, but all he could see was her.

Aurora, beaten and bleeding. Aurora, struggling to stay conscious. Aurora, reaching for him in silent desperation.

He let his head fall against the tiled wall, his hands braced on either side.

He had done everything he could for her medically. But the uneasy feeling in his chest told him that walking away from this—from her—wasn't going to be that simple.

It wasn't just the horror of what had happened to her or the injustice of it. It was something deeper. A pull he couldn't quite explain.

He felt protective of her in a way that went beyond his duty as a doctor. It was irrational—he barely knew her—but that didn't change the fact that the thought of her alone, vulnerable, and afraid made something in him tighten.

Anthony hoped the hospital would track down a relative or friend—someone who cared about Aurora, someone who would sit by her bedside and reassure her that she wasn't alone. Surely, there had to be someone out there anxiously waiting for news of her.

A father, a sibling, a best friend. A boyfriend. A husband.

The thought made him tense. He didn't know why. It wasn't his business— who she belonged to, who she would wake up asking for. But the idea of another man pacing outside her hospital room, desperate to hold her hand, made something sharp and unfamiliar coil in his chest.

Jealousy? No, that was ridiculous. He barely knew her. And yet, the thought of Aurora turning to someone else, leaning on someone else, needing someone else—he couldn't explain why it bothered him.

And somehow, that felt like it meant something.

Early the next morning, Anthony walked into the trauma ward, the familiar scent of antiseptic and coffee lingering in the air. The hospital was already buzzing with activity—nurses making their rounds, doctors reviewing charts, the occasional murmur of patients waking up to another day of recovery.

The head nurse, a no-nonsense woman named Helen, spotted him as he approached the nurses' station. She gave him a knowing look over the rim of her coffee cup. "Morning, Doctor Hardwick."

"Morning, nurse," he replied, rubbing the tension from his neck. "Busy night?"

Helen let out a long-suffering sigh, rolling her eyes. "Mary has been driving us crazy."

Anthony barely suppressed a groan. Of course, she has.

"Oh? Why's that?" he asked, though he wasn't sure he wanted to know.

Helen crossed her arms. "She's constantly complaining about that poor girl in the next bed."

His stomach tightened. Aurora.

"What's wrong with her?" His voice came out sharper than he intended.

Helen's expression softened, her exasperation shifting into something more sympathetic. "Nothing wrong with her, poor thing. She must be having nightmares—probably reliving whatever horror put her here in the first place." She shook her head. "But Mary's acting like it's some personal offence. She's been whining all night that Aurora's restlessness is keeping her from getting a good sleep."

Anthony's jaw clenched. He shouldn't be surprised—Mary's self-centredness was nothing new—but something about her complete lack of compassion for Aurora made irritation simmer beneath his skin.

"She was brutally attacked," he said, his tone controlled but firm. "Of course she's going to be unsettled."

Helen huffed. "Tell that to Mary. She keeps buzzing the nurses, demanding to be moved or to have us 'do something' about the noise. As if we can just flip a switch and make the poor girl's trauma disappear."

Anthony exhaled slowly, pinching the bridge of his nose. So much for bedside manner, Mary.

His concern shifted back to Aurora. She was reliving the nightmare in her sleep—probably trapped in the memories of last night, unable to escape them. The thought unsettled him more than it should have.

"I'll check on her," he said finally, already turning toward the patient rooms.

Helen nodded, her expression knowing. "I figured you would."

Anthony didn't respond, but he could tell from her tone that she assumed he was going to check on Mary. It made sense—after all, Mary was his girlfriend. But she was the last person on his mind right now.

It was Aurora he needed to see.

As he made his way down the hall, he tried to ignore the way his pulse quickened. He told himself it was concern, nothing more. She had been through hell, and if she was suffering from nightmares, someone needed to make sure she was okay.

Still, a part of him knew there was something else at play—something he wasn't ready to examine just yet.

When he reached the door, he braced himself for Mary's whining, already anticipating the exaggerated sighs, the dramatic complaints about how she was the one suffering.

Taking a deep breath, he pushed open the door.

When he entered the room, his heart clenched at the sight before him.

Aurora lay tangled in the hospital sheets, her body shifting restlessly. Even in sleep, she looked tormented—her hands twitching as if trying to defend herself, her lips parted in soft, pained whimpers. Every so often, she let out a small, distressed sound, the kind that made his chest tighten with something he didn't quite understand. She was obviously having a nightmare, reliving the horror of what had happened to her.

Before he could take a step toward her, Mary's voice cut through the room like nails on glass.

"Oh, thank goodness," she huffed, throwing her arms up as if she were the real victim here. "Maybe now you can finally arrange for my transfer to another room."

She shot a pointed look at Aurora's bed, her nose wrinkling in distaste.

No Good morning, Anthony. No How are you? No I missed you last night.

Just straight into complaining.

Anthony exhaled slowly, forcing himself to keep his expression neutral. But irritation simmered just beneath the surface.

"Mary," he said, his voice low and controlled. "Surely you must understand what she's been through." He turned his gaze back to Aurora, his chest aching at how small and fragile she looked despite the bruises and bandages. "Look at her."

Mary made a dismissive noise, folding her arms across her chest. "I have been looking at her all night. She's been keeping me awake with her tossing and moaning." She gestured vaguely toward Aurora, like she was some sort of nuisance rather than a woman who had barely survived an attack. "I need my rest too, Anthony. You know how exhausting my job is."

Anthony slowly turned his head to look at her. His patience, already worn thin from the night before, stretched even tighter.

Mary was a nurse. She had seen victims of violence before. She knew what trauma did to the body and mind. And yet, she had no empathy for the woman lying broken in the bed beside her.

It made something inside him shift. A realisation he had been avoiding for too long.

Mary wasn't the woman he thought she was.

Maybe, deep down, he had always known that.

Their relationship had been unravelling for a while now, in ways so subtle he hadn't fully acknowledged them until this moment. The forced conversations. The moments of silence that used to feel comfortable but had started to feel suffocating. The way she dismissed his concerns, rolling her eyes whenever he spoke about his long shifts or the emotional toll of his job.

And then there was the intimacy—or lack thereof.

They hadn't been together in over a month. Every time Mary had asked him to stay over, he had made an excuse. Too tired, early shift, need to catch up on paperwork. He told himself it was just exhaustion, the stress of the hospital wearing him down. But now, standing in this room, listening to her whine about something so insignificant in the grand scheme of things, he knew the truth.

He had already checked out of this relationship.

Maybe he'd done it the first time he caught her rolling her eyes at an elderly patient. Or when he realised, she was more interested in looking like a compassionate nurse than being one.

Or maybe it had happened even before that—somewhere between their first date and now, when the spark that had drawn him to her had quietly burned out, leaving nothing but embers.

And yet, he had stayed. Out of habit? Convenience? Because breaking up meant admitting they had been wrong for each other all along?

Whatever the reason, it no longer mattered.

Because in this moment—seeing her utter lack of empathy, her complete disregard for the woman fighting demons in the next bed—he knew one thing with absolute certainty.

This was over.

It had to be.

Chapter Four

Anthony made it to his office just before eight, his mind still tangled in the events of the morning. He had spoken to Mary briefly before leaving, though the conversation had been as strained as ever. She had been irritated that he hadn't requested a room transfer for her, pouting in a way that once might have amused him but now only exhausted him.

Helen had been just as surprised. "I thought you would have had her moved," she remarked as he passed the nurses' station.

"She'll be fine," was all he had said.

The truth was, he didn't care about Mary's complaints. Aurora was the one on his mind. That's why, before leaving, he had asked Helen to let him know when Aurora woke up. The request had clearly caught her off guard, her brow lifting slightly.

"I'll keep an eye on her," Helen had promised. "And if she wakes up after my shift, I'll make sure the next nurse informs you."

He had thanked her and walked away without another word.

Anthony knew he needed to end things with Mary, but the hospital wasn't the place for it. It would be messy, dramatic, and far too public. She wouldn't take it well, and he had no intention of letting their relationship—or whatever was left of it—turn into gossip for the entire staff. No, that conversation would have to wait.

For now, he had a full day ahead.

Stepping into his office, he exhaled slowly, rolling his shoulders to release the tension that had taken root there. He barely had time to gather his thoughts before his receptionist, Cindy, greeted him with a bright smile.

"Morning, Dr. Hardwick."

He forced himself to return the gesture, though his mind was elsewhere.

"Morning, Cindy. How are you this morning?"

"Can't complain," she said cheerfully, handing him his schedule for the day. "You've got a full patient load, plus a consult at ten and a meeting with Dr. Patel this afternoon."

He nodded, scanning the list quickly, but his thoughts kept drifting. No matter how busy the day ahead was, he knew his mind would keep circling back to Aurora—wondering if she was still asleep, if she was in pain, if she would wake up afraid and alone.

And why, despite everything else demanding his attention, he couldn't seem to shake the need to be there when she did.

It was after five by the time Anthony had finished with all his patients and the mountain of paperwork that had been waiting for him. The day had been relentless—back-to-back consultations, difficult diagnoses, and a particularly emotional discussion with a patient's family. Normally, he would take a moment to breathe, to clear his head before leaving his office. But today, his thoughts weren't on his usual post-shift routine.

Aurora.

As soon as he finished his last task, he picked up his phone and dialled the trauma ward. He hadn't heard anything all day, and part of him worried that Helen had forgotten to pass along his request.

A different voice answered this time—one of the evening nurses.

"This is Nurse Keira speaking."

"Hi, this is Dr. Hardwick." Anthony adjusted his grip on the phone, his voice steady despite the unease curling in his chest. "I asked Helen to inform me when Aurora—uh, Miss Vincent—woke up. I haven't heard anything, so I wanted to check in."

"Oh, yes, Dr. Hardwick. Helen let us know." The nurse's voice was warm but professional. "Aurora is still asleep. She's been out all day."

Anthony exhaled slowly, leaning back in his chair. His fingers drummed absently against the desk.

"She hasn't woken up at all?"

"No, not yet. Her body must need the rest," Keira replied. "Her vitals have been stable, and she's responding normally to the pain medication. We've been monitoring her closely."

That was a relief, but it didn't ease the knot of concern in his stomach. She needed sleep to heal, but if nightmares were keeping her mind in turmoil, was she truly resting?

"Has she been restless?" he asked, his voice quieter now.

There was a brief pause before Keira answered. "A little. She's moved around in her sleep, some tossing and turning, but nothing too alarming. We suspect she's having nightmares, but she hasn't woken up from them."

Anthony's jaw tightened. Of course, she was. After what she had endured, nightmares were inevitable. But the thought of her suffering—even in sleep— unsettled him in a way he couldn't quite explain.

"I see." He hesitated, debating his next question. "Has anyone contacted her family?"

Another pause.

"She has no family, Doctor." Keira's voice softened slightly. "She's an orphan."

Anthony's fingers stilled against the desk.

"We did manage to reach her boss," Keira continued. "He said he'd inform some of her friends, but… he was quite upset. Apparently, he was the one who asked her to work late that night. If she had left earlier, well…" She trailed off, but the implication was clear.

Anthony swallowed.

"I see," he said, his voice quieter now. "If she wakes up, please call me."

"We will," Keira assured him. Then, after a brief hesitation, she asked, "Would you like us to pass on any message?"

He opened his mouth, then closed it. What could he say? That she wasn't alone. That someone cared? That he cared.

But that wasn't his place. Was it?

"No message," he finally said after a pause. "Just… let me know."

Hanging up, Anthony stared at the phone for a long moment, his jaw tense.

He should go home. But the thought of Aurora waking up alone, with no one there, sat heavy in his chest. He exhaled sharply, already knowing he wasn't leaving just yet.

Anthony tapped his fingers against the desk, staring at the phone long after the call had ended. The knowledge that Aurora had no family to contact settled heavily in his chest. No parents, no siblings—just a boss who sounded like he was carrying a great deal of guilt. No one sat by her bedside. No one waited for news.

He sighed and pinched the bridge of his nose. Why did that bother him so much? He barely knew her.

But he did know what it was like to wake up in a hospital room, disoriented and in pain, with no familiar face waiting to comfort you. He knew how loneliness could creep in even when people surrounded you. And something about Aurora—her strength, her resilience—made the thought of her going through that unbearable.

Maybe that was why he couldn't bring himself to leave just yet.

He pushed back from his desk and stood, grabbing his coat. He told himself he was only going to check in—to make sure everything was fine with his own eyes. It wasn't unusual for doctors to do rounds after hours, and no one would question it. If anything, it would look like he was visiting Mary.

That excuse sat uneasily with him, but it would have to do.

As he made his way toward the trauma ward, he told himself he wasn't overstepping. He wasn't doing anything inappropriate. He was simply making sure his patient was okay.

That was all.

At least, that was what he kept telling himself.

Anthony opened the door to the hospital room, stepping inside quietly. Mary looked up from her bed, her lips curving into a smile that didn't quite reach her eyes.

"Oh, Anthony. Finally, you come to visit me," she said, her tone laced with something between amusement and irritation.

"Yes," he replied, his voice even. "How are you? Did they find anything?"

As he spoke, his gaze drifted toward the other bed. Aurora lay still, her face wrapped in bandages, resting against the pillow. But despite her motionlessness, the tangled sheets and the faint indentations in the mattress told another story—she had been restless, trapped in whatever turmoil haunted her even in sleep.

Mary sighed, pulling his attention back to her. "The X-rays didn't show anything definitive, but they're pretty sure it's fractured. I have to get scans tomorrow." She paused, then flicked a dismissive glance at Aurora's bed, rolling her eyes.

"Another night of that," she muttered, gesturing toward the sleeping woman.

Anthony frowned. "What do you mean?"

"She's been moving around all night and all day," Mary said, irritation threading through her voice. "Not fully awake, but tossing, turning… mumbling things. It's exhausting just watching her."

Anthony's jaw tightened. He didn't doubt Mary was in pain, but the sheer lack of sympathy in her voice when she spoke about Aurora made his stomach turn.

His gaze returned to Aurora. Even in sleep, she looked troubled, her brows faintly furrowed, her breathing uneven, as if she were fighting something unseen.

He exhaled slowly, his concern deepening. "She's been through a lot," he said quietly.

Mary scoffed, crossing her arms. "Haven't we all? I mean, she's lucky, really—people are paying attention to her." She let out a small laugh. "Though I doubt she'll want the attention once they take those bandages off."

"Why?"

She cast another glance at Aurora, this time with a smirk tugging at her lips. "With all those bandages, she probably looks unrecognisable. Can you imagine?" She smirked. "I'd hate to see what's underneath."

Anthony's head snapped toward her, disbelief flashing in his eyes. "What?"

Mary shrugged, completely unbothered. "I mean, come on, Anthony. Can you imagine what's under there? I'd hate to see what she looks like when they take them off. Probably scarred… mutilated." She let out a small, almost amused laugh.

Anthony was stunned. "You need to show a bit more compassion," he said, his voice low and edged with controlled anger.

Mary rolled her eyes. "Oh, please—"

"No," he cut her off sharply, his patience wearing thin. "She's a patient, Mary. A victim. And she doesn't deserve your cruelty."

Mary blinked, clearly caught off guard by his tone. For the first time, a flicker of unease crossed her face.

Anthony shook his head, glancing at Aurora again. She deserved kindness. Care. And right now, looking at Mary, he realised—maybe for the first time—that she wasn't capable of either.

Anthony stared at her for a beat, his jaw tightening. A muscle in his cheek twitched as he exhaled sharply, shaking his head—not in anger, but in finality. Without another word, he turned on his heel and walked out.

"Anthony, don't go," Mary called after him, her voice laced with frustration.

He didn't stop. Didn't even look back. The door swung shut behind him, cutting her off mid-sentence.

Her protests faded behind him as he stepped into the hallway, his mind still clouded with anger and something deeper—something heavier.

Aurora was suffering, and Mary's callousness had only confirmed what he had been trying to ignore for too long.

He needed to put distance between himself and Mary.

Chapter Five

Aurora woke in pain. A deep, aching pain that radiated through her entire body, as if she had been crushed beneath something heavy and left to mend itself in slow, agonising pieces. Her head throbbed in dull, rhythmic pulses, and her chest felt tight, each breath sending sharp stabs of discomfort through her ribs.

She tried to open her eyes, but they barely parted—swollen, heavy, resisting her every effort. The dim light filtering into the room was hazy, blurred at the edges. She blinked sluggishly, trying to make sense of her surroundings. The steady beeping of machines filled the air, rhythmic and unyielding, grounding her in the reality of where she was. A hospital. That much was clear.

She tried to take a deeper breath, but a sharp, searing pain tore through her ribs, forcing a small whimper from her lips. Even that hurt. Everything hurt.

"Hello there."

The voice was warm, gentle—comforting in a way that made her feel slightly less alone.

Aurora tried to turn her head toward the sound, but even the smallest movement sent fresh waves of pain rippling through her body. She let out a weak groan, frustration curling inside her at her own helplessness.

"Moving is going to hurt for a little while," the voice continued, still calm, still reassuring.

A shadow moved at the edge of her vision, and a cool hand rested lightly on her arm—a touch so light she might not have noticed it if she weren't so attuned to every sensation.

"You're safe," the voice added softly. "You're in the hospital. I'm nurse Kiera. You've been through a lot, but you're going to be okay."

Aurora swallowed, her throat dry and raw, as if she hadn't spoken in days. She wanted to ask what had happened, but the words wouldn't come. They tangled in the back of her mind, just out of reach.

What had happened?

Memories flickered at the edges of her consciousness—darkness, fear, pain— but they slipped away before she could grasp them. All she knew was the present moment. The beeping machines, the cool touch on her arm, the ache that wrapped around her like a vice.

She forced her lips to part, her voice barely a whisper. "W-what...?"

The hand on her arm gave a gentle squeeze. "You were hurt, but you're safe now. Do you remember anything?"

Aurora's brows knitted together, another faint pulse of pain blooming in her temple at the effort. She tried to remember, but the more she reached for the past, the further it seemed to slip away.

"I…" She swallowed again, her throat burning. "I don't…"

"That's okay," the voice reassured her. "Don't push yourself."

"Water?" Aurora's voice was barely more than a rasp, her throat dry and scratchy.

The nurse moved swiftly, her motions smooth and practiced. A moment later, she gently pressed a straw to Aurora's lips. "Here you go, sweetheart. Small sips."

Aurora's cracked lips closed around the straw, and she sucked in a cool trickle of water. The relief was instant, soothing the raw burn in her throat, though even the simple act of swallowing sent a dull ache radiating through her chest. She took as much as she could manage before pulling back with a weak exhale.

"Thank you," she murmured, her voice a little stronger now.

"You're welcome, sweetie." The nurse placed the cup back on the tray beside the bed. "You've had visitors, you know. But you were asleep."

Visitors? A faint spark of warmth flickered in Aurora's chest. People had come to see her. Even in her foggy state, the thought warmed her.

"Who?" she asked, her voice still hoarse.

"Your boss, Mr. Greene. Poor thing, he's been worried sick about you."

Aurora tried to smile, though the simple movement felt strained. "He's a lovely man," she said, her voice soft but full of sincerity.

The nurse nodded, returning her smile. "Yes, he is. He sat by your bed for an hour. Said he blamed himself for what happened."

Aurora's brows furrowed slightly. Mr. Greene had always been kind to her— more than just a boss, he treated his employees like family. The idea of him carrying guilt over this made her heart twist.

"He shouldn't blame himself," she whispered.

"I told him the same thing, but you know how people are when they care."

Aurora swallowed, her throat still sore but no longer unbearable. "Who else?"

The nurse's expression softened. "Two of your friends—Sarah and Emily. They stopped by earlier and wanted you to know they'll be back later."

Aurora's chest tightened, but this time it wasn't from pain. Sarah and Emily. Her two best friends in the world. She hadn't expected anyone to visit—hadn't even allowed herself to hope—but knowing they had been here, that they had sat by her bedside, waiting for her to wake up, sent a wave of unexpected emotion crashing over her. The back of her eyes burned.

"They came?" she whispered, barely believing it.

"They did." The nurse smiled warmly. "Sat right here for a while, talking about how much they missed you. I think they would have stayed all day if they could."

Aurora blinked, her vision slightly blurry now. She had spent so much of her life feeling like she had to face things alone. The idea that someone had been here—that three people had cared enough to come and wait for her—made something deep inside her chest ache.

"They wanted to be here when you woke up," the nurse continued, "but they had to leave for work. They told me to tell you that as soon as their shifts are over, they'll be back."

Aurora let out a shaky breath, relief settling in her bones. Sarah and Emily had always been there for her, even when she'd tried to keep her troubles to herself. They were her family in every way that mattered.

"They'll be back," the nurse assured her gently. "You're not alone, honey."

Aurora inhaled slowly, feeling the truth of those words settle over her. Not alone.

For the first time since waking up, she didn't feel quite so lost.

"Just rest for now," the nurse murmured, adjusting the blankets around her with careful hands.

Aurora exhaled, her body sinking deeper into the pillows. Rest. That was all she could do. As much as she hated the weakness consuming her, she had no choice but to surrender to it.

For now.

She let her head fall back against the pillow, the cool fabric soothing against her overheated skin of her neck. The rhythmic beeping of the machines around her felt distant now, fading into the background as exhaustion tugged at her.

The door creaked open a few moments later, and a doctor stepped inside. He was an older man, his salt-and-pepper hair neatly combed back, his face lined with the kind of experience that only came from years of practice. Despite the weariness in his sharp blue eyes, he carried himself with an air of quiet confidence, his presence steady and reassuring.

"Hello, Aurora," he greeted warmly, stepping up to her bedside. "I was glad when the nurse let me know you were awake. You gave us quite a scare."

Aurora swallowed, her throat still raw, but she managed a faint, "Hello."

The doctor pulled a chair closer and sat down, his expression kind but serious. "I'm Dr. Whitmore. I've been overseeing your care since you were brought in." He studied her for a moment, as if assessing how much she could handle. "I know you must be confused and in a lot of pain, so I'll do my best to explain things clearly."

Aurora nodded slightly, wincing at the movement.

He sighed, his voice gentle but firm. "You suffered multiple injuries—some more severe than others. You have a concussion, which is why your head is aching so much. The swelling around your eyes should go down in a few days, but for now, it may be difficult to see clearly."

She felt a lump form in her throat, but she forced herself to listen.

"You also sustained several fractured ribs," he continued, "which is why breathing deeply hurts. We have you on pain medication to help manage the discomfort, but you'll need to be careful with sudden movements."

Aurora's fingers curled weakly against the sheets. The weight of his words settled over her, heavier than she'd expected.

"You have some bruising and soft tissue injuries. But the most significant concern was the damage to your face." His voice softened, as if he was trying to prepare her. "There were deep lacerations, and we had to perform surgery to repair some of the damage. The bandages will need to stay in place for now to aid the healing process."

Aurora swallowed hard, her stomach twisting. She didn't want to ask, but the question pressed at the back of her mind like a sharp blade.

"Will there… be scars?" Her voice was barely above a whisper.

Dr. Whitmore hesitated before answering. "It's too early to say for certain. The surgeons did everything they could to minimise long-term scarring, and with time, much of it should fade. There are treatments available to help improve the appearance of any lasting marks, but for now, the focus is on healing."

Aurora's chest tightened. She wanted to be brave, to tell herself that scars didn't matter, that she was lucky to be alive—but fear still gnawed at her. What would she see when they finally removed the bandages? Would she even recognise herself?

Sensing her distress, Dr. Whitmore's expression softened. "I know this is a lot to take in, but you're strong, Aurora. You survived something terrible, and now you're on the road to recovery. You're not alone in this. The medical team, your friends—we're all here to help you through it."

She nodded faintly, the reassurance easing some of the weight pressing on her chest.

"For now, the best thing you can do is rest," he continued. "Your body needs time to heal, and pushing yourself too soon will only slow the process."

Aurora let out a shaky breath, the exhaustion tugging at her again. "Okay."

Dr. Whitmore stood, giving her a small but reassuring smile. "If you need anything, just press the call button. A nurse will be in to check on you regularly."

She nodded again, and as he turned to leave, she let her eyes drift closed.

She had survived.

That was what mattered.

And no matter what came next, she would face it.

The next time she opened her eyes, a presence beside her caught her attention. The quiet hum of the hospital faded into the background as she turned her head slowly, her body protesting even the smallest movement.

And then she saw him.

Her rescuer.

He sat in the chair next to her bed, his broad shoulders slightly hunched forward, as if he had been there for a while. When their eyes met, he smiled—a warm, breathtaking smile that made the sterile hospital room feel just a little less cold.

His hair was dark, thick, and slightly tousled, as though he had run his fingers through it more than once. His features were strong and defined—a chiselled jawline, high cheekbones, and a straight nose that gave him an air of quiet confidence. But it was his eyes that held her attention the longest. Deep brown, rich and warm, filled with something that made her breath catch. Kindness. Concern.

He was handsome, undeniably so, but there was something more to him—something steady and grounding. He exuded a quiet strength; the kind that made her feel safe despite the vulnerability of her current state.

"You're awake," he said softly, his voice deep and soothing.

Aurora swallowed, still feeling groggy, but she managed to whisper, "You saved me."

His smile faltered, his fingers flexing slightly where they rested on his knee. Something flickered in his eyes—something unspoken, unreadable. "I just did what anyone would have done."

But somehow, she knew that wasn't true.

Chapter Six

Anthony had been relieved when Nurse Kiera called to tell him Aurora was awake. He had been carrying the weight of worry since the night he found her—bruised, broken, barely clinging to consciousness. Every time he had checked on her, she had been lost in the haze of pain and medication. But now, she was awake. She was talking. That was enough to let him breathe a little easier.

He was also relieved to hear that she had visitors. Three people had come to see her—her boss, Mr. Greene, and two friends, Sarah and Emily. That meant she had people who cared about her, people who would help her heal. She wouldn't be alone in this.

Anthony had wanted to see her immediately, but his schedule had been packed. As a doctor, he had responsibilities—patients who needed him, surgeries that couldn't wait. So, he had pushed through his day with a gnawing impatience, waiting for the moment he could finally check on her himself.

By the time he arrived, Dr. Whitmore had already been in to see her, explaining the extent of her injuries and what the hospital was doing to help her recover. From what Anthony had heard, she had taken the news quietly, processing each word with a calmness that both impressed and concerned the medical staff. She hadn't asked many questions.

Now, as he sat beside her, he could see the exhaustion still clinging to her, the battle between relief and uncertainty playing across her delicate features.

"How are you feeling?" he asked, keeping his voice gentle.

Aurora hesitated before answering, as if she had to sift through everything, she was feeling just to find the right words. "Like I got hit by a truck," she admitted, her voice hoarse.

Anthony chuckled softly, the corners of his mouth lifting. "That's actually not too far from the truth."

She attempted a weak smile, but it faded quickly. "Dr. Whitmore said I was lucky."

His expression grew serious again. "You are." His gaze swept over her, lingering on the bruises that still marred her skin. "What happened to you…" He hesitated, then shook his head. "You shouldn't have had to go through that."

Aurora looked away, her throat working as she swallowed. There was something haunted in her eyes, a flicker of fear and uncertainty that made Anthony's chest tighten. She wanted to say something—needed to—but the weight of it held her back.

He didn't push. He had seen enough trauma in his years as a doctor to know that some wounds took longer to surface. That silence was often a shield, a fragile barrier between fear and the truth. She would speak when she was ready. Until then, all he could do was be here.

And he would be.

Aurora's fingers curled weakly against the blanket, gripping it as if to steady herself. The gaps in her memory were terrifying. She remembered the attack in flashes—blurry, disjointed pieces that refused to fit together. She remembered the man's shadow looming over her, the impact of his blow. She remembered the pain, the cold ground beneath her. And she remembered her rescuer. The warmth of his touch, the calmness of his voice. But beyond that, there was darkness.

And it was the unknown that scared her the most.

She forced herself to meet Anthony's gaze, her voice barely above a whisper. "Can I ask you a question about that night?"

His expression shifted instantly, his warm brown eyes sharpening with concern. "Of course."

Aurora hesitated, bracing herself. Her heart pounded against her ribs, every beat a painful reminder of how fragile she felt. The words tasted bitter on her tongue, but she had to ask. She needed to know.

"Was I..." She swallowed hard, her voice barely above a whisper. "Was I sexually assaulted?"

The room seemed to shrink around them, the air thick with unspoken tension. The steady hum of the hospital monitors faded into the background, leaving only the sharp, unbearable silence between them.

Anthony's jaw tightened. For a moment, something flickered in his eyes— something raw, something fierce. But it wasn't pity. It wasn't hesitation.

It was certainty.

"No," he said firmly. "You weren't."

Aurora exhaled sharply, the breath she hadn't realised she was holding leaving her in a rush. Her fingers loosened their grip on the blanket, her knuckles no longer white from the pressure. The relief that flooded her chest was immediate, but it wasn't pure—it was tangled with remnants of fear, with the knowledge that while one nightmare had been avoided, another had still taken place.

Anthony leaned forward slightly, his voice gentler now, as if he knew how fragile she felt. "I understand why you were afraid to ask. But I promise you, Aurora, nothing like that happened."

She searched his face, needing to be sure. Anthony wouldn't lie to her. She knew that much. Even if the truth was painful, even if it was something she didn't want to hear, he would give it to her straight. That was who he was.

"How do you know?" she whispered, her voice trembling.

His gaze never wavered. "Because I was the one who found you and stopped the attack."

Her stomach clenched. The words settled heavily between them, each syllable carrying weight she wasn't sure she was ready to bear.

"I can't lie to you," he continued, his voice steady but laced with something taut—something restrained. "Their intentions were… to do that." He hesitated, as if the words themselves were too vile to say aloud. "But they didn't get the chance."

She shivered, her mind spinning.

"When I got to you," he went on, his hands clenching into fists at his sides, "your clothes were still in place. And the doctors who examined you afterward confirmed there was no sign of sexual assault." His jaw flexed, as if the memory itself was unbearable. "Your injuries were severe, but they were from blunt force trauma, not…" He trailed off, unwilling to finish the sentence.

Aurora's throat tightened, her hands curling into the sheets. The thought of what could have happened—of what almost happened—was enough to make her feel sick.

But it hadn't.

She had been hurt. Badly. But at least that horror hadn't been added to the rest.

"Thank you," she murmured, her voice barely audible.

Anthony's expression softened, his eyes holding something unreadable. "You don't have to thank me."

But she did. Not just for answering her, but for the way he had done it—with honesty, with care, with a steadiness that made her feel, for the first time in what felt like forever, that maybe she wasn't completely lost.

She let out another shaky breath, closing her eyes briefly. The fear wasn't gone—not entirely. It still curled in the pit of her stomach, whispering reminders of the things she couldn't remember, of the things she had survived.

But it had loosened its grip.

Just a little.

And right now, that was enough.

Anthony watched her, his expression unreadable, but there was something in his gaze—something quiet yet unwavering. Without a word, he reached out, his fingers brushing against hers before gently taking her hand in his. His grip was warm, firm but careful, as if he knew she was fragile but refused to let her feel alone.

She glanced down at their joined hands, her breath catching. It was such a simple gesture, yet it carried more comfort than words ever could, a silent promise that she wasn't alone in this.

Before Anthony could speak, the sharp sound of wheels rolling across the floor shattered the fragile moment like glass.

His entire body tensed.

Aurora turned her head just as the door swung open, revealing a woman being wheeled into the room. The air seemed to shift, the warmth of comfort replaced by something cold and sharp. The woman's dark eyes swept over them, calculating, assessing. Then her lips curved into a smirk—one that never reached her eyes.

"Well," Mary drawled, her gaze locking onto Anthony's hand still wrapped around Aurora's. "What exactly is going on here?"

Anthony released Aurora's hand as if burned, but the damage was already done. Mary had seen enough. Her expression darkened, her eyes narrowing with a mix of suspicion and something far more cutting.

"What are you doing here?" she demanded, her voice like the crack of a whip. Her gaze flicked between them, her lips curling. "Are you here to see me—or her?"

Aurora stiffened at the way Mary said her—like she was something insignificant, something that didn't belong.

Anthony's face hardened, his jaw tightening with barely restrained irritation. He had been relieved when Mary wasn't around to disrupt Aurora's recovery, but clearly, their luck had just run out.

"I'm here as a doctor, Mary." His tone was clipped, professional, but there was an unmistakable edge to it.

Mary let out a low, humourless chuckle, shaking her head. "Oh, please," she sneered. "You're here for her." She turned her gaze to Aurora, and the smirk on her lips sharpened into something cruel. "I hope you're enjoying all the attention. Poor little victim, making everyone trip over themselves to take care of her."

Aurora's stomach twisted at the venom in her voice. What had she ever done to this woman?

Anthony's eyes darkened with fury. "That's enough, Mary." His voice was low, controlled—but there was no mistaking the warning in it. Even Mary hesitated for the briefest moment.

Then, just as quickly, she pasted on an innocent smile. "Relax, I'm just saying what everyone else is thinking." She gave Aurora a slow, deliberate once-over before turning back to Anthony. "I mean, it's convenient, isn't it? All this sympathy? All this attention? Especially from you."

Aurora's pulse thundered in her ears. She felt the weight of Mary's accusation, even if she didn't fully understand it. The hostility in the woman's eyes made her uneasy.

Anthony stepped closer, his posture rigid with anger. "If you have a problem with me, take it up with me," he said, his voice dangerously calm. "But don't you dare speak to Miss Vincent that way again."

The nurse pushing Mary looked deeply uncomfortable, shifting from foot to foot, her expression tight with disapproval.

Mary's smirk faltered—just for a fraction of a second—before she scoffed, masking whatever emotion had flickered in her eyes. "So protective," she mused, tilting her head. "Tell me, Anthony… do you want to save her again?"

His jaw tightened. "I don't know what you're trying to get at, but I'm not playing this game with you."

Mary's gaze gleamed with something close to triumph. "I'm just glad I'm getting out of here. At least I won't have to listen to her whimpering in her sleep anymore."

Aurora's breath hitched.

She hadn't realised. Had she been crying out in the night? Had her nightmares bled into reality for everyone to hear?

Embarrassment flared hot in her chest, shame creeping up her spine. She knew it wasn't her fault—logically, she knew. But the idea that she had been so vulnerable, so exposed, made her stomach twist. The last thing she wanted was to be seen as weak.

"I… I'm sorry," she murmured, her voice barely above a whisper.

Mary let out a sharp laugh. "Bit late for that, isn't it?" she said coldly, her smirk widening.

No one noticed the door opening again. The tension in the room was thick, suffocating—until a sharp voice cut through it like a blade.

Chapter Seven

"Don't you dare apologise to this witch, Aurora."

Aurora flinched at the sudden voice, her head snapping toward the door just as two women strode into the room. Their presence was a force in itself—fierce, unyielding. Sarah's eyes burned with indignation, her posture stiff with barely restrained anger.

Beside her, Emily scoffed, folding her arms tightly over her chest. "Yeah, she doesn't deserve it."

Both women pinned Mary with unfiltered disdain, their gazes sharp enough to cut. The contrast between their righteous fury and Mary's smug expression was stark.

For the first time since rolling into the room, Mary's confidence flickered. Her smirk wavered—only slightly—but she quickly recovered, rolling her eyes with a theatrical sigh. "Oh, great," she muttered, slumping back in her wheelchair. "The rescue squad has arrived."

Aurora blinked, a rush of emotion tightening her throat. Her friends. They were standing up for her, defending her. But unlike Anthony—who approached conflict with careful restraint—Sarah and Emily wielded their words like weapons. They weren't just here to protect her; they were ready to fight for her.

Mary, however, remained unfazed. The smirk slid back into place as she tilted her head mockingly. "At least I won't have to listen to you two rambling on about nonsense anymore. This morning was bad enough."

Sarah arched a brow, unimpressed. "No. You're just used to people letting you get away with your toxic nonsense."

Emily nodded sharply, taking a step forward. "But that ends right now. You treat our friend with respect, or you'll have us to deal with. And we are not as forgiving or as kind as Aurora."

Mary's eyes flickered with something almost like worry. For the first time, she actually seemed to hesitate. Then, as if realising she was outnumbered, she turned her attention to the nurse pushing her wheelchair. "Get my stuff. I'm out of here."

She shot Anthony a look, her expression darkening. "We need to talk."

Anthony crossed his arms, his face impassive. "Not now. Just go, Mary."

For a moment, Mary looked like she might argue. But then, with one last glare at Aurora and her friends, she huffed and looked away. "Fine."

As the nurse wheeled her out, silence settled over the room, thick and heavy. Then, Sarah turned to Aurora, her face softening.

"Are you okay?"

Aurora let out a shaky breath. She wasn't entirely sure what she felt—relief, gratitude, exhaustion—all of it tangled together in a way that made her chest feel tight. But when she looked at Sarah and Emily, at the fire in their eyes and the unwavering support etched into their expressions, she knew one thing for certain.

She wasn't alone.

A wry smile ghosted across her lips. "I'm alive." She tried to make it sound light, like a joke, but her voice was still hoarse, the weight of everything she had been through pressing down on her.

Sarah and Emily immediately responded in unison. "Thank God you are."

Sarah stepped closer, reaching for Aurora's hand and squeezing it gently. "You're going to get through this, Rory. We've got you."

Aurora swallowed hard, the lump in her throat making it impossible to speak for a moment.

Emily, meanwhile, had turned her attention to Anthony, her sharp eyes scanning him from head to toe with the scrutiny of someone evaluating whether to trust him or not.

Anthony, ever composed, offered a polite smile.

Emily raised a single eyebrow, crossing her arms. "And you are?"

He extended his hand toward them. "Dr. Anthony Hardwick." His tone was warm but professional, his grip firm as he shook their hands.

Aurora's gaze softened as she looked at him. "He saved me." The words came out quieter than she intended, almost reverent.

Sarah's expression shifted, her wariness melting into gratitude as she shook Anthony's hand firmly. "Then we owe you our thanks, Doctor. Thank God you were there."

Emily nodded, still watching him carefully. "Yeah, really. We can never repay you for that."

Anthony glanced at Aurora, something unreadable flickering across his face before he turned back to the two women. "There's no debt to repay. I was just doing my job."

Sarah smiled, but there was something knowing in her eyes, a quiet understanding that said she saw more than he let on. "I don't think so. I doubt scaring off violent thugs is listed under medical duties in your contract." Her expression softened as she looked at Aurora. "But we're grateful. Aurora is very important to us."

Anthony's gaze flickered to Aurora again, lingering for a heartbeat longer than necessary. "I can see that." His voice was quiet, steady. "I'm glad she has such good friends."

Emily crossed her arms, tilting her head as she studied him. "You didn't just save her, did you?"

Anthony met her gaze, his expression unreadable. "What do you mean?"

Sarah exchanged a look with Emily before turning back to him. "I mean, you're here. You care."

Anthony hesitated, just for a moment, before replying. "She's been through something terrible. Of course, I care."

Sarah and Emily shared another glance, something knowing passing between them. It was subtle, but Aurora caught it—the way they saw something she wasn't ready to acknowledge yet.

Emily smirked, nudging Sarah. "He's being humble."

Sarah nodded, her smile widening. "Very."

Anthony let out a small chuckle, shaking his head. "I better be going."

But instead of immediately leaving, he turned to Aurora, moving to her bedside. His presence was steady, grounding, and for a moment, she didn't want him to go.

"I'll let you visit with your friends." His voice was warm, but there was a reluctance there, a hesitation that made Aurora's chest tighten.

She looked up at him, her throat suddenly dry. "Thank you again." Her voice was barely above a whisper, but she knew he heard it.

His lips curved into a soft smile. "Get better, Aurora."

For a second, neither of them moved. Then, with one last lingering glance, he turned and walked toward the door.

Aurora exhaled, not realising she had been holding her breath.

Sarah waited until the door clicked shut before turning to her with a grin. "Well. That was interesting."

Emily smirked. "Very."

Her friends stayed for an hour, filling the room with warmth and easy laughter. Even though Aurora couldn't talk much, Sarah and Emily's banter was exactly what she needed—a distraction from the pain, from the fear, from the whirlwind of emotions still settling inside her.

They told her stories, some ridiculous, some heartwarming, all meant to make her smile. Sarah dramatically recounted a disastrous date, complete with exaggerated impressions, while Emily threw in sarcastic commentary that had Aurora shaking with silent laughter. It was the first time in days that she felt something close to normal, even if only for a little while.

When it was time for them to leave, Sarah squeezed Aurora's hand gently. "We'll be back tomorrow, okay? No getting rid of us."

Emily leaned in, giving her a mock-stern look. "And if you need anything, anything at all, you call. I don't care if it's the middle of the night."

Aurora's heart swelled. "Thank you," she whispered, emotion thick in her voice.

"Always." Sarah smiled, and with one last glance, they slipped out of the room, leaving behind a lingering sense of comfort.

Not long after, there was a soft knock at the door, and Aurora looked up to see Mr. Greene stepping inside.

His face was lined with worry, his usual confident demeanour clouded with guilt. He hesitated before walking closer, wringing his hands together. "Aurora… I—" He let out a heavy sigh, his voice thick with emotion. "I am so sorry. I don't even know what to say."

Aurora managed a weak but reassuring smile. "Mr. Greene, you have nothing to apologise for."

He shook his head, his jaw tightening. "I should have made sure you got home safely. I should have—" He stopped himself, running a hand through his greying hair. "I keep thinking of all the things I could have done differently."

"Please," Aurora said softly, "this wasn't your fault."

His shoulders sagged, but the guilt didn't fade from his expression. "You've always been one of the best employees I've ever had. Seeing you like this…" He trailed off, swallowing hard. "I just want you to know that whatever you need—time off, financial help, anything at all—it's yours."

Aurora's throat tightened. She hadn't expected that, and the generosity in his voice nearly broke her. "That's very kind of you."

"It's the least I can do." He exhaled deeply. "Just focus on getting better. The entire staff is thinking about you."

The words warmed her, a reminder that even in the darkness of what happened, there were still people who cared. People who wanted to help.

And for the first time in days, Aurora truly believed she would get through this.

By the next morning, her hospital room had transformed into something of a garden. Bouquets of flowers in every colour filled the space, their soft fragrance a stark contrast to the sterile scent of disinfectant. Some were arranged neatly on the small table beside her bed, others placed carefully along the windowsill, catching the early morning sunlight.

Aurora blinked in surprise as Nurse Helen walked in, carrying yet another bouquet—her third delivery of the morning. The older woman shook her head with an amused smile. "Someone is very popular," she teased, setting the vase down.

Aurora managed a small smile, her voice still hoarse but touched with warmth. "Where are those from?"

"Your colleagues," Nurse Helen said, glancing at the attached note. "Seems like everyone at work is thinking about you."

Aurora's chest tightened at the thought. She had always gotten along with everyone at work, but she had never been the type to stand out or draw too much attention. Yet here was proof that she was more valued than she had ever realised.

Swallowing past the lump in her throat, she reached for the small card nestled between the petals, her fingers brushing against the delicate blooms. The handwritten message inside was simple yet deeply heartfelt.

We miss you, Aurora. Take your time to heal—we'll be here when you're ready.

Her vision blurred as emotion swelled within her, the unexpected kindness wrapping around her like a warm embrace.

Nurse Helen, ever observant, gave her a gentle pat on the arm. "You're loved, dear. Don't forget that."

Aurora swallowed past the lump in her throat and whispered, "Thank you."

Because, for the first time in a long time, she truly felt it.

Chapter Eight

Anthony decided that during his lunch break, he would visit Aurora. It had been a long morning filled with back-to-back consultations and procedures, but she had been on his mind more than he cared to admit. The hospital didn't have official visiting hours in the middle of the day, which meant he could stop by without interruptions—no concerned visitors hovering, no nurses bustling in and out. Just a quiet moment to check on her.

As he made his way down the hall, the scent of antiseptic lingered in the air, mingling with the faint floral aroma that had become unmistakably linked to Aurora's room. The closer he got, the stronger it became.

Passing the nurses' station, Nurse Helen glanced up from her notes and offered him a warm smile. "Good afternoon, Dr. Hardwick."

He returned the smile with a polite nod, slowing his steps as she leaned slightly forward, lowering her voice as if sharing a secret. "She's quite the popular girl, that one," Helen mused, her eyes twinkling with something close to fondness. "You should see her room—it looks more like a florist than a hospital suite." She chuckled lightly. "Cards, flowers, even a few teddy bears. It's lovely to see how many people care about her."

Anthony's lips twitched slightly, the corner of his mouth lifting in a barely-there smile. Of course, people cared. Aurora had that effect—quiet, unassuming, but impossible to ignore once you truly saw her.

Nurse Helen tilted her head, studying him with the kind of knowing expression that made him brace himself. "Dr. Whitmore mentioned that you were the one who found her that night."

Anthony stiffened slightly. It wasn't a secret, but hearing it spoken aloud still sent an uncomfortable ripple through him. He met Helen's gaze, nodding once. "Yes," he confirmed simply.

Her expression softened. "That must have been difficult."

Difficult wasn't the word he would have used. Haunting, maybe. The image of Aurora—battered, unconscious, barely clinging to life—had been burned into his mind, a memory that refused to fade no matter how many times he tried to push it away. He had seen countless patients teeter on the edge between life and death, but that night had been different. It had lodged itself deep within him, unsettling in a way he couldn't fully explain.

Instead of acknowledging the weight of it, he exhaled quietly, forcing himself to focus on the present. "She's recovering," he said, his voice measured, clinical. A simple truth, yet it barely scratched the surface of what he really felt.

Helen studied him for a moment, her eyes soft with understanding. She had worked in the hospital long enough to recognise when a case was more than just another patient. "She's lucky you were there," she said gently.

Anthony's jaw tightened almost imperceptibly. He wasn't sure if it was luck. Or fate. Or something else entirely. All he knew was that from the moment he had found her, Aurora had become impossible to forget.

With a small nod to Helen, Anthony continued down the hall, his footsteps echoing softly against the polished floor. As he approached Aurora's room, he pushed open the door, immediately enveloped by the rich, floral scent of fresh bouquets. The air was thick with the mingling fragrances of roses, lilies, and peonies, a stark contrast to the clinical sterility of the hospital corridors.

All thoughts of flowers and well-wishes vanished. His gaze landed on her.

Aurora sat upright in bed, her posture slightly tense, her expression carefully composed, yet her eyes held a shadow of something he couldn't quite place. The fresh bandages on her face stood out starkly against her skin, a reminder of just how fragile she had been the night he found her. The swelling had gone down slightly, allowing her features to emerge from beneath the bruises, but the evidence of her ordeal remained.

Dr. Whitmore stood beside her, his expression calm and professional as he finished adjusting the gauze on her arm. A nurse hovered nearby, efficiently disposing of used bandages and tidying up the medical tray. At the sound of the door opening, all three turned their attention to him.

"Ah, Dr. Hardwick," Dr. Whitmore greeted, offering a brief nod of acknowledgment. "We just finished changing Miss Vincent's bandages on her face and arms."

Anthony's gaze flickered to the fresh white dressings on her arm, his jaw tightening. He had treated countless injuries in his career, seen people in far worse conditions—but something about seeing her like this made it feel different. Personal.

He forced himself to push past the tightness in his chest, offering a measured nod as he stepped further into the room. "How's the pain?" His voice was steady, though softer than usual as his attention remained fixed on her.

Aurora hesitated for a moment before offering a small, almost apologetic smile. "Manageable," she replied, though the slight strain in her voice betrayed her discomfort.

But there was something else—something that made his chest tighten for an entirely different reason. Her voice. It was stronger than it had been before, no longer raspy from the trauma. For the first time, he heard its true tone—rich, smooth, with a hint of warmth that was strangely… sensual.

Dr. Whitmore adjusted his glasses, glancing between them before speaking. "She's healing well, but she still needs rest. No overexerting yourself, Miss Vincent." His tone was light but firm, the warning clear.

Aurora sighed, shifting slightly in the bed. "When can I get out of this bed and take a walk?"

Dr. Whitmore chuckled at her impatience. "Maybe tomorrow, okay?"

She nodded, though it was clear she would rather it be sooner.

The nurse finished gathering the discarded bandages and turned to Dr. Whitmore. "Shall I take these out?"

"Yes, thank you," he replied before turning back to Anthony. "Well, I'll leave you to it, Dr. Hardwick. I'm sure Miss Vincent has had enough of my lectures for the day." He sent Aurora a good-natured smile before heading toward the door, the nurse following closely behind.

As they left, the room settled into a quieter hum, the door clicking shut behind them.

Anthony remained standing near the foot of the bed, watching her carefully. Even with the signs of healing, exhaustion still clung to her features. But for the first time in what felt like days, she was looking at him—really looking at him. Her eyes weren't as swollen now, and though bruises still shadowed her delicate features, they didn't diminish the quiet strength in her gaze.

"You didn't have to come," she said softly, her fingers idly tracing the edge of the blanket, her nails skimming over the fabric in slow, absent movements.

Anthony let out a quiet breath, stepping closer. "I wanted to."

Her lips curved slightly; the first real hint of a smile he'd seen from her since that night. Even through the small opening in her bandages, he could see the deep cut on her bottom lip, healing but still tender. The sight stirred something in him—relief that she was improving, but also a lingering anger at whoever had done this to her.

"Well," she said, tilting her head slightly, "you better sit. You're making the room feel smaller, looming over me like that."

The teasing lilt in her voice wasn't lost on him, and he felt the tension in his shoulders ease ever so slightly.

"Thank you," he murmured, pulling the chair closer to her bedside before lowering himself into it.

For a moment, silence settled between them—not uncomfortable but weighted with something unspoken. He studied her carefully, noting the faint traces of exhaustion in her posture, the way her fingers still absently toyed with the blanket as if grounding herself.

"How are you really feeling?" he asked, his voice quieter now, more personal.

Aurora exhaled, her gaze drifting for a moment before returning to him. "Tired," she admitted. "But better than yesterday. And a lot better than the day before that." A soft breath of laughter escaped her. "That's progress, right?"

His lips twitched, almost smiling. "It is."

She watched him then, as if trying to read something in his expression. "And you?"

He frowned slightly. "Me?"

"Yes, you," she said, her voice quiet but insistent. "I know that night must not have been easy for you either."

His jaw tightened, his fingers curling slightly against the armrests of the chair. The memory was never far from his mind—her crumpled form on the ground, blood staining her pale skin, the eerie stillness that had nearly made his heart stop. He had seen more than his share of trauma, but nothing had unsettled him quite like that moment.

"I'm just glad I was there for you," he said finally, his voice even, controlled.

Aurora studied him, her eyes searching his face, as if trying to see past the carefully measured words. "That sounds like something someone says when they don't want to talk about something."

Anthony exhaled through his nose, shaking his head slightly. "You shouldn't be worrying about me."

She gave him a pointed look, one brow arching ever so slightly. "Says the man who came all the way here during his lunch break to check on me."

He didn't respond right away, his fingers drumming lightly against the chair's armrest. He hadn't planned on staying long—just a quick visit to see how she was doing. But now, sitting here, looking at her, he realised he wasn't quite ready to leave.

"I guess we're both a little stubborn," he finally admitted, a hint of amusement flickering in his eyes.

Aurora smiled again, small, and tired but genuine. "I think we are."

Anthony let the silence linger between them for a moment, comfortable and unhurried. But then his gaze softened, and his voice dropped slightly. "How are the nightmares?"

Aurora's smile faltered, just a little. She glanced down, fingers idly toying with the blanket as if considering her answer. "Oh… you know about them."

"Yes," he said. "The nurses mentioned them."

She exhaled, nodding slightly. "They're getting less and less, which is good." Her voice was steady, but he caught the flicker of hesitation in her eyes. "They got a lot better after you told me that they didn't… you know."

Anthony's chest tightened. He knew exactly what she meant. As brutal as the attack had been, they hadn't taken that from her.

"I'm glad," he said, his voice quiet, firm.

Aurora let out a slow breath, lifting her gaze to meet his again. "Me too."

A pause. Silence stretched between them, but it wasn't uncomfortable. It was the kind of quiet that came when words weren't needed—when just being there was enough.

Then, after a moment, she tilted her head slightly. "So… what type of doctor are you?"

He blinked, caught off guard by the shift in topic. "An oncologist."

Her brows lifted. "Oh, that must be hard."

"It can be," he admitted. "But when I get to tell someone good news, when I can look them in the eye and say their fight is over—it makes it all worthwhile."

Aurora studied him, her expression thoughtful. "You care a lot," she said softly. "I can see that. It's in your eyes."

Anthony held her gaze, something unreadable flickering across his face. He wasn't sure what it was about her words that affected him so much—maybe it was the simplicity of them, the quiet sincerity.

He cleared his throat lightly. "I think you'd make a good doctor," he said, attempting to steer the attention away from himself.

She let out a small, breathy laugh. "Me? Oh no, I don't think so."

"You have a way of seeing people," he countered. "Not just what they say, but what they mean. That's a rare thing."

Aurora's lips parted slightly, as if she were about to say something, but then she hesitated, pressing them together again. Instead, she simply watched him, her expression unreadable, as if she were trying to decide how much to say.

Anthony tilted his head slightly, studying her. "What do you do for a living?" he asked, genuinely interested.

"I'm an office coordinator at a medical equipment company," she replied.

His brows lifted. "How long have you been doing that? Do you like it?"

A small smile touched her lips. "A few years now. I love my job, and Mr. Greene is a wonderful boss."

But then, just as quickly, her expression shifted, a faint frown settling on her face.

Anthony didn't miss it. His gaze sharpened. "What's wrong?"

Aurora hesitated before sighing softly. "Mr. Greene came to visit me yesterday. He feels terrible about what happened to me."

Anthony's jaw tightened slightly. "Why would he blame himself?"

She lowered her gaze, absently tracing a fold in the blanket. "Because I was walking home from work when it happened. He asked me to work back that night, he said if he hadn't, none of this would have happened."

A flicker of something dark crossed Anthony's expression. He understood guilt—how it could twist inside a person, convincing them they should have done more. But there was only one person responsible for what had happened to Aurora—the one who had hurt her.

"He shouldn't blame himself," Anthony said firmly, his voice steady and unwavering. "And neither should you."

Aurora sighed, her fingers idly twisting the edge of the blanket. "I know," she murmured. "I tried to convince him, but I could see it in his eyes—he feels responsible." Her gaze flickered to Anthony's, worry shadowing her features. "I'm worried about him."

Anthony studied her for a moment, the way her concern for someone else outweighed her own suffering. Even after everything she had been through, she was still thinking of others. A slow, knowing smile tugged at the corner of his lips.

"You really care," he said, his voice softer now, filled with something unspoken.

Aurora blinked, her expression flickering with something like surprise before she let out a small, breathy laugh. "Of course, I do. Mr. Greene has always been kind to me. He's more than just my boss—he's a good person."

Anthony nodded, his smile lingering as he watched her. "It says a lot about you, you know."

She tilted her head slightly. "What do you mean?"

"That after everything you've been through, you're still more concerned about how someone else is feeling than yourself."

Aurora held his gaze, something unspoken passing between them. Then, almost shyly, she lowered her eyes, a small smile playing at her lips. "It's just who I am, I guess."

Anthony's expression softened. "Yeah," he said quietly. "I can see that."

Anthony rose from the chair, smoothing a hand over his coat. "I should go— my patients are waiting."

Aurora nodded, her fingers still idly tracing the edge of her blanket. "Thank you for coming," she said softly, a hint of shyness in her tone.

He hesitated for a moment, then met her gaze. "Would you mind if I came back tomorrow?"

Her eyes widened slightly, surprise flickering across her face before it softened into something warmer. "I'd like that," she admitted, a small, genuine smile touching her lips.

Anthony returned her smile, a quiet satisfaction settling in his chest. "Then I'll see you tomorrow." With one last glance at her, he turned and headed for the door, already looking forward to their next conversation.

Chapter Nine

For the next ten days, Anthony visited Aurora every lunch break, even on weekends when he wasn't scheduled to work. At first, he had told himself he was simply checking on her recovery, ensuring that her condition continued to improve. But by the third or fourth day, he knew that wasn't the real reason. He enjoyed her company—more than he cared to admit. There was something about her presence that made his world feel a little lighter, a little less burdened by the weight of his work. She was warm, generous, and endlessly kind in a way that wasn't performative but simply a part of who she was.

They talked about everything. She told him about her life before the attack—how she had grown up in the foster system, never knowing her biological parents. How, despite that, she had found a family in her closest friends, people who had stood by her in ways blood relatives often didn't.

"I used to wonder," she admitted one afternoon, as they sat by the window in her hospital room, watching the rain streak against the glass, "if I would ever feel like I belonged somewhere. But then I met Sarah, and later Emily, and suddenly… it didn't matter that I didn't have a traditional family. I had them, and that was enough."

He listened intently, his attention never wavering. It struck him how deeply she felt things; how much she cared.

In turn, he told her about his own family—his parents, who still lived in Melbourne, thousands of miles away. He called them often but rarely saw them in person, relying on video calls to maintain their connection. He was an only child, something he had never minded much, though he sometimes wondered what it might have been like to have a sibling, someone who truly understood the weight of family expectations.

"Do they ever visit?" she asked one day, tilting her head slightly as she studied him.

He exhaled quietly. "Not as often as they'd like to. My schedule makes it difficult. And, well… my father and I don't always see eye to eye."

Aurora didn't press, didn't demand details. Instead, she simply nodded, as if to say, I understand.

On the second day of his visits, she had finally been cleared to take gentle walks. He had been there when she took her first steps outside of her hospital bed, his hand hovering just near her back—not quite touching, but close enough to catch her if she needed support.

She had been determined, but her movements were slow, careful. He walked beside her through the corridors, guiding her past nurses and patients, pausing whenever she needed a break.

"You're doing great," he murmured when she sighed in frustration at how weak her legs felt.

Aurora huffed out a breath, glancing at him. "I feel like a baby deer."

He smirked. "A very graceful baby deer."

That made her laugh, the sound warm and soft, curling around him like something tangible.

Then, on another afternoon, the mood had shifted. He had arrived at her room quieter than usual, his usual easy confidence weighed down by something heavy. She noticed immediately.

"What's wrong?" she asked, her voice gentle, concerned.

He hesitated, debating whether he should even say anything at all. But Aurora had a way of drawing things out of him, of making him feel like it was safe to unburden himself, if only for a little while.

So, he told her. He told her about the young mother he had seen earlier that day, about how he had to sit across from her and tell her that she had breast cancer. About how she had gripped his hand so tightly, her eyes wide with fear, as she asked if she would get to see her daughter grow up.

Aurora listened without interrupting; her eyes filled with quiet understanding. And when he finally exhaled, as if letting go of the weight of it all, she reached out—hesitant at first, but then firmer—and placed her hand over his.

"I can't imagine how hard that must be," she said softly. "Having to deliver that kind of news. Carrying the weight of it."

He looked down at their hands, at the warmth of her touch. "You get used to it," he murmured.

But she shook her head. "No, you don't. Not really. If you did, you wouldn't be the doctor you are."

Something about the way she said it, so certain, so sincere, made his chest tighten.

He hadn't realised how much he needed to hear that.

By the tenth day, Aurora's stitches had been removed, and the bandages on her face had gradually lessened. Yet, he still hadn't seen her face completely. Not that it mattered. He had already seen her true beauty—the kindness in her eyes, the warmth in her smile, the quiet strength in the way she carried herself.

Her appearance was irrelevant to him. Aurora's beauty wasn't just skin deep; it radiated from within, and that was all he cared about.

On one hand, there was Aurora—warm, kind, and effortlessly genuine. Spending time with her had become the highlight of his days, something he looked forward to more than he cared to admit. There was an ease between them, a quiet understanding that didn't need to be spoken aloud.

And then there was Mary.

He had broken things off with her the day after the scene in Aurora's hospital room. Anthony could still remember the moment with perfect clarity—the day he had finally severed ties with Mary. It had been inevitable, yet the confrontation had been even more explosive than he'd anticipated.

She had demanded they talk, cornering him in his office before his shift had even started. He had barely shut the door before she launched into accusations, her face red with rage.

"So that's it?" she spat, arms crossed over her chest. "You're just throwing us away? After everything we've been through?"

Anthony had stood calmly by his desk, arms at his sides, no longer feeling the guilt that had once plagued him. The clarity in his mind was unwavering. "Mary, we haven't been anything for a long time."

That had sent her into a frenzy. "Oh, don't give me that! You're breaking up with me because of her, aren't you?" Her voice wavered with bitterness. "Aurora. The little patient you've been so concerned about."

Anthony clenched his jaw. He could have corrected her, told her that his decision had nothing to do with Aurora—that their relationship had been doomed long before Aurora had ever stepped into his hospital. But he didn't owe her an explanation. Not after the way she had treated Aurora. Not after she had stood in that hospital room, looking down at a vulnerable woman, and still chosen cruelty.

He met her gaze, his voice measured and firm. "I'm ending this because it should have ended a long time ago. You and I both know that."

Mary let out a harsh laugh, but there was a tremor in it. "You're pathetic," she hissed. "Throwing away a stable relationship for what? A fantasy? A woman you barely know?"

Anthony exhaled, shaking his head. "You're angry. I get it. But this isn't about anyone else, Mary. This is about us. And we haven't been right for a long time."

She scoffed. "You're delusional. We were fine until she showed up."

"Were we?" he asked, tilting his head slightly. "Because from where I'm standing, we were just two people holding onto something that stopped working a long time ago."

Her eyes burned with unshed tears; her hands clenched into fists. "You'll regret this, Anthony. You'll see. One day, you'll realise what you've lost."

But as he looked at her—truly looked at her—he realised something. He felt nothing. No sadness, no remorse, no second-guessing. Just relief.

For the first time in a long while, he felt free.

A weight had lifted from his shoulders, one he hadn't fully realised he had been carrying until it was gone.

So, as Mary stormed out of his office, slamming the door behind her, Anthony didn't stop her. He didn't chase after her. He simply exhaled, squared his shoulders, and moved forward.

Because for the first time in six months, he could. A weight had lifted from his shoulders, one he hadn't fully realised he had been carrying until it was gone.

Mary, of course, hadn't taken it well. She hadn't broken her ankle—it had only been a sprain—so within days, she was back at work, walking through the hospital corridors with her usual sharp confidence. Their paths inevitably crossed, but she refused to acknowledge him, her demeanour cold and distant. That suited him just fine.

What didn't suit him, however, was the way she looked at Aurora.

Whenever she saw Aurora in the hallways—slowly regaining her strength, still wrapped in bandages but growing stronger each day—her expression would darken. It wasn't outright hostility, not yet, but there was a sharpness to her gaze, something calculating. Anthony noticed it, and he didn't like it.

Mary wasn't the type to let things go easily. And something told him this wasn't over yet.

On the fourteenth day after Aurora's attack, Anthony visited her during his lunch break, as had become his habit. He told himself it was just concern for a patient, but deep down, he knew the truth—his feelings for Aurora had grown into something more. He didn't just care about her recovery; he wanted to be around her, to hear her laugh, to see the light in her eyes when she spoke about something she loved.

When he arrived at her hospital room, he found her sitting beside her new roommate, an elderly woman who had suffered a fall at her nursing home. Aurora was gently holding the woman's hand, listening intently as she spoke, her voice filled with warmth and reassurance.

Anthony lingered in the doorway, simply watching. It was a sight that touched something deep inside him. Despite everything she had been through, Aurora still had so much kindness to give. She wasn't just surviving—she was still caring, still giving, still making the world a little softer for those around her.

It warmed him in a way he hadn't expected, stirring something in his soul. At that moment, he realised just how much she had come to mean to him.

When Aurora realised Anthony was in the room, she turned toward him, wincing slightly as a twinge of pain shot through her ribs. They were still healing, but each day was better than the last. Despite the discomfort, her eyes lit up with warmth.

"Oh, hello, Anthony! I didn't see you there," she said with a smile. "I've got some wonderful news."

She gently patted her elderly roommate's hand and told her she would be back soon before pushing herself to her feet. Though her movements were careful, she was eager, already ready for the walk they had started taking together every time he visited.

Anthony stepped forward instinctively, always ready to help if she needed him. "What's your news?" he asked, his curiosity piqued.

"Dr. Whitmore said I can get my bandages off tomorrow," she said, her excitement evident.

Anthony's smile was immediate and genuine. "Oh, that's great news, Aurora."

She nodded, a flicker of nervousness crossing her face. "Yeah... I'm a little nervous, but I can't wait."

Anthony could understand why. It would be the first time she would see herself since the attack. He wanted to reassure her, to tell her that no matter what, she was still the same incredible woman he had come to admire—but he held back, sensing this was something she needed to process in her own way.

Instead, he simply held out his arm in silent invitation. "Shall we?"

Aurora looped her arm through his, leaning into his quiet strength. "Let's go."

They walked together in comfortable silence, the soft hum of the hospital around them. He kept his pace slow, matching hers, always attuned to her movements. Every now and then, she would glance up at him with a small smile, and he found himself wishing their walks didn't have to end.

When they returned to her room, he hesitated at the door. "I'll see you tomorrow," he said, reluctant to leave but knowing she needed rest.

Before he could step away, she surprised him by wrapping her arms around him in a hug. It was sudden, unexpected—but he liked it. More than that, he needed it. He hesitated only for a moment before hugging her back, savouring the warmth of her touch.

She pulled back slightly and met his gaze. "Whatever I look like, it doesn't matter," she said softly, her voice filled with quiet determination. "My friends will still care about me. That's the main thing."

Anthony looked at her, admiration swelling in his chest. "They will," he agreed, his voice steady. "And so will I."

She smiled at him, a silent thank you in her eyes, before stepping back into her room. He watched her for a moment longer before turning away, already counting the hours until tomorrow.

When Anthony left, Aurora sat on the edge of her bed, her fingers absently touching her arm where his warmth still lingered. She hadn't planned to hug him—it had just happened. But now that she had, she couldn't stop thinking about it.

It felt nice. Safe. Right.

She cared about Anthony—a lot more than she should. At first, she had convinced herself it was just gratitude for his kindness, for being there when she needed someone. But that wasn't the truth, and deep down, she knew it.

She was kidding herself.

She had fallen for him. Hard.

And now, as she sat in her hospital room, the reality of tomorrow settled over her like a heavy weight. She wasn't really worried about seeing her own reflection for the first time since the attack. She had already accepted that she might not look the same as before. What truly scared her was Anthony's reaction.

Would he care that she was scarred?

Would the warmth in his eyes change when he finally saw her face?

Aurora knew Anthony wasn't shallow—he had already shown her that he cared about who she was on the inside. But still, an uneasy doubt crept in. It was one thing to say scars didn't matter. It was another to see them.

Chapter Ten

Aurora was awake early the next morning, long before the sun had fully risen, lying in bed and staring at the ceiling. Her heart thrummed with nervous anticipation, her fingers twisting the edge of her blanket as she tried to calm her racing thoughts. Today was the day. The day she would finally see her face again.

Would she recognise herself?

Would she feel like a stranger staring back at her in the mirror?

A gentle knock on the door pulled her from her thoughts. Nurse Helen stepped in, her usual warm smile in place as she carried a tray with Aurora's morning medication and a fresh set of bandages.

"Big day, Aurora?" Helen asked, setting the tray down on the small table by the bed.

Aurora forced a smile, though she wasn't sure if it reached her eyes. "Yes," she admitted, shifting slightly in bed. "I'm a bit nervous."

Helen sat on the edge of the bed and gave her a reassuring look. "That's completely normal, love. But you have nothing to be nervous about. Dr. Whitmore said everything is healing beautifully. You're going to be just fine."

Aurora exhaled slowly, nodding. "I know," she murmured, though deep down, she wasn't entirely convinced.

Helen studied her for a moment, her expression softening. "It's not just about the healing, is it?"

Aurora looked down at her hands, hesitating. "It's silly," she said after a moment. "I know scars don't define me. I know that I'm lucky to even be alive. But… what if I don't look like me anymore?"

Helen reached out and squeezed her hand gently. "Scars tell a story, Aurora. They show that you survived something that could have broken you. But they don't change who you are." She patted Aurora's hand before standing. "And for what it's worth, I think you'll still be just as beautiful as ever."

Aurora swallowed against the lump forming in her throat, touched by the kindness in Helen's voice. "Thank you," she whispered.

Helen winked. "Now, let's get you ready. Dr. Whitmore will be in soon, and I have a feeling you have a certain visitor who won't want to miss this moment."

Aurora's stomach flipped. Anthony.

Would he be here? Would he want to see her before or after the bandages came off?

The thought both thrilled and terrified her.

Taking a deep breath, she steeled herself. No matter what happened today, she would face it with strength.

She had come this far. She could do this.

Aurora exhaled deeply, her heart hammering in her chest as she tried to steady her nerves. The anticipation coiled tight in her stomach, but she forced herself to focus on the positive. No matter what she saw in the mirror, she was still her.

Soon after breakfast, the door opened, and Dr. Whitmore strode in with a reassuring smile, followed closely by another nurse carrying a medical tray.

"Morning, Aurora," Dr. Whitmore greeted warmly. "Are you ready to be rid of those bandages?"

Aurora sat up straighter, her hands gripping the blanket in her lap. "Oh yes, very ready," she said, determination lacing her voice.

Dr. Whitmore chuckled. "That's what I like to hear."

He pulled on a pair of gloves while the nurse set the tray beside him, laying out scissors, antiseptic wipes, and fresh gauze in case they were needed.

"Alright," he said gently, stepping closer. "Let's take this nice and slow. If at any point you feel dizzy or uncomfortable, let me know, alright?"

Aurora nodded, swallowing hard as he reached for the first strip of bandages.

The air felt thick with anticipation as he carefully snipped the edge of the gauze at her forehead, loosening the fabric before slowly unwinding it. The sensation was strange—her skin tingling as cool air brushed across it for the first time in weeks. She held still, forcing herself to breathe evenly as layer after layer was peeled away.

Dr. Whitmore worked methodically, his expression calm and professional, though a glint of satisfaction shone in his eyes as he examined her skin.

When the last of the bandages fell away, he leaned in slightly, studying her face with a critical yet pleased expression.

"Well," he said, his smile widening, "I think you're going to be pleasantly surprised."

Aurora's breath hitched. "Really?"

He nodded. "Your wounds have healed exceptionally well. There's some scarring, as expected, but overall... you still look like you, Aurora."

The nurse handed him a mirror, and he turned to her. "Would you like to see for yourself?"

Aurora hesitated for a fraction of a second before nodding.

Dr. Whitmore passed her the mirror, and with a steadying breath, she lifted it, bracing herself for the reflection that awaited her.

Her heart pounded as her gaze met her own.

And then, relief flooded through her.

Her face was still hers.

Her features, her eyes, her expression—it was all the same. There were scars, yes, but they were far less severe than she had feared.

A small, thin scar ran just above her upper lip, barely noticeable unless you were looking for it. Another lined the left side of her jaw, but it was faint, tucked just beneath the natural curve of her face. The largest scar was on her forehead, but it wasn't as prominent as she had dreaded. With a slight tilt of her head, she realised it could easily be hidden beneath her hair.

Tears pricked her eyes, but not from sorrow. From sheer, overwhelming relief.

"I... I still look like me," she murmured, touching her fingers lightly to her cheek, tracing over the smooth skin where the bandages had once been.

Dr. Whitmore chuckled. "Of course you do. You were always going to, Aurora. You healed beautifully."

She let out a shaky laugh, a mix of disbelief and gratitude washing over her. "I really thought..." She trailed off, shaking her head. "I was so scared I wouldn't recognise myself."

The nurse patted her shoulder kindly. "You've been through a lot, love. It's natural to worry. But you're still as beautiful as ever."

Aurora bit her lip, a wave of emotions crashing over her. She hadn't realised just how much weight she had been carrying until now, until this moment of clarity, of reassurance.

"Thank you," she whispered, gripping the mirror tightly for a second before lowering it.

Dr. Whitmore nodded approvingly. "Now, you'll still need to keep up with proper skincare and sun protection for a while, and the scars may continue to fade over time. But overall, I'd say you're in fantastic shape."

Aurora exhaled, her shoulders finally relaxing.

She was okay.

More than okay.

And for the first time in a long while, she truly believed it.

Anthony found it impossible to concentrate that morning. His mind was consumed by one thought—he would finally see Aurora's face.

He had imagined her features countless times, piecing them together from the glimpses he had caught. He knew she had striking blue eyes, the kind that held depth and emotion, and honey-golden hair that shimmered in the light. He had memorised the curve of her lips, full and inviting, the kind that made a man wonder how they would feel against his own. But beyond all of that, it was her presence, her resilience, that had captivated him.

Still, a lingering worry gnawed at him. Would she be disappointed by the results? Would she struggle to accept the face she saw in the mirror? He didn't care about scars or imperfections—Aurora was beautiful to him, with or without them. He only hoped she would see herself the way he did.

By the time his lunch break arrived, he was more nervous than he had ever been. His usual confident stride felt forced as he made his way to the trauma ward, a place he had visited more than two dozen times since Aurora had been admitted. Today, however, was different.

As he passed the nurses' station, Nurse Kiera glanced up and grinned.

"Hello, Dr. Hardwick." There was a knowing twinkle in her eye. "You're going to be very surprised."

She walked off before he could respond, leaving him standing there, his heart hammering.

Was that good or bad?

He didn't have time to dwell on it. Taking a steadying breath, he continued down the hall until he reached Aurora's door. He braced himself, fingers curling around the handle, willing his emotions into check before pushing it open.

The moment he stepped inside, his world tilted.

Aurora looked up from where she was sitting in the chair beside her bed, and surprised wasn't the word he would have used.

He was stunned.

She was breathtaking.

Her features were delicate yet strong, a striking blend of beauty and resilience. Her blue eyes were even more vivid without the barrier of bandages, framed by thick lashes that made them appear almost otherworldly. Her golden hair cascaded over her shoulders, catching the light in soft waves.

And her scars…

They were there, yes. A small one above her upper lip, another along her jawline, and the most prominent one on her forehead—but they did nothing to diminish her beauty. If anything, they only added to it, a testament to her strength, her survival.

His throat went dry.

Aurora's gaze searched his, as if bracing herself for his reaction. A hint of vulnerability flickered across her face, but she lifted her chin, meeting his eyes with quiet determination.

"Hi," she said softly.

Anthony swallowed hard. "Hi."

His voice was rougher than he intended, thick with something he couldn't quite name.

Aurora shifted, tucking a strand of hair behind her ear, her fingers lingering over the scar on her forehead. "It's not as bad as I thought," she admitted, a small, tentative smile playing on her lips. "Dr. Whitmore did a great job."

Anthony finally found his voice, stepping closer. "You look…" He exhaled, shaking his head slightly. "Aurora, you look incredible."

Her cheeks flushed, and she ducked her head for a moment before looking back up at him. "You don't have to say that."

"I'm not just saying it." He knelt beside her chair so that they were eye level. "I mean it. You were always beautiful. This"—he reached out, hesitating before lightly tracing his fingers along the edge of the scar on her jaw— "doesn't change that."

Her breath hitched at his touch, and for a moment, neither of them moved.

Then she let out a small, shaky laugh. "You're just saying that because you're a doctor. You have to be reassuring."

He smirked. "Aurora, I'd be saying it even if I wasn't in a white coat."

A soft silence stretched between them.

Then, with a teasing tilt of her head, she asked, "So… do I look anything like you imagined?"

Anthony huffed a laugh, running a hand through his hair. "Not even close."

Aurora arched a brow. "Oh?"

He met her gaze, a slow smile tugging at his lips. "Because no matter how many times I tried, I never could have imagined someone as stunning as you."

Aurora blinked, her expression caught between disbelief and something softer, something warmer.

Before she even realised what she was doing, she leaned forward, her lips brushing against Anthony's in a fleeting, hesitant kiss.

It was quick—just a whisper of contact—but it was enough to make her heart race.

Anthony froze, caught completely off guard. His breath hitched, his entire body going still as he processed what had just happened.

Their eyes met, searching, questioning, as the air between them grew charged with something unspoken.

Then, slowly—deliberately—Anthony raised his hand, his fingers threading gently through the hair at the nape of her neck. His touch was warm, steady, sending shivers down her spine. His gaze flickered to her lips, dark with intent, and this time, when he brought her mouth back to his, there was nothing hesitant about it.

The second kiss was deep, filled with unspoken emotions—longing, relief, desire.

Aurora gasped against his lips, and Anthony took advantage of the moment, tilting his head to deepen the kiss. His other hand found her waist, pulling her closer as their bodies melted into each other. His lips moved over hers with a perfect blend of tenderness and hunger, as if he had been waiting for this moment longer than he was willing to admit.

Aurora's hands slid up his chest, grasping at the fabric of his white coat, anchoring herself as the world around them blurred into nothing.

Heat coiled low in her stomach as Anthony's fingers traced slow, reverent patterns at the base of her skull, his thumb stroking lightly against her jaw. The sensation sent a shiver down her spine.

She had never been kissed like this before.

It wasn't just a kiss—it was a confession, a promise, a breath-stealing, soul-deep kind of need that neither of them had expected but both had craved.

Anthony shifted, angling his mouth over hers, drawing another soft sound from deep in her throat. The kiss grew more desperate, more consuming, as if they were both trying to make up for all the moments they had resisted, for every second they had convinced themselves this couldn't happen.

But it was happening.

Aurora felt herself sinking into it, into him, until a soft knock on the door made them jolt apart.

Breathless, lips swollen, Aurora stared at Anthony, her chest rising and falling rapidly.

His own breathing was uneven, his pupils blown wide as he dragged his gaze over her face.

Neither of them spoke.

But in that moment, with their hearts pounding in sync, they both knew— there was no going back from this.

Chapter Eleven

Anthony paced his office, running a hand through his hair, his mind spinning. That kiss…

It was amazing.

No, amazing wasn't enough. It had been earth-shattering.

It had unravelled him, set his very soul on fire in a way he hadn't thought possible. He could still feel the warmth of Aurora's lips, the way she had melted into him, the way her fingers had clutched at his coat as if she needed him as much as he needed her.

And that realisation hit him like a freight train.

He had been kidding himself.

Convincing himself that his feelings for Aurora were nothing more than concern, admiration, attraction even. But it was all a lie. A desperate attempt to suppress what had been growing inside him since the moment he first saw her lying in that hospital bed, bruised yet still so strong.

He loved her.

God help him, he loved Aurora.

The thought both exhilarated and terrified him. Love wasn't something he had ever allowed himself to consider—not like this, not with this kind of intensity. It wasn't supposed to happen. He had told himself that over and over again. But one kiss had shattered every wall he had so carefully built.

He stopped pacing and exhaled sharply, gripping the edge of his desk. His heart was still racing, his pulse erratic. He needed to see her again. Needed to talk to her.

Did she feel the same way?

Had that kiss meant as much to her as it had to him?

Or had it been a moment of impulse—one she would regret?

The thought made his stomach twist, but deep down, he knew what he had felt in that kiss. He had felt her hesitation, her surprise… but then, he had felt her give in. The way her body had responded to him, the way her breath had hitched, the way she had pressed closer as if she couldn't bear to be apart from him.

It meant something.

Anthony clenched his jaw, determination settling in.

He had to know.

He had to find Aurora.

But before he could leave his office, there was a sharp knock at the door.

Anthony exhaled, irritated by the interruption. "Come in," he called, already halfway to the door.

The last person he expected to see walked in.

"Hello, Anthony," Mary said smoothly, leaving the door ajar behind her.

Anthony's jaw tightened. He had successfully avoided any direct interaction with her since their breakup, and he had no desire to change that now.

"What do you want, Mary?" he asked, keeping his voice even, though his patience was already thinning.

Mary crossed her arms over her chest. Her expression was unreadable—neither angry nor upset. If anything, there was a calculating gleam in her eyes, one that put him on edge.

"I heard about Aurora's bandages coming off today," she said, her tone almost casual. "I imagine you were very eager to see the results."

Anthony's jaw clenched. "That's none of your business."

Mary gave a small, knowing smirk. "Oh, but it is my business, isn't it?" She tilted her head. "But it makes me wonder—would you be so enamoured with her if her face had been ruined? If she was covered in scars?"

Anthony's fists curled at his sides, his anger rising swiftly. "Aurora is not just a face to me," he bit out.

Mary's eyes gleamed with something cold and triumphant. "No, she's a patient of this hospital," she countered, her voice sharp. "That's why I've decided to report you to the hospital administrator for unethical conduct."

His stomach dropped. "What?"

"You heard me." She folded her arms. "You've been having an affair with a patient. You know it's not allowed."

Anthony took a step closer, his voice firm. "I have not been having an affair with Miss Vincent."

Mary's lips curled into a sneer. "Oh, so it's Miss Vincent now?"

He clenched his jaw. He knew Mary too well—when she made a threat, she followed through. If she went to the hospital board with this, even without proof, it could damage his career. And worse, it could hurt Aurora.

He had to think fast.

Anthony forced his expression into one of indifference, ignoring the sharp pain in his chest as he looked Mary directly in the eye.

"I have no feelings for Miss Vincent." The lie burned as it left his lips.

Mary narrowed her eyes. "Don't give me that, Anthony. I see the way you look at her. The way you protect her."

He exhaled slowly, forcing himself to stay calm. "You're imagining things," he said, his voice cold. "I checked on her because she was my patient—nothing more. And now that she's recovering, I have no further interest in her."

Mary studied him for a long moment, as if searching for any crack in his façade. He fought to keep his expression neutral, even as his heart pounded painfully in his chest.

Finally, she smirked. "Well. That's disappointing," she said, feigning boredom. "For a moment, I thought I had something juicy to use against you."

Anthony shrugged, though every part of him was screaming to push her out of his office and find Aurora. "I'm sorry to disappoint you," he said coolly.

Mary tapped a manicured finger against her chin, considering him. "Fine. If you're telling the truth, I suppose I'll let it go."

He nodded once, keeping his relief hidden.

Mary lingered another second, then turned toward the door. "But just so you know," she said over her shoulder, "if I do find proof that you're involved with her, I will make sure the entire hospital knows."

She left, her heels clicking against the floor as she disappeared down the hall.

The moment the door shut behind her, Anthony let out a slow breath and sank into his chair.

He had convinced her. For now.

But the cost was steep.

Lying about his feelings for Aurora—denying what he knew was real—felt like a betrayal. His hands curled into fists as he shut his eyes.

It didn't matter. The only thing that mattered now was protecting Aurora.

And if that meant pretending, she meant nothing to him until Aurora has been discharged... then so be it.

Aurora's steps faltered as she reached Anthony's office, her heart fluttering with nervous anticipation. She hadn't seen him since that kiss—since the moment that had left her breathless, dizzy, and filled with hope. Now, as she stood outside his door, ready to say goodbye, she realised just how much she wanted to see him to see if they had a future.

But then—voices.

She froze, her fingers resting lightly on the doorframe. The door was slightly ajar, and inside, she heard Anthony's deep, steady voice.

Then—her name.

Aurora's stomach tightened.

'I have no feelings for Miss Vincent.'

The words struck her like a physical blow. Her breath caught in her throat.

Mary's voice followed, sharp and knowing.

'Don't give me that, Anthony. I see the way you look at her. The way you protect her.'

Aurora's heart leaped—maybe Mary was right, maybe he would contradict his own words, admit that he did feel something for her.

She held her breath, waiting, praying.

But then Anthony spoke again, his tone distant, detached—cold.

'You're imagining things, I checked on her because she was a patient—nothing more. And now that she's recovering, I have no further interest in her.'

The world tilted beneath her feet.

Aurora felt her entire chest cave in, as if something inside her had been ripped apart.

Nothing more.

Her fingers trembled as she pressed them against the doorframe for support.

She had let herself believe—just for a moment—that there had been something real between them. That he had felt it too.

That she mattered to him.

But she had been wrong.

Biting her lip to hold back the sting of tears, she turned and walked away, her heart shattering with every step.

Anthony had to calm himself before making the call. His pulse thundered in his ears, his mind a whirlwind of frustration and regret. He needed to hear Aurora's voice—to explain why he hadn't come to see her and to tell her that, once she was released, he wanted a future with her.

But he couldn't risk seeing her in person. Not with Mary lurking, waiting for any excuse to ruin him.

Taking a steadying breath, he picked up the phone and dialled.

"Trauma ward, Nurse Kiera speaking."

"This is Dr. Hardwick," he said, his voice edged with urgency. "I need to speak to Miss Vincent."

There was a brief silence, and then Kiera's voice came back, gentle but firm.

"Sorry, doctor… she was discharged this morning."

Anthony froze. His grip on the phone tightened as his chest constricted.

"What?" His voice came out sharper than he intended. "She's gone?"

"Yes," Kiera confirmed. "Dr. Whitmore signed her release papers earlier today. She left about an hour ago."

A heavy weight settled in Anthony's stomach. He had known she would be leaving soon, but not this soon. Not before he had the chance to talk to her, to tell her how he felt.

Now, she was gone.

And she hadn't even said goodbye.

The realisation cut deep, an ache settling in his chest. He had been so sure that what they had meant something. But maybe he had been wrong. Maybe Aurora didn't want a future with him after all.

His heart twisted painfully at the thought.

Chapter Twelve

One year later…

Dr. Anthony Hardwick walked into his new office at Royal Prince Alfred Hospital in Sydney, the sleek, modern interior a stark contrast to the place he had called home for years. It was only his third day, and though he was still adjusting, he already knew this had been the right decision. The hospital had made him a generous offer—one too good to refuse—but the real reason he had left St. Vincent's was far more personal.

Mary.

She had become unbearable, her obsession with rekindling their relationship growing more desperate by the day. At first, he had ignored it, hoping she would move on. But she hadn't. The subtle manipulations, the unexpected run-ins, the carefully placed remarks about their past—it had all become too much. And Anthony refused to live under her scrutiny any longer.

But even as he settled into his new hospital, far from the tangled mess of St. Vincent's, he knew there was another reason he had left. A reason that had nothing to do with Mary.

Aurora.

Her name still echoed in his mind, as fresh as if he had seen her yesterday.

She had left the day after they had kissed.

That kiss.

It was still imprinted on his soul. The way she had melted into him, the way her fingers had clutched at his coat, as if she needed him just as much as he needed her. The way the world had ceased to exist for those few stolen seconds.

But it hadn't meant the same to her.

She had walked away without a word.

He had tried to forget her. God knows he had tried. He had thrown himself into his work, gone on dates, even convinced himself that maybe she had been nothing more than a passing fantasy. But how could he forget when she was everywhere? In the quiet moments between surgeries. In the scent of a passing perfume that reminded him of her. In the ghost of her touch that still haunted his dreams.

After four weeks of agonising over what had happened, he had finally broken. He had gone to her records, found her address, and driven to her home, fully prepared to fight for her—to convince her that they belonged together.

But she was gone.

She had moved.

No forwarding address. No trace of where she had gone.

It had been a year. A long, torturous year. And yet, the pain still lingered.

Anthony exhaled sharply, dragging a hand through his hair. He needed to move on. She had.

But no matter how much time passed, no matter how much he told himself to let go—

He knew the truth.

Aurora Vincent had been the only woman he had ever loved.

And he wasn't sure he would ever stop.

Anthony sat at his desk, fingers drumming absently against the polished wood as he glanced at the clock. His new colleague, Dr. Harry Young, was due any moment now. Harry had offered to show him around, introduce him to key staff, and help him settle in. A courtesy, but also a chance to get to know the man he'd be working alongside.

A sharp knock on the door pulled him from his thoughts.

"Come in," he called.

The door swung open, and Harry stepped inside with an easy smile. He was in his early thirties, tall and athletic, with neatly styled blond hair and striking green eyes. Though not as broad as Anthony, he had an effortless confidence, the kind that made people gravitate toward him.

"Hey, mate," Harry greeted, extending a hand.

Anthony stood and shook it firmly. "Thanks for taking the time to show me around."

"No problem." Harry grinned. "Welcome to RPA. Ready to meet the team?"

As Anthony grabbed his hospital ID, he noticed the excitement radiating off Harry. The man practically vibrated with energy.

"I have to say, this week has been incredible," Harry continued as they walked down the hall. "New colleague, new fiancée… I finally convinced my girlfriend to become my fiancée."

Anthony raised an eyebrow. "You convinced her?"

Harry chuckled, rubbing the back of his neck. "Yeah, she was hesitant at first, but I made her see we belong together. Proposed again over the weekend, and she said yes." He beamed. "She actually works here at the hospital."

Anthony cringed slightly but kept his expression neutral. After the mess with Mary, he had vowed never to mix his professional and personal life again. He wasn't about to share that bit of advice, though—Harry seemed too overjoyed to hear it.

"Congrats," he said simply.

"Thanks, mate. She's amazing," Harry said, practically glowing with pride. "You'll meet her soon enough."

Anthony nodded, pushing aside the flicker of unease curling at the edges of his thoughts.

The introductions went smoothly. Harry led Anthony through the hospital, introducing him to senior staff, nurses, and specialists. Everyone seemed to warm to Anthony instantly—everyone was professional and friendly.

After nearly an hour of handshakes and polite conversations, Harry glanced at his watch.

"Just one more person to meet," he said, leading Anthony down a quieter hallway. "The Patient Liaison. You'll work with her a lot—she handles patient concerns, advocacy, administrative coordination. Honestly, she's a lifesaver."

Anthony nodded. "Sounds like an important role."

"Oh, it is," Harry said, grinning. "And trust me, she's the best."

He pushed open the door to the Patient Liaison's office and stepped aside, letting Anthony enter first.

The moment Anthony's eyes landed on the woman standing inside, the air was sucked from his lungs.

Time stopped.

Aurora.

She was standing behind the desk, flipping through a file, her golden-blonde hair tumbling over one shoulder. When she heard them enter, she looked up— her warm blue eyes locking onto his.

Anthony forgot how to breathe.

The hospital, the people outside, even Harry beside him—all of it blurred.

It was her.

The woman who had haunted his thoughts for a year. The woman he had searched for, longed for. The woman who had disappeared from his life without a word.

Aurora.

She looked different, yet exactly the same. Strong. Beautiful. Unforgettable.

His heart pounded so violently it hurt.

Aurora froze, the file slipping slightly in her grasp. Shock flickered in her gaze, followed by something unreadable.

Then Harry's voice shattered the suffocating silence.

"There she is!" he said brightly, stepping forward.

Anthony barely processed what happened next.

Harry wrapped an arm around Aurora's waist, pressing a quick kiss to her temple.

Aurora stiffened.

Anthony's world tilted dangerously.

Harry turned to him, oblivious to the tension crackling in the air.

"Anthony, meet my fiancée," he said proudly. "Aurora Vincent."

Anthony's mind reeled.

Aurora.

Engaged.

To Harry.

The room felt too small, the walls pressing in. His chest constricted with something sharp and agonising.

Aurora swallowed hard, her gaze locked onto his, her expression unreadable.

And in that moment, Anthony realised one thing with absolute clarity—

He couldn't let her marry Harry.

Aurora just stared.

Anthony.

The man who had never left her mind. The man she had tried so desperately to forget.

But he had forgotten her first.

She had left his life as soon as she was healed, as if she had never mattered. And clearly, she hadn't.

Harry's arm slipped around her waist, a casual, familiar gesture. She froze, her body rigid under his touch, but she couldn't move, couldn't speak.

Her throat tightened as she swallowed the storm raging inside her. She forced herself to stand tall, to breathe, to keep her voice even.

"Hello, Anthony," she said, though it barely came out above a whisper.

Anthony exhaled slowly, as if savouring the sound of her voice. His dark eyes burned into hers, intense, unreadable. "Hello, Aurora."

Harry's gaze bounced between them, his brow furrowing. "Wait—you two know each other?"

Aurora spoke before Anthony could. Her voice was steady, but her fingers clenched at the fabric of her blouse. "Remember when I told you I was saved from that attack?" She gestured toward Anthony, her movements sharp and controlled. "Anthony was the one who saved me."

A heavy silence settled over the room.

Harry looked surprised, glancing at Anthony as if seeing him in a completely new light. "Seriously? You have my thanks, mate."

Anthony barely heard him. His entire focus was on Aurora.

She had spoken about him.

He shouldn't care.

But he did.

"How have you been, Aurora?"

Anthony kept his voice even, but inside, he was unravelling. He wanted to know everything. Had she been happy? Had she missed him at all? Why had she disappeared without a word?

Most of all—had she ever cared for him, even a little?

Aurora straightened, her expression unreadable. "I'm good, thank you, Anthony."

He searched her face for any sign of emotion, but she was guarded, distant. It sent a sharp pang through him.

"You work here now?" she asked, her tone polite, almost detached.

"Yes." He let out a slow breath. "And so do you."

She gave a small nod.

"What happened to your job with Mr. Greene?" he asked, remembering how much she had cared about her work there.

For the first time, something flickered in her eyes. Sadness.

"Unfortunately, he passed away about six months ago," she said quietly.

He remembered. She shouldn't be happy about Anthony remembering anything about her. But she was.

Anthony's chest tightened. He remembered how highly she had spoken of Mr. Greene, how she had admired him.

"I'm sorry," he said sincerely.

Aurora gave a small, bittersweet smile. "Thank you." She shifted slightly, as if shaking off the emotion. "When the new management took over, I was let go. And, well… here I am."

Harry glanced at his watch and let out a small sigh. "I have an appointment. I'll leave you two to catch up."

Before Aurora could respond, he pressed a quick kiss to her temple. "I'll see you tonight, darling."

Aurora stiffened slightly but nodded. "Ah… yes, okay."

Anthony clenched his jaw, his fists tightening at his sides. He forced himself to keep his expression neutral, but inside, a storm was raging.

She was engaged.

To Harry.

And yet, the way she had tensed at his touch, the hesitation in her voice… it didn't seem right with him.

As soon as Harry left her office, Anthony turned to Aurora, his piercing gaze locking onto hers. He didn't waste a second.

"Why did you leave without saying goodbye?" His voice was low, edged with the bitterness that had simmered inside him for a year.

Chapter Thirteen

Aurora's grip tightened on the file. She looked away, searching for words—but what could possibly ease the ache he'd carried since she left?

"I—" She hesitated, exhaling slowly before meeting his gaze again. "I didn't think there was anything left to say."

Anthony let out a humourless laugh, shaking his head. "Nothing left to say?" His jaw tightened. "After everything? After that kiss?"

Aurora flinched, but she lifted her chin. "It was just a kiss, Anthony."

Just a kiss.

Her words were like a blade, sharp and merciless, cutting straight through him.

He stepped closer, his voice quiet but laced with something raw, something undeniable. "It wasn't just a kiss to me."

Aurora's gaze flickered with doubt. "No," she whispered. "It meant nothing to you."

His jaw tightened. "It meant everything, Aurora. I had feelings for you… I have feelings for you."

She let out a shaky breath, turning away from him, her arms wrapping around herself as she stared out the window. "No, you didn't. No, you don't."

Anthony took another step, but she didn't turn back.

"I heard you," she said, her voice barely above a whisper. "I heard you tell Mary that I meant nothing to you."

His brow furrowed. "When?"

"In your office." She swallowed hard. "I came to tell you I was being discharged… but then I heard how you really felt."

Anthony's entire body went rigid. "No, no, Aurora, you have it all wrong."

"I heard you, Anthony," she said, her voice breaking slightly, though she quickly steadied it. "I heard everything."

He took a deep breath, his frustration barely concealed. "I only said that to Mary because she was going to report me to the hospital board for inappropriate behaviour toward a patient…" He exhaled sharply, his voice thick with emotion.

"You."

Aurora's breath hitched, but she refused to turn around. She clenched her hands at her sides, staring out the window as if the view could somehow steady her.

"I don't believe you," she said quietly, but her voice lacked conviction.

Anthony exhaled sharply, running a hand through his hair. "Aurora, look at me."

She didn't. She couldn't.

"Aurora," his voice was gentler this time, almost pleading. "Please."

Slowly, she turned, her expression carefully composed, but her eyes—those betrayed her. There was hurt there, buried deep, but it was still there.

Anthony took another step forward, closing the space between them. He needed her to understand. Needed her to believe him.

"I never meant a single word of what I said to Mary that day," he said, his voice low but firm. "I had to make her think you didn't matter to me. Because if she had reported me, I could have lost my career. I could have lost everything, Aurora—including you."

She inhaled sharply, her brows drawing together.

"I didn't care about the risk," he admitted. "Not at first. But then I thought about you—about what they might do to you. They would have questioned you, investigated us, twisted everything into something ugly. You had already been through so much, and I—" He let out a rough breath, shaking his head. "I couldn't let that happen to you."

Aurora swallowed hard, her fingers tightening against the windowsill. "So, you lied."

He nodded. "Yes. But only to protect you."

She searched his face, looking for any sign of deception, any hint of dishonesty. But there was none. Only raw, unfiltered truth staring back at her.

A part of her wanted to believe him. God, she wanted to. But the pain of that moment—of hearing him say she meant nothing—had left a wound so deep, she wasn't sure it could ever fully heal.

"Anthony…" She shook her head, stepping back. "It doesn't change anything."

His jaw tensed. "Doesn't it?"

"No." She forced herself to stand tall, to ignore the way her heart ached. "Because I moved on."

His dark eyes darkened, a storm brewing beneath them. "Did you?"

"Yes."

A slow, bitter smile tugged at his lips. "Then why can't you look me in the eye when you say that?"

Her breath caught. He still read her too easily. Still held her too tightly—without even touching her.

But it didn't matter. It couldn't matter.

Because she was engaged to Harry.

And Anthony Hardwick was her past.

She turned to look at him, her expression unreadable. "I'm engaged, Anthony."

His gaze darkened. "Yes. Harry told me he had to convince you to say yes."

Aurora's breath hitched, but she quickly masked it, turning back toward the window. Silence stretched between them, thick with unspoken words.

Then, softly, Anthony asked, "Do you love him?"

"Yes," she whispered.

Anthony reached for her; his touch impossibly gentle as he turned her to face him. His dark eyes burned into hers, filled with an intensity that made it impossible to look away.

"Tell me that you're happy," he said, his voice low, unwavering. "That you're in love with him, and I'll walk away."

He lifted his hand, the pad of his finger tilting her chin up, so she had no choice but to meet his gaze.

"Tell me," he murmured. "Then I'll leave and never bother you again."

Aurora's breath shuddered. He was too close, too overwhelming, making it impossible to think.

"Anthony, please…"

"Tell me," he repeated, his voice a whisper now, rough with emotion. His face inched closer, his breath warm against her lips. "If you're certain that Harry is the one…"

Closer.

"Anthony, I…"

His lips hovered over hers, a breath away. One tilt, one moment of surrender, and he'd be hers—and she'd be his.

Without another word, Aurora leaned in.

The moment their lips met; it was as if the world around them ceased to exist. The soft, hesitant brush of her mouth against his sent a shiver down Anthony's spine, but that single touch wasn't enough—not after a year of wanting, of longing. A quiet, desperate sound escaped him as he pulled her closer, his hands sliding to her waist, gripping her as if he was afraid, she might disappear again.

And then restraint shattered.

Anthony deepened the kiss, pouring a year's worth of pent-up love emotion into it. His fingers tangled in her hair, tilting her head back as he kissed her with all the hunger, all the longing he had tried so hard to suppress. She responded just as fiercely, her hands gripping the fabric of his shirt, pulling him closer, needing more, giving more.

The kiss was fire and desperation, a battle between want and need, between everything unsaid and everything they were too afraid to admit. Their breaths mingled, their bodies pressing against each other as if trying to close every inch of space between them.

Aurora's heart pounded so hard she swore he could feel it. The taste of him—warm, intoxicating—drowned her senses, making it impossible to think of anything but him. Anthony groaned softly against her lips, his grip tightening, as if he was terrified, she might slip away.

He kissed her like a man starved, like she was the only thing that had ever mattered. And Aurora kissed him back just as desperately because, in that moment, she knew—she had never stopped wanting him.

She never could.

As his lips moved from hers, trailing along her jaw, her breath hitched. He whispered her name against her skin, reverent, almost broken. It sent a shiver down her spine, a reminder that this—whatever this was—had never truly ended between them.

And maybe… it never would.

His lips trailed back up to hers, his breath warm against her skin.

She barely managed to whisper his name— "Anthony, please…"—before his mouth claimed hers again.

This kiss was different. It was no longer just passion; it was desperation, raw and consuming. Anthony groaned deep in his throat, pulling her closer, as if he could fuse them together. Aurora's arms wrapped around his neck, her fingers threading through his hair, holding on as though letting go would break her.

His hand cradled the back of her head, his fingers tangling in her hair, while the other gripped her waist with an almost bruising intensity. Heat radiated between them, every frantic kiss speaking of all they had denied for too long.

Their breaths came in ragged gasps between stolen kisses, but neither could stop. The world outside this moment ceased to exist—there was only them. Only the longing, the hunger, the undeniable truth neither had dared to face.

And then—

Aurora tore herself away, her breath unsteady, her hands still fisting the fabric of his shirt as though she needed the strength to keep from reaching for him again.

"Anthony," she whispered, her voice thick with emotion.

He searched her face, his breath uneven, his hands still resting against her as if letting go would make this moment—make her—disappear.

She swallowed hard, forcing herself to meet his gaze, even as her heart waged war against her mind.

"This is wrong."

Anthony's jaw tensed. "Aurora—"

"No, Anthony." Her voice wavered, but she steeled herself. "I can't do this. I won't cheat on Harry. He doesn't deserve that. He's a good man."

Anthony exhaled sharply, dragging a hand through his hair, his desperation evident. "I don't want you to cheat. I want to be the only man in your life."

Her lips parted, but no words came.

He stepped closer, his voice raw. "I want you to choose me, Aurora. Because you want to. Because you can't imagine spending your life with anyone else."

Her throat tightened. "I can't break his heart."

Anthony's gaze darkened. "So, you're going to marry a man you don't love?"

She hesitated, her breath hitching—but then she lifted her chin, forcing the words out.

"I do love him."

And she did. She wouldn't have agreed to marry him if she didn't.

It just wasn't this. It wasn't breathless and all-consuming. It wasn't fire and longing tangled in a single touch.

It wasn't Anthony.

Anthony let out a quiet, bitter laugh, shaking his head in disbelief. "Do you kiss him the way you just kissed me?" His voice was low, rough with emotion.

She opened her mouth, but no words came.

"Aurora," he pressed, stepping closer. "Tell me." His gaze burned into hers, searching, demanding the truth. "Do you?"

Her throat tightened. She could lie to herself, but not to him.

Softly, she whispered, "No."

His jaw clenched. "Doesn't that tell you something?" He let the question hang between them, the air thick with unspoken truths. Then, after a beat, he asked, "Tell me this—if Mary hadn't been there that day, when you came to say goodbye… I was going to ask you to stay. I was going to tell you I wanted to see where this could go." His voice dropped to a whisper, hesitant yet filled with longing. "Would you have stayed with me?"

"Anthony…" Aurora's voice trembled, uncertainty warring with the emotions swirling between them.

But before she could say more, a sharp knock at the door shattered the moment.

Aurora exhaled, blinking as if pulling herself back to reality. "Come in," she called, her gaze flickering to Anthony.

The door opened, and a young doctor stepped inside.

Anthony's frustration was palpable. His jaw tensed, his hands curling into fists at his sides. "Thank you for your help," he said stiffly, barely sparing the doctor a glance. "I'll come back later."

Without another word, he turned and walked out, leaving Aurora standing there, her heart pounding, her unspoken answer lingering in the air between them.

Chapter Fourteen

Anthony walked back to his office, each step heavier than the last. His mind was a storm, thoughts crashing into each other, refusing to settle.

How the hell was he supposed to work alongside the man engaged to the woman he loved?

And he did love her.

That kiss had shattered any lingering doubts. Feeling Aurora in his arms again, tasting the soft, desperate way, she had responded to him—it had been earth-shattering. Mind-blowing. It was everything he had tried to forget, only to realise he never could.

His hands curled into fists as he pushed open his office door. The room felt suffocating, as if the air had been sucked out, leaving behind only the weight of his emotions.

He wanted her. Aurora. Desperately.

But she wouldn't hurt Harry. And the worst part? Anthony didn't want to hurt him either.

He liked the guy. Harry was a good doctor, a good person. But he had the one thing Anthony wanted more than anything in this world.

And that was a hard pill to swallow.

Running a hand through his hair, he exhaled sharply, pacing the length of the room. He had to get a grip. Be professional. Accept that Aurora was engaged.

But how was he supposed to pretend?

How was he supposed to stand in the same room as Harry, shake his hand, work alongside him—knowing he had kissed Aurora? Knowing she had kissed him back?

And worst of all… knowing that if he pushed—just a little—she might kiss him again?

Anthony dragged a hand down his face, exhaling shakily. His mind wavered between reason and desire, between the moral weight of stepping back and the unbearable ache of losing her again.

Maybe he should walk away. Maybe he should respect her choice.

But the thought of it—of watching her slip through his fingers without a fight—made his chest tighten like a vice.

The past year had been torture. The nights spent wondering what if, the hollow ache of missing her, the regret that had clung to him like a shadow. And now, after that kiss, after the way she had melted into him, as if the distance between them had never existed…

How could he pretend she wasn't still his?

No.

He couldn't let her go.

He wouldn't.

Anthony straightened, jaw set with newfound resolve. He would fight for her—not in a way that would hurt Harry. He wasn't that kind of man.

But he had to make her see. Make her feel what he felt.

Because deep down, he knew she already did.

And if there was even the smallest chance, she loved him…

Then he was damn sure not going to lose her without a fight.

Aurora sank into her chair the moment the door closed behind the young doctor, her hands trembling in her lap.

Her heart was still racing. Her lips still tingled from that kiss.

Anthony cared.

If only she had known that a year ago.

She had spent so long convincing herself that what they had was fleeting, that she had built it up into something more than it really was. She had told herself that their kiss—the one she had clung to in her darkest moments—was nothing more than a fantasy. That moving on was the right thing to do.

And she had moved on.

Hadn't she?

She had said yes to Harry. A good man. A man who had been there when she needed someone to hold her steady. A man who was safe, kind, and steady.

When he proposed, she had told herself she was happy. That she loved him the way a fiancée should. That she could build a life with him.

But now…

Now she wasn't so sure.

Because the moment Anthony's lips touched hers, every rational thought had vanished.

The world had narrowed to him—his touch, his warmth, the way he kissed her like he had been starving for her.

And worse… she had kissed him back.

She squeezed her eyes shut.

This isn't fair.

Not to her. Not to Harry.

Harry deserved more than half of her heart. He deserved a woman who could kiss him with the same passion she had just given to another man.

He deserved someone who didn't hesitate.

Someone who didn't feel another man's hands on her skin long after he had let go.

She swallowed hard, her decision settling in her chest like a stone.

She couldn't do this to Harry.

Whatever she had felt with Anthony—whatever was still lingering between them—it didn't change the fact that she had made a choice.

And she wouldn't hurt Harry.

She refused to.

No matter what it cost her.

Anthony's afternoon was relentless—back-to-back patients, endless consultations—but through it all, his mind kept circling back to her. Every quiet moment, every second of stillness between appointments, was filled with the memory of Aurora's lips on his, the way she had melted into him before pulling away. Before telling him, she couldn't.

She's engaged.

The thought sat heavy in his chest, a dull, unrelenting ache that refused to subside.

By the time the day finally ended, exhaustion clung to him, but it wasn't just from work. His head felt cluttered; his emotions frayed. He needed a drink. A distraction. Anything to stop himself from thinking about her.

Gathering his things, he left his office, his footsteps echoing against the polished floor. As he rounded the corner, he spotted Harry at the reception desk, flashing his usual easy smile as he said goodnight to Harriet, the older receptionist who had been working there for years. She smiled warmly, responding with a motherly fondness.

Anthony slowed his steps, adjusting his expression as he approached.

"Goodnight, Harriet," he said with a polite nod.

"Goodnight, dear," she responded, her sharp eyes flickering between him and Harry with quiet curiosity.

Anthony pushed open the door, stepping outside just as Harry fell into step beside him.

"Hey, Anthony. How was your day?" Harry asked cheerfully, his voice carrying that effortless warmth that made him so damn likeable.

Anthony forced a small smile, one that didn't quite reach his eyes. "Busy but good."

Harry, as always, didn't seem to notice. He was the kind of man who wore his thoughts on his sleeve, who never hesitated to fill silences with easy conversation. Maybe too open, too willing to share.

"I'm off to dinner with Aurora," he added casually.

Anthony's grip tightened around the handle of his briefcase, his jaw clenching for the briefest second before he forced himself to school his expression.

His lips pressed into a thin line at the mention of her.

He knew it was ridiculous to react this way—Aurora is his fiancée, of course they're having dinner—but knowing it didn't make it easier to hear.

It didn't stop the slow burn of jealousy curling in his chest.

Forcing a neutral tone, he replied, "Sounds nice."

Harry chuckled. "Yeah, it's been a crazy week, so I thought it'd be good to spend some quality time together."

Quality time.

Anthony swallowed hard, his mind flashing back to the way Aurora had kissed him, the way she had clung to him as if she had forgotten everything—forgotten Harry, forgotten her engagement, forgotten the life she had built without him.

But she had remembered soon enough.

And now, she was going to sit across from Harry at dinner, smile at him, hold his hand—maybe even kiss him goodnight.

The thought made Anthony's stomach twist.

He should let it go. He should accept it.

But the problem was—he couldn't.

Aurora sat across from Harry at a cozy corner table in an intimate Italian restaurant, the warm glow of candlelight flickering between them. The scent of garlic and fresh basil filled the air, mingling with the low hum of conversation around them. A soft melody played in the background; the kind of slow, romantic music that should have made this moment feel special.

But it didn't.

Aurora stirred the pasta on her plate absentmindedly, twirling her fork through the noodles but barely eating. Her mind was elsewhere—on a kiss that had happened hours ago but still lingered on her lips. A kiss that wasn't Harry's.

"Are you okay, Aurora?" Harry's voice pulled her from her thoughts, his brow furrowing with concern. "You seem distant tonight."

She blinked, realising she had been staring at her plate for too long. Looking up, she forced an apologetic smile. "Sorry, just a little tired."

Harry nodded, accepting her answer, but his eyes studied her carefully. He wasn't the type to pry, but she could tell he wasn't convinced.

They made small talk throughout dinner—he told her about his day at the hospital, a difficult patient, a colleague's blunder in surgery. Normally, she would have been engaged, asking questions, laughing at his dry humour. But tonight, she found herself nodding along, offering polite responses without really absorbing what he was saying.

More than once, she felt his gaze linger on her, as if waiting for her to say something—to be the woman he knew.

She wasn't sure who she was right now.

By the time the waiter cleared their plates, Harry glanced at his watch. "You want dessert? We could split the tiramisu?"

Aurora hesitated, then shook her head. "I think I'd rather call it a night. I'm just exhausted."

His brows lifted slightly, surprised. They had only been here for an hour, and usually, she loved lingering over dinner, sipping wine, drawing out the night.

"Of course," he said easily, signalling for the check. But there was a flicker of something in his expression—uncertainty, maybe even disappointment.

The drive home was quiet, a stark contrast to their usual effortless conversation. Harry kept glancing at her, but she stared out the window, watching the city lights blur past.

When they pulled up in front of her apartment, he shifted in his seat, looking at her expectantly. She knew what he was waiting for—he always kissed her goodnight before she got out of the car. A soft, lingering kiss that made her feel safe and cared for.

Tonight, she couldn't do it.

Leaning over, she pressed a quick kiss to his cheek instead.

"Goodnight, Harry." Her voice was soft, but there was an undeniable distance in it.

When she pulled back, she saw the confusion flicker across his face. His lips parted slightly, as if he wanted to say something—but he didn't.

Instead, he nodded slowly. "Goodnight, Aurora."

She stepped out of the car, closing the door behind her. As she walked toward her building, she resisted the urge to look back.

Because if she did, she knew she'd see him still sitting there, watching her, trying to figure out why tonight felt different.

Anthony spent a restless night, tossing and turning in his bed, his thoughts consumed by Aurora. Every time he closed his eyes, he saw her—her wide, startled gaze when he kissed her, the way she had melted against him for just a moment before pulling away. Did she regret it? Was she thinking about him right now, the same way he was thinking about her?

Or was she trying to forget him?

The thought twisted like a knife in his chest.

Was she still with Harry? Had she gone to dinner with him, let him hold her hand, kiss her goodnight? Had she let him in—into her apartment, into her bed? The idea made Anthony sit up, running a hand through his already tousled hair, frustration burning in his chest.

He rubbed his face, exhaling sharply. He had no right to feel like this. Aurora wasn't his. Not anymore. He had let her slip through his fingers once, and in the time, he had been gone, Harry had stepped in. He had been the one to hold her, to love her, to build a future with her.

But after that kiss—Anthony knew the truth.

Aurora might have convinced herself she loved Harry. She might have convinced herself she had moved on. But when she was in his arms again, she felt something. Something real. Something she couldn't ignore.

Neither could he.

The past year had been torture, missing her, regretting every moment he hadn't fought for her. Now, fate had given him another chance.

But was Aurora willing to take it?

Anthony lay back against his pillows, staring at the ceiling, his heart pounding. He didn't have the answers. But one thing was certain—he wasn't going to let her go without a fight.

Aurora spent the weekend at Sarah's house, needing space to think—away from Harry, away from the hospital, away from the turmoil in her heart. She had lied to Harry, telling him she was going away with both Sarah and Emily, when in reality, she had holed up in Sarah's cozy guest room, trying to make sense of everything.

By Saturday morning, Emily arrived, barely through the door before she dropped her bag and folded her arms. "Okay, spill, Aurora. Why are you hiding out here the week after you got engaged?" She arched a brow. "Have you finally worked out that Harry's not the guy for you?"

Aurora, who had been curled up on Sarah's couch with a cup of tea, sighed. "Why don't you like him?"

Sarah sat down beside her and exchanged a glance with Emily before answering. "It's not that we don't like him. He's nice, polite, treats you well... but we don't think he's right for you."

Aurora frowned. "Why?"

Emily sat on the armrest of the couch, looking down at her. "Because we know you, Aurora. You had to think about his proposal. A lot." She gave her a pointed look. "You were torn about it for weeks. If Harry was really the one, would it have been that hard to say yes?"

Sarah nodded. "You weren't excited, Aurora. You were anxious. You told us you cared about him, that you thought you loved him. But thinking you love someone isn't the same as knowing."

Aurora looked down at her tea, tracing the rim of the mug with her finger. "I do care about him. He's been there for me. He helped me move on with my life."

"Which is why you convinced yourself this was the right thing," Emily said gently. "But now? A week after saying yes, you're hiding here instead of spending the weekend with your fiancé."

Aurora exhaled sharply, running a hand through her hair. "It's not just that..." she admitted, her voice barely above a whisper.

Sarah and Emily leaned in. "Then what is it?" Sarah prompted.

Aurora hesitated for a long moment, then finally met their eyes. "Anthony is back."

There was a beat of silence. Then Emily blinked. "Wait... Anthony? As in Dr. Tall, Dark, and Broody Anthony?"

Aurora let out a dry laugh. "Yes. That Anthony."

Sarah's lips parted in surprise. "And?"

Aurora swallowed, gripping the mug tighter. "He... He has feelings for me. After all this time." She took a shaky breath. "I misheard him that day with Mary. He wasn't dismissing me. He cared. He still does."

Sarah and Emily exchanged another glance, this one sharper, more knowing.

"And how do you feel?" Emily asked.

Aurora opened her mouth, then closed it, her heart twisting painfully. "I don't know," she whispered. "I thought I loved Harry the way a fiancée should. I thought I was happy. But after seeing Anthony again... after—" She stopped herself, shaking her head.

Sarah's eyes narrowed. "After what?"

Aurora hesitated. Then, in a barely audible voice, she admitted, "After he kissed me."

Emily let out a dramatic gasp. "Aurora!"

Sarah's expression softened, understanding dawning in her eyes. "And now everything you thought you knew is in question."

Aurora nodded, her throat tightening. "I don't want to hurt Harry. He doesn't deserve that."

"But do you love him?" Sarah pressed. "Or do you just not want to hurt him?"

Aurora looked down again, unable to answer. Because deep down, she already knew the truth.

Chapter Fifteen

Anthony avoided Aurora for a few days, keeping himself busy with patients and paperwork. He told himself it was for the best—he needed to clear his head, figure out what to do. No matter how much he tried to focus, his mind betrayed him, dragging him back to that kiss. Had she thought about it as much as he had? Or had she already dismissed it as a mistake?

By Monday morning, the start of his second week at RPA, Anthony had come to one conclusion: avoiding Aurora wasn't making anything easier. He had to face her eventually.

He walked into the office, shrugging off his coat, and spotted Harry through his open door, already at his desk.

"Morning, Anthony. You have a good weekend?" Harry asked, though his usual cheerfulness was noticeably absent.

"Fine, thanks. You?"

Harry sighed, rubbing the back of his neck. "Not really. Aurora went away with her friends this weekend."

Anthony tensed but forced himself to keep his expression neutral. Sarah and Emily. He remembered the two women well—the way they had stood by Aurora's side after the attack, their fierce loyalty to her. And how they had defended her against Mary, cutting through the nurse's cruelty without hesitation. He had liked them instantly.

"Sarah and Emily?" Anthony kept his tone even. "Yeah. I met them when Aurora was recovering."

Harry let out a small chuckle, but it lacked humour. "Yeah, well… they aren't exactly my biggest fans. I'm not sure why."

Anthony frowned, processing this. Sarah and Emily had been warm and welcoming to him. They had appreciated the way he had cared for Aurora. But Harry?

He watched the other man closely, trying to piece it together.

"Did something happen between you?" Anthony asked carefully.

Harry shook his head. "Not that I know of. They're just… cold toward me. Polite, but distant. Aurora says they'll warm up eventually, but I don't know." He sighed. "It's just weird, you know? They're her best friends, her family. You'd think they'd be happy for her."

Anthony didn't reply right away. Instead, he leaned against Harry's door jam, his thoughts racing. If Sarah and Emily didn't like Harry, there had to be a reason.

And if they weren't happy about Aurora's engagement… maybe they knew something Aurora wasn't willing to admit to herself.

Anthony didn't want to think about that right now. Instead, he focused on the conversation with Harry, keeping it strictly professional. They went over a few patient cases, discussing treatment plans and upcoming surgeries, until a voice interrupted them—a voice that sent a cold shiver down Anthony's spine.

"Morning, Dr. Hardwick."

A chill ran down Anthony's spine. That voice. Smooth, self-assured, laced with amusement. The same voice that had destroyed everything.

Slowly, he turned, and there she was. Mary.

She stood before them, her dark eyes glinting with amusement, a smirk playing on her lips as if she had been waiting for this moment. She was dressed in crisp scrubs, her ID badge clipped neatly to her pocket.

Before he could stop himself, the words shot out of his mouth. "What the hell are you doing here?"

Mary's smirk widened. "Now, is that any way to greet an old friend?" She tilted her head, studying him. "I work here now. Today's my first day."

Anthony clenched his jaw.

Of course.

Harry, oblivious to the tension crackling between them, got up from his desk and walked to them, turned to Anthony. "You two know each other?"

Before Anthony could respond, Mary placed a hand on her hip and flashed Harry a charming smile. "Oh, we go way back."

Harry glanced between them, then grinned. "Well, I'm Harry Young. And you are…?"

Mary extended her hand. "Mary Moore. Nice to meet you, Dr. Young."

Harry shook her hand, then looked at Anthony. "Anthony, you didn't tell me there was a pretty nurse around here you already knew."

Anthony barely resisted the urge to roll his eyes. Harry had no idea. He had no idea the kind of person Mary really was, the manipulation, the lies, the destruction she had left in her wake.

He forced his expression into something neutral, but inside, irritation churned in his gut. Mary had transferred here. To this hospital. It wasn't a coincidence. Not with Mary.

Anthony's gaze locked onto hers. "Didn't know you were looking to make a change," he said coolly.

Mary gave him an infuriating smile. "Oh, you know me, Anthony. I like to keep things… interesting."

Anthony's stomach twisted. She was acting like a stalker.

She was up to something. He didn't know what yet, but he was damn sure going to find out.

He excused himself leaving Harry and Mary talking. She flirted with him as she usually did with doctors. He should warn Harry about Mary, but would he even listen?

Anthony stepped into his office, closing the door behind him with more force than necessary. He raked a hand through his hair, exhaling sharply. Mary. Just when he thought she was finally out of his life, she had found a way back in. And not just anywhere—here. At the very hospital where Aurora worked.

Coincidence? Not a damn chance.

He sank into his chair, staring blankly at the patient files in front of him. His mind wasn't on work anymore. It was on Aurora. On Harry. And now, on Mary, weaving her way into their lives like a snake waiting for the right moment to strike.

A knock on his door snapped him out of his thoughts. He straightened, expecting a nurse or another doctor, but instead, Harry poked his head in.

"Hey, man, you okay? You left in a hurry."

Anthony forced a neutral expression. "Yeah, just had some things to do."

Harry stepped inside, leaning against the doorway. "So… Mary." He let out a low whistle. "She's something, huh?"

Anthony tensed. Here we go.

"She's… charming," Harry continued, rubbing his jaw. "Bit of a flirt too." He chuckled. "She wasted no time, that's for sure."

Anthony's grip tightened on his pen. "Harry, listen to me." His voice was calm, but firm. "Be careful with her."

Harry raised an eyebrow. "Why? You two have history or something?"

Anthony hesitated. How much should he say? If he warned Harry too strongly, it might come off as jealousy. But if he said nothing, Harry could walk right into Mary's trap.

"She's not who she seems," Anthony said carefully. "She's manipulative. She knows how to twist things to her advantage."

Harry frowned. "That's a pretty strong accusation."

"It's the truth."

There was a pause. Then Harry shrugged. "Well, she seems fine to me so far. I mean, I'm taken, so if she's flirting, it's wasted on me." He grinned, clearly missing the real warning. "Aurora would kill me if I even looked at another woman the wrong way."

Anthony's stomach turned at the mention of her name.

Harry gave a half-smile, shrugging. "Look, I appreciate the warning, but she seems fine to me."

Anthony wasn't so sure.

As Harry left, Anthony exhaled heavily, rubbing his temples. He had no doubt Mary was already calculating her next move. He had to stay one step ahead of her.

And more than anything, he needed to talk to Aurora.

Anthony tapped his fingers impatiently against his desk as he stared at his computer screen. The hospital portal confirmed his appointment—Aurora Vincent, Patient Liaison, two p.m.

It was the earliest available slot, and though waiting until the afternoon frustrated him, it was better than nothing. This wasn't a conversation they could have in passing. He needed privacy, a setting where they wouldn't be interrupted. Where she would actually listen.

Because she had to listen.

Mary was here now, working under the same roof, breathing the same air, circling like a vulture. And Anthony had no doubt she was already scheming. He didn't know her plan yet, but he had learned the hard way—Mary didn't move without an agenda.

With a sigh, he leaned back in his chair and rubbed a hand over his jaw.

Would Aurora even believe him?

The last time he had tried to protect her from Mary, it had blown up in his face. Aurora had overheard a twisted version of events, leading her to believe he had never truly cared about her. And when he had finally found her again, she was already engaged to Harry.

He had lost her.

But if Mary had transferred here—if she had deliberately positioned herself close to them—then Aurora needed to know the kind of woman they were dealing with.

The day dragged. Anthony saw patients, reviewed charts, performed rounds, but his mind wasn't on his work. He kept checking the time, waiting for two o'clock like a man counting down to a storm.

Finally, when the hour arrived, he left his office and made his way toward the Patient Liaison department.

He passed nurses, doctors, patients—colleagues who now unknowingly worked alongside a woman capable of tearing lives apart.

By the time he reached Aurora's office, he was on edge.

Her door was slightly ajar, and he could hear her voice inside.

"I'll get that request processed by the end of the day," she was saying. "Yes, of course. Let me know if there's anything else you need."

A pause. Then, "You too. Take care."

Anthony knocked lightly on the doorframe.

Aurora turned, her expression shifting the moment she saw him. Surprise flickered in her eyes, followed quickly by something more guarded.

"Dr. Hardwick." Her voice was polite, professional. "Come in."

He stepped inside and closed the door behind him.

Aurora gestured to the chair across from her desk. "I saw your name on my schedule. What can I do for you?"

He sat but didn't lean back, his posture tense. "I needed to talk to you."

She folded her hands on the desk. "About what?"

He took a breath. No easy way to say this.

"Mary," he said. "She works here now."

Aurora's expression didn't change immediately, but he saw it—the brief flicker of something in her eyes. Shock. Unease.

Then, just as quickly, she masked it. "I know," she said simply.

Anthony frowned. "You know?"

Aurora nodded, exhaling. "She introduced herself to me this morning. Told me she's starting as part of the nursing staff."

Anthony clenched his jaw. "Did she say why?"

Aurora tilted her head, studying him. "Does it matter?"

"Yes." His voice was sharper than he intended, but he didn't care. "Aurora, she didn't come here for a fresh start. She came here for a reason."

Aurora sighed and leaned back in her chair. "Anthony, I get it. I know you don't trust her. And I know what she did to me—to us. But what do you expect me to do? She has every right to work here."

"She has a right," Anthony agreed, forcing his tone to stay level. "But that doesn't mean she doesn't have an agenda. You need to be careful."

Aurora hesitated, just for a second. Then she shook her head. "I'm not afraid of her."

Anthony leaned forward, his gaze locking onto hers. "You should be."

Aurora exhaled sharply, crossing her arms. "I don't see why I should be. I hardly know her."

Anthony's jaw tightened. "She ruined our chance to be together, Aurora. I will never forgive her for that. She threatened to report me to the hospital board— blackmailed me into staying away from you. She's capable of anything."

"I know what she did." Her voice softened, the sadness in her eyes unmistakable. "I hate it as much as you do, but she can't hurt us now."

Anthony let out a bitter laugh and pushed to his feet, pacing the small office. "Why? Because you're engaged to a man you don't love?"

Aurora stiffened. "That's not fair."

"No?" He turned to face her, frustration burning in his chest. "Tell me, then. Look me in the eye and tell me you're in love with Harry."

Her lips parted, but no words came.

That silence was all the answer he needed.

Anthony exhaled sharply, his frustration simmering beneath the surface. "Aurora, you don't have to say it. I already know."

She swallowed hard, shaking her head. "Anthony, I thought I was in love with him. I care for Harry, I do. I wouldn't have agreed to marry him if I didn't." Her voice wavered, as if she were trying to convince herself as much as him.

Anthony folded his arms, his gaze steady. "You don't build a life with someone out of obligation, Aurora. Love isn't a duty. It's a choice. And you haven't chosen him—you've settled for him."

"I know that now." She looked away, guilt flickering in her expression. "I didn't even realise it until you turned up. And I feel terrible about all of this, but I can't hurt Harry. It's not fair to him. He's done nothing wrong."

Anthony ran a hand through his hair, exhaling. "And you think staying with him when your heart isn't in it is fair? To either of you?"

Aurora's shoulders sagged. "It's not that simple."

"Yes, it is," he said, stepping closer. "You don't love him, Aurora. And no matter how hard you try to convince yourself otherwise, it won't change the truth."

Her breath hitched as she met his eyes, and for the first time, Anthony saw it— the war waging inside her. The guilt, the fear, the undeniable pull between them.

He softened his tone. "You deserve more than settling for someone just because it feels safe."

She blinked rapidly, as if holding back tears. "And what if it's too late? What if I've already made my choice?"

Anthony's voice was quiet but firm. "Then make a new one."

Aurora let out a shaky breath, wrapping her arms around herself as if trying to hold in the storm raging inside her. "And what should that be, Anthony? To dump Harry and be with you?" Her voice was laced with frustration, but beneath it, uncertainty trembled. "Do you have any idea how that would look? To him? To everyone?"

Anthony's jaw tightened. "I don't care how it looks." His voice was firm, his eyes burning with intensity as he stepped closer. "I care about what's real, Aurora. And this—" he gestured between them, his gaze locked onto hers, unwavering "—this is real. You know it just as much as I do."

Aurora swallowed hard, her heart pounding against her ribs. "Even if it is," she admitted in a whisper, "it doesn't change the fact that I said yes to him."

A muscle ticked in Anthony's jaw. "Did you, though? Or did he talk you into it?"

Her breath hitched, but before she could respond, he continued. "I know your friends don't approve of you and Harry being engaged."

Her brows pulled together in shock. "How do you know that?"

"Harry mentioned it." He studied her reaction before adding, "Sarah and Emily? Do they approve?"

She hesitated, her fingers curling against her arms. "No," she admitted, the word barely audible.

Anthony nodded as if he already knew. "And why is that, Aurora? They know you better than anyone. They love you. If they were truly happy for you, they wouldn't have hesitated." He paused, his voice quieter now, but no less piercing. "I bet it's because Harry had to convince you to marry him."

Aurora looked away, but the flicker of guilt in her expression told him he was right.

A deep breath left his lips, controlled but weighted. "When I ask the person, I want to spend the rest of my life with," he said, his voice thick with emotion, "I don't want to convince her. I don't want her to have doubts. I want her to want it as much as I do."

His words struck something deep inside her, something she had been trying so hard to ignore. Because the truth was, she hadn't been certain when she said yes to Harry. She had told herself it was the right choice, that love—her version of love—wasn't supposed to be all-consuming or terrifying. It was supposed to be steady. Safe. Predictable.

But standing here now, with Anthony looking at her like she was the only thing that mattered, Aurora felt the weight of the truth settle over her. She had been lying to herself all along—telling herself that love was meant to be steady, safe, and predictable. But with Anthony, it was none of those things. It was intense. Unshakable. Undeniable.

Anthony took a slow step closer, his voice low but firm. "Our future was stolen from us by circumstances beyond our control, but now—now we've been given another chance." His gaze searched hers, pleading without words. "I don't want to squander it. I want to grab it with both hands." He swallowed hard. "Don't you?"

Aurora's breath hitched, her vision blurring as tears welled in her eyes. Her heart screamed yes, but her mind—her logic, her fear—refused to let the word slip from her lips.

"I… I need time, Anthony." The words came out as a plea, barely more than a breath.

His jaw tightened, and for a moment, he just studied her, his expression unreadable. Then, with quiet resolve, he nodded. "Okay." His voice was soft, but there was steel beneath it. "You know where I stand. I want you, Aurora. And I know you want me." His gaze held hers, a quiet promise burning in his eyes. "But I won't stop fighting for you. For us."

With that, he turned, his departure slow and deliberate, as if waiting for her to call him back.

She didn't.

Aurora stood frozen, her hands trembling at her sides as she watched him walk away, her heart twisting painfully in her chest. And as the door clicked shut behind him, she pressed a shaking hand to her lips—because she knew.

She knew.

Her time was running out.

Chapter Sixteen

A week had passed, and still, Aurora hadn't reached out.

Anthony told himself he was giving her space, respecting her silence—but every day without a word felt unbearable. It was getting harder to stay away, harder to resist the urge to track her down and demand to know what she was thinking. Had she already decided to stay with Harry? Was she trying to forget him?

His jaw tightened at the thought.

Last week, as he had been leaving her office, Mary had intercepted him in the hallway, her presence like an unwelcome shadow. She leaned against the wall, arms crossed, a knowing smirk curling her lips.

"Still chasing after little miss victim?" she had taunted, voice dripping with mock sympathy.

Anthony barely spared her a glance. Not today, Mary. He was done playing her games.

"Go away," he said coldly. "And don't come near me unless it's about work."

But Mary, never one to take a hint, only stepped closer. Her perfume clung to the air, sickly sweet. Her fingers trailed up his arm.

"Oh, come on, Anthony." Her voice was silk laced with poison. "You know you want me."

She reached up, trying to loop her arms around his neck, but before she could, Anthony shoved her back—hard enough to make her stumble. His patience had long since run out.

"Nothing," he bit out, voice like steel, "makes me sicker than that prospect."

For a split second, something flickered across Mary's expression—something ugly beneath her curated seduction. But she masked it just as quickly, her smirk settling back into place.

"You'll regret that."

Anthony didn't dignify her with a response. He turned on his heel and walked away, leaving her standing there.

Even now, a week later, her words echoed in his mind. Not because he feared her—but because he knew Mary well enough to recognise a threat when he heard one.

Another day passed without a word from Aurora.

Anthony buried himself in work—patient files, surgeries, anything to keep his mind from drifting back to her. But it was a losing battle. Was she avoiding him? Had she already chosen Harry?

With a weary sigh, he grabbed his coat and stepped out of his office, ready to leave for the day.

As he walked down the hall, he noticed Harry emerging from his own office.

Anthony frowned immediately.

Harry looked rough. His usual neatness was gone—his shirt wrinkled, tie loosened like he hadn't even bothered to fix it. His face was pale, nearly grey under the fluorescent lighting, dark circles shadowing his eyes. He looked like a man unravelling.

"You okay, Harry?" Anthony asked.

Harry jolted slightly, as if he hadn't even noticed him there.

"Oh… yeah… no, I'm fine."

But he didn't look fine. His voice lacked its usual ease, and when he met Anthony's gaze, something flickered in his expression—something raw and guilty.

Anthony narrowed his eyes. "You sure? You look like hell."

Harry let out a weak chuckle, dragging a hand over his face. "Rough night," he muttered.

There was something in his tone that made Anthony's stomach tighten.

"You sick or something?"

Harry hesitated for half a second—barely noticeable, but Anthony caught it.

"No, no. Just… bad decisions and worse company, I guess."

Anthony's brow furrowed. "What does that mean?"

Harry let out a hollow laugh. "Just saying, sometimes a guy should listen to a friend's advice."

Something about the way he said it sent a warning chill through Anthony.

"Advice about what?"

Harry finally looked up, and for the first time, Anthony saw it clearly—the unmistakable weight of guilt in his eyes.

"Mary."

Anthony's expression hardened instantly.

"Harry," his voice was low, edged with warning, "please don't tell me—"

Harry shook his head quickly. "I don't want to talk about it." His voice was sharp, defensive.

Anthony clenched his jaw. "I told you to stay away from her."

Harry let out a dry, bitter laugh. "Yeah, well. Maybe I should've listened."

For a brief second, he looked like he wanted to say more—but then he just shook his head and turned away.

"See you around, Anthony."

And with that, he walked off, leaving Anthony standing in the empty hallway, a bad feeling settling deep in his chest.

Whatever had happened, it wasn't just a mistake. It was something worse.

Aurora stepped into her office Tuesday morning, exhausted.

The dark circles under her eyes told the story of another sleepless night. It had been over a week since her conversation with Anthony, and yet his words still echoed in her head.

She knew she had to decide. She couldn't keep drifting between two men, trapped in emotional limbo. But how could she walk away from Harry? He was good. He was steady. He didn't deserve to be hurt.

But Anthony…

Her chest tightened at the thought of him. She loved him. She had loved him since the moment he pulled her back from the brink of death. No matter how much she tried to deny it, she felt it every time he was near.

No matter what choice she made, someone would get hurt. And it would be her fault.

Harry had to sense something was wrong. He hadn't asked her out all weekend, hadn't even suggested they spend time together. That wasn't like him. Normally, he went out of his way to make her feel loved. Now, it was as if he was avoiding her.

Maybe, deep down, he already knew.

Aurora sighed, sinking into her chair. She had come in early, hoping the quiet would help clear her mind.

She had just reached for her laptop when there was a knock at the door.

Her brows furrowed. It was too soon for patients or meetings.

"Come in," she called.

The door creaked open—and the last person she expected stepped inside.

Aurora froze.

Mary.

A smug, twisted smile stretched across her lips as she sauntered in like she owned the place.

"Morning, Miss Vincent," she said, her voice syrupy sweet. Then her smile widened. "Or should I say… soon-to-be Mrs. Young?"

Aurora clenched her jaw. She was far too tired for this.

"What do you want, Mary?" she asked flatly.

Mary hummed, running a hand through her sleek, styled hair. "Oh, nothing really. Just thought I'd check in. After all, wedding plans must be so stressful." She paused, tilting her head. "Or… maybe it's something else keeping you up at night?"

Aurora stiffened.

Mary grinned. "You know, I ran into Harry on Saturday."

Aurora's stomach twisted.

"Did you?" she said cautiously.

"Mmm. He looked so tense. Poor thing. So, being the caring person I am, I helped him unwind."

Aurora's breath caught.

Mary leaned in slightly, voice a conspiratorial whisper. "We had a very long night together."

Aurora's body went cold.

She wanted to believe it was a lie. That Mary was just trying to get under her skin.

Mary smirked. "He didn't tell you, did he?"

Aurora swallowed, her throat dry. She couldn't show weakness. Not in front of her.

"You're lying."

Mary let out a laugh—light, taunting. "Oh, sweetheart." She reached into her bag and pulled out her phone, tapping the screen a few times before flipping it around.

Aurora's stomach dropped.

There, in the dim glow of a bedside lamp, was Harry. Shirtless. Asleep. In Mary's bed.

Mary gasped, putting a hand over her heart. "Oops. Guess I forgot to mention—he stayed all night."

Aurora's chest tightened.

This couldn't be happening.

This wasn't happening.

She felt like the air had been sucked from the room, like the walls were closing in on her.

Mary chuckled, clearly amused by Aurora's reaction. She took her time scrolling through her phone, dragging out the moment with deliberate cruelty.

"Oh, but you might want to see this one," she teased, tilting the screen slightly in Aurora's direction but never quite letting her see. "You see, after Harry snuck out of my bed like the guilty little coward he is, I just so happened to run into

Anthony. And let's just say…"—she let out a dramatic sigh, her eyes glittering with malice— "one man's regret is another man's opportunity."

Aurora's stomach twisted. It was bad enough seeing Harry in Mary's bed. The thought of Anthony anywhere near her—let alone in the same scenario—was unbearable. Her hands curled into fists, nails biting into her palms.

"No!" Her voice was sharp, cutting through the air, but it didn't shake Mary's smirk.

With a slow, satisfied hum, Mary slipped her phone back into her purse, as if she'd already won.

"Suit yourself," she said breezily, taking a step back. "But you know what I'd do if I were you? I'd stop pretending like you have the moral high ground. I mean, really, Aurora—look at you. You've been stringing along poor, oblivious Harry while pining for Anthony like some tragic little heroine in a bad romance novel."

Aurora's breath hitched, but she forced herself to stay still, to keep her expression unreadable.

Mary leaned in, lowering her voice to a whisper laced with venom. "The difference between you and me? I don't pretend to be something I'm not. I take what I want. And I don't waste time feeling guilty about it. You had your chance with Anthony, and guess what? He's sick of waiting."

She straightened, flipping her hair over one shoulder with a slow, deliberate motion, savouring every second of Aurora's silence.

"Enjoy your wedding planning—oh, wait." A wicked little giggle escaped her lips. "That is, if Harry's still interested. I know Anthony isn't."

And with that, she sauntered out, her heels clicking against the floor like a victory march.

Aurora stood frozen, her mind spinning, her heart shattering.

The moment the door clicked shut behind Mary, the silence in the room became deafening, pressing in on her like a suffocating weight.

No.

She forced in a breath—shallow, unsteady—as if oxygen alone could steady her thoughts. This was just another one of Mary's games, another cruel attempt to destroy her. It had to be.

But the image of Harry in that bed was burned into her mind, seared into her memory like an inescapable truth. And Anthony—

Aurora's fingers dug into the edge of her desk.

Anthony.

The name was both a lifeline and a death sentence. She had told herself that even if she couldn't have him, even if she had chosen Harry, Anthony had been hers in some quiet, unspoken way. A love she hadn't allowed herself to claim.

She wanted to scream—to lash out and break something, anything, just to release the unbearable pressure building inside her. But she couldn't move. She couldn't breathe. She could only stand there, drowning in the tidal wave of betrayal crashing over her.

Harry.

Her stomach twisted painfully at the thought of him in Mary's bed, the image burned into her mind like a cruel brand. The proof had been right there in front of her, undeniable. She wanted to believe there was an explanation, some justification that would make it all a terrible misunderstanding. But deep down, she knew.

She had suspected something was off for days. The distance. The avoidance. She had tried to tell herself it was just her own guilt projecting onto him, but the truth had been staring her in the face all along.

Harry had betrayed her.

The man who had been her safe place, her steady ground, had slipped away the moment temptation whispered in his ear. And he hadn't even told her. He had let her walk around, blind and trusting, while he carried this secret like a weightless thing.

She should be furious. She should hate him.

But the pain in her chest told her she didn't.

Because this wasn't what truly shattered her.

It was Anthony.

Aurora's hands trembled as she reached for the edge of her desk, gripping it as if it were the only thing keeping her upright.

Anthony.

Mary's words echoed like a dagger twisting deeper into an already open wound. One man's regret is another man's opportunity.

Her stomach lurched.

She had expected Mary to use Harry's betrayal against her, but this—this was a different kind of pain. A deeper, more unbearable kind.

Anthony was supposed to be different.

Even when she had doubted, even when she had tried to push him away, some part of her had clung to the belief that what they had—the connection that had burned so intensely between them—was real. That no matter how much she hurt him, no matter how much she resisted, she mattered to him.

But if Mary was telling the truth… if Anthony had turned to her of all people—

There was no if.

Mary had been ready to show her the proof, to flaunt another cruel, damning image just like the one of Harry. Aurora knew that if she had looked, it would have shattered whatever was left of her. She couldn't do it. She wouldn't do it.

Because once that image was in her head, it would never leave.

A sharp, broken breath escaped her lips.

She pressed a trembling hand to her chest, as if she could hold herself together, as if she could stop the aching, splintering feeling inside her. But it was useless.

She had been fighting her feelings for so long, telling herself she couldn't have Anthony, that she shouldn't want him. She had buried her love for him beneath guilt and obligation, convinced that she was making the right choice.

And now?

Had she hesitated for too long? Had she pushed him away until there was nothing left?

Aurora squeezed her eyes shut, but it didn't stop the images from invading her mind. Anthony's hands on Mary. His lips against hers. The same touch, the same kiss that had once unravelled her.

Her stomach twisted violently.

No.

Her mind rejected it, but the fear had already taken root.

She had spent so much time trapped between two men, torn between duty and desire, and now—

Now she has lost both.

Chapter Seventeen

Aurora knew she had to confront Harry.

As for Anthony…

She swallowed hard, her throat tight.

Anthony wasn't hers.

So, she wasn't going to confront him.

Her heart clenched painfully at the thought, but she forced herself to push it aside. Right now, she needed answers—the truth, from the one person who owed it to her.

Steeling herself, she turned on her heel and left her office.

The walk to Harry's door felt endless, the steady click of her heels against the polished hospital floor the only sound filling the quiet hallway. With every step, she tried to convince herself she wasn't about to break apart. That she was in control. That she wasn't walking straight into the confirmation of her worst fears.

But she already knew.

Mary had made sure of that.

Aurora stopped in front of Harry's office, hesitating for only a second before raising her fist and knocking twice.

A pause. Then—

"Come in," Harry called, his voice steady. Too steady.

Aurora pushed the door open, stepping inside.

Harry sat behind his desk, flipping through a file. When he looked up and saw her, his expression flickered—just for a second—before he plastered on a smile. It was tight. Forced.

"Hey," he said casually, as if nothing had changed. As if he didn't look like a man who hadn't slept in days. "Didn't expect to see you this early."

Aurora didn't return his smile. She closed the door behind her, pressing her back against it for support.

Harry's brows furrowed. "Aurora?"

He was trying so hard to act normal. To pretend.

Her chest ached at the sight of him, at the way he was still trying to protect whatever illusion they had left.

She took a slow breath. "I know, Harry."

His entire body stiffened.

Aurora held his gaze, watching as his fingers clenched around the file in his hands. He didn't speak, didn't move, but she saw it—the slight shift in his expression, the crack in his carefully built facade.

Still, he played dumb. "Know what?"

A hollow laugh escaped her. She shook her head, dropping her gaze for a moment before looking back at him, her voice quiet but sharp.

"Mary enjoyed telling me."

Harry's face drained of colour.

His jaw tensed, and for the first time, he broke eye contact. He set the file down, his fingers still curled into fists on top of it.

"Aurora…" His voice was low, rough. "It's not—"

"Please, don't lie to me."

The words came out stronger than she expected, and she hated how her voice wavered at the end.

Harry looked at her then, really looked at her, and whatever excuse he had been about to give died on his lips.

His shoulders sagged. His face crumpled, guilt tightening every line.

Aurora's throat burned.

"I didn't mean for it to happen," he whispered.

"But it did."

He exhaled sharply, dragging a hand down his face. "It was a mistake."

Aurora clenched her jaw, biting back the sting of tears. "Was it?"

"Of course it was!" Harry snapped, before his expression softened. He ran a hand through his dishevelled hair, looking at her with something close to desperation. "Aurora, you have to believe me. I—I wasn't thinking. She—she got into my head."

Aurora's stomach twisted. She didn't want to hear this.

"Why didn't you tell me?" Her voice was cold now, sharp with betrayal. "Or were you just hoping I'd never find out?"

Harry flinched. That was answer enough.

She let out a slow, measured breath, steadying herself against the storm of emotions crashing inside her.

"I never would have expected this from you," she admitted, her voice barely above a whisper. "Never in a million years."

Harry's face twisted with something close to regret, but regret wouldn't change what he'd done.

"What now?" he asked, though they both already knew the answer.

Aurora's heart ached.

She had spent so much time convincing herself that Harry was the right choice. That he was safe, steady, good.

But he had broken her trust in the worst possible way.

And there was no coming back from that.

Silently, she slipped the engagement ring from her finger. The weight of it felt heavier than it ever had before.

"Goodbye, Harry," she said, setting it down on his desk.

His eyes widened in desperation. "Aurora, no. Can't you—" His voice cracked as he reached for her, his face pleading.

She met his gaze, her expression unreadable.

"No."

The single word sealed everything between them.

Harry exhaled sharply, running a hand through his hair. His next words came out almost like a confession, quiet and bitter.

"Anthony warned me about her. I should have listened."

Aurora's head snapped up.

"He did?"

Harry nodded, his mouth pressing into a tight line. "Yeah. I thought it was because he was jealous, but he was right." His voice was thick with regret as he dropped his head into his hands before looking back up at her. "I'm so sorry, Aurora. I never meant for it to happen."

Tears burned in her eyes now, but she blinked them away.

"I know," she whispered. "But it did."

With that, she turned and walked out, leaving behind the man she once thought she loved.

Anthony had just come from Aurora's office, only to find it empty. His chest tightened with frustration—he had hoped to see her, to talk to her. It had been too long. A whole week, but it felt like an eternity.

As he turned the corner, he nearly collided with someone. His hands instinctively came out to steady them.

Aurora.

She looked up at him, her eyes shimmering with unshed tears. The moment recognition dawned on her, she flinched away, jerking out of his grasp as if his touch burned her.

"Aurora?" His brows knitted in concern. "Are you okay?"

Her lips parted, but whatever she wanted to say died on her tongue. Instead, she shook her head sharply and stepped back.

"Go away, Anthony," she muttered, her voice thick with emotion.

That only made his concern deepen. He took a step closer. "What's wrong?"

"I said go away." She turned abruptly, heading down the hall.

Anthony wasn't about to let her walk away like this. Not when she was clearly upset. Not when something had put that devastated look in her eyes.

He followed her, ignoring the way her shoulders tensed at his presence.

"Aurora, talk to me," he urged. "What happened?"

She didn't answer.

He kept pace beside her, watching her face carefully. "Was it Harry?" His voice was sharper now, tinged with something possessive. "Did he do something?"

She let out a bitter laugh, shaking her head.

"Just leave me alone, Anthony." She reached her office door and pushed it open. But before she could shut it in his face, he caught the edge, keeping it from closing.

"Not until you tell me what's wrong," he said, his voice gentler now.

Aurora's patience snapped. She spun around, her eyes flashing with anger and pain.

"I know," she blurted, her chest rising and falling rapidly. "I know about you and Mary. About you and Harry both sleeping with her."

Anthony froze.

His entire body went rigid, his expression one of pure shock.

"What?" he breathed, staring at her as if she had just spoken a foreign language.

Aurora let out a humourless laugh. "Don't bother denying it. Mary enjoyed telling me."

For a moment, Anthony just stood there, as if trying to process what he had just heard. Then, his brows drew together, his jaw tightening.

"That's a lie," he said, his voice low and firm. "Aurora, I never—"

"Don't," she cut him off, wrapping her arms around herself. "Just don't."

But Anthony wasn't letting this go.

He stepped closer, his eyes locked onto hers with an intensity that made her heart pound. "I don't know what Mary told you, but I swear to you, I never touched her."

Aurora wanted to believe him. She really did. But after everything—after the lies, the heartbreak, the betrayal—how could she?

She swallowed the lump in her throat, her fingers gripping the edge of her desk as if it was the only thing keeping her upright. "At least Harry admitted it." Her voice was quieter now, laced with exhaustion rather than anger.

Anthony took a step closer, his expression dark with frustration. "I didn't touch her, Aurora. I would never."

She let out a hollow laugh, shaking her head. "She had photos, Anthony."

That stopped him cold.

For a moment, something flickered in his eyes—shock, then disbelief. His jaw tightened, the muscle ticking as he fought to contain the storm of emotions brewing beneath the surface.

"Photos?" he repeated, his voice dangerously low, as if the very word disgusted him.

Aurora crossed her arms, bracing herself against the pull he still had on her, against the way his presence unravelled her defences. "Yes. Of Harry. Of you. Of her. Together." Her throat constricted, but she forced the words out. "She showed them to me."

Anthony went completely still, his body rigid, hands clenching into fists at his sides. "That's impossible."

"She looked pretty damn pleased with herself when she told me," Aurora said bitterly. The memory of Mary's smug smile sent a fresh wave of anger through her. "And after everything that's happened, can you really blame me for believing it?"

"Yes," he snapped, his voice cutting through the air, edged with something dangerously close to desperation. "Because it's not true."

She scoffed, turning away.

"Then explain the photos."

Anthony exhaled sharply, running a frustrated hand through his hair. "I don't know what she showed you, but I swear on my life, Aurora, I never touched her." His voice was raw now, pleading. "Not since a month before I even met you."

Aurora squeezed her eyes shut. She wanted to trust him—to believe the conviction in his voice, the sincerity in his gaze. But those images... Mary had shown her pictures of Harry, but she hadn't looked at Anthony's. She couldn't.

And yet... she knew he'd gone out with Mary before they met. Could the photo have been from then?

She wanted to believe Anthony wasn't like that. But wanting and knowing weren't the same thing. And she had been wrong before.

Her chest tightened, confusion pressing in from all sides. "How do I know that?" she whispered, her voice barely audible. "How do I know you're not just trying to convince me it didn't happen, like Harry did?"

Chapter Eighteen

Anthony took a slow step forward, closing the distance between them. His voice, though softer now, carried no less intensity. "Because I wouldn't lie to you about this." He swallowed hard, his eyes searching hers. "I can't stand the thought of you believing I would ever betray you like that."

Aurora's heart twisted painfully. Her emotions were at war—her mind screaming caution, her heart aching to believe him.

Her throat tightened. What if he's telling the truth?

"I don't know what to think," she admitted finally, lifting her gaze to his. Her voice trembled under the weight of it all. "This is too much."

Anthony stepped closer, his movements slow and deliberate, as if afraid she might pull away. Gently, he placed his hands on her shoulders, his touch warm but tentative. His eyes, dark with intensity, searched hers.

"Aurora, I swear to you, I have never slept with Mary since I've known you." His voice was low, almost raw, heavy with emotion. "I would never do that to you... ever."

Her hands curled into fists at her sides, nails biting into her palms, as if pain could anchor her.

Something inside her cracked. The walls she had tried to keep up, the ones meant to shield her from more pain, crumbled under the sheer desperation in his voice.

A sob escaped her lips before she could stop it. Her resolve shattered, and she broke down, her body trembling as the weight of everything crashed over her. Without thinking, she fell into Anthony's arms.

He held her tightly, his embrace firm and steady, as if anchoring her. One hand cradled the back of her head, the other splayed against her back, as though he could shield her from the pain threatening to consume her.

She wanted to believe him. She truly did. But trust, once broken, wasn't easily repaired.

And yet, in his arms, the world didn't feel quite so unbearable.

Anthony held her as if he was afraid, she might slip away if he let go. His fingers twitched against her back, reluctant to break the fragile moment between them. His brows drew together, his expression torn between duty and the overwhelming need to stay.

"I don't want to leave you," he murmured, his voice rough with emotion. "But I have a patient in five minutes."

Regret flickered in his eyes, as if he was silently begging her to ask him to stay.

Aurora forced herself to step back, putting some much-needed space between them. She needed to breathe, to think. "Go," she said softly, trying to sound steady even though she felt anything but. "Your patients are important."

He studied her for a long moment, then reached out, gently cupping her face. His thumb brushed against her cheek, his touch warm and grounding.

"We'll talk later," he promised, his voice low, intimate. Then he leaned in, pressing a soft, lingering kiss to her lips—one that left her heart aching in its wake.

She nodded, unable to find the words to respond.

With one last reluctant glance, Anthony turned and walked away. Aurora watched him disappear through the door, out of her office, a part of her wanting to call him back, to ask him to stay.

But she couldn't.

As soon as he was gone, the weight of everything pressed down on her, threatening to crush her. The hospital walls suddenly felt too bright, too constricting, too loud. She couldn't be here. Not now.

Her feet moved on autopilot as she made her way to her supervisor's office. Knocking lightly, she stepped inside when called.

Her supervisor looked up, brows raising at the sight of her. "Aurora? You okay?"

"I'm not feeling well," she said, and for once, it wasn't a lie. Her voice came out softer than she intended, the exhaustion bleeding through. "I think I need to go home."

A frown of concern crossed her supervisor's face. "You do look a little pale." She studied Aurora for a beat longer, then nodded. "Go home and rest. Let me know if you need more time."

Aurora barely managed a nod of thanks before turning and heading for the exit.

Each step felt heavier than the last, her emotions threatening to overwhelm her. The moment she stepped outside and felt the cool air on her skin, she exhaled shakily, but it did little to ease the tightness in her chest.

She needed someone.

Without thinking, she pulled out her phone and dialled.

"Hey, it's me," she said the moment Emily picked up.

"What's wrong?" Emily's voice was immediately filled with concern.

Aurora swallowed the lump in her throat. "Can you come over?" Her voice wavered. "Please?"

"I'm already grabbing my keys," Emily said without hesitation. "I'll be there soon."

Aurora barely had time to murmur a quiet "thank you" before ending the call.

The moment she stepped inside her apartment, she shut the door behind her and leaned against it, eyes squeezing shut.

She had held it together as long as she could.

But now, in the quiet safety of her own home, with Emily on her way…

She finally let herself break.

The moment Emily stepped through the door; she didn't hesitate. She pulled Aurora into a tight embrace, wrapping her arms around her like a shield against the pain. Aurora clung to her, silent sobs shaking her body. Emily didn't ask any questions, didn't push for explanations—she simply held her, letting her cry until the worst of the storm had passed.

When Aurora finally pulled back, sniffling and wiping at her damp cheeks, she let out a shaky breath. "I'm sorry for dragging you here on your day off."

Emily gave her a pointed look. "Oh, please. You know I'd drop everything for you." She tucked a strand of Aurora's hair behind her ear. "Now tell me—what happened?"

Aurora hesitated, her throat tightening. Then, in a quiet voice, she asked, "Do you remember that nurse from the hospital? The nasty one you and Sarah had words with?"

Emily's eyes immediately darkened. "Yes. How could I forget her?"

Aurora swallowed hard. "Harry slept with her."

Emily's jaw dropped. For a moment, she just stared. Then— "Are you kidding me?"

Aurora gave a humourless laugh, wiping at her damp cheeks. "I wish I was."

Emily shook her head, pacing the living room. "I mean, I always knew she was trouble, but Harry? What the hell was he thinking?"

Aurora sank onto the couch, wrapping her arms around herself as if trying to hold herself together. "I don't know," she admitted. "He said it was a mistake. That he never meant for it to happen." Her throat tightened. "But it did."

Emily stopped pacing and sat beside her, squeezing her hand. "I'm so sorry, babe. You don't deserve this."

Aurora gave her a small, watery smile. "I know." She exhaled, staring at her hands. "And that's not even the worst part."

Emily's brow furrowed. "What do you mean?"

Aurora hesitated, her pulse hammering in her ears. Saying it out loud made it feel even more real.

"Mary told me…" She took a steadying breath. "She told me Anthony slept with her too."

Emily blinked, then scoffed. "Oh, please. You can't seriously believe that."

"She showed me photos, Em," Aurora said, her voice cracking. "Of Harry. Of Anthony. Of her."

Emily's mouth fell open. "Are you serious?"

Aurora nodded. "I didn't even look at Anthony's—I couldn't. But Mary... she was so smug about it. She wanted me to believe it."

Emily sat back, her expression thoughtful. "And Anthony? What did he say?"

Aurora swallowed hard. "He denied it. He swore he hadn't touched her since before he met me."

Emily's eyes narrowed. "And do you believe him?"

Aurora's heart twisted painfully. "I want to," she admitted. "But after everything... how can I be sure?"

Emily considered this for a long moment, then shook her head. "You know, Mary is the kind of person who lives to stir up drama. I wouldn't put it past her to fake something just to mess with you."

Aurora let that thought settle but doubt still gnawed at her.

Emily gave her a reassuring squeeze. "You said you didn't even look at the ones of Anthony, right?"

Aurora nodded.

"Then maybe you should."

Aurora stiffened. "I don't know if I can."

Emily tilted her head. "If he's telling the truth, then seeing them might prove it. And if he's lying... then at least you'll know instead of torturing yourself with what–ifs."

Aurora clenched her jaw, her stomach twisting at the mere thought of those photos. Just the idea of seeing them made her feel sick. But Emily was right.

She couldn't keep running from the truth.

Steeling herself, she exhaled slowly and straightened her shoulders. There was only one way to put this torment to rest.

She needed to confront Mary—once and for all.

Chapter Nineteen

Anthony arrived at the hospital early Wednesday morning, his mind consumed by one thought—Aurora. He had to see her.

Yesterday, he had gone to her office, only to be told she had left early, feeling unwell. The news had unsettled him. He hated the idea of her going home alone, hurting, with no one to comfort her. If only he knew where she lived. If only he had her number.

Seeing Aurora so devastated yesterday had been unbearable. He wished he could take her pain away; undo the betrayal she had suffered.

Instead, he had spent the afternoon talking to Harry. As much as he despised what Harry had done, Anthony knew they needed to have an honest conversation.

When he walked into Harry's office, he immediately saw the weight of regret on the man's face. Harry sat slumped behind his desk, his usually composed demeanour shattered.

Anthony shut the door behind him and leaned against the frame. "How are you holding up?"

Harry sighed heavily, rubbing a hand over his tired face. "You know, then?"

"Yes. Aurora told me."

Harry exhaled, shaking his head. "I stuffed up. You warned me, and I didn't listen." His voice was thick with remorse.

Anthony stepped forward, lowering himself into the chair across from Harry's desk. "Harry, I know this probably isn't the best time, but I need to be honest with you."

Harry frowned, looking at him warily. "About what?"

Anthony hesitated for a brief moment before meeting his gaze head-on. "You know Aurora and I knew each other before I started working here."

"Yes," Harry said slowly.

Anthony exhaled, rubbing his jaw before looking Harry in the eye. "Well… we were more than just friends. At least, I wanted us to be." His voice was quiet but steady.

Harry's posture stiffened, his expression hardening. "Are you telling me Aurora was cheating on me with you?" His tone carried a sharp edge, as if he wanted to shift some of the blame.

"No." Anthony's voice was firm, leaving no room for doubt. "Aurora has done nothing wrong. But I need to tell you the truth—I wanted to be with Aurora a year ago. I cared about her. More than I should have, given the circumstances." He ran a hand through his hair before adding, "But Mary came between us."

Harry's eyes narrowed slightly before understanding dawned on his face. "This is why you warned me about her," he realised.

"Yes," Anthony confirmed. "Mary manipulated the situation—made it look like I didn't care about Aurora. And by the time I figured it out, it was too late. Aurora left the hospital, and I didn't see her again."

Harry leaned back in his chair, running a hand over his face again. "So… Mary played us both." His voice was bitter, filled with self-loathing.

"She did," Anthony agreed. "And I should have tried to stop her before she had the chance to do the same to you."

Silence settled between them, thick with unspoken emotions. Harry stared at his desk, his jaw tight, while Anthony sat across from him, waiting for the reality of the situation to fully sink in.

Finally, Harry let out a humourless laugh, shaking his head. "You love Aurora, don't you?"

Anthony didn't hesitate. "Yes."

Harry exhaled sharply, nodding to himself. He seemed to be processing everything, the weight of his actions settling over him like a heavy fog. Then, looking Anthony straight in the eye, he admitted, "I think you might love her more than I ever did. If I had loved her the way you do… I wouldn't have done what I did." His voice was raw, edged with guilt and regret.

Anthony ran a hand through his hair, frustration flickering across his face. "I still want to be with Aurora," he admitted. "But she doesn't want to hurt you."

Harry let out a small, sad chuckle. "That's Aurora," he murmured, shaking his head. "Always thinking of others, even when she's the one who's been hurt."

Anthony nodded. "She deserves better than what she's been through. And I don't just mean with you," he added, his tone softening. "She's been through so much already. I don't want to add to her pain."

Harry leaned forward, resting his elbows on the desk. "Then don't," he said simply. "If you love her, show her she's worth fighting for."

Anthony's jaw clenched as he absorbed Harry's words. He had spent so much time holding back, afraid of making things worse for Aurora. But maybe that was the mistake. Maybe he needed to show her, without hesitation, that she was the most important thing to him.

Harry sighed and rubbed his temples, the weight of his actions evident in his slumped posture. "Look, I know I don't deserve her forgiveness. And I definitely don't have the right to decide what's best for her. But if she loves you—even a little—don't let her push you away just because of me."

Anthony studied him for a long moment, searching for any sign of resentment, but all he saw was regret. "Are you sure you're okay with this?"

Harry let out a quiet, almost self-deprecating chuckle. "I'm the one who messed up, Anthony. I let my own insecurities ruin something good. Aurora deserves better. And from the way you talk about her, it sounds like that's you."

Anthony's chest tightened at the sincerity in Harry's voice. He stood and extended his hand. "I appreciate that."

Harry hesitated only for a second before rising to his feet and shaking Anthony's hand firmly. His grip was steady, but there was a sadness in his eyes. "Make her happy, Anthony. She deserves it."

Anthony gave a nod, determination settling in his gut. "I'm going to try."

Anthony was relieved that he had cleared the air with Harry. The last thing he wanted was tension at work because of his feelings for Aurora. Now, all that remained was convincing her that Mary had lied about him sleeping with her. The mere thought of Mary feeding Aurora that lie made his blood boil.

A sharp knock at his office door pulled him from his thoughts.

"Come in," he called, already feeling on edge.

The door swung open, and his stomach tightened in irritation.

Mary.

She sauntered in as if she owned the place, leaving the door ajar behind her.

Anthony's jaw clenched. "What the hell are you doing here?" His voice was cold, sharp. "Get out."

Mary ignored him, her lips curling into a smirk. "I heard Aurora's not too happy with you."

He stared at her in disbelief, his anger bubbling to the surface. "What is wrong with you, Mary? Why do you enjoy ruining people's lives?"

Her expression darkened. "You hurt me, Anthony," she snapped. "When Aurora showed up, you dropped me like a hot potato."

He let out a humourless chuckle, shaking his head. "You can't be serious." His eyes narrowed. "I was going to break things off with you long before I even met Aurora."

"I don't believe you!" she cried, her voice rising with desperation.

Anthony exhaled sharply, trying to keep his frustration in check. "Think about it, Mary. For the last month before we broke up, did I ever want to be intimate with you?" He let the words hang between them before continuing. "I always had an excuse, didn't I? And do you know why?" His gaze hardened. "Because I knew we were wrong for each other. I knew we'd never be serious."

Mary's breath hitched, but instead of backing down, she stepped closer, reaching for his arm.

"Anthony," she whispered, her fingers clutching at his sleeve. "I can be better. I can be what you want." Her eyes shimmered with unshed tears. "I love you."

He looked at her in disbelief. "You can't be serious. After knowing someone like Aurora, why would I ever want to be with a manipulative woman like you?"

Mary's expression darkened as she dropped her hand from his arm. "Aurora isn't as perfect as you think," she sneered. "She believed me when I told her you slept with me." A cold, satisfied laugh escaped her lips. "You should've seen her face. Oh, she was devastated about Harry cheating, but when I told her you did too?" She smirked, her eyes gleaming with malice. "She was shattered. She'll never believe you now—not after I offered to show her the photos."

"The photos that don't exist," Anthony shot back.

Mary tilted her head, unfazed. "Oh, after I showed her the one of Harry, she didn't even want to see one of you."

Anthony's jaw clenched. "And you counted on that, didn't you? You preyed on her kindness, her trust."

Mary grinned wickedly. "She's so gullible. She believed me instantly."

"No, I didn't."

A new voice cut through the tension.

Mary froze.

Anthony turned sharply, his breath catching for half a second.

Aurora.

She stood with her arms crossed, her expression unreadable. But her voice— calm and controlled—held a quiet fury.

Mary stiffened, but it was only for a second before she plastered on her usual smirk. "Well, well, well," she purred, flipping her hair over her shoulder. "How much did you hear?"

"Enough," Aurora said coolly, stepping further into the room.

Anthony barely took his eyes off her, relief washing over him at her words. He had feared she had truly believed Mary's lies, that her trust in him had been permanently shattered. But now, seeing the fire in her eyes, the way she held her ground, he realised she wasn't as easily fooled as Mary had assumed.

Mary let out a fake laugh, tilting her head. "Oh, come on, Aurora. You were devastated when I told you Anthony slept with me. And now you want to pretend you didn't believe it?"

Aurora met her gaze without flinching. "I was devastated, yes," she admitted. "But I never fully believed you. Not deep down." She took another step closer, her voice steady. "You see, Mary, there's a difference between being hurt and being fooled. You knew how much I cared about Anthony, and you used that to try and break me. You knew I was already reeling from Harry's betrayal, and you twisted the knife."

Mary's smirk faltered for the first time.

Aurora exhaled, shaking her head. "I won't lie—I was scared. Scared that it might be true, because the thought of Anthony betraying me hurt more than I was willing to admit. But something didn't add up." She glanced at Anthony, her voice softening. "I thought about how you cared for me when I was attacked. The way you held me when you kiss me. And I remembered what you said to me yesterday in my office—you told me you would never hurt me like that." She turned back to Mary, her voice firm. "But you miscalculated. The more I thought about it, the more I realised the truth."

Mary's eyes narrowed. "And what truth is that?"

"That you're a liar," Aurora said simply. "A bitter, manipulative liar who thrives on hurting others because you can't stand to see people happy."

Anthony stepped forward then, his gaze locked on Mary, his voice cold. "You played your last card, Mary. And you lost."

Mary clenched her jaw, her hands balling into fists. For a moment, she looked as though she might lash out, but then, something flickered in her eyes—was it regret? No, not regret. Frustration. She had lost. She knew it. Yet she forced a smirk, lifting her chin as if she were the one in control. "This isn't over," she muttered. Then, with one last glare at Aurora, she turned on her heel and stormed out of the office, her footsteps echoing down the hall.

Silence filled the room in her absence.

Anthony turned to Aurora, searching her face. "Are you okay?"

Aurora let out a slow breath. "I will be."

His chest tightened. "I'm so sorry she did this to you."

Aurora finally met his gaze, and something in her eyes softened. "I should have trusted you."

Anthony stepped closer, hesitant, his voice barely above a whisper. "Do you?"

Aurora exhaled slowly, her eyes searching his. Then, she nodded. "Yes." A small, almost tentative smile ghosted across her lips. "I do."

Chapter Twenty

Relief flooded through Anthony, but he didn't rush forward. Instead, he let Aurora close the final distance between them. And when she did, when she reached for his hand, he pulled her into his arms, his grip firm yet reverent, as if afraid she might slip away again.

His lips found hers in a kiss that was both a plea and a promise. It wasn't hurried or frantic—no, it was something deeper, something weighted with all the emotions he had held back for so long. His hands slid up her back, pulling her impossibly closer, as if by sheer proximity he could erase the pain of the past.

Aurora melted into him, her fingers threading through his hair, anchoring him to this moment. The heat between them burned slow and steady, like embers stirred back to life. She could feel his heart pounding against her own, could taste the quiet desperation in his kiss—an unspoken vow that he wouldn't let her go this time.

When they finally broke apart, their foreheads pressed together, their breaths mingling in the charged space between them. Anthony cupped her face, his thumb tracing the delicate curve of her cheek.

"I thought I was going to lose you again," he murmured, his voice rough with emotion.

Aurora's lips curved into the faintest smile, her fingers tightening in his hair. "You never did."

And then she kissed him again—not out of hesitation, not out of doubt, but with the certainty of a woman who knew exactly where she belonged.

Aurora left Anthony's office happier than she had felt in a long time. A weight she hadn't realised she'd been carrying had finally lifted. She called Emily as soon as she was back in her office, excitement bubbling in her voice as she recounted everything that had happened.

"I knew Anthony was a good guy," Emily said, her voice warm with approval. "He'll treat you right."

Aurora smiled, leaning back in her chair. "Thanks, Em."

The rest of her day flew by, her mind only half-focused on work. Every glance at the clock made her heart race a little faster. She just wanted to be with Anthony again, to hold onto the happiness she had found in his arms. So, when five o'clock neared, she was already gathering her things, eager to leave.

A sharp knock at her office door pulled her from her thoughts.

"Come in," she called.

The door opened, and her supervisor, Marie Winters, stepped inside. But the moment Aurora saw her expression—lips pressed into a thin line; brows furrowed with tension—her stomach sank.

Marie closed the door behind her, her movements stiff with authority. "Aurora, we need to talk."

Aurora straightened in her chair, forcing a calm smile. "Of course." She gestured for Marie to sit, but Marie remained standing.

"We've received a complaint," Marie said, her voice heavy with disapproval. "A serious complaint."

Aurora blinked in confusion. "A complaint?"

Marie nodded, crossing her arms. "An allegation has been made against you… regarding inappropriate behaviour in the workplace."

Aurora's stomach twisted. "I don't understand."

Marie inhaled sharply, then spoke with careful precision. "You've been accused of engaging in sexual misconduct on hospital grounds—specifically, in your office."

Aurora felt as if the air had been knocked from her lungs. "What? That's not true!"

"The complaint states that you were caught in a… compromising position with Dr. Harry Young." Marie's gaze was unreadable, but there was an unmistakable weight behind her words.

Aurora's blood ran cold.

Harry?

This had to be some kind of sick joke.

Marie continued, "It's also been alleged that when confronted about the situation, you threatened or pressured the individual to stay quiet—to not report what they saw."

Aurora's pulse thundered in her ears. This was insane. Who would say something like this? And why?

"Marie, I swear to you, this never happened." Her voice shook slightly, but not with guilt—with sheer disbelief.

Marie studied her for a long moment before finally sitting down across from her. Her gaze softened just a fraction, but her voice remained firm.

"Aurora, I want to believe you. You've been an exemplary employee since you started here. Your record is spotless." She hesitated, then sighed. "But this is a formal complaint. I have to investigate."

Aurora's heart pounded as the weight of the accusation settled over her, cold and suffocating. Someone was trying to destroy her reputation. Someone who wanted to see her fall. And she had a sickening feeling she knew exactly who was behind it.

Marie continued, her voice laced with regret. "The hospital board will launch an investigation immediately. Until then, Aurora, you will be placed on administrative leave while they review the claims."

Aurora's breath caught in her throat. "Administrative leave?" The words felt foreign, like they belonged to someone else's nightmare, not hers.

Marie gave a slow nod. "Effective immediately. You'll need to turn in your badge and leave the premises today."

Aurora shook her head in disbelief. "This can't be happening."

But the grim set of Marie's expression told her otherwise.

Aurora packed her things in silence, her hands shaking as she stuffed her belongings into her bag. Each movement felt surreal, as if she were watching herself from the outside. Her heart pounded relentlessly, the weight of the accusation pressing down on her chest like a heavy stone.

She took a deep breath, squared her shoulders, and handed Marie her hospital badge. The loss of it felt oddly symbolic, as if a piece of her identity was being stripped away.

Marie took the badge gently, her expression conflicted. "Aurora, I am sorry about this," she said, her voice softer now. "I don't know what's really going on, but I have to follow protocol."

Aurora swallowed hard, her throat tight. "I understand."

Marie hesitated, then gave her a small nod. "You can make a phone call before you leave. Security will escort you out once you're done. They're just outside the door."

Aurora stiffened. Security. The implication stung. She was being treated like a threat, like a criminal.

Marie must have noticed the flicker of pain in her expression because she sighed. "I truly hope this gets sorted out quickly."

With that, she turned and left, the door clicking shut behind her.

Aurora exhaled shakily and reached for the phone, her fingers gripping the receiver tightly as she dialled the number of the person, she needed the most.

It barely rang twice before a deep, familiar voice answered.

"Dr. Hardwick."

Relief flooded through her at the sound of his voice, steady and grounding.

"Anthony?"

His tone immediately shifted, laced with concern. "Aurora? What's wrong?"

She took a shaky breath. "I—I need to see you. Something's happened."

The tension in his voice sharpened instantly. "Tell me."

Aurora closed her eyes, forcing herself to stay calm as she explained everything—the false accusation, the complaint, the forced administrative leave. The moment she finished, she heard his sharp intake of breath.

"Where are you now?" he asked, his voice tight with controlled anger.

"In my office. Security is waiting to escort me out." The last part tasted bitter on her tongue.

A heavy silence stretched between them before he finally spoke, his voice firm and unwavering.

"I'll meet you in the car park."

Aurora gripped the phone tighter. "Anthony—"

"I'm on my way," he said, leaving no room for argument.

The line went dead.

Aurora slowly replaced the receiver, then took one last glance around the office that had become her safe haven these past six months. Now, it felt tainted.

Squaring her shoulders, she took a steadying breath and walked to the door.

The security guards waiting outside straightened at her approach. Without a word, they gestured for her to follow.

Keeping her head high, Aurora stepped forward.

She wasn't going to let them see her break.

Anthony hung up the phone, his jaw clenched so tightly it ached. Aurora had sounded devastated—shaken in a way he had never heard before. The accusation itself was absurd. Sexual misconduct? Aurora would never do something like that. Anyone who truly knew her would see how ridiculous it was.

His frustration surged as he grabbed his briefcase, stuffing papers inside with little care. He needed to get to her. Now. He strode out of his office, his mind racing with possible ways to fight this. Whoever had orchestrated this lie was going to regret it.

As he turned the corner, he nearly collided with Harry.

"Everything alright, Anthony?" Harry asked, frowning. "You look stressed."

Anthony hesitated for the briefest moment, studying him. He was almost certain he knew exactly who had filed the complaint against Aurora. But on the slim chance that Harry had played a role, he needed to be sure.

Keeping his voice calm but firm, he asked, "You didn't have anything to do with the complaint made against Aurora, did you?"

Harry's brows furrowed. "Aurora? Complaint?" His confusion was genuine, his expression open. "No. What complaint?"

Anthony held his gaze, searching for any flicker of dishonesty. But before he could answer, realisation dawned in Harry's eyes.

His face hardened.

"Mary." His voice was laced with disbelief and disgust.

Anthony exhaled sharply, nodding. "That's my guess too."

Harry shook his head, a muscle twitching in his jaw. "That vindictive little—" He exhaled sharply, reigning in his temper. "I noticed she had some sort of grudge against Aurora, but this? This is low, even for her."

Anthony's expression darkened. "If she thinks she's going to get away with this, she's dead wrong."

Harry straightened, his own anger simmering beneath the surface. "I'll back Aurora up in any way I can. If Mary's behind this, I'll make damn sure the board knows the truth."

Anthony gave him a curt nod. He had no time for grudges right now—Aurora needed him. Without another word, he pushed past, making his way toward the parking lot, his determination burning hotter with every step.

Chapter Twenty-One

When Anthony walked into the car park, his eyes immediately found Aurora. She stood next to her car, arms wrapped tightly around herself, her shoulders shaking. Even from a distance, he could see the unshed tears shimmering in her eyes, the weight of betrayal pressing down on her.

The moment he reached her; he pulled her into his arms without hesitation. She clung to him, her fingers gripping the fabric of his shirt as if he were the only thing keeping her grounded. He held her close, his arms tightening around her, willing his strength into her trembling frame.

"Why would anyone do this?" she whispered, her voice raw with disbelief and hurt. "I would never do the things they've accused me of."

Anthony's chest ached at the desperation in her voice. He cupped the back of her head, pressing a firm kiss to her hair. "I know, sweetheart," he murmured against her temple. "I know."

She pulled back slightly, her wide, tear-filled eyes searching his. "I've worked so hard to build my career, my reputation. And now… one lie could destroy everything." Her breath hitched. "I don't understand how someone could be this cruel."

Anthony brushed his thumb across her cheek, wiping away a stray tear. His jaw tightened with controlled fury. "We will fight this, Aurora. You're innocent, and I won't let them take anything from you. Not your job, not your dignity, nothing."

Her lips trembled as she looked up at him. "But what if they don't believe me?"

"They will," he said with unwavering certainty. "And if they don't, we'll make them."

Aurora let out a shaky breath and nodded, leaning into him again. His arms remained locked around her, protective, unwavering. He wasn't just going to stand by while she was torn down by a vindictive lie.

Whoever had done this had made a grave mistake. And Anthony was certain it was Mary.

His jaw clenched as he held Aurora close, feeling the slight tremble in her body. The thought of her suffering because of some malicious lie made his blood boil. He wasn't going to rest until the truth came out. Until everyone knew exactly what kind of person Mary was.

But first, he needed to get Aurora somewhere safe. Somewhere she could breathe without the walls of the hospital closing in on her.

"I'll follow you in my car to your place, okay?" Anthony said, his voice gentle yet firm as he searched her eyes for any hesitation.

Aurora hesitated only for a second before nodding. "Okay."

Relief flickered across his face. He leaned in, pressing a soft, lingering kiss to her forehead, as if trying to silently reassure her that she wasn't alone in this. When he finally pulled away, he waited, watching as she slid into her car before getting into his own.

As he drove, his mind raced. He was already strategising—who he needed to speak to, what evidence they could gather, and how they could clear Aurora's name as quickly as possible. He wouldn't rest until the truth came out.

When they arrived at Aurora's apartment building, Anthony parked beside her and followed her inside. The space was small but warm, filled with little touches that made it uniquely hers. He took in the soft lighting, the bookshelf filled with well-loved novels, and the faint scent of lavender lingering in the air.

"This is nice," he said, looking around with genuine appreciation.

"I like it." Aurora smiled as she set her bag down.

Anthony turned to her, his expression unreadable for a brief moment before he closed the distance between them. Without a word, he pulled her into his arms, wrapping her in a firm, protective embrace. She let out a shaky breath as she melted against him, her arms circling his waist.

He tilted her chin up, his eyes dark and intense as they searched hers. Then, with slow, deliberate tenderness, he kissed her.

It wasn't rushed or desperate. It was deep, unhurried, and full of emotion—a kiss that spoke of everything they had been through, of everything unspoken between them. His lips moved over hers with reverence, as if committing her to memory.

Aurora responded just as slowly, her fingers gripping the fabric of his shirt as she let herself fall into the moment. This wasn't just comfort. It wasn't just relief. It was something more, something raw and real.

When they finally pulled apart, their breaths mingled in the space between them, the weight of the day momentarily forgotten.

"You're safe with me," he whispered, his forehead resting against hers.

She closed her eyes, holding onto him as if he were the only solid thing in her world. "As long as I'm with you," she murmured, "I know I am."

Anthony tightened his hold on her, his hand stroking gently along her back, grounding her. They stood there in silence, wrapped in each other's warmth, as the weight of the day slowly melted away. The steady rhythm of his heartbeat beneath her cheek was comforting, a quiet reassurance that she wasn't alone in this fight.

Minutes passed, neither of them willing to break the moment. Aurora felt the tension in her body ease as she let herself breathe him in, his scent—a mix of clean soap and something uniquely him—filling her senses.

Anthony pressed a lingering kiss to her temple, his lips barely moving as he whispered, "I'll protect you, Aurora. No matter what."

Emotion swelled in her chest. She had been fighting for so long, standing strong on her own. But with Anthony, she didn't have to carry the weight alone.

She pulled back slightly, just enough to look up at him. His dark eyes were filled with a fierce determination, but there was something else, too—something softer. Love.

Her fingers traced the side of his face, memorising the feel of him. "I know you will," she whispered. "And I trust you."

A small, almost relieved smile touched his lips. He leaned down, brushing another slow, reverent kiss against hers—one that wasn't about passion, but about promise.

Just as they were pulling apart, a sharp knock echoed through the apartment. Aurora blinked, momentarily disoriented before realisation dawned. "Oh, that'll be Sarah and Emily," she murmured, stepping back from Anthony with a mix of reluctance and fond amusement.

Anthony arched a brow. "They're coming over now?"

Aurora offered him an apologetic smile. "They come every week for dinner. It's our tradition."

His expression softened instantly. "That's nice." He reached up, tucking a loose strand of hair behind her ear before letting his fingers trail away. "Go on, let them in."

She nodded and made her way to the door, pulling it open to reveal Sarah and Emily standing there, their arms weighed down with bags of takeaway. The delicious scent of Chinese food immediately filled the air, making Aurora's stomach growl in response.

Sarah, the taller of the two, with dark brown curls and sharp green eyes, grinned. "We come bearing gifts," she announced, lifting the bags as if they were priceless treasures.

Emily, shorter and sporting a sleek blonde bob, peeked past Aurora and immediately spotted Anthony standing in the middle of the living room. Her lips curled into a knowing smile as she nudged Sarah. "Well, well, what do we have here?"

Sarah's eyes followed Emily's gaze, and the moment she saw Anthony, her eyebrows shot up. "Aurora, you didn't mention we'd be having company tonight."

Aurora let out a small laugh, stepping aside to let them in. "Anthony just—"

Emily cut her off with a teasing grin. "Just happened to be here when we arrived. How convenient."

Aurora rolled her eyes. "It's not like that."

Sarah smirked, giving Anthony an appraising look. "It's good to see you Dr. Hardwick."

Anthony chuckled, his gaze flicking to Aurora. "Anthony, please."

"Hello Anthony," Emily said, setting the food down on the small dining table. "You should stay and eat with us. We got way too much food anyway."

Anthony glanced at Aurora, silently asking if she was okay with it. She gave him a small, appreciative smile. "You should stay. It's been a long day."

"Alright," he agreed easily, rolling up his sleeves as he moved toward the table. "Chinese food sounds great."

Sarah and Emily exchanged another cheeky look before unpacking the food. They arranged the containers, filling the table with dumplings, sweet and sour pork, stir-fried vegetables, and fried rice.

They all sat down, and for a while, the conversation was light hearted—filled with laughter and stories about work. But as the meal went on, Aurora's smile faded, the weight of the day creeping back in.

Sarah was the first to notice. "Alright," she said, setting down her chopsticks. "Something's wrong. Spill."

Aurora hesitated, glancing at Anthony before taking a deep breath. "There's been an accusation made against me at the hospital."

Emily frowned. "What kind of accusation?"

Aurora swallowed hard. "Sexual misconduct. Someone claimed I was… involved with a colleague in my office."

Sarah and Emily's jaws dropped simultaneously.

"What?!" Sarah practically shouted. "That's ridiculous!"

Emily shook her head in disbelief. "Who would say something like that?"

Anthony's expression darkened. "We have a pretty good idea."

Sarah narrowed her eyes. "Mary."

Aurora nodded, her fingers tightening around her chopsticks. "It has to be her."

Emily's face twisted in anger. "That bitter little—"

Sarah cut her off, her expression fierce. "Aurora, this won't stick. Everyone knows you'd never do something like that."

Anthony reached for Aurora's hand under the table, squeezing it reassuringly. "We'll fight it. And we'll win."

Aurora glanced around the room, taking in the fierce expressions of her friends—Sarah and Emily, outraged on her behalf, and Anthony, steady and unwavering in his support. A deep sense of gratitude swelled in her chest. No matter what lay ahead, she wasn't alone.

They finished their meal, the conversation shifting between strategising how to clear Aurora's name and light-hearted distractions meant to ease the tension. Laughter occasionally broke through the heaviness of the night, especially as Sarah and Emily recounted a particularly disastrous dating story involving a man who spoke exclusively in movie quotes.

By the time the last of the Chinese food was gone and the bottle of wine had been emptied, Sarah stretched with a yawn. "Alright, we should head out," she announced, exchanging a glance with Emily.

Emily smirked, shooting a look between Aurora and Anthony before standing. "Yeah, we'll leave you two to… talk."

Aurora rolled her eyes, but warmth crept into her cheeks. "Thanks for coming guys. Really."

Sarah pulled her into a quick, fierce hug. "Always."

As they left, closing the door behind them, Aurora turned back to Anthony. For a moment, she hesitated, shifting on her feet. Then, taking a deep breath, she met his gaze.

"Stay," she said softly. "I don't want to be alone tonight."

Anthony stepped closer, his fingers brushing against hers. "I wasn't planning on going anywhere."

Aurora melted into Anthony's embrace, pressing her face against his chest as his arms tightened around her. His warmth, his strength, the steady rhythm of his heartbeat—all of it grounded her in a way nothing else could. She tilted her head up, and he cupped her cheek, his thumb brushing away the last traces of the evening's turmoil from her skin.

"I've got you," he murmured.

She reached for him then, her fingers threading into his hair as she pulled him down into a slow, lingering kiss. It started gentle, filled with unspoken promises, but as the tension of the day unravelled, a different kind of urgency took its place.

Anthony deepened the kiss, his hands exploring the curve of her back before sliding lower, lifting her effortlessly. Aurora wrapped her legs around his waist, feeling the solid strength of him as he carried her toward the bedroom.

The moment they reached the bed, he laid her down carefully, hovering over her as his eyes traced every inch of her face. "Are you sure?" he asked, his voice husky but controlled.

Aurora nodded, her heart hammering. "I've never been surer of anything."

A slow, devastating smile curved his lips before he kissed her again, this time with nothing held back. His hands moved with deliberate reverence, sliding beneath the fabric of her dress, mapping her skin as if committing every inch of her to memory. She arched beneath him, sighing his name as heat unfurled low in her belly.

Clothes were removed piece by piece, soft laughter mingling with breathy gasps as they rediscovered each other in the dim glow of the city lights filtering through the window. Anthony worshipped her with his touch, his lips tracing the delicate lines of her collarbone, her shoulders, the dip of her waist.

Aurora trembled beneath him, not from nerves, but from the sheer intensity of the moment. She had wanted this—wanted him—for so long. And now, as he joined their bodies in a slow, unhurried rhythm, she knew this wasn't just desire. It was something deeper, something that reached into her very soul.

Their movements were tender yet consuming, a dance of whispered confessions and unspoken emotions. He held her close, his forehead resting against hers as he murmured her name like a vow. Aurora clung to him, matching each movement, every sensation overwhelming in the best way.

When they finally found release together, Aurora buried her face in Anthony's neck, pressing a soft, lingering kiss against his skin as their breaths slowed. His arms tightened around her, holding her close, as if he never wanted to let go.

In the quiet aftermath, tangled in the warmth of his embrace, Aurora knew—this was where she belonged.

Anthony lay there, his fingers tracing slow, idle patterns along her back. The words sat heavy on his tongue, threatening to spill out—I love you. He felt it in every breath, in every touch, in the way his heart ached just holding her. But was it too soon? They had only reconnected a few weeks ago.

So instead, he pressed a kiss to her hair and held her a little tighter, silently promising that when the moment was right, she would hear the words he longed to say.

Chapter Twenty-Two

Unbeknownst to Anthony and Aurora, Mary was already setting a sinister plan in motion. She stood in the dimly lit corner of a rundown bar, her fingers drumming impatiently against the wooden table as she eyed the man across from her. He was rough-looking, with a permanent sneer etched onto his scarred face, his eyes cold and calculating. The kind of man who had long since abandoned any shred of morality.

Mary slid an envelope across the table, her lips curling into a twisted smirk. "Here is her address," she said, her voice low and laced with satisfaction. "And this is a picture of her."

The man took the items, studying the photograph with a leer before pocketing them. "Pretty girl," he mused, his voice rasping with amusement. "Shame she's about to have a very bad night."

Mary leaned in, her expression dark and venomous. "I don't care what you do—just make sure she knows she messed with the wrong person. Scare her. Humiliate her. Make her regret ever crossing me."

He chuckled, a slow, menacing sound. "You really got it out for this chick, huh?" He tapped the envelope against the table. "Did you bring the money?"

"Yes," Mary snapped, reaching into her purse and producing a thick wad of cash. She shoved it into his waiting hand, watching as he thumbed through the bills with a satisfied grin.

"Pleasure doin' business," he drawled, tucking the cash away. He leaned back in his chair, regarding Mary with a look that sent a shiver down even her spine. "This girl… she's not gonna be the same after I'm done."

Mary's smile widened, her heart pounding with cruel anticipation. "Good," she whispered. "Make sure she never forgets it."

The man stood, cracking his knuckles as he gave her one last, knowing smirk. "Oh, don't worry, sweetheart. This chick's in for a real surprise."

Mary watched as he disappeared into the night, a sick satisfaction curling in her chest. Aurora had taken everything from her—her reputation, her relationship, and now, it was time for payback.

And this time, there would be no coming back from it.

The morning light spilled through the bedroom window, casting a soft glow over the room. Aurora stirred beneath the covers, stretching with a satisfied sigh as she felt the warmth of Anthony's body beside her. Last night had been everything—comforting, passionate, and filled with the quiet understanding that neither of them wanted to be apart.

Anthony shifted beside her, propping himself up on one elbow. His dark eyes roamed over her face, memorising every curve, every expression. "I don't want to leave," he admitted, brushing a stray lock of hair behind her ear.

Aurora smiled sleepily, reaching up to trace his jaw with her fingers. "I don't want you to go either."

He pressed a lingering kiss to her forehead before reluctantly sitting up. "I have a long shift today, and after that, I'm meeting a friend to discuss your situation with the hospital. Once that's done, I'll come straight back here." His dark eyes searched hers. "Are you sure you're okay with that?"

Aurora sat up as well, wrapping her arms around her knees. A soft smile touched her lips as she nodded. "Of course. I'd rather have you here than be alone."

Anthony smirked. "I'm starting to think you might actually like having me around."

She rolled her eyes playfully. "Don't get ahead of yourself, Dr. Hardwick."

He chuckled, then leaned in to steal one last lingering kiss before forcing himself out of bed. As he dressed, his gaze lingered on her, filled with quiet affection. "Just try to relax and not worry too much, okay?"

Aurora smiled softly, tilting her head as she watched him. "I'll try."

Satisfied, Anthony kissed her again—this time with a hesitation that made her heart squeeze. Then he was gone, leaving Aurora to spend the day wrapped in the warmth of his lingering presence, counting down the hours until he returned.

Aurora spent the day tackling long-overdue housework, determined to keep her mind off the hospital and Mary. She scrubbed, dusted, and reorganised, anything to keep herself busy. As the sun dipped below the horizon, she decided to cook dinner, hoping to have everything ready by the time Anthony arrived.

The evening stretched on, the city beyond her window alive with the hum of distant traffic and the occasional laughter of passersby. Wrapped in a soft blanket, Aurora curled up on the couch with a book resting on her lap. Every few minutes, her gaze flickered to the clock, anticipation stirring in her chest.

Anthony had texted her half an hour ago, saying he'd be leaving soon—and that he had good news.

A knock at the door made her heart skip a beat. Finally.

Smiling, she set her book aside and padded toward the door. "Took you long enough," she teased as she unlocked it and swung it open.

The smile vanished.

The man standing in the doorway was not Anthony.

He was tall, broad-shouldered, his weathered face marred by deep scars. But it was his eyes that froze her in place—cold, empty, devoid of anything human.

A slow, predatory grin stretched across his lips as he took her in.

"Hey there, sweetheart," he murmured.

Aurora's stomach turned to ice.

Instinct screamed at her to slam the door shut, but before she could react, he lunged.

A gasp caught in her throat as he shoved the door open, forcing his way inside. The impact sent her stumbling backward, her hands scrambling for anything to steady herself.

The door slammed shut behind him, the sound echoing through the apartment like a gunshot.

Aurora's breath came in sharp, panicked gasps as she backed away, but he advanced with slow, deliberate steps, like a predator toying with its prey.

"W-What do you want?" Her voice trembled, barely above a whisper.

The man chuckled darkly, rolling his shoulders as if preparing himself for a long, enjoyable night. "Let's just say… I want to have a bit of fun."

Aurora's heart pounded against her ribs, her mind racing for an escape. But she was trapped. She prayed that Anthony would be here soon.

The man took another step forward, cracking his knuckles, his lips curling into a sneer.

"Now," he murmured, his voice laced with cruel amusement, "let's have some fun."

Aurora's breath came in short gasps, her back pressing against the wall as the man advanced. Fear gripped her, but survival instinct kicked in. She grabbed the closest object—a glass from the counter—and hurled it at him. It shattered against his shoulder, making him grunt in irritation rather than pain.

"Feisty," he mused, rolling his neck. "I like that."

Heart pounding, Aurora darted toward the kitchen, her eyes locking on the knife block. If she could just—.

A rough hand yanked her back before she could reach it, slamming her against the wall so hard that stars exploded in her vision.

Aurora's heart pounded violently in her chest, her pulse roaring in her ears. The only thing she could think to do was scream. And she did—loud and piercing, the sound ripping through the air.

The man lunged.

Anthony jogged up the steps to Aurora's apartment, he just come from having a drink with Graham. His friend, a lawyer, had agreed to help Aurora sort out her issue with the hospital, and Anthony couldn't wait to tell her the good news.

"You love this girl?" Graham had asked earlier.

"Yep. She's the one, mate," Anthony had answered, a grin spreading across his face.

"That's great. Can't wait to meet her."

"You'll love her," Anthony had said with certainty. "She's sweet, kind, and beautiful."

He was nearly at her door when he heard it.

A scream.

Aurora's scream.

His heart slammed against his ribs as he sprinted the rest of the way, reaching her door in seconds. He grabbed the handle and twisted. Locked.

Another scream, sharp and terrified.

Panic surged through him. Anthony rammed his shoulder into the door, pain jolting through him as it held firm.

"Hang on, Aurora!" he shouted, taking a step back before throwing his full weight into it again.

The doorframe splintered.

The lock gave way.

The door flew open just in time for Anthony to see a hulking figure rear back and slap Aurora across the face. The force sent her flying. She crashed into the kitchen counter, her head striking the edge with a sickening crack before she crumpled to the floor.

Everything inside Anthony went cold.

Rage unlike anything he had ever felt surged through him, drowning out every rational thought. He charged at the man, his fist connecting with his jaw in a brutal punch. The man staggered, but Anthony didn't stop. He hit him again, harder this time, and the man barely had time to register what was happening before Anthony's fist met his face one final time.

The intruder collapsed, unconscious.

Breathing hard, Anthony turned to Aurora.

Aurora lay motionless on the floor, her golden hair fanned out around her, stark against the crimson trickle of blood slipping down her temple. Anthony's stomach twisted violently, fear coiling in his chest like a vice.

"Aurora?" His voice was raw, desperate.

He dropped to his knees beside her, his trembling fingers pressing against her wrist, searching for a pulse. Relief crashed over him when he found it—faint, but steady. Yet she wasn't moving. She wasn't waking up.

Panic clawed at his throat. His hands shook as he yanked his phone from his pocket, fumbling to dial emergency services.

"Come on, baby, don't do this to me," he pleaded, his voice thick with emotion. "Stay with me. Just stay with me."

The moment the dispatcher answered, Anthony forced himself to stay calm enough to relay the situation—home invasion, unconscious victim, possible head trauma.

Minutes stretched into eternity as he cradled Aurora's face, brushing his thumb over her cheek, his mind racing with worst-case scenarios.

Then, sirens.

Red and blue lights flooded through the windows, casting flickering shadows across the walls. The sound of heavy boots echoed in the hallway.

The door, already battered from Anthony's forced entry, was pushed open further as uniformed officers stormed in.

"There!" Anthony barked, his head snapping toward the unconscious intruder sprawled on the floor. "He attacked her."

The police moved swiftly. Within moments, the man was yanked to his feet, barely conscious. One officer secured his hands behind his back with zip ties before cuffing him properly.

"Name?" one of them demanded.

Anthony barely heard them. His focus was on the paramedics now kneeling beside Aurora.

"She hit her head pretty hard," he told them hoarsely as they checked her vitals. "She was attacked—she fought back, but he overpowered her."

One paramedic shined a light into her eyes, frowning. "Possible concussion," she murmured.

Another pressed gauze to the wound on Aurora's temple to slow the bleeding. "We need to get her to the hospital."

Anthony clenched his jaw, barely holding himself together. "I'm coming with her."

The paramedics lifted Aurora onto a stretcher, securing her in place as they moved toward the waiting ambulance.

Anthony didn't spare the bastard who hurt her another glance. The officers could deal with him—his only focus was Aurora. He climbed into the ambulance beside her, his grip tightening around her limp hand as the doors shut behind them.

His mind reeled, flashing back to that morning. The way she had kissed him, slow and sweet, her smile lingering against his lips. She had been happy. Safe. Completely unaware that within hours, she'd be fighting for her life.

Anthony pressed a trembling kiss to her knuckles. "I'm right here, baby," he whispered. "I'm not going anywhere."

Then he saw it.

Blood.

Dark, seeping into her golden hair, staining the gauze the paramedics pressed against her temple. The stark contrast against her pale skin sent a sharp jolt of nausea through him. His stomach twisted violently. He had seen her injured before—had seen her fight through pain with quiet resilience—but nothing prepared him for this. Seeing her like this again. Hurt. Unconscious. Because he hadn't been there to stop it.

"Her pulse is steady," one of the paramedics assured him. "She's stable for now."

The words barely registered. He gave a stiff nod, his jaw locked so tight it ached, but the crushing weight in his chest refused to lift. Stable wasn't enough. Stable still meant she was hurt. Still meant she had been terrified, alone, and at the mercy of that monster before he got there.

He had arrived just in time to stop the bastard—but not in time to stop this. Not in time to protect her.

And that failure would haunt him.

His fingers curled around her hand, desperate for any sign of warmth, any flicker of movement that might tell him she was coming back to him. But she remained still, her breathing shallow, her face eerily peaceful in unconsciousness.

Anthony leaned closer, brushing his lips against her bruised knuckles, his voice hoarse with guilt. "I should have been there."

But he wasn't.

And now, all he could do was pray that she would wake up.

Chapter Twenty-Three

Through the swirling mists of pain, there were voices.

Distant, muffled, floating in and out of the darkness. Some were calm, measured, clinical. But one voice rose above the others.

Deep, husky, laced with quiet desperation.

"Don't leave me, baby. Don't let go. You need to fight. Don't leave me, sweetheart."

Aurora felt herself reaching for it, clinging to the sound even as the void pulled at her. Warmth wrapped around her hand—firm, steady, familiar. Something solid in the haze. Then, cool hands touched her—efficient, gentle. The sharp edges of pain dulled, and for a moment, she thought she could surface.

But the blackness swallowed her whole.

The next time consciousness stirred; the world was softer. The beeping of machines, the hushed murmur of voices. She blinked slowly, her vision blurring, then sharpening.

Sarah was there, her face tight with worry.

Aurora tried to speak, but her throat felt raw. She made a feeble attempt to lift her head, but Sarah was already leaning over her, pressing her gently back against the pillows.

"No, don't move," Sarah said firmly. "You're going to have a sore head for a while."

Aurora swallowed, forcing out the only name that mattered. "Anthony?"

Sarah exhaled, her features softening. "He's been here for two days, Rory. Never slept, never left your bedside." She shook her head, a mix of fondness and exasperation in her tone. "They threw him out this morning—practically had to drag him. He finally went to get a shower and a few hours of sleep, but not until the doctor came in personally to tell him you'd be all right." She gave Aurora's hand a gentle squeeze. "You got a good one there, Rory."

Aurora let her head fall back against the pillow, her body heavy with exhaustion. Sleep pulled at her again, a fog of painkillers dragging her under before she could even respond.

When she woke again, the room was bathed in dim light. The shadows stretched across the walls, the sterile hospital air oddly still.

And then she felt it—him.

Warm, strong fingers wrapped around hers.

Aurora turned her head, her eyes misting as she took in the dark head resting against their joined hands. Anthony sat beside her, his body slumped forward, exhaustion pulling him under even as his grip on her remained unyielding.

Her fingers trembled as she moved them, slipping from his hold to touch his hair. Silky strands, rich brown, gleamed under the soft light. The usually perfect waves fell across his forehead, softening the harsh lines of his face. He looked so tired. The thick black lashes that framed his eyes cast deep shadows against his cheekbones. And for the first time, she saw it—vulnerability. The weight of something deeper than exhaustion.

She stroked his hair gently, an ache blooming in her chest. He had been here, fighting for her, worrying for her.

Loving her.

"Anthony…" She whispered his name, a world of longing wrapped in those three syllables.

The reaction was instant.

His body jerked awake, his head snapping up, those stormy brown eyes locking onto hers in an instant. His breath hitched, and then his hands were on her— cradling hers, pressing it against his cheek as though reassuring himself she was real.

"Aurora." His voice was hoarse, thick with emotion. He turned his face into her palm, squeezing his eyes shut before opening them again, like he couldn't bear to look away. "Aurora, sweetheart. I'm sorry, so sorry."

Her fingers traced the sharp lines of his jaw, her heart twisting at the raw torment in his gaze. "I'm all right, Anthony," she murmured, her voice barely above a breath. "It wasn't your fault."

His grip on her hand tightened. "It was," he rasped. "I should have protected you."

Her eyes softened, her fingers brushing over the faint stubble shadowing his face. "You were there when it mattered."

His throat bobbed as he swallowed hard, but his gaze never left hers. "I can't lose you, Aurora."

She squeezed his hand. The weight of everything unsaid pressed between them, heavy, inescapable. "You won't."

His breath shuddered out, his forehead dropping to her hand as he held it to his lips. And for the first time in days, the tightness in his chest loosened.

Over the next few days, Aurora's strength steadily returned. The pounding ache in her head dulled until it was nothing more than a faint throb, and each morning she found herself able to sit up a little longer, speak a little more, and feel a little less fragile.

Through it all, Anthony remained by her side.

He spent every possible moment with her, reluctant to leave even when the nurses insisted, he needed rest. If he wasn't sitting beside her, his fingers loosely intertwined with hers, he was adjusting her pillows, making sure she was comfortable, or coaxing her into eating the hospital meals she stubbornly avoided.

She had plenty of visitors—Emily, Sarah, and even Harry had stopped by, their concern filling the room with warmth and familiarity. Their presence was a comfort, a reminder that she wasn't alone. She was grateful for all of them, for their kindness and support, but the most unexpected visit came on her fourth day of recovery, just after lunch.

Aurora had just finished picking at her meal when a firm knock sounded at the door. She looked up as two uniformed officers stepped into the room. Their expressions were serious, their presence casting a shadow over the quiet peace of the afternoon.

Anthony, who had been sitting beside her, immediately straightened, his protective instincts sharpening like a blade. His grip on her hand tightened, grounding her.

"Miss Vincent," one of the officers—a middle-aged man with greying hair and a solemn face—began. "I'm Detective Marshall, and this is my partner, Detective Liu. We're sorry to disturb you, but we have important information regarding your attack."

Aurora felt her stomach twist. The attack. The bruises on her skin were fading, the sharp pain in her head had dulled, but the memory still lingered like a phantom, refusing to be forgotten. She forced herself to nod, swallowing against the sudden dryness in her throat.

"What is it?" Anthony's voice was calm, but there was an unmistakable edge beneath it.

Detective Liu stepped forward, her eyes sympathetic yet firm. "Your attacker has been cooperating with us since his arrest. We questioned him extensively, and this morning, he finally gave us a full confession."

Aurora's fingers curled into the sheets. "What did he say?"

The detectives exchanged a glance before Marshall spoke again. "He admitted that he was hired. Someone paid him to go to your apartment, to *teach you a lesson.*"

Aurora felt the blood drain from her face. She barely registered the way Anthony's entire body went rigid beside her.

"Who?" His voice was low, dangerous.

Detective Liu's jaw tightened. "Mary Moore."

A stunned silence filled the room.

Aurora's breath hitched. "Mary?" she whispered, the name barely forming on her lips.

Anthony shot to his feet, his chair scraping violently against the floor. "That bitch—"

"Anthony," Aurora whispered, squeezing his hand in an effort to anchor him, but he was shaking with barely restrained fury.

Detective Marshall cleared his throat. "We've arrested her. She's facing multiple charges, including conspiracy to commit assault and endangerment. Given the evidence, we expect a strong case against her."

Aurora struggled to process it. The woman who had made her life miserable, who had tried to ruin her career—had she really gone this far? A chill ran down her spine.

Anthony let out a sharp, disbelieving laugh. "She hired someone to attack Aurora. What the hell is wrong with her?" His hands clenched into fists, his entire body radiating anger.

Detective Liu smiled grimly. "Justice will be served. She won't be walking away from this."

Aurora exhaled shakily, trying to steady the whirlwind of emotions crashing through her. She had feared that Mary would continue her campaign of cruelty, but she never imagined it would come to this.

"She's in custody now?" she asked, her voice steadier than she felt.

"Yes," Detective Liu confirmed. "And the man she hired will be serving time as well. You're safe now."

Safe. The word settled over her like a fragile promise.

Anthony ran a hand through his hair, his jaw still tight with rage. "She better not get away with this," he muttered. "She put Aurora through hell. She could have killed her."

Detective Marshall nodded. "The legal system will take it from here. If you decide to pursue further legal action, your lawyer can guide you through the process. But for now, we just wanted you to know—she can't hurt you anymore."

Aurora swallowed the lump in her throat, then looked up at Anthony. His brown eyes were still dark with fury, but beneath it, there was something else. Relief.

Chapter Twenty-Four

Soon after the detectives left Marie, her supervisor, entered the room with a small smile. Aurora straightened in bed, her fingers instinctively curling around Anthony's. His grip tightened in silent support.

"Aurora, I'm so glad you're feeling better," Marie said warmly, stepping closer to the bed. Her expression was kind, but there was something more in her eyes—an urgency, as if she'd been waiting for this conversation.

"Thank you," Aurora said, her voice steady, though her heart picked up slightly.

Marie hesitated for only a second before taking a deep breath. "I wanted to tell you in person—the complaints against you have been dismissed."

Aurora blinked. "What?"

Marie nodded. "The board conducted a thorough review, and I'm happy to inform you that the allegations were treated as completely unworthy of consideration."

Relief crashed over Aurora so suddenly that she sagged against the pillows. She hadn't realised just how much weight she'd been carrying until it lifted.

Marie continued, her voice firm. "Dr. Young—Harry—stood by you completely. He assured the board that no such incident ever occurred. His statement was crucial, but ultimately, the truth came to light through the police investigation of your attack."

Aurora exchanged a glance with Anthony, who was watching Marie with sharp, unreadable eyes. "What do you mean?" she asked.

Marie's expression darkened slightly. "We know the police arrested Mary Moore—the individual who filed the complaints—on charges of soliciting someone to harm you."

Aurora stiffened, her breath catching.

Marie nodded grimly. "Under these circumstances, the board has determined that this was nothing more than an act of vengeance against you. A personal vendetta, not a professional misconduct case. Given this, your suspension has been fully lifted."

Aurora exhaled shakily, her mind reeling. "So… I can come back?"

Marie's face softened. "Not only can you come back, but we want you back. You've been reinstated with our apologies, Aurora. The hospital deeply regrets how this situation unfolded, and you are welcome to return as soon as you feel well enough."

Anthony's thumb brushed soothing circles against the back of her hand, grounding her as she processed everything. The injustice, the fear, the anger— it was all behind her now. Mary had tried to destroy her, but she had failed.

Aurora met Marie's gaze, gratitude and quiet determination settling in her chest. "Thank you," she said, meaning every word.

Marie gave a small smile. "Take your time to heal, Aurora. We'll be waiting when you're ready."

As she left the room, Aurora exhaled slowly, her grip on Anthony's hand still firm.

He studied her, his expression unreadable, before finally speaking. "It's over."

She turned to him, meeting those intense brown eyes. "Yeah," she whispered. "It is."

On the fifth day, Anthony took her home—to his home. He insisted she would be safer with him, and more than that, he wanted her there. Aurora didn't argue. Deep down, she wanted it too.

He was careful with her. Every movement was measured, deliberate. To him, she was something fragile. Something precious. His touch was gentle yet steady, his presence an unspoken promise of protection. When they arrived, he helped her through the grand entrance of his building and into the private lift, his hand never leaving hers.

The elevator doors slid open with a soft chime, revealing the stunning space beyond. Aurora took one step inside and froze.

Her breath caught as she took in the breathtaking panorama of Sydney Harbour. Floor-to-ceiling windows framed the dazzling city skyline, the golden glow of the setting sun casting a warm hue over the water. Ferries glided across the harbour, their lights flickering like fireflies, while the Opera House stood proudly in the distance, a masterpiece against the twilight sky.

"You live here?" she asked, her voice barely above a whisper.

Anthony watched her, a small, almost sheepish smile playing on his lips. "Yeah."

She turned slowly, taking in the space. The penthouse was sleek yet inviting, modern yet warm. Dark wood floors stretched beneath her feet, complementing the plush furniture and minimalist elegance that somehow still felt unmistakably him. Yet, despite the refined luxury surrounding her, it was the view that captivated her most.

Aurora drifted toward the window and pressed a hand against the cool glass. Below her, the city spread like a living painting—golden sun flickering off the other buildings, water shimmering. For a moment, she felt weightless, as if she were floating above it all.

"It's beautiful," she murmured.

Anthony stepped up behind her, his warmth wrapping around her before his arms did. He pulled her gently against him, his chest solid and reassuring against her back. When he dipped his head, his lips brushed the crown of her head in a featherlight touch.

"You're beautiful," he whispered, reverence lacing his voice.

Aurora exhaled, the last of her tension melting away. For the first time since her ordeal, the weight pressing on her chest lifted. Here, in his arms, she felt safe. Whole. It was just the two of them—standing together against the world.

Anthony shifted, turning her gently until she was facing him. His deep, unwavering gaze searched hers.

"Aurora, I know this probably isn't the best time to say this, but I can't hold it back any longer." He cupped her face, his thumb tracing the curve of her cheek with aching tenderness. "I love you."

Her breath hitched, her heart stuttering in her chest. For twelve long months, she had yearned for those words, dreamed of hearing them. Emotion swelled inside her, overflowing as tears welled in her eyes.

A trembling smile graced her lips. "I love you too, Anthony."

The air between them shifted, charged with something deep and unspoken. Anthony let out a slow, unsteady breath, his grip on her tightening as if anchoring himself to the moment. He had waited so long to say those words, and now that he had, hearing them echoed back filled him with a sense of rightness he hadn't thought possible.

Aurora's fingers trembled as she reached up to cup his face, tracing the sharp angles of his jaw as though committing him to memory. "You have no idea how long I've wanted to hear you say that," she whispered.

Anthony covered her hands with his, his eyes never leaving hers. "I should have said it sooner," he admitted, his voice raw with emotion. "I don't want to waste another second. Not after everything we've been through."

A single tear slipped down her cheek, and he caught it with his thumb, brushing it away with a tenderness that sent her heart soaring.

Then, unable to hold back any longer, he lowered his head and kissed her.

It wasn't a desperate, urgent kiss—it was something deeper. Something that spoke of love, of permanence, of the unbreakable bond between them. His lips moved over hers slowly, reverently, as though savouring the taste of forever.

Aurora melted into him, her arms winding around his neck as she kissed him back with equal tenderness. Every emotion she had bottled up over the past year poured into that moment—her longing, her heartbreak, her hope.

When they finally pulled apart, their foreheads remained pressed together, their breaths mingling in the quiet, intimate space between them. The world outside faded, leaving only the steady rhythm of their hearts and the undeniable pull between them.

Anthony traced his fingers along her jaw, then tucked a loose strand of hair behind her ear, his touch lingering. His dark eyes, filled with unwavering certainty, held hers.

"Marry me, Aurora," he murmured, his voice steady, sure—like a vow already made in his heart.

Aurora searched his face, looking for hesitation. Doubt. A single crack in his certainty. But there was none. Just love. Just him.

This man, who had fought for her, waited for her, loved her without question—he was hers. And she was his.

Forever.

A slow, radiant smile broke across her lips, her eyes shimmering with emotion.

"Yes, please," she whispered, the words wrapped in joy, in quiet disbelief, in everything she had ever dreamed of.

Anthony exhaled a breath he hadn't realised he was holding, then pulled her close again, holding her as if he never intended to let go. And this time, he wouldn't.

Epilogue

Two years later…

The hospital room was quiet except for the soft beeping of monitors and the occasional murmur of nurses outside the door. The air smelled of antiseptic and fresh linen, but to Anthony, it was the scent of a new beginning.

He sat beside Aurora's bed, cradling their newborn son in his arms. The tiny boy was swaddled in a pale blue blanket, his delicate features barely visible beneath the soft fabric. His little fingers curled into a fist, one resting against Anthony's chest, as if already seeking the steady beat of his father's heart.

Aurora watched them, exhaustion evident in her features, but her eyes shimmered with warmth. She looked radiant despite the long hours of labour, her hair slightly damp, her body still recovering from the miracle it had just performed. Yet, she smiled at him, at them, as though the world had never held anything more perfect.

Anthony couldn't speak at first. His throat was tight, his emotions a tangled mess. He had thought he understood love before. But nothing—*nothing*—had ever prepared him for this.

Carefully, he shifted their son in his arms and turned to Aurora, his voice husky when he finally managed to speak.

"He's perfect," he whispered, awe thick in his tone.

Aurora's smile softened as she reached for him, her fingers brushing against his wrist. "So are you," she murmured.

He let out a shaky breath, shaking his head slightly. "I don't know how I got this lucky."

Aurora's gaze held his, steady and sure. "Because you never gave up on us."

His grip on their son tightened just slightly, as if grounding himself in the reality of the moment. He had almost lost her once—had almost let fear and circumstance pull them apart. But now, here she was, their child in his arms, their future spread out before them.

A flicker of memory crossed Aurora's mind, and for a brief moment, she was transported back to that day—the day she had walked down the aisle toward him, her heart full and her future certain.

It had been six months after Anthony proposed, a ceremony filled with love and laughter. Sarah and Emily had been by her side as bridesmaids, their joy infectious as they helped her prepare for the most important moment of her life. She had never felt more beautiful than she had that day, wrapped in ivory lace, Anthony waiting for her at the end of the aisle with that soft, reverent look in his eyes.

She could still hear the whispers of excitement, the sound of vows exchanged in a room full of people who loved them, and the way Anthony had held her as they swayed to their first dance. It had been magical, not because of the grandeur, but because of the love that surrounded them. Every moment had been a promise, a beginning, a homecoming.

And now, as she lay in this hospital bed, gazing at her husband and son, she realised that her love story had only just begun.

Anthony leaned forward, pressing a tender kiss to her forehead before resting his against hers. "You've given me everything, Aurora," he whispered. "Everything I never even knew I needed."

Her fingers curled around his, their wedding bands glinting under the dim hospital lights. "And you've given me the kind of love I never thought I'd find."

A small, sleepy sound escaped their son, and Anthony pulled back just enough to look down at him again. A surge of protectiveness swelled in his chest, an unbreakable promise forming in his heart.

No matter what, he would always be there. For Aurora. For their son. For the family they had built against all odds.

As the first rays of morning light filtered through the hospital blinds, Anthony knew—this was only the beginning.

Their love had been tested, broken, rebuilt. And in the end, it had endured.

It had won.

The End

Before You Go...

If you fell for these characters and want more love stories filled with emotion, passion, and second chances, my newsletter is where I share them first.

You'll receive:

💕 Early access to new releases

💕 Exclusive reader-only content and extras

👉 **Join my reader list here:** https://alisonreidauthor.com

I'd love to welcome you.

Alison Reid

Thank you for reading Torn Between Hearts!

If you enjoyed this collection of emotionally charged romances, keep an eye out for more upcoming romance collections by Alison Reid, including:

Alpha Kings - *A Billionaire Alpha Male Romance Collection*

Cautious Hearts - *A Trust-After-Heartbreak Romance Collection*

Dark & Dangerous - *Brooding Heroes Romance Collection*

Final Surrender - *Alpha Heroes Yielding to Love Collection*

Forbidden Hearts - *A Forbidden Love Romance Collection*

Forever Mine - *A Longing-for-Love Romance Collection*

Guarded Hearts - *A Surrender to Love Romance Collection*

Hearts & Secrets - *Small Town Romance Collection*

Hearts in Peril - *A Suspenseful Romance Collection*

Hidden Truths - *A Secret Identity Romance Collection*

Lies & Hearts - *A Lies, Secrets & Betrayal Romance Collection*

Love After Regret - *A Second-Chance Redemption Romance Collection*

Misjudged Hearts - *A Love After Judgement Romance Collection*

All of Alison Reid's books feature standalone stories, swoon-worthy heroes, and guaranteed happily-ever-afters.

Books by Alison Reid

A Billionaire for Christmas

A Heart in Florence

After The Storm

Always You

Before I Fell

Before the Thaw

Beneath the Lies

Billionaire Bodyguard

Billionaire Rancher

Blueprints of the Heart

Branlow

Collide

Echoes of Deception

Falling for the Billionaire

Forever Yours

Heart of the Outback

Hearts on the Line

Hidden Gem

Kept Promises

Mended Hearts

Mistaken Hearts

New Year's Eve Kiss

Quiet Danger

Reckless Hearts

Reflections of Deception

Second Glance

Shadows of the Past

Shattered Dreams

Shattered Hope, Stolen Kisses

Still Yours

The Billionaire's Accidental Legacy

The Billionaire's Bargain

The Billionaire's Mistake

The Billionaire's Regret

The Billionaire's Secret Baby

The Billionaire's Unexpected Heir

The Blood Debt

The Playboy's Surrender

The Wrong Sister

Trust in Time

Undercover Billionaire

Until you Loved Me

Vows of Vengeance

Wife in Name Only

Find all my books on Amazon:

https://www.amazon.com/author/alisonreid1970

About the Author

Alison Reid writes contemporary and small-town romance filled with heart, passion, and second-chance love stories. Her novels feature strong heroines, irresistible heroes, and the happily-ever-afters readers adore.

Before turning her love of storytelling into a publishing career, Alison spent thirty-five years working as an engineer—proof that happily-ever-afters can be built as carefully as any blueprint. She began writing as a hobby during the COVID lockdowns and quickly discovered a passion she couldn't ignore.

Alison is happily married, has two grown children, and shares her home with two beautiful dogs who are convinced they deserve to be her main characters. When she's not writing, she enjoys reading, spending time with her family, and imagining new love stories. She hopes her books give readers a few hours of escape, joy, and swoon-worthy romance they won't soon forget.

www.ingramcontent.com/pod-product-compliance
Lightning Source LLC
Chambersburg PA
CBHW050955180726
48291CB00006B/1828